AS THE CROW FLIES

BY MELANIE GILLMAN

nquiry@ironcircus.com   www.ironcircus.com

IRON
CIRCUS
COMICS

trange and amazing

first printing: August 201
ISBN: 978-1-945820-06-9   printed in Canada   second printing: March 201

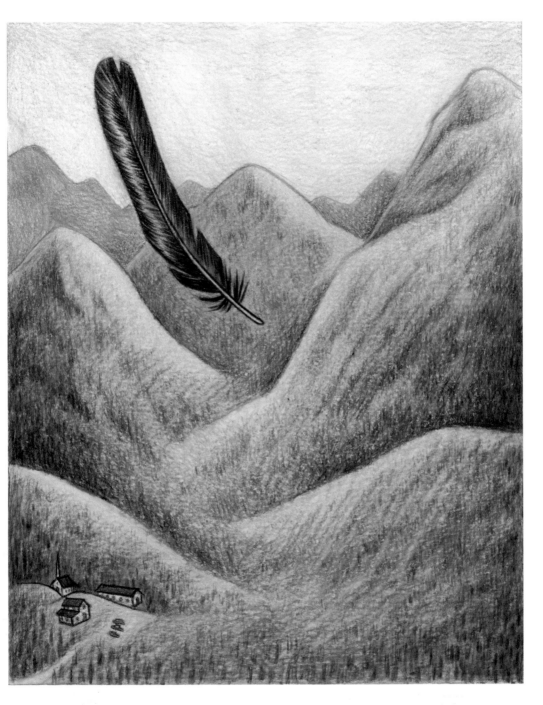

3

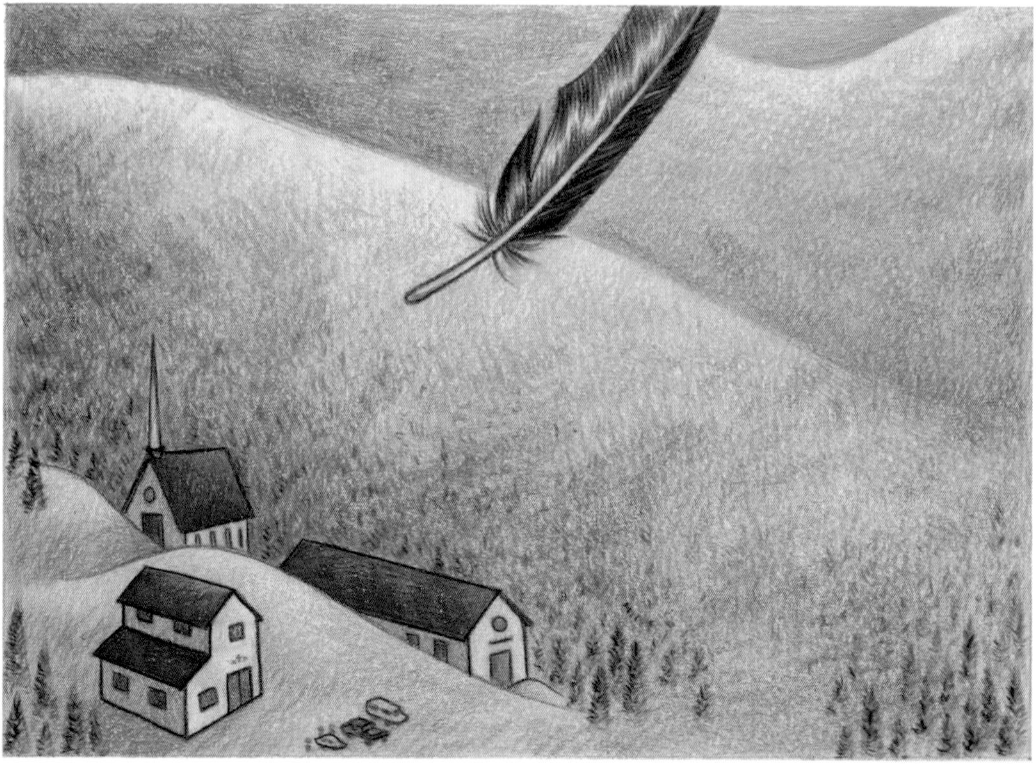

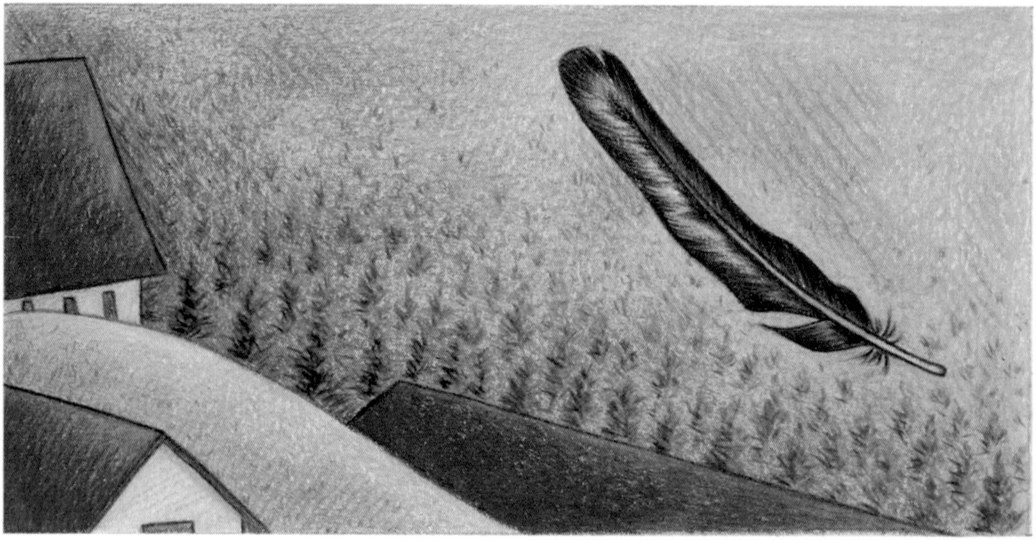

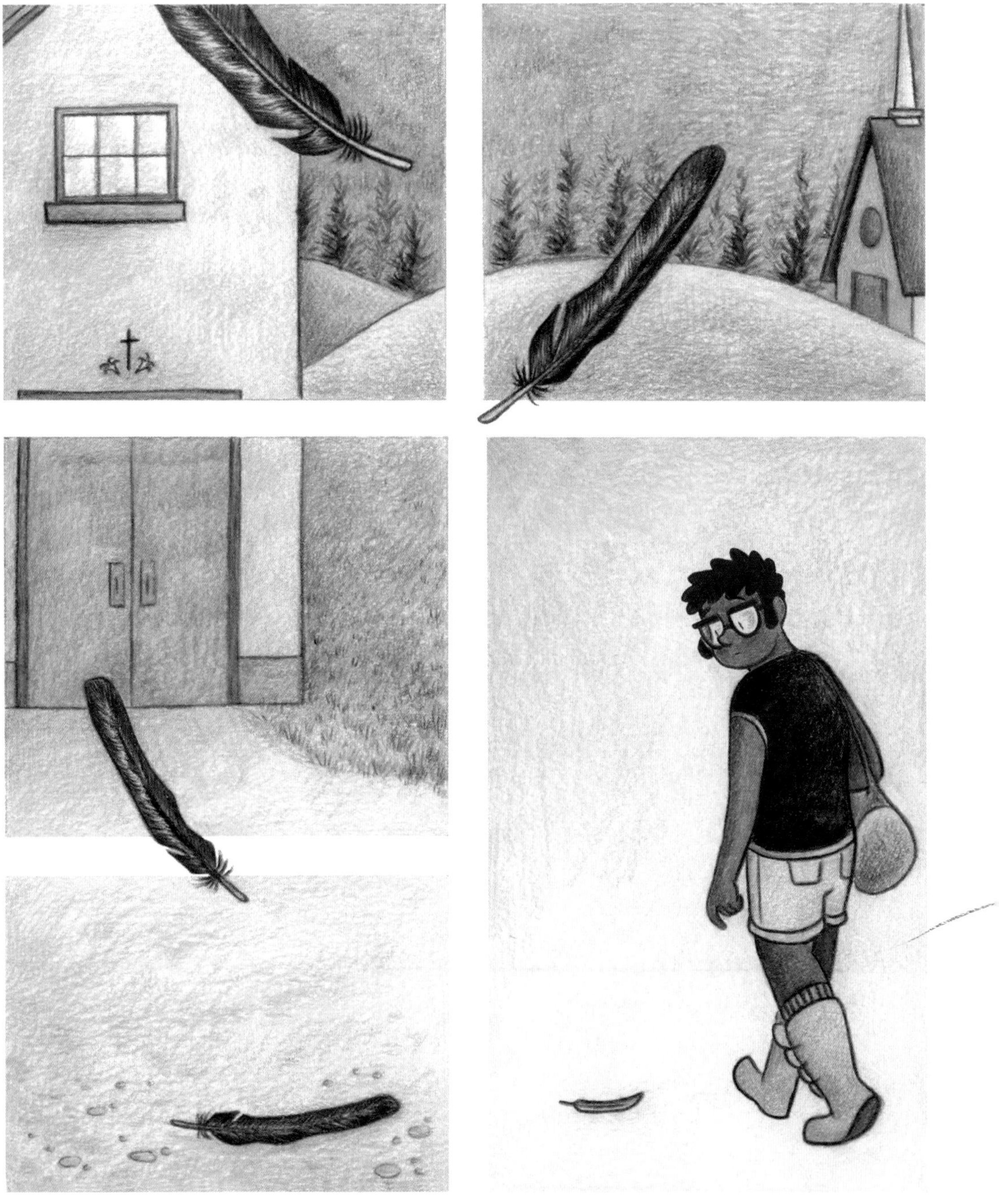

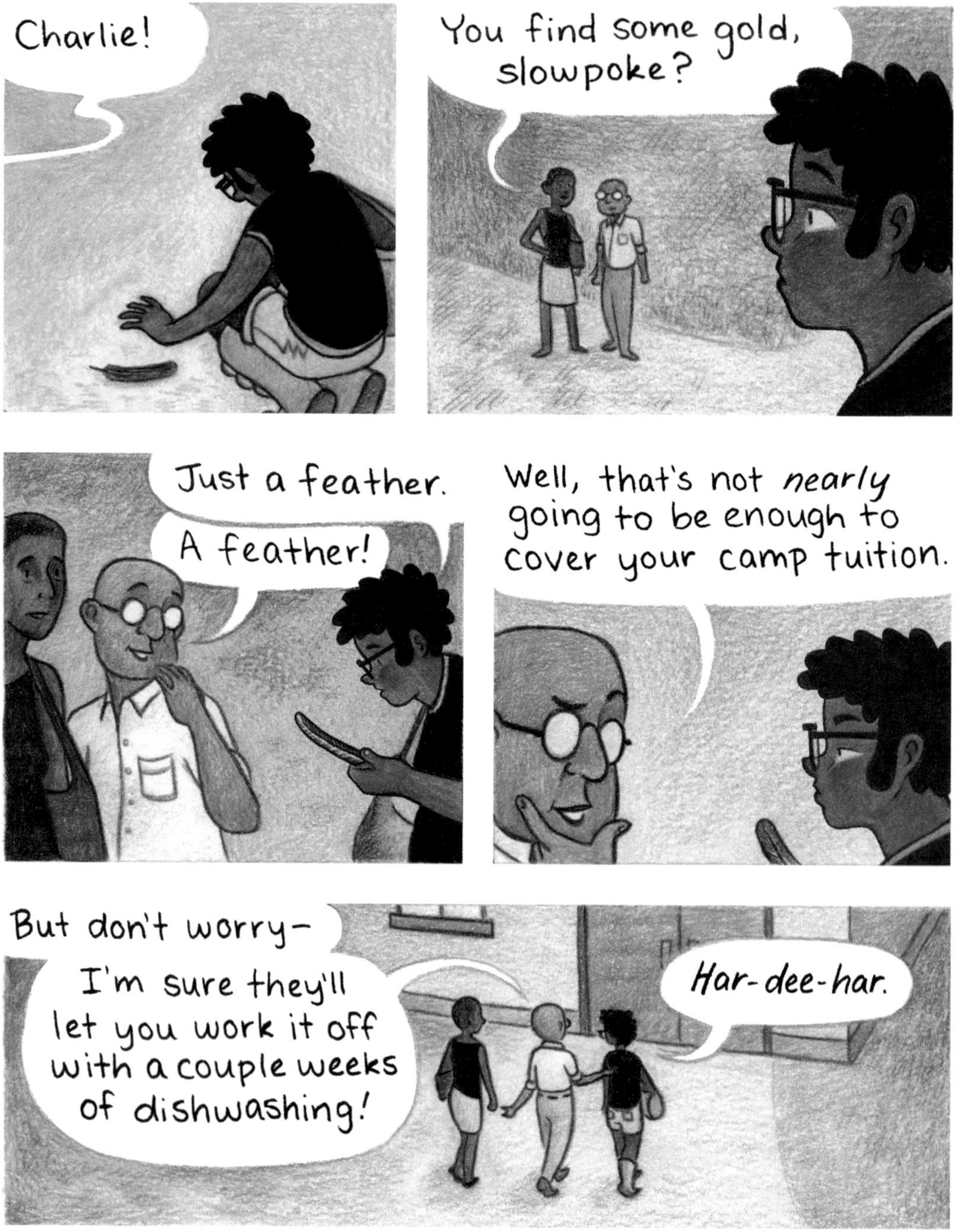
Charlie!
You find some gold, slowpoke?
Just a feather.
A feather!
Well, that's not *nearly* going to be enough to cover your camp tuition.
But don't worry—
I'm sure they'll let you work it off with a couple weeks of dishwashing!
Har-dee-har.

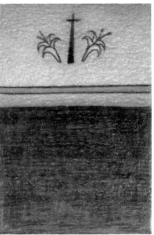

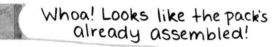

Whoa! Looks like the pack's already assembled!

There's the check-in.

Hi there! Sorry we're so late—

—Charlie. Should be under "Lamonte."

That's L-A-M-

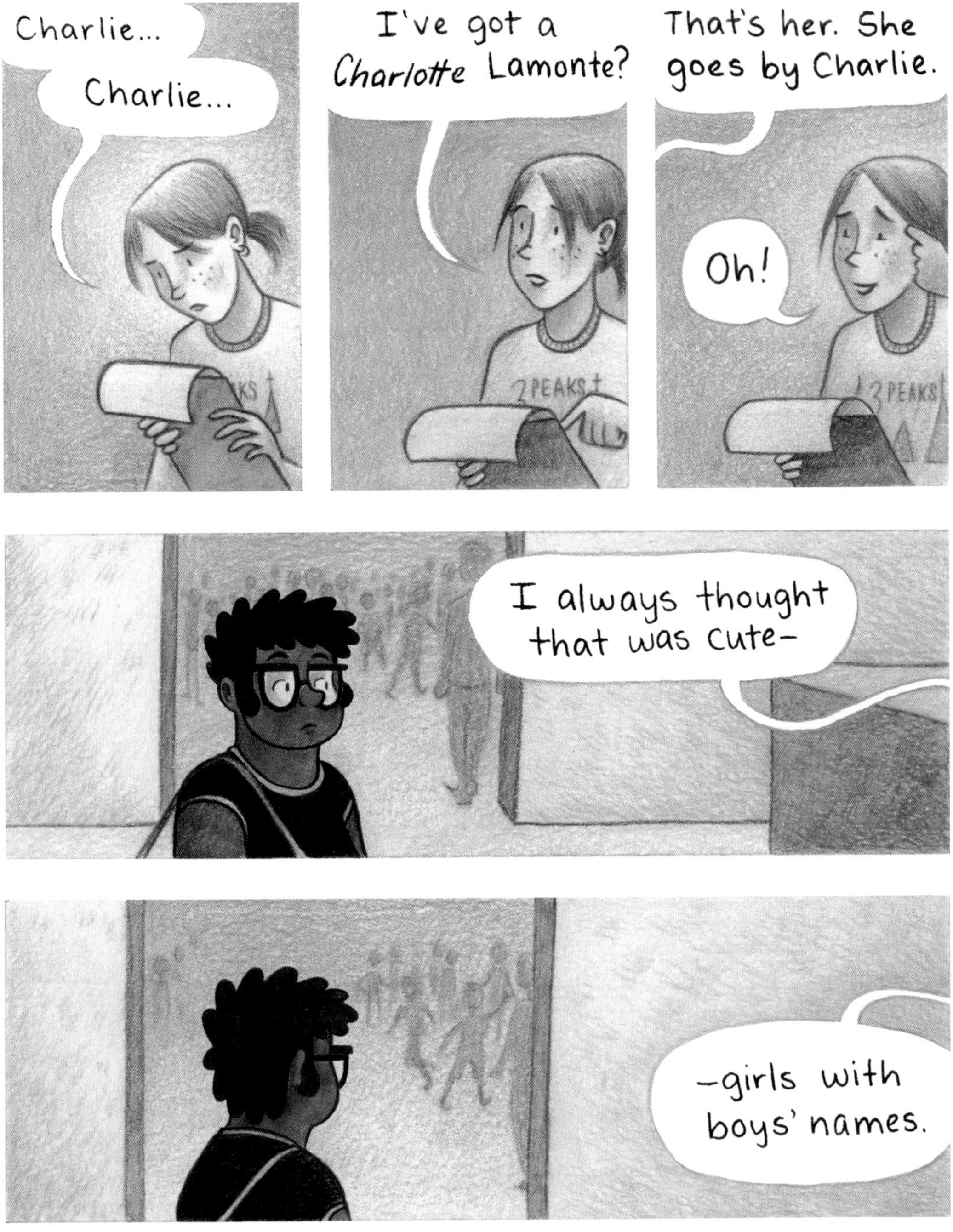

Charlie...
Charlie...
I've got a *Charlotte* Lamonte?
That's her. She goes by Charlie.
Oh!
2 PEAKS
I always thought that was cute-
-girls with boys' names.

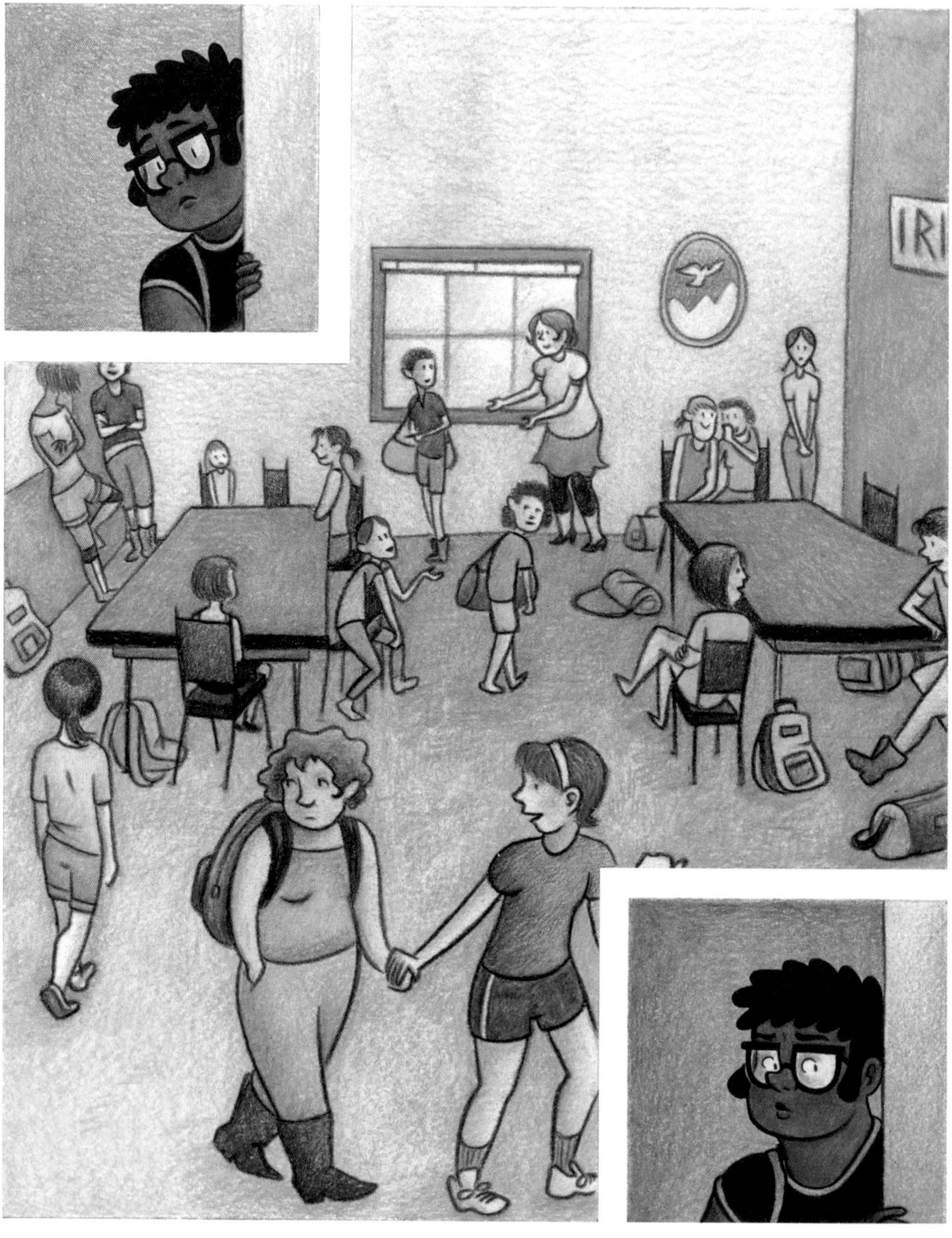

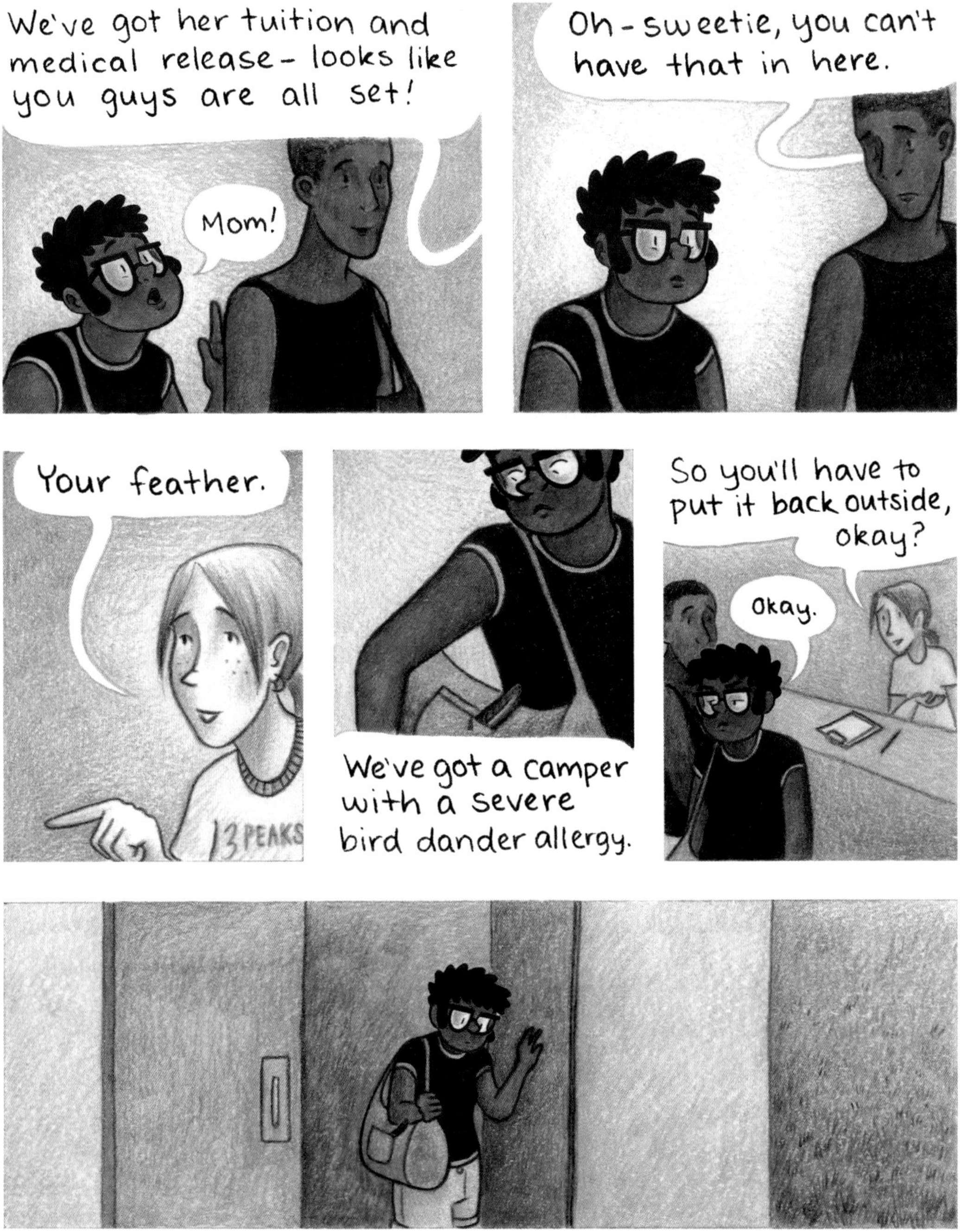
We've got her tuition and medical release- looks like you guys are all set!
Mom!
Oh-sweetie, you can't have that in here.
Your feather.
3 PEAKS
We've got a camper with a severe bird dander allergy.
So you'll have to put it back outside, okay?
Okay.

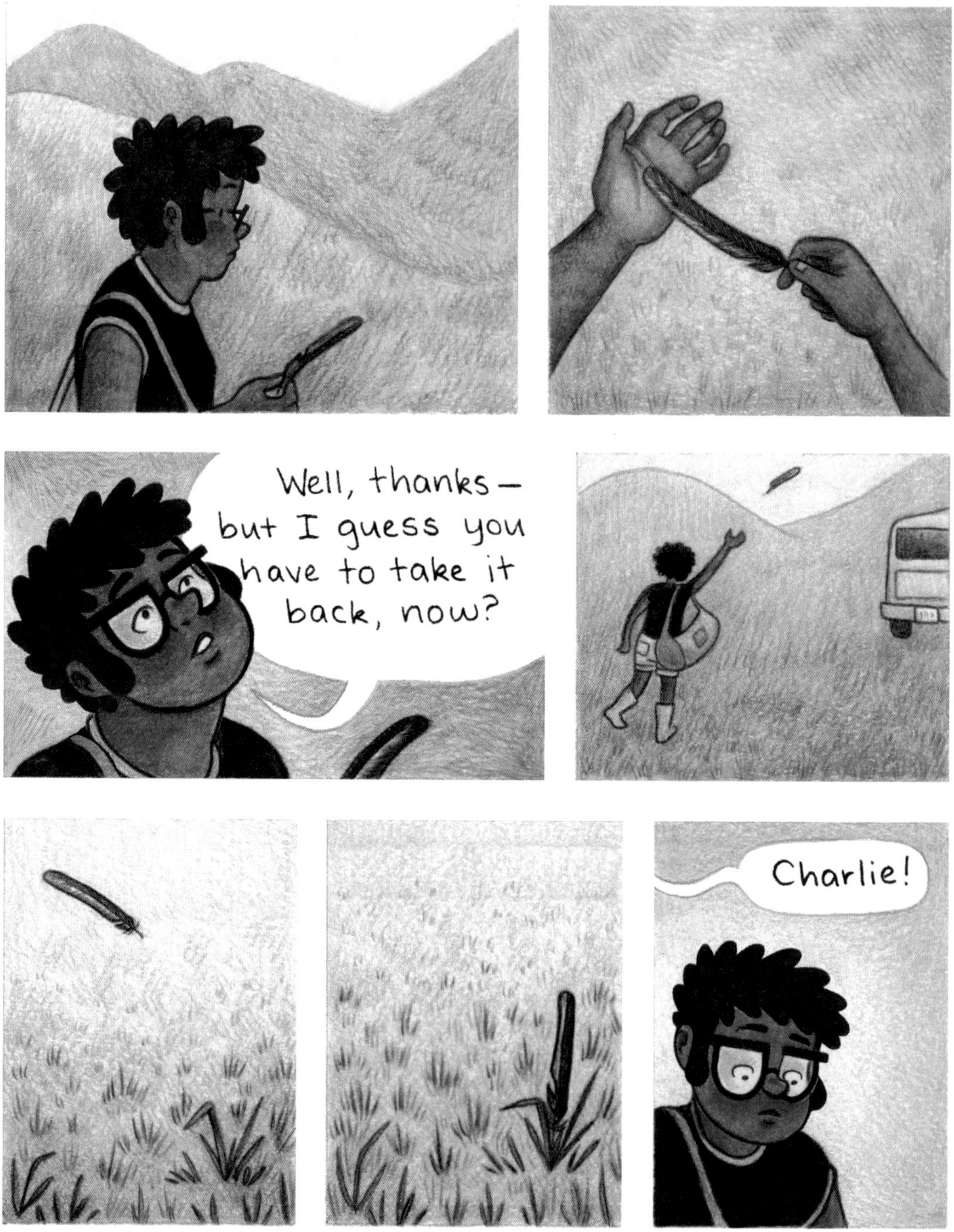
Well, thanks—but I guess you have to take it back, now?
Charlie!

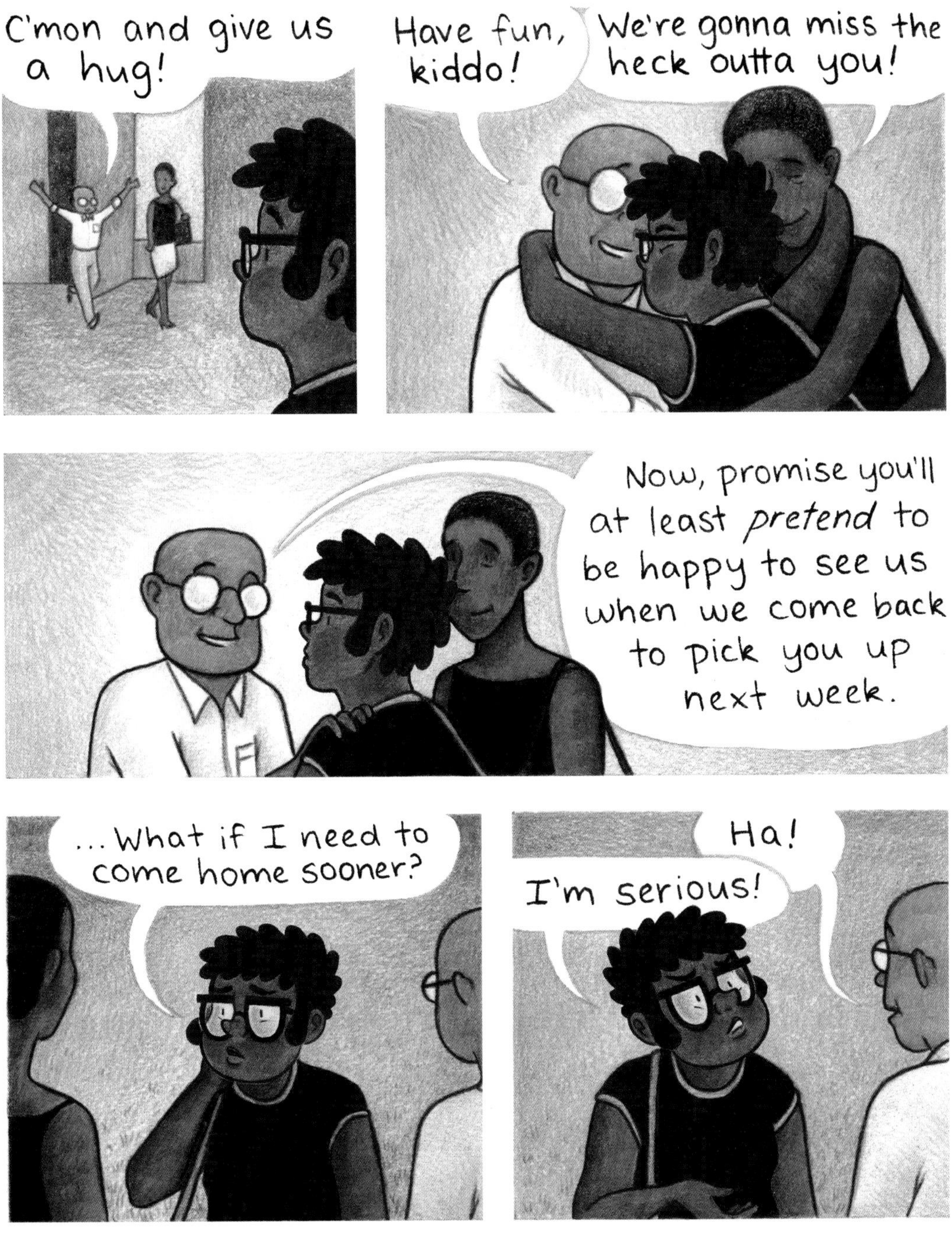

C'mon and give us a hug!
Have fun, kiddo!
We're gonna miss the heck outta you!
Now, promise you'll at least *pretend* to be happy to see us when we come back to pick you up next week.
...What if I need to come home sooner?
Ha!
I'm serious!

I'm just not sure I'm going to fit in here.

Aww, honey, you're just nervous!

But-

I'm sure you'll make plenty of friends!

No, really-

All the other girls are *WHITE!*

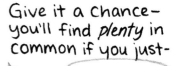

Is *that* what this is all about?

Give it a chance- you'll find *plenty* in common if you just-

All white, Charlie?

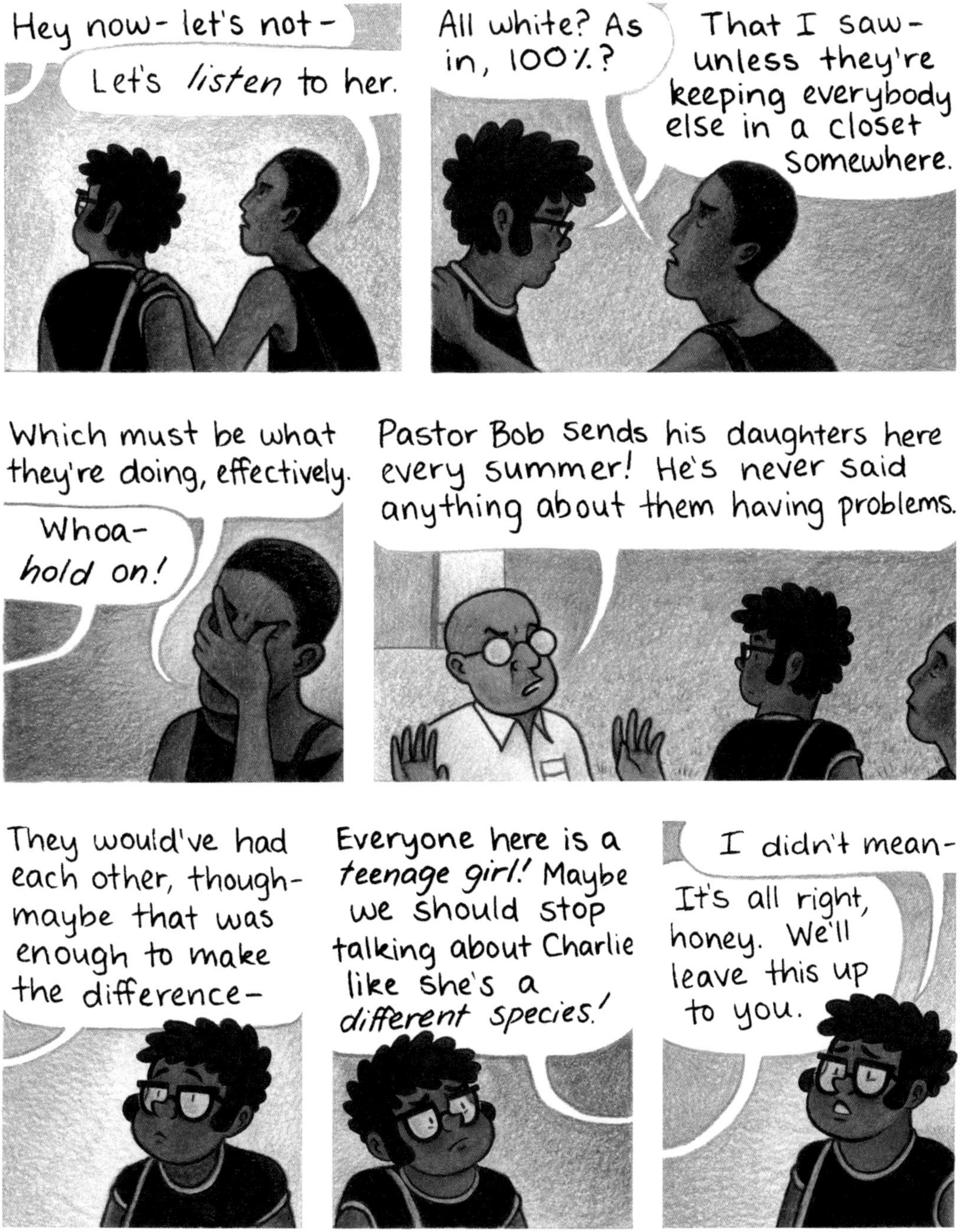
Hey now- let's not-
Let's *listen* to her.
All white? As in, 100%?
That I saw- unless they're keeping everybody else in a closet somewhere.
Which must be what they're doing, effectively.
Whoa- *hold on!*
Pastor Bob sends his daughters here every summer! He's never said anything about them having problems.
They would've had each other, though- maybe that was enough to make the difference-
Everyone here is a *teenage girl!* Maybe we should stop talking about Charlie like she's a *different species!*
I didn't mean-
It's all right, honey. We'll leave this up to you.

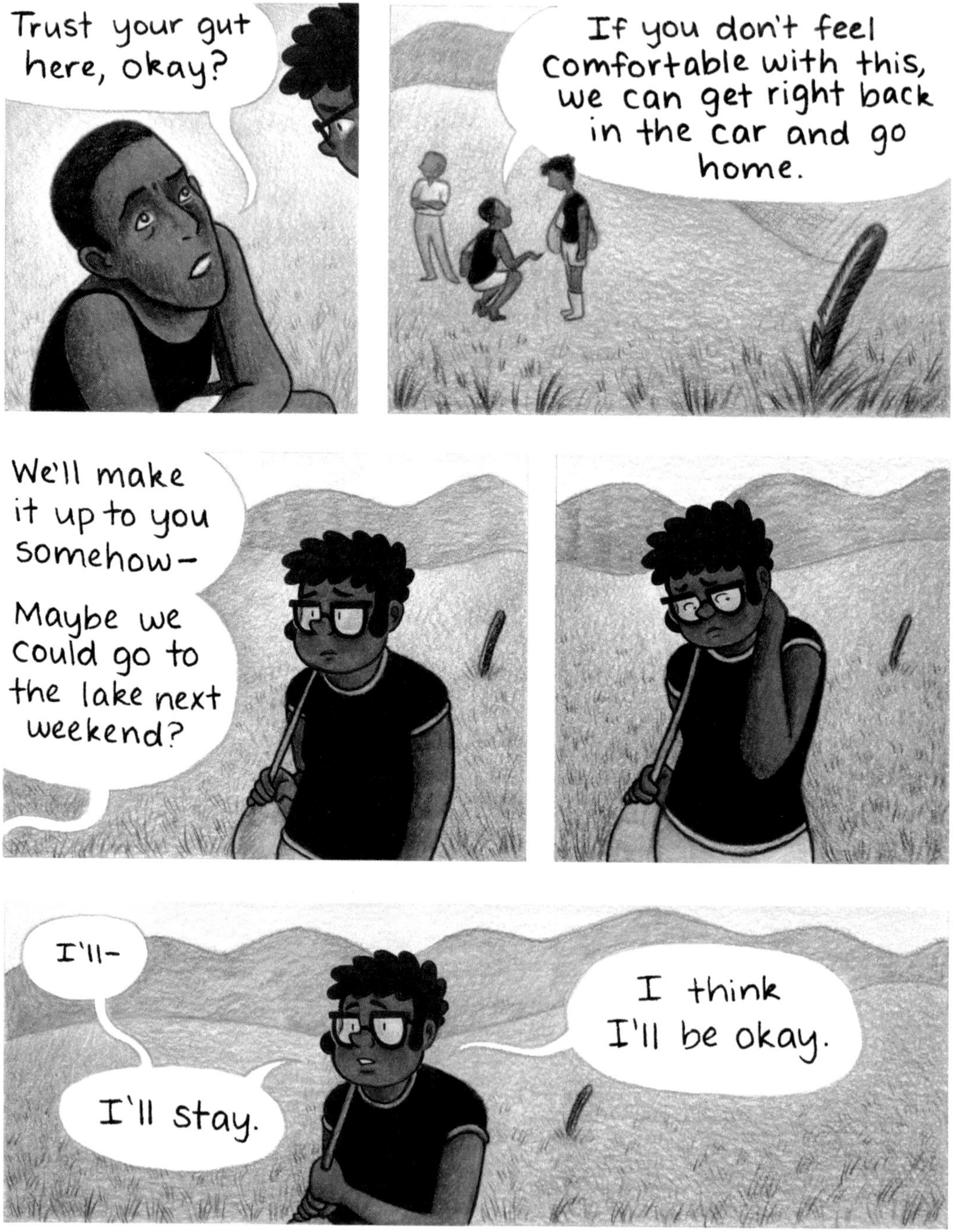
Trust your gut here, okay?
If you don't feel comfortable with this, we can get right back in the car and go home.
We'll make it up to you somehow-
Maybe we could go to the lake next weekend?
I'll-
I'll stay.
I think I'll be okay.

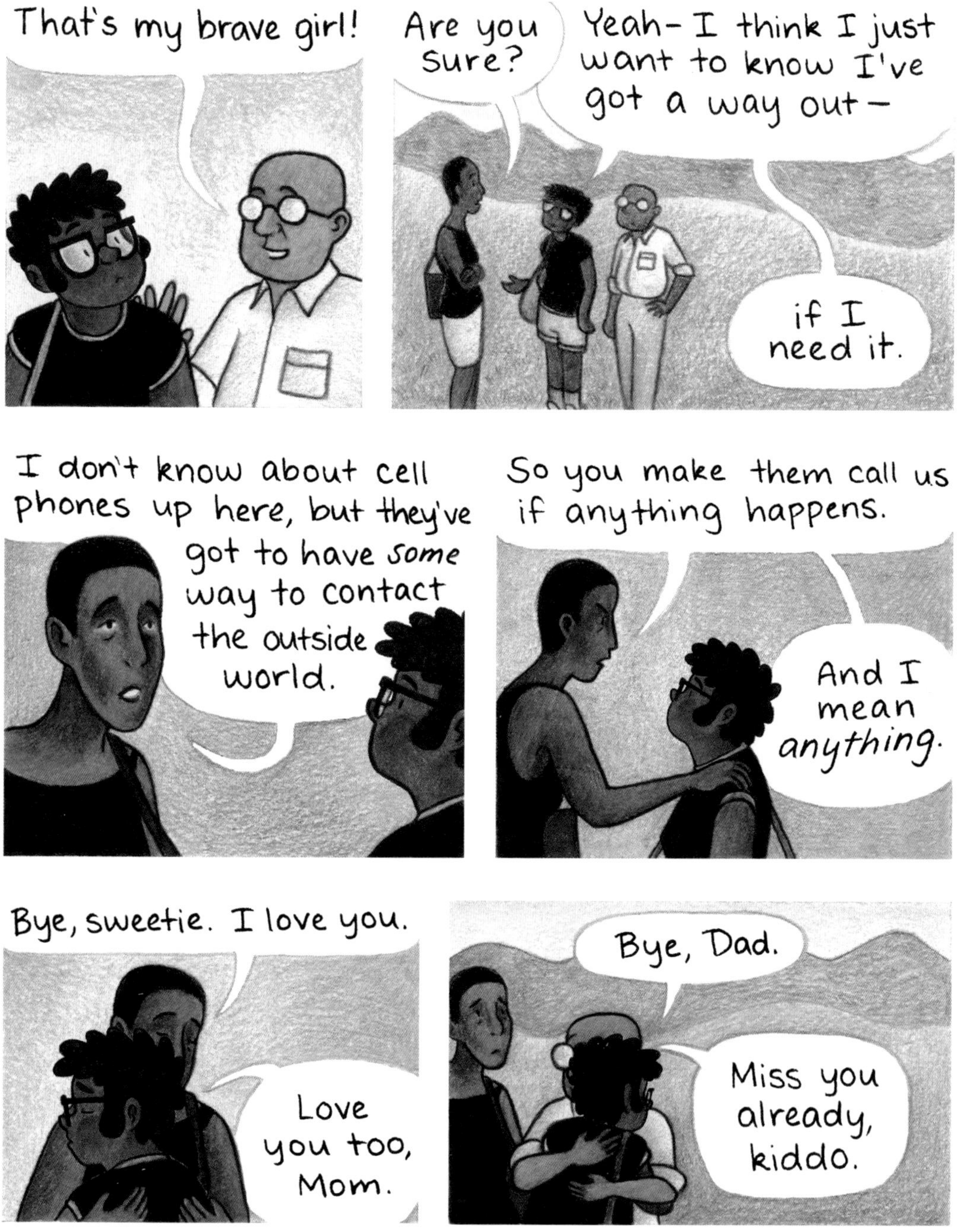
That's my brave girl!
Are you sure?
Yeah- I think I just want to know I've got a way out-
if I need it.
I don't know about cell phones up here, but they've got to have *some* way to contact the outside world.
So you make them call us if anything happens.
And I mean *anything*.
Bye, sweetie. I love you.
Love you too, Mom.
Bye, Dad.
Miss you already, kiddo.

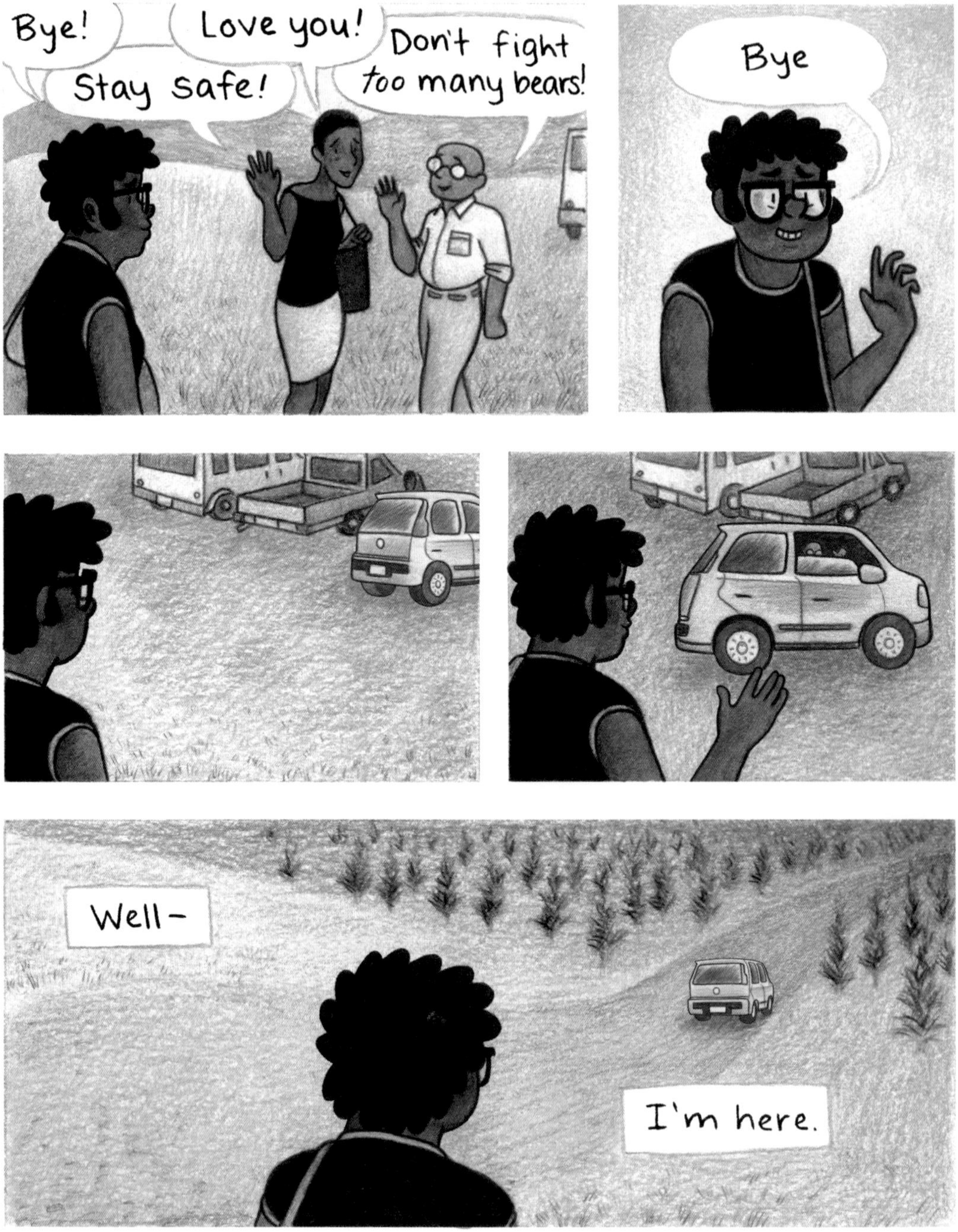
Bye!
Stay safe!
Love you!
Don't fight too many bears!
Bye
Well-
I'm here.

Where I'm supposed to be—

Right?

Where you

asked me to be.

No, this is silly.

There's no way you'd deliberately put me in harm's—

There you are!

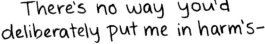

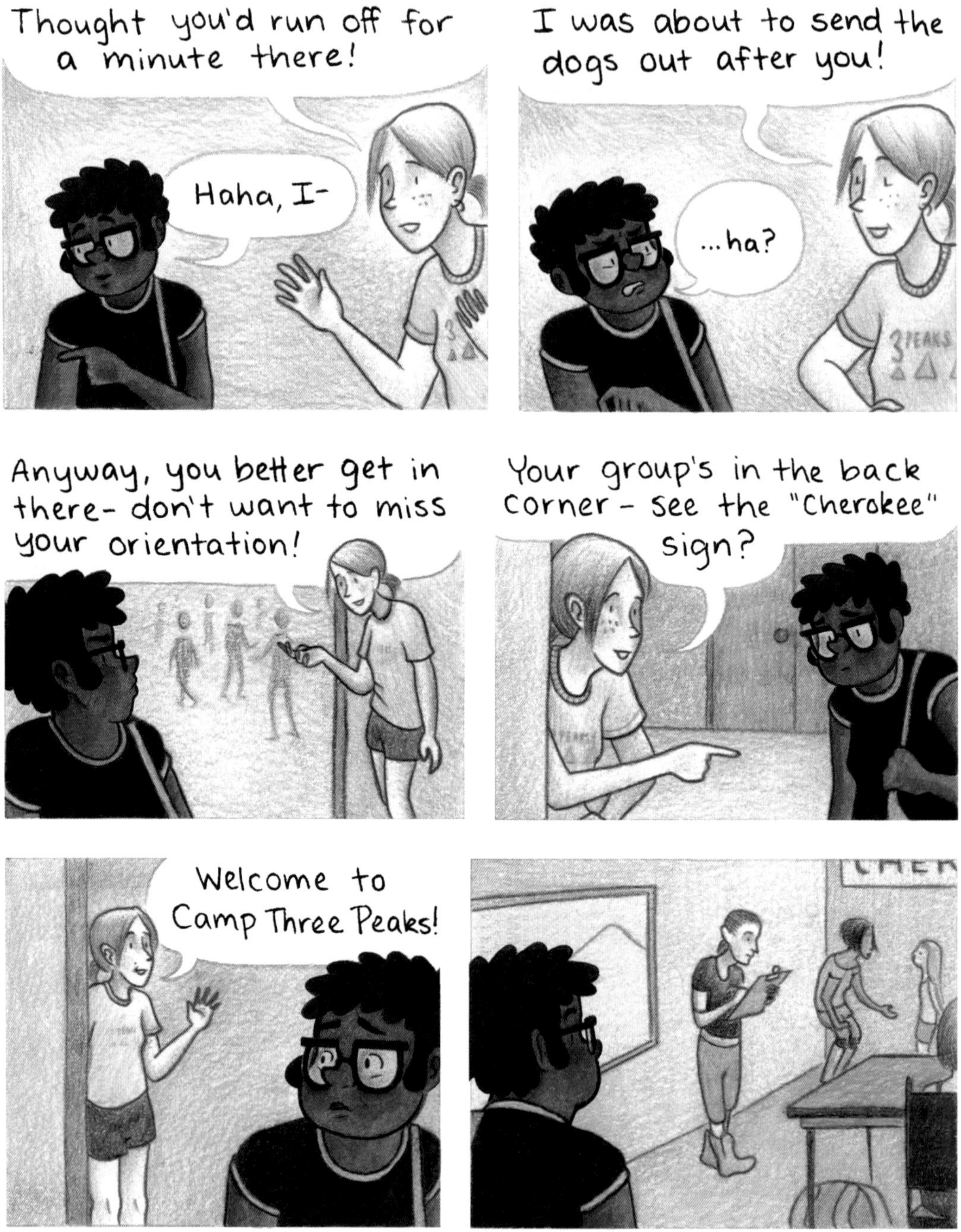
Thought you'd run off for a minute there!
Haha, I-
I was about to send the dogs out after you!
...ha?
Anyway, you better get in there- don't want to miss your orientation!
Your group's in the back corner - see the "Cherokee" sign?
Welcome to Camp Three Peaks!

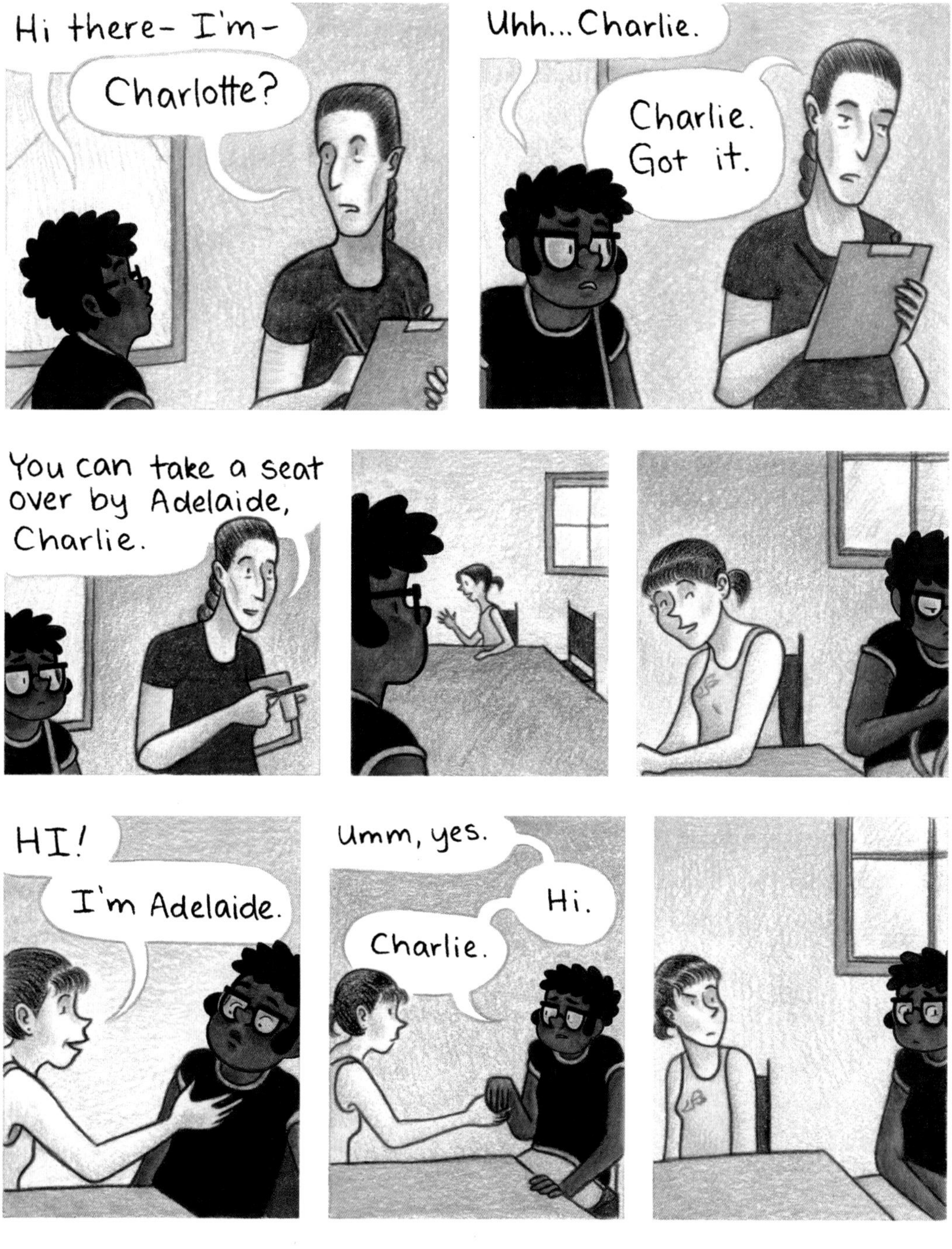
Hi there- I'm-
Charlotte?
Uhh... Charlie.
Charlie. Got it.
You can take a seat over by Adelaide, Charlie.
HI!
I'm Adelaide.
Umm, yes.
Hi.
Charlie.

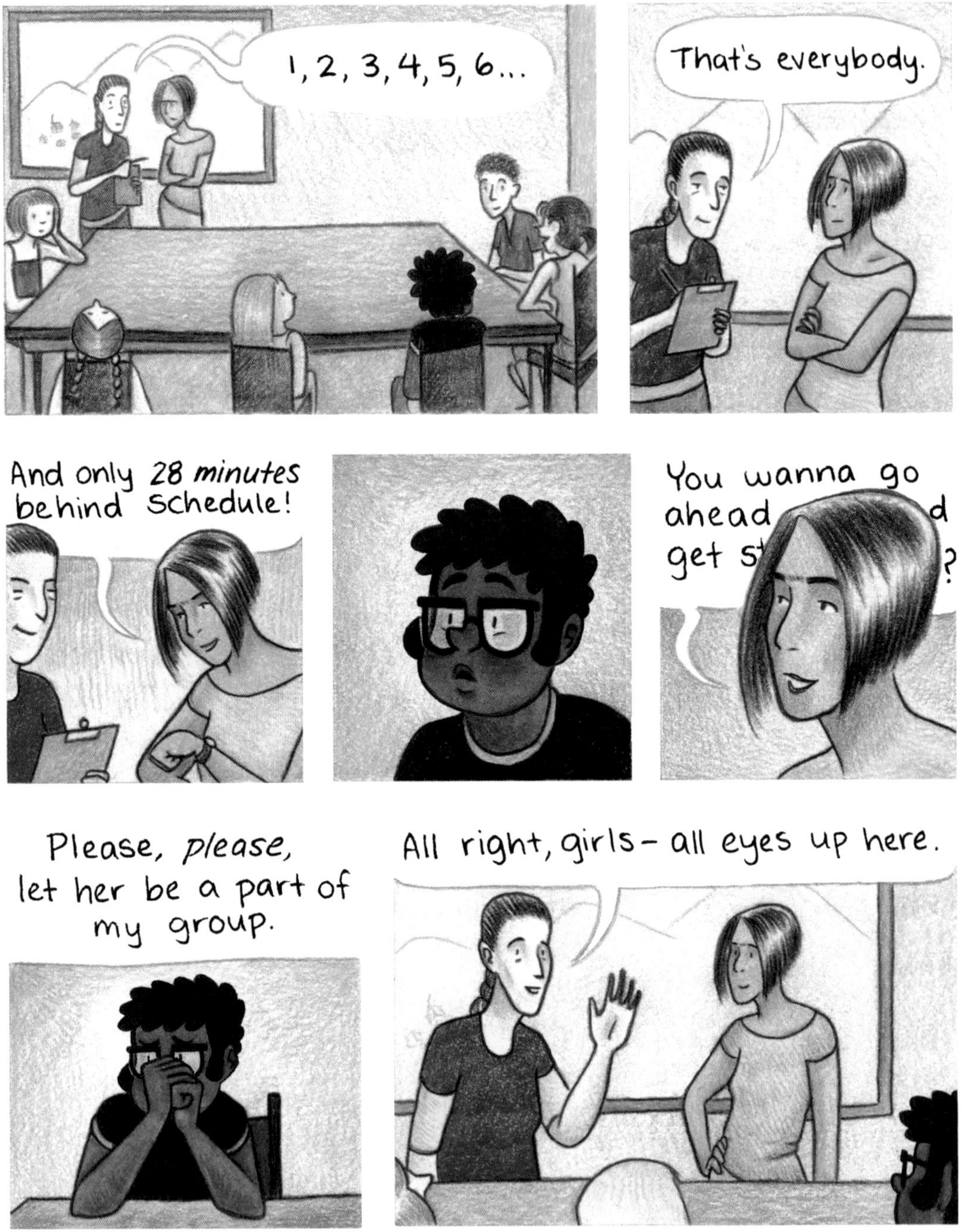
1, 2, 3, 4, 5, 6...
That's everybody.
And only *28 minutes* behind schedule!
You wanna go ahead
Please, *please,* let her be a part of my group.
All right, girls– all eyes up here.

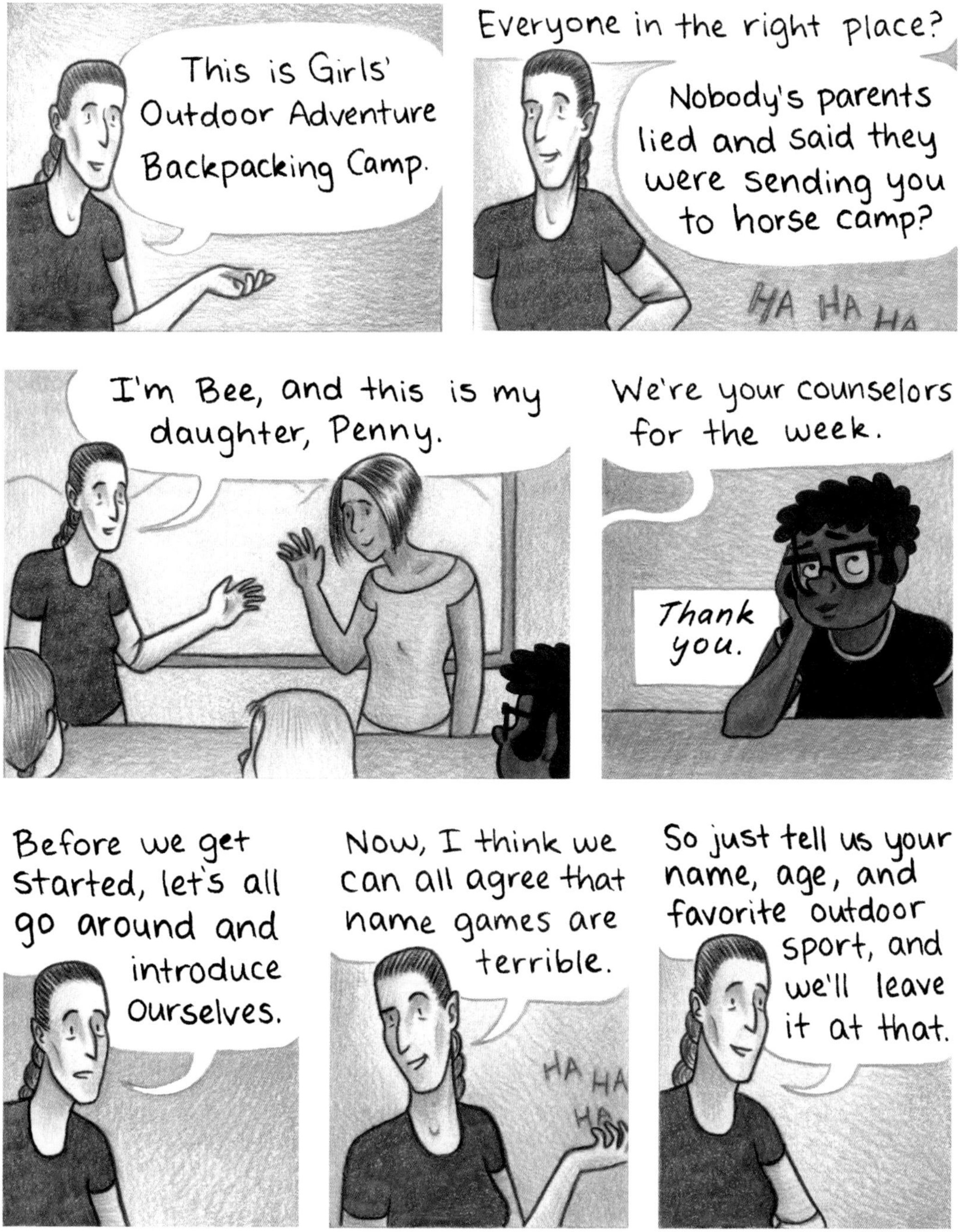

This is Girls' Outdoor Adventure Backpacking Camp.
Everyone in the right place?
Nobody's parents lied and said they were sending you to horse camp?
HA HA HA
I'm Bee, and this is my daughter, Penny.
We're your counselors for the week.
Thank you.
Before we get started, let's all go around and introduce ourselves.
Now, I think we can all agree that name games are terrible.
HA HA HA
So just tell us your name, age, and favorite outdoor sport, and we'll leave it at that.

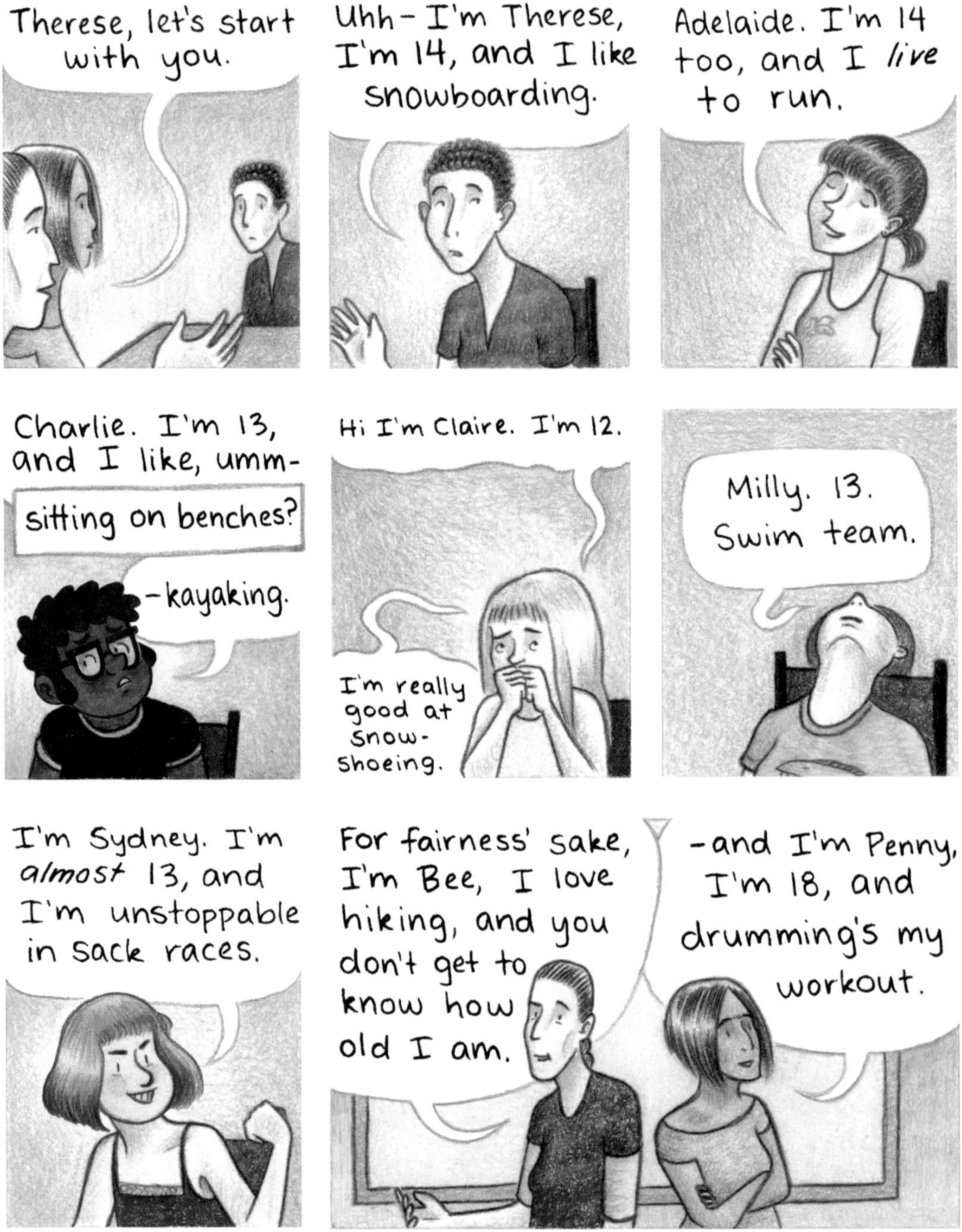

Therese, let's start with you.
Uhh- I'm Therese, I'm 14, and I like snowboarding.
Adelaide. I'm 14 too, and I *live* to run.
Charlie. I'm 13, and I like, umm-
sitting on benches?
-kayaking.
Hi I'm Claire. I'm 12.
I'm really good at snow-shoeing.
Milly. 13. Swim team.
I'm Sydney. I'm *almost* 13, and I'm unstoppable in sack races.
For fairness' sake, I'm Bee, I love hiking, and you don't get to know how old I am.
-and I'm Penny, I'm 18, and drumming's my workout.

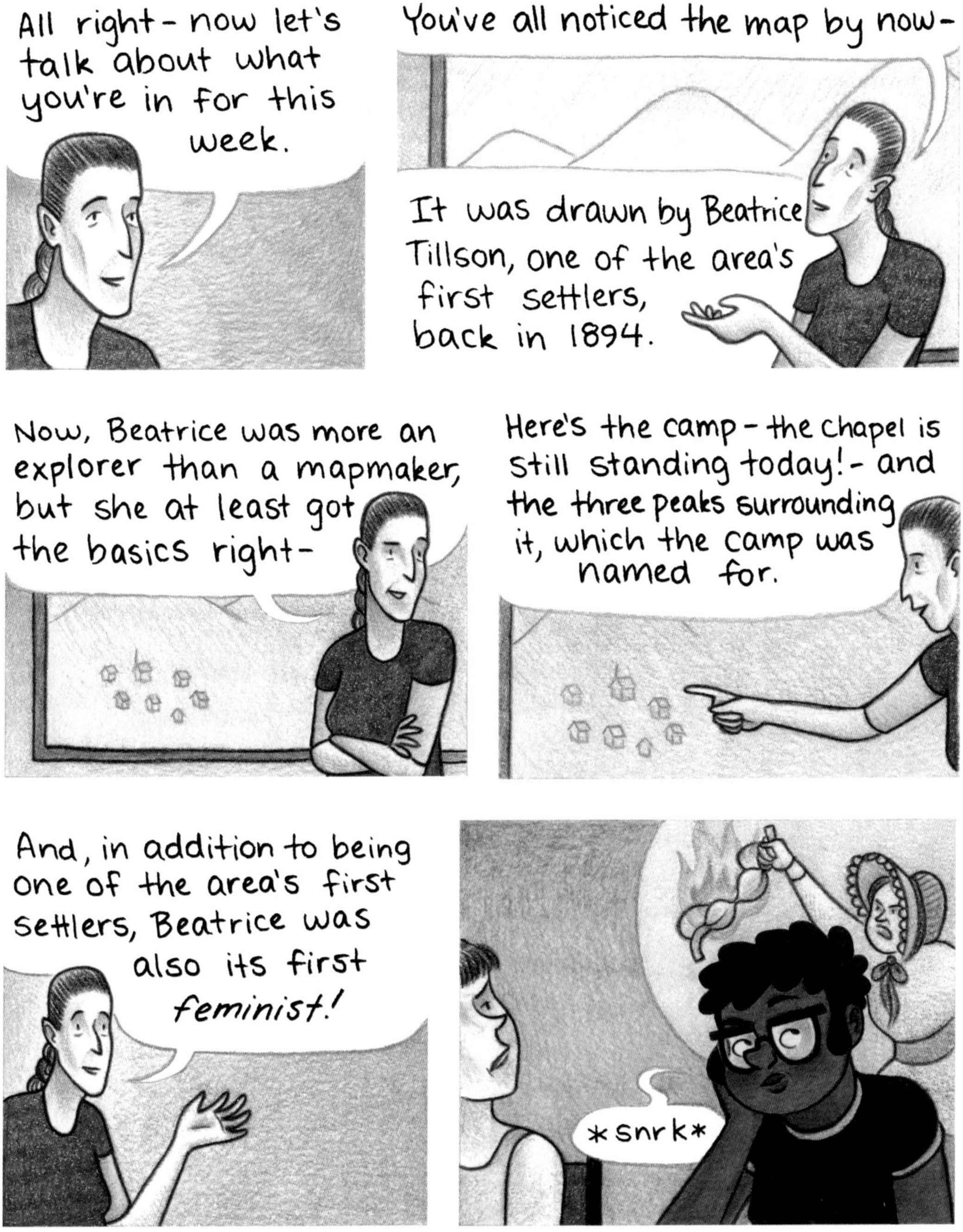
All right - now let's talk about what you're in for this week.
You've all noticed the map by now-
It was drawn by Beatrice Tillson, one of the area's first settlers, back in 1894.
Now, Beatrice was more an explorer than a mapmaker, but she at least got the basics right-
Here's the camp - the chapel is still standing today! - and the three peaks surrounding it, which the camp was named for.
And, in addition to being one of the area's first settlers, Beatrice was also its first *feminist*!
snrk

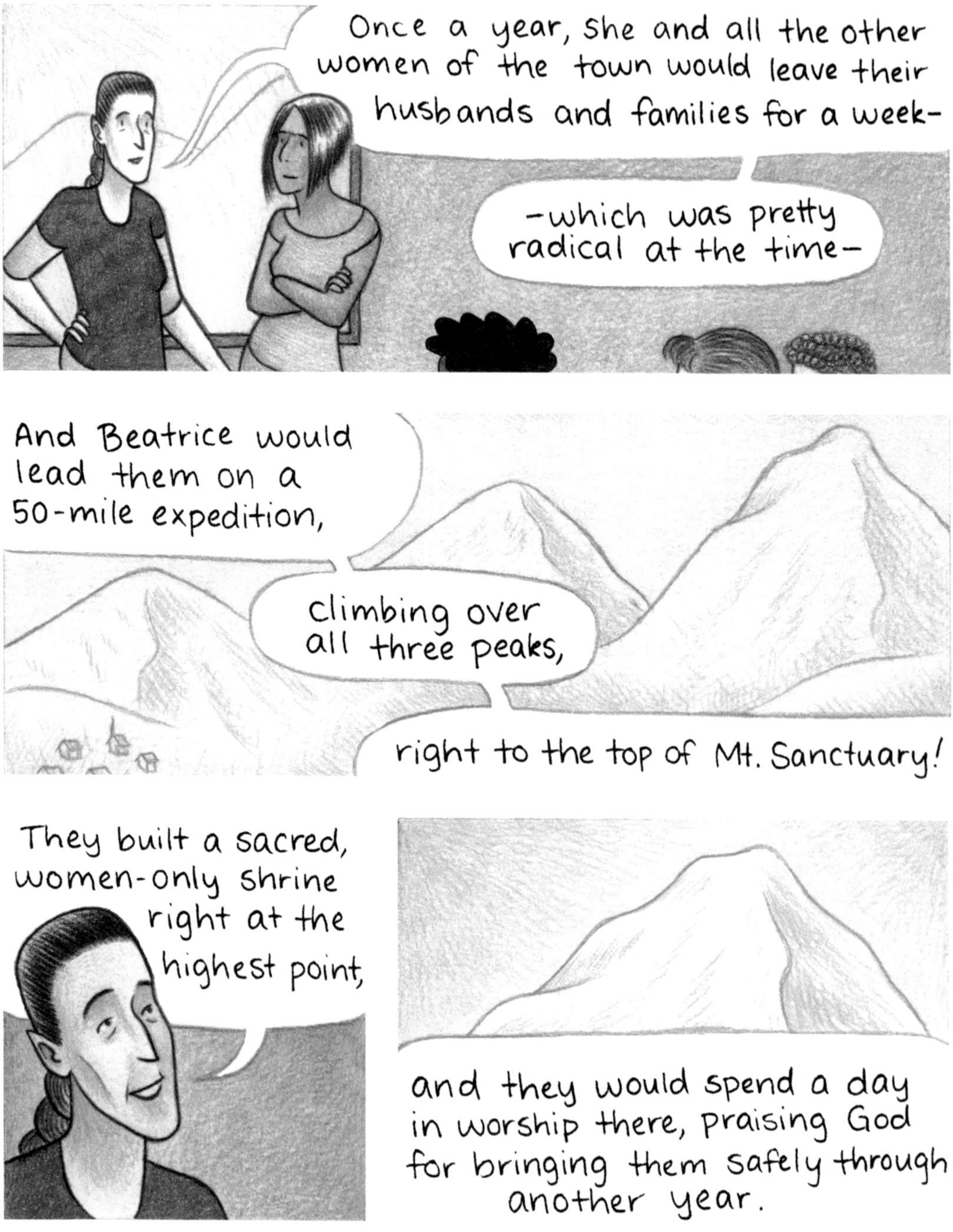

Once a year, she and all the other women of the town would leave their husbands and families for a week-
-which was pretty radical at the time-
And Beatrice would lead them on a 50-mile expedition,
climbing over all three peaks,
right to the top of Mt. Sanctuary!
They built a sacred, women-only shrine right at the highest point,
and they would spend a day in worship there, praising God for bringing them safely through another year.

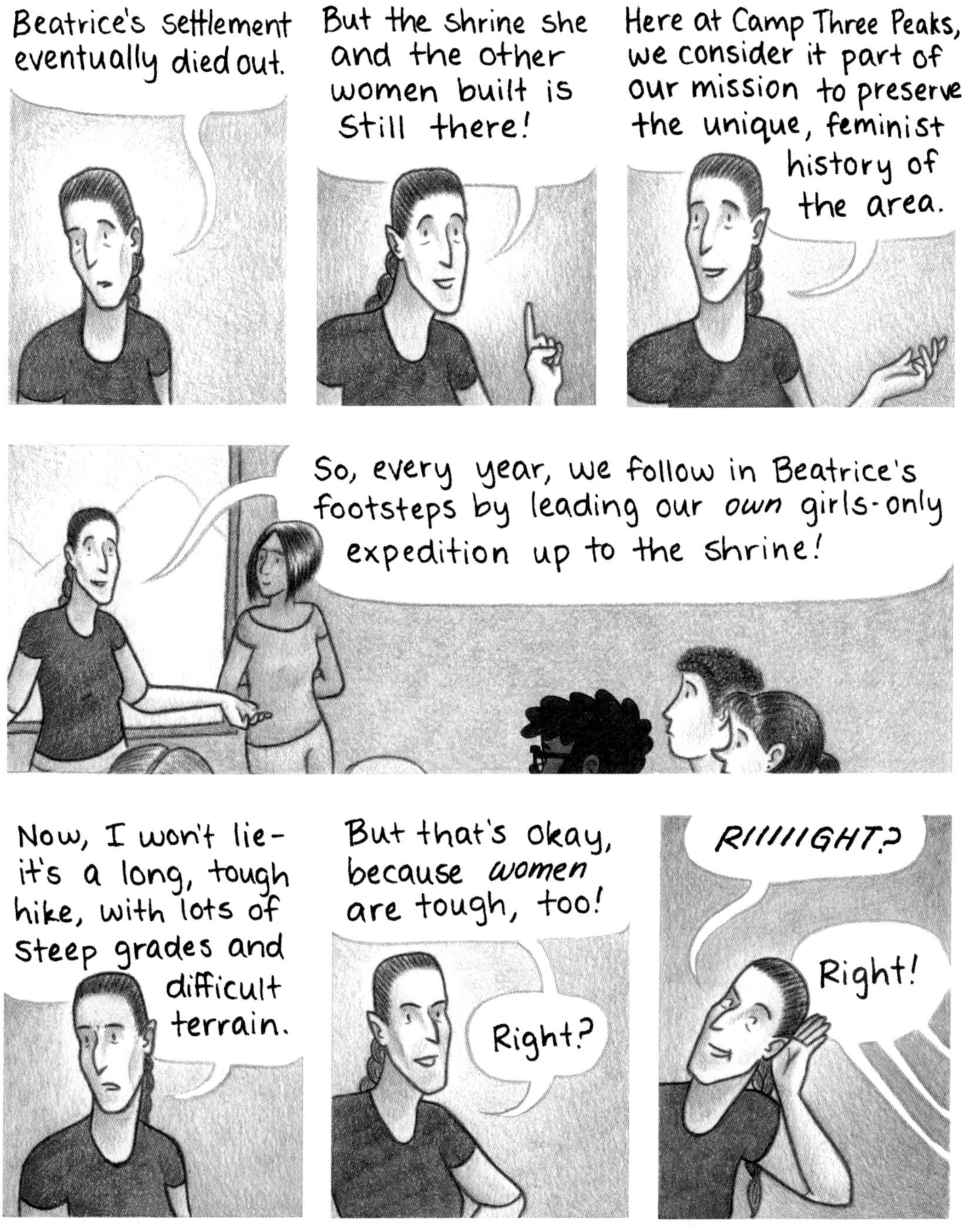
Beatrice's settlement eventually died out.
But the shrine she and the other women built is still there!
Here at Camp Three Peaks, we consider it part of our mission to preserve the unique, feminist history of the area.
So, every year, we follow in Beatrice's footsteps by leading our *own* girls-only expedition up to the shrine!
Now, I won't lie- it's a long, tough hike, with lots of steep grades and difficult terrain.
But that's okay, because *women* are tough, too!
Right?
RIIIIIGHT?
Right!

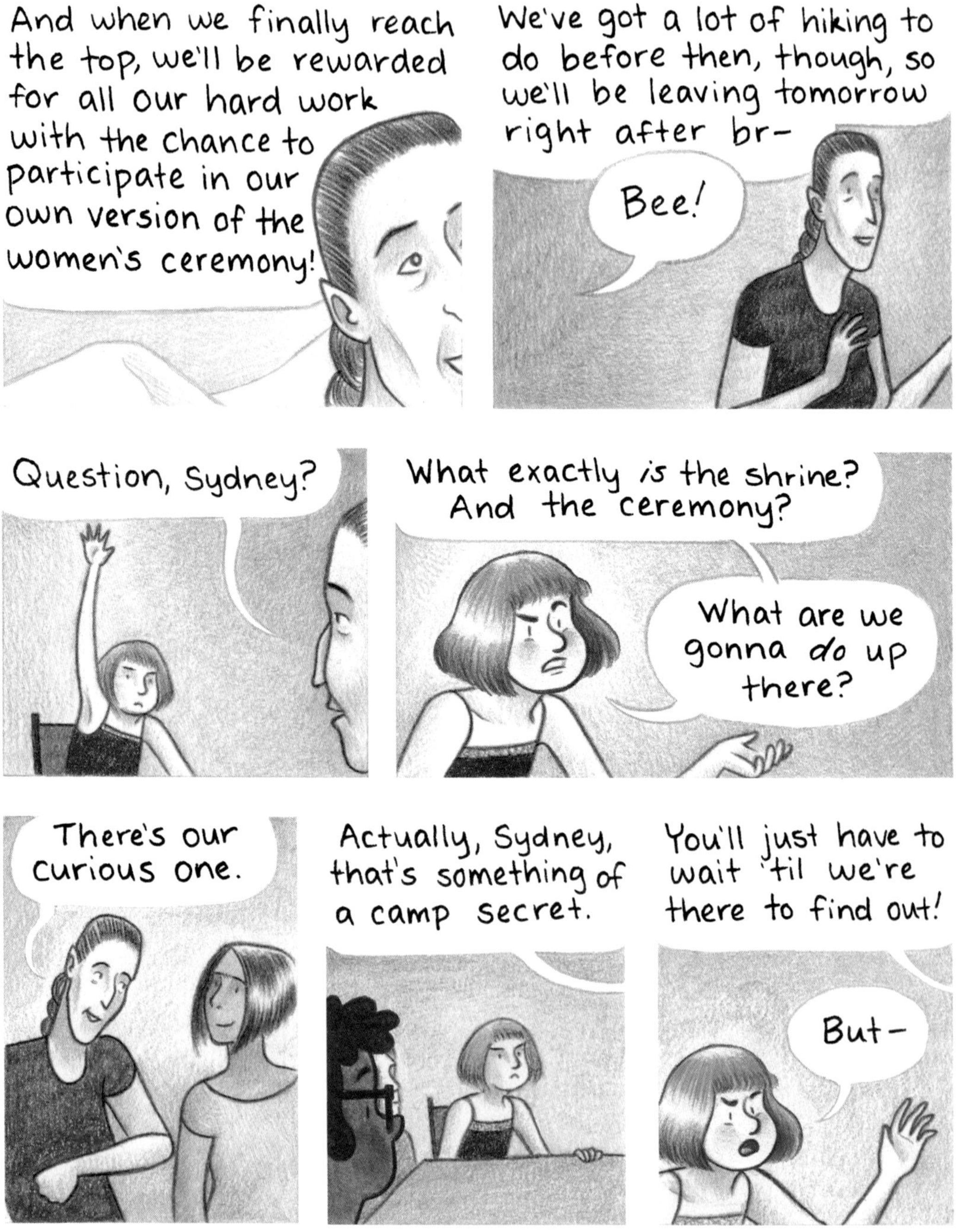
And when we finally reach the top, we'll be rewarded for all our hard work with the chance to participate in our own version of the women's ceremony!
We've got a lot of hiking to do before then, though, so we'll be leaving tomorrow right after br–
Bee!
Question, Sydney?
What exactly *is* the shrine? And the ceremony?
What are we gonna *do* up there?
There's our curious one.
Actually, Sydney, that's something of a camp secret.
You'll just have to wait 'til we're there to find out!
But–

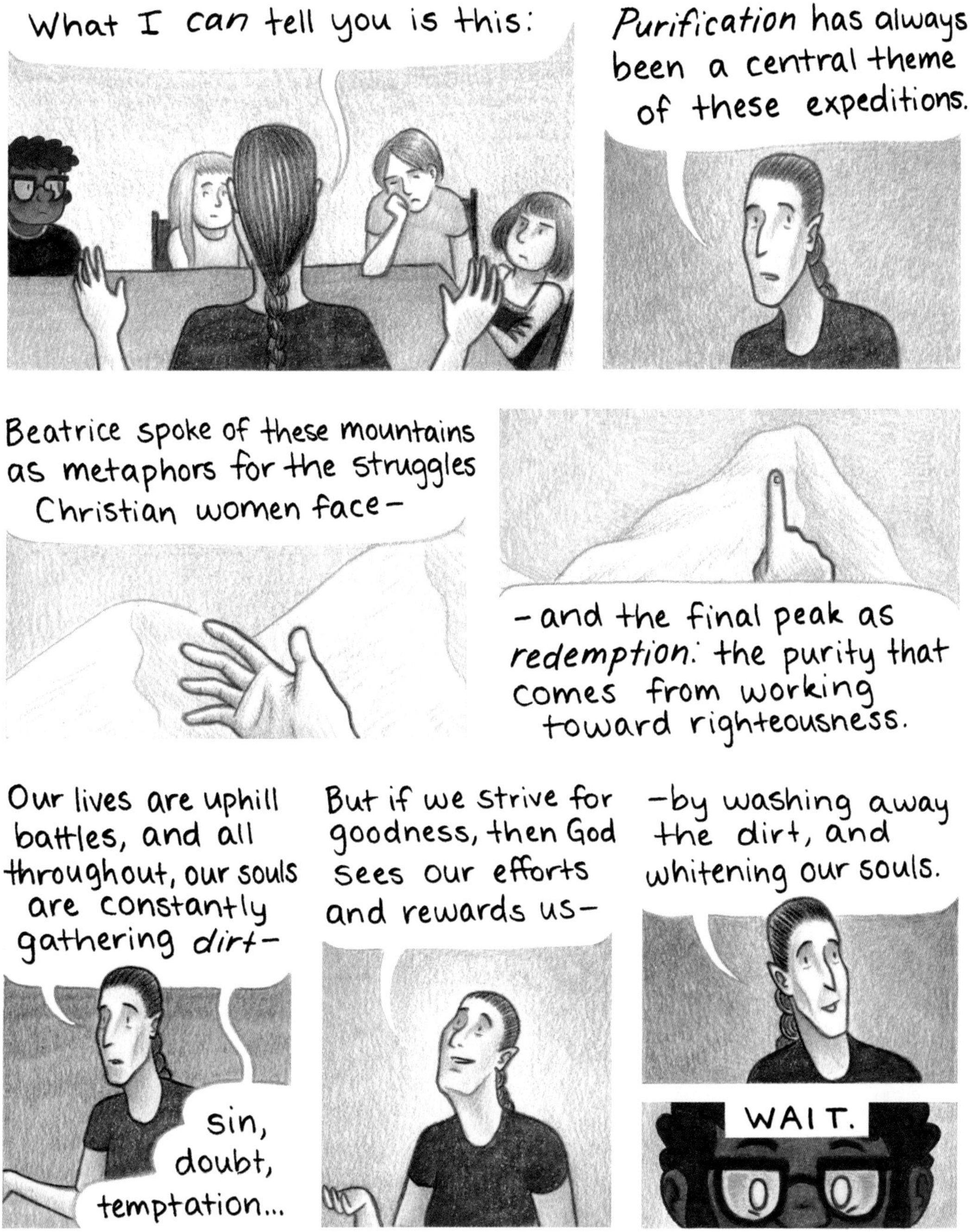
What I *can* tell you is this:
Purification has always been a central theme of these expeditions.
Beatrice spoke of these mountains as metaphors for the struggles Christian women face-
-and the final peak as *redemption*: the purity that comes from working toward righteousness.
Our lives are uphill battles, and all throughout, our souls are constantly gathering *dirt*-
sin, doubt, temptation...
But if we strive for goodness, then God sees our efforts and rewards us-
-by washing away the dirt, and whitening our souls.
WAIT.

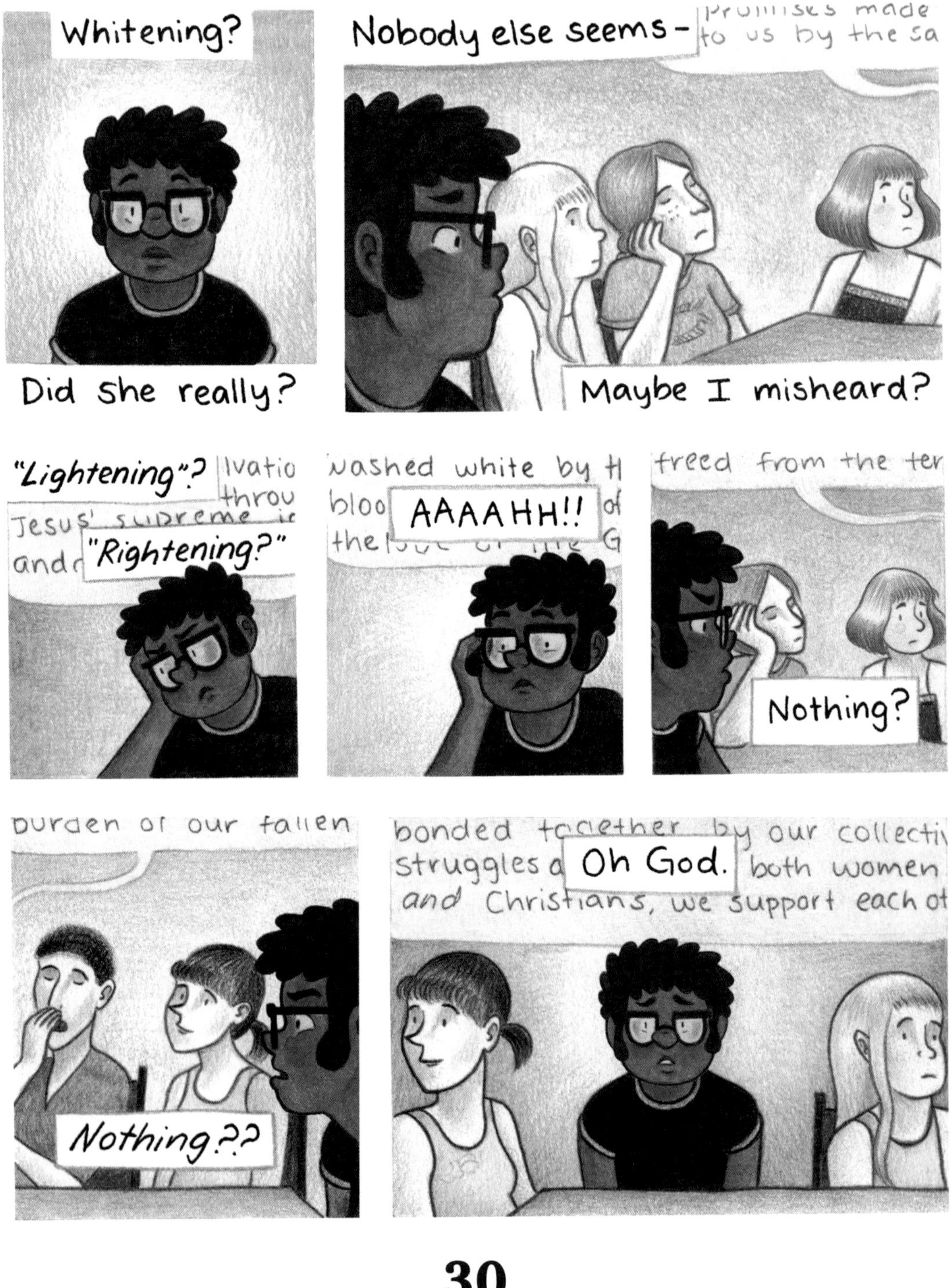

Whitening?
Did she really?
Nobody else seems-
to us by the sa
Maybe I misheard?
"Lightening"?
Jesus' supreme
"Rightening?"
washed white by th
AAAAHH!!
freed from the ter
Nothing?
burden of our fallen
Nothing??
bonded together by our collecti
struggles a
Oh God.
both women
and Christians, we support each ot

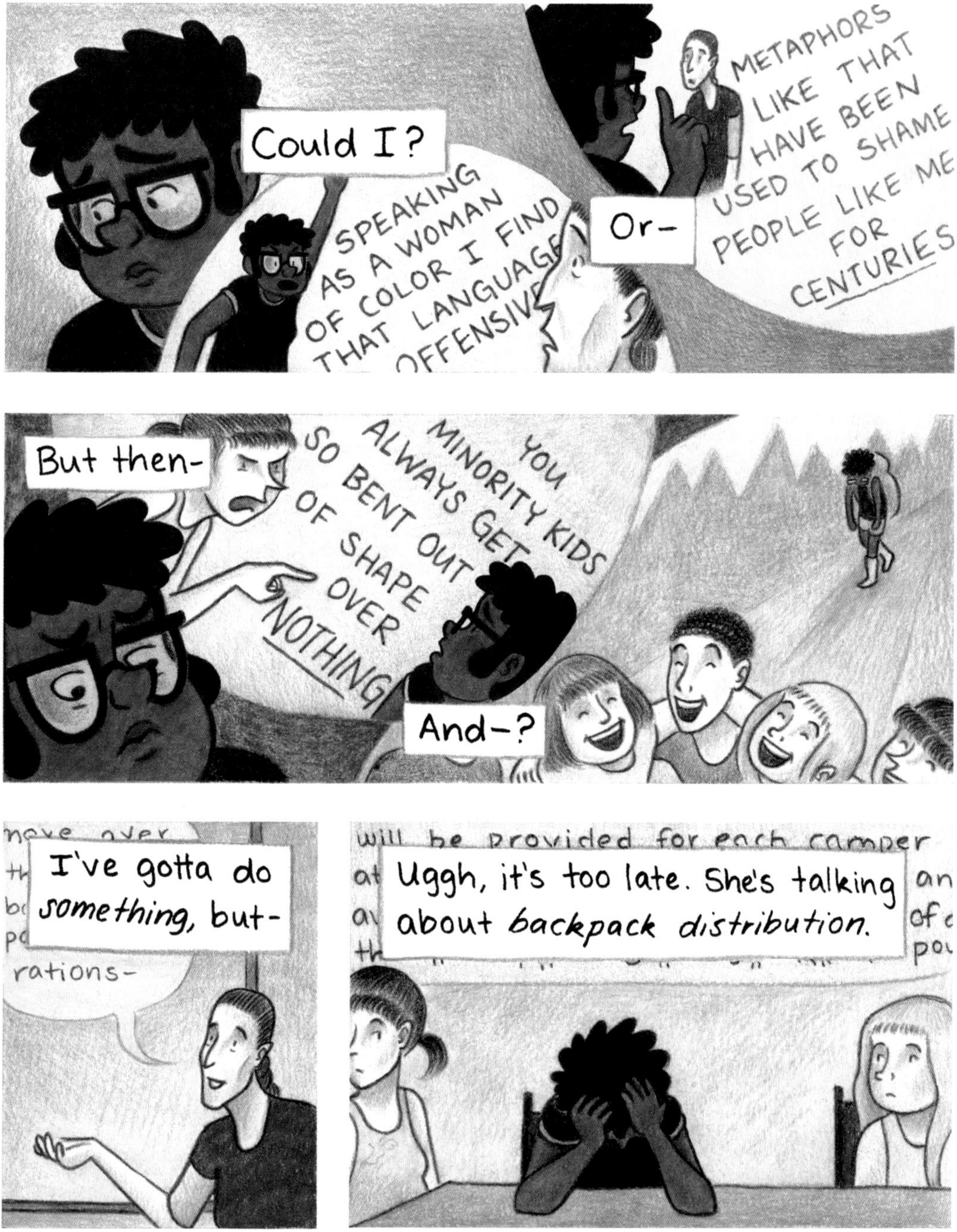
Could I?
SPEAKING AS A WOMAN OF COLOR I FIND THAT LANGUAGE OFFENSIVE
Or-
METAPHORS LIKE THAT HAVE BEEN USED TO SHAME PEOPLE LIKE ME FOR CENTURIES
But then-
YOU MINORITY KIDS ALWAYS GET SO BENT OUT OF SHAPE OVER NOTHING
And-?
I've gotta do *something*, but-
rations-
will be provided for each camper
Uggh, it's too late. She's talking about *backpack distribution*.

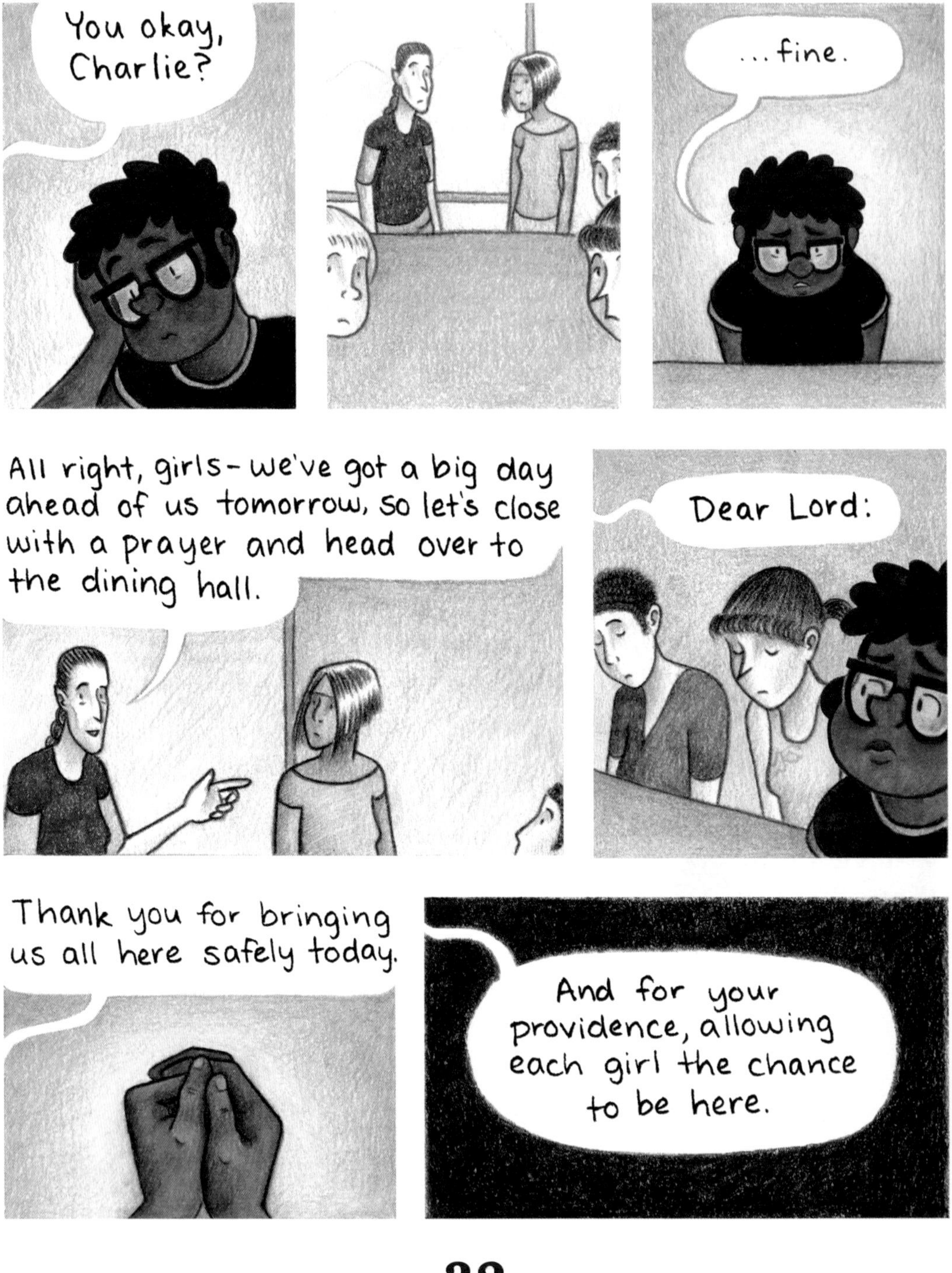
You okay, Charlie?
...fine.
All right, girls- we've got a big day ahead of us tomorrow, so let's close with a prayer and head over to the dining hall.
Dear Lord:
Thank you for bringing us all here safely today.
And for your providence, allowing each girl the chance to be here.

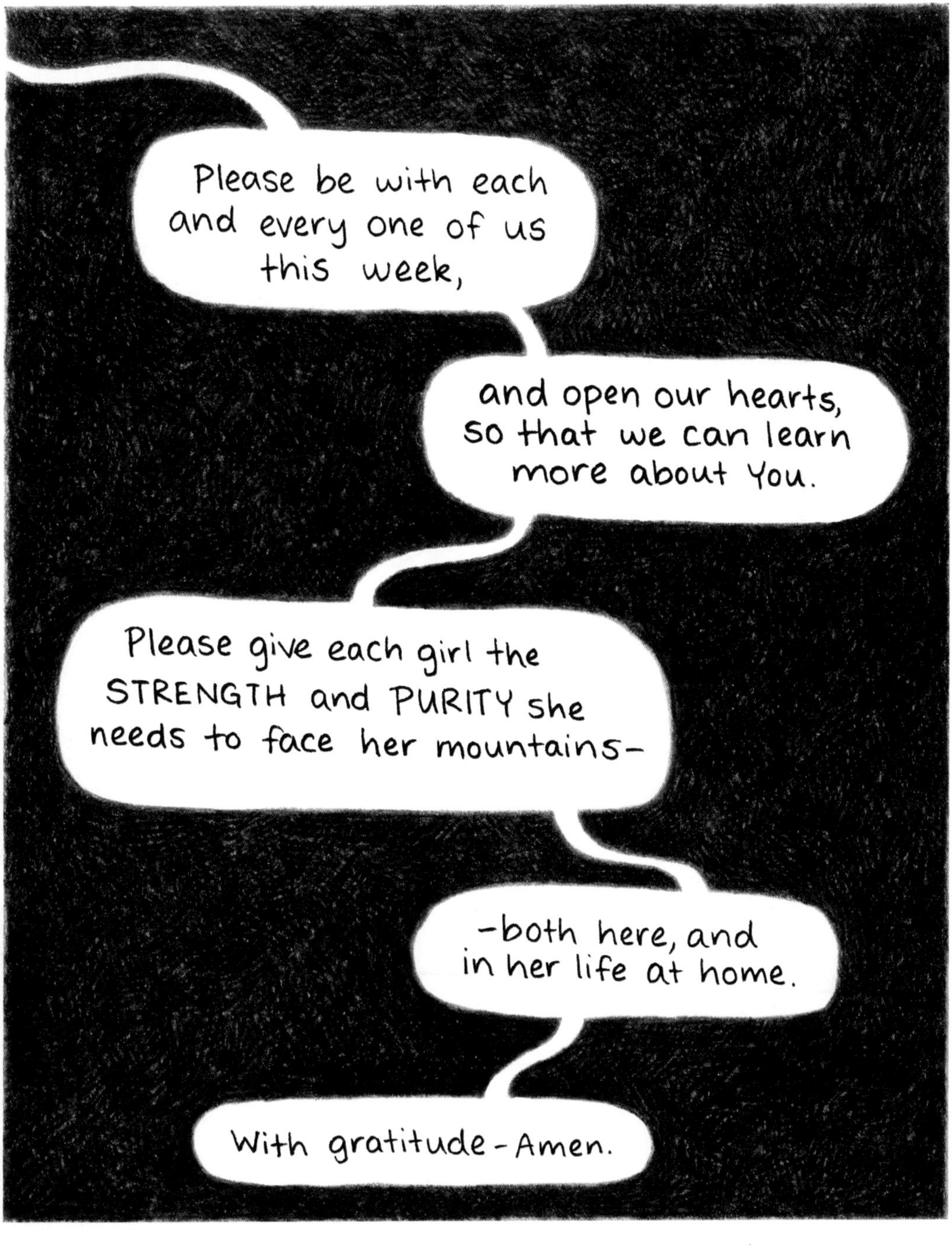
Please be with each and every one of us this week,
and open our hearts, so that we can learn more about You.
Please give each girl the STRENGTH and PURITY she needs to face her mountains-
-both here, and in her life at home.
With gratitude-Amen.

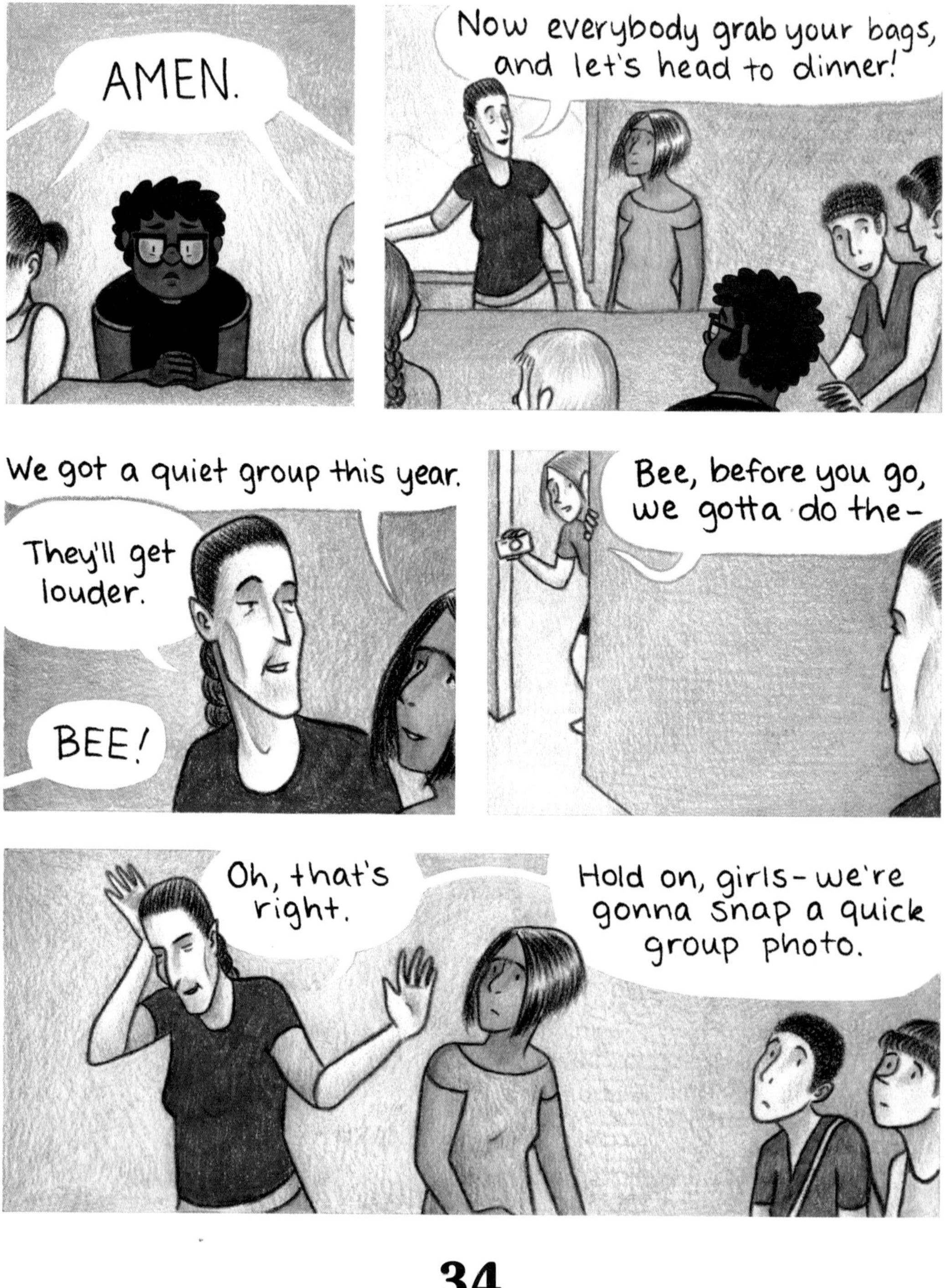
AMEN.
Now everybody grab your bags, and let's head to dinner!
We got a quiet group this year.
They'll get louder.
BEE!
Bee, before you go, we gotta do the-
Oh, that's right.
Hold on, girls- we're gonna snap a quick group photo.

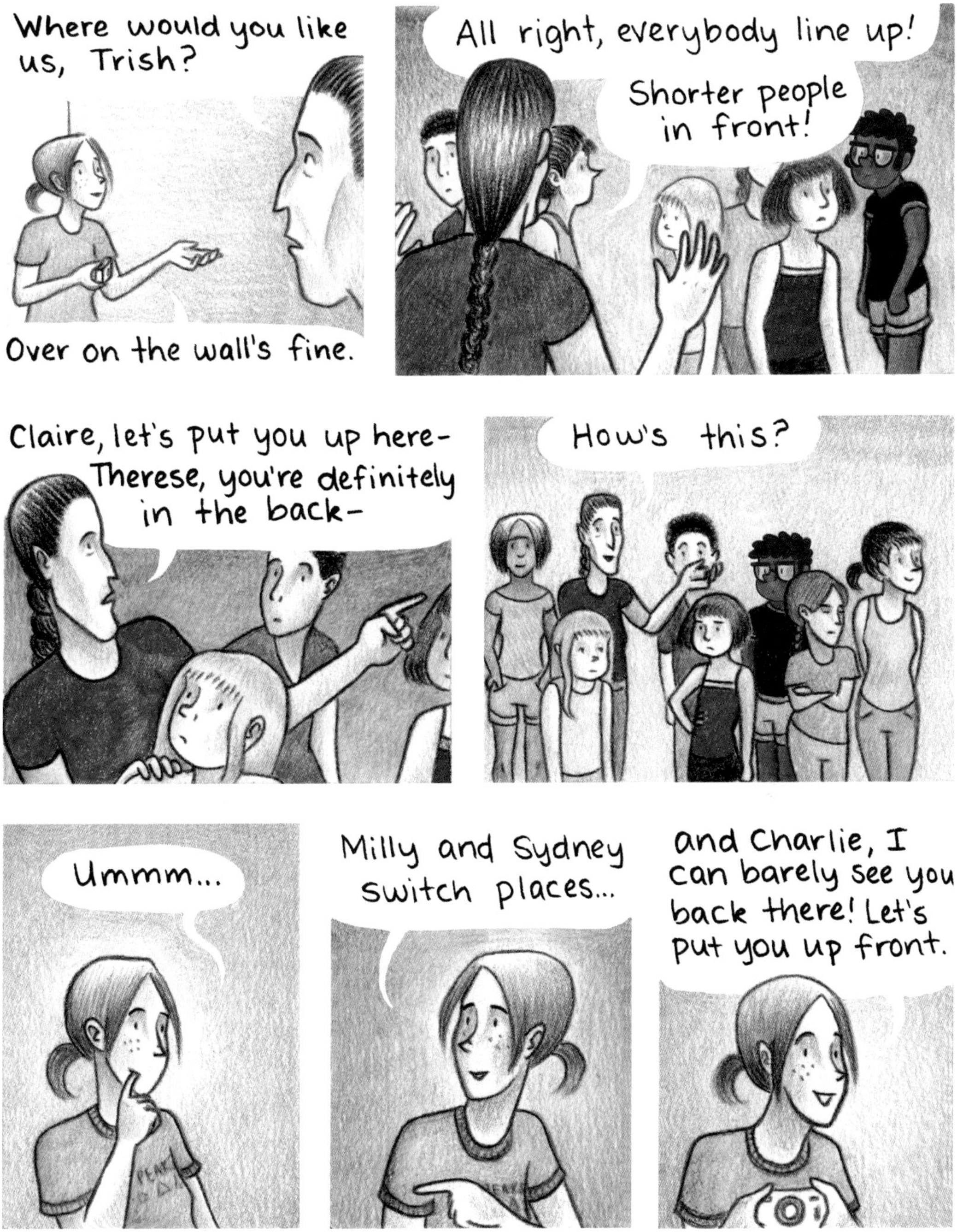
Where would you like us, Trish?
Over on the wall's fine.
All right, everybody line up!
Shorter people in front!
Claire, let's put you up here-
Therese, you're definitely in the back-
How's this?
Ummm...
Milly and Sydney switch places...
and Charlie, I can barely see you back there! Let's put you up front.

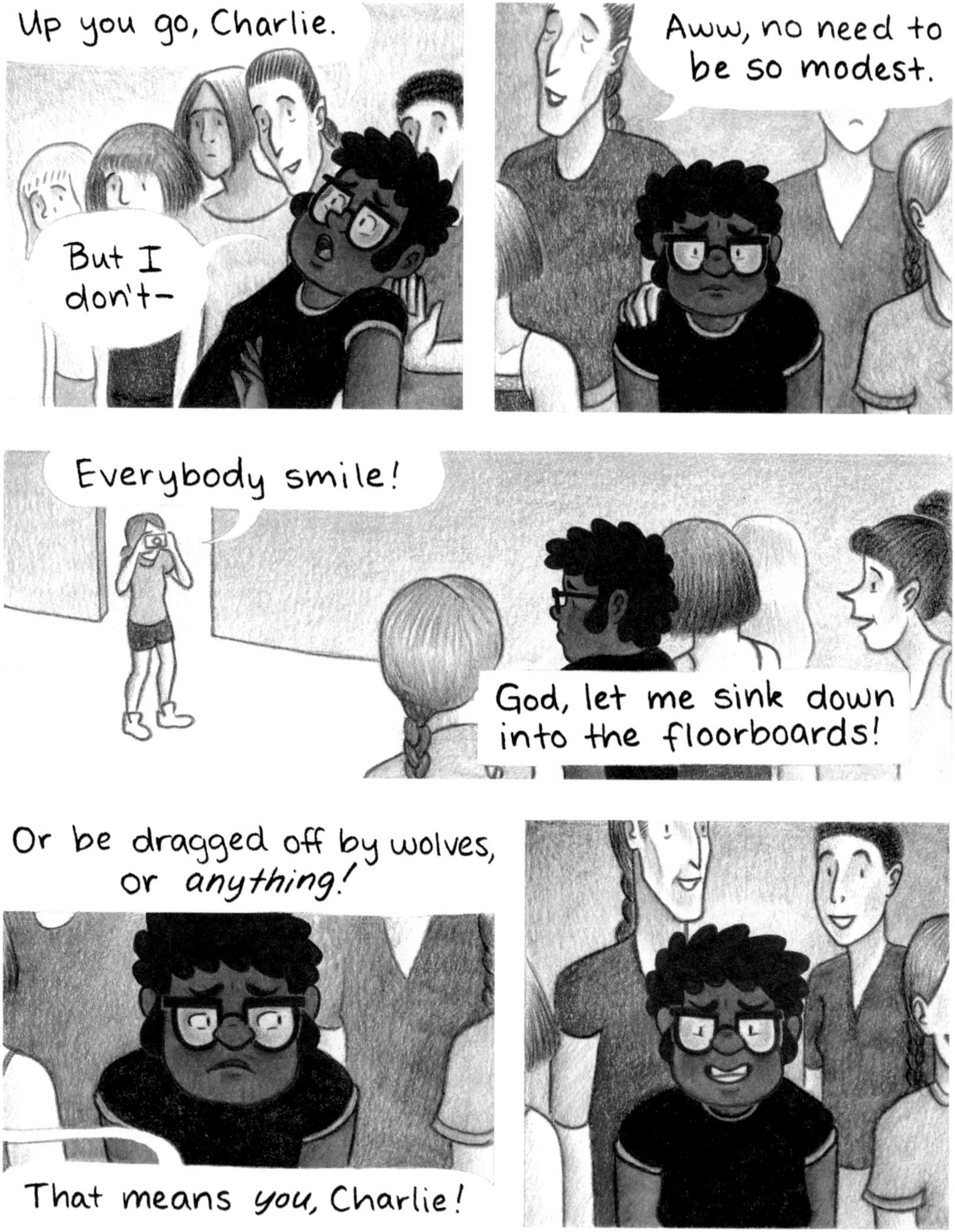
Up you go, Charlie.
But I don't-
Aww, no need to be so modest.
Everybody smile!
God, let me sink down into the floorboards!
Or be dragged off by wolves, or *anything*!
That means *you*, Charlie!

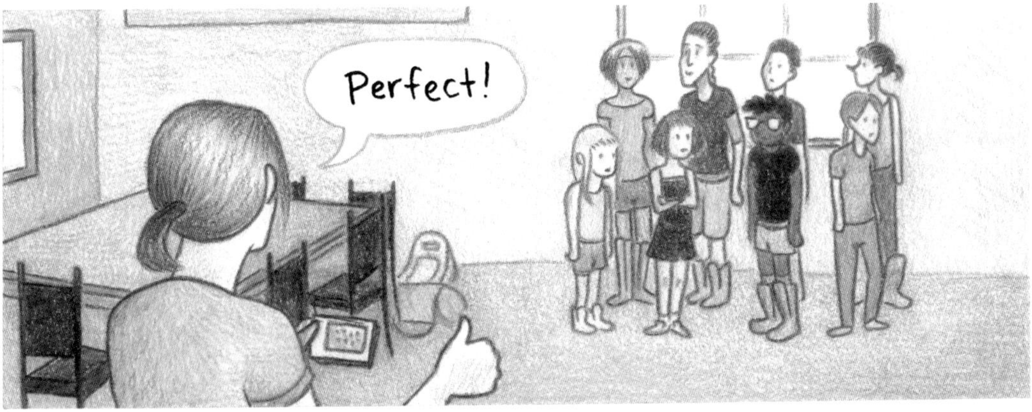
Perfect!

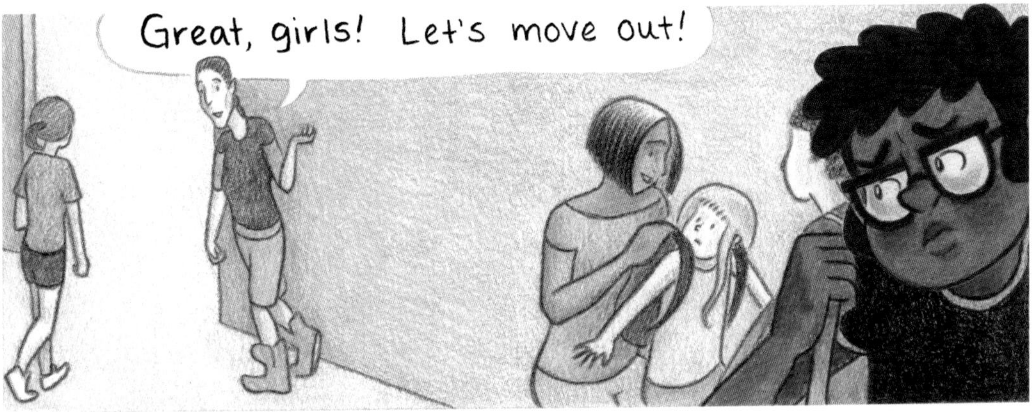
Great, girls! Let's move out!

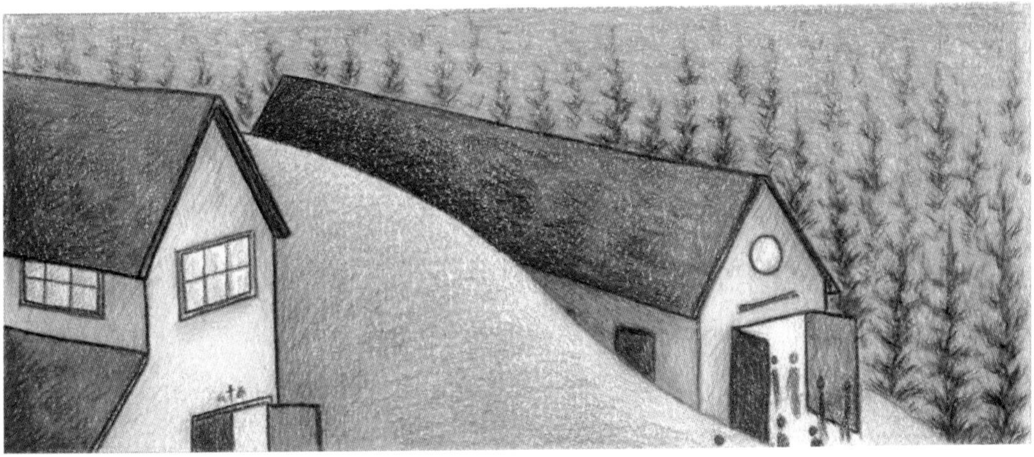

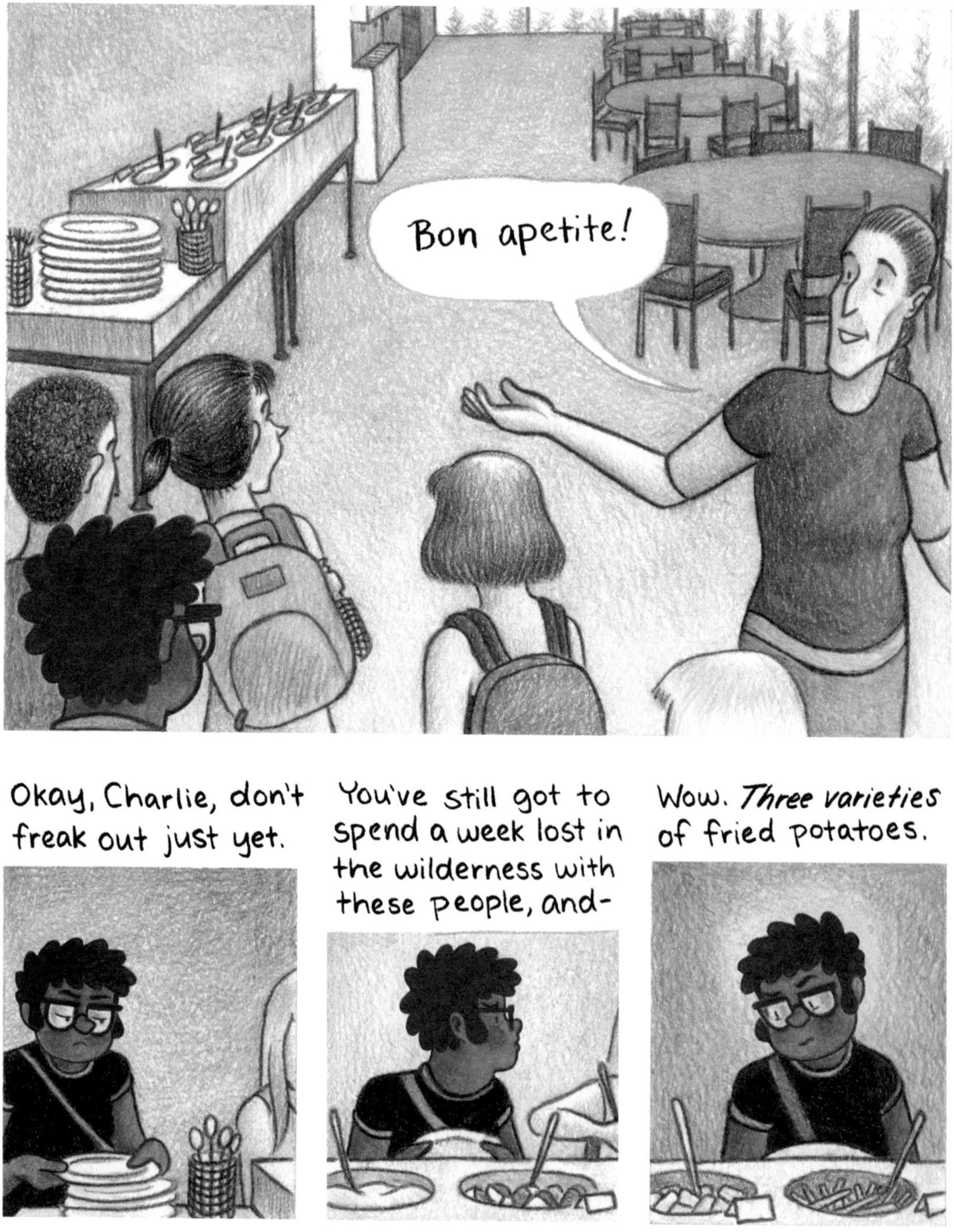
Bon apetite!
Okay, Charlie, don't freak out just yet.
You've still got to spend a week lost in the wilderness with these people, and-
Wow. *Three varieties* of fried potatoes.

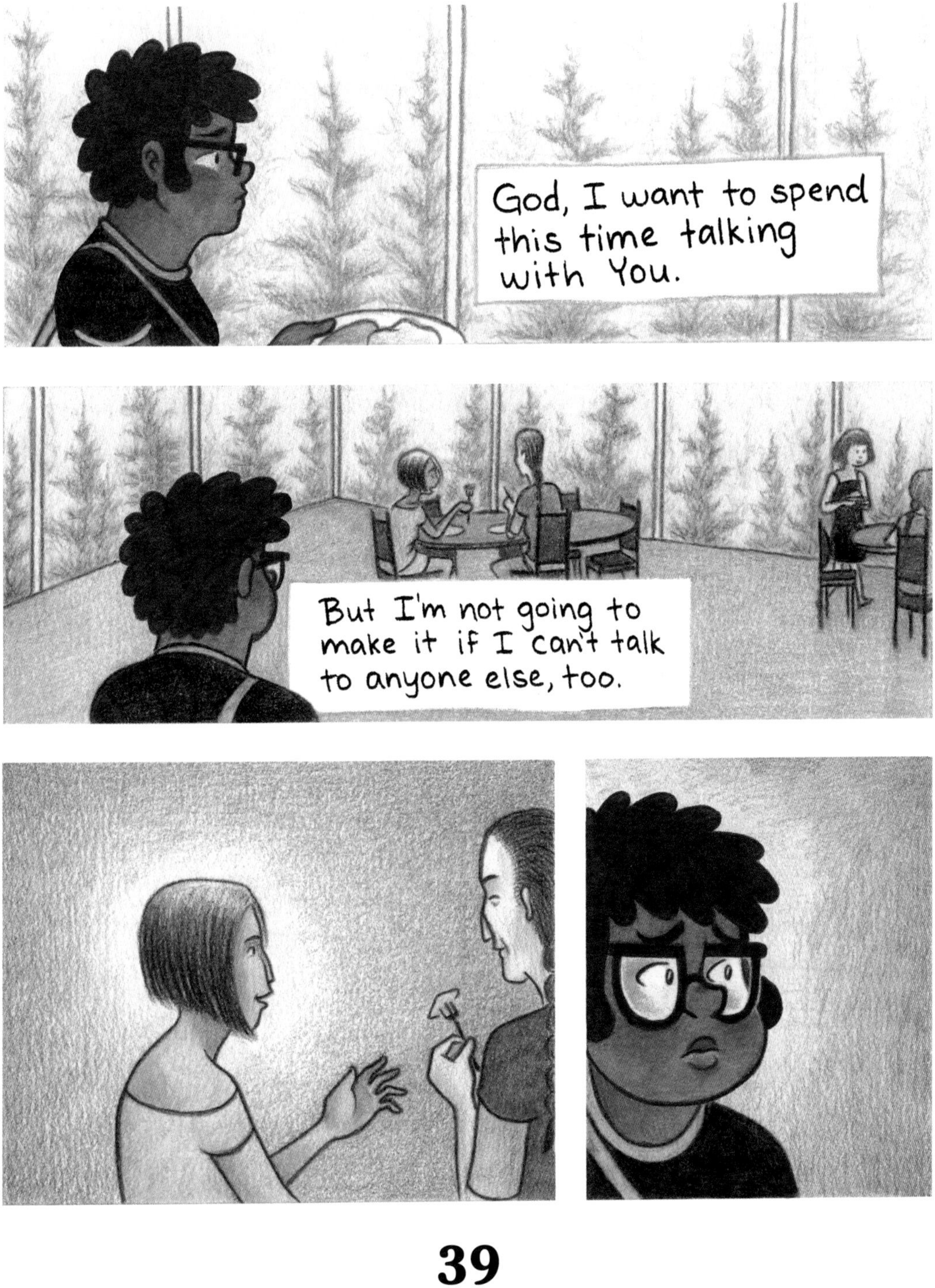
God, I want to spend this time talking with You.
But I'm not going to make it if I can't talk to anyone else, too.

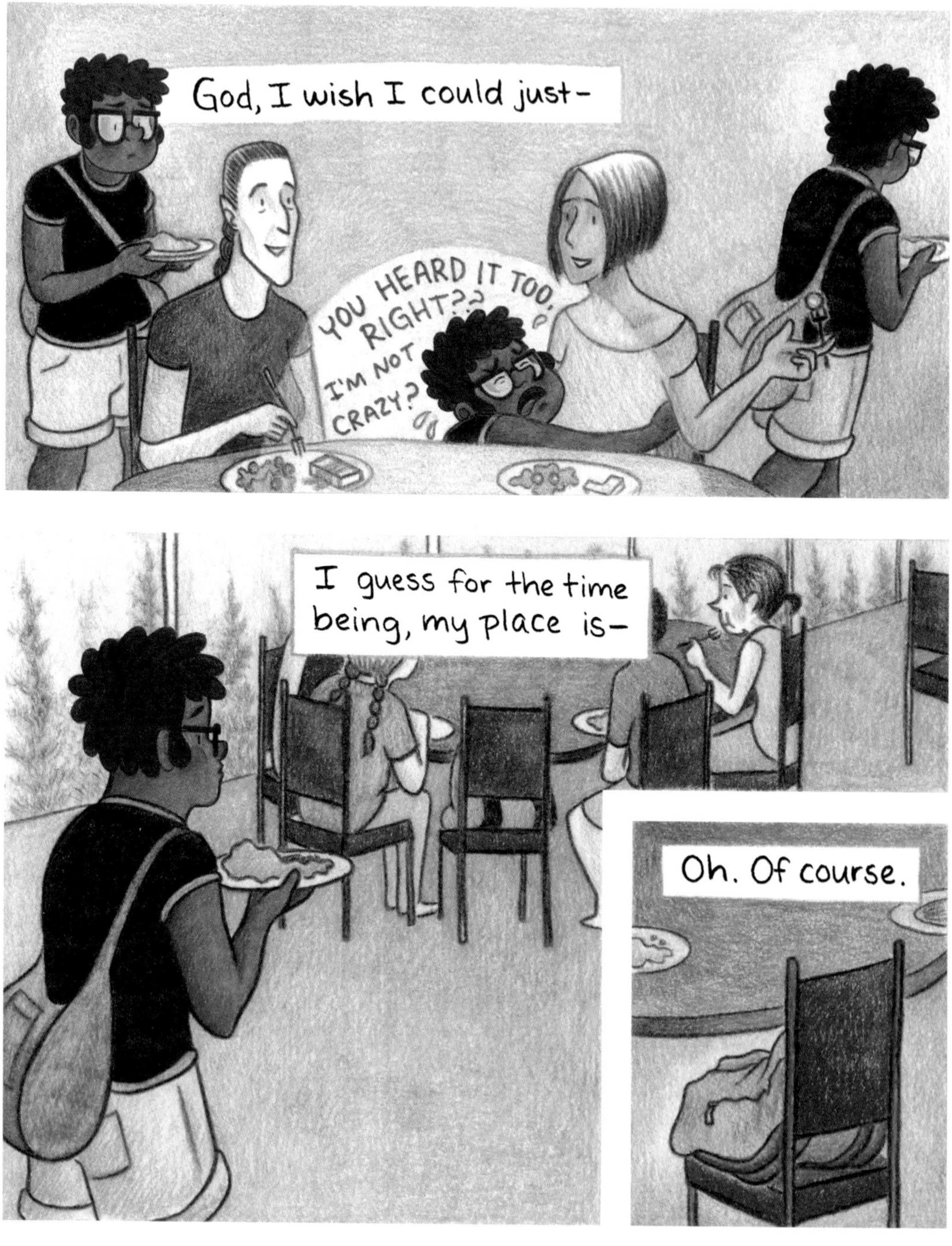
God, I wish I could just-
YOU HEARD IT TOO, RIGHT??
I'M NOT CRAZY?
I guess for the time being, my place is-
Oh. Of course.

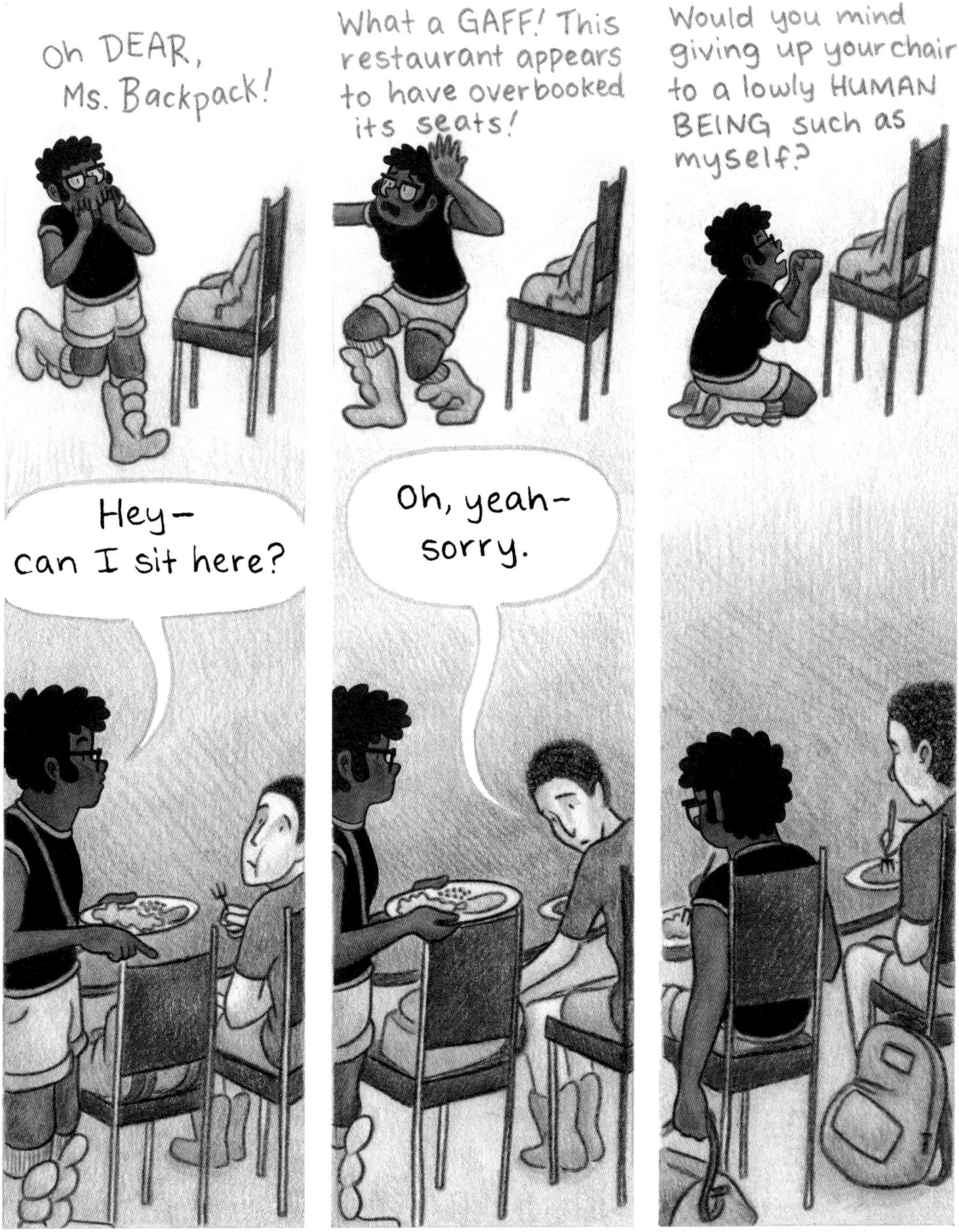
Oh DEAR, Ms. Backpack!
Hey- can I sit here?
What a GAFF! This restaurant appears to have overbooked its seats!
Oh, yeah- sorry.
Would you mind giving up your chair to a lowly HUMAN BEING such as myself?

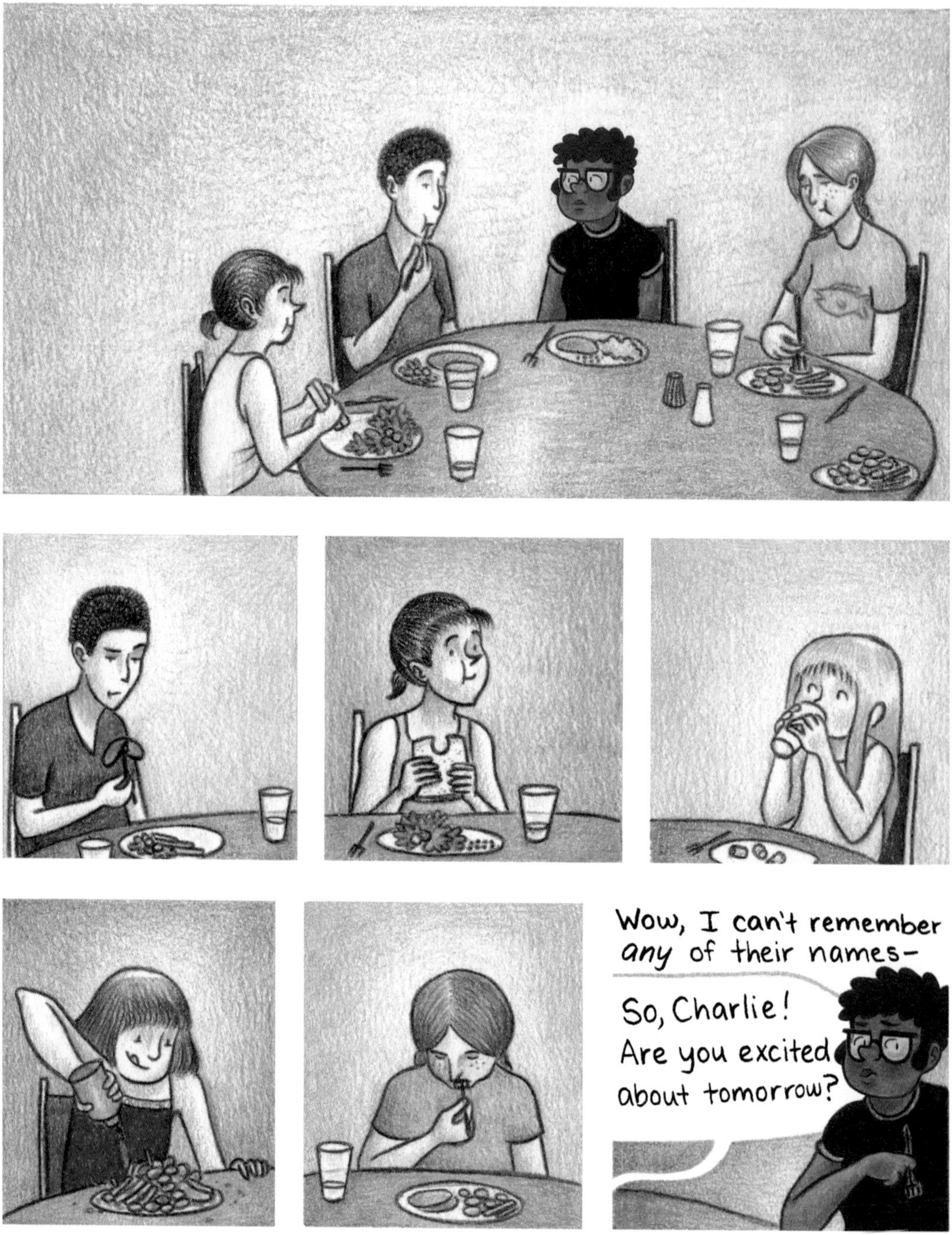
Wow, I can't remember *any* of their names-
So, Charlie! Are you excited about tomorrow?

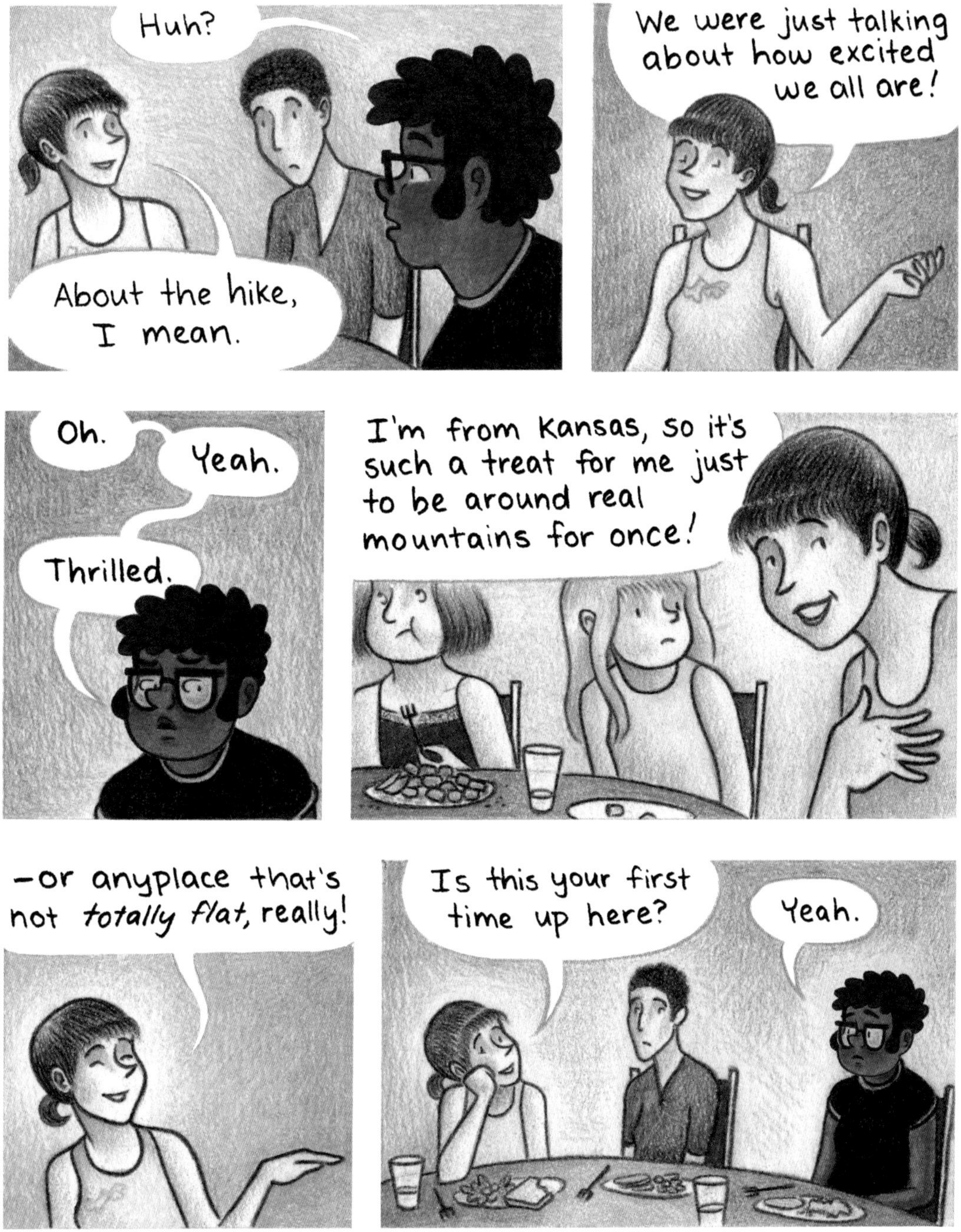

Huh?
About the hike, I mean.
We were just talking about how excited we all are!
Oh.
Yeah.
Thrilled.
I'm from Kansas, so it's such a treat for me just to be around real mountains for once!
—or anyplace that's not *totally flat*, really!
Is this your first time up here?
Yeah.

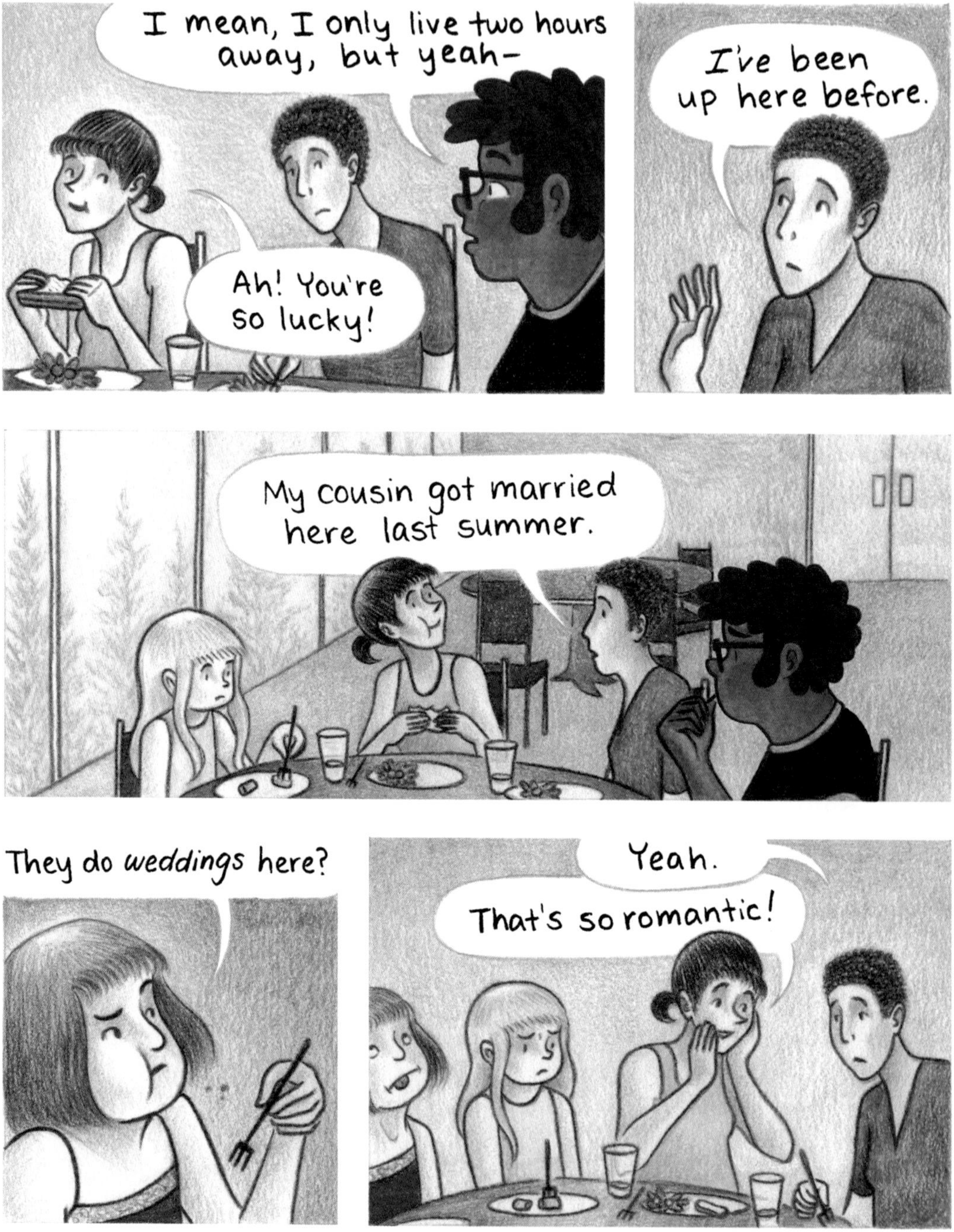
I mean, I only live two hours away, but yeah–
Ah! You're so lucky!
I've been up here before.
My cousin got married here last summer.
They do *weddings* here?
Yeah.
That's so romantic!

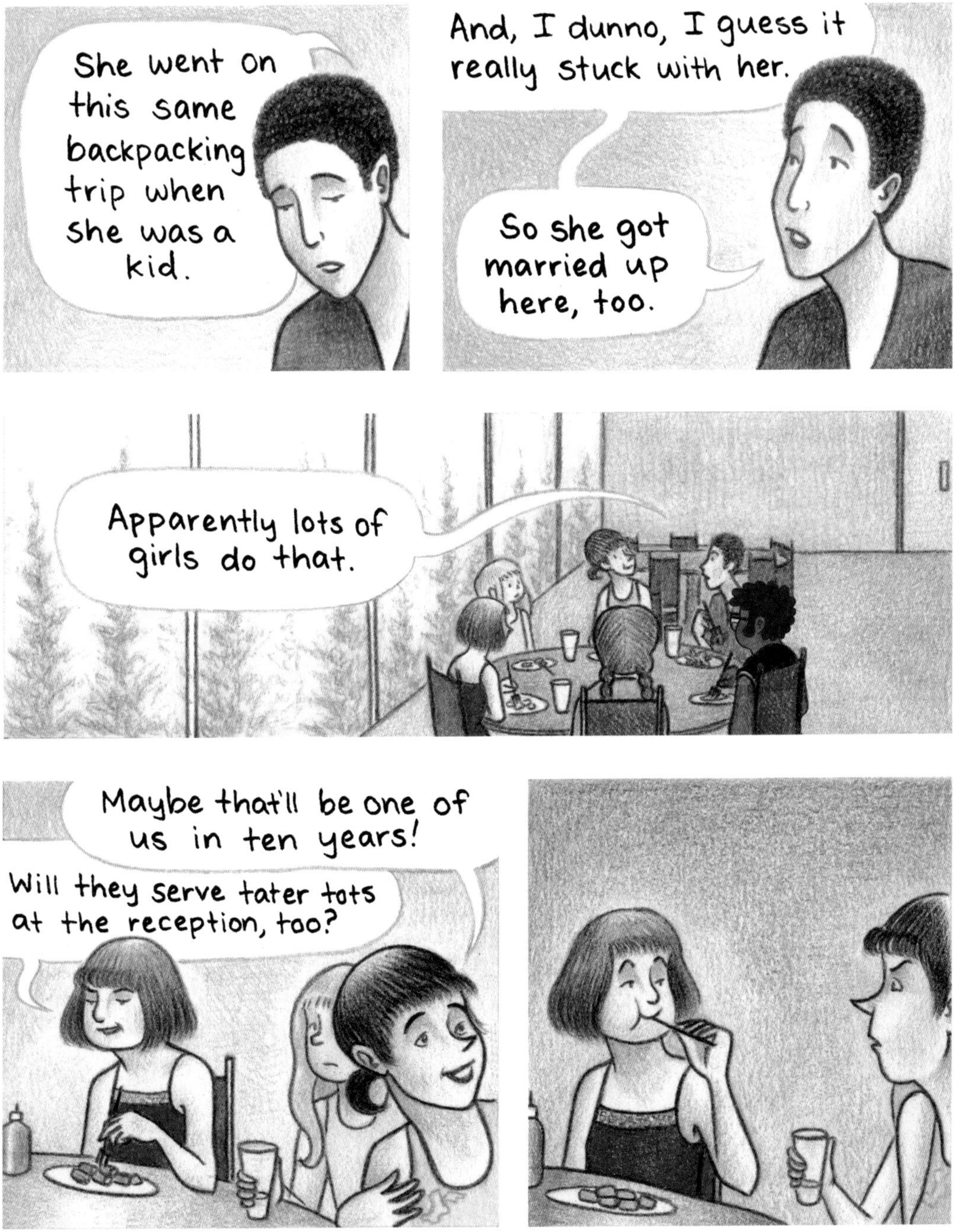
She went on this same backpacking trip when she was a kid.
And, I dunno, I guess it really stuck with her.
So she got married up here, too.
Apparently lots of girls do that.
Maybe that'll be one of us in ten years!
Will they serve tater tots at the reception, too?

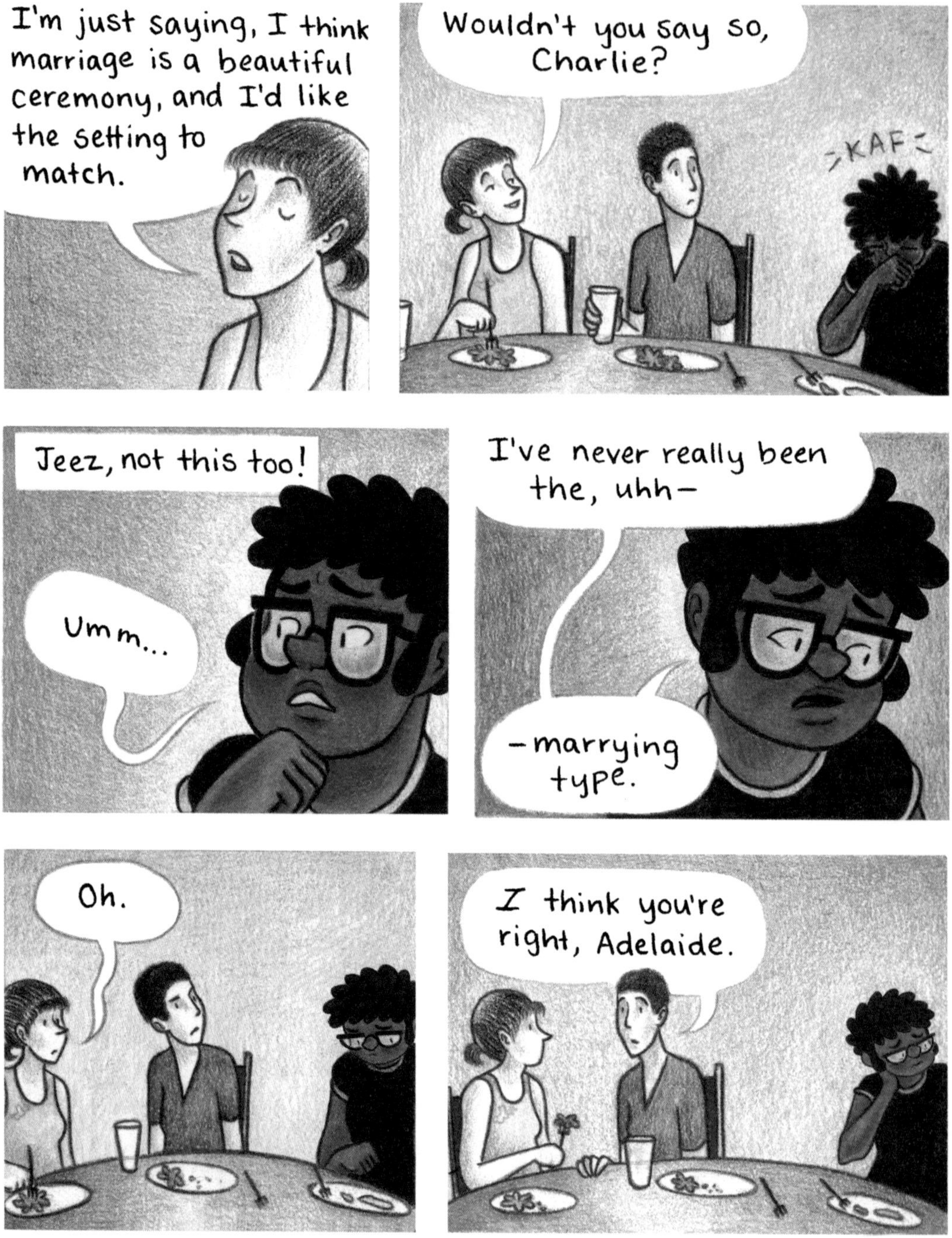
I'm just saying, I think marriage is a beautiful ceremony, and I'd like the setting to match.
Wouldn't you say so, Charlie?
KAF
Jeez, not this too!
Umm...
I've never really been the, uhh–
–marrying type.
Oh.
I think you're right, Adelaide.

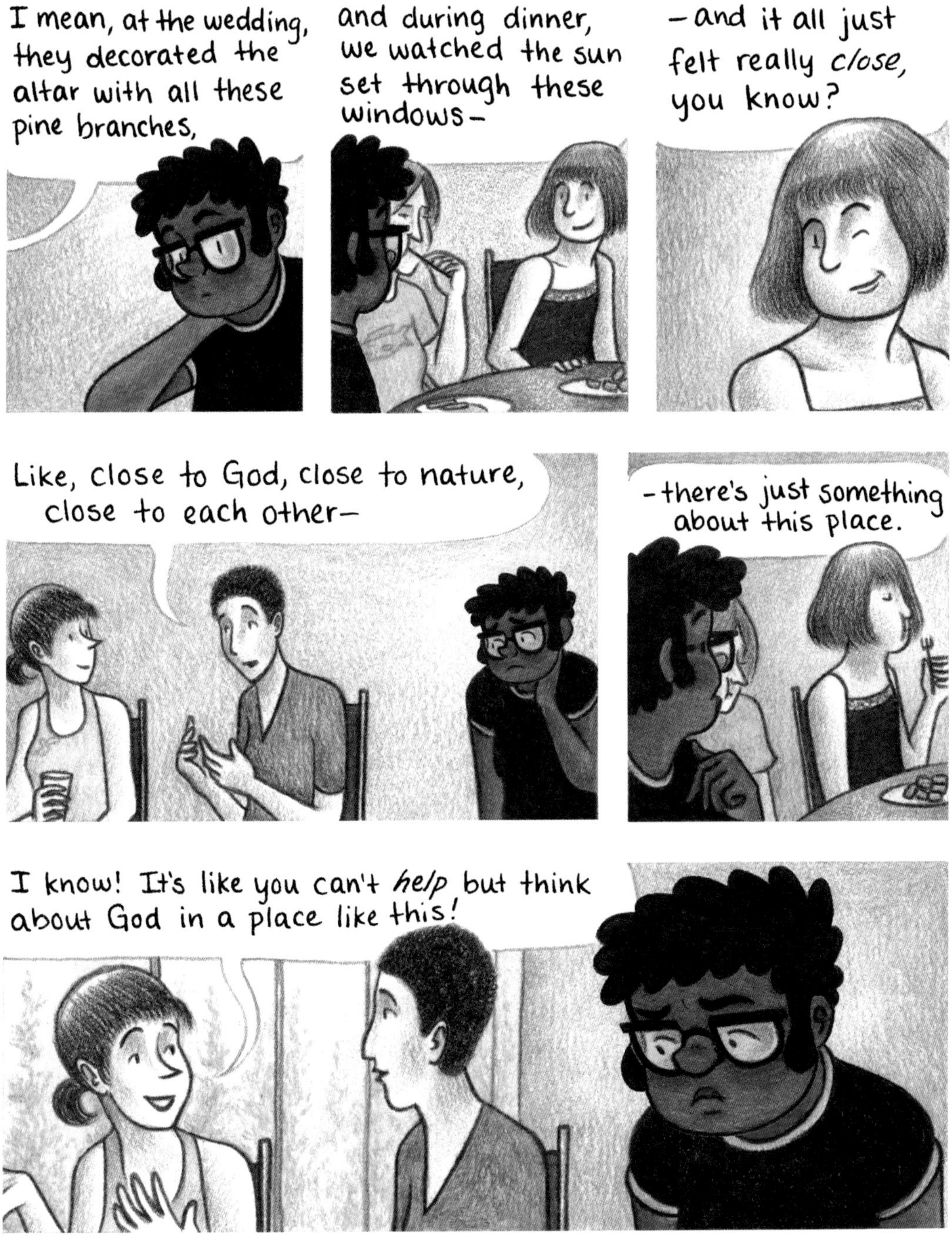
I mean, at the wedding, they decorated the altar with all these pine branches,
and during dinner, we watched the sun set through these windows–
–and it all just felt really *close*, you know?
Like, close to God, close to nature, close to each other–
–there's just something about this place.
I know! It's like you can't *help* but think about God in a place like this!

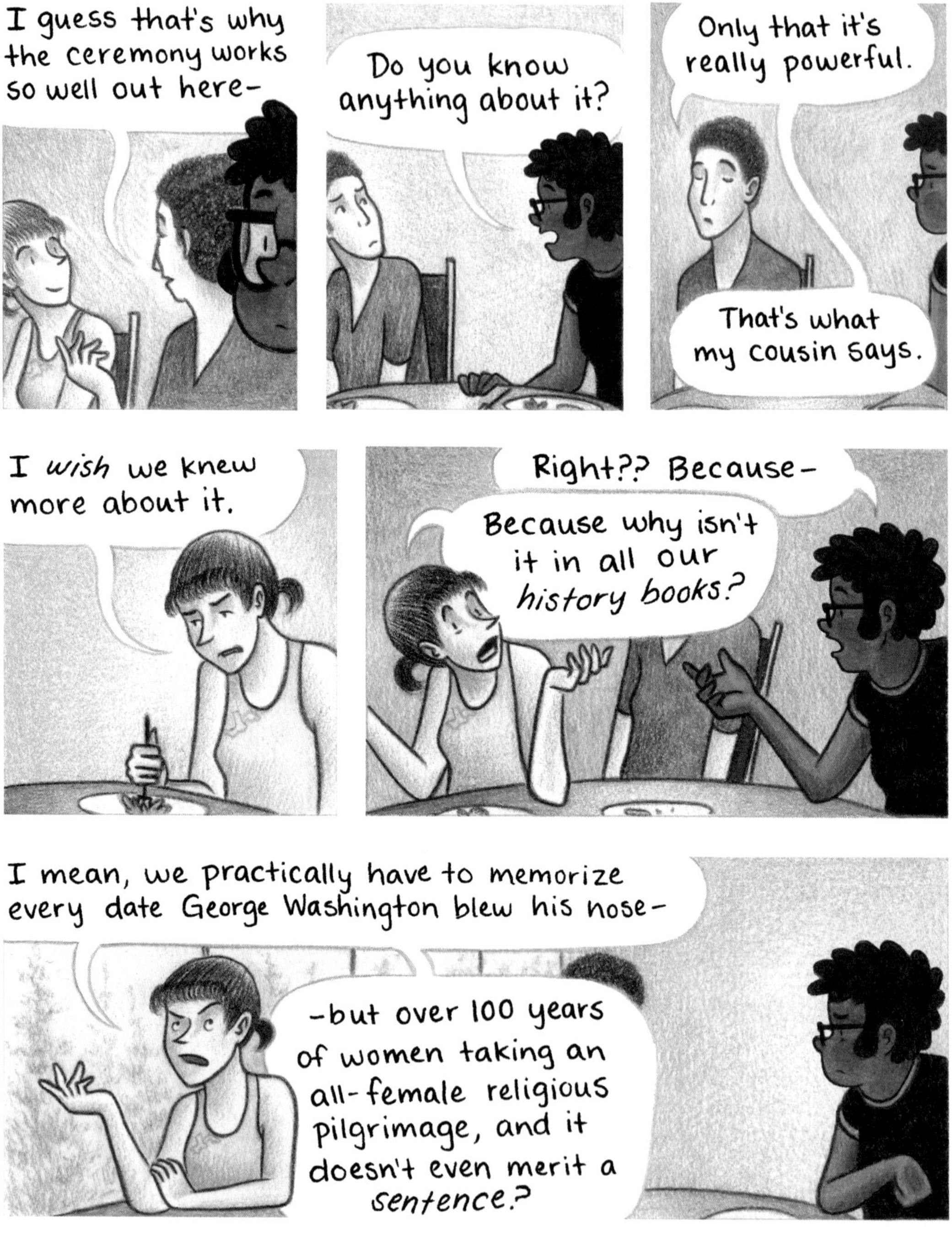
I guess that's why the ceremony works so well out here-
Do you know anything about it?
Only that it's really powerful.
That's what my cousin says.
I *wish* we knew more about it.
Right?? Because-
Because why isn't it in all our *history books?*
I mean, we practically have to memorize every date George Washington blew his nose-
-but over 100 years of women taking an all-female religious pilgrimage, and it doesn't even merit a *sentence?*

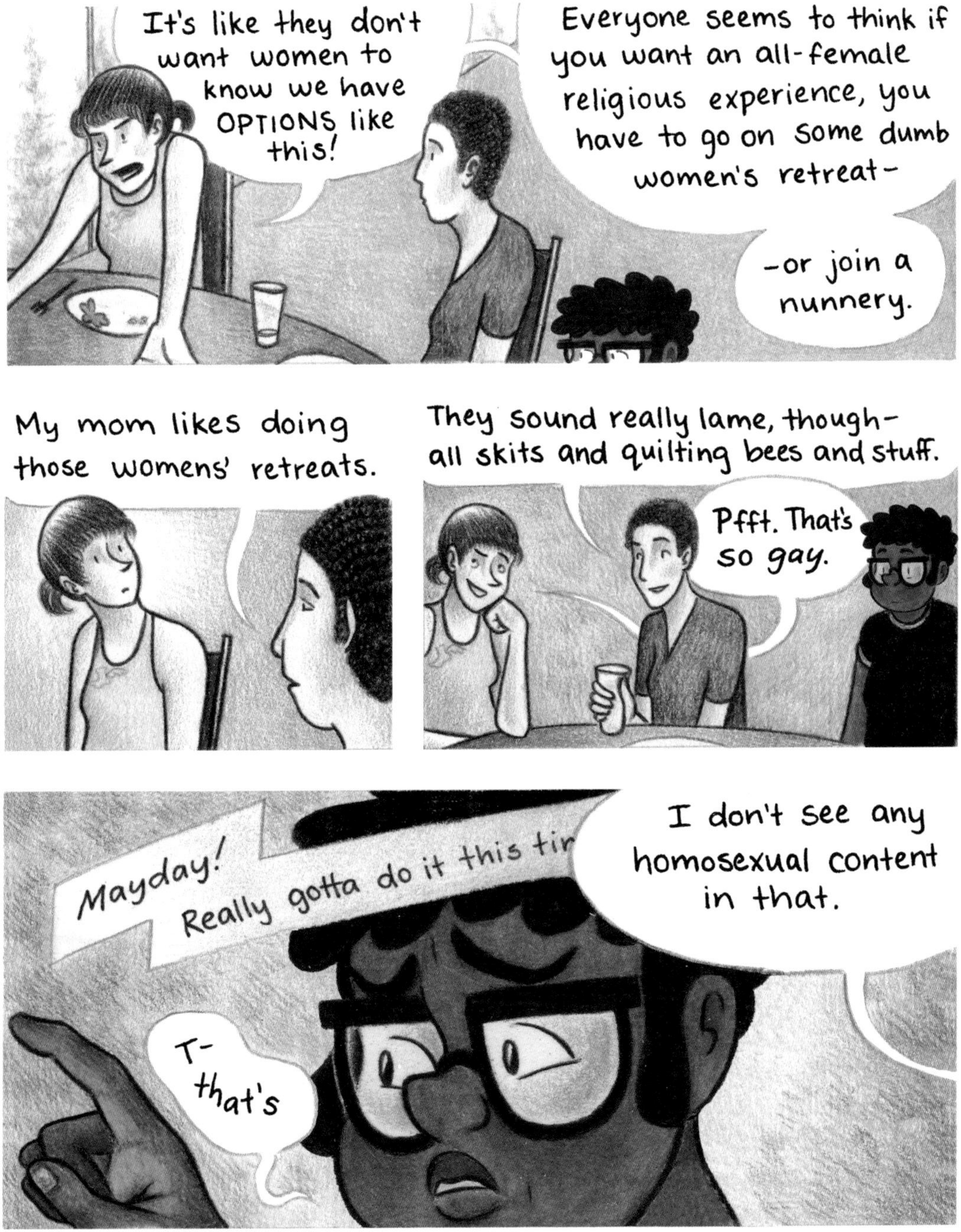
It's like they don't want women to know we have OPTIONS like this!
Everyone seems to think if you want an all-female religious experience, you have to go on some dumb women's retreat-
-or join a nunnery.
My mom likes doing those womens' retreats.
They sound really lame, though- all skits and quilting bees and stuff.
Pfft. That's so gay.
I don't see any homosexual content in that.
Mayday! Really gotta do it this tir
T- that's

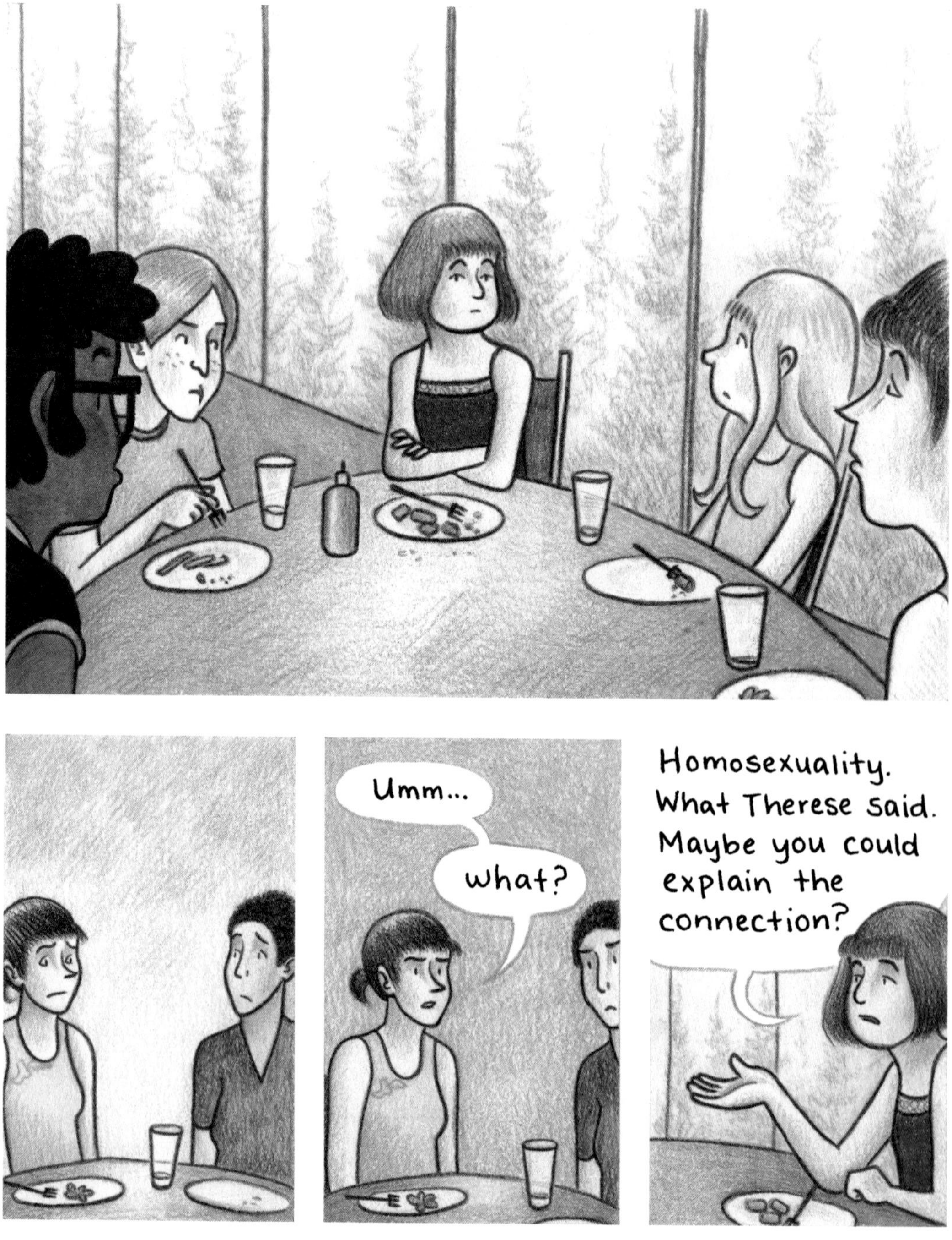
Umm...
what?
Homosexuality. What Therese said. Maybe you could explain the connection?

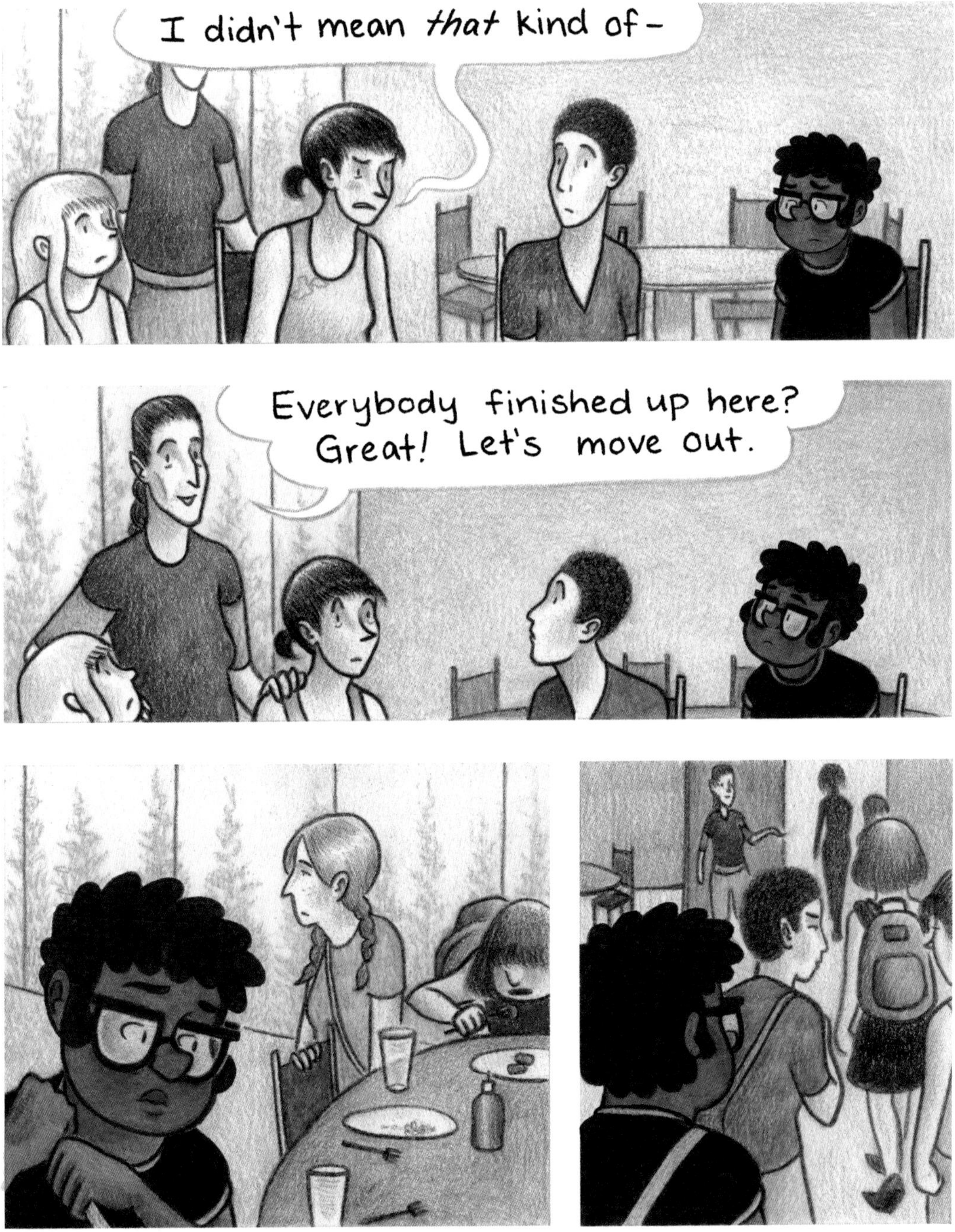
I didn't mean *that* kind of-
Everybody finished up here? Great! Let's move out.

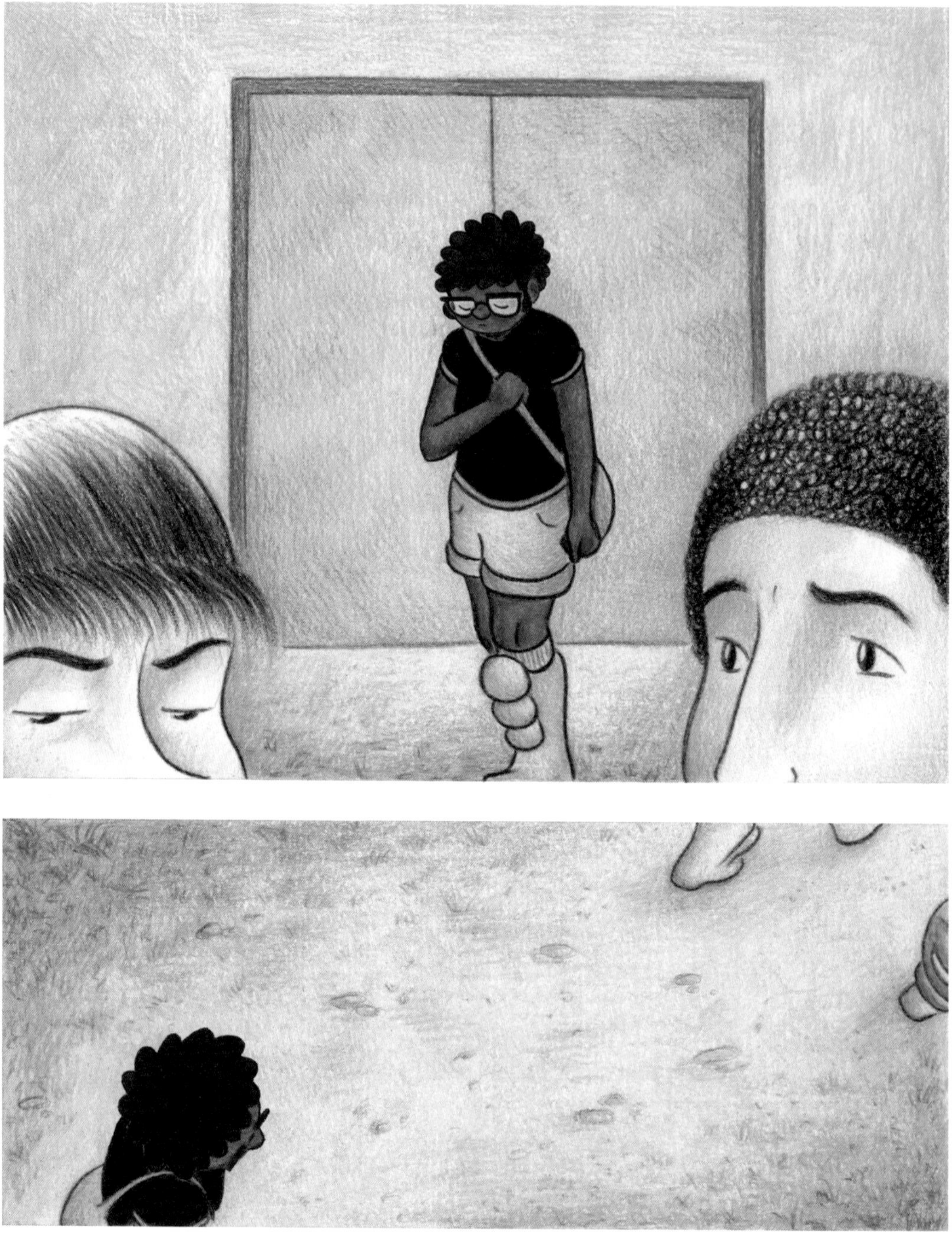

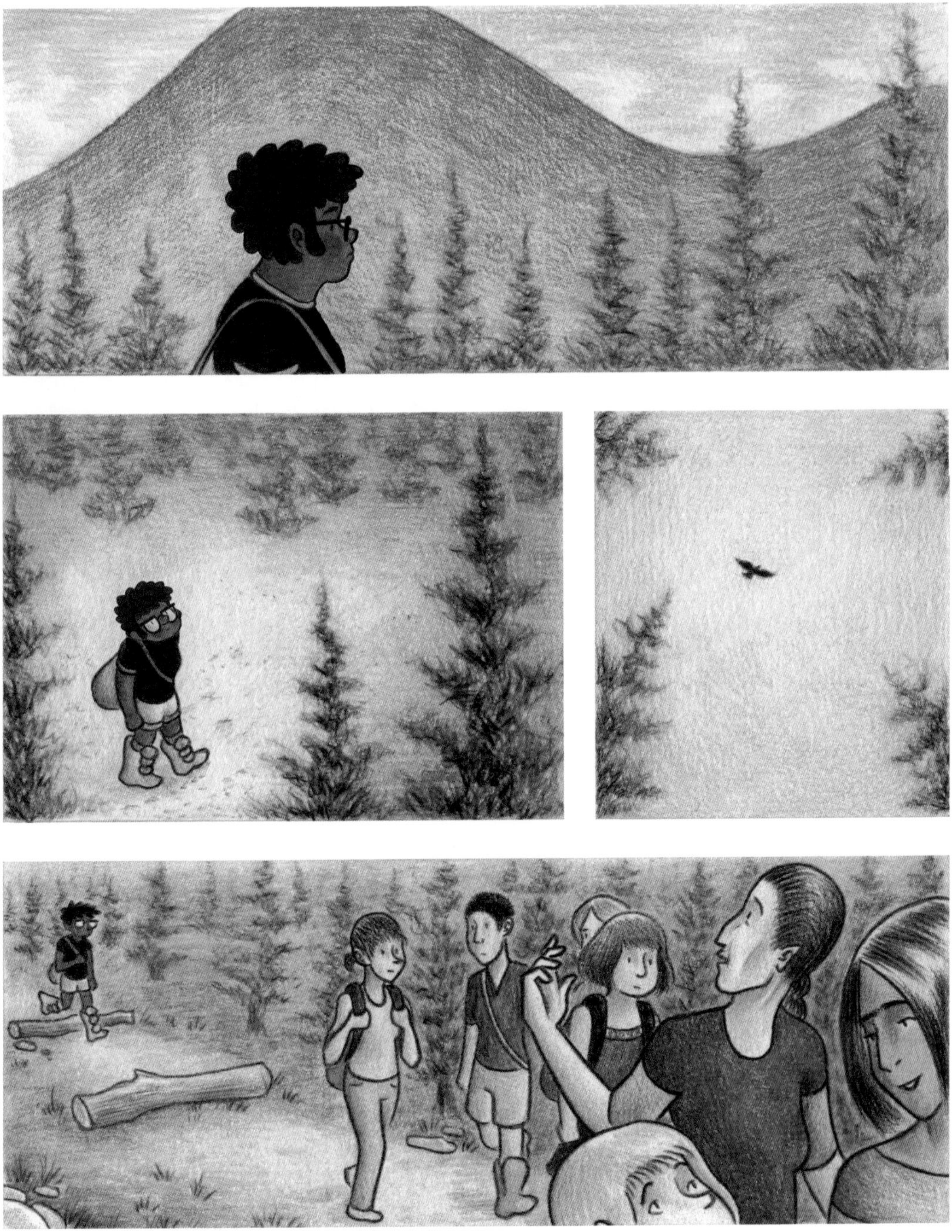

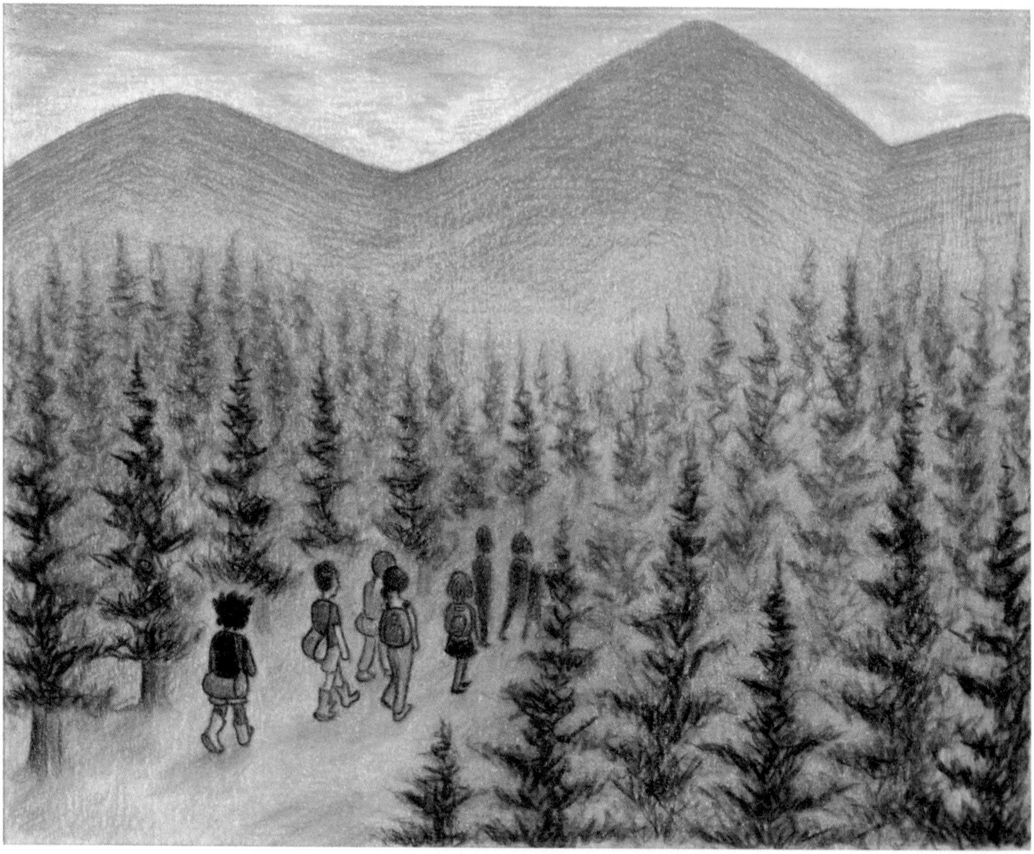

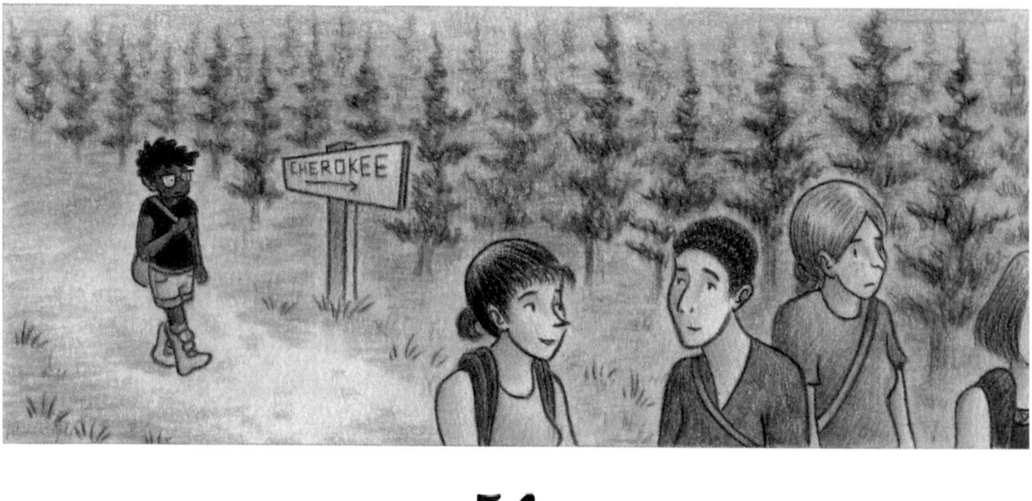
CHEROKEE

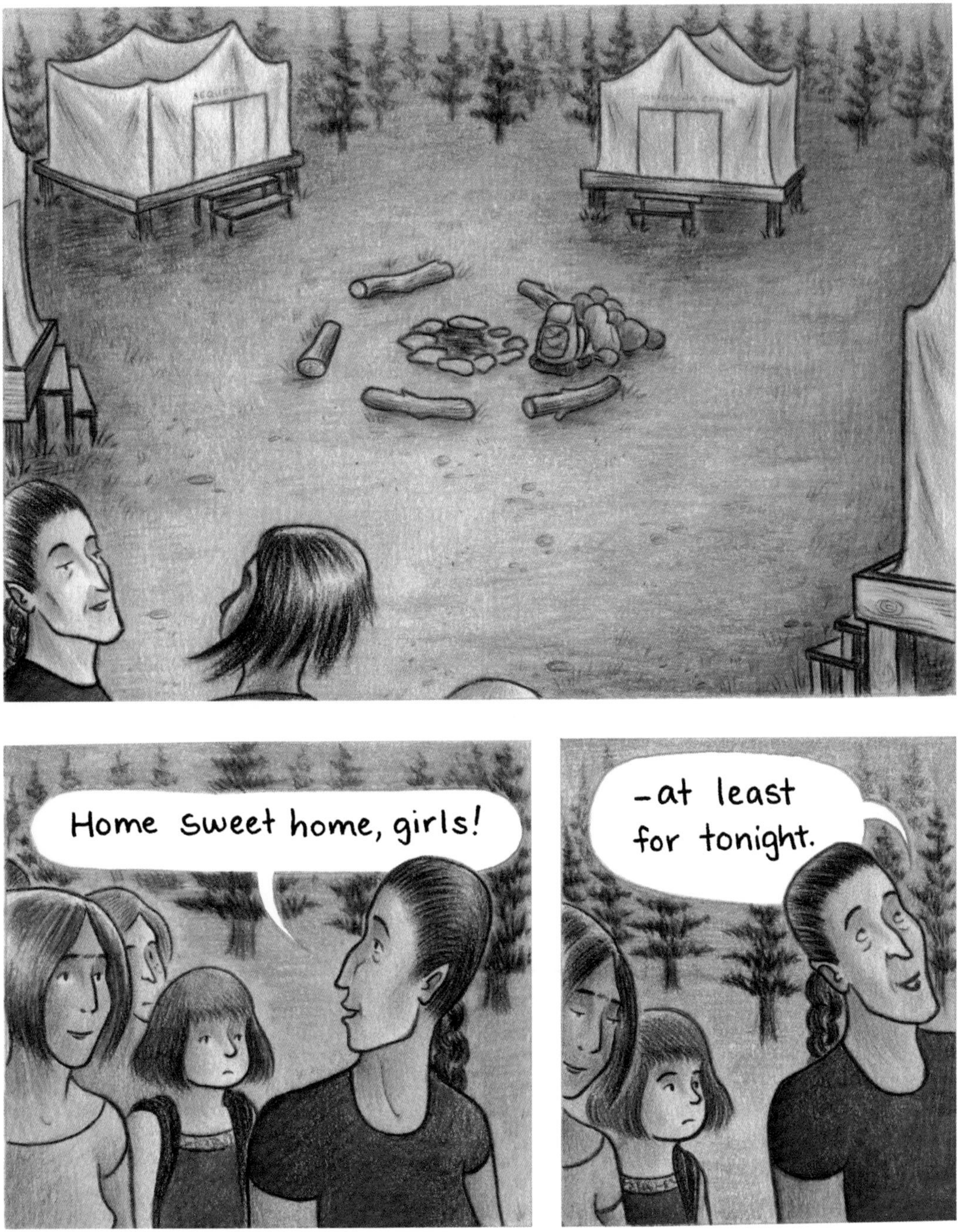
Home sweet home, girls!
-at least for tonight.

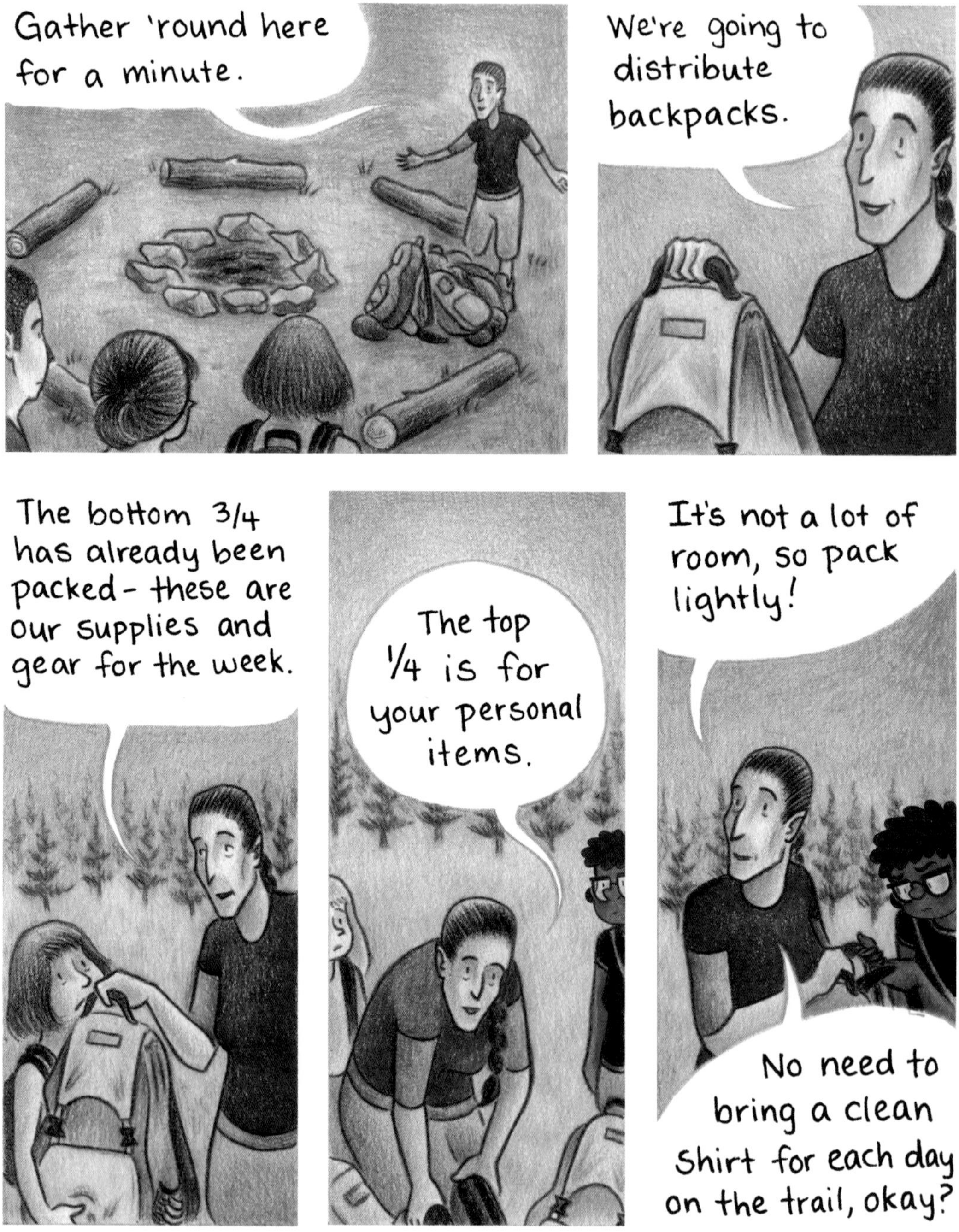
Gather 'round here for a minute.
We're going to distribute backpacks.
The bottom 3/4 has already been packed - these are our supplies and gear for the week.
The top 1/4 is for your personal items.
It's not a lot of room, so pack lightly!
No need to bring a clean shirt for each day on the trail, okay?

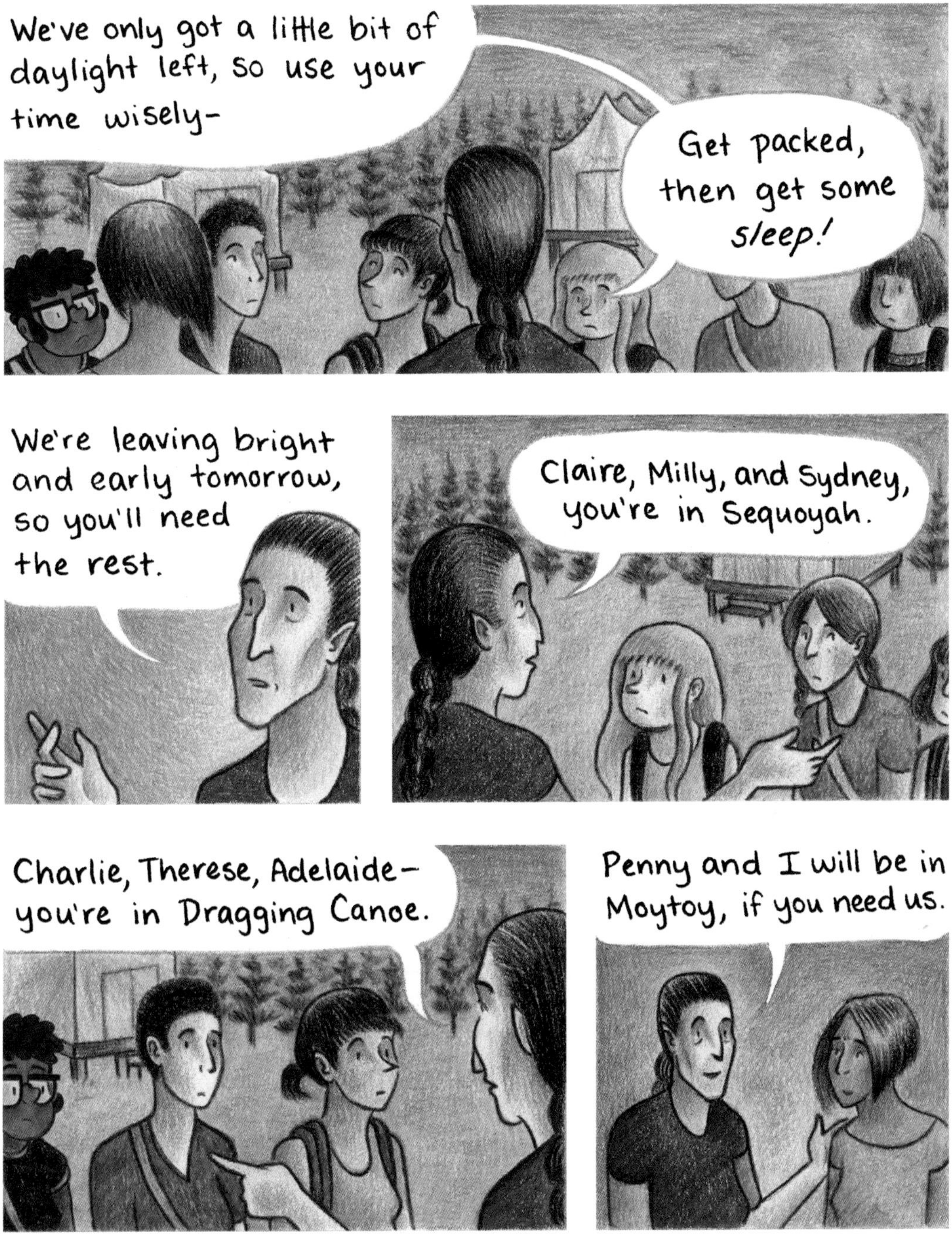
We've only got a little bit of daylight left, so use your time wisely-
Get packed, then get some *sleep!*
We're leaving bright and early tomorrow, so you'll need the rest.
Claire, Milly, and Sydney, you're in Sequoyah.
Charlie, Therese, Adelaide- you're in Dragging Canoe.
Penny and I will be in Moytoy, if you need us.

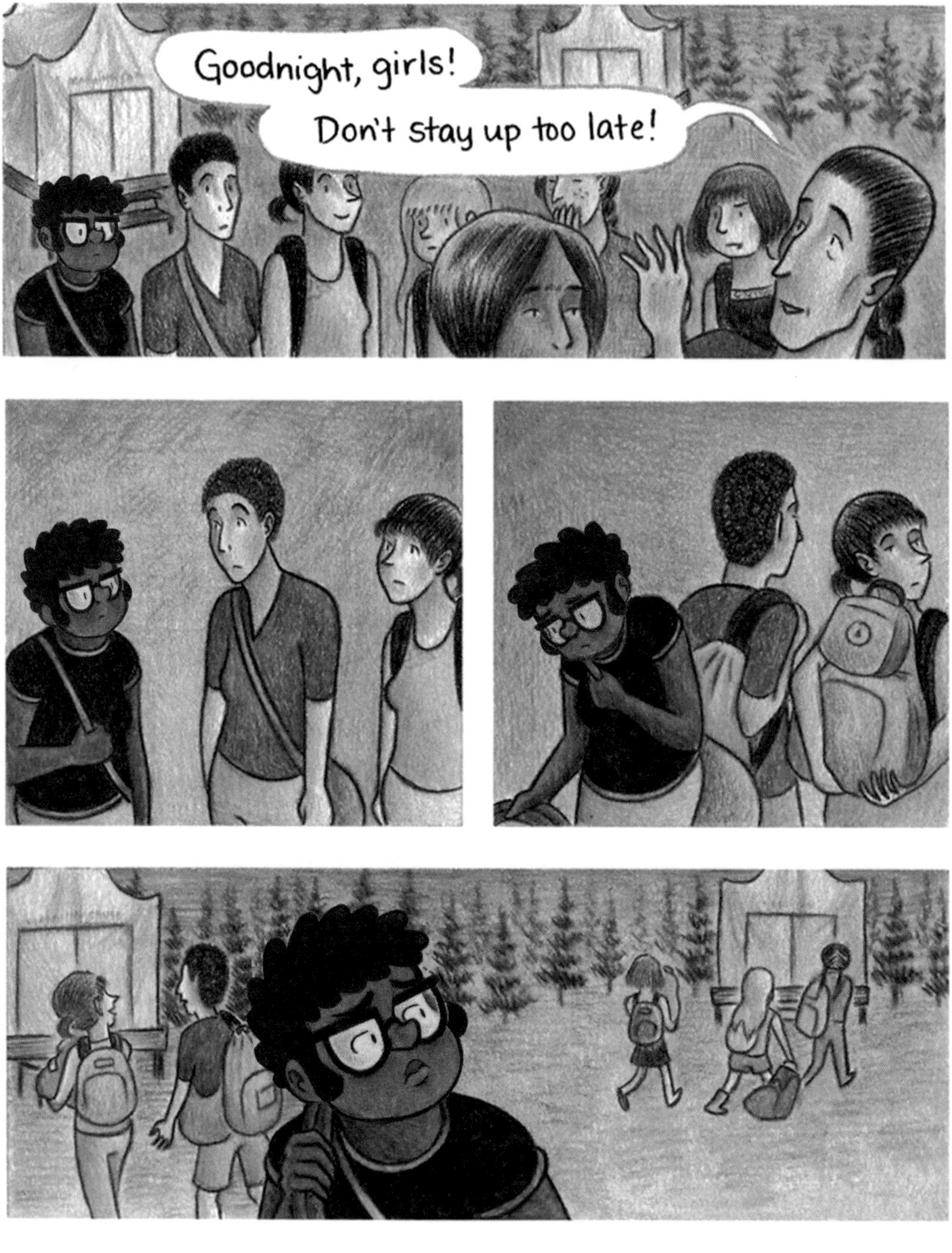
Goodnight, girls!
Don't stay up too late!

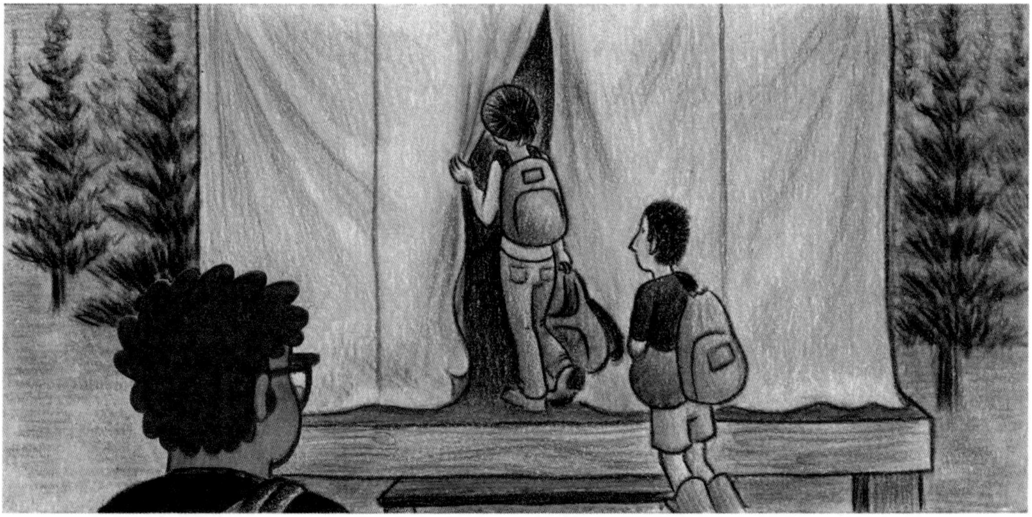

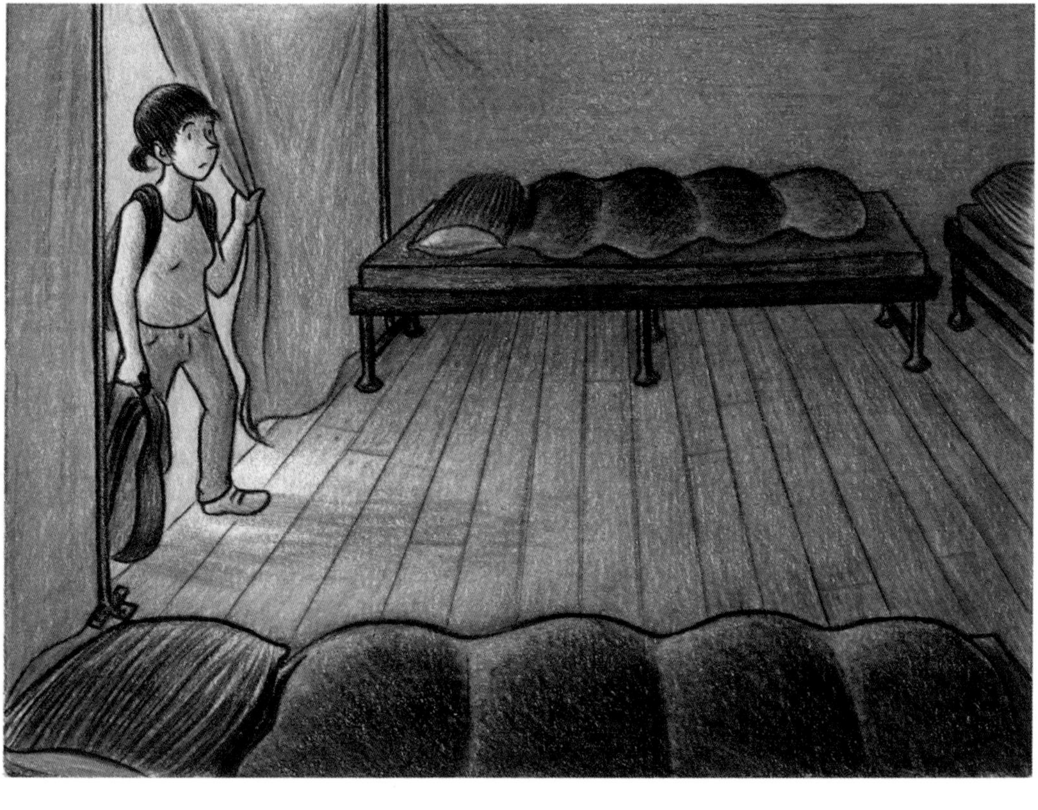

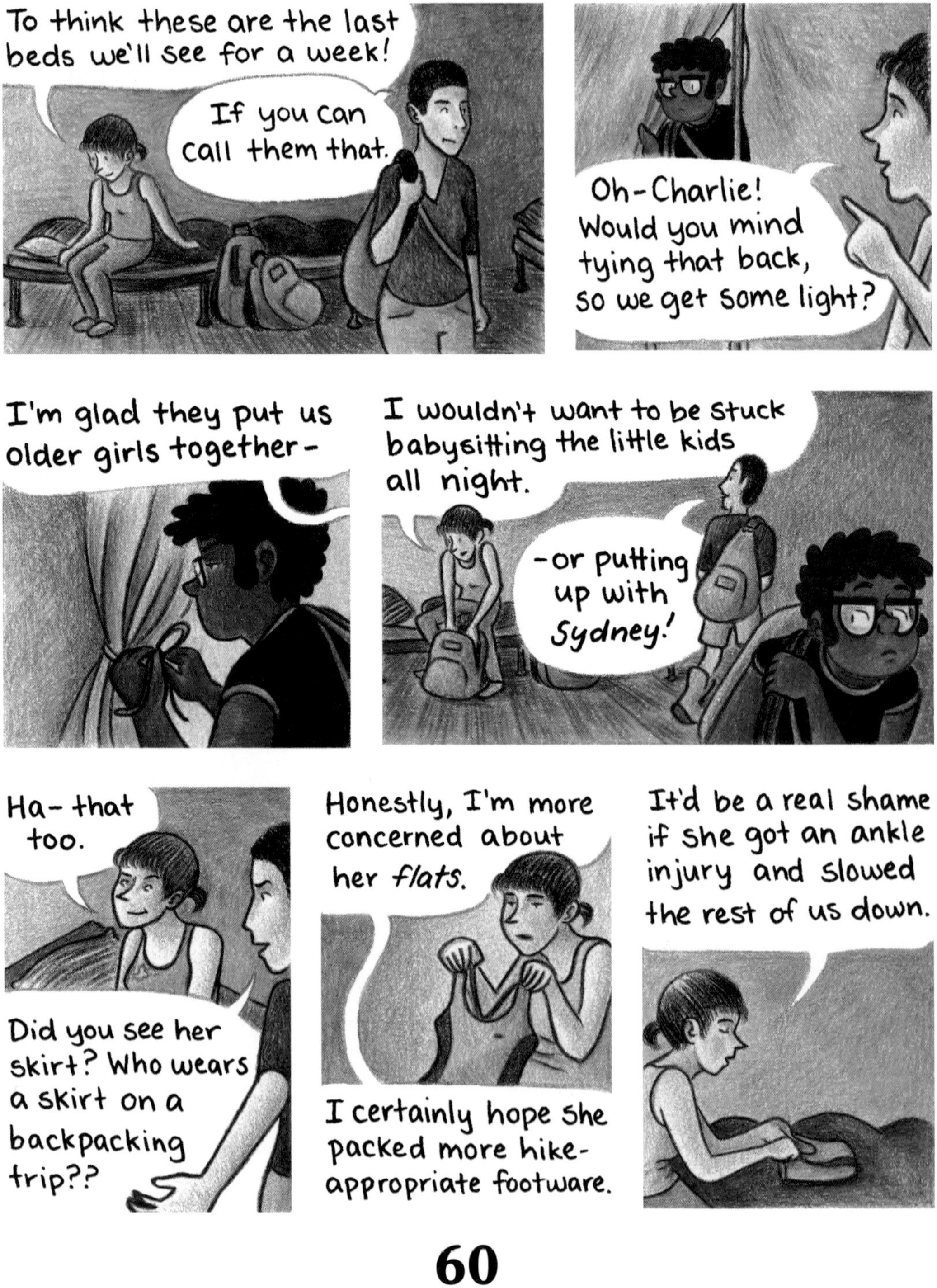

To think these are the last beds we'll see for a week!
If you can call them that.
Oh-Charlie! Would you mind tying that back, so we get some light?
I'm glad they put us older girls together-
I wouldn't want to be stuck babysitting the little kids all night.
-or putting up with *Sydney!*
Ha- that too.
Did you see her skirt? Who wears a skirt on a backpacking trip??
Honestly, I'm more concerned about her *flats*.
I certainly hope she packed more hike-appropriate footware.
It'd be a real shame if she got an ankle injury and slowed the rest of us down.

How many shirts are you gonna pack, Adelaide?

Just three.

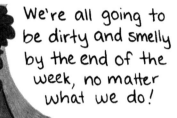

Really?

Yeah!

We're all going to be dirty and smelly by the end of the week, no matter what we do!

Might as well not overpack.

But I tell you—

the first shower once we get back will feel AMAZING.

—like a baptism.

Ha ha, totally...

61

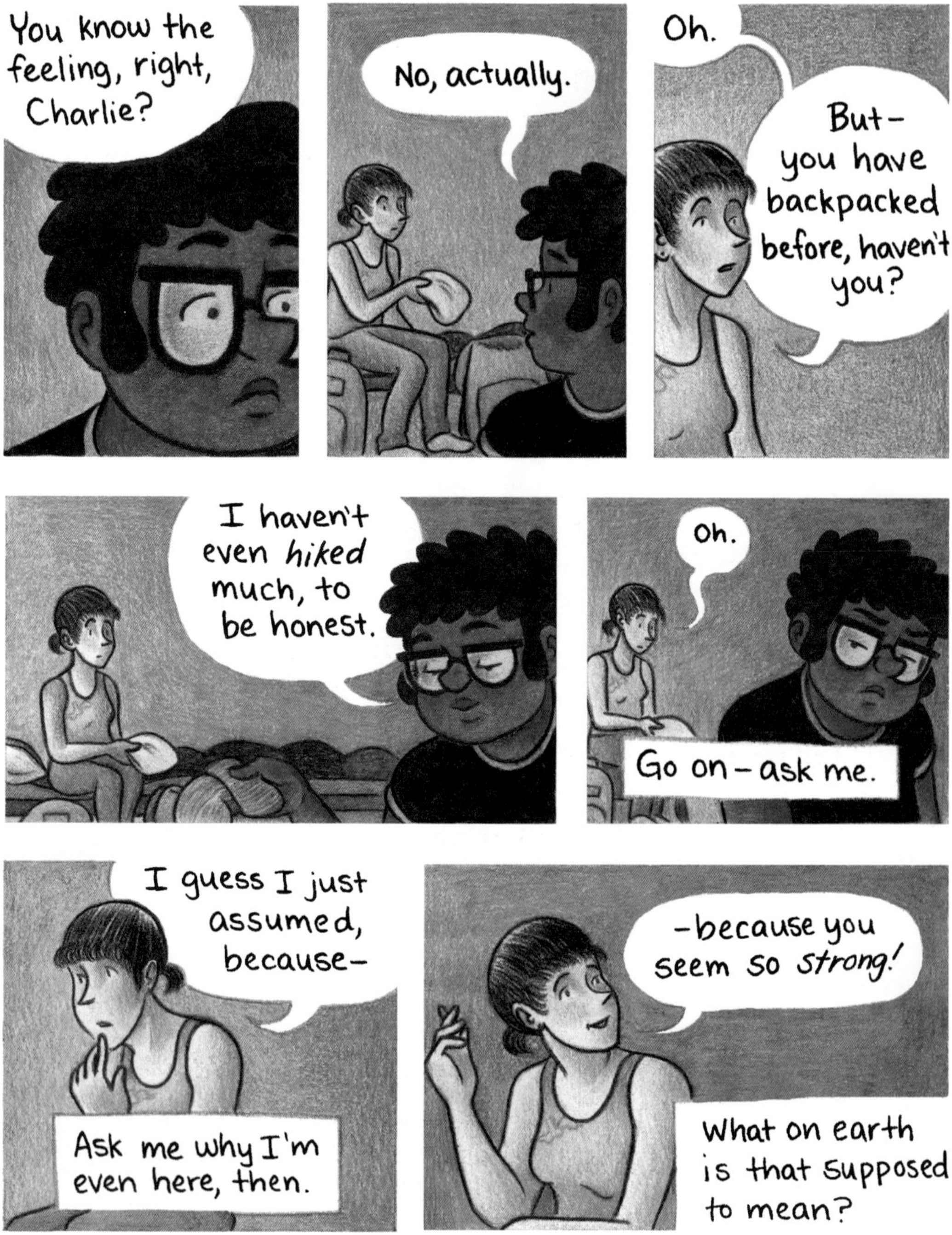
You know the feeling, right, Charlie?
No, actually.
Oh.
But- you have backpacked before, haven't you?
I haven't even *hiked* much, to be honest.
Oh.
Go on-ask me.
I guess I just assumed, because-
Ask me why I'm even here, then.
-because you seem so *strong*!
What on earth is that supposed to mean?

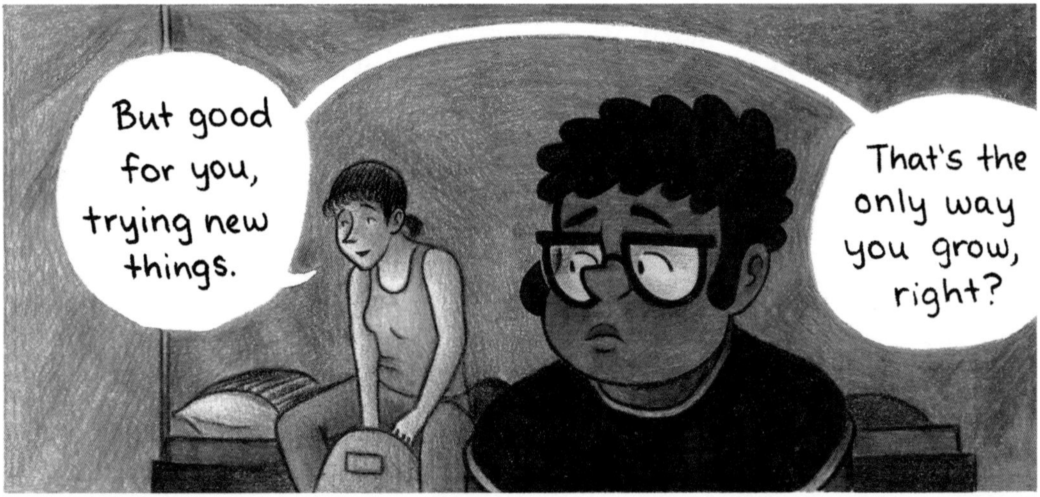
But good for you, trying new things.
That's the only way you grow, right?

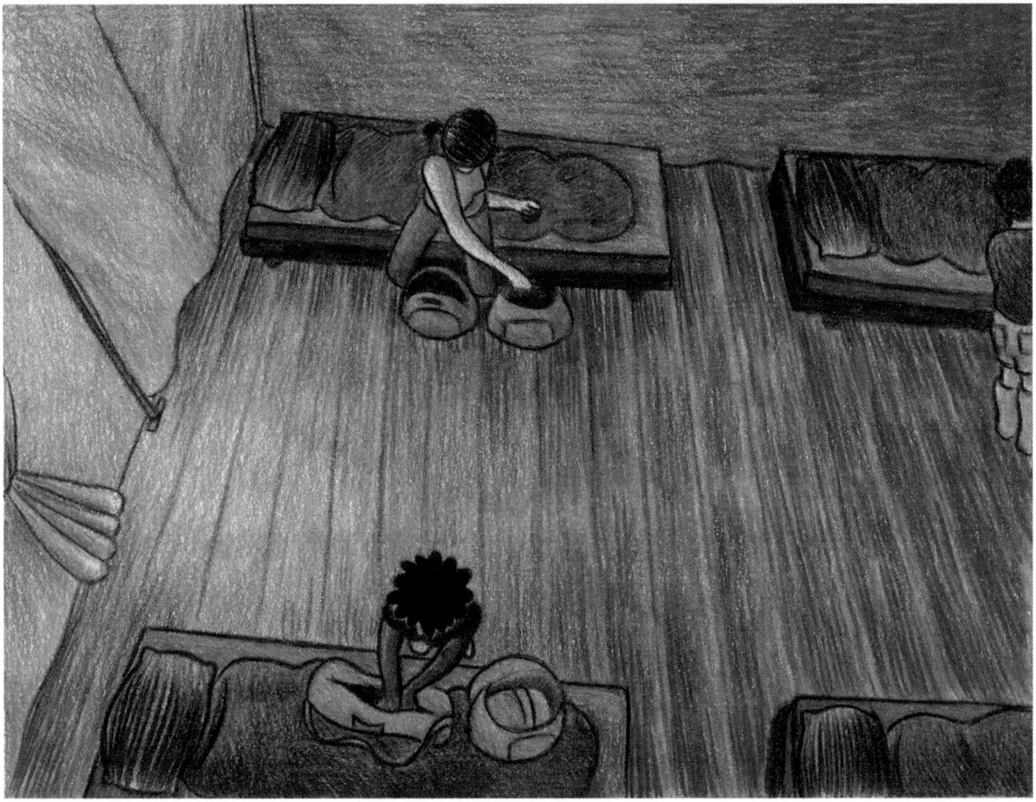

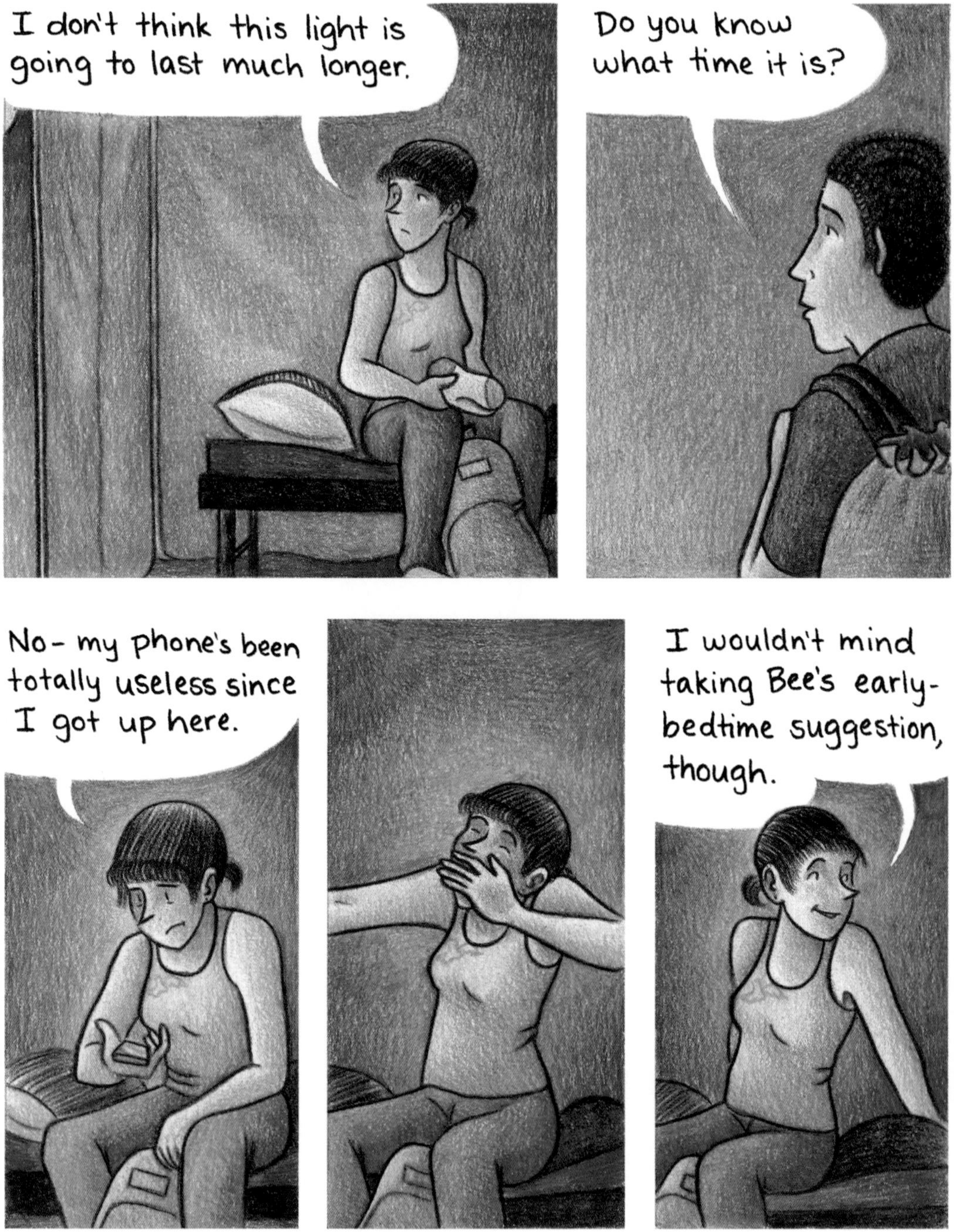

I don't think this light is going to last much longer.
Do you know what time it is?
No- my phone's been totally useless since I got up here.
I wouldn't mind taking Bee's early-bedtime suggestion, though.

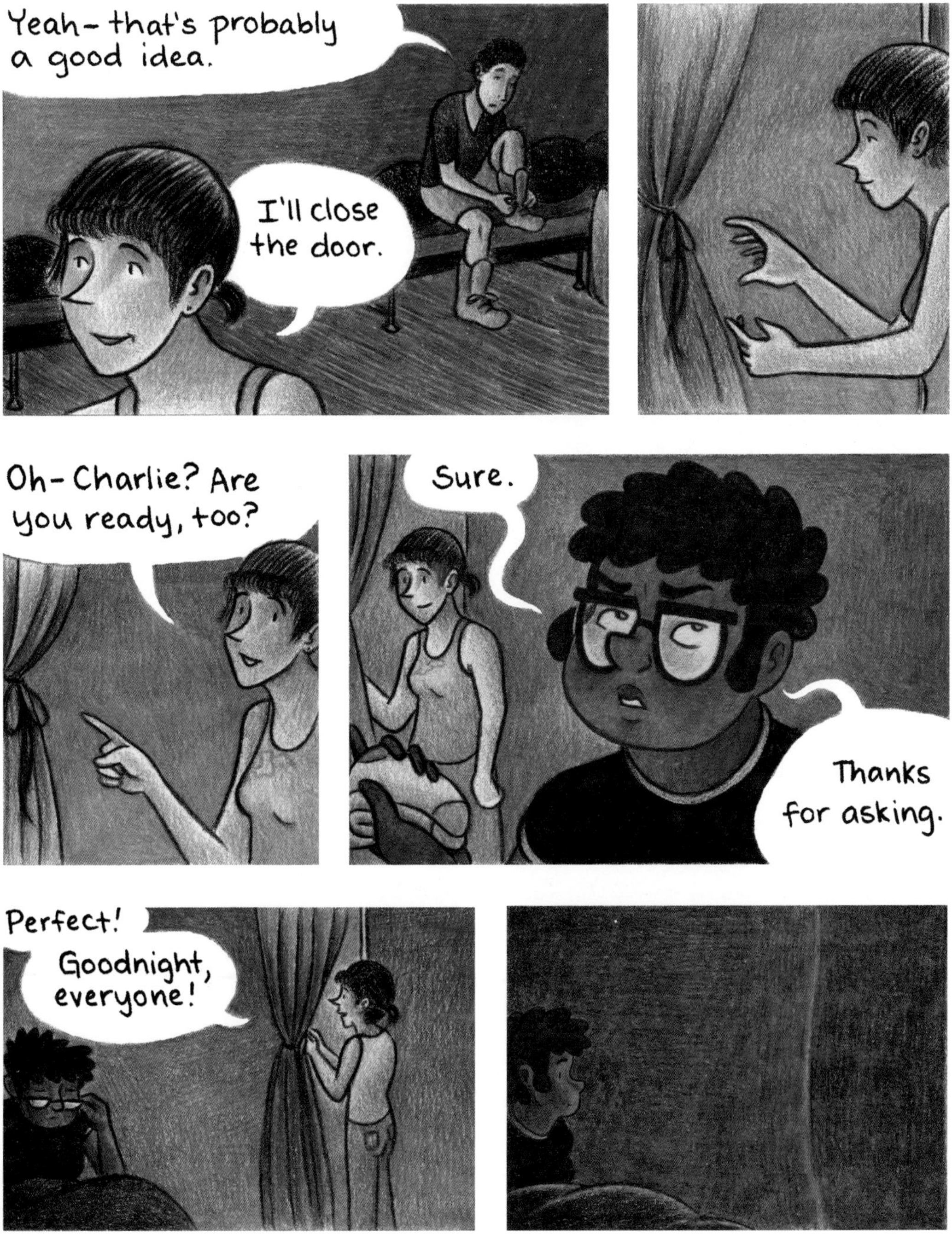
Yeah- that's probably a good idea.
I'll close the door.
Oh-Charlie? Are you ready, too?
Sure.
Thanks for asking.
Perfect!
Goodnight, everyone!

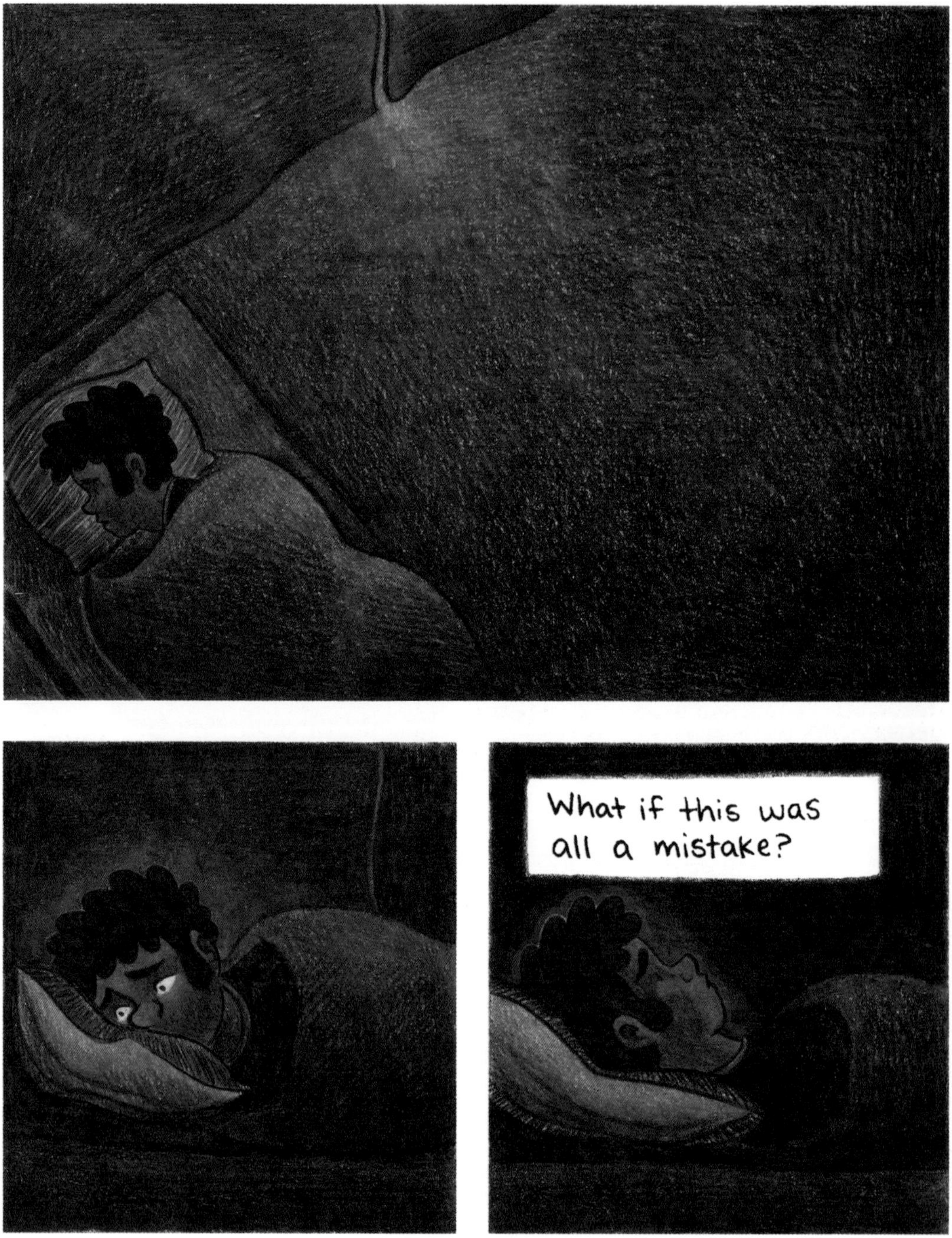
What if this was all a mistake?

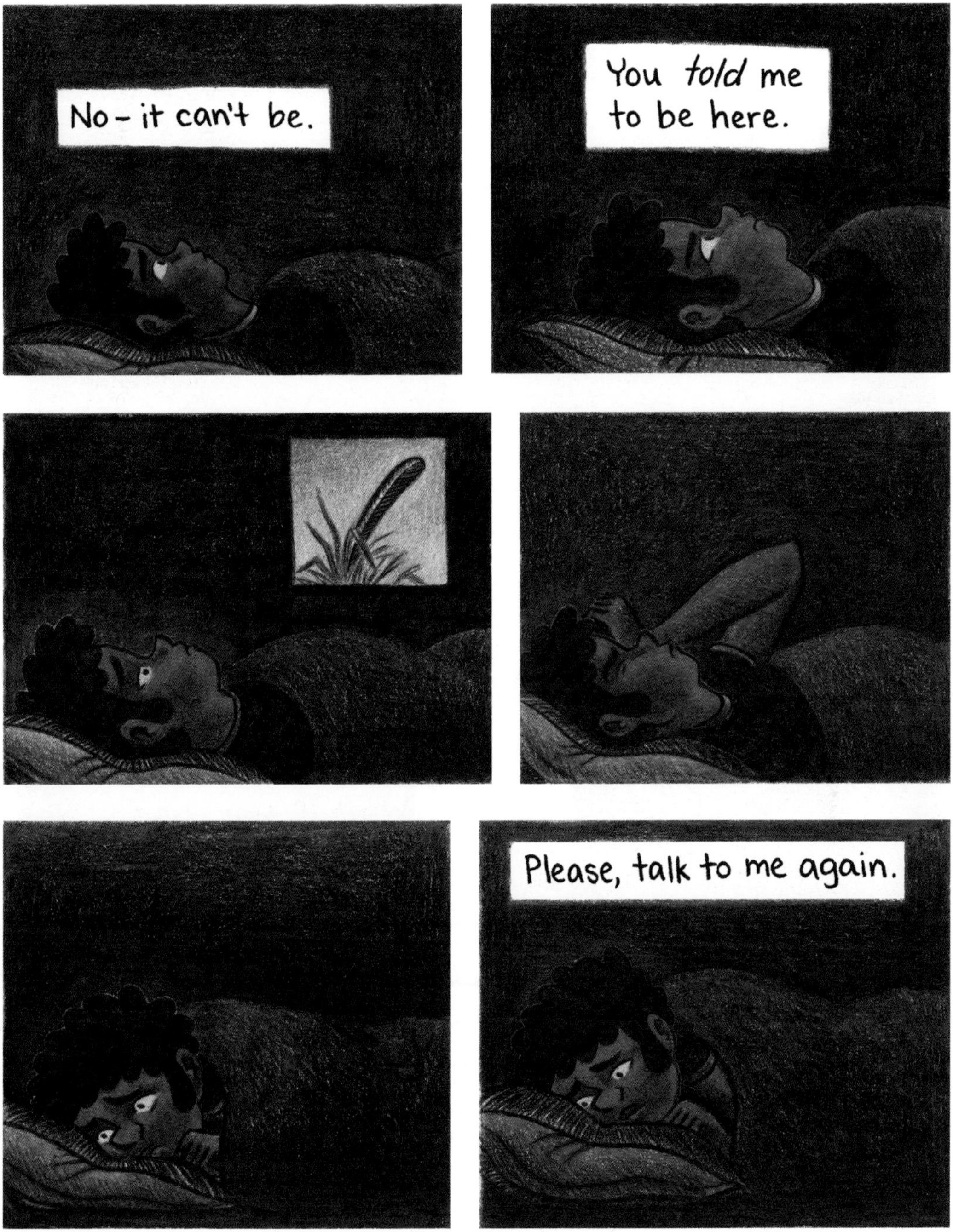
No - it can't be.
You *told* me to be here.
Please, talk to me again.

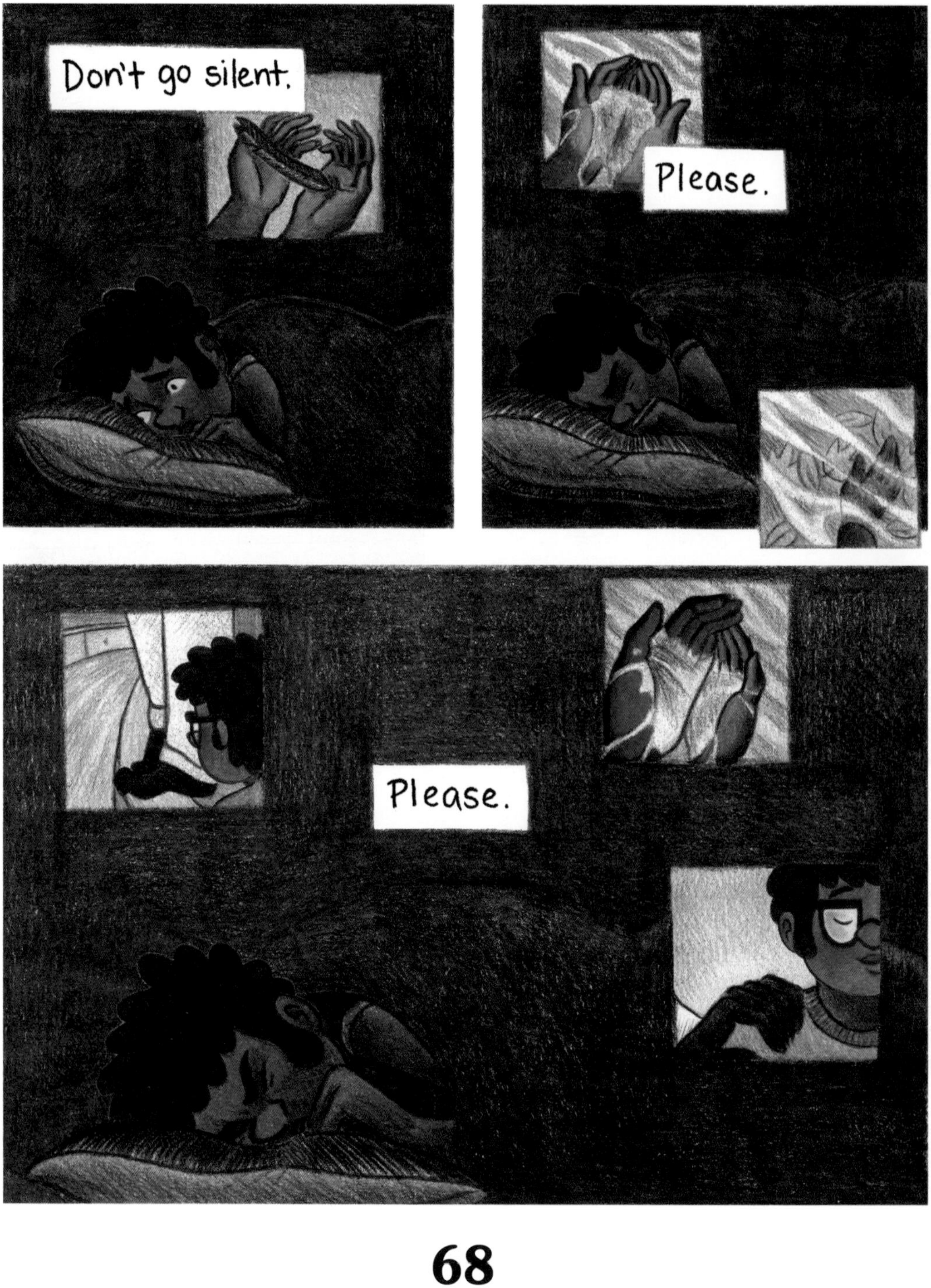
Don't go silent.
Please.
Please.

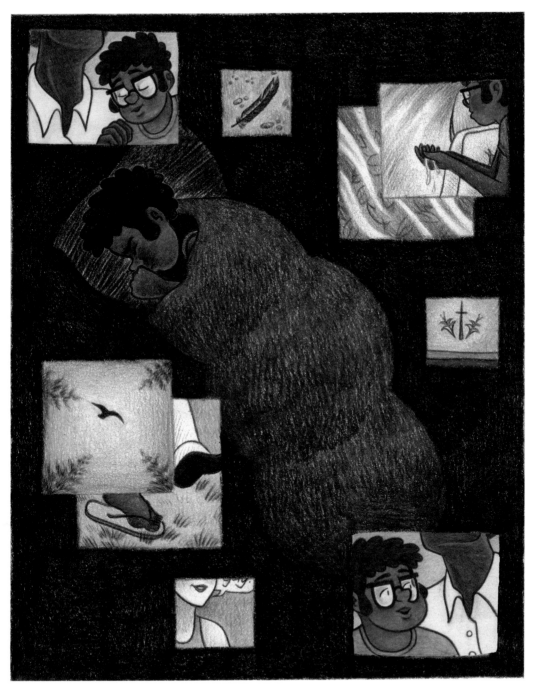

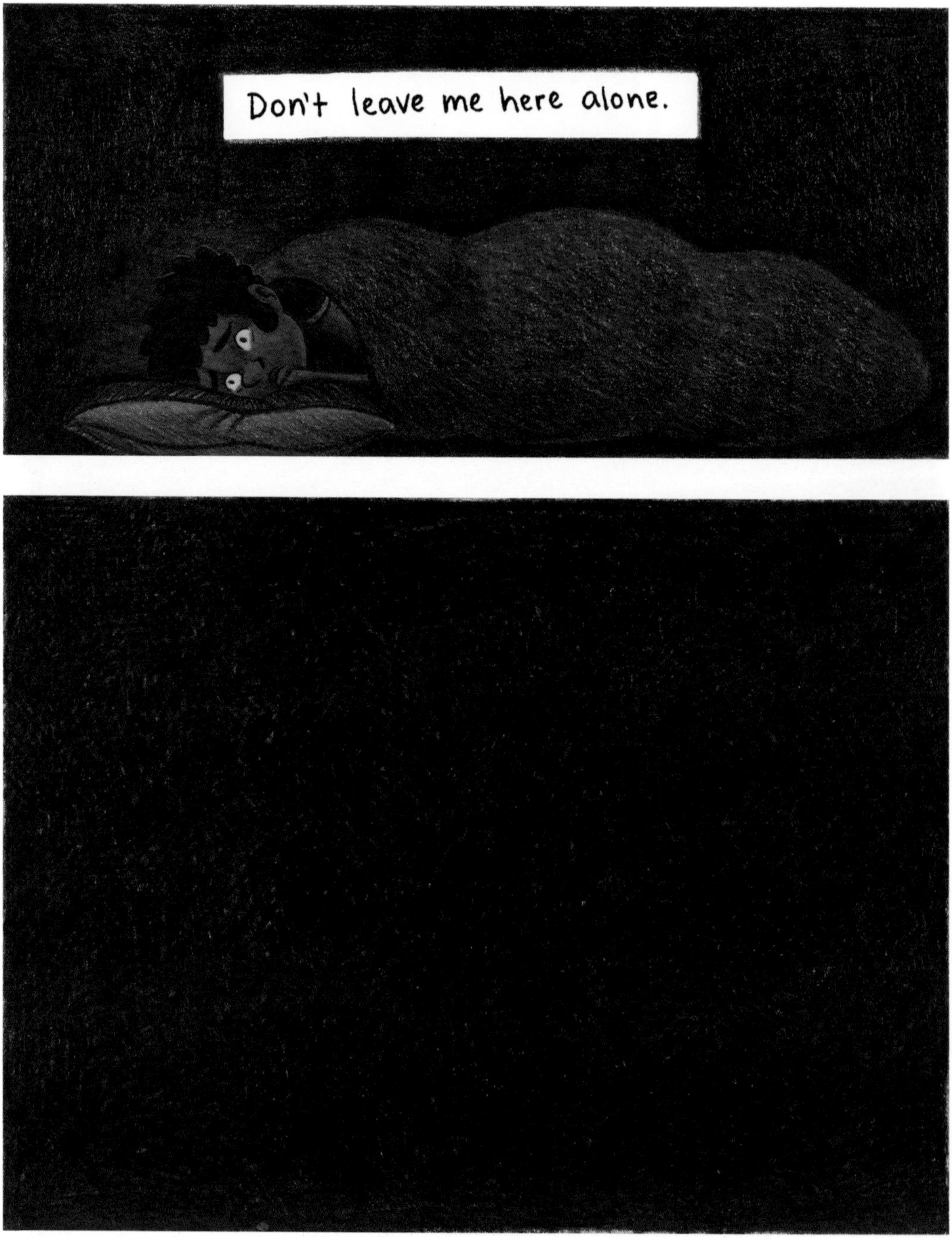
Don't leave me here alone.

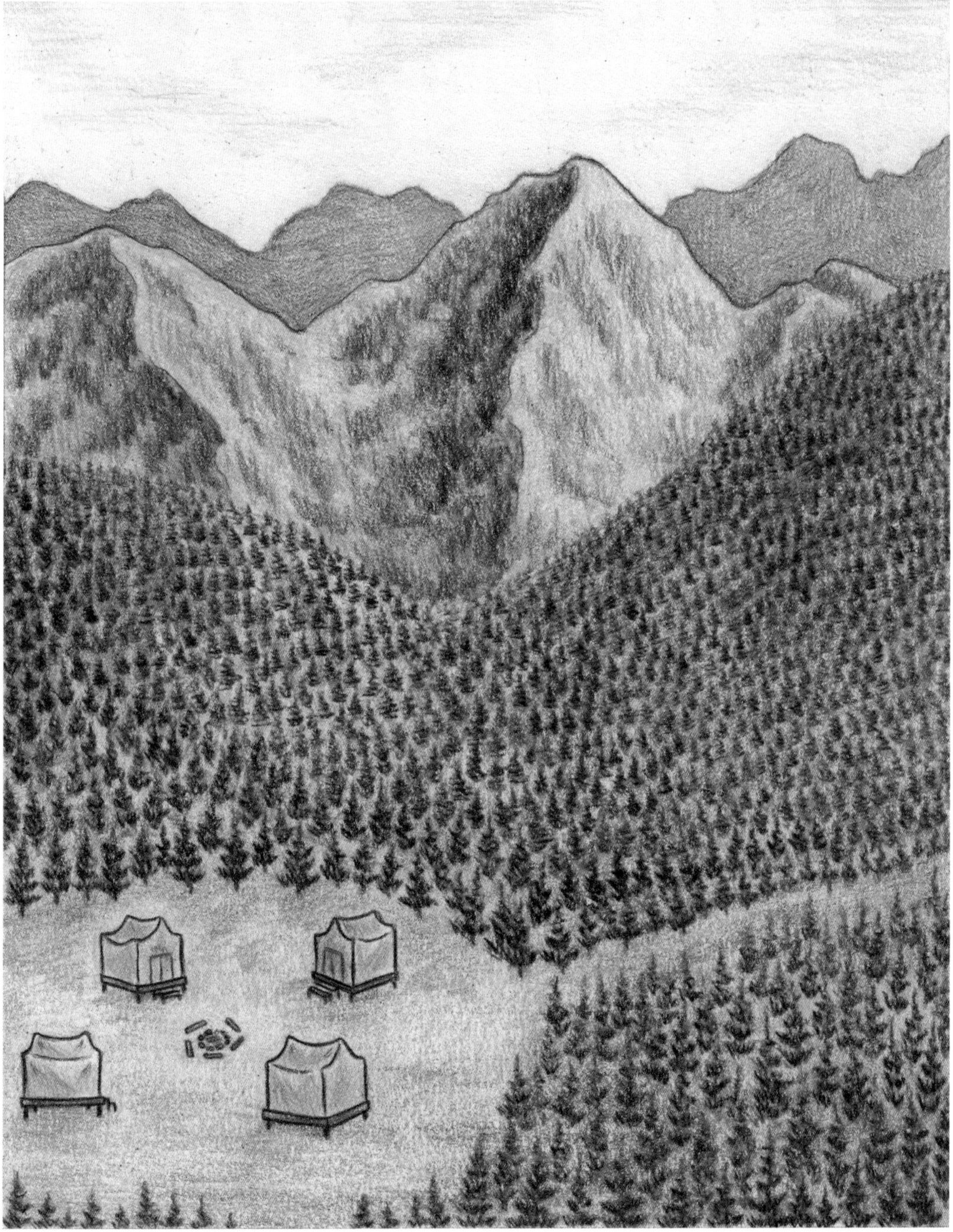

72

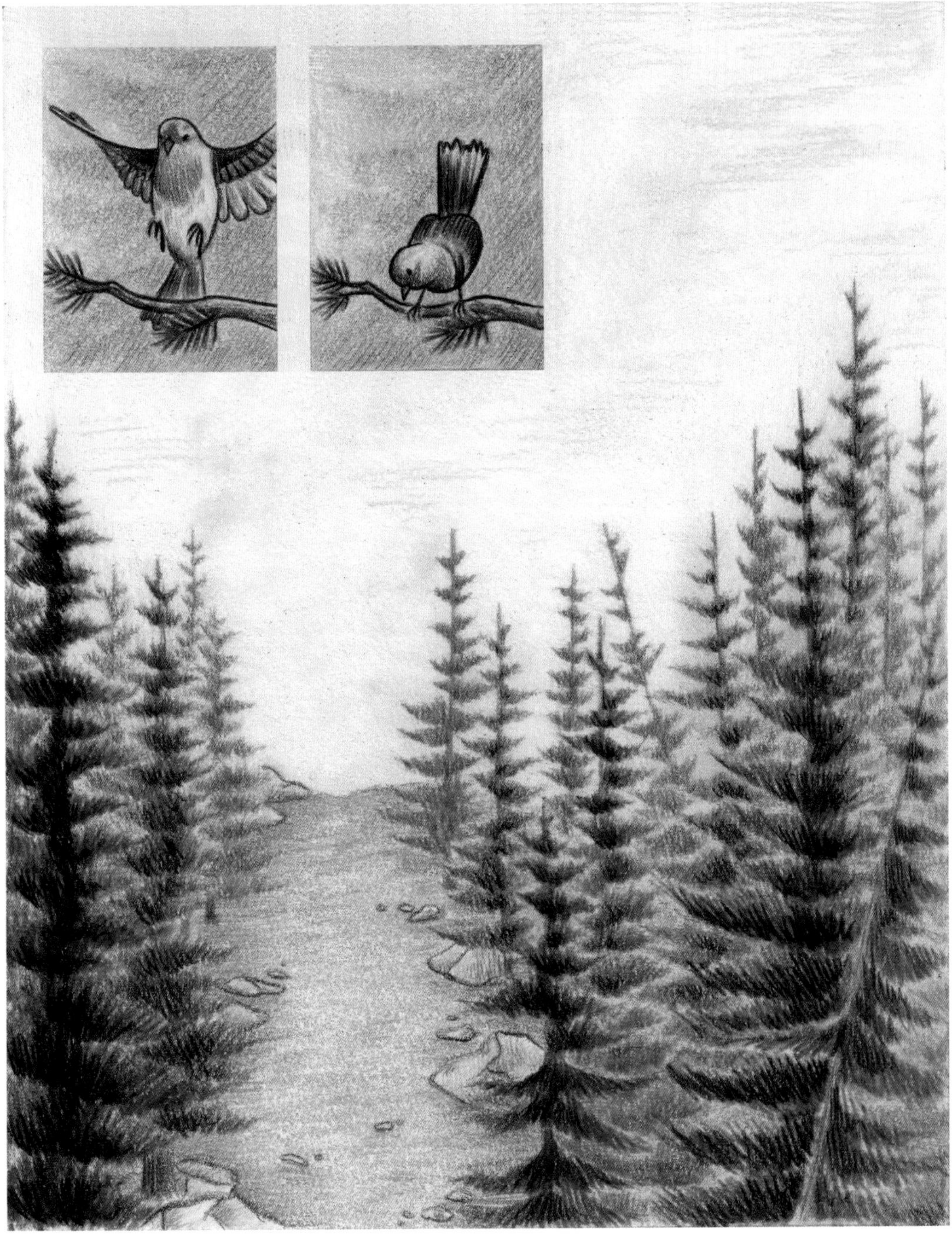

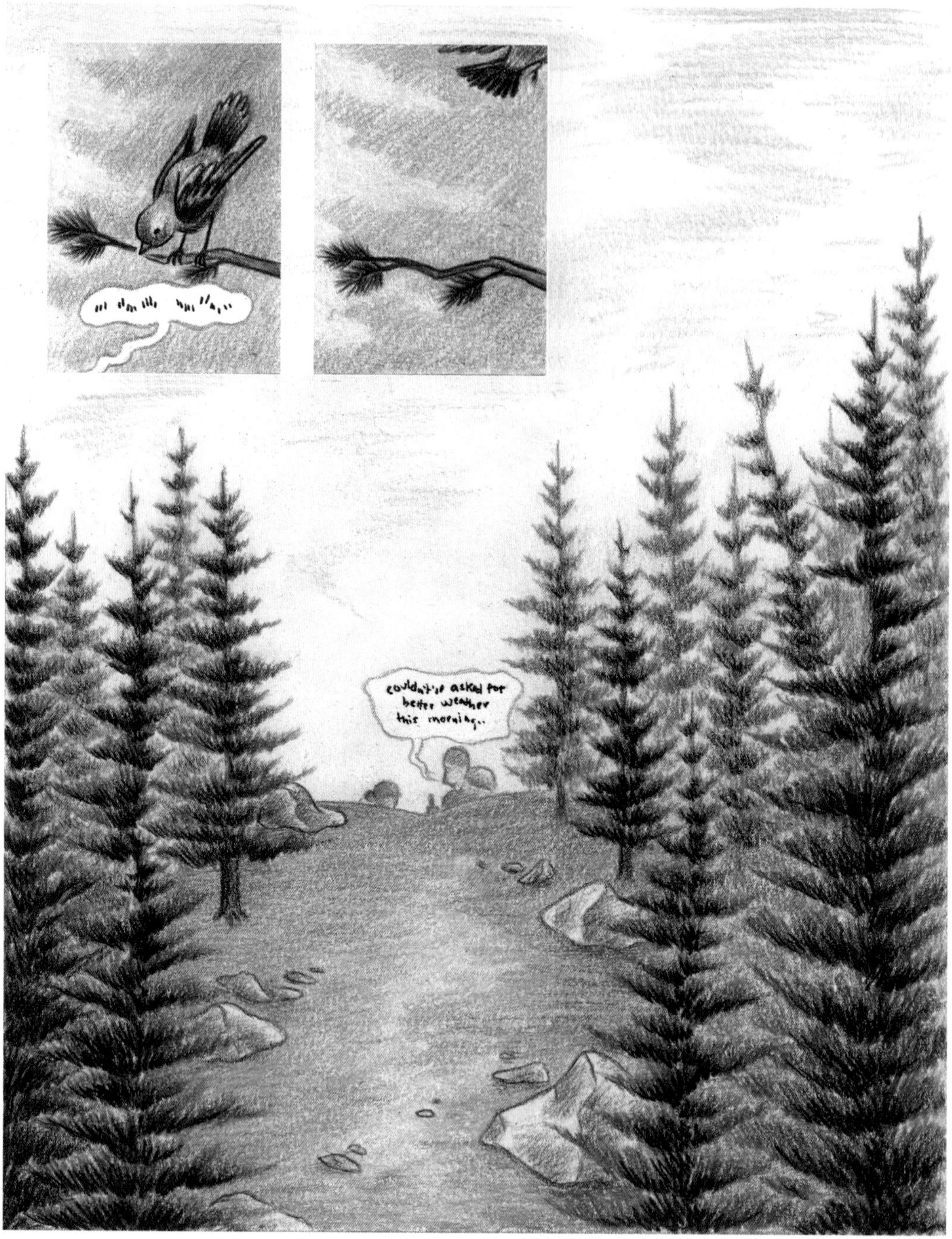
couldn't've asked for better weather this morning..

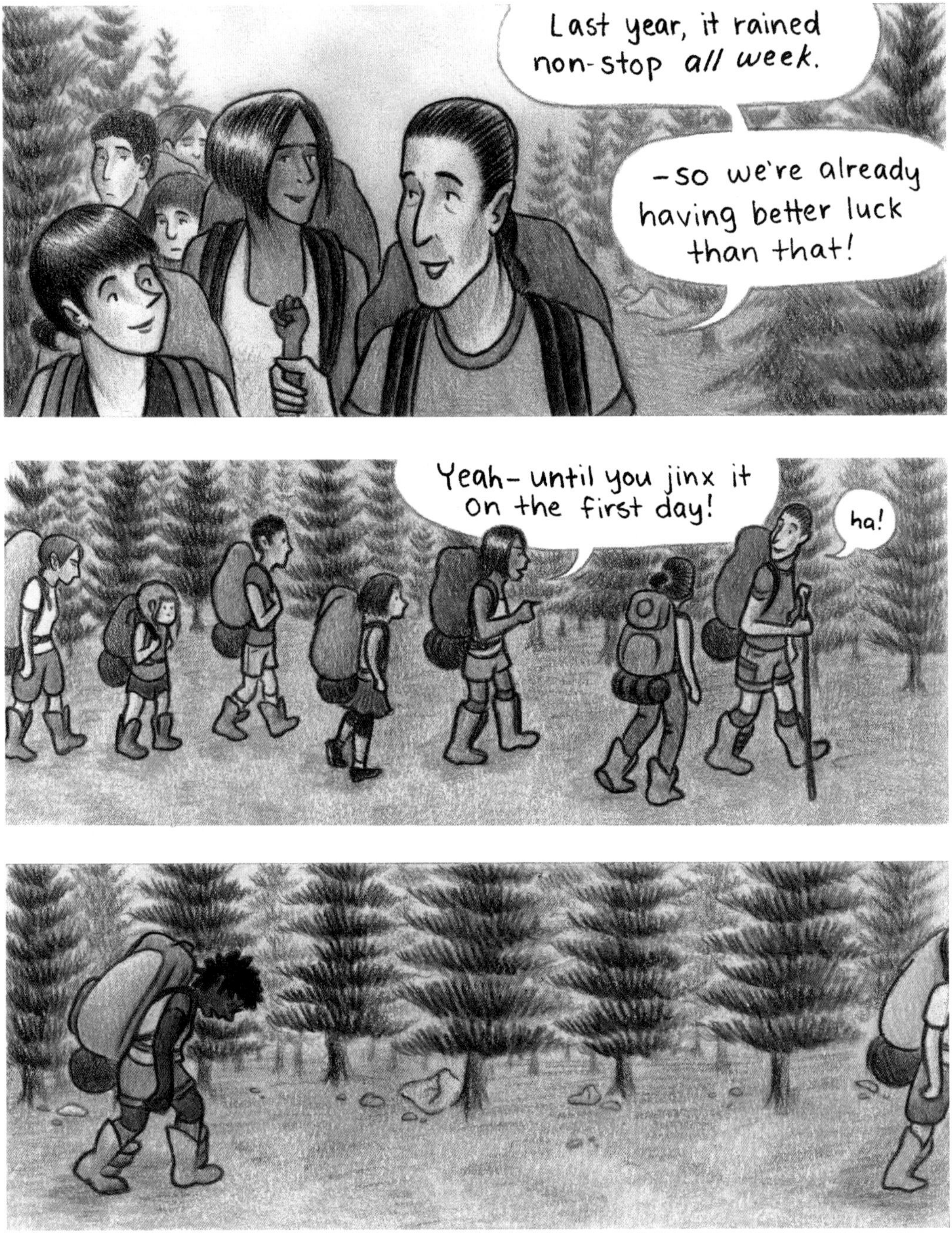

Last year, it rained non-stop *all week.*
-so we're already having better luck than that!
Yeah- until you jinx it on the first day!
ha!

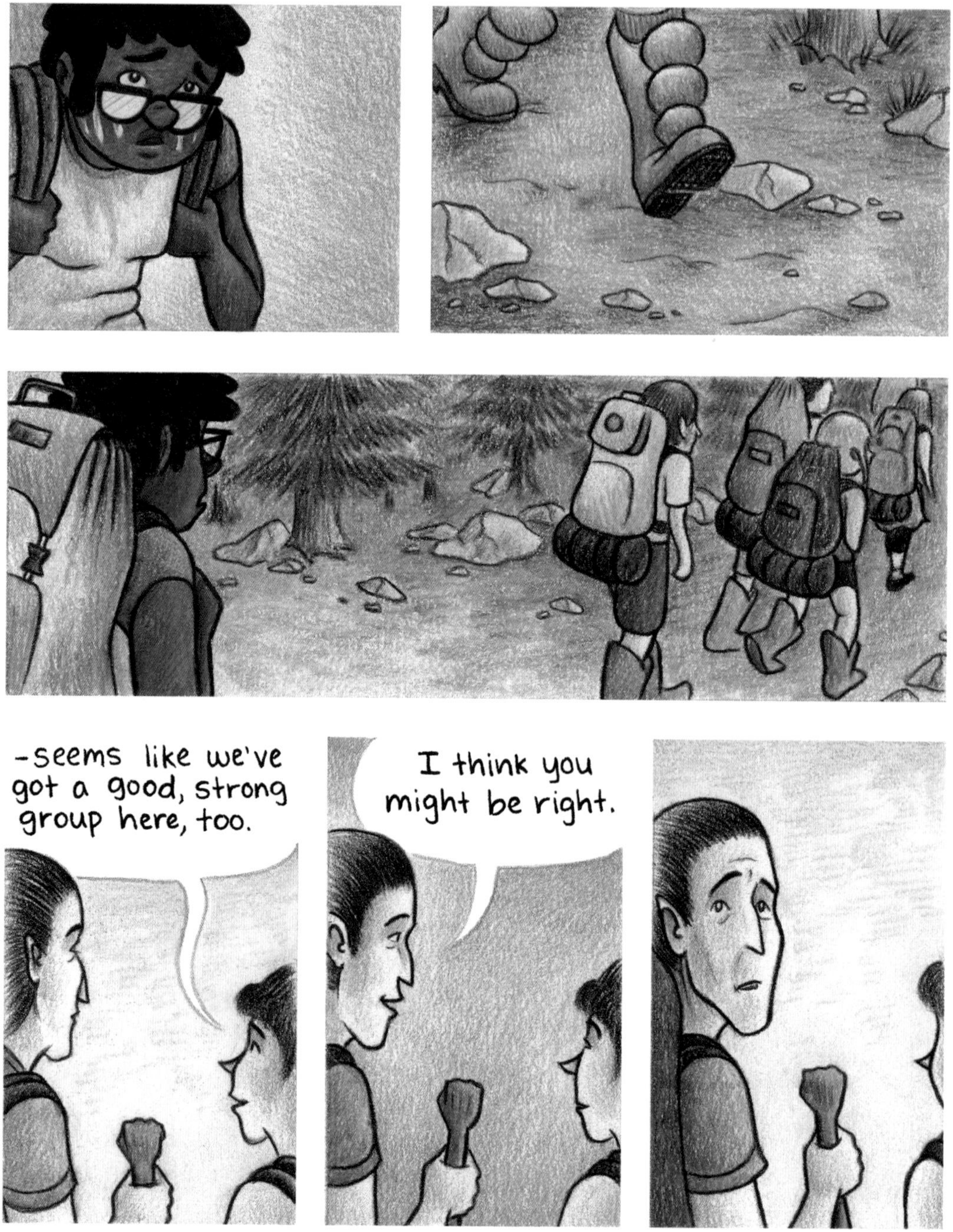
-seems like we've got a good, strong group here, too.
I think you might be right.

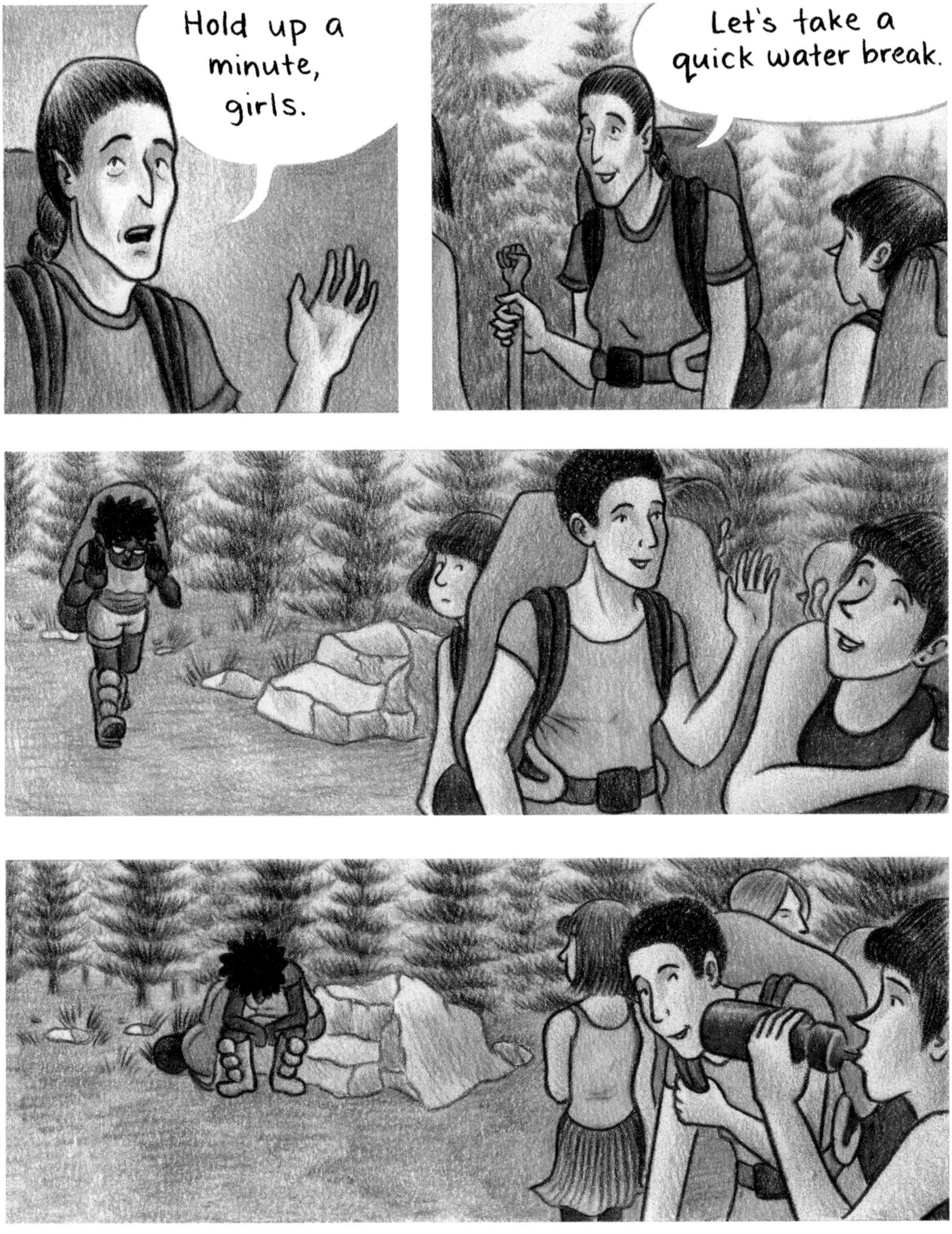
Hold up a minute, girls.
Let's take a quick water break.

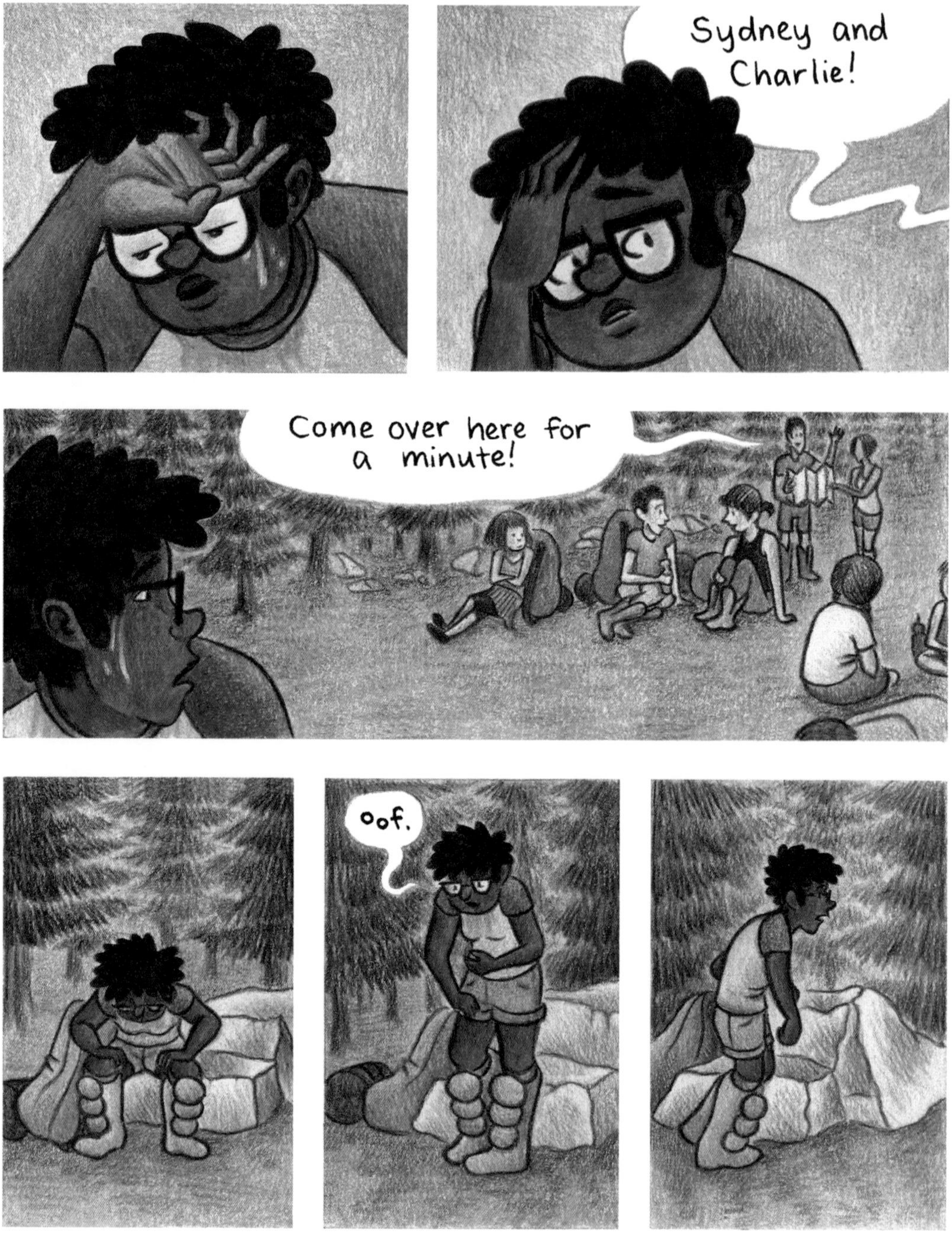
Sydney and Charlie!
Come over here for a minute!
oof.

-it should be just down the hill- couple hundred yards or so?

We won't get lost- you can even hear it a little from here.

You can? I must be getting older than I think!

Are we in trouble?

'Cuz if we are, I wanna hear some Miranda rights first.

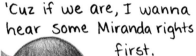

No - I've got a job for you two.

Maybe even the most important job!

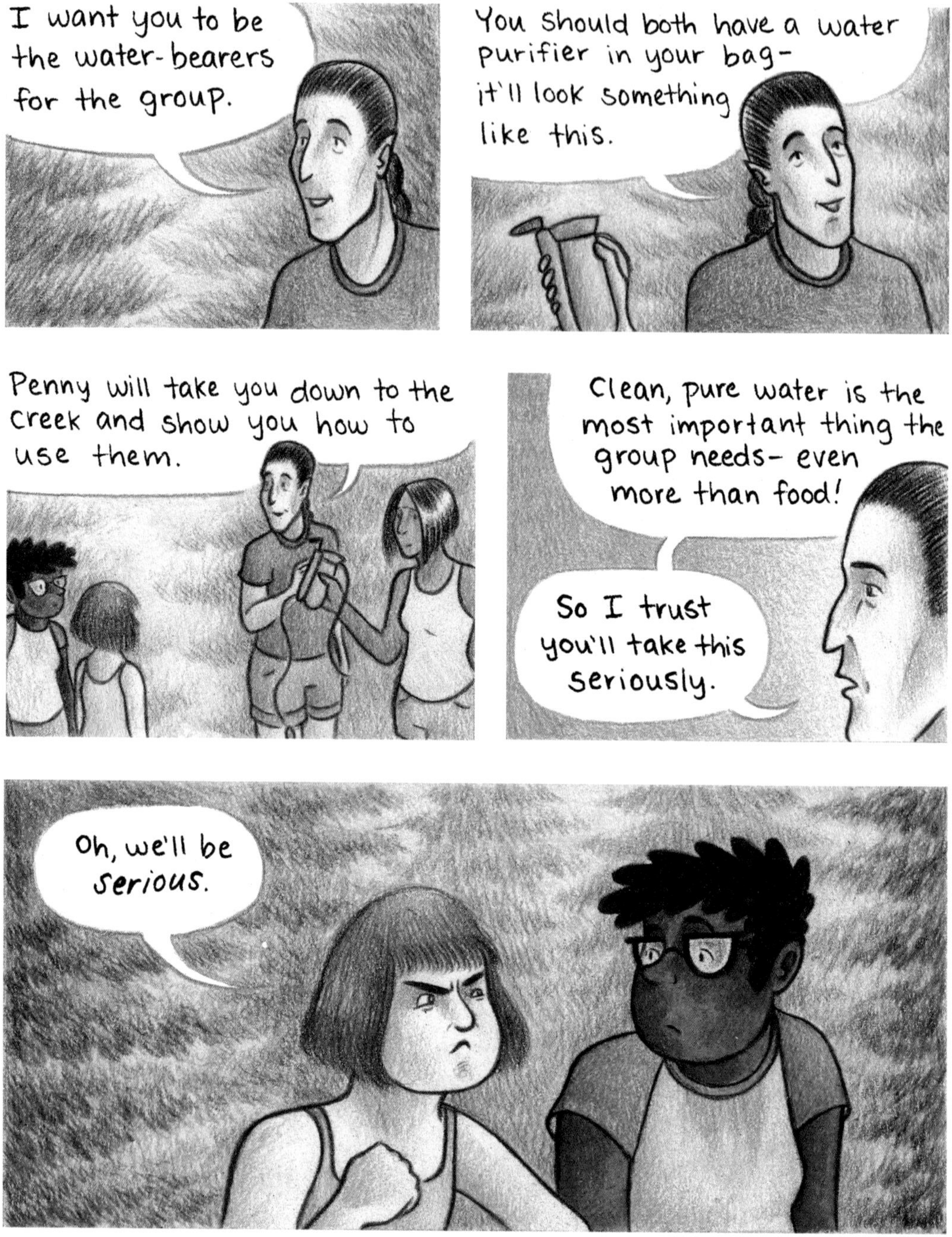
I want you to be the water-bearers for the group.
You should both have a water purifier in your bag- it'll look something like this.
Penny will take you down to the creek and show you how to use them.
Clean, pure water is the most important thing the group needs- even more than food!
So I trust you'll take this seriously.
Oh, we'll be *serious*.

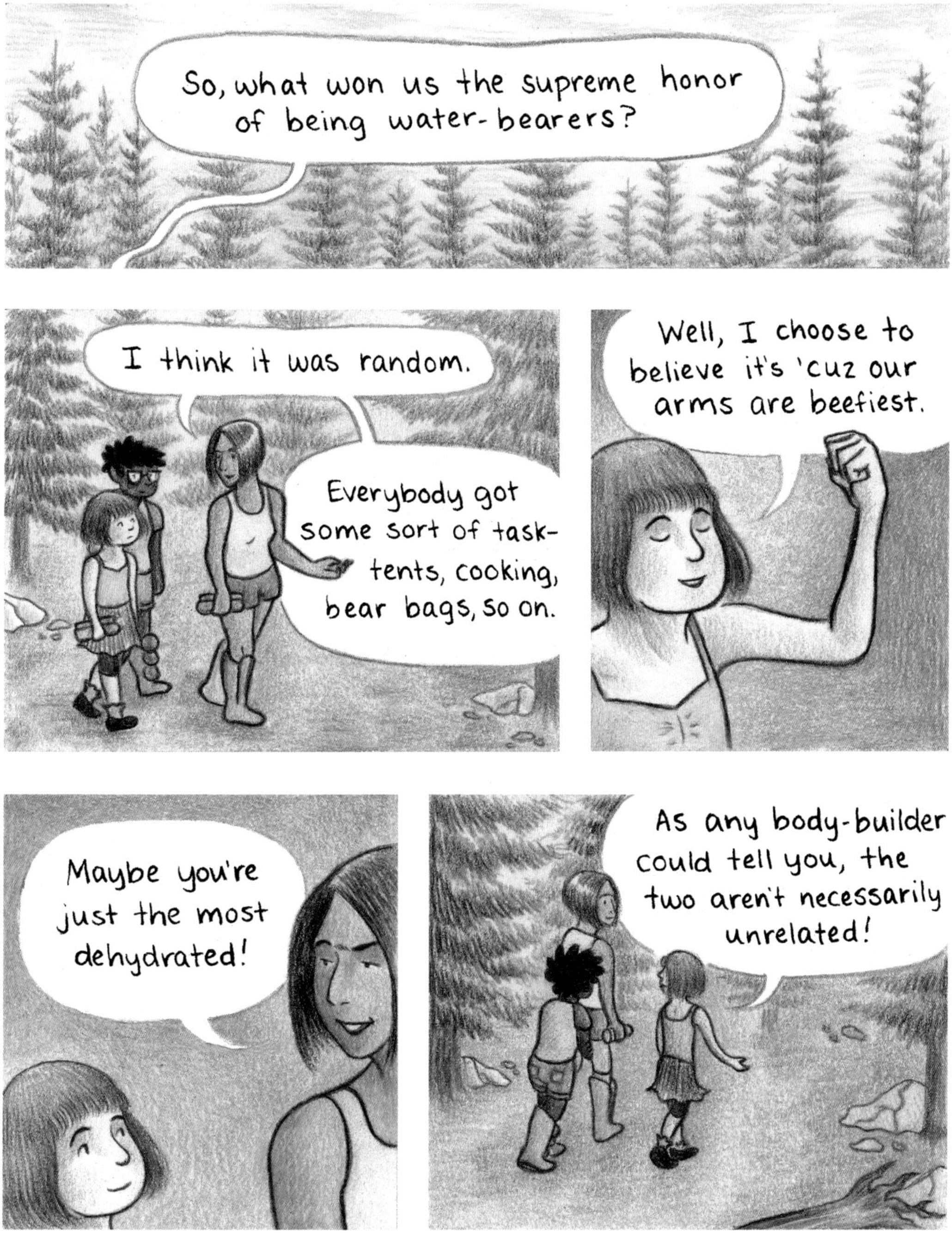
So, what won us the supreme honor of being water-bearers?
I think it was random.
Everybody got some sort of task- tents, cooking, bear bags, so on.
Well, I choose to believe it's 'cuz our arms are beefiest.
Maybe you're just the most dehydrated!
As any body-builder could tell you, the two aren't necessarily unrelated!

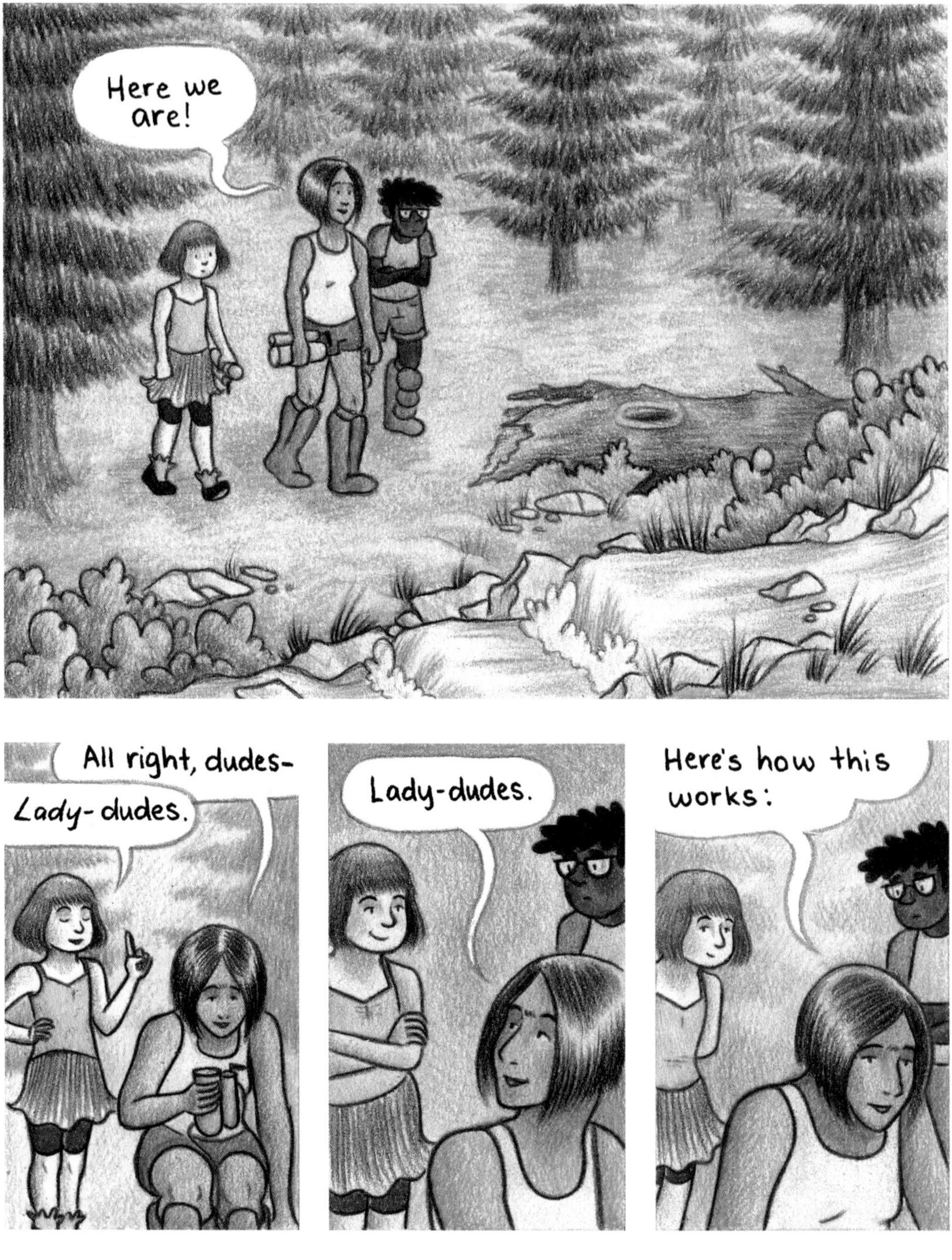
Here we are!
All right, dudes-
Lady-dudes.
Lady-dudes.
Here's how this works:

The black part is what goes in the water.

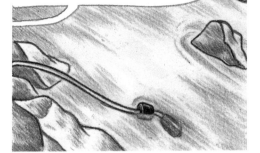

Try to aim for the fast-moving water- germs and gunk like to congregate in the still areas.

The other tube attaches to your water bag like so—

— then you use those beefy arms to PUMP SOME IRON.

And once it's full, you can distribute water to all your adoring, parched campmates.

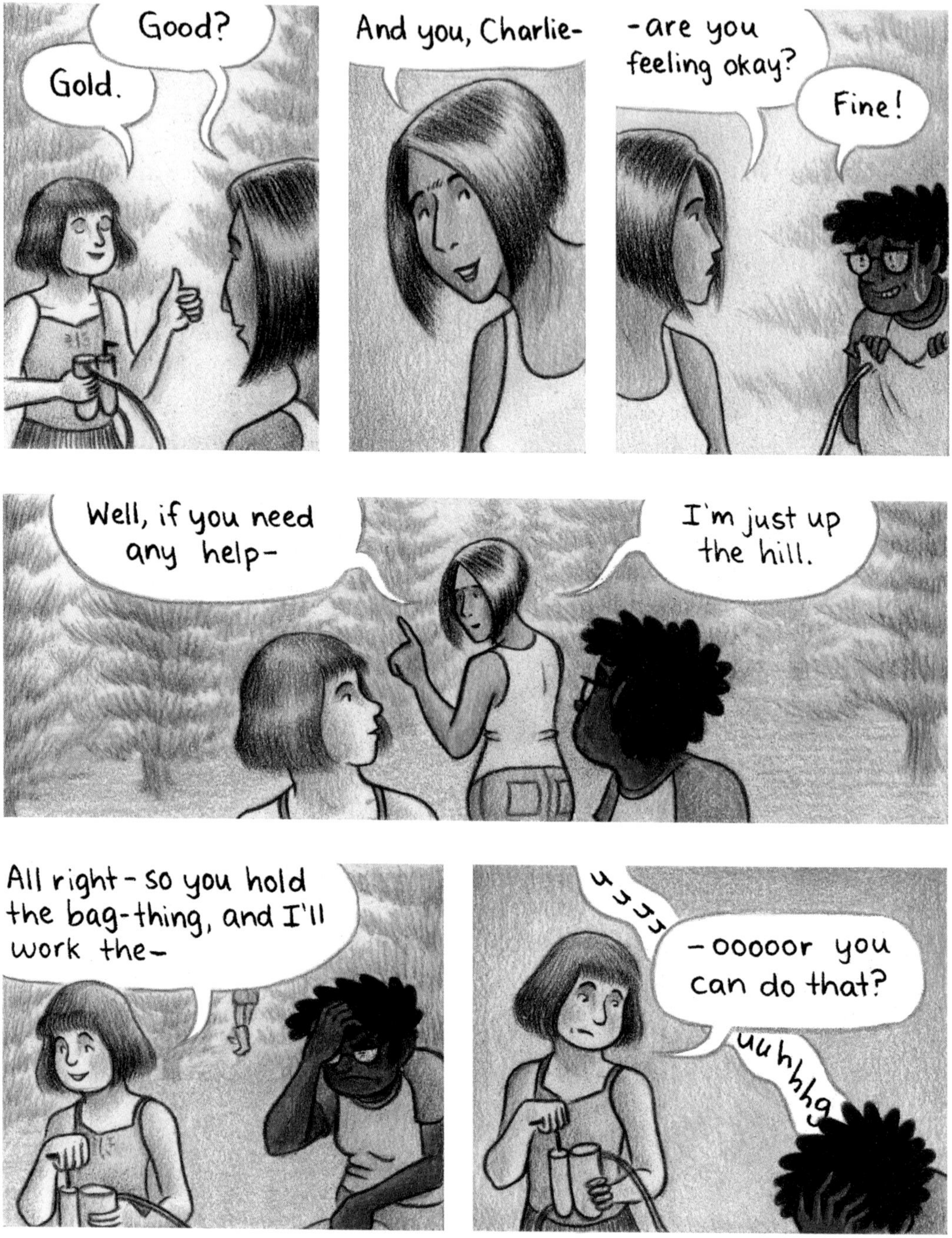
Good?
Gold.
And you, Charlie-
-are you feeling okay?
Fine!
Well, if you need any help-
I'm just up the hill.
All right- so you hold the bag-thing, and I'll work the-
uuuu
-oooor you can do that?
uuhhhg

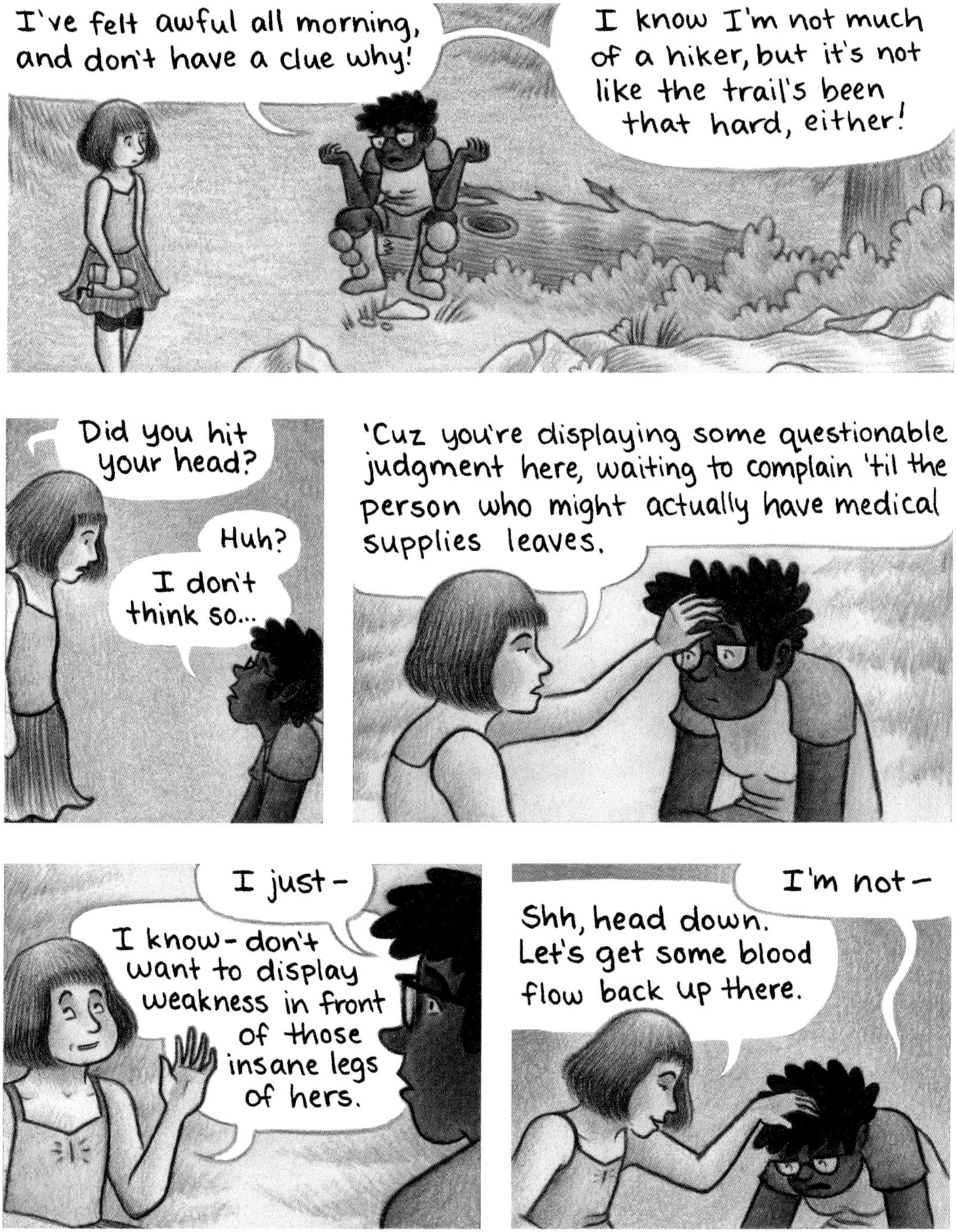
I've felt awful all morning, and don't have a clue why!
I know I'm not much of a hiker, but it's not like the trail's been that hard, either!
Did you hit your head?
Huh?
I don't think so...
'Cuz you're displaying some questionable judgment here, waiting to complain 'til the person who might actually have medical supplies leaves.
I just-
I know- don't want to display weakness in front of those insane legs of hers.
I'm not-
Shh, head down. Let's get some blood flow back up there.

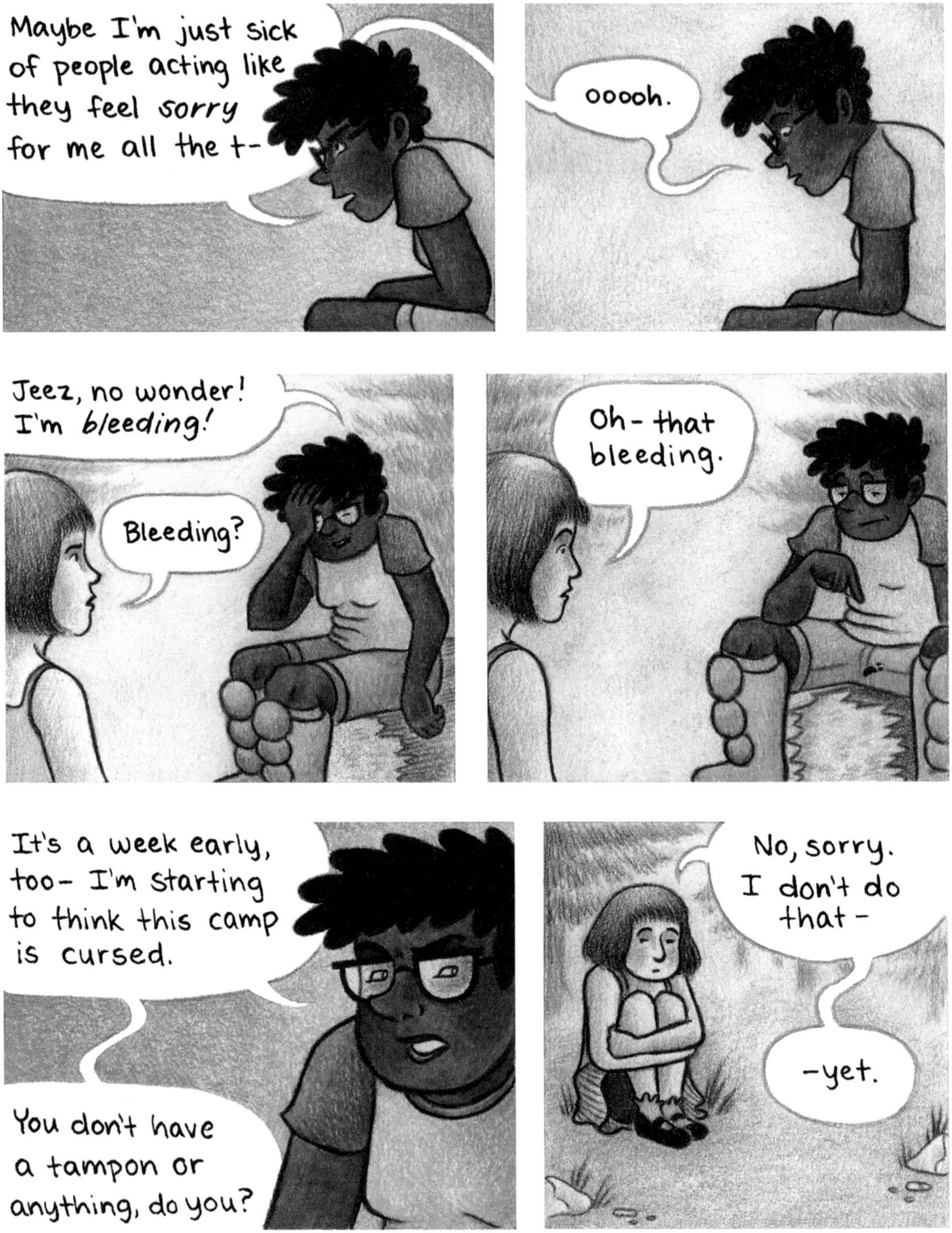

Maybe I'm just sick of people acting like they feel *sorry* for me all the t-
ooooh.
Jeez, no wonder! I'm *bleeding!*
Bleeding?
Oh- that bleeding.
It's a week early, too- I'm starting to think this camp is cursed.
You don't have a tampon or anything, do you?
No, sorry. I don't do that-
-yet.

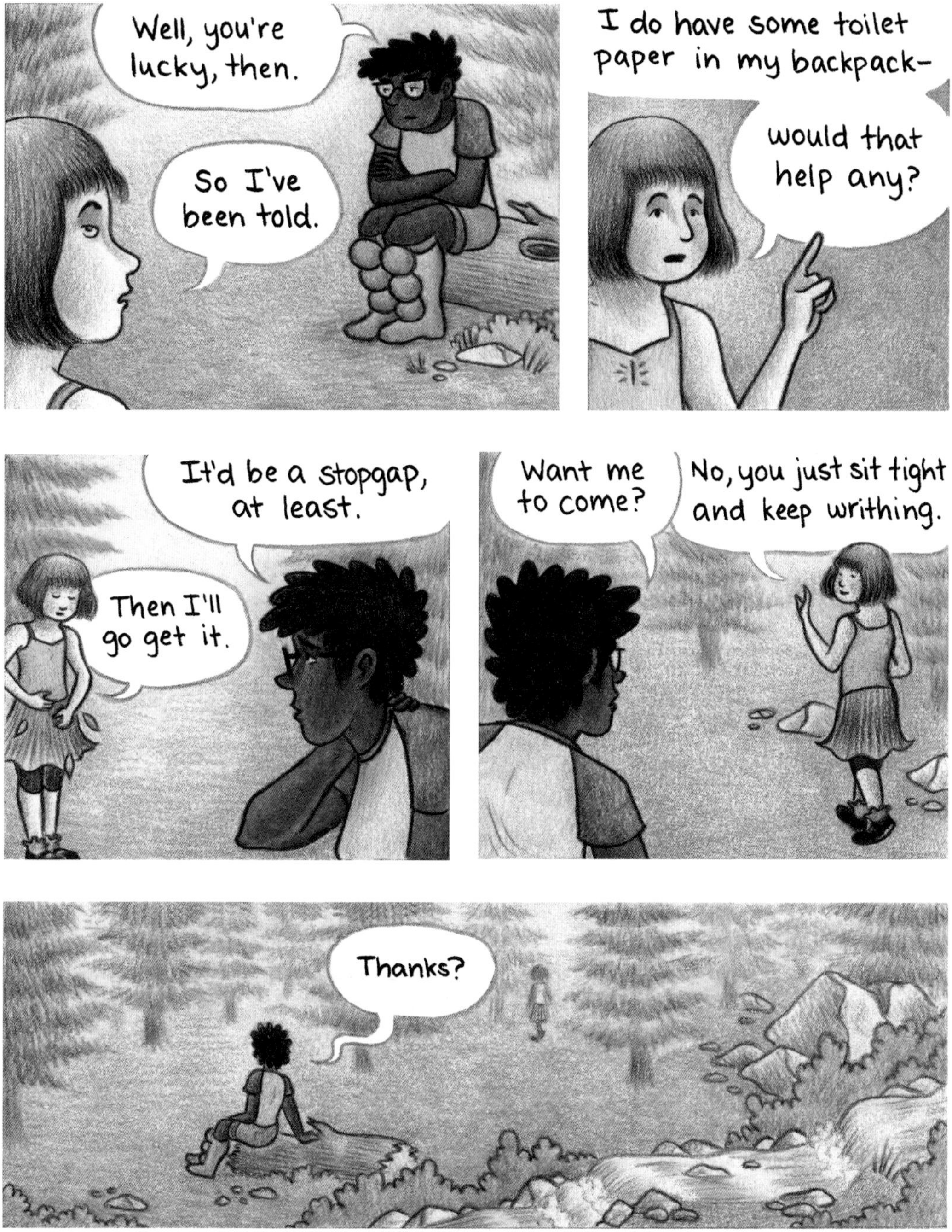
Well, you're lucky, then.
So I've been told.
I do have some toilet paper in my backpack-
would that help any?
It'd be a stopgap, at least.
Then I'll go get it.
Want me to come?
No, you just sit tight and keep writhing.
Thanks?

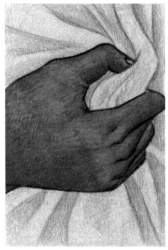

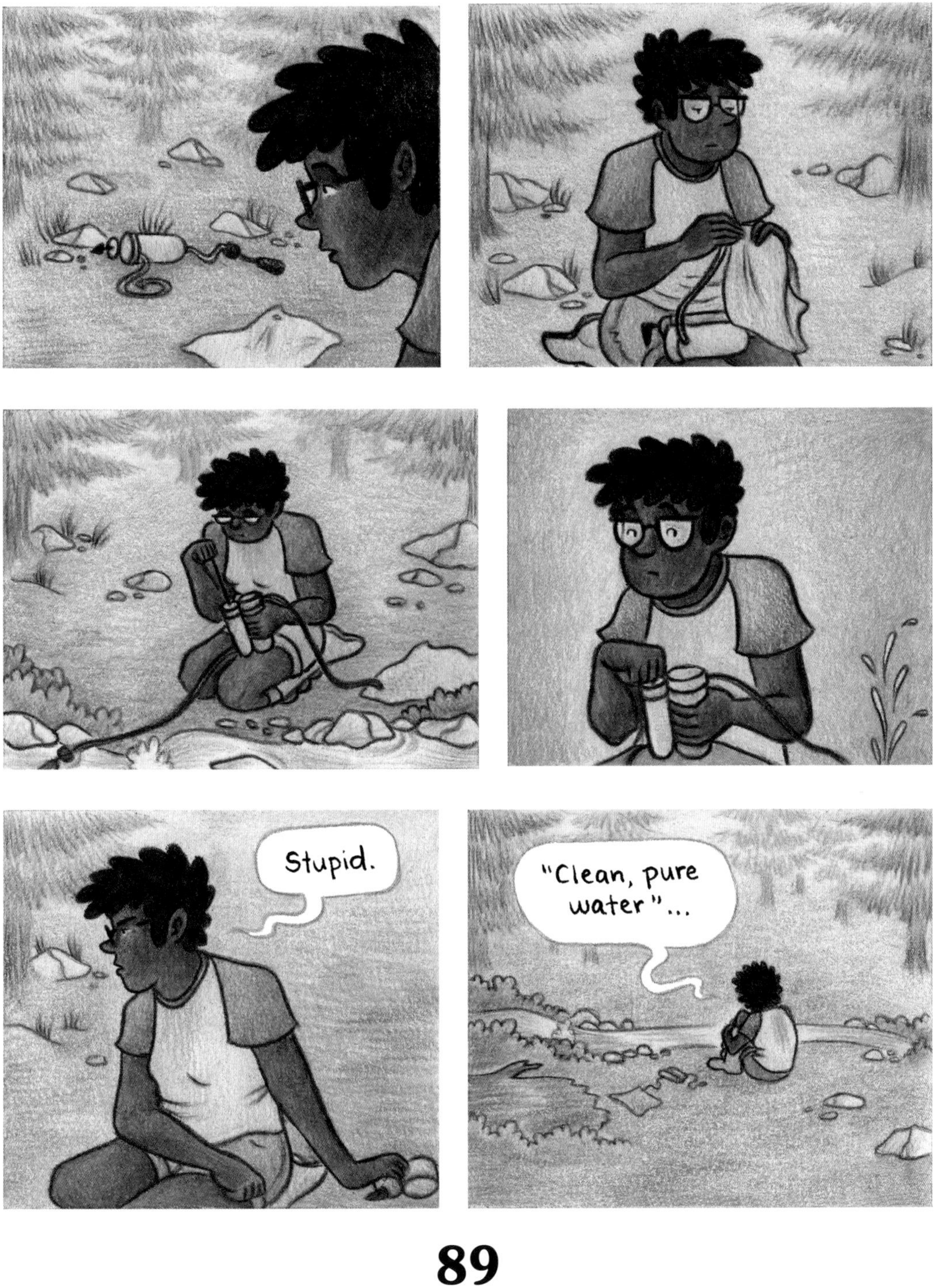
Stupid.
"Clean, pure water"...

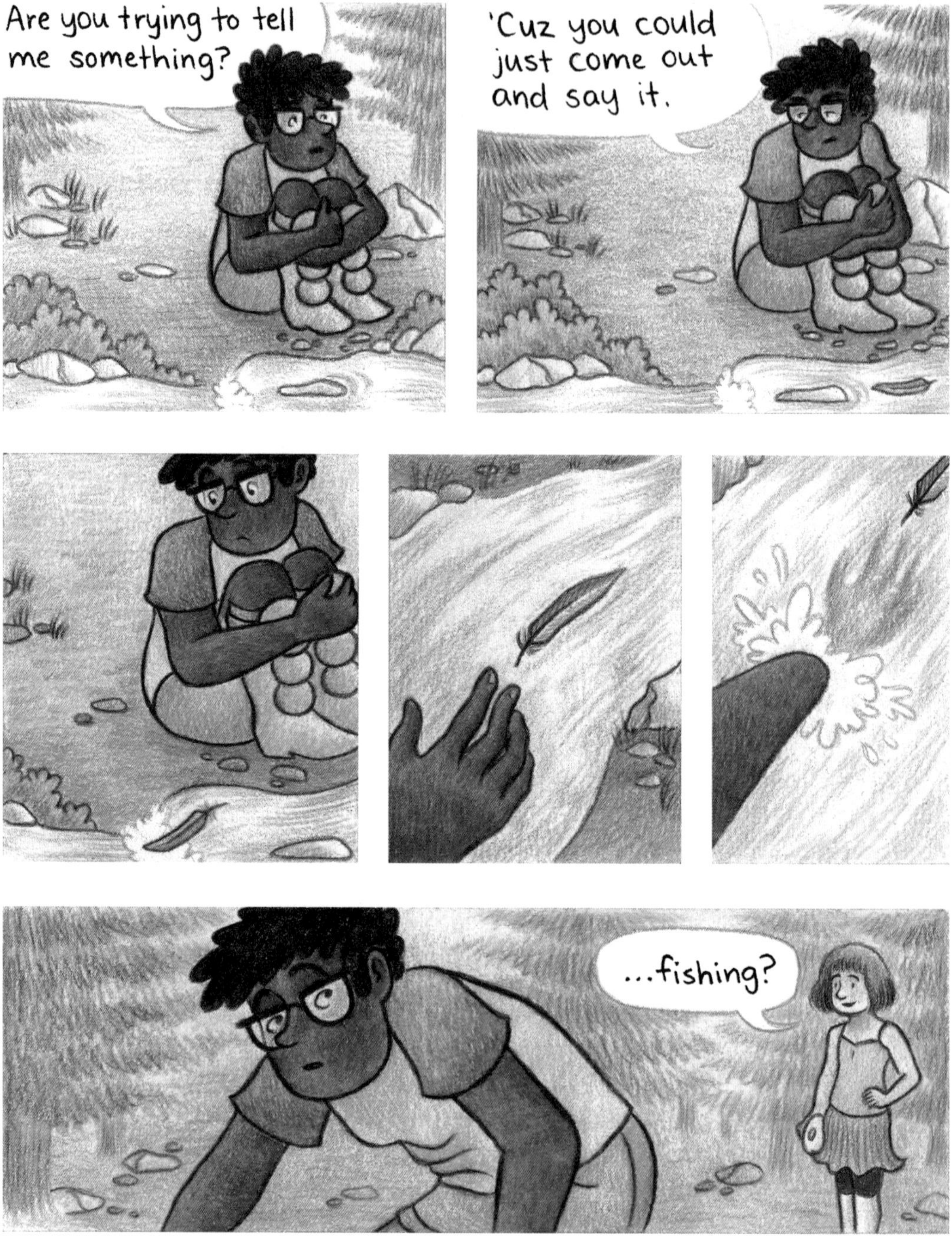
Are you trying to tell me something?
'Cuz you could just come out and say it.
...fishing?

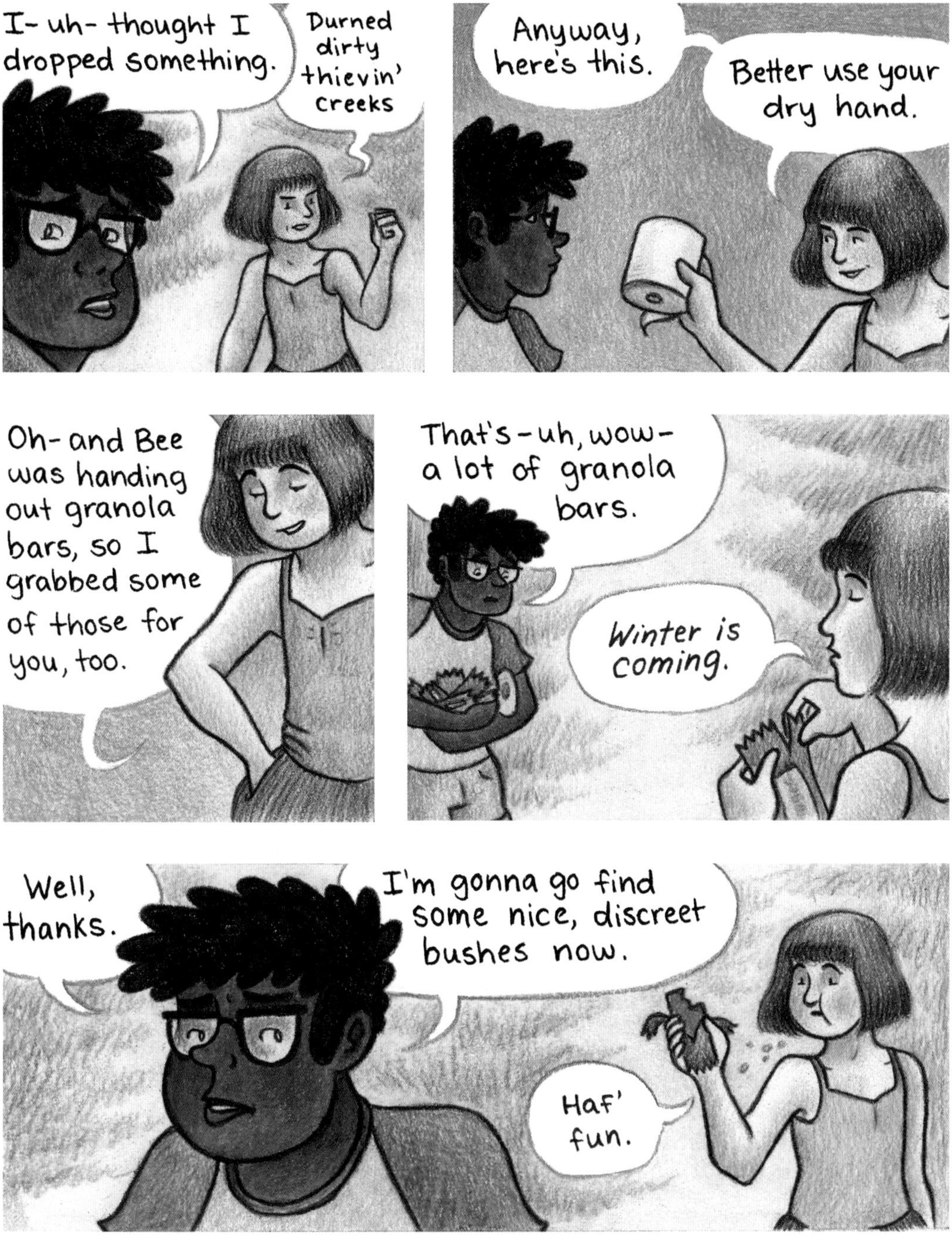
I- uh- thought I dropped something.
Durned dirty thievin' creeks
Anyway, here's this.
Better use your dry hand.
Oh- and Bee was handing out granola bars, so I grabbed some of those for you, too.
That's- uh, wow- a lot of granola bars.
Winter is coming.
Well, thanks.
I'm gonna go find some nice, discreet bushes now.
Haf' fun.

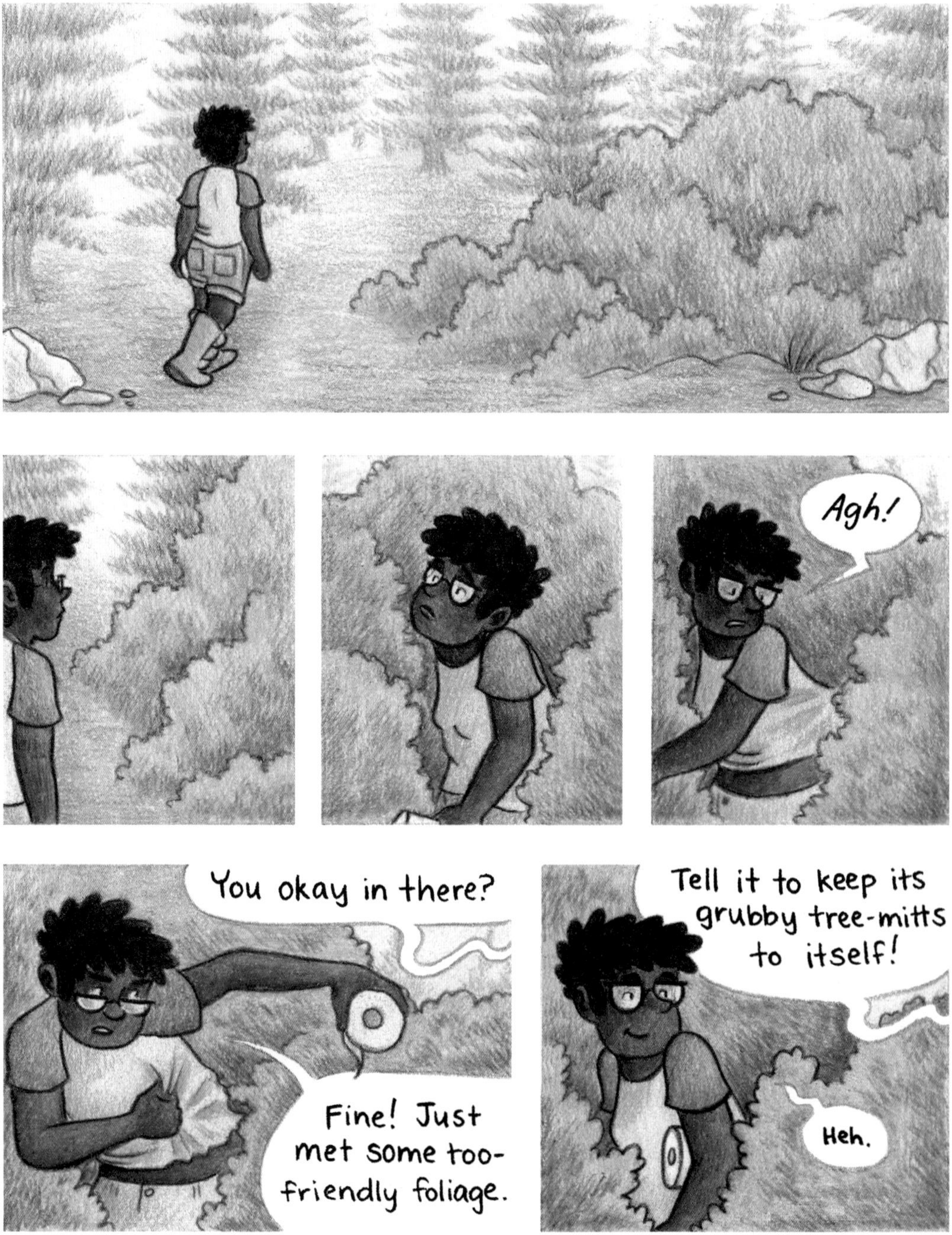
Agh!
You okay in there?
Fine! Just met some too-friendly foliage.
Tell it to keep its grubby tree-mitts to itself!
Heh.

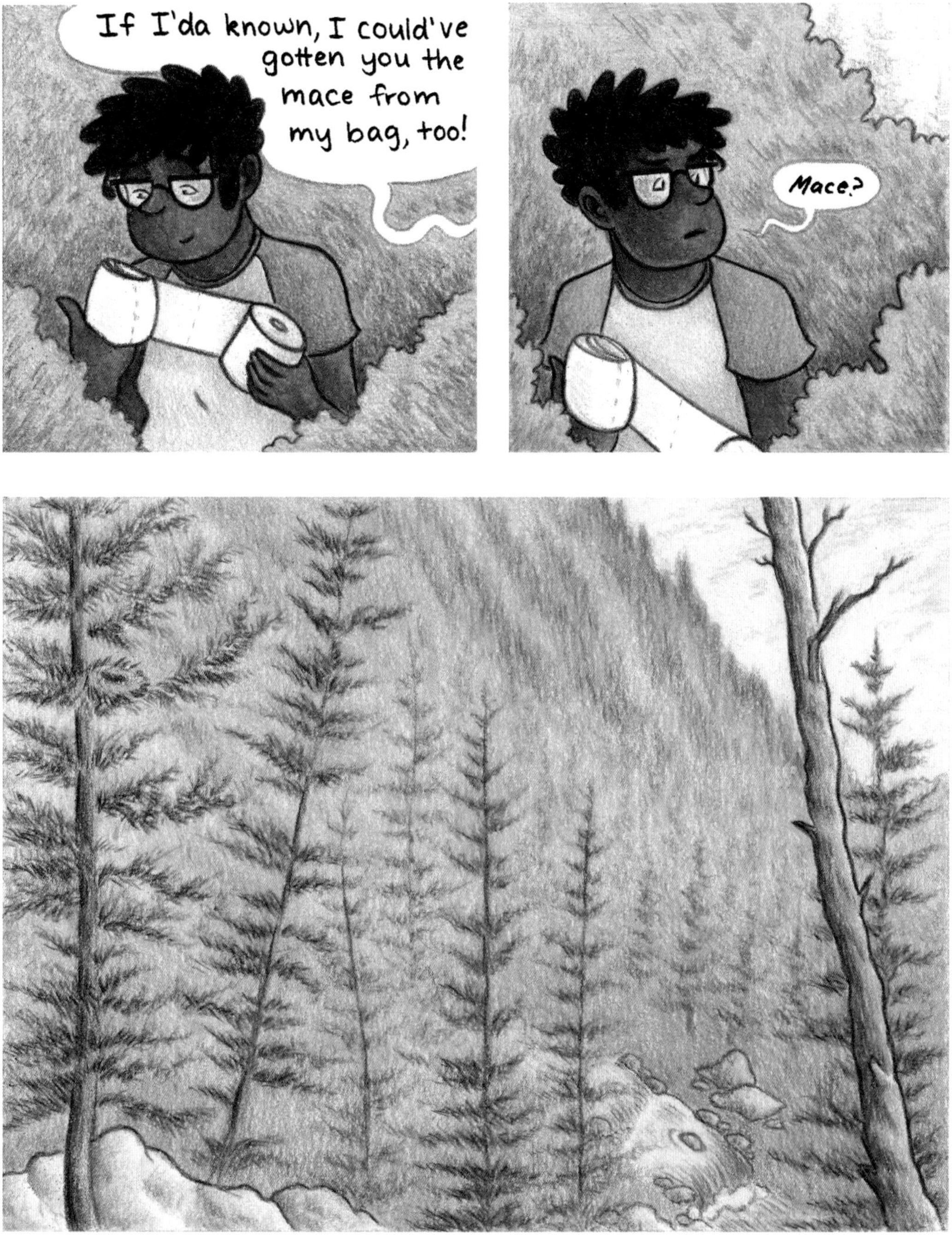
If I'da known, I could've gotten you the mace from my bag, too!
Mace?

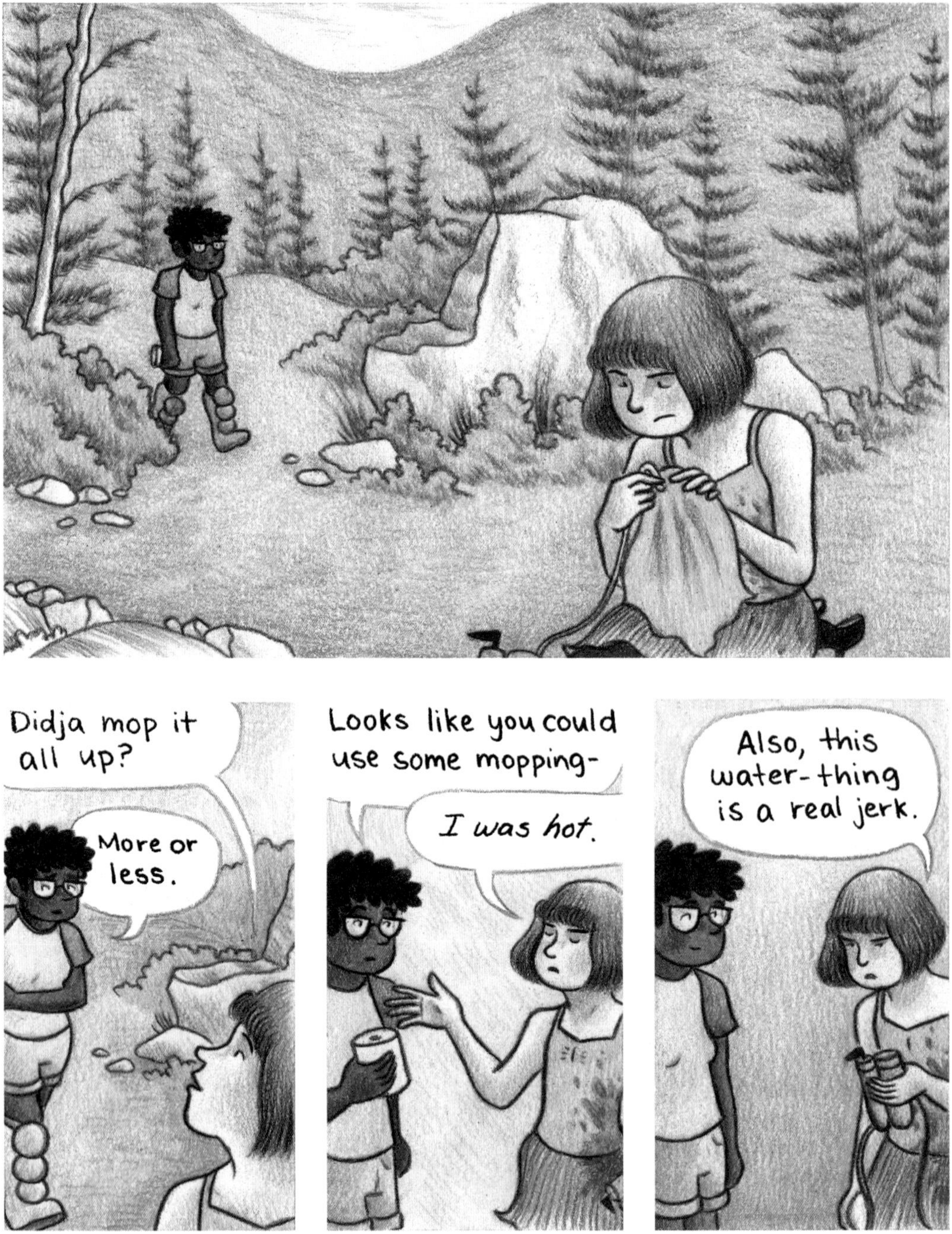
Didja mop it all up?
More or less.
Looks like you could use some mopping-
I was hot.
Also, this water-thing is a real jerk.

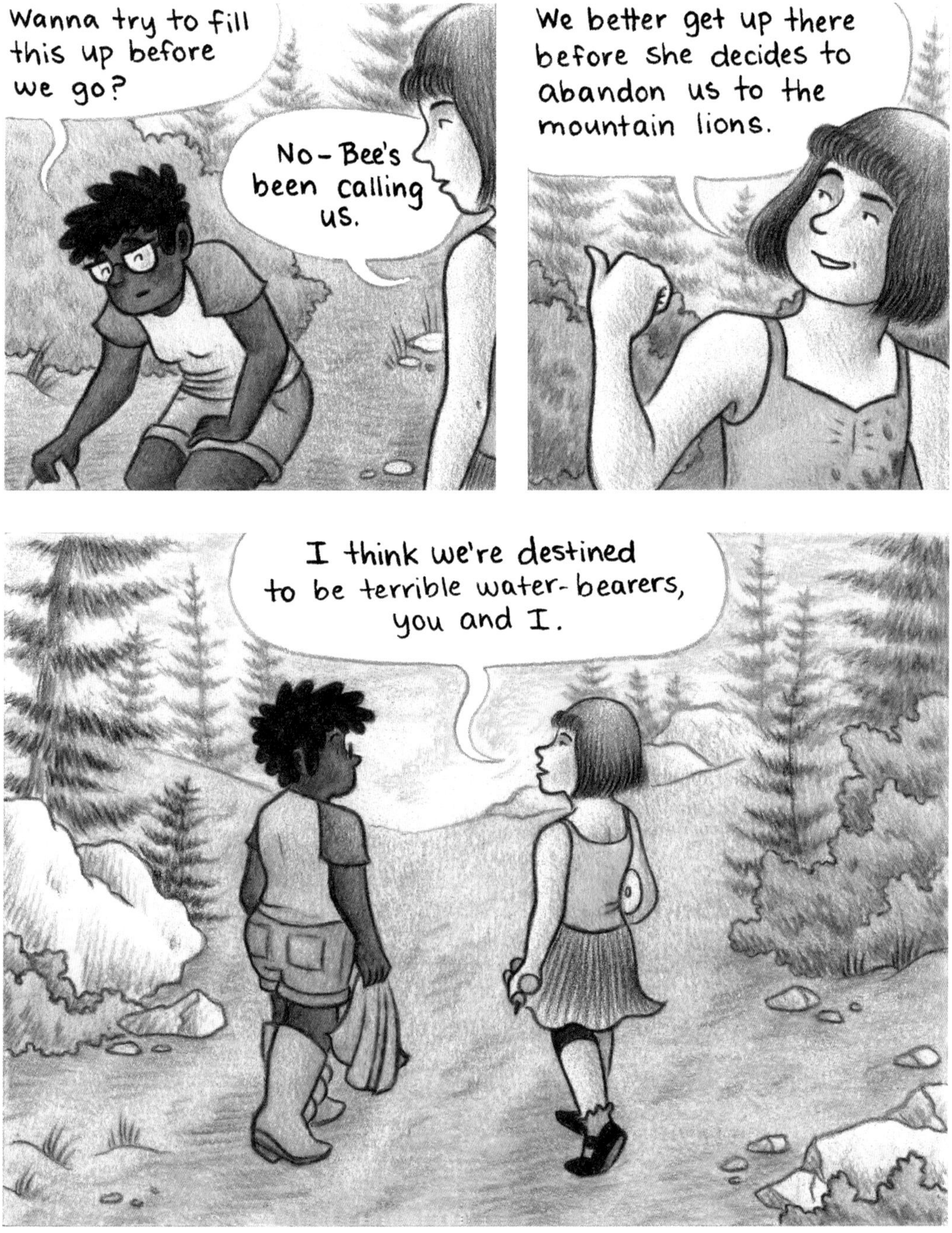
Wanna try to fill this up before we go?
No-Bee's been calling us.
We better get up there before she decides to abandon us to the mountain lions.
I think we're destined to be terrible water-bearers, you and I.

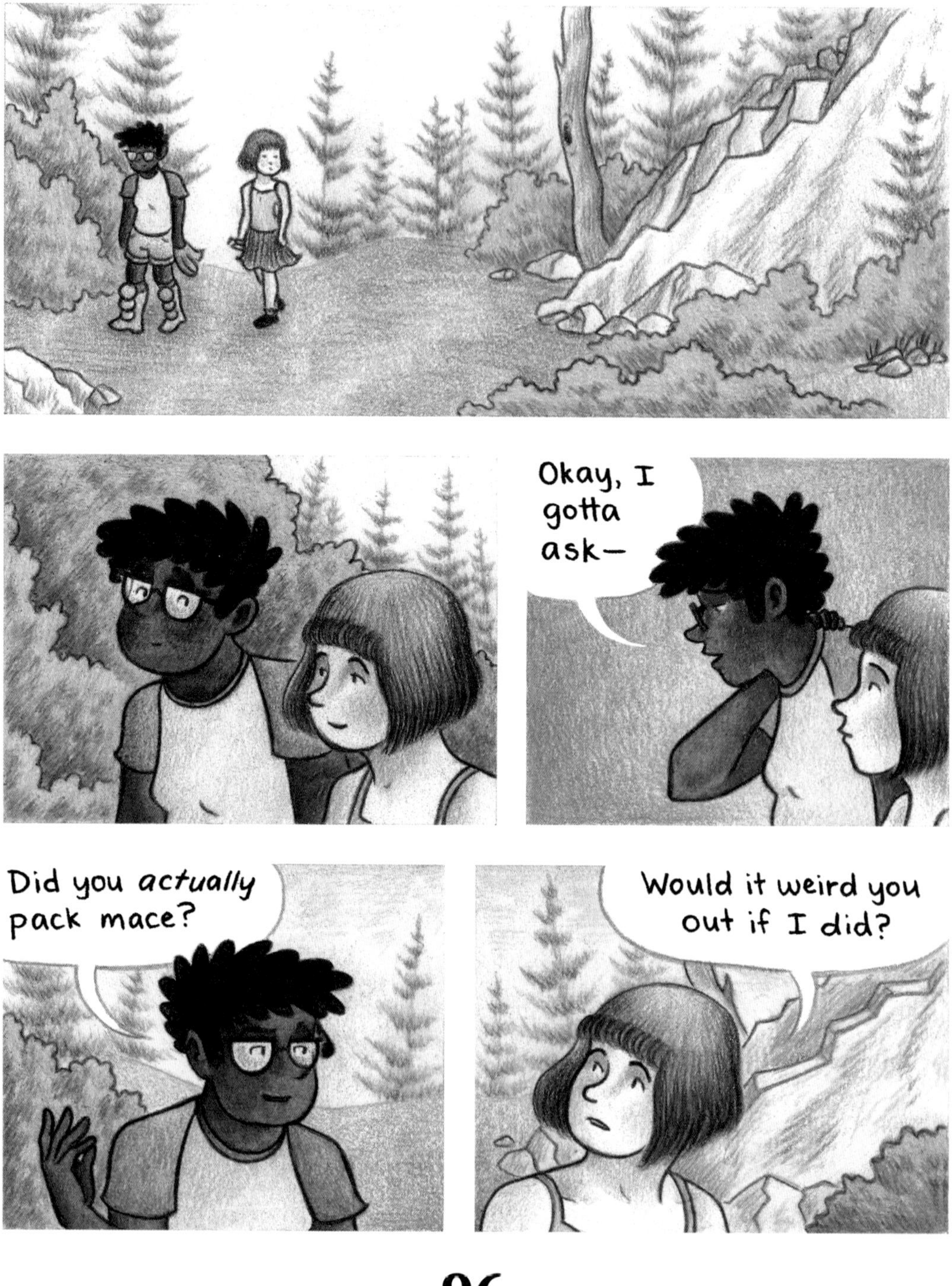
Okay, I gotta ask—
Did you *actually* pack mace?
Would it weird you out if I did?

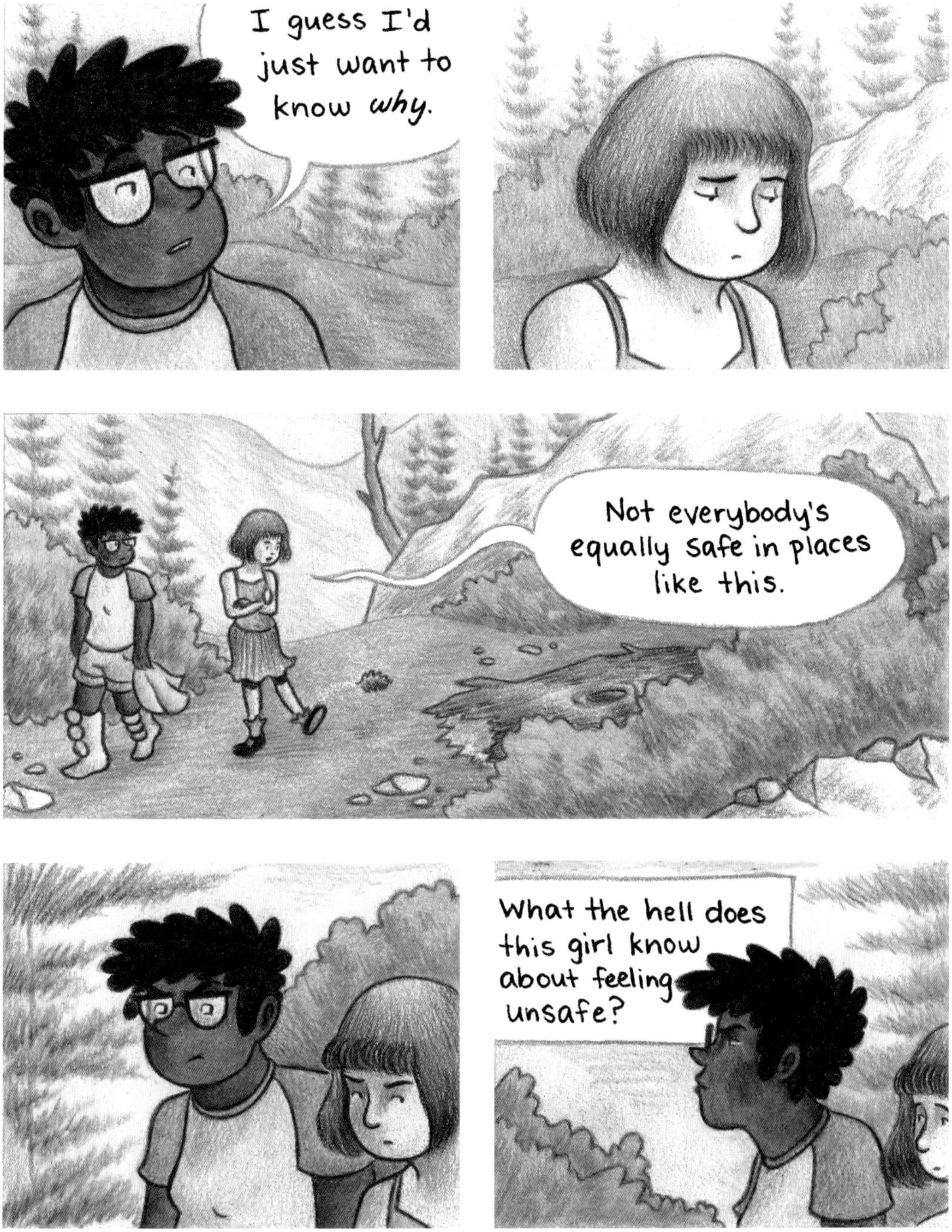
I guess I'd just want to know *why*.
Not everybody's equally safe in places like this.
What the hell does this girl know about feeling unsafe?

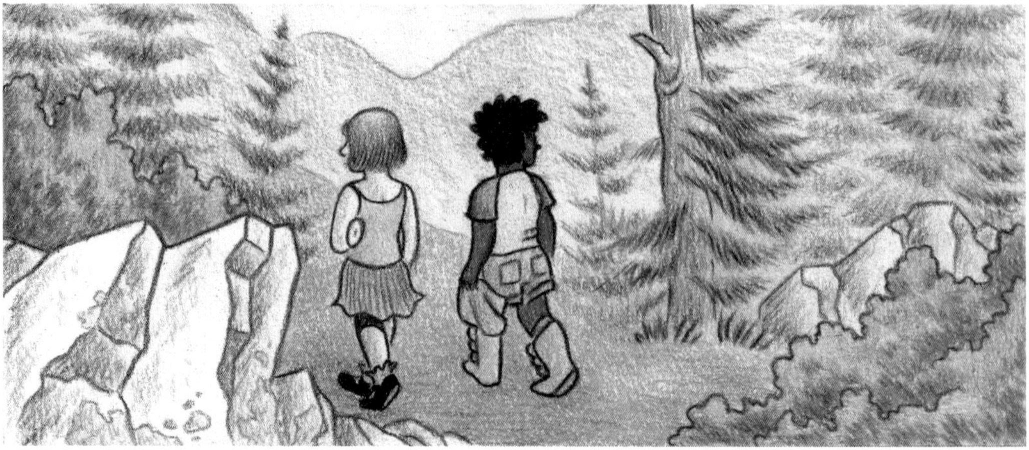

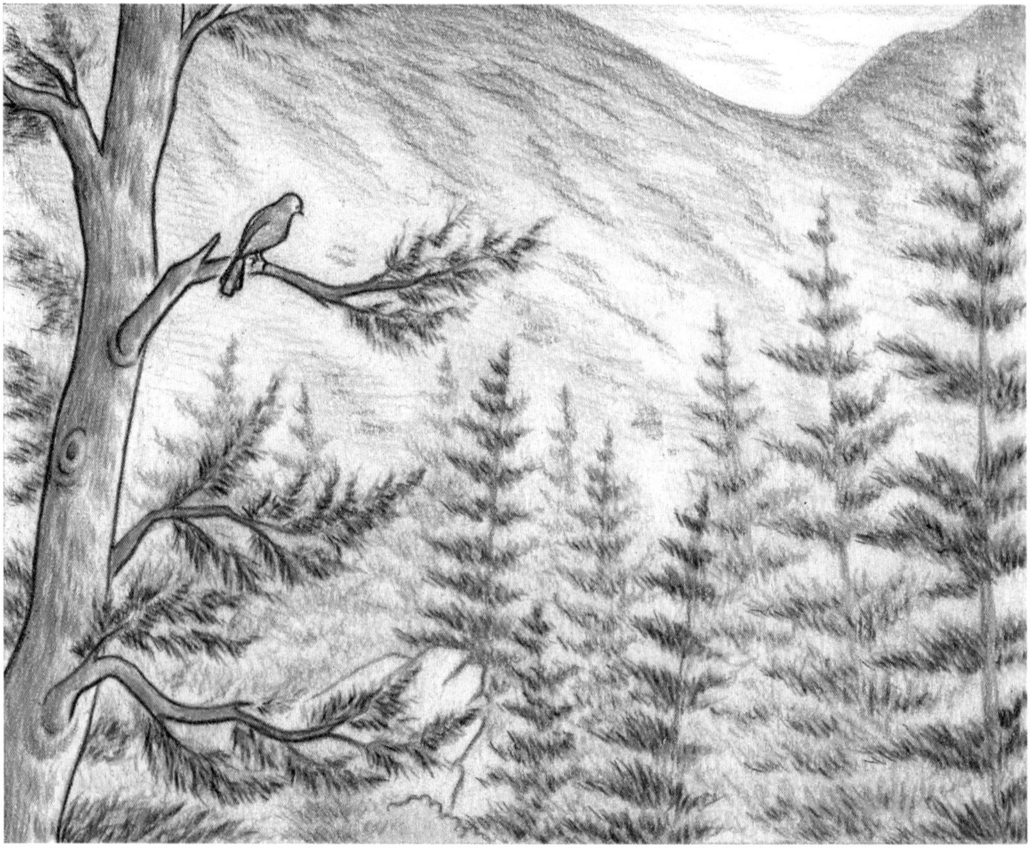

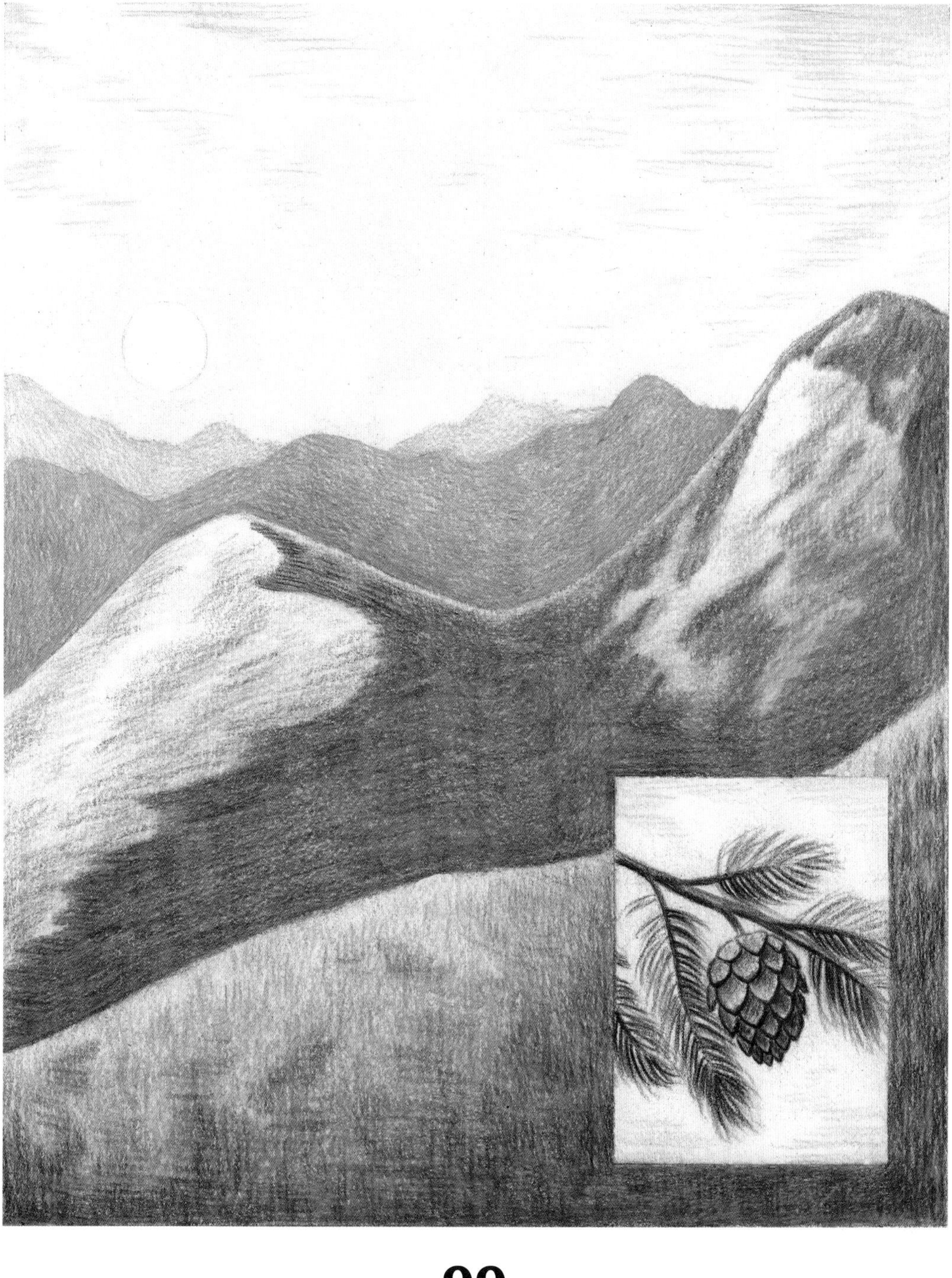

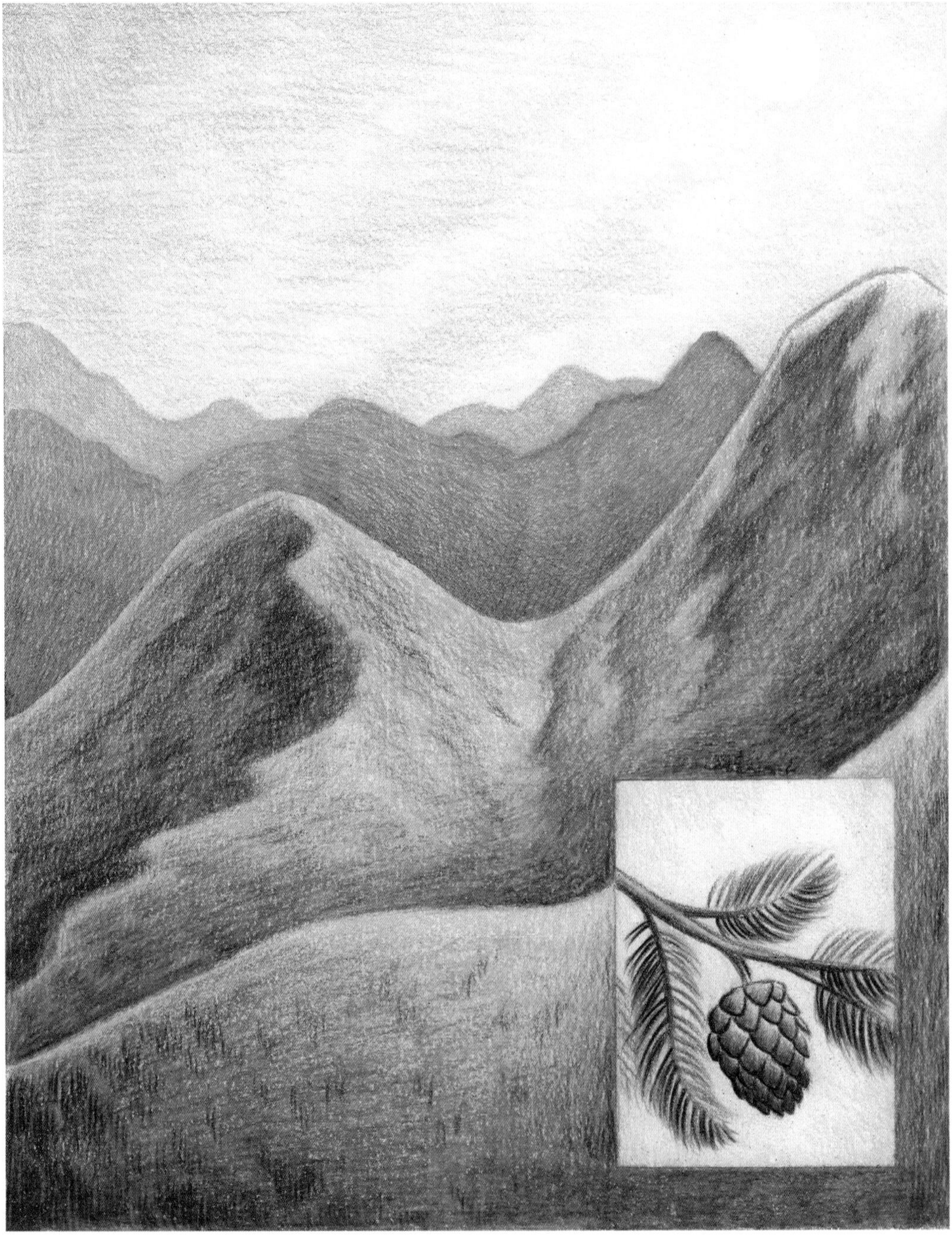

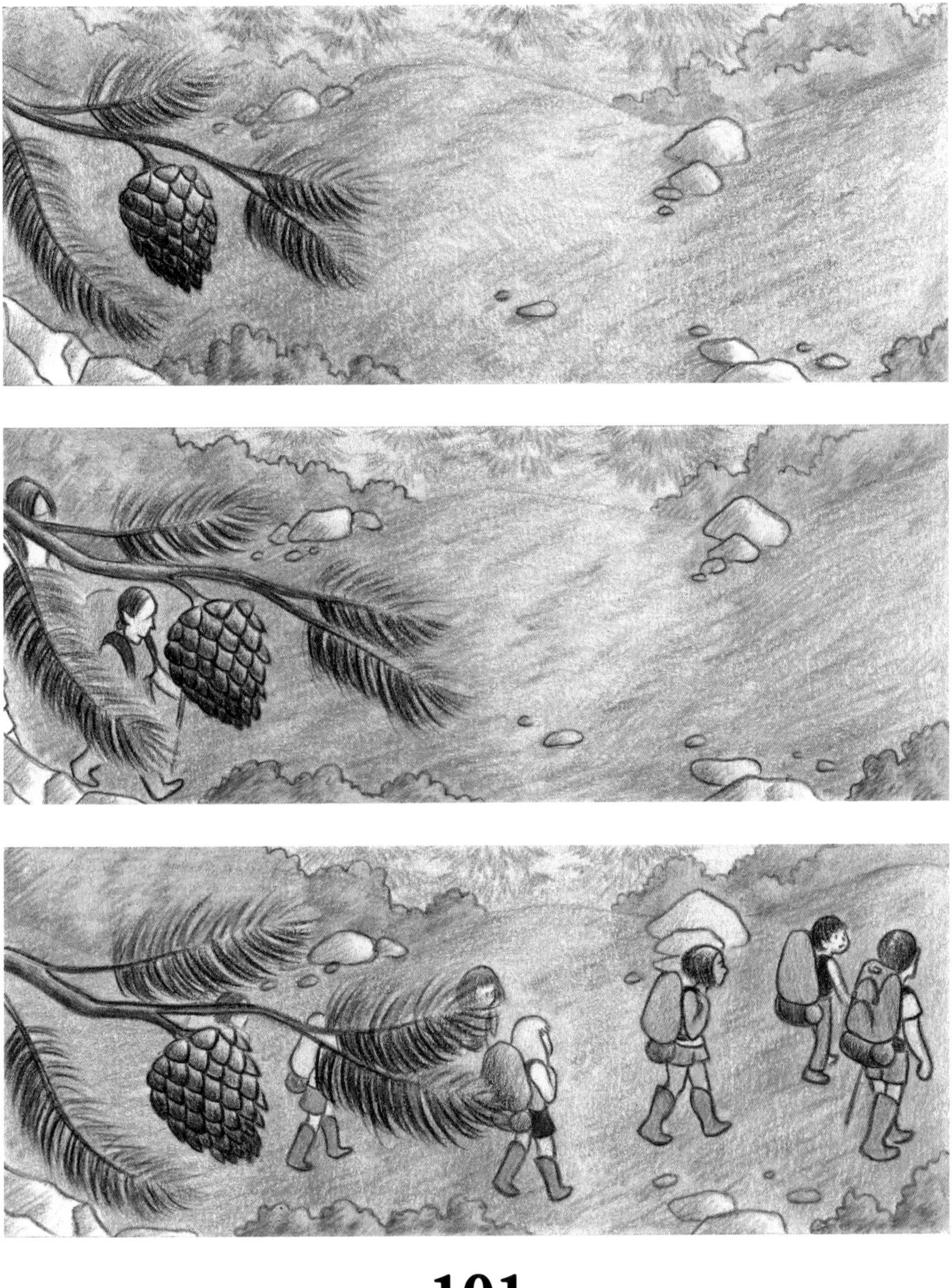

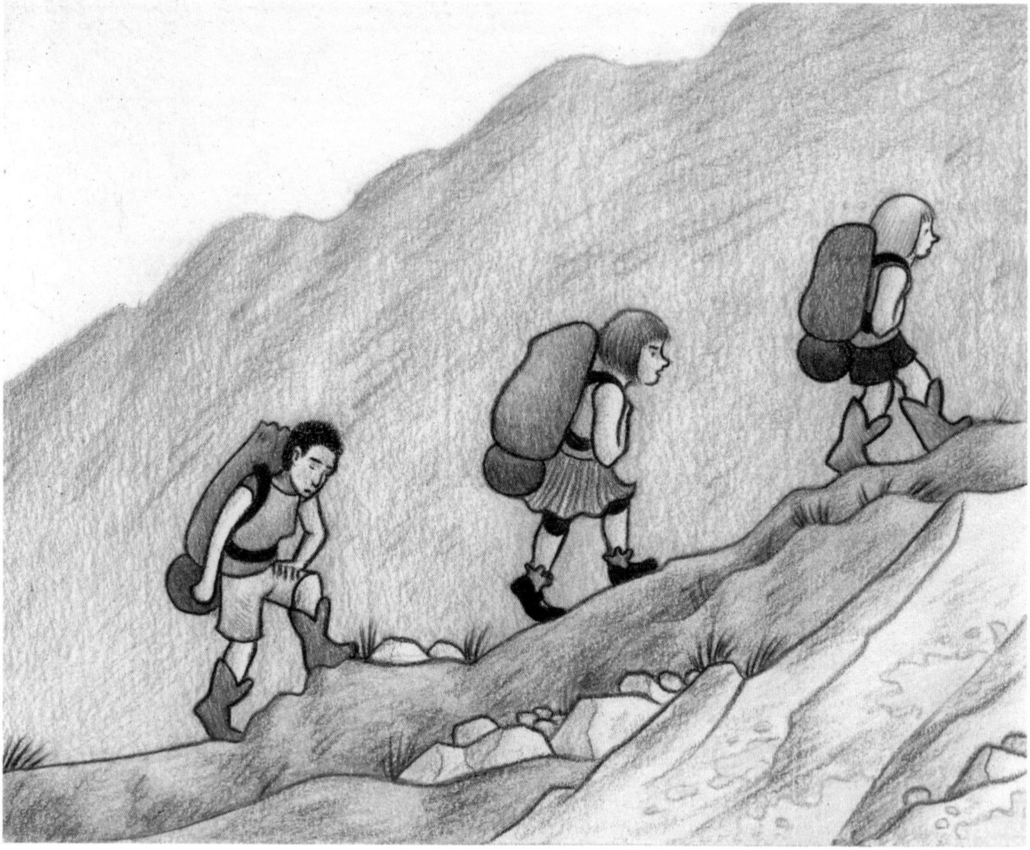

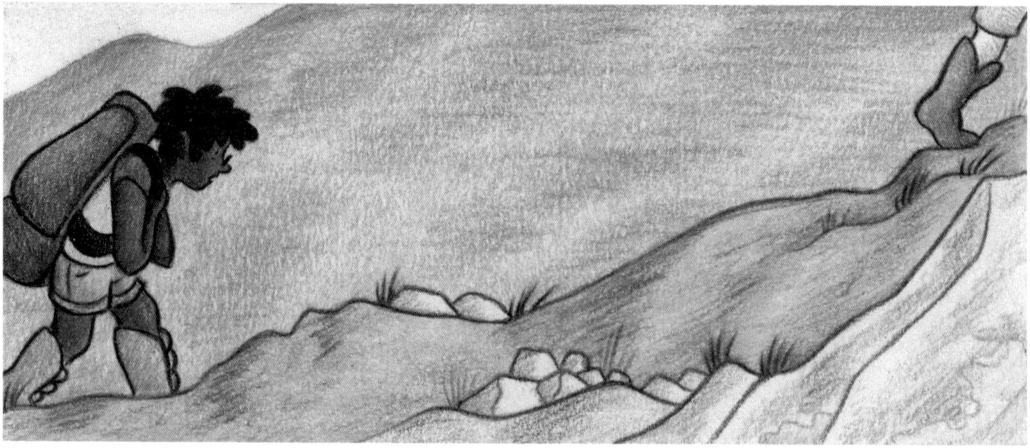

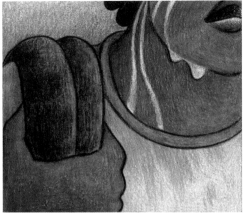

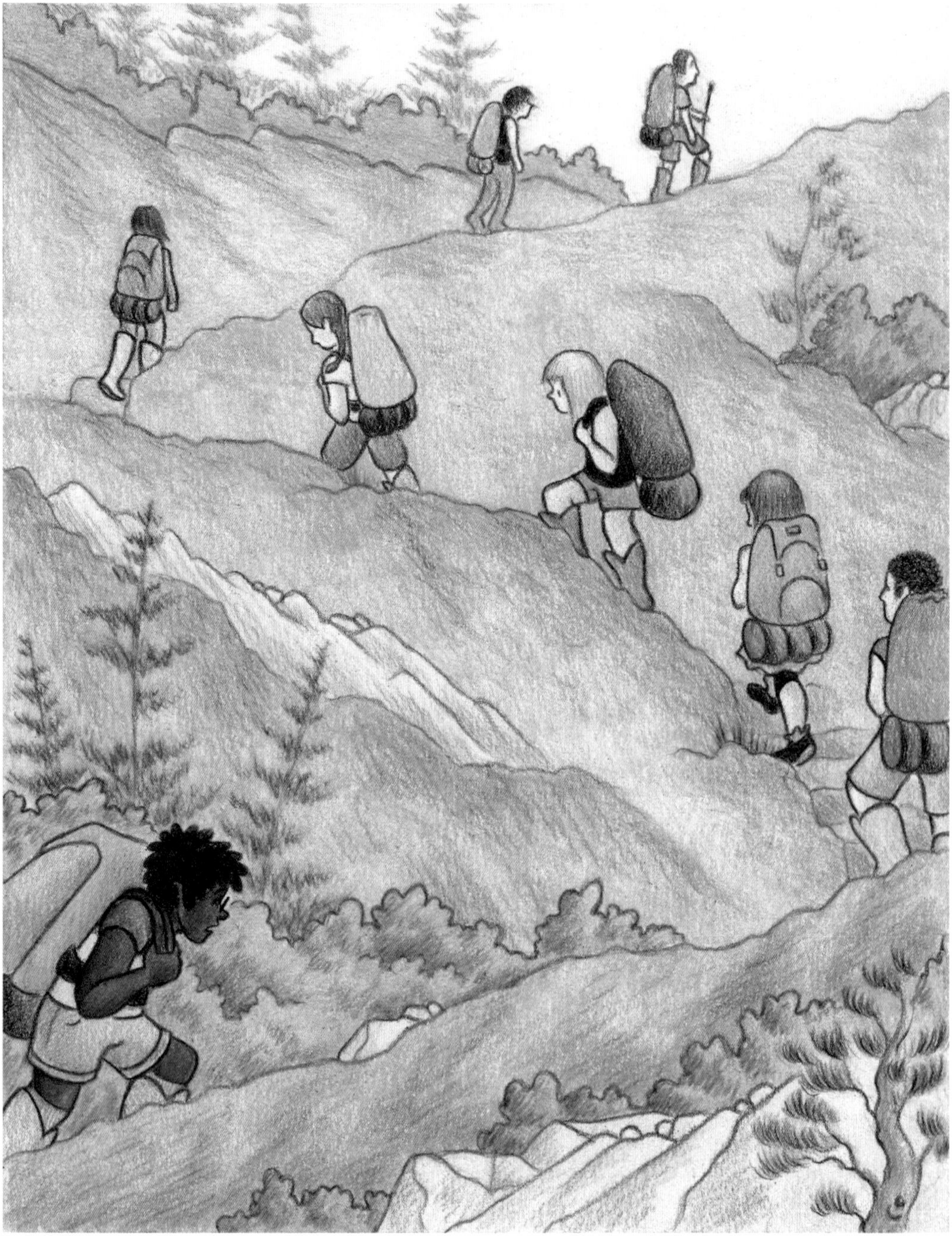

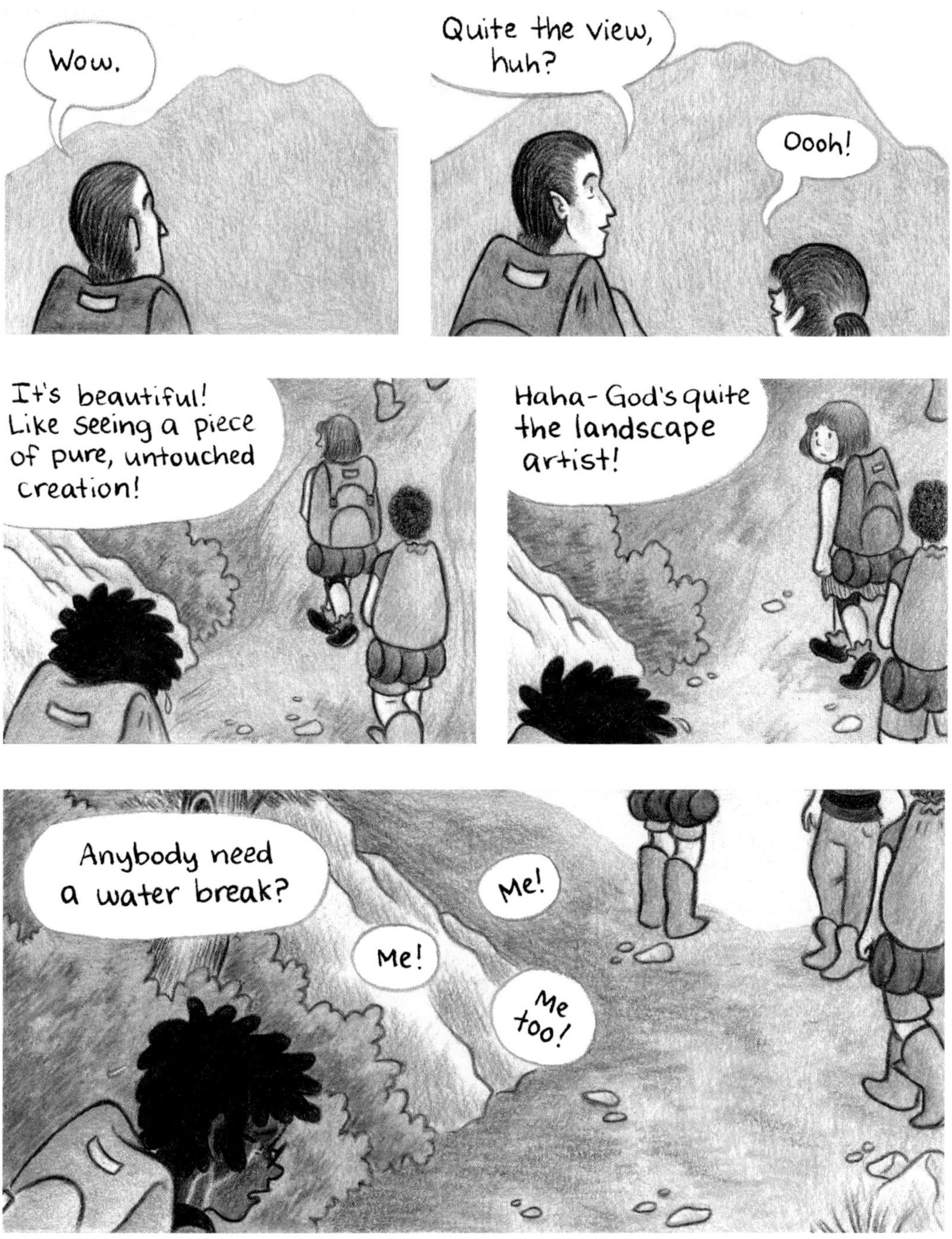
Wow.
Quite the view, huh?
Oooh!
It's beautiful! Like seeing a piece of pure, untouched creation!
Haha- God's quite the landscape artist!
Anybody need a water break?
Me!
Me!
Me too!

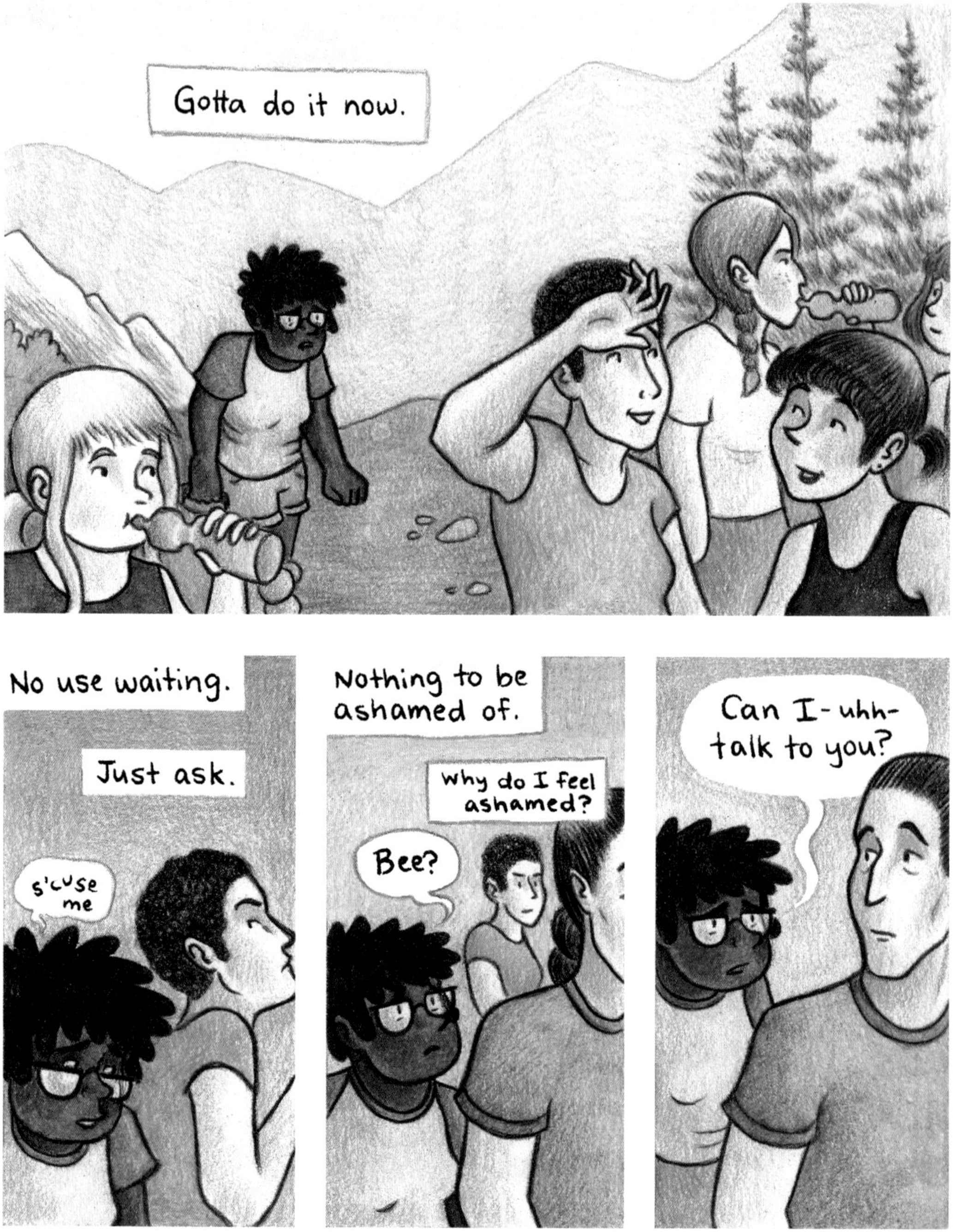
Gotta do it now.
No use waiting.
Just ask.
s'cuse me
Nothing to be ashamed of.
Why do I feel ashamed?
Bee?
Can I- uhh- talk to you?

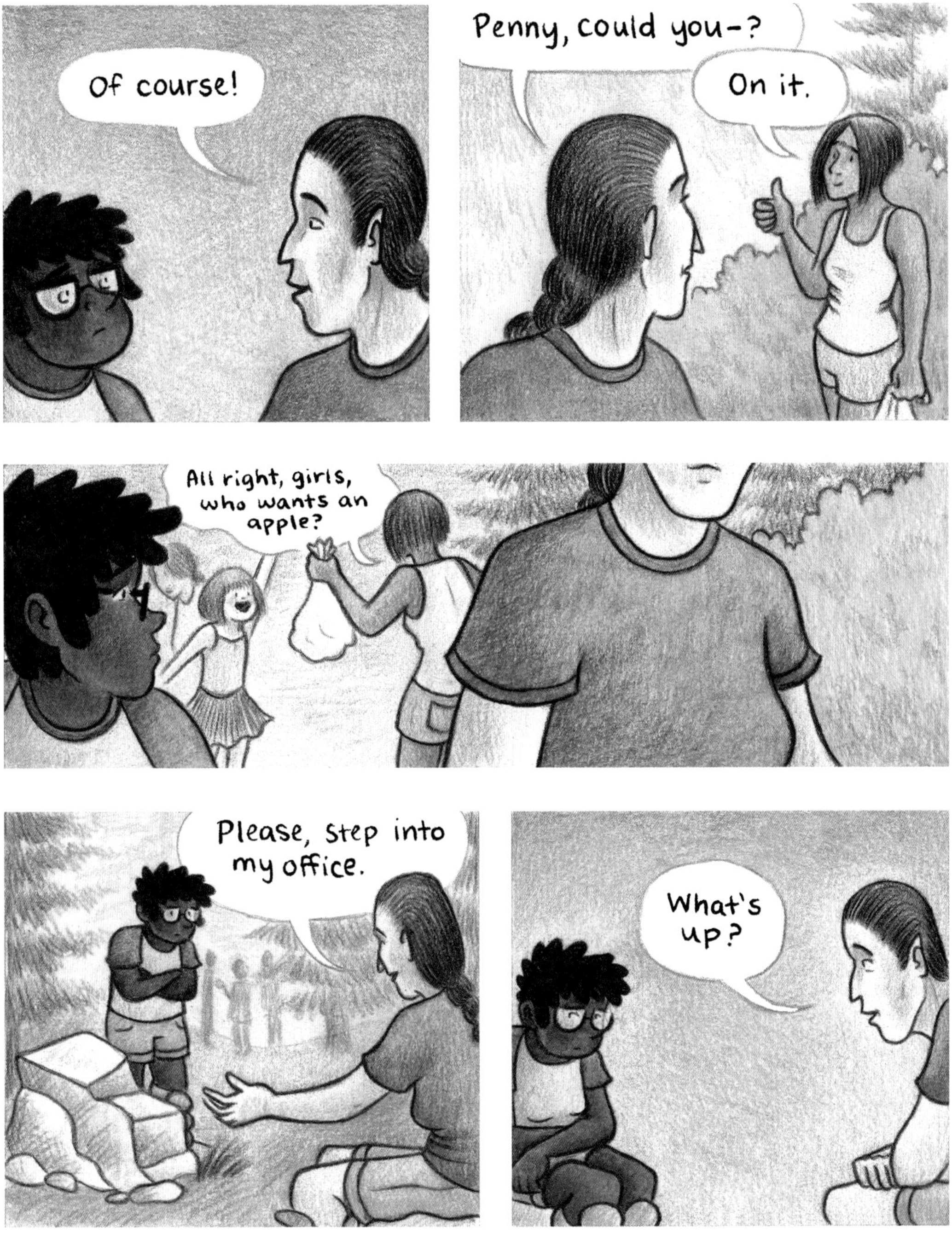
Of course!
Penny, could you-?
On it.
All right, girls, who wants an apple?
Please, step into my office.
What's up?

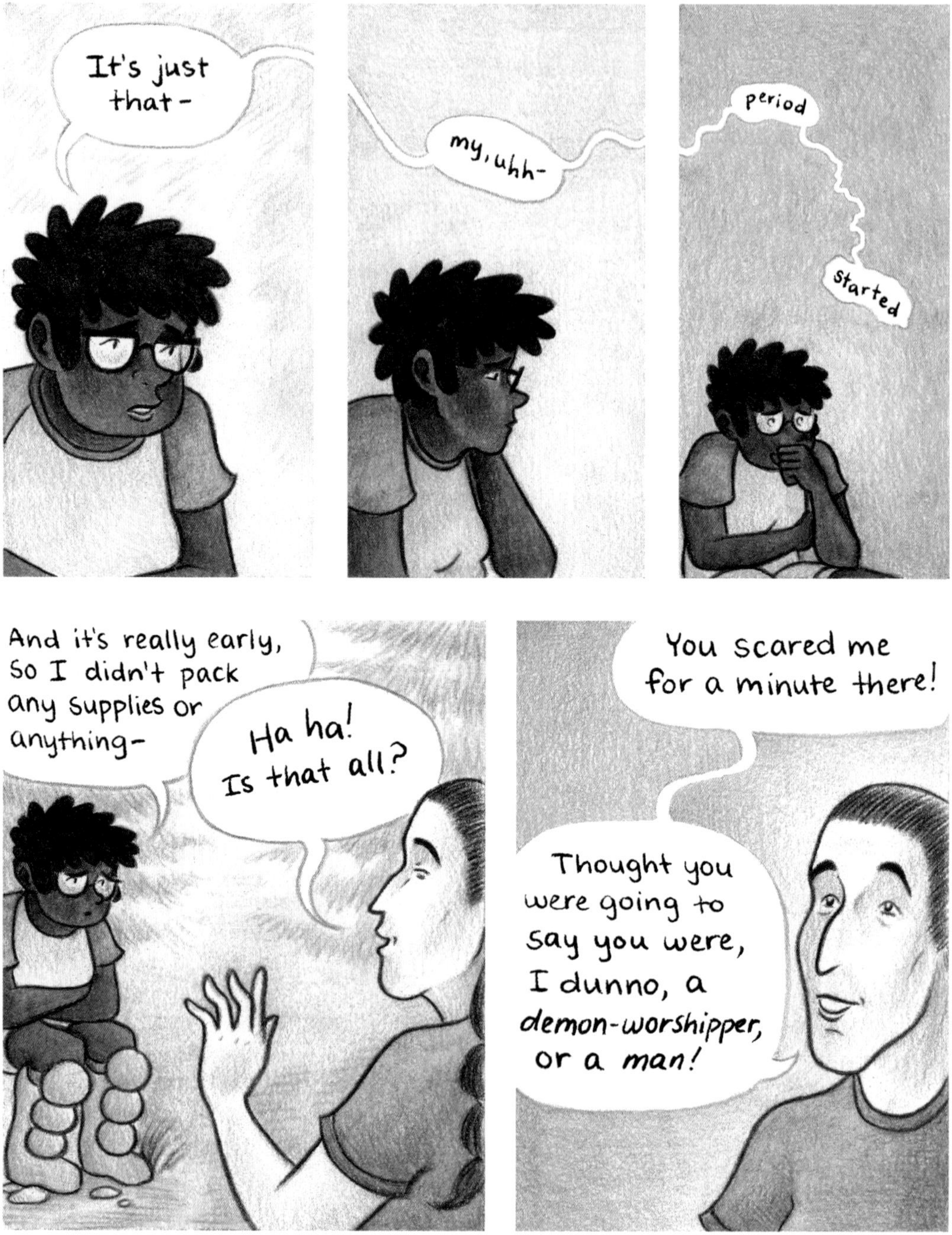
It's just that-
my, uhh-
period
started
And it's really early, so I didn't pack any supplies or anything-
Ha ha! Is that all?
You scared me for a minute there!
Thought you were going to say you were, I dunno, a *demon-worshipper*, or a *man*!

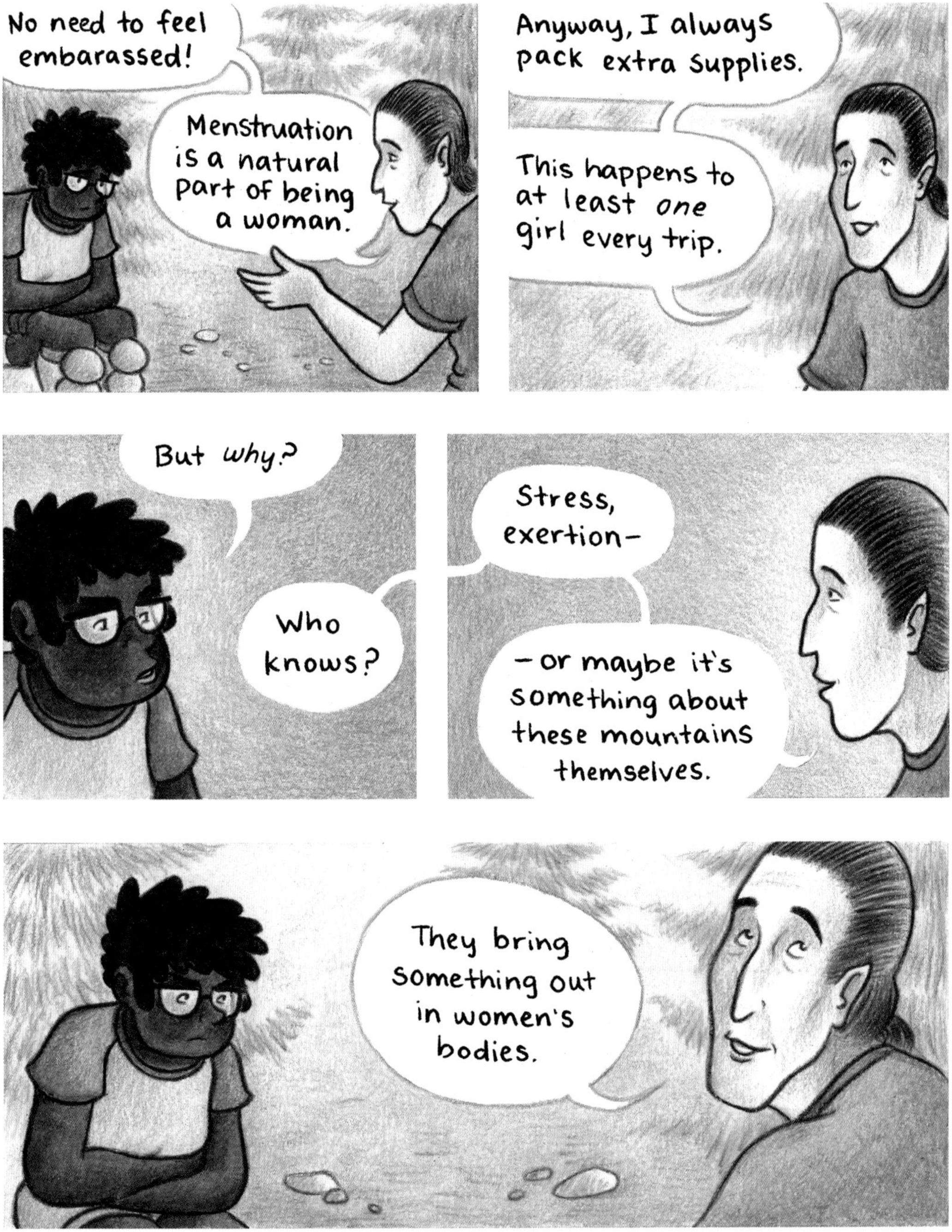
No need to feel embarassed!
Menstruation is a natural part of being a woman.
Anyway, I always pack extra supplies.
This happens to at least *one* girl every trip.
But *why?*
Who knows?
Stress, exertion—
—or maybe it's something about these mountains themselves.
They bring something out in women's bodies.

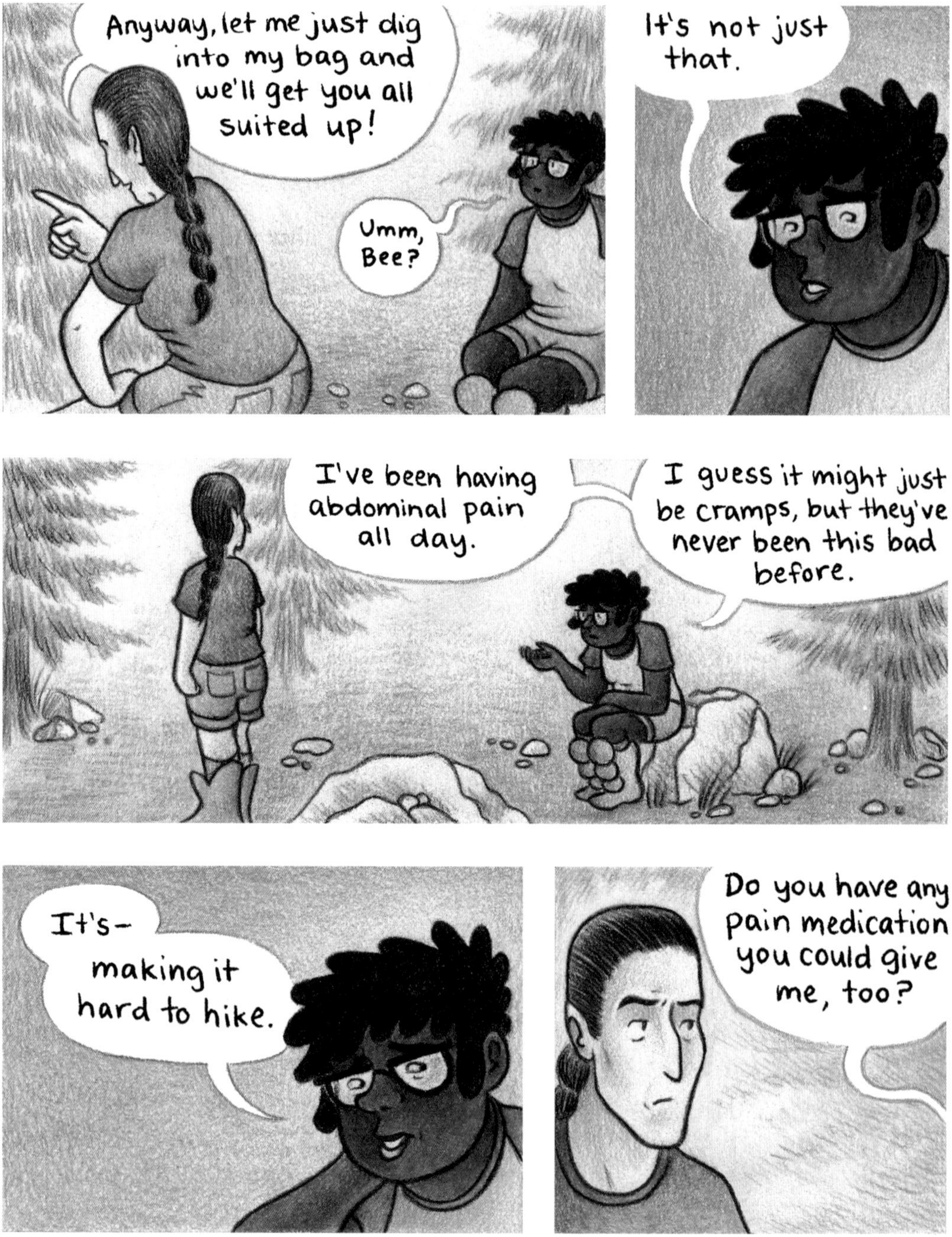
Anyway, let me just dig into my bag and we'll get you all suited up!
Umm, Bee?
It's not just that.
I've been having abdominal pain all day.
I guess it might just be cramps, but they've never been this bad before.
It's—
making it hard to hike.
Do you have any pain medication you could give me, too?

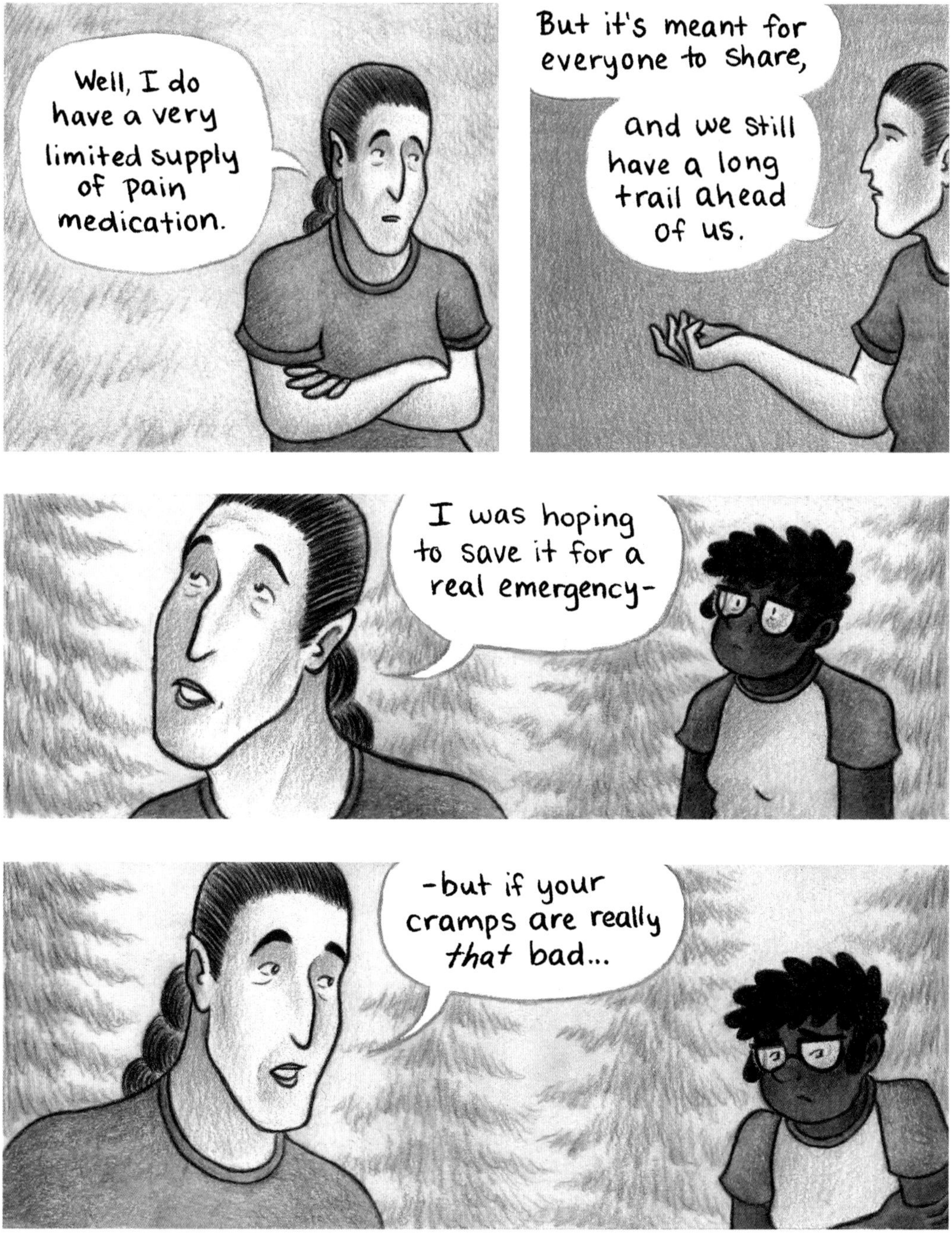
Well, I do have a very limited supply of pain medication.
But it's meant for everyone to share,
and we still have a long trail ahead of us.
I was hoping to save it for a real emergency-
-but if your cramps are really *that* bad...

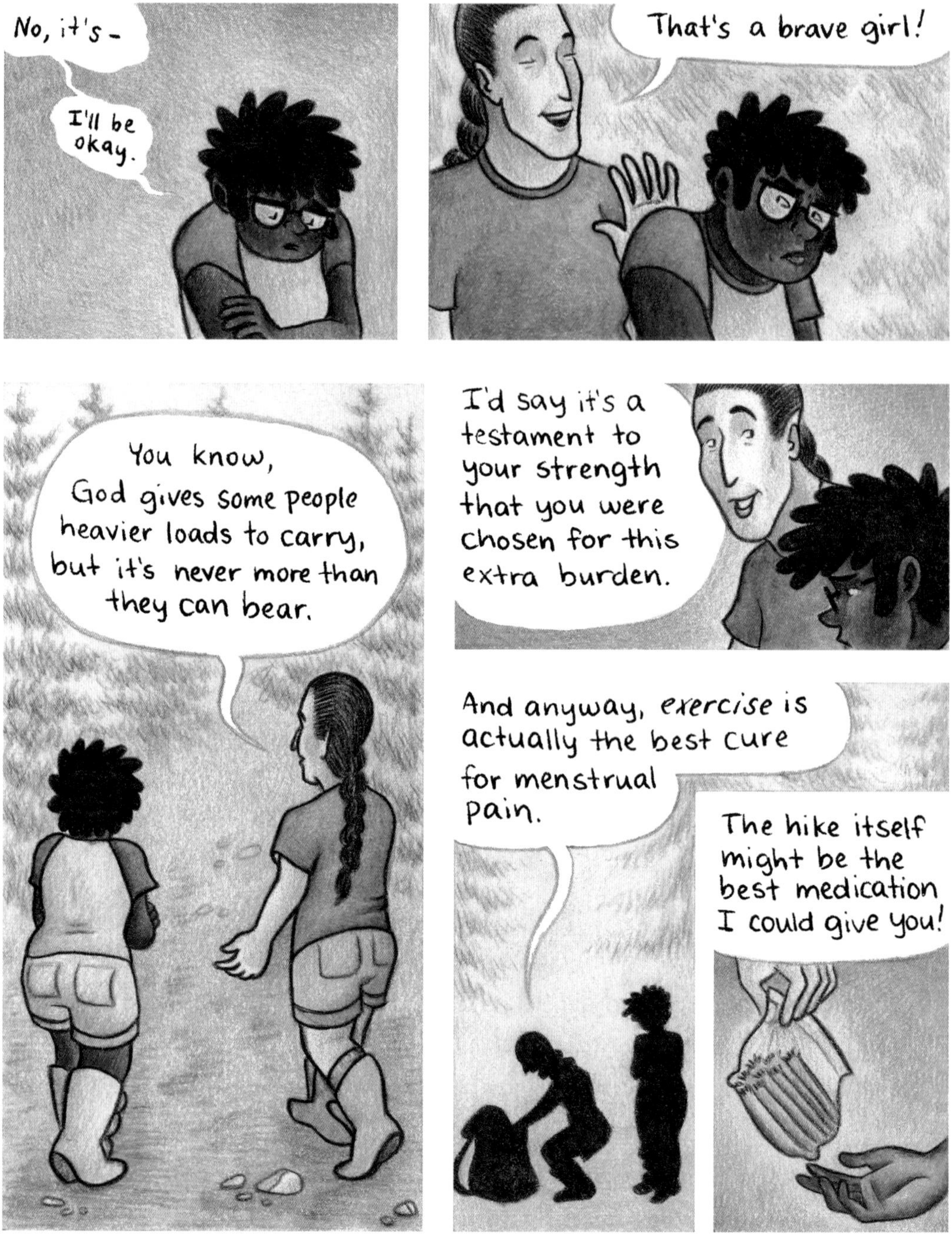
No, it's -
I'll be okay.
That's a brave girl!
You know, God gives some people heavier loads to carry, but it's never more than they can bear.
I'd say it's a testament to your strength that you were chosen for this extra burden.
And anyway, exercise is actually the best cure for menstrual pain.
The hike itself might be the best medication I could give you!

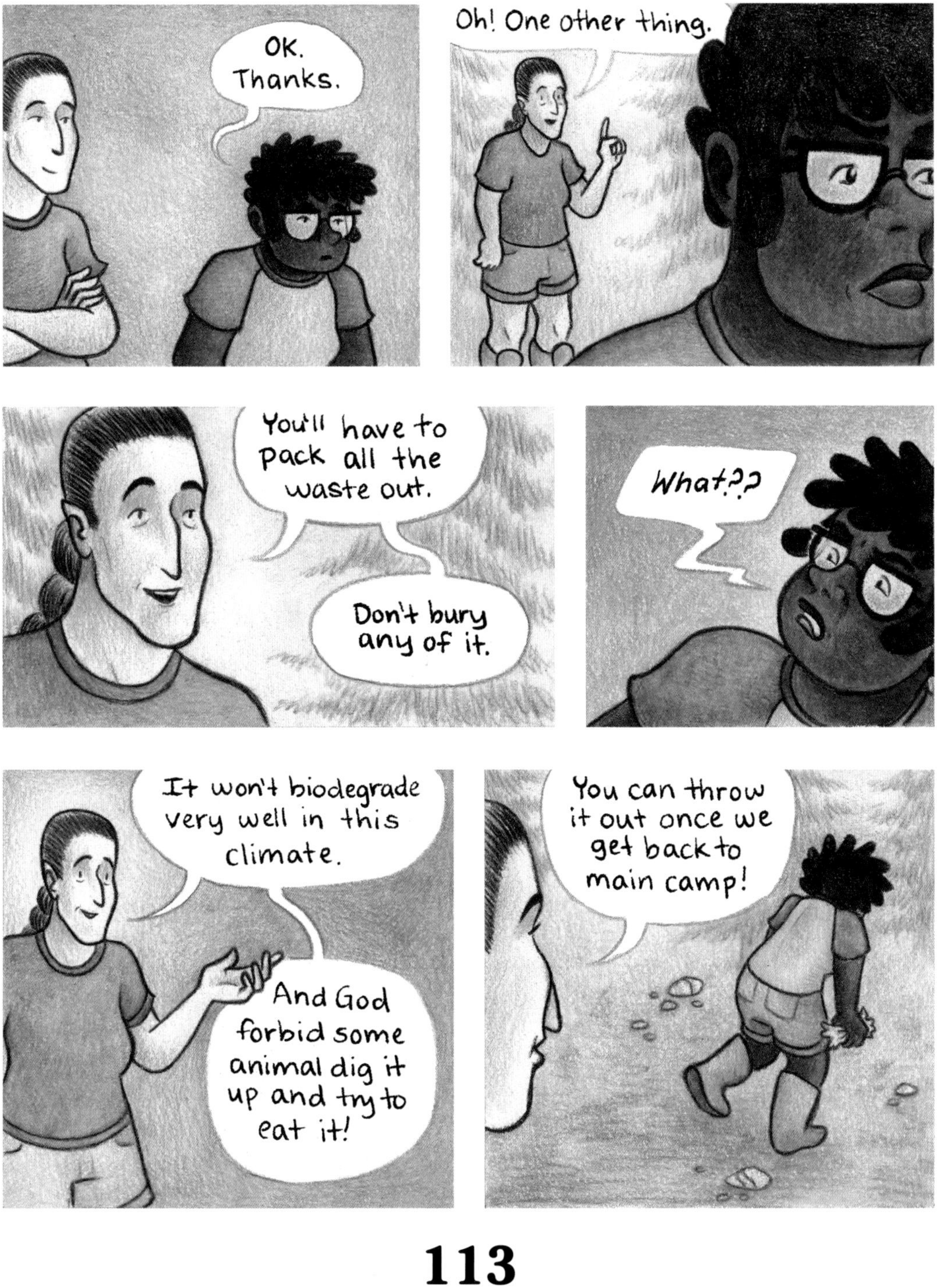
OK. Thanks.
Oh! One other thing.
You'll have to pack all the waste out.
Don't bury any of it.
What??
It won't biodegrade very well in this climate.
And God forbid some animal dig it up and try to eat it!
You can throw it out once we get back to main camp!

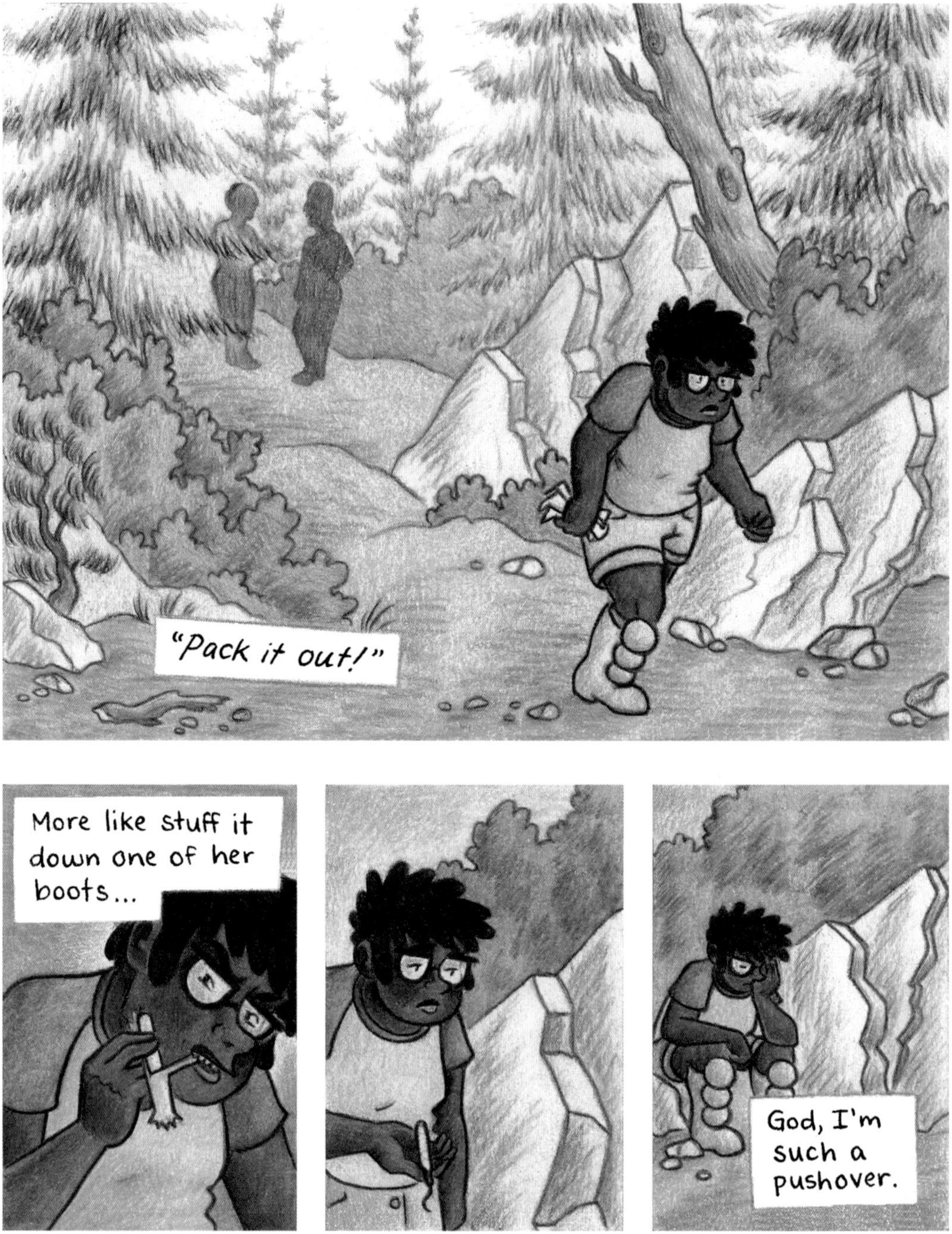
"Pack it out!"
More like stuff it down one of her boots...
God, I'm such a pushover.

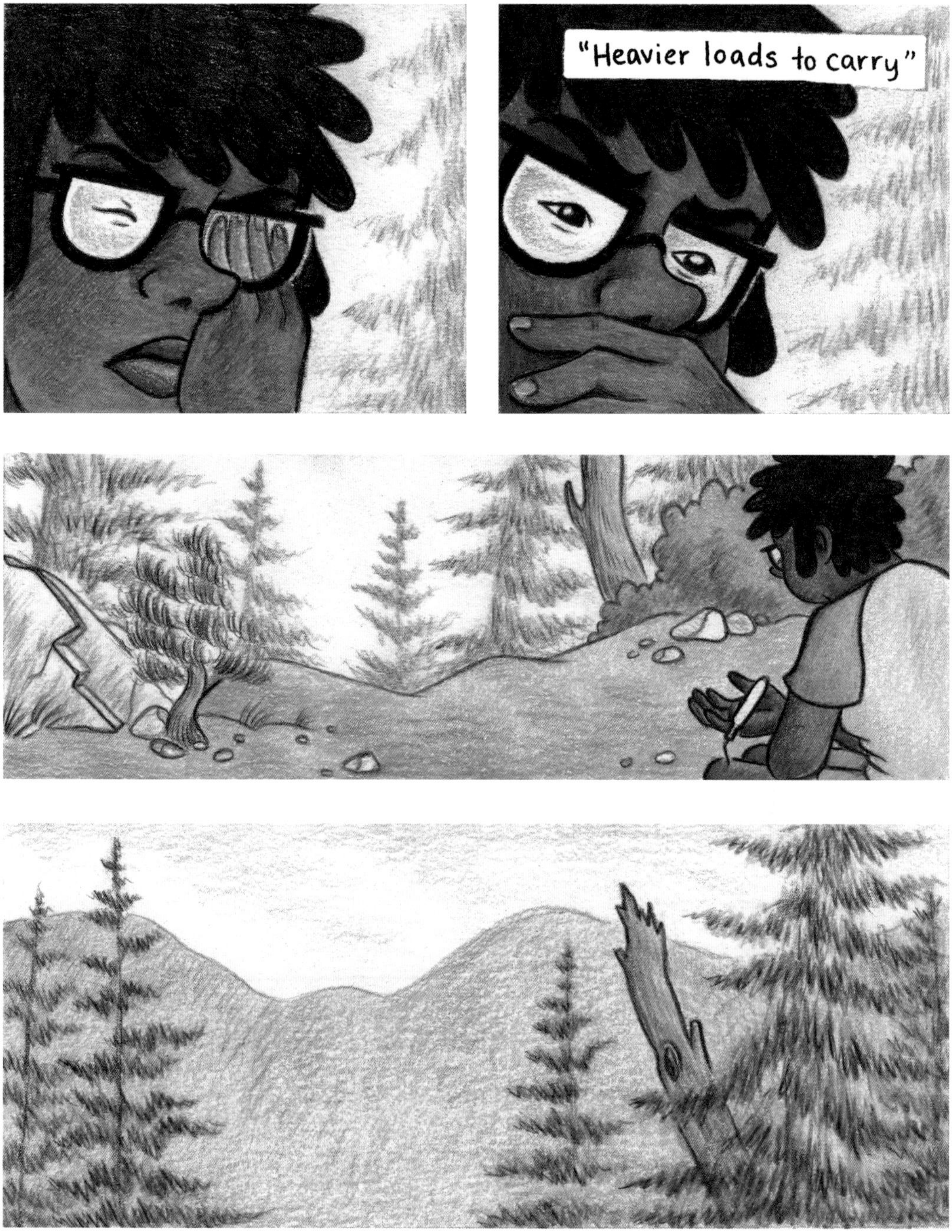
"Heavier loads to carry"

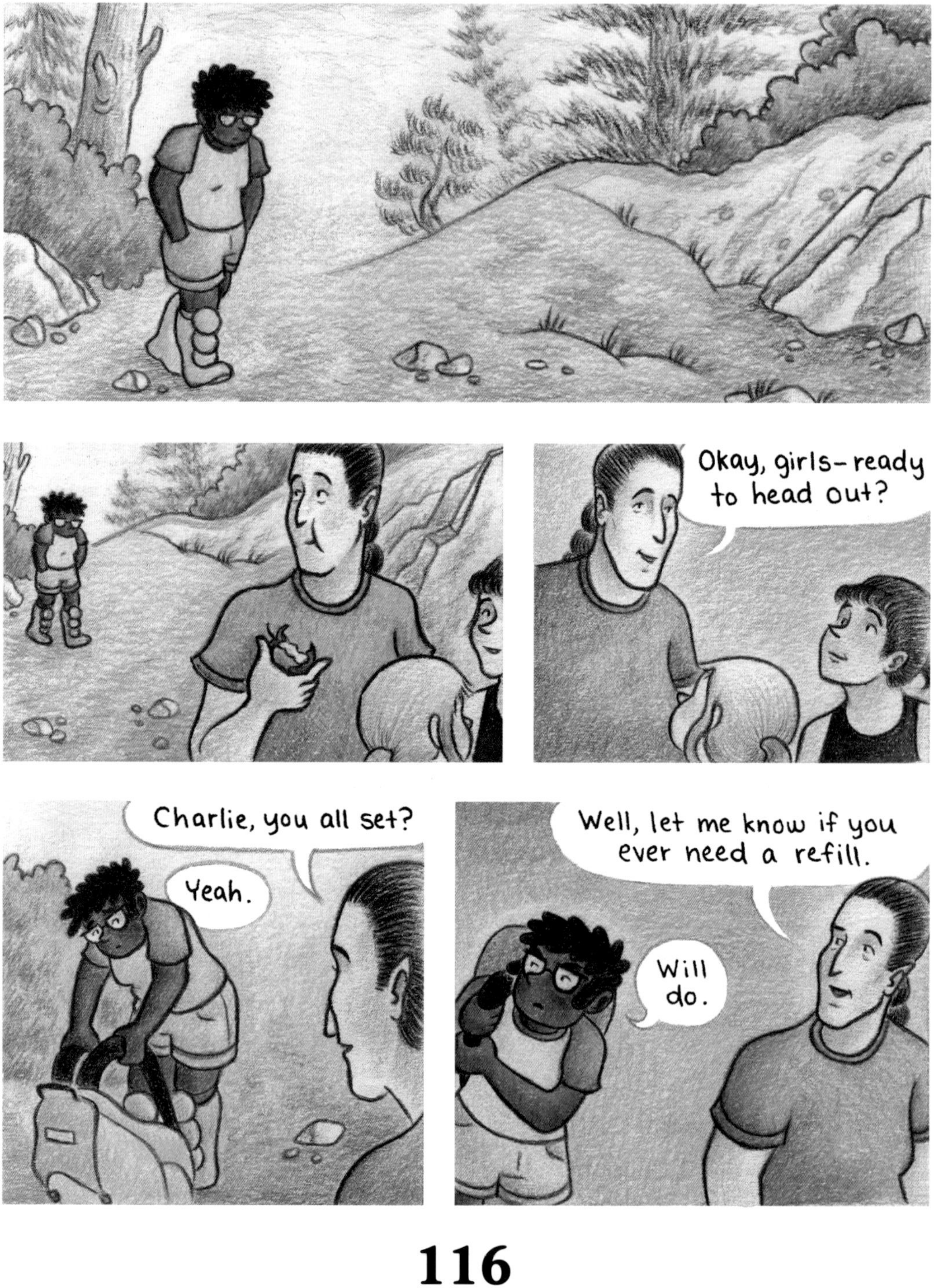
Okay, girls–ready to head out?
Charlie, you all set?
Yeah.
Well, let me know if you ever need a refill.
Will do.

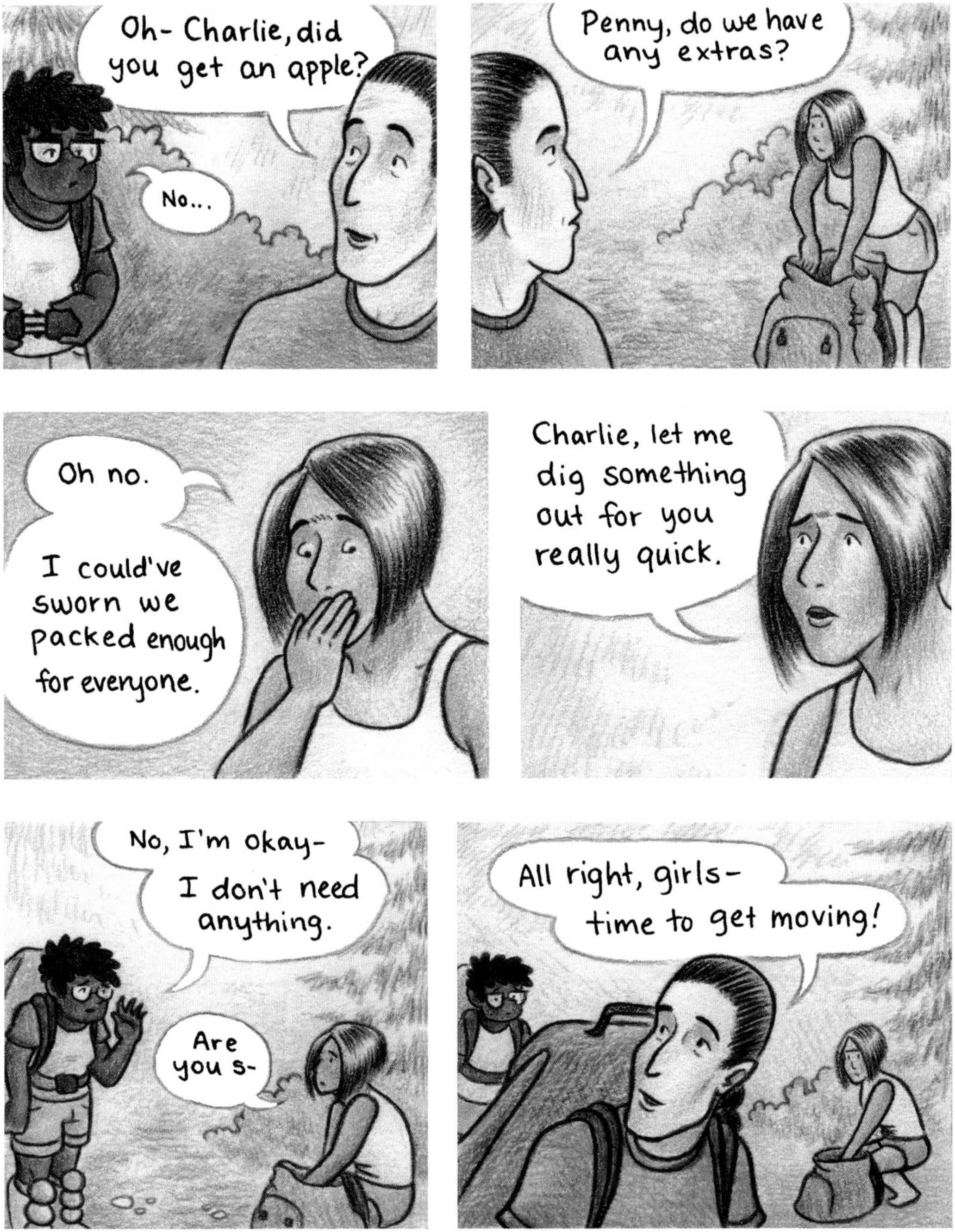
Oh- Charlie, did you get an apple?
No...
Penny, do we have any extras?
Oh no.
I could've sworn we packed enough for everyone.
Charlie, let me dig something out for you really quick.
No, I'm okay-
I don't need anything.
Are you s-
All right, girls- time to get moving!

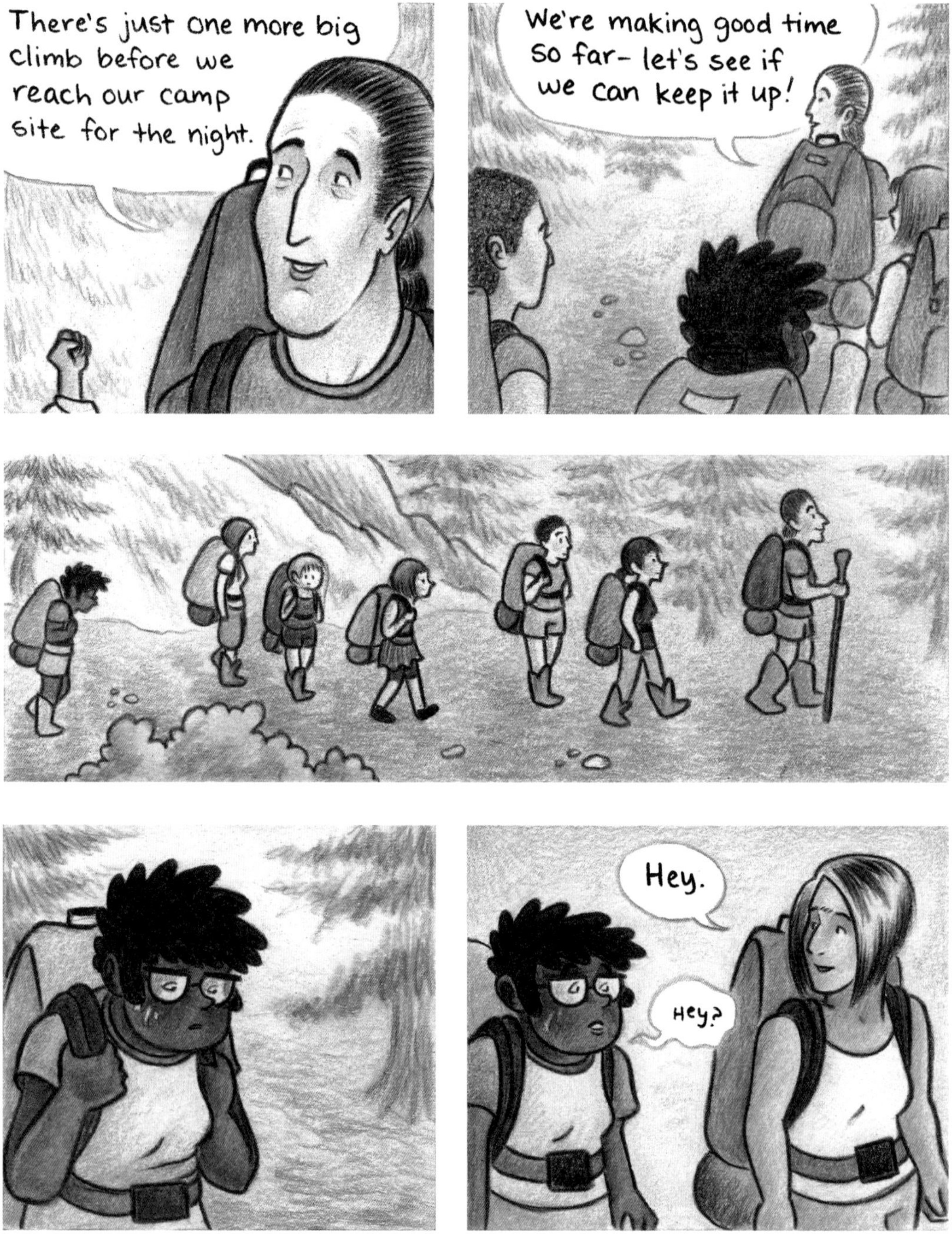
There's just one more big climb before we reach our camp site for the night.
We're making good time so far- let's see if we can keep it up!
Hey.
Hey?

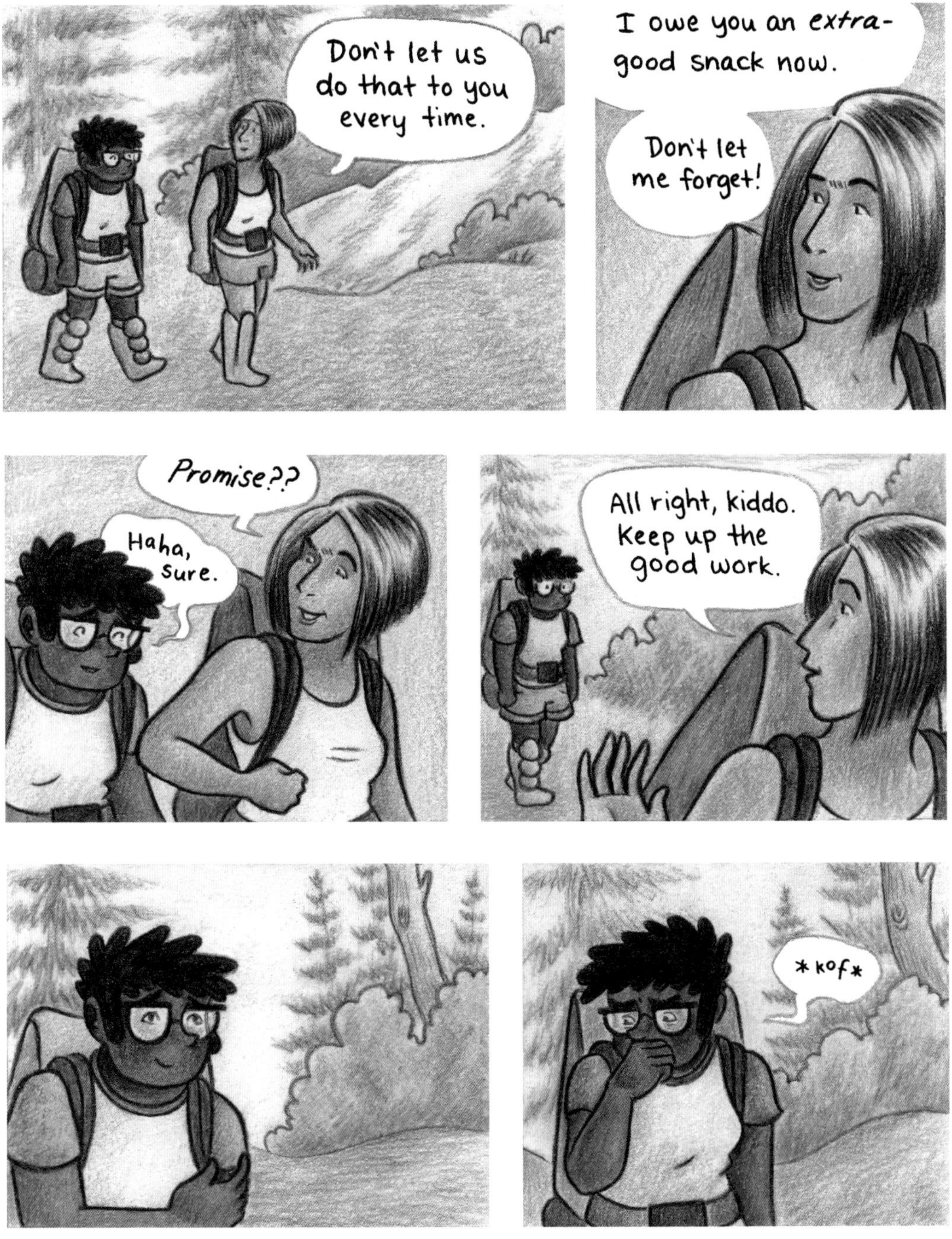
Don't let us do that to you every time.
I owe you an *extra-*good snack now.
Don't let me forget!
Promise??
Haha, sure.
All right, kiddo. Keep up the good work.
kof

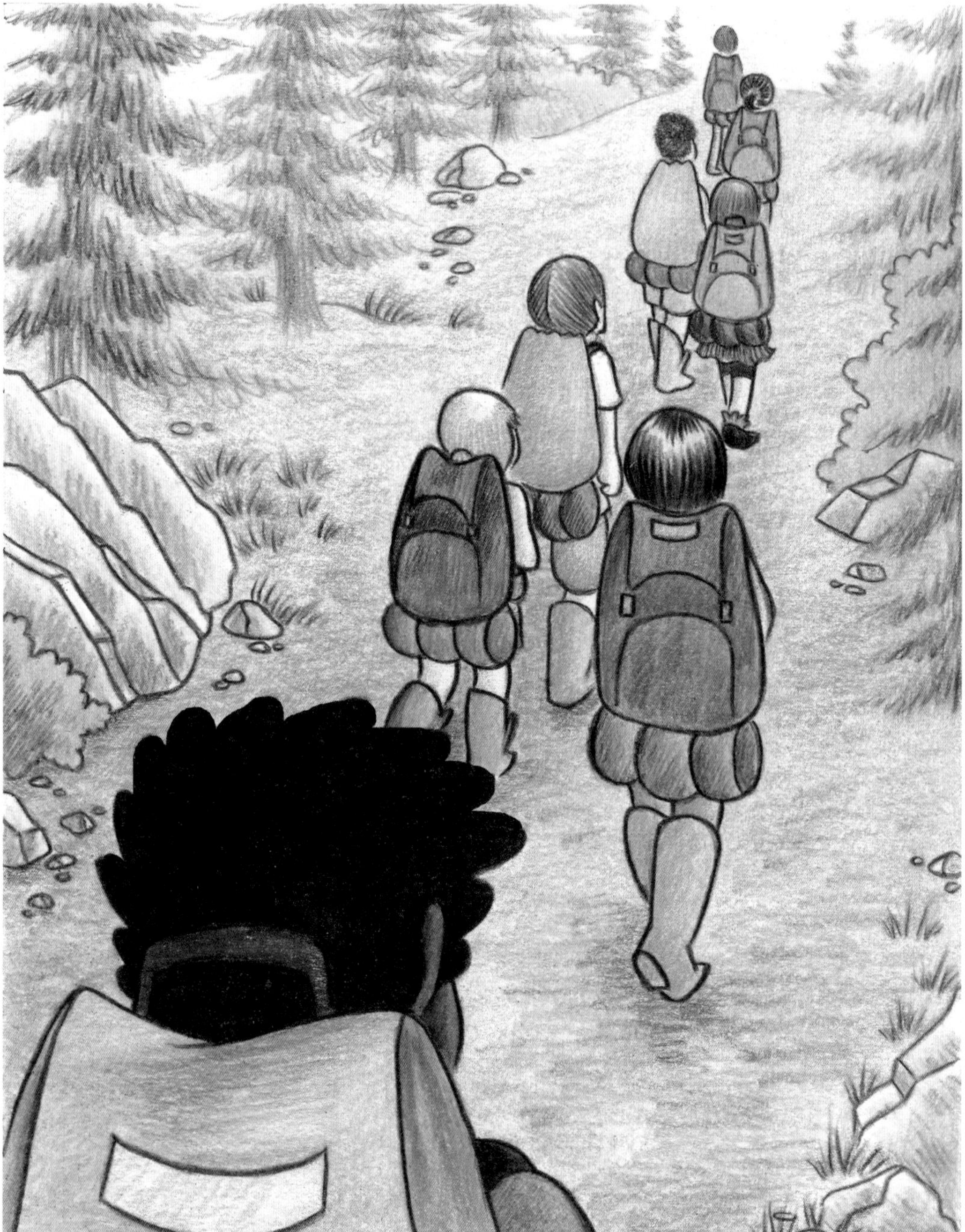

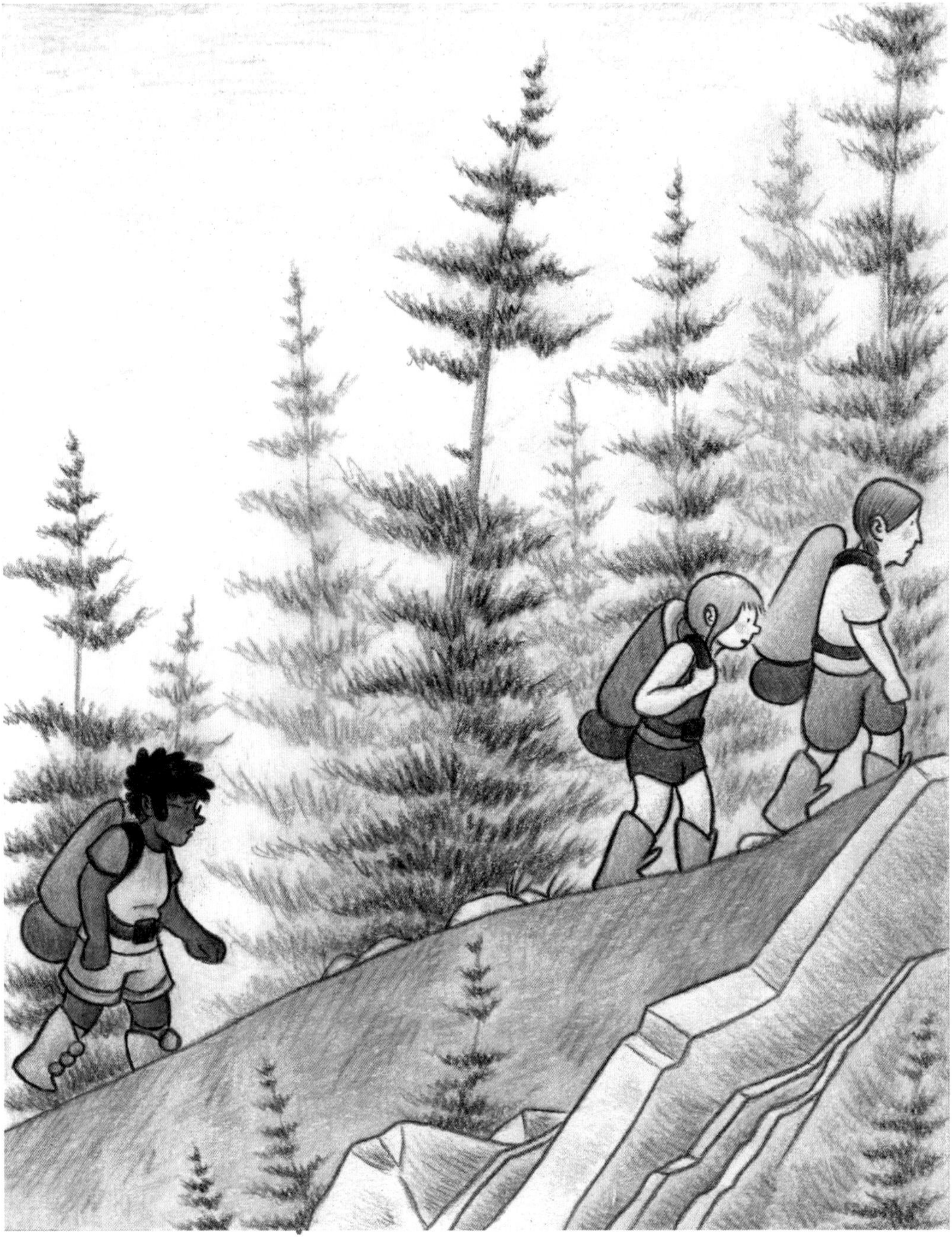

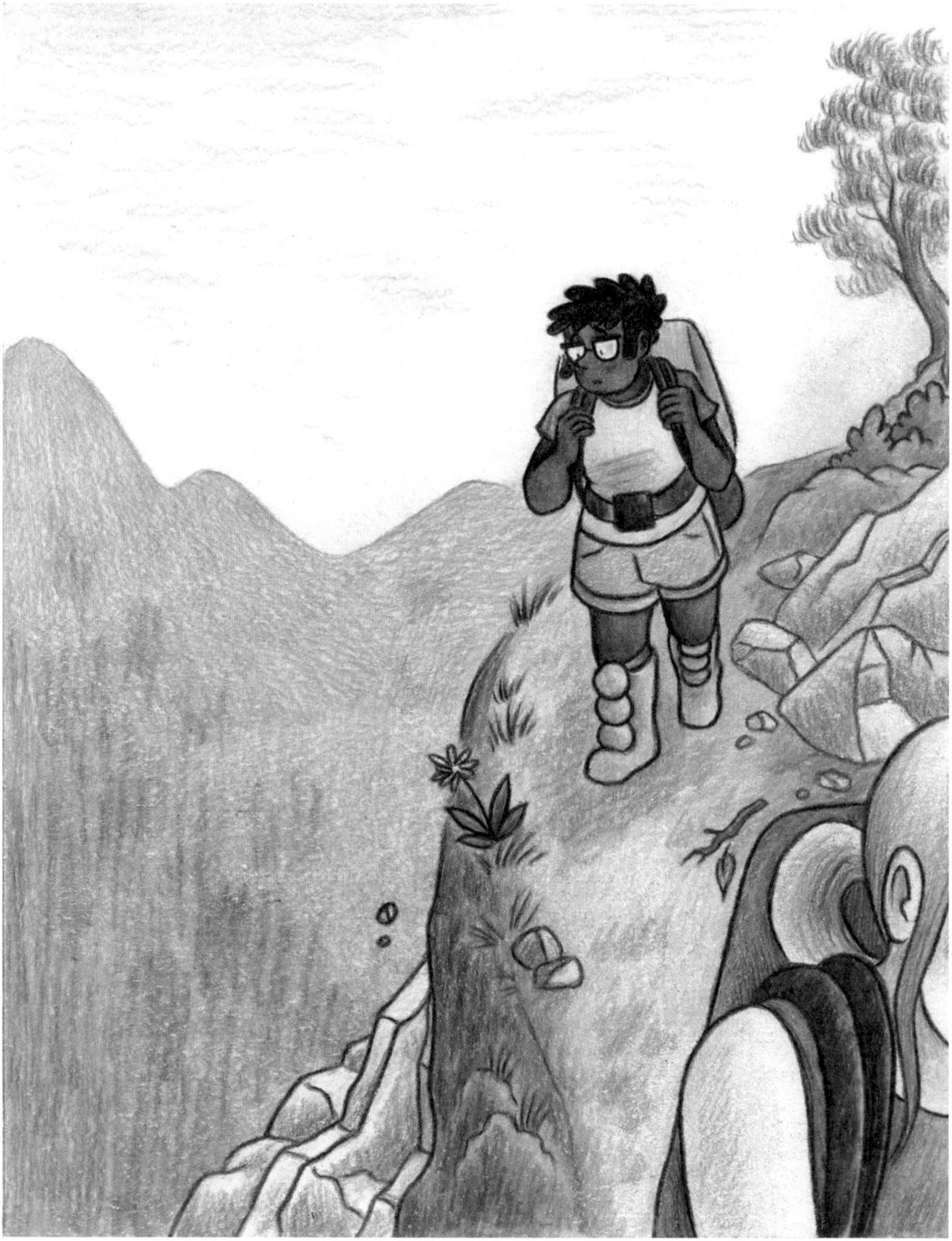

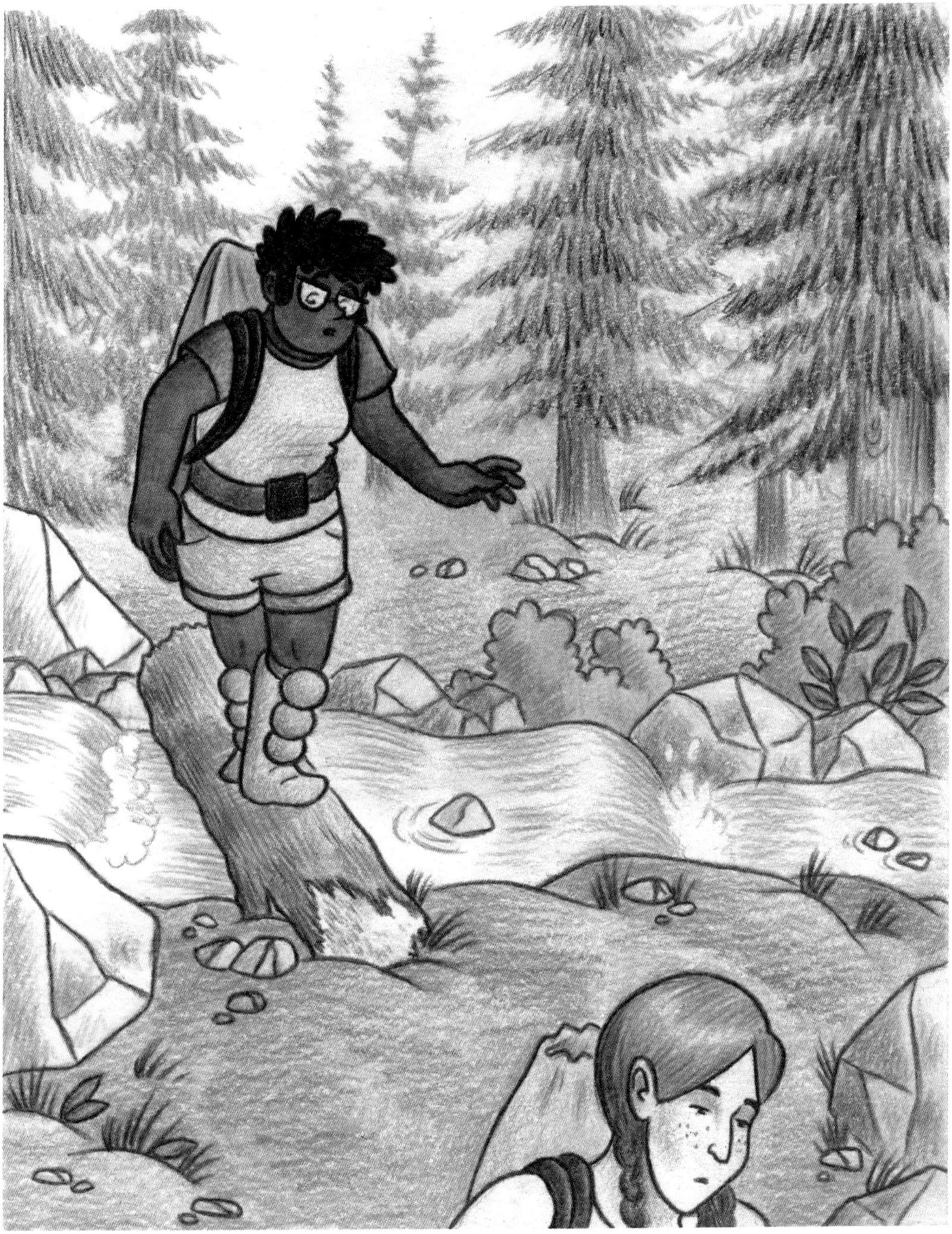

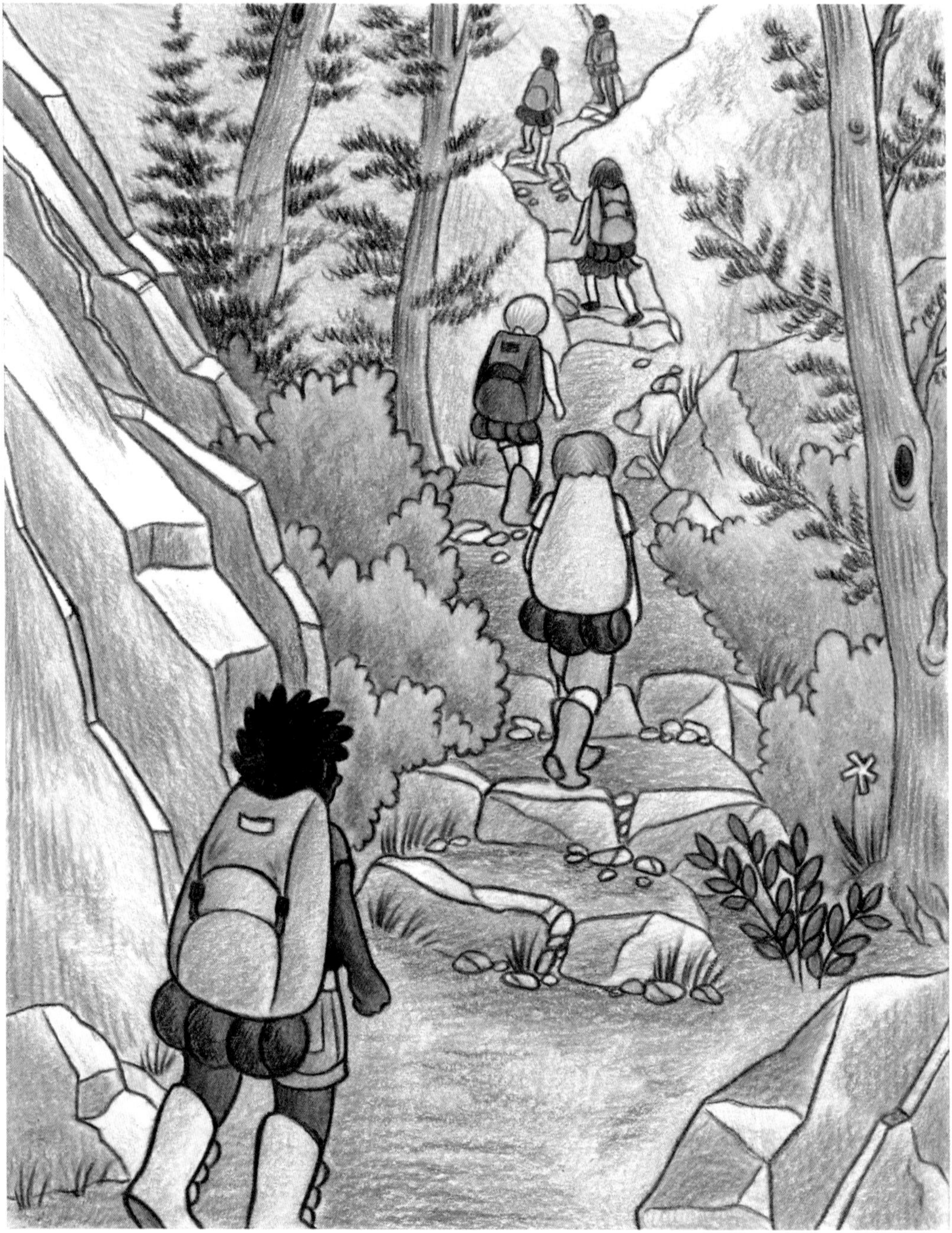

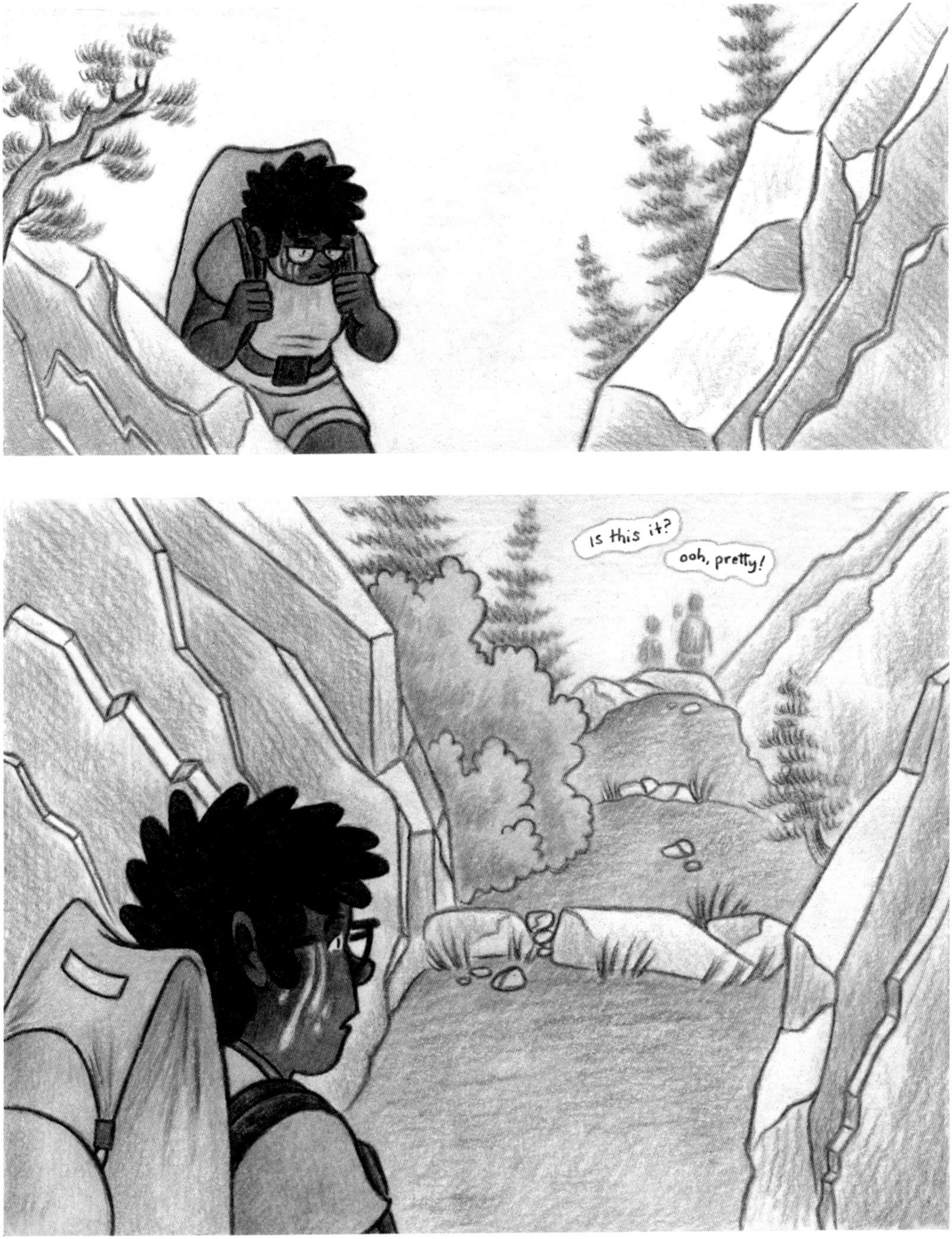
Is this it?
ooh, pretty!

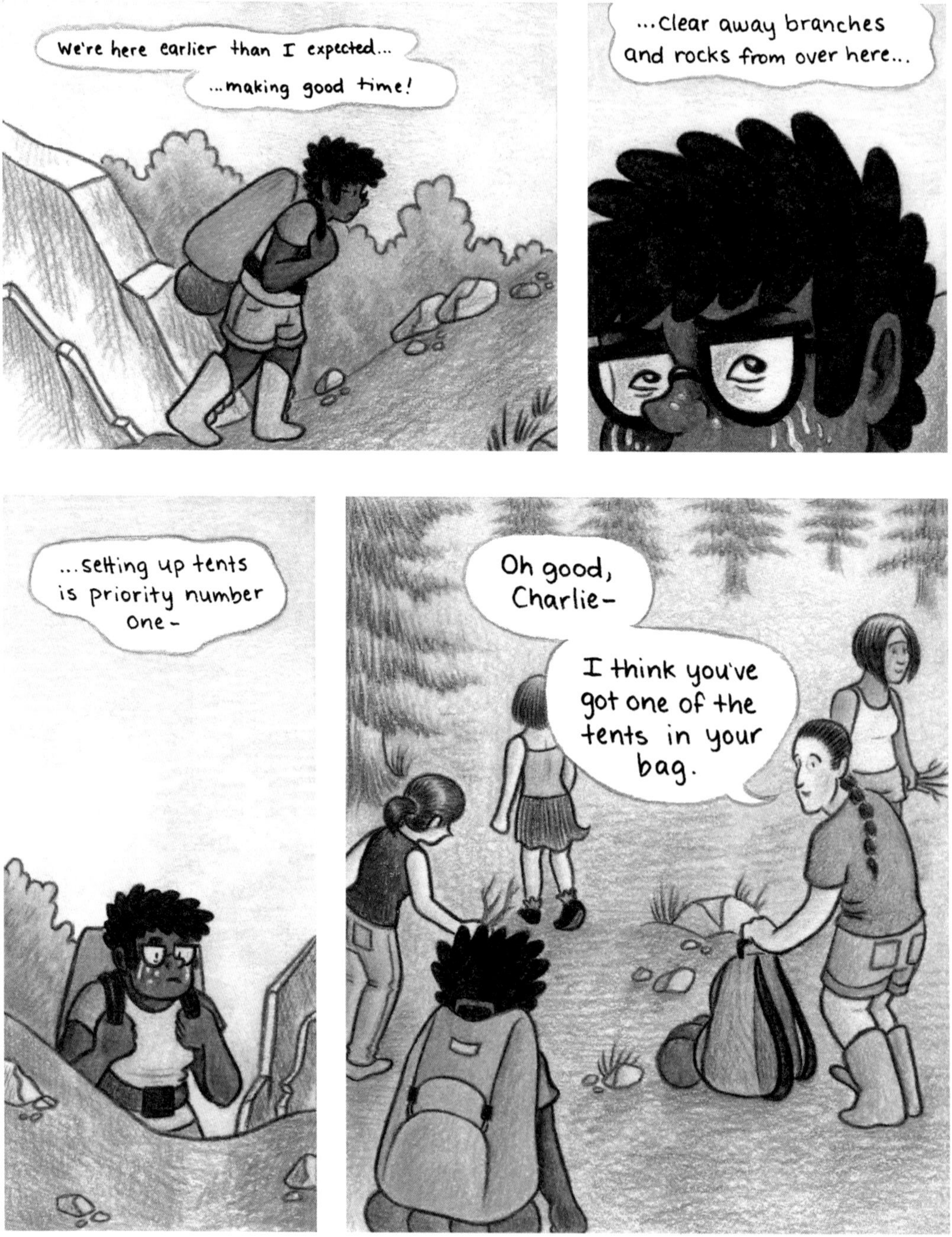

We're here earlier than I expected...
...making good time!
...Clear away branches and rocks from over here...
...setting up tents is priority number one-
Oh good, Charlie-
I think you've got one of the tents in your bag.

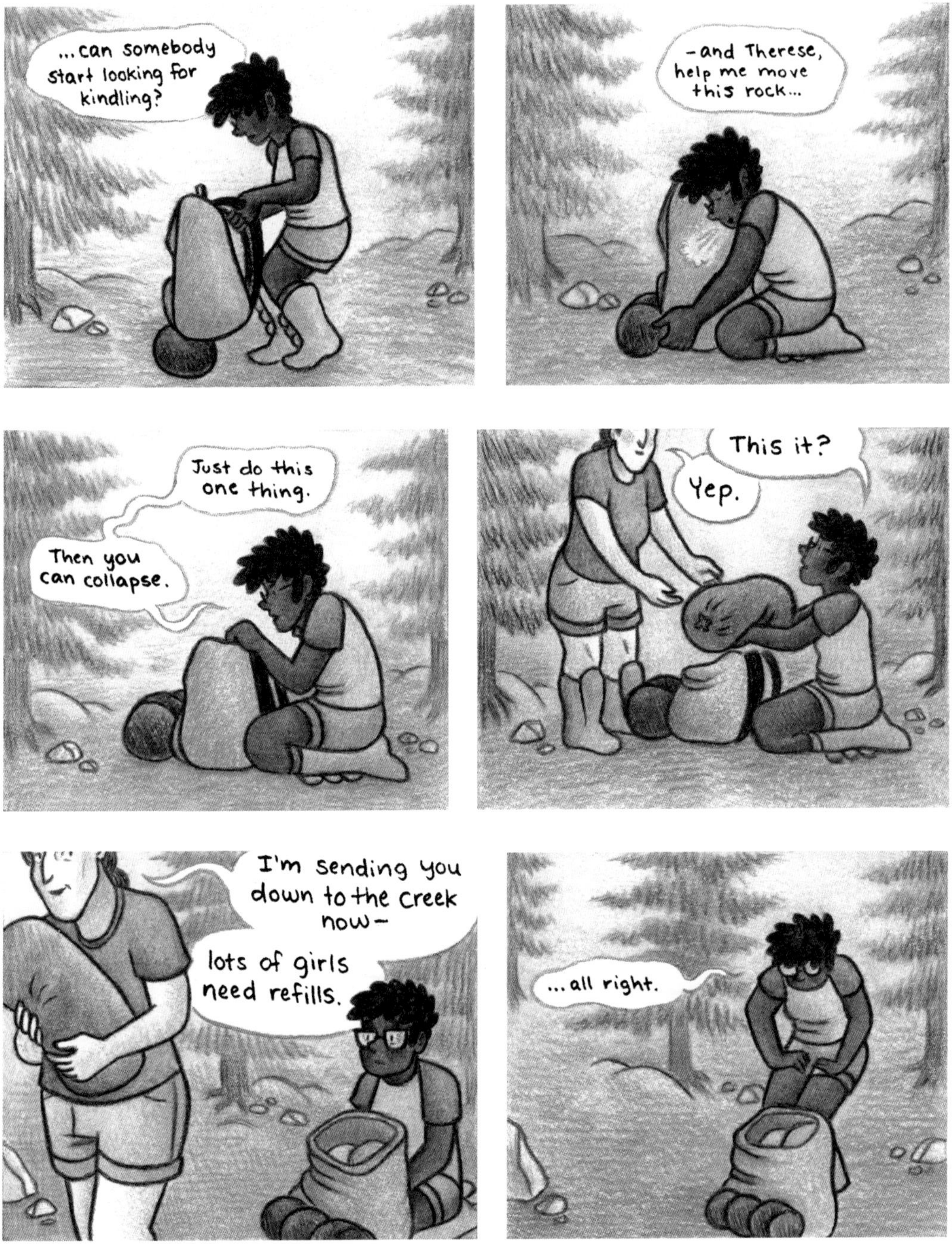
...can somebody start looking for kindling?
-and Therese, help me move this rock...
Just do this one thing.
Then you can collapse.
This it?
Yep.
I'm sending you down to the creek now-
lots of girls need refills.
...all right.

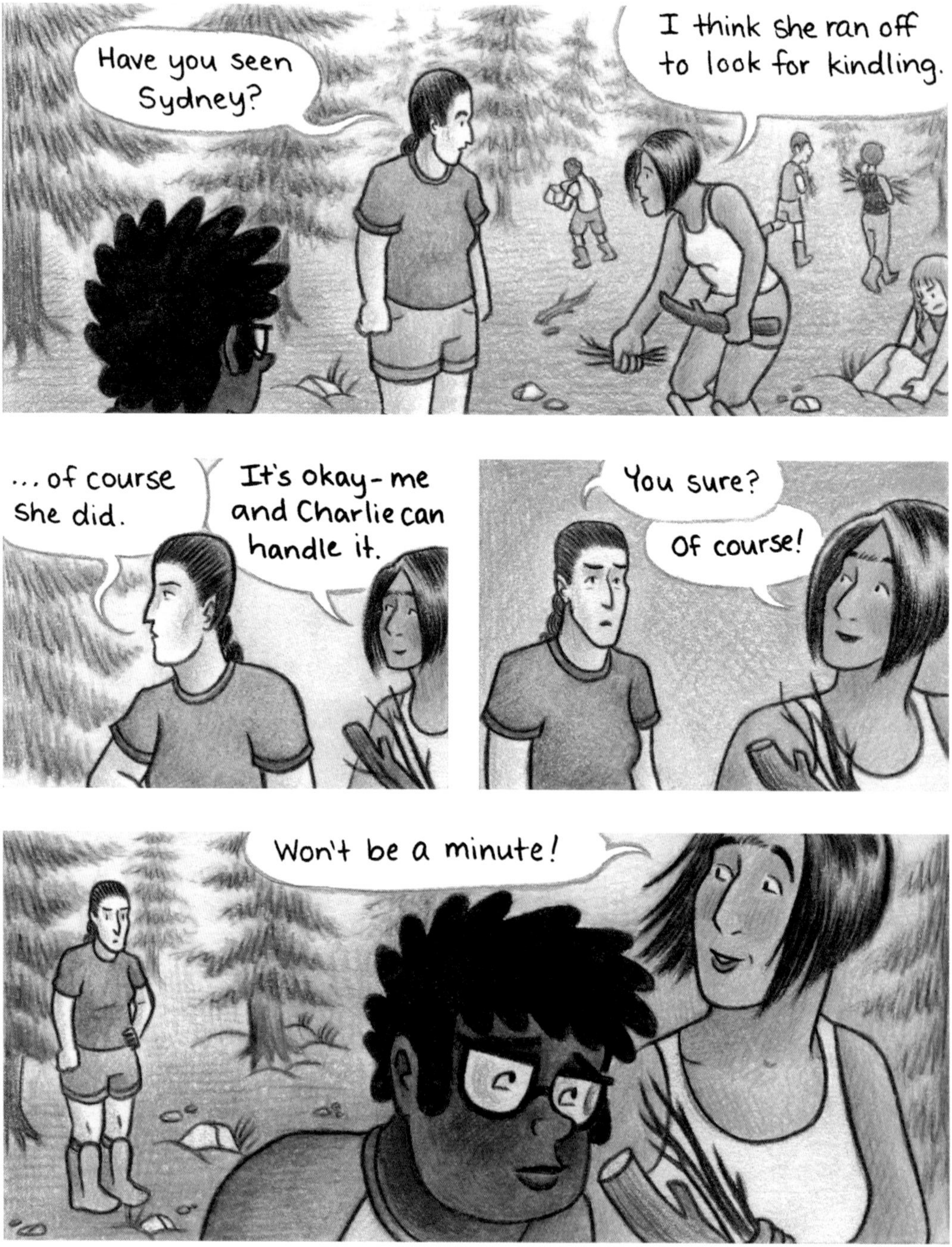
Have you seen Sydney?
I think she ran off to look for kindling.
... of course she did.
It's okay- me and Charlie can handle it.
You sure?
Of course!
Won't be a minute!

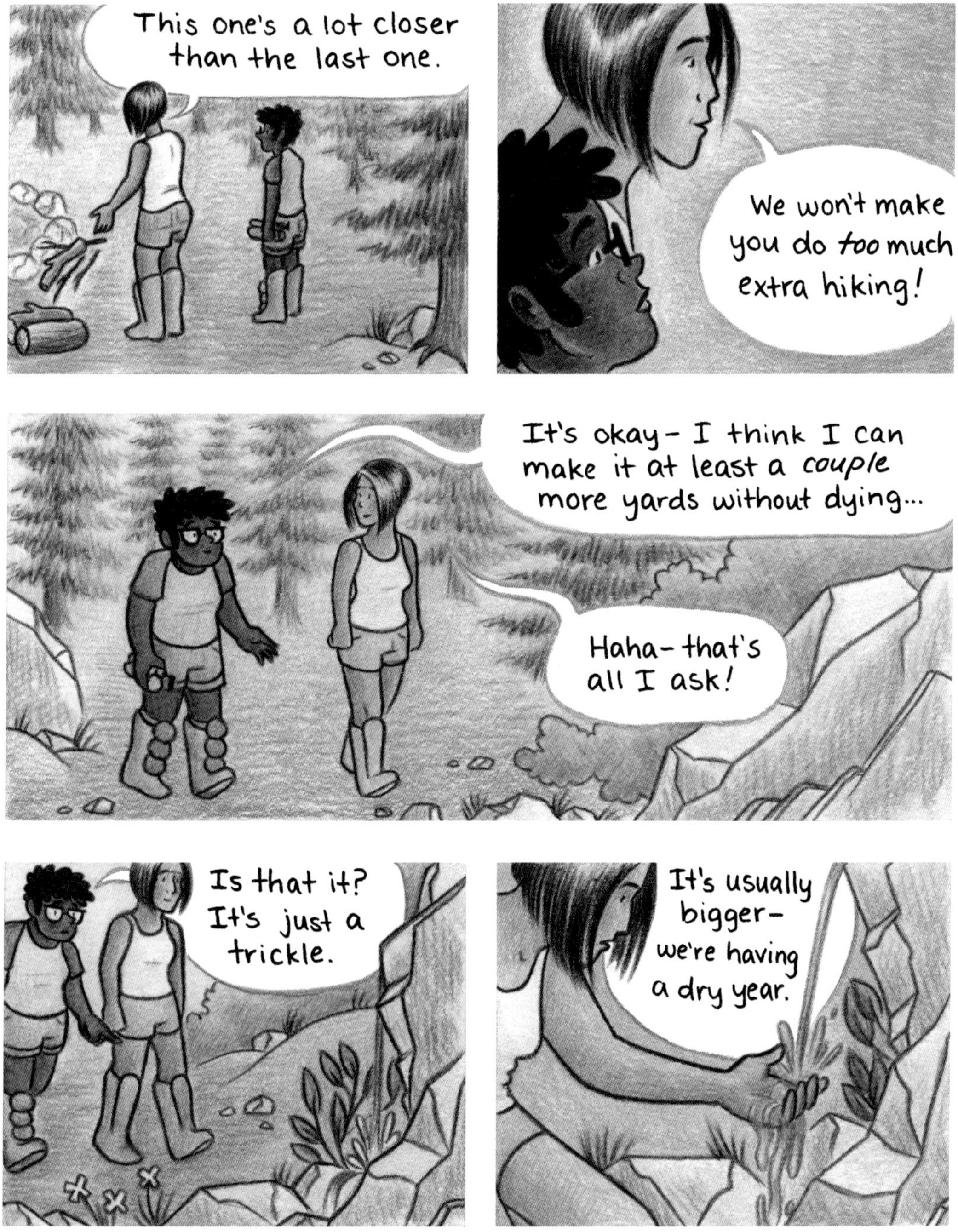
This one's a lot closer than the last one.
We won't make you do *too* much extra hiking!
It's okay- I think I can make it at least a *couple* more yards without dying...
Haha- that's all I ask!
Is that it? It's just a trickle.
It's usually bigger- we're having a dry year.

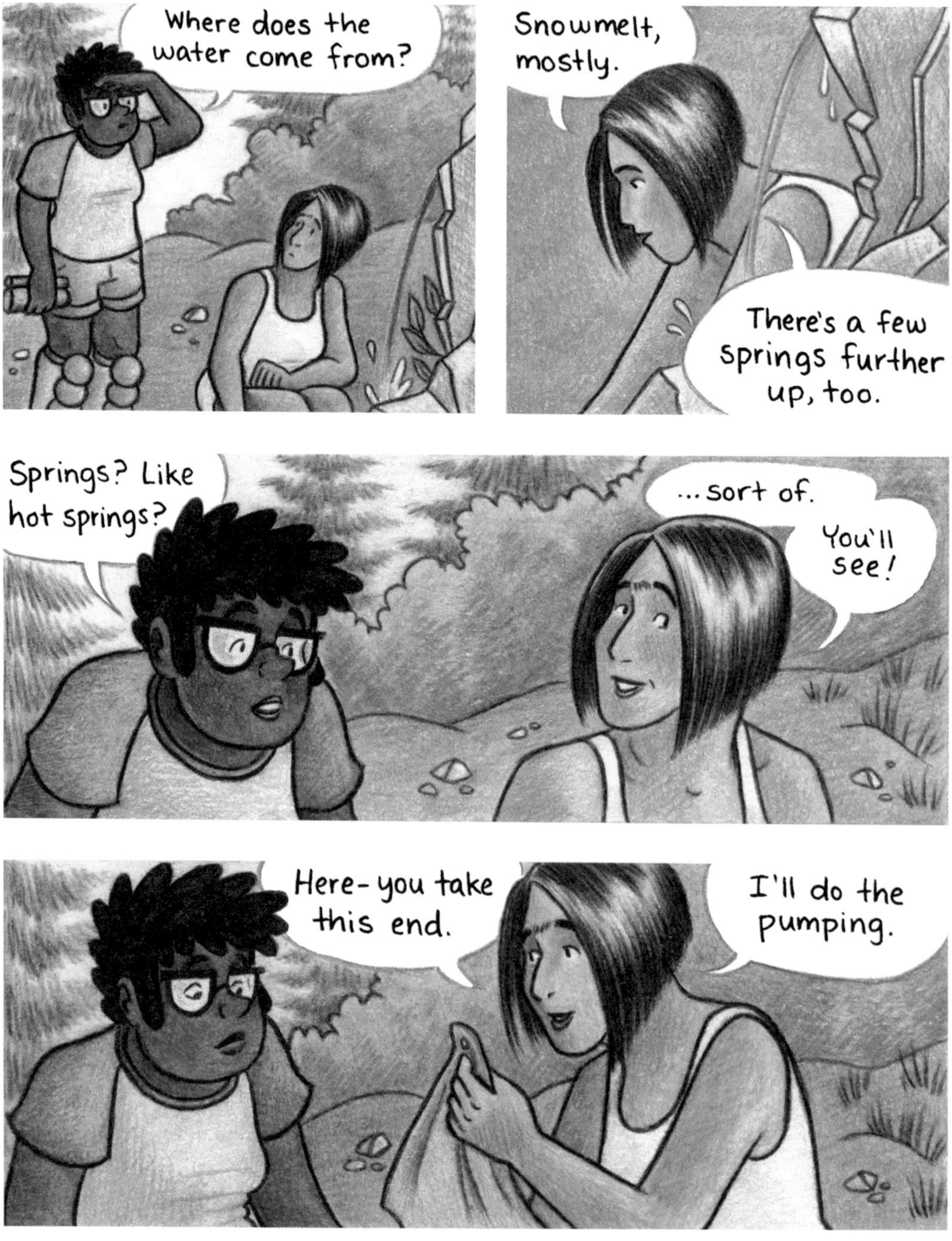
Where does the water come from?
Snowmelt, mostly.
There's a few springs further up, too.
Springs? Like hot springs?
...sort of.
You'll see!
Here- you take this end.
I'll do the pumping.

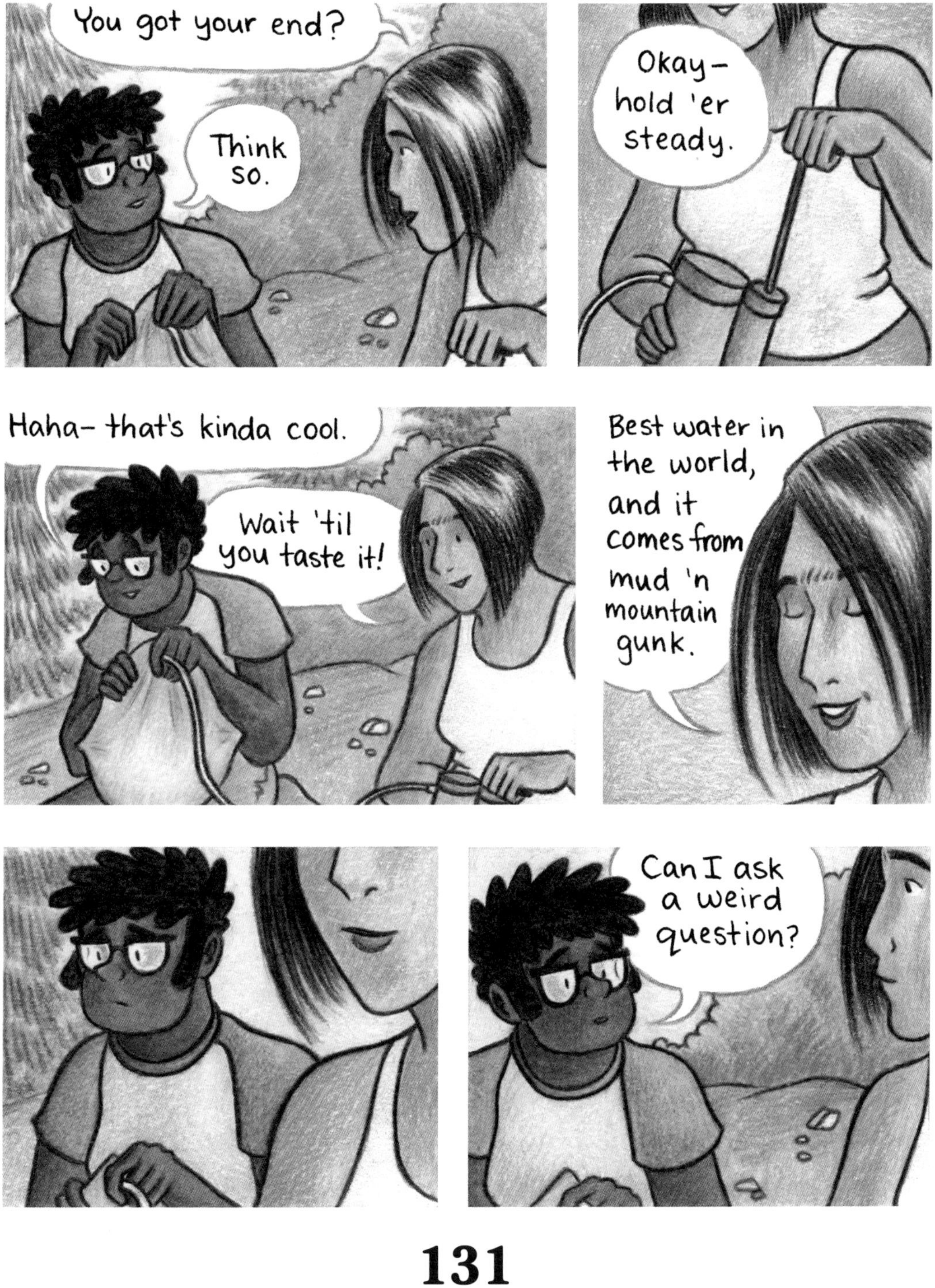
You got your end?
Think so.
Okay– hold 'er steady.
Haha– that's kinda cool.
Wait 'til you taste it!
Best water in the world, and it comes from mud 'n mountain gunk.
Can I ask a weird question?

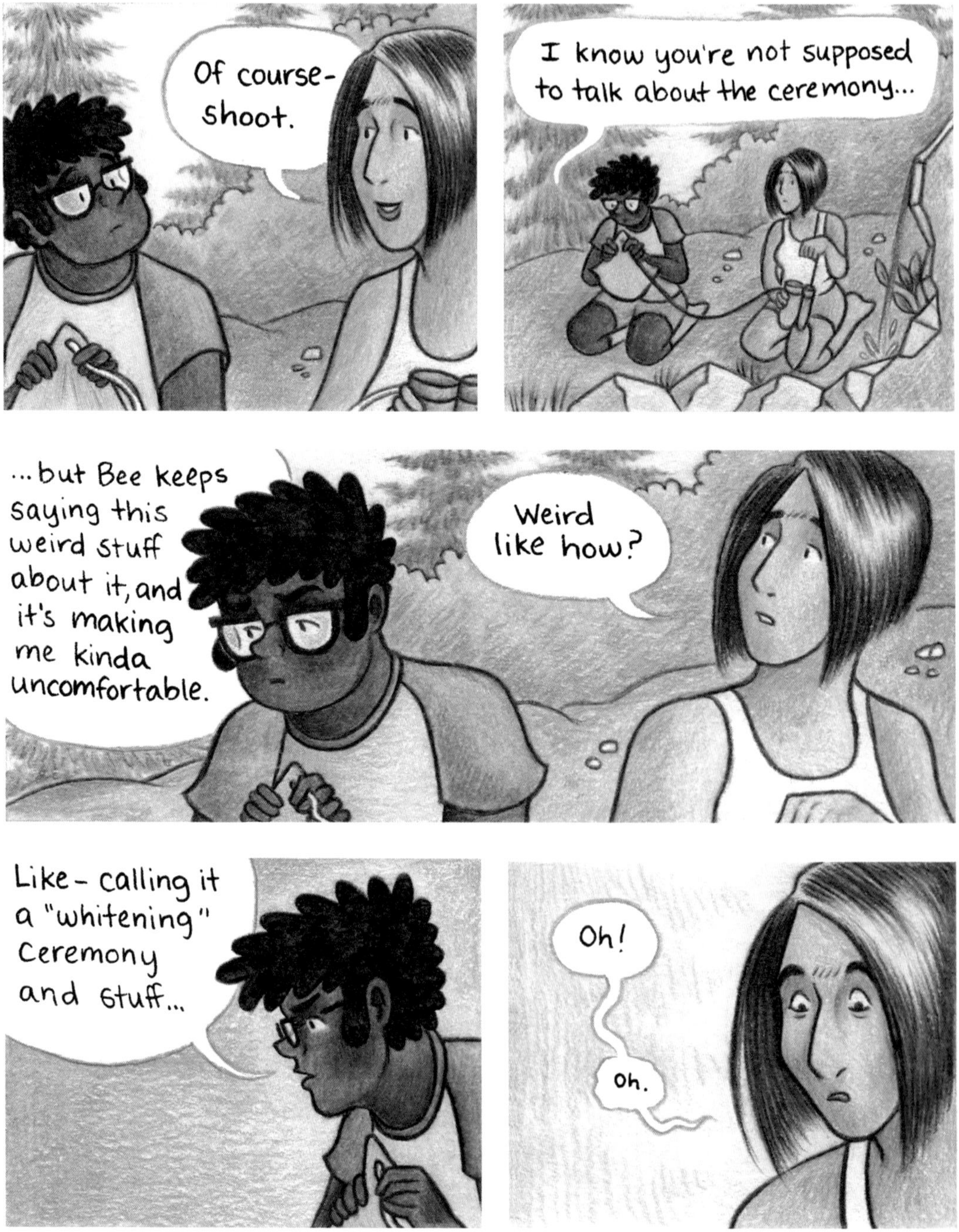
Of course- shoot.
I know you're not supposed to talk about the ceremony...
...but Bee keeps saying this weird stuff about it, and it's making me kinda uncomfortable.
Weird like how?
Like- calling it a "whitening" ceremony and stuff...
Oh!
Oh.

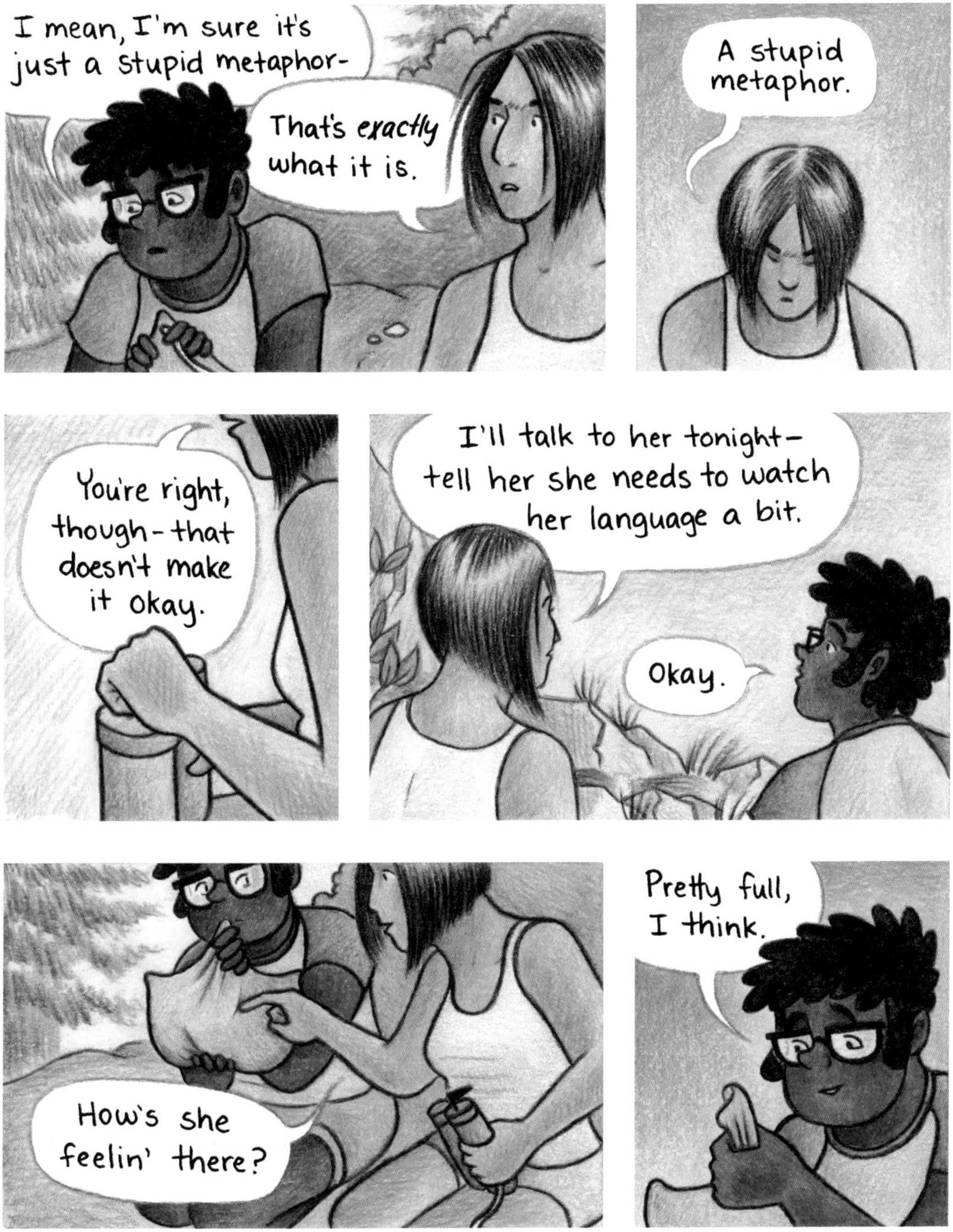
I mean, I'm sure it's just a stupid metaphor-
That's *exactly* what it is.
A stupid metaphor.
You're right, though- that doesn't make it okay.
I'll talk to her tonight- tell her she needs to watch her language a bit.
Okay.
How's she feelin' there?
Pretty full, I think.

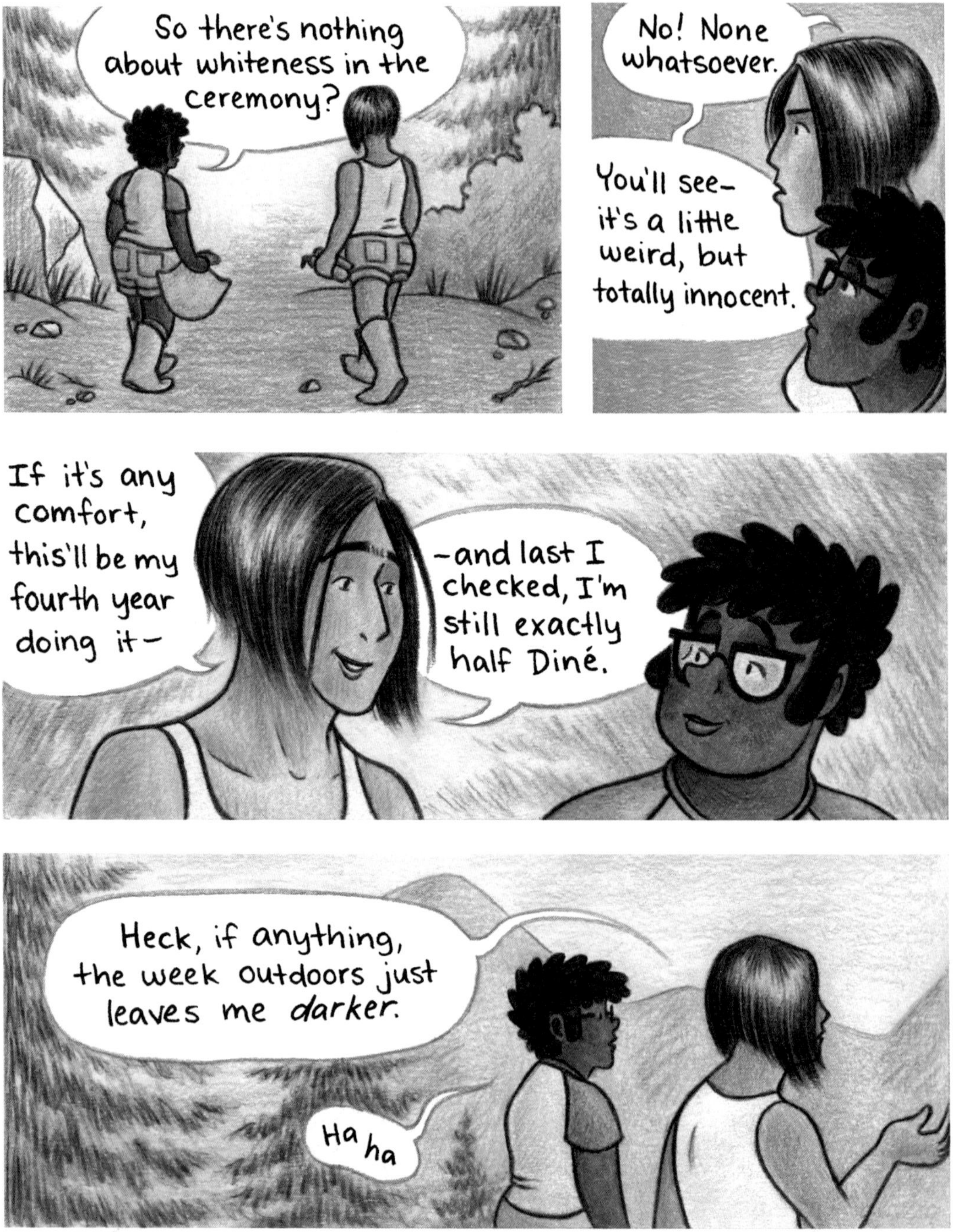
So there's nothing about whiteness in the ceremony?
No! None whatsoever.
You'll see– it's a little weird, but totally innocent.
If it's any comfort, this'll be my fourth year doing it–
–and last I checked, I'm still exactly half Diné.
Heck, if anything, the week outdoors just leaves me *darker*.
Ha ha

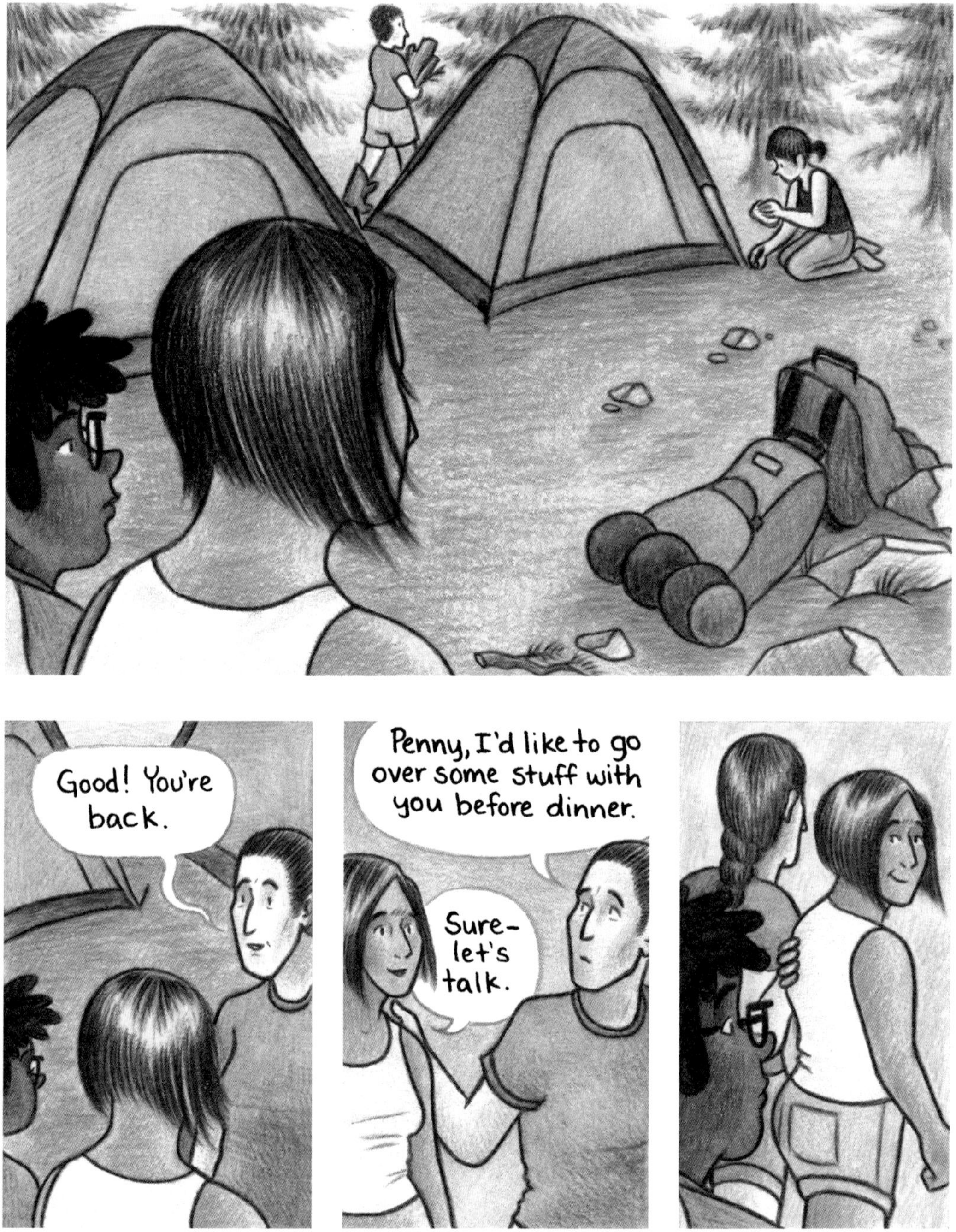
Good! You're back.
Penny, I'd like to go over some stuff with you before dinner.
Sure- let's talk.

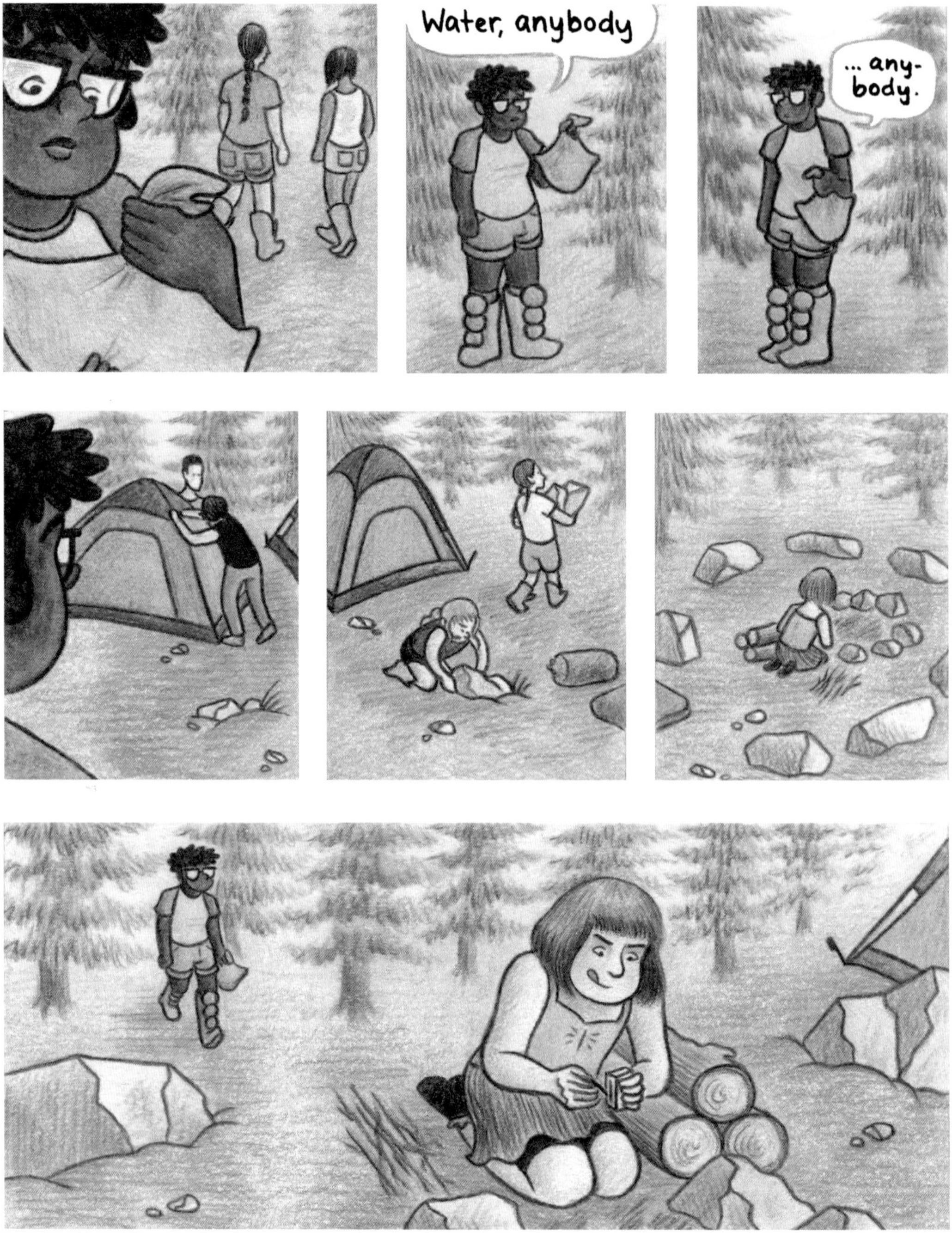
Water, anybody
... any-body.

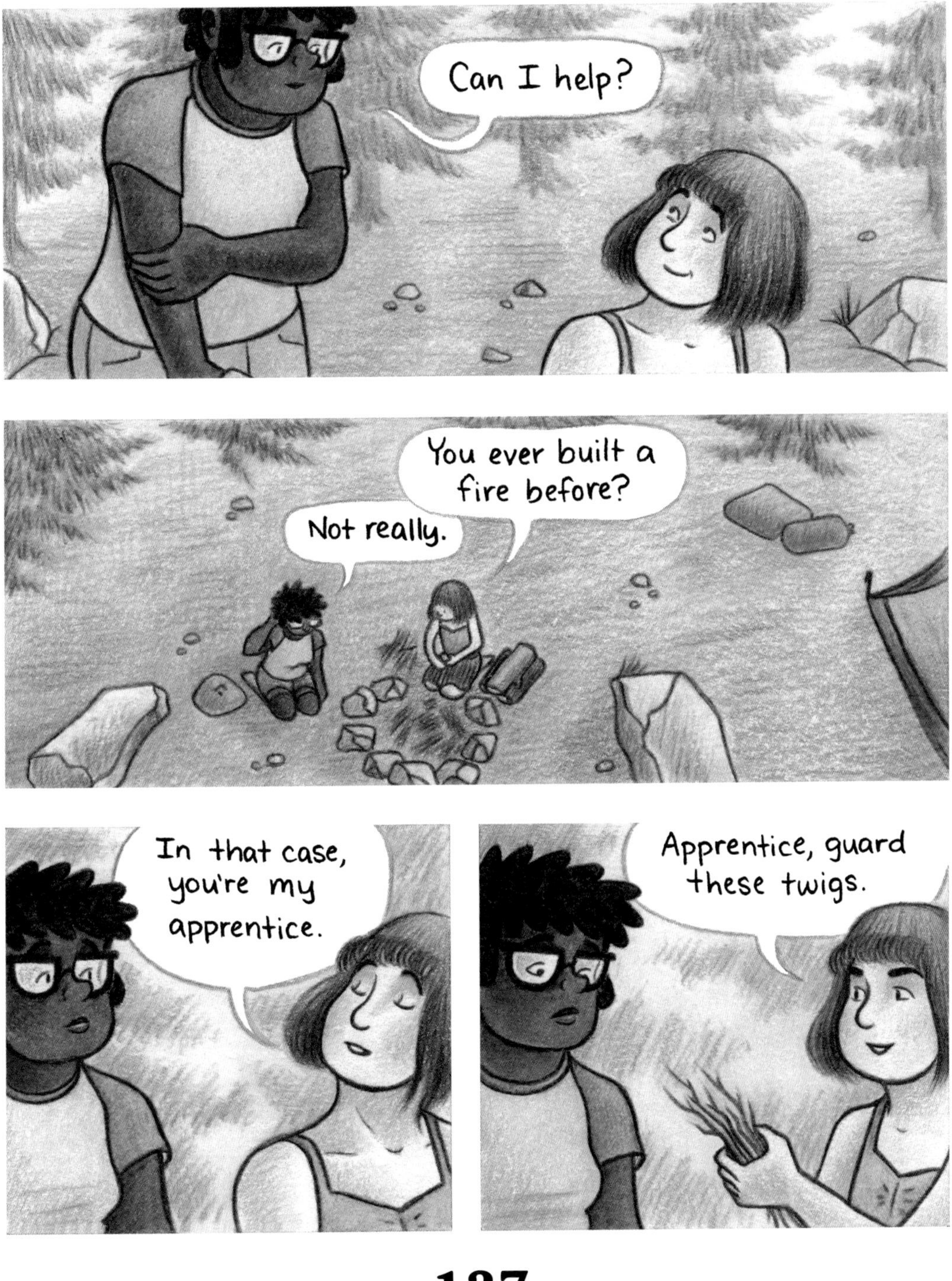
Can I help?
You ever built a fire before?
Not really.
In that case, you're my apprentice.
Apprentice, guard these twigs.

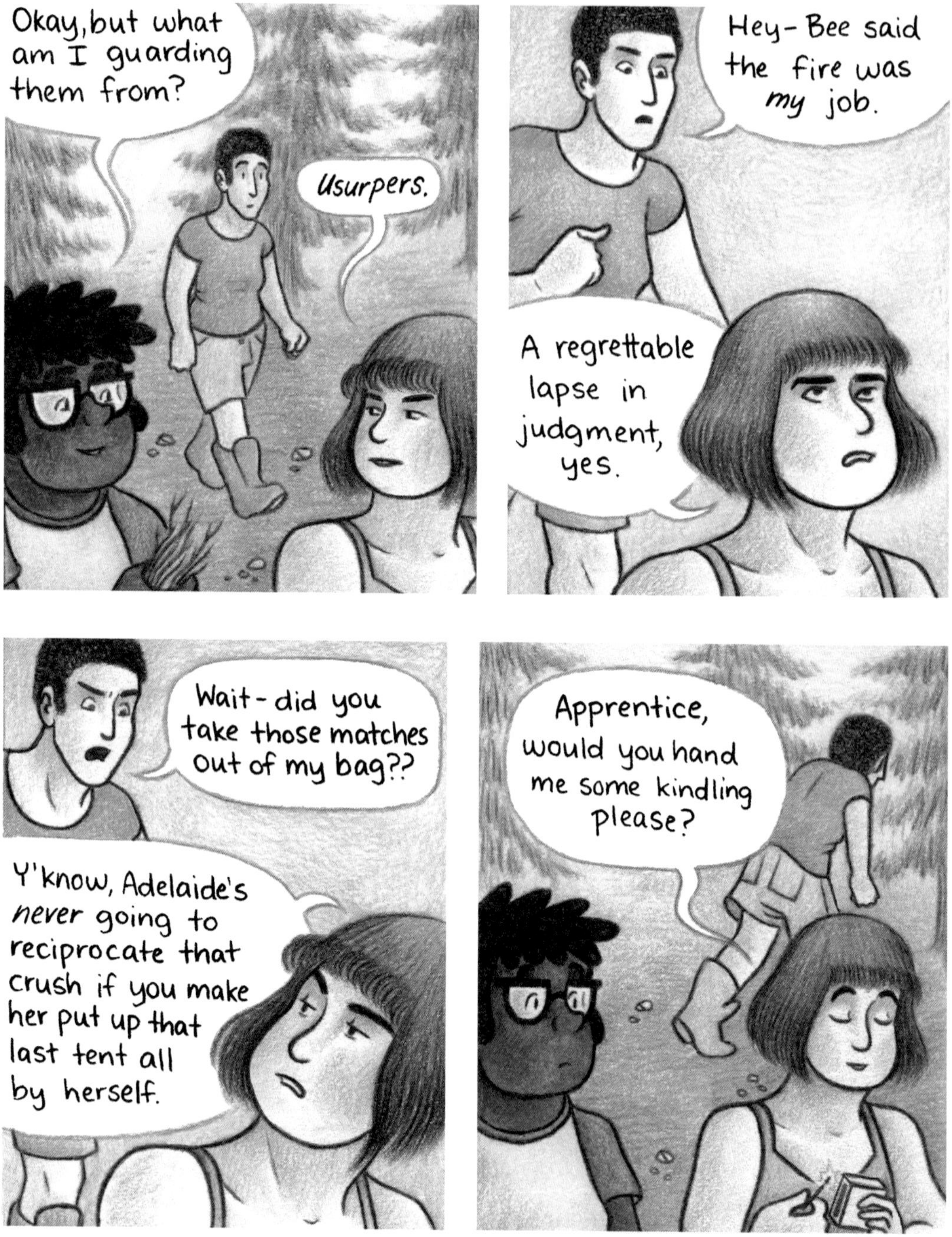
Okay, but what am I guarding them from?
Usurpers.
Hey- Bee said the fire was *my* job.
A regrettable lapse in judgment, yes.
Wait- did you take those matches out of my bag??
Y'know, Adelaide's *never* going to reciprocate that crush if you make her put up that last tent all by herself.
Apprentice, would you hand me some kindling please?

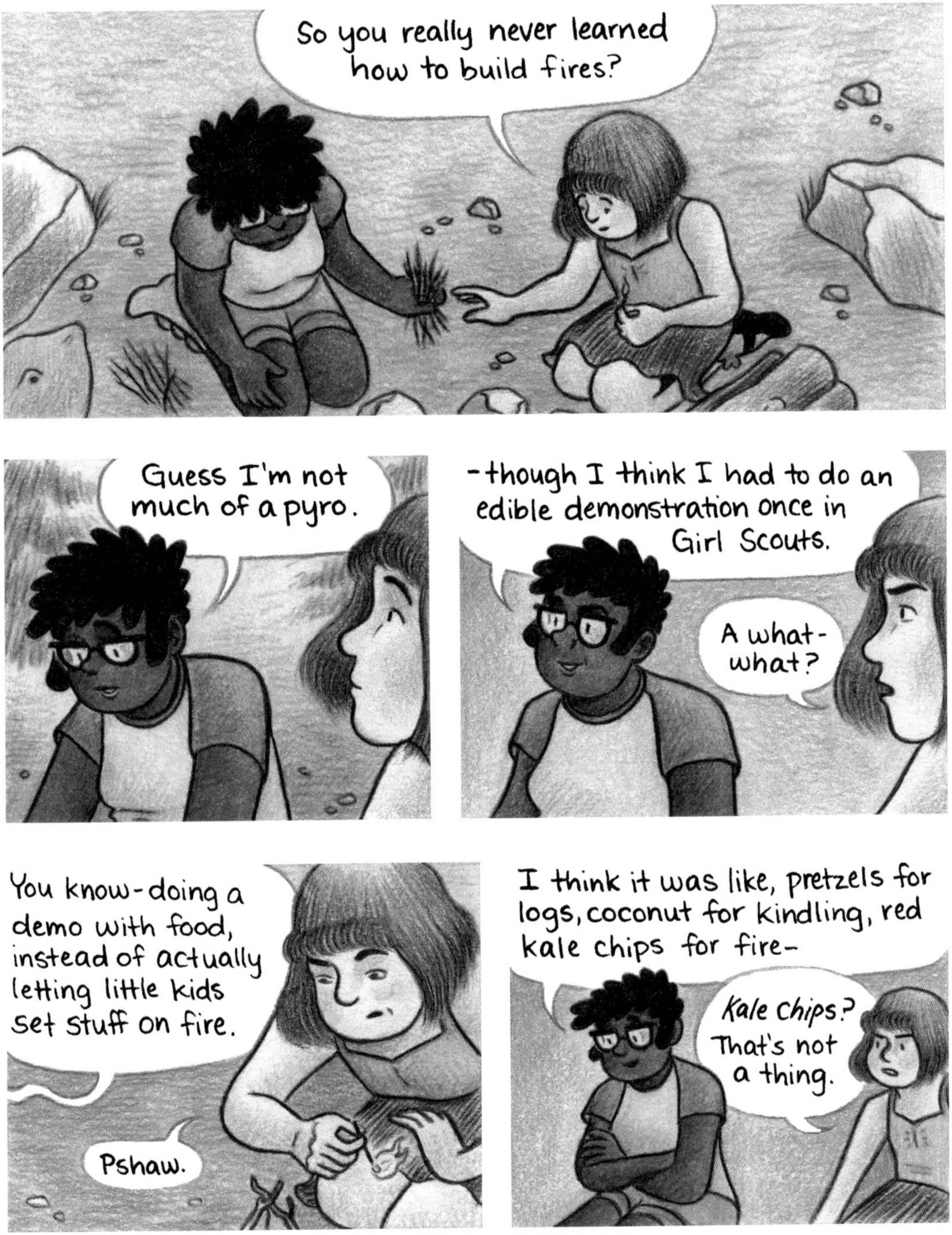
So you really never learned how to build fires?
Guess I'm not much of a pyro.
-though I think I had to do an edible demonstration once in Girl Scouts.
A what-what?
You know-doing a demo with food, instead of actually letting little kids set stuff on fire.
Pshaw.
I think it was like, pretzels for logs, coconut for kindling, red kale chips for fire-
Kale chips? That's not a thing.

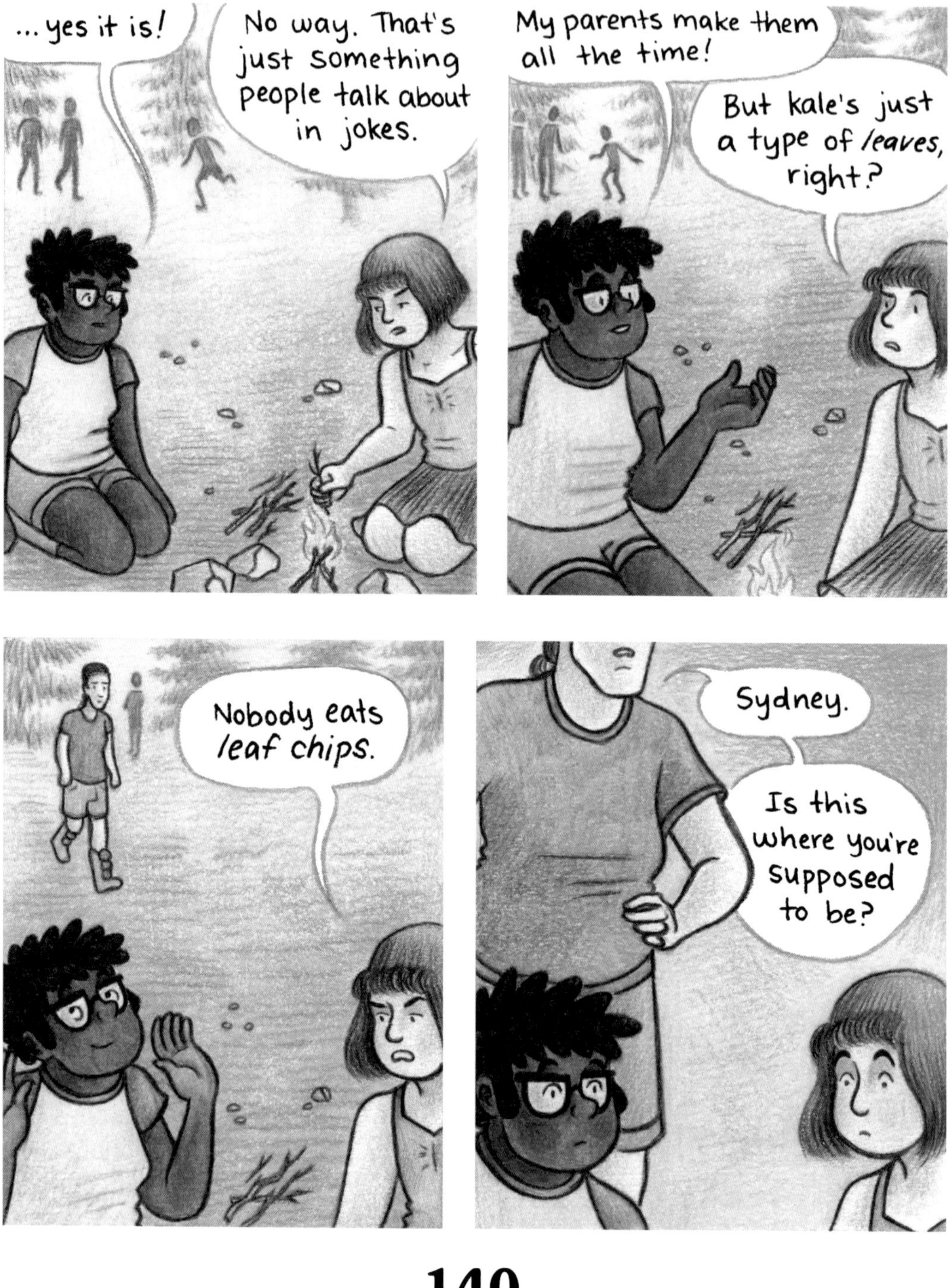
...yes it is!
No way. That's just something people talk about in jokes.
My parents make them all the time!
But kale's just a type of *leaves*, right?
Nobody eats *leaf chips*.
Sydney.
Is this where you're supposed to be?

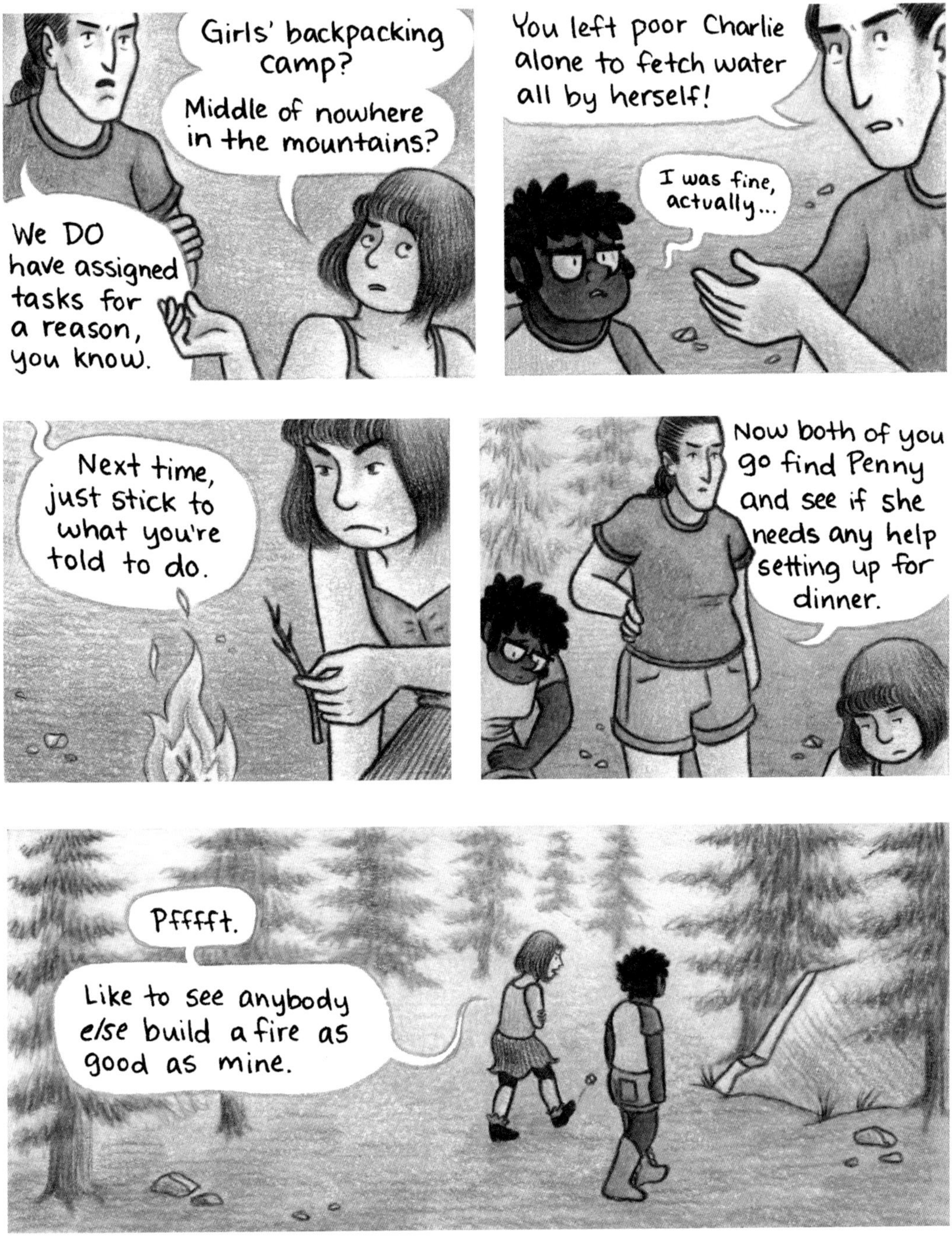

Girls' backpacking camp?
Middle of nowhere in the mountains?
We DO have assigned tasks for a reason, you know.
You left poor Charlie alone to fetch water all by herself!
I was fine, actually...
Next time, just stick to what you're told to do.
Now both of you go find Penny and see if she needs any help setting up for dinner.
Pfffft.
Like to see anybody *else* build a fire as good as mine.

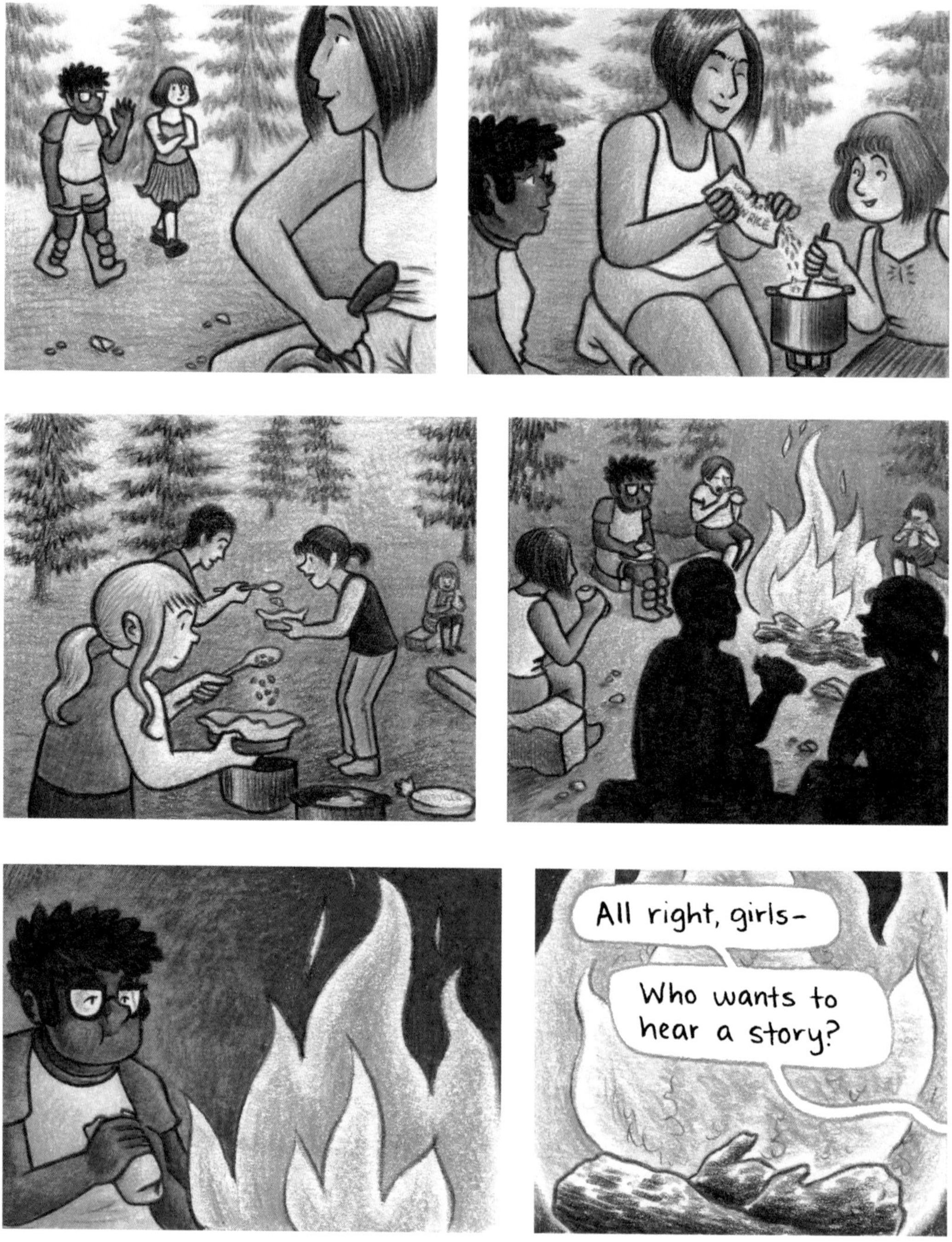
All right, girls-
Who wants to hear a story?

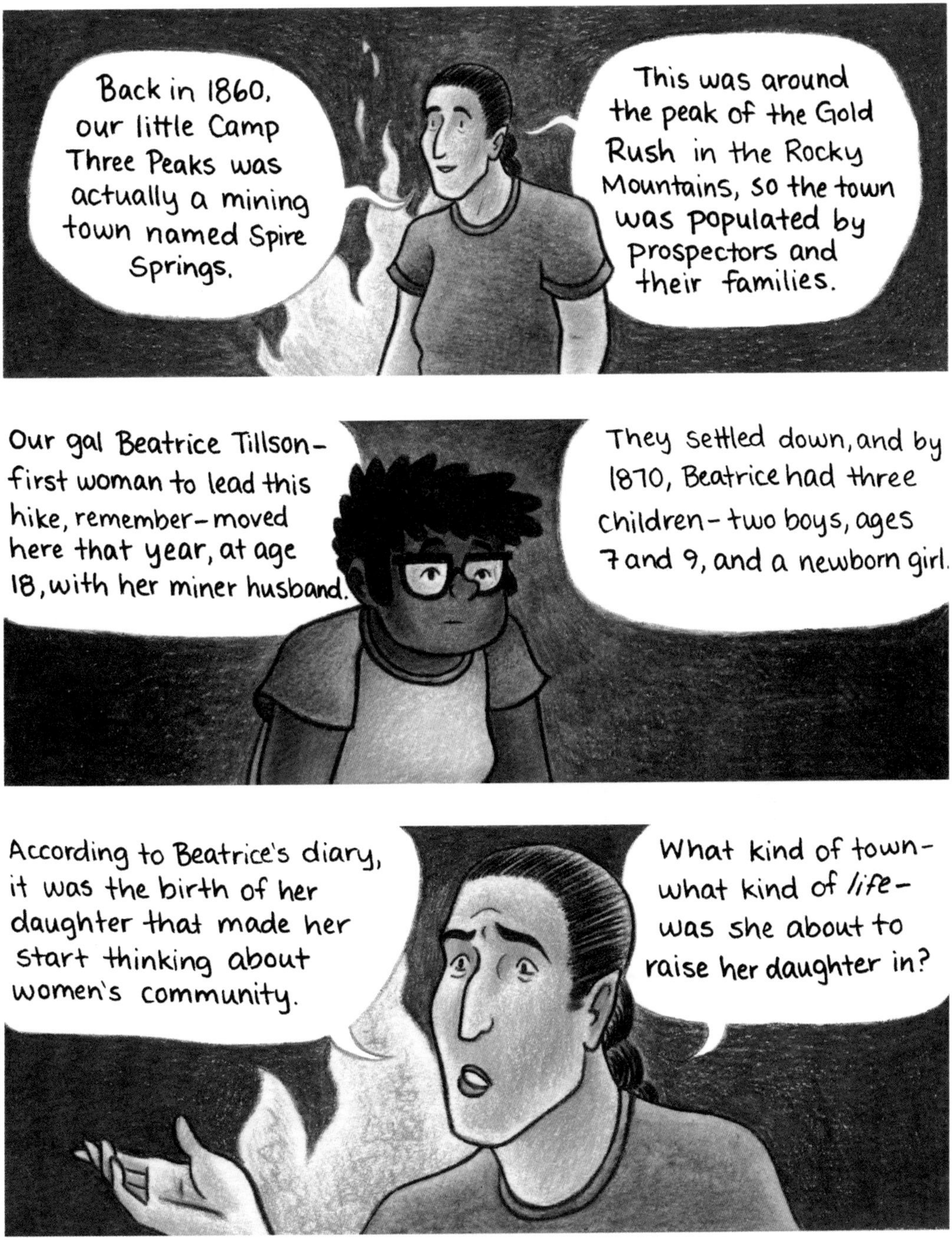
Back in 1860, our little Camp Three Peaks was actually a mining town named Spire Springs.
This was around the peak of the Gold Rush in the Rocky Mountains, so the town was populated by prospectors and their families.
Our gal Beatrice Tillson– first woman to lead this hike, remember– moved here that year, at age 18, with her miner husband.
They settled down, and by 1870, Beatrice had three children– two boys, ages 7 and 9, and a newborn girl.
According to Beatrice's diary, it was the birth of her daughter that made her start thinking about women's community.
What kind of town– what kind of *life*– was she about to raise her daughter in?

Living in such a remote area, it took a lot of work to keep a family alive.

-and women were expected to do most of the heavy lifting.

Women grew and harvested all the crops to feed their families—

Did all the cooking, cleaning, and any other household chores—

-and raised as many as 6 or 7 children!

The men of the town had their mining work, their hunting trips, their after-work visits to the trading post or saloon, to build community with.

But what about their wives?

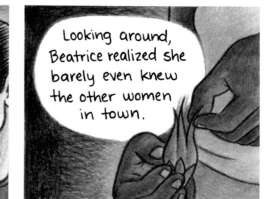

Looking around, Beatrice realized she barely even knew the other women in town.

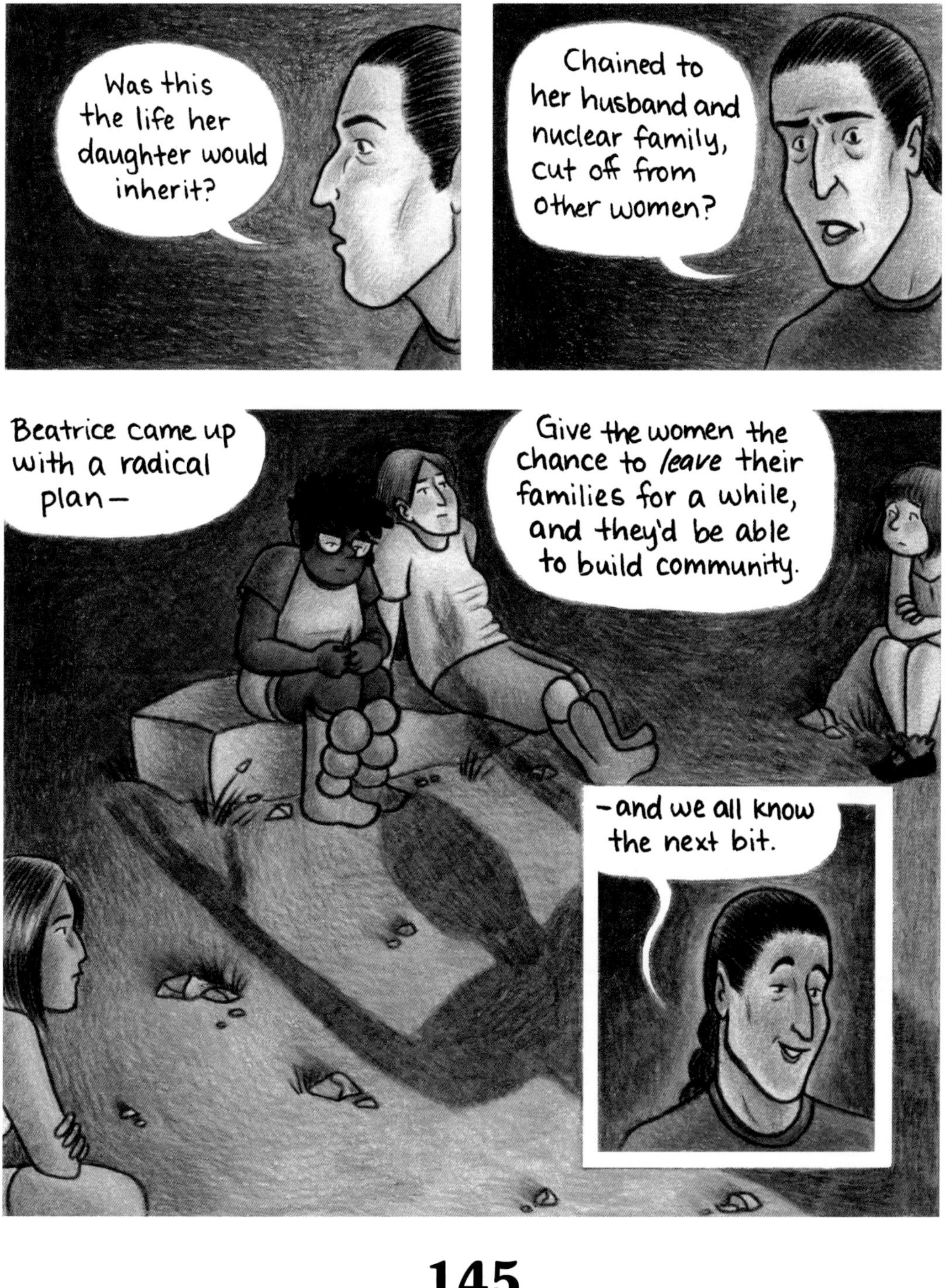
Was this the life her daughter would inherit?
Chained to her husband and nuclear family, cut off from other women?
Beatrice came up with a radical plan—
Give the women the chance to *leave* their families for a while, and they'd be able to build community.
—and we all know the next bit.

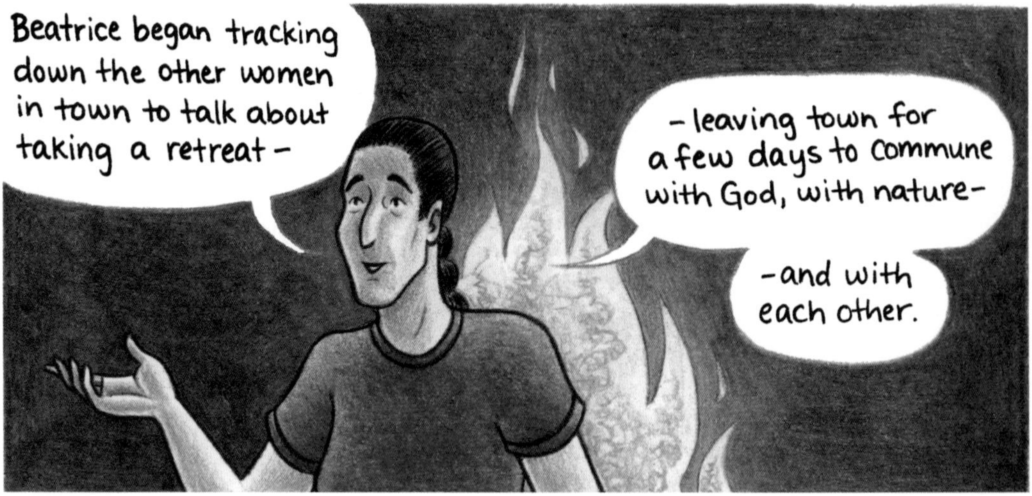
Beatrice began tracking down the other women in town to talk about taking a retreat–
–leaving town for a few days to commune with God, with nature–
–and with each other.

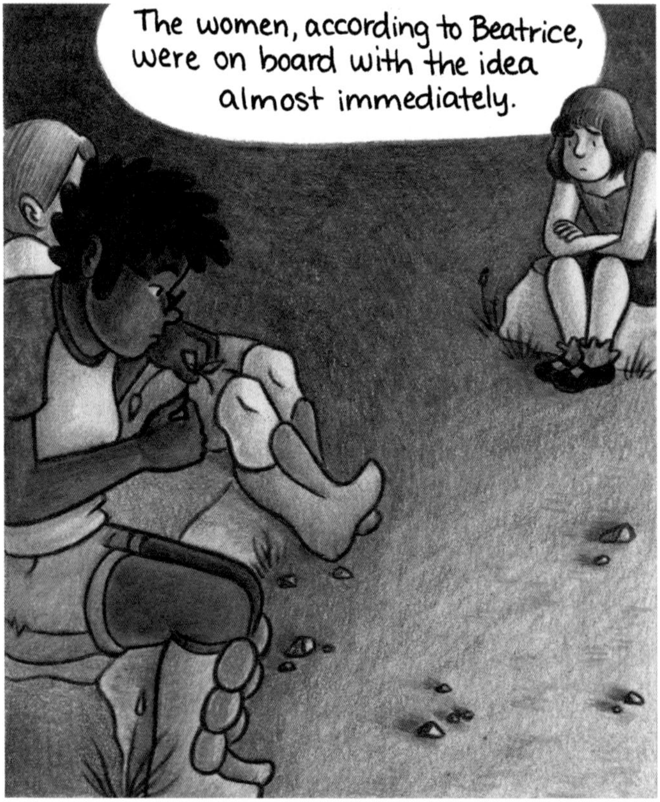
The women, according to Beatrice, were on board with the idea almost immediately.

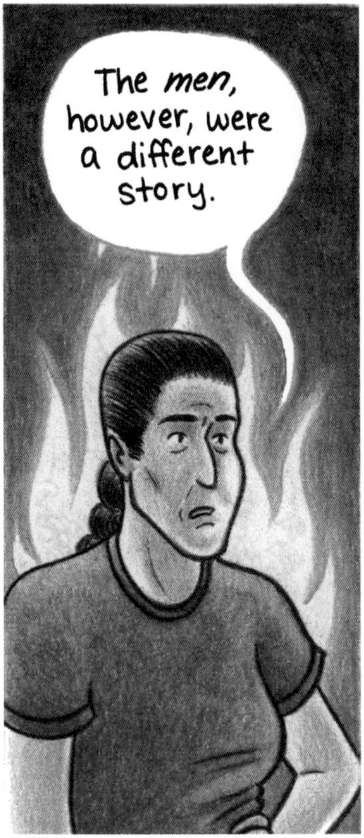
The *men*, however, were a different story.

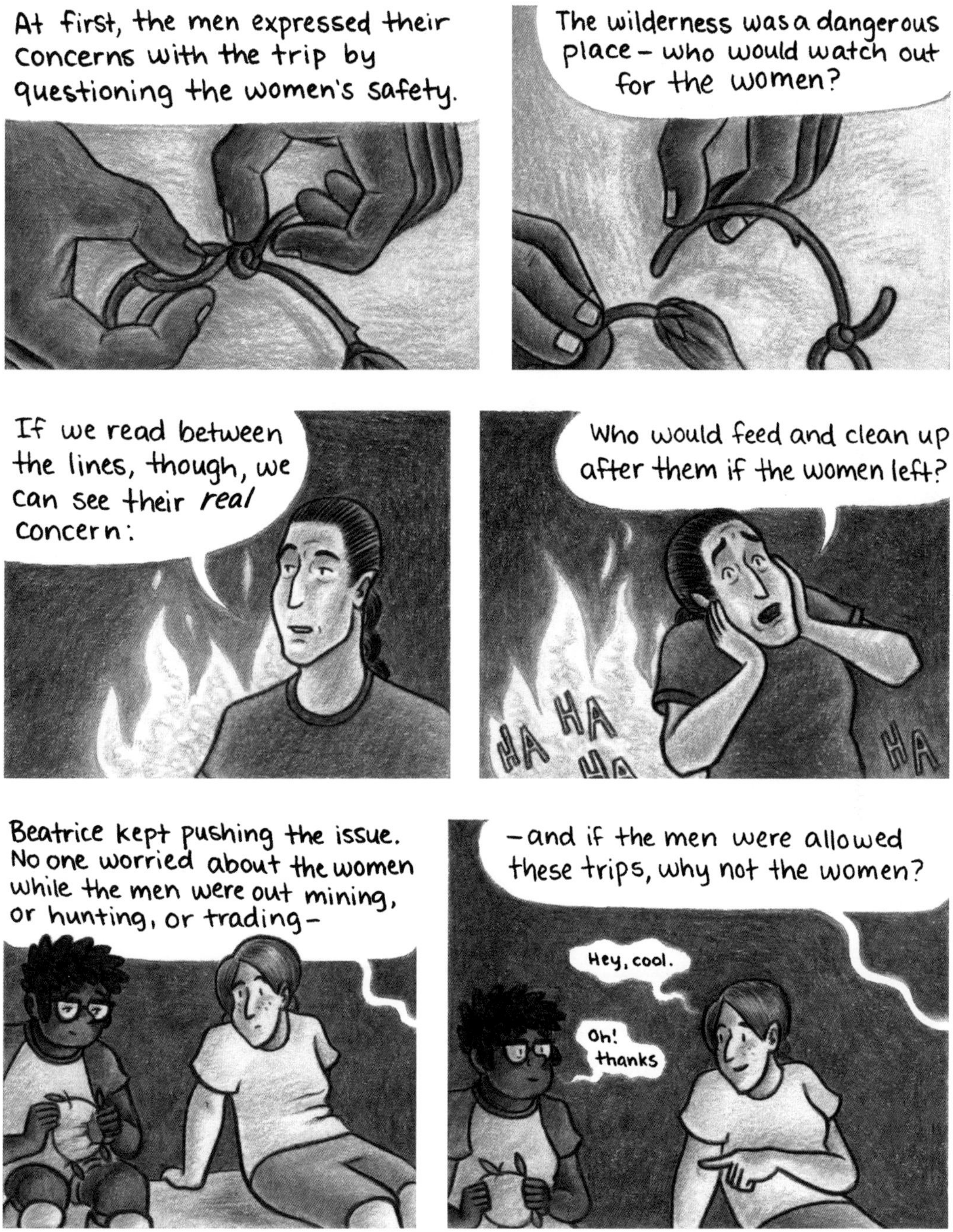
At first, the men expressed their concerns with the trip by questioning the women's safety.
The wilderness was a dangerous place – who would watch out for the women?
If we read between the lines, though, we can see their *real* concern:
Who would feed and clean up after them if the women left?
HA HA HA HA HA
Beatrice kept pushing the issue. No one worried about the women while the men were out mining, or hunting, or trading–
–and if the men were allowed these trips, why not the women?
Hey, cool.
Oh! thanks

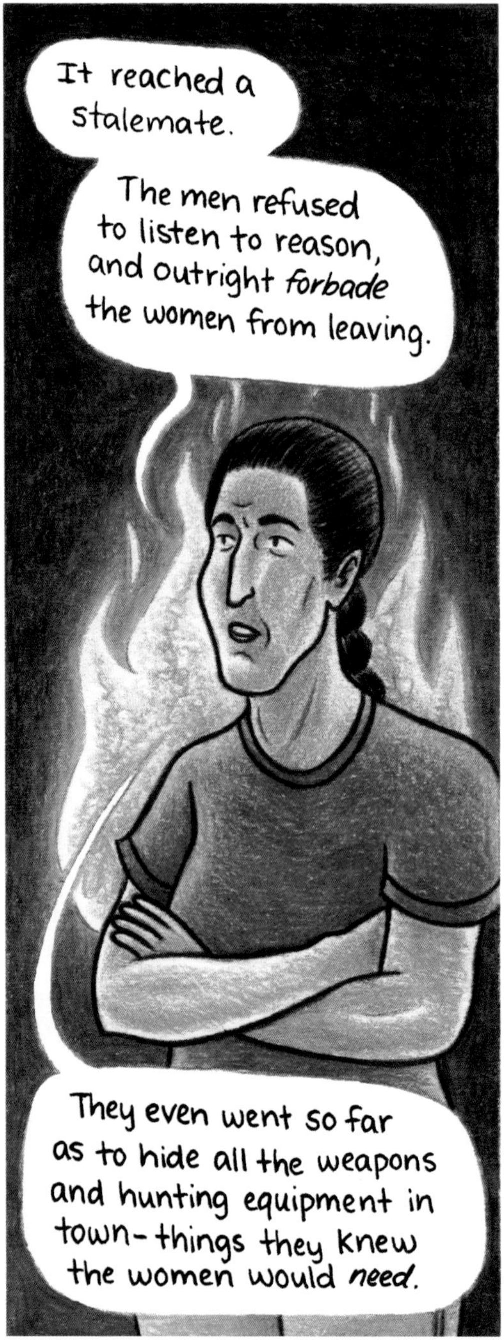
It reached a stalemate.
The men refused to listen to reason, and outright *forbade* the women from leaving.
They even went so far as to hide all the weapons and hunting equipment in town- things they knew the women would *need*.

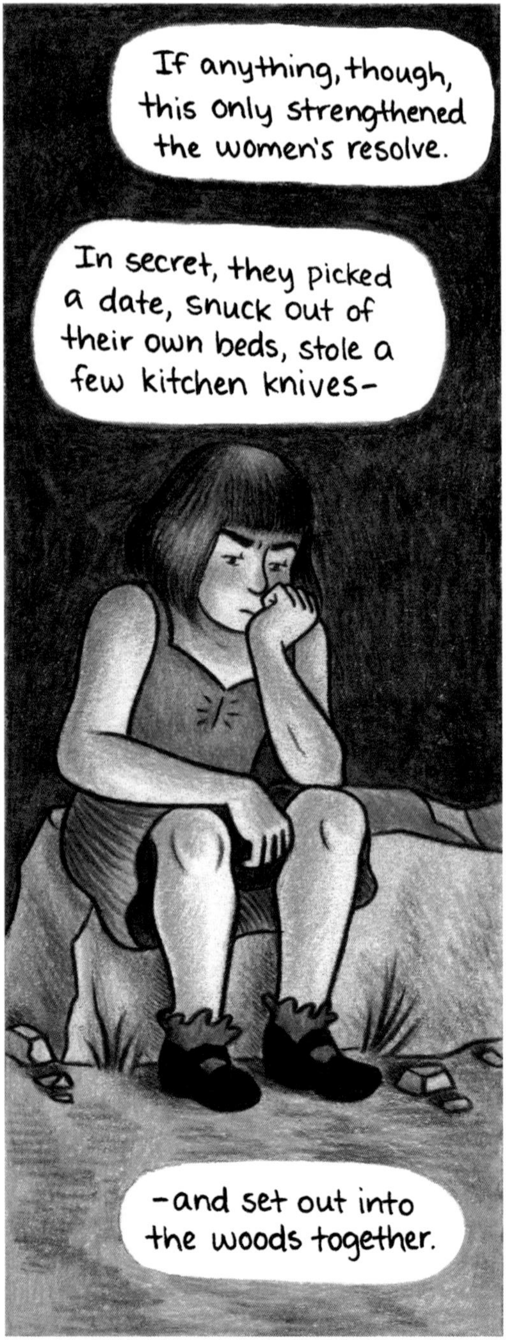
If anything, though, this only strengthened the women's resolve.
In secret, they picked a date, snuck out of their own beds, stole a few kitchen knives-
-and set out into the woods together.

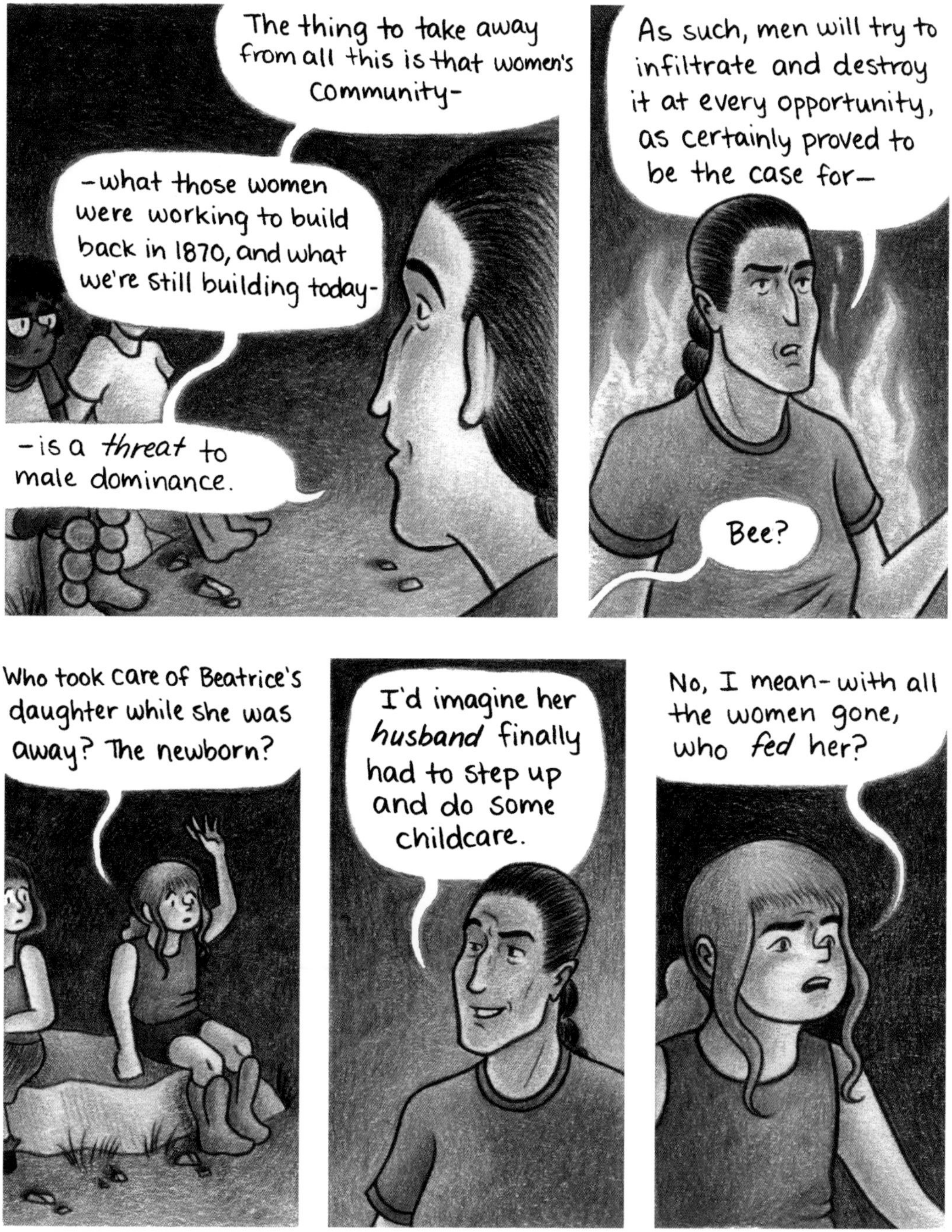
The thing to take away from all this is that women's community-
-what those women were working to build back in 1870, and what we're still building today-
-is a *threat* to male dominance.
As such, men will try to infiltrate and destroy it at every opportunity, as certainly proved to be the case for—
Bee?
Who took care of Beatrice's daughter while she was away? The newborn?
I'd imagine her *husband* finally had to step up and do some childcare.
No, I mean- with all the women gone, who *fed* her?

Oh.

Well, ah—

We have to remember, this was a very different time in American history.

Uh-oh.

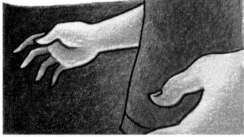

Beatrice does make a few references in her journal to— well, what she calls "servant" women.

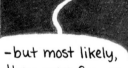

We don't know who they were, exactly—

—but most likely, they were former slaves— brought here at the start of the Gold Rush.

For most towns in the area, these people were either African-American or Ute— but that's all the records say.

It's likely Beatrice found a wetnurse among them.

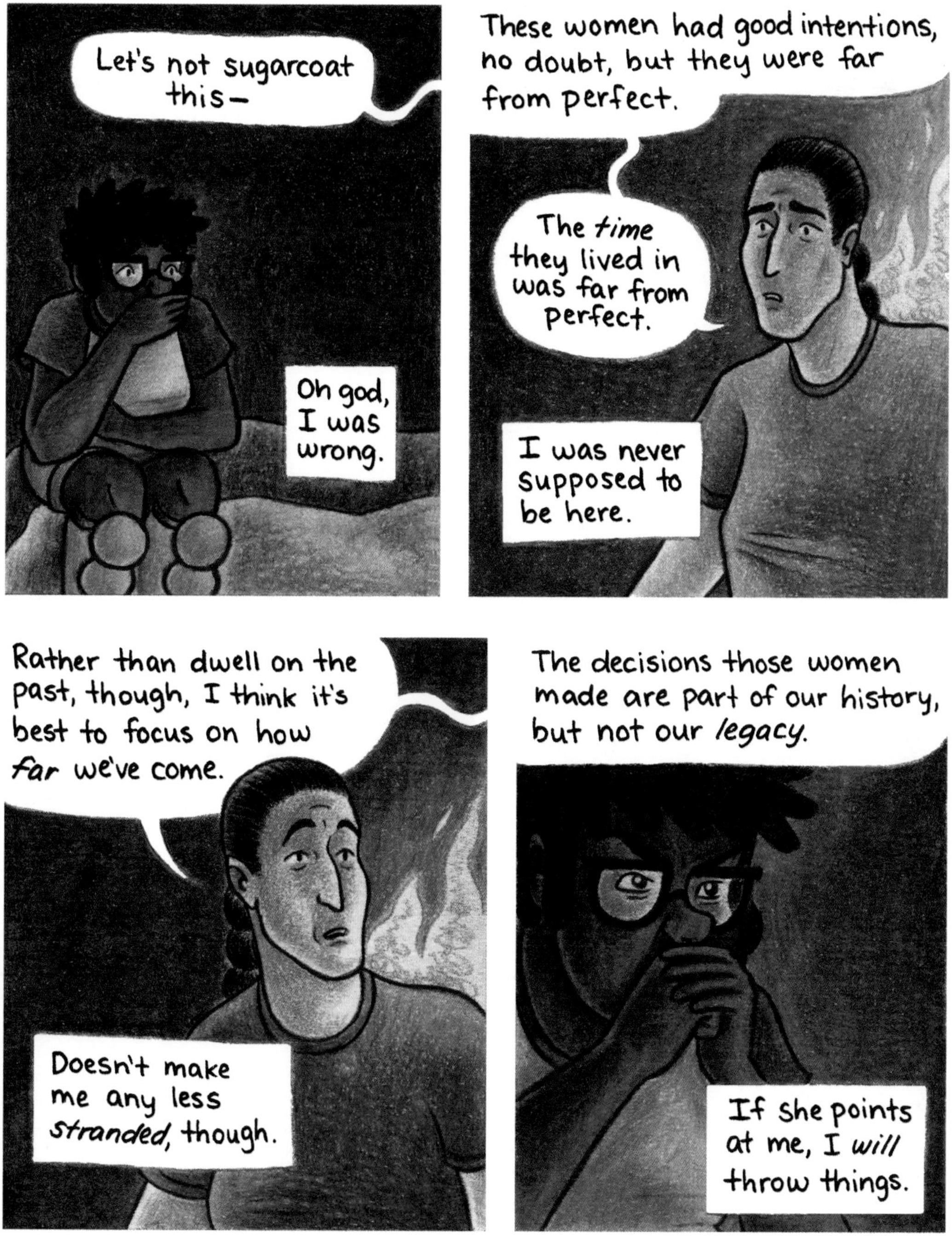
Let's not sugarcoat this—
Oh god, I was wrong.
These women had good intentions, no doubt, but they were far from perfect.
The *time* they lived in was far from perfect.
I was never supposed to be here.
Rather than dwell on the past, though, I think it's best to focus on how *far* we've come.
Doesn't make me any less *stranded*, though.
The decisions those women made are part of our history, but not our *legacy*.
If she points at me, I *will* throw things.

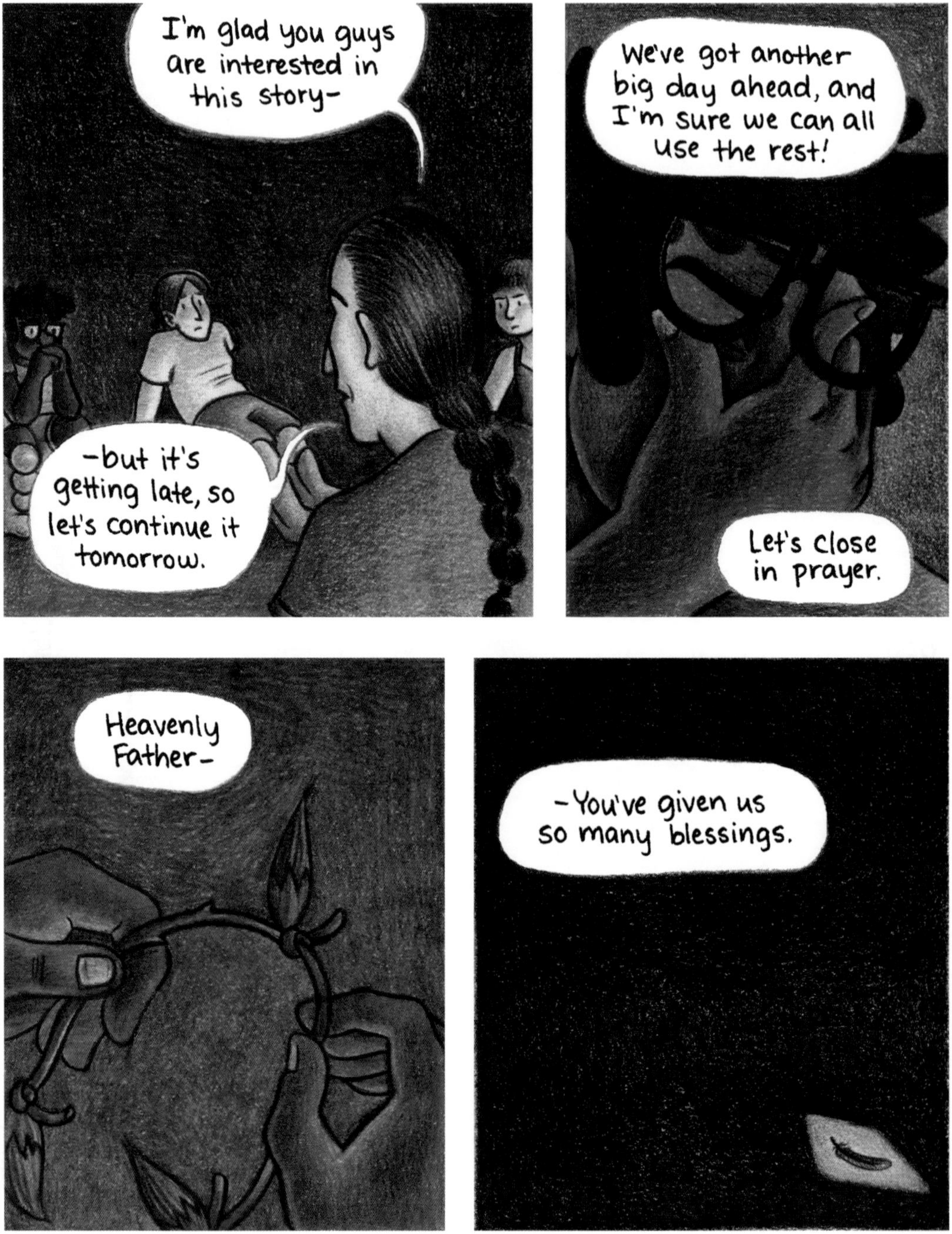
I'm glad you guys are interested in this story-
-but it's getting late, so let's continue it tomorrow.
We've got another big day ahead, and I'm sure we can all use the rest!
Let's close in prayer.
Heavenly Father-
-You've given us so many blessings.

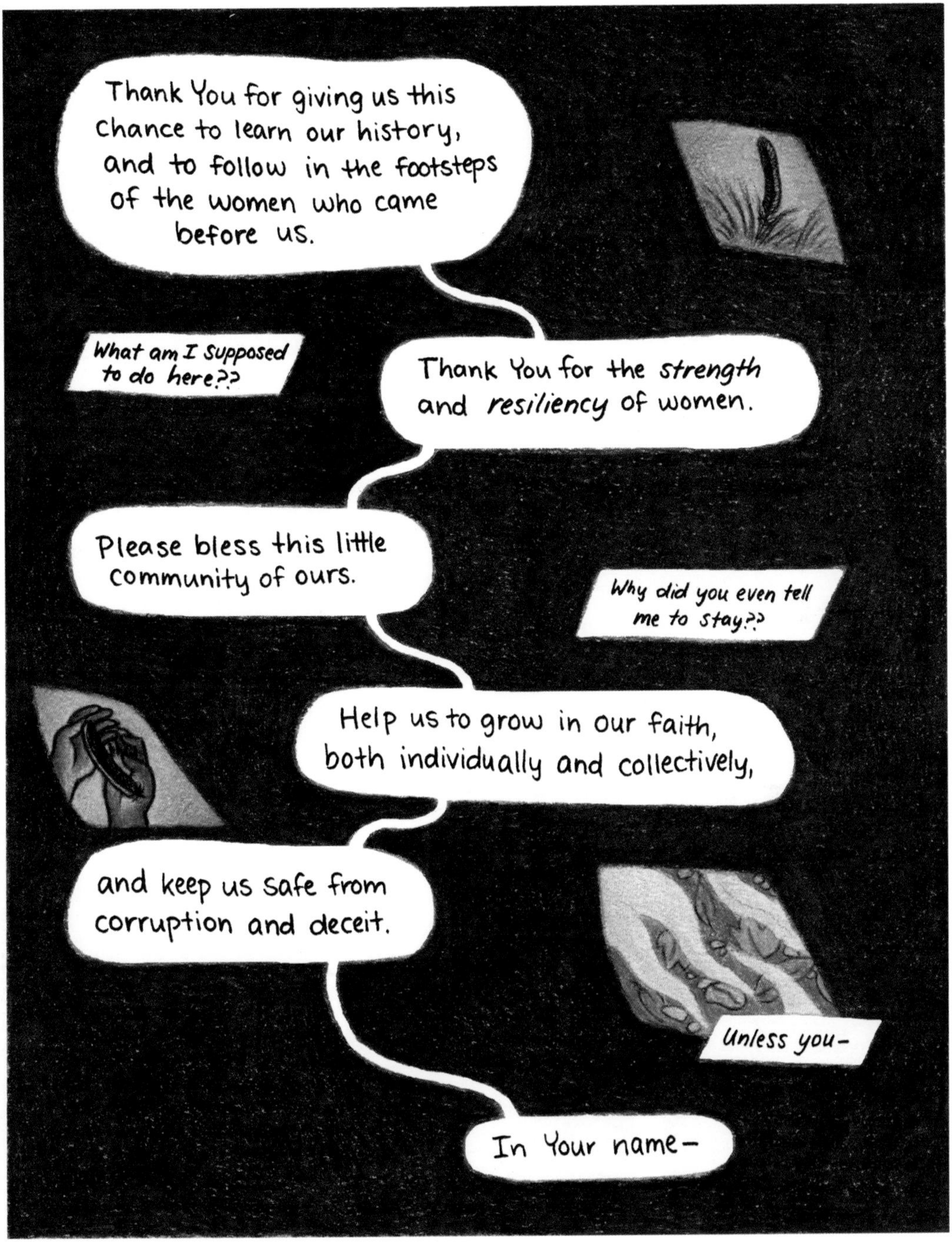
Thank You for giving us this chance to learn our history, and to follow in the footsteps of the women who came before us.
What am I supposed to do here??
Thank You for the *strength* and *resiliency* of women.
Please bless this little community of ours.
Why did you even tell me to stay??
Help us to grow in our faith, both individually and collectively,
and keep us safe from corruption and deceit.
Unless you-
In Your name-

-didn't.

All right, girls – now off to bed with you!

– and no staying up late chattering!

I've *gotta* talk to somebody.

–if you have enough energy to chatter, that means we gotta work you harder!

Claire, I think you're in the middle tent–

No faci content whatsoe

Nah, better put my sleeping bag on the side. I'm a kicker.

154

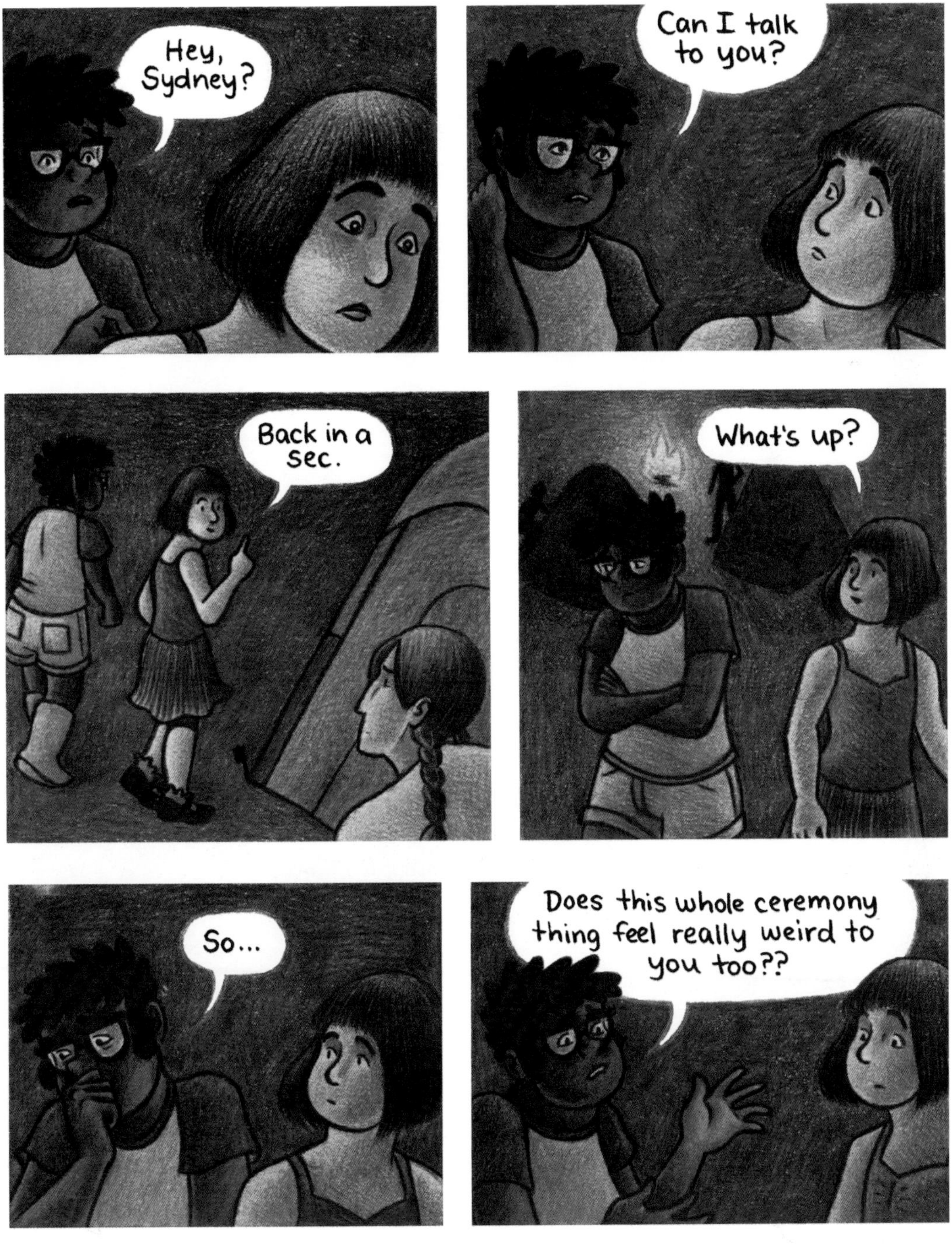
Hey, Sydney?
Can I talk to you?
Back in a sec.
What's up?
So...
Does this whole ceremony thing feel really weird to you too??

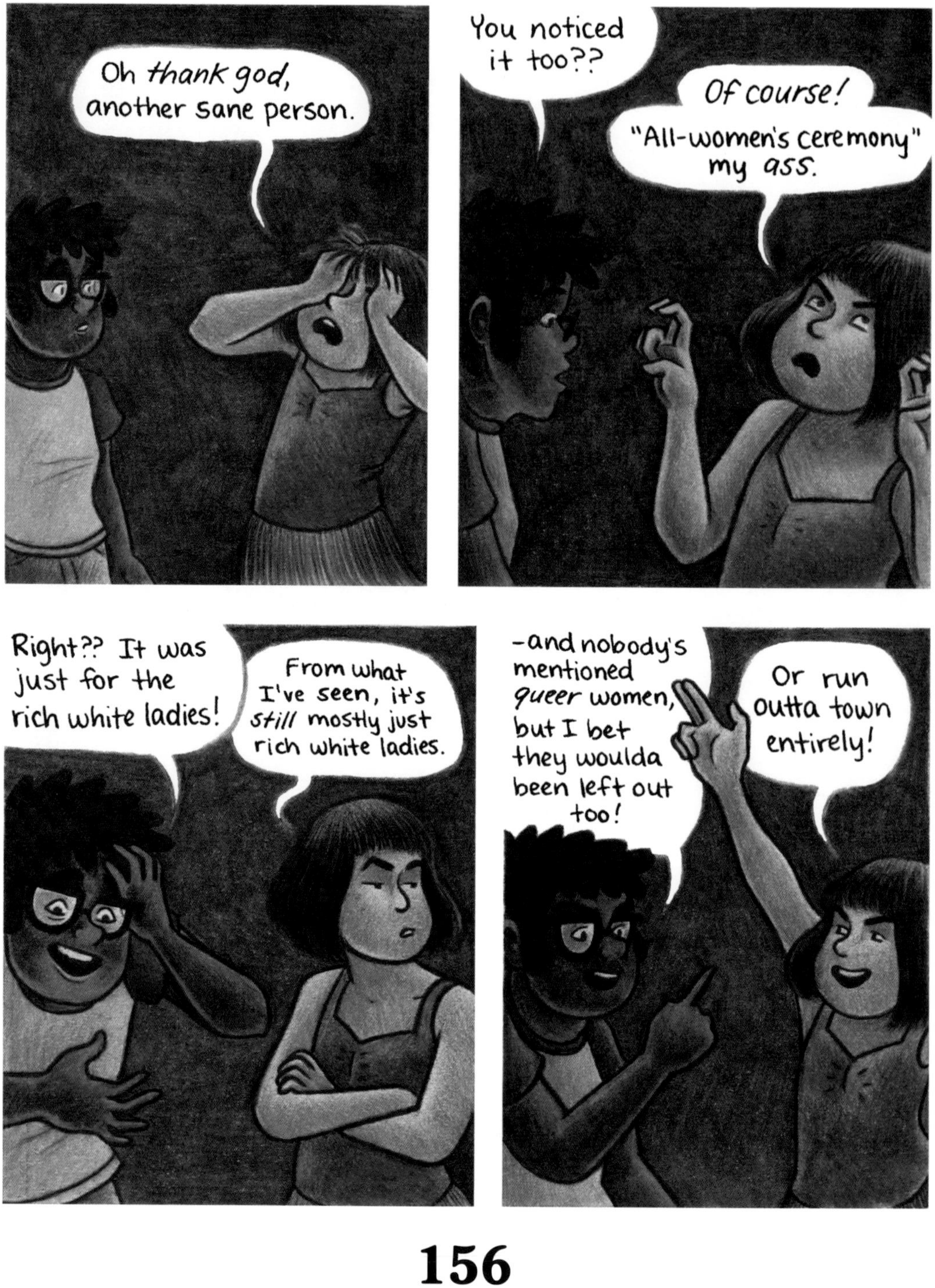

Oh *thank god*, another sane person.
You noticed it too??
Of course!
"All-women's ceremony" my *ass*.
Right?? It was just for the rich white ladies!
From what I've seen, it's *still* mostly just rich white ladies.
-and nobody's mentioned *queer* women, but I bet they woulda been left out too!
Or run outta town entirely!

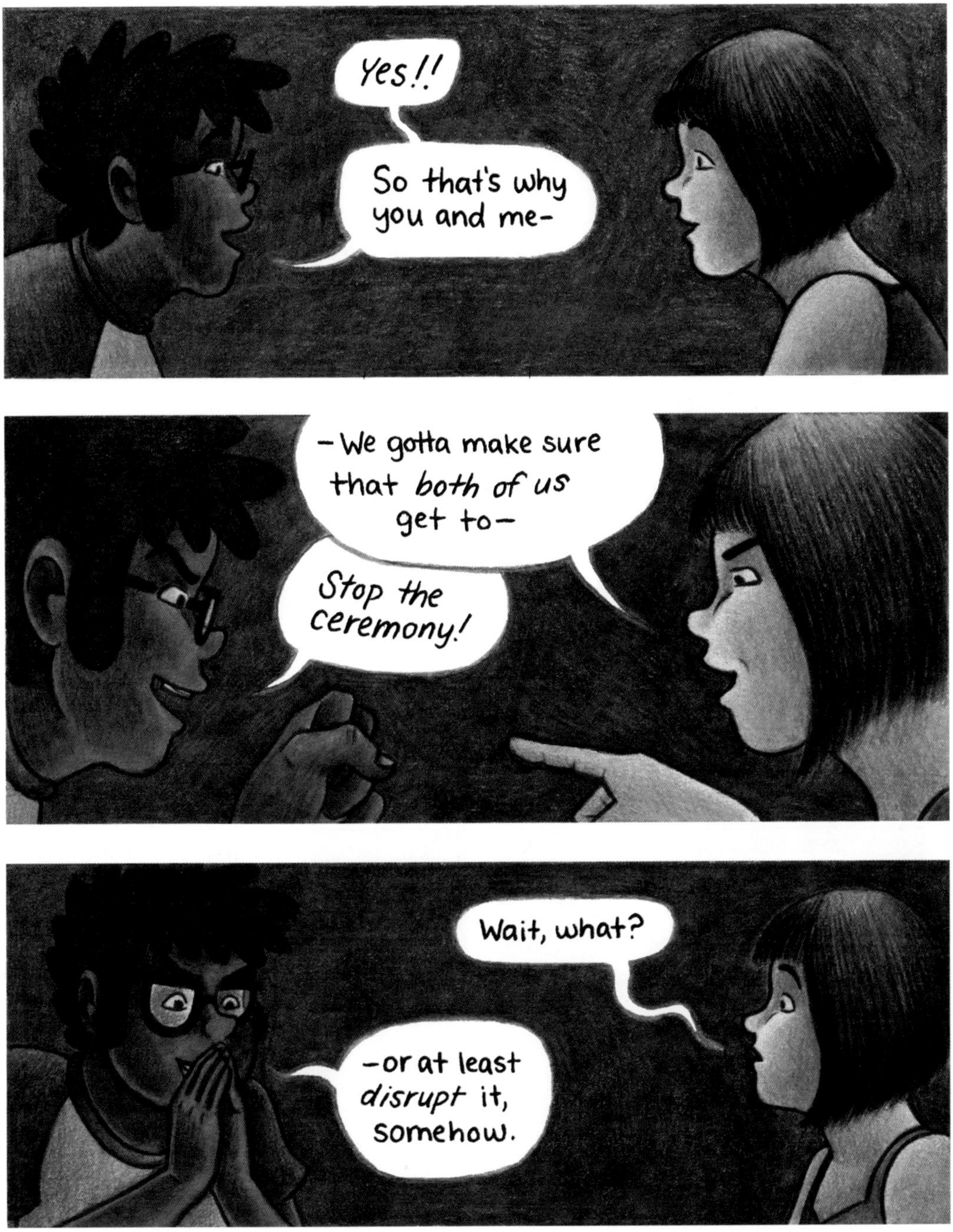
Yes!!
So that's why you and me-
-We gotta make sure that both of us get to-
Stop the ceremony!
Wait, what?
-or at least disrupt it, somehow.

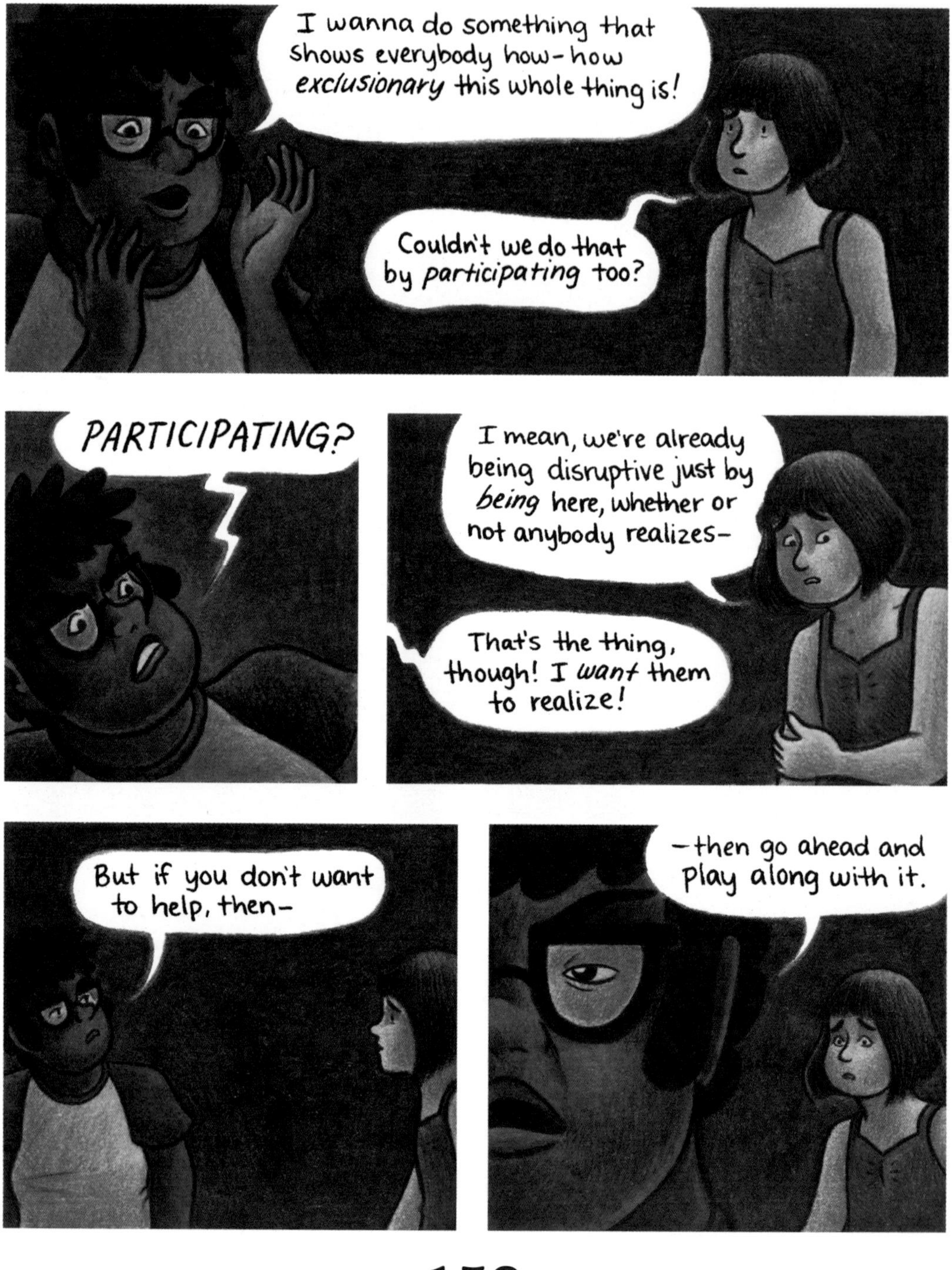
I wanna do something that shows everybody how-how *exclusionary* this whole thing is!
Couldn't we do that by *participating* too?
PARTICIPATING?
I mean, we're already being disruptive just by *being* here, whether or not anybody realizes-
That's the thing, though! I *want* them to realize!
But if you don't want to help, then-
-then go ahead and play along with it.

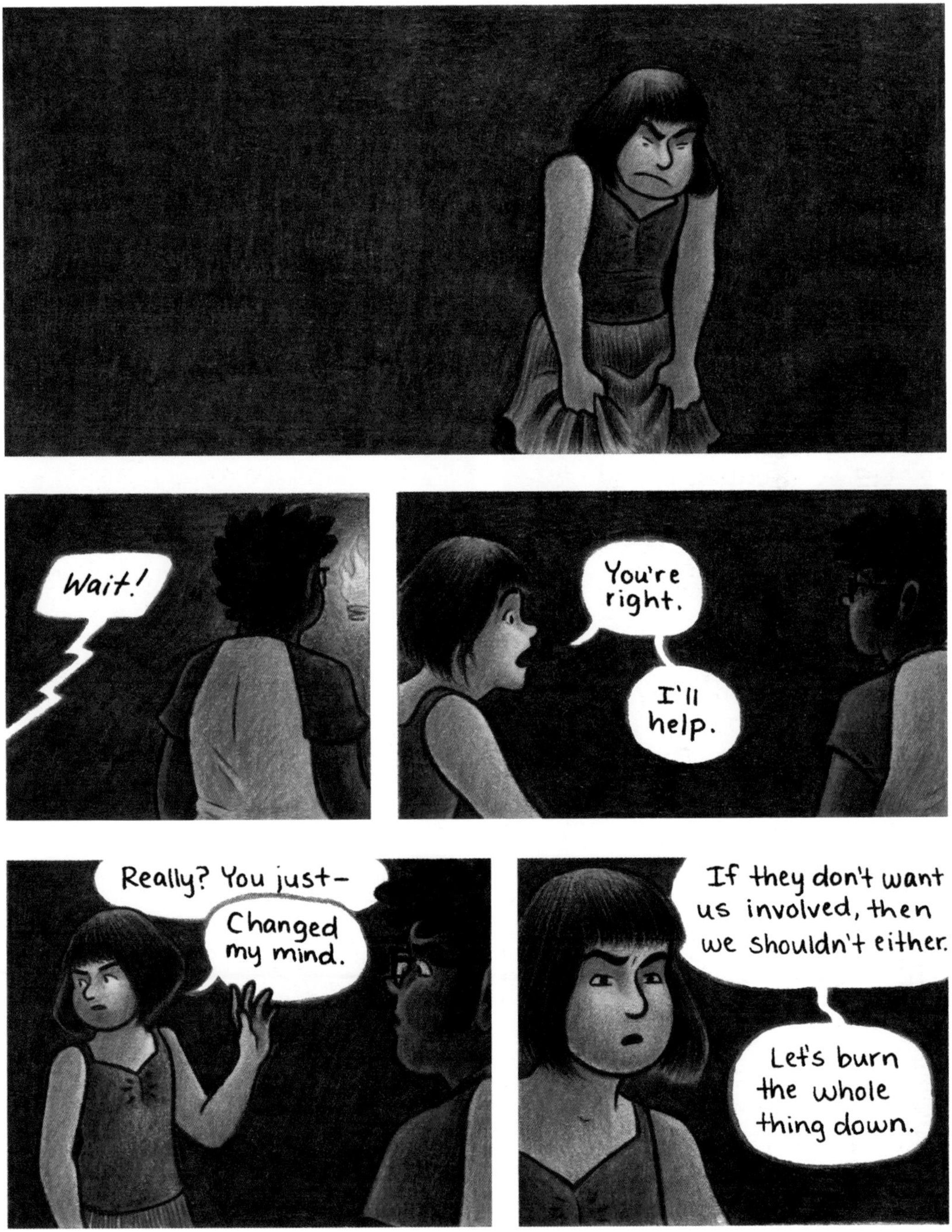
Wait!
You're right.
I'll help.
Really? You just-
Changed my mind.
If they don't want us involved, then we shouldn't either.
Let's burn the whole thing down.

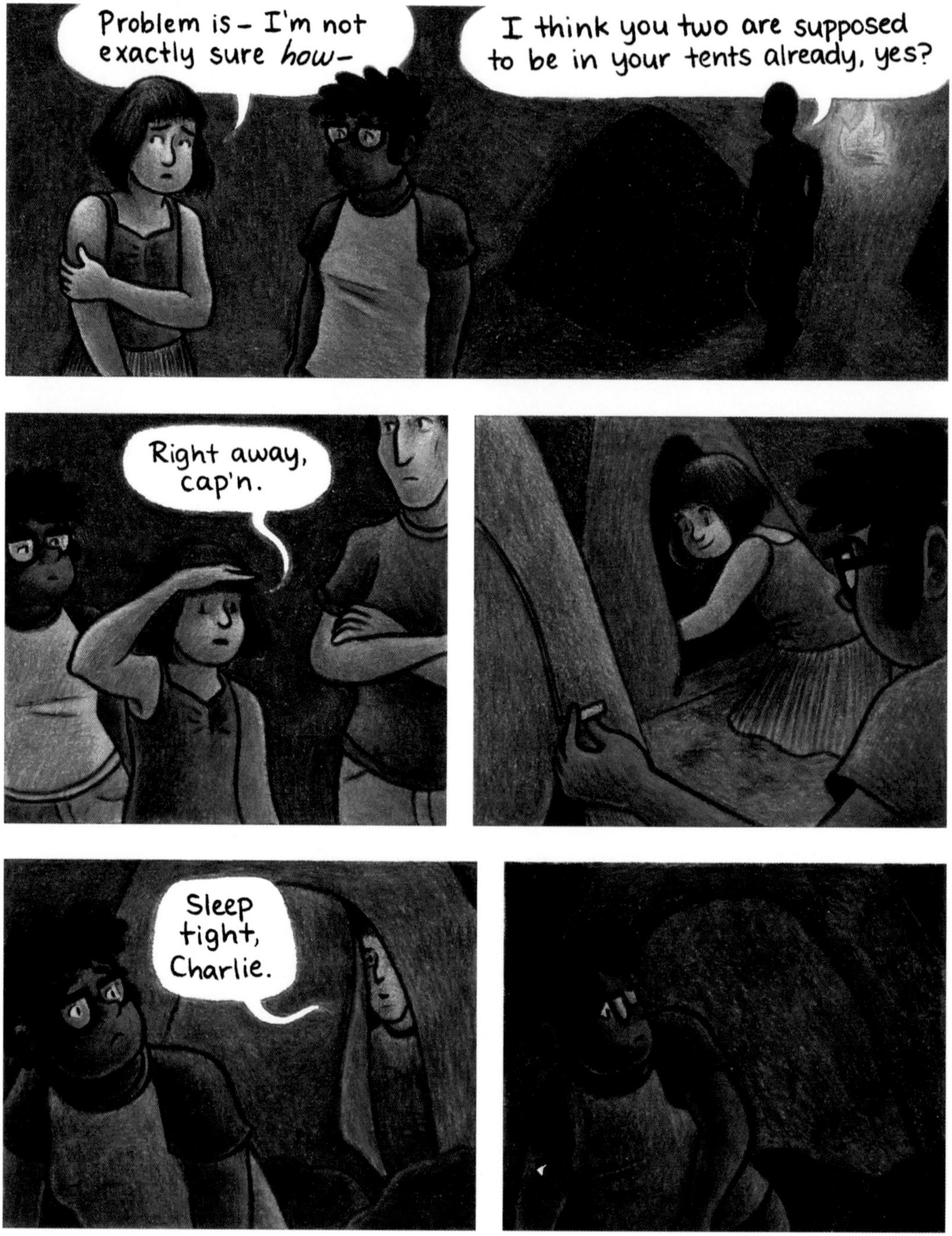
Problem is - I'm not exactly sure *how*-
I think you two are supposed to be in your tents already, yes?
Right away, cap'n.
Sleep tight, Charlie.

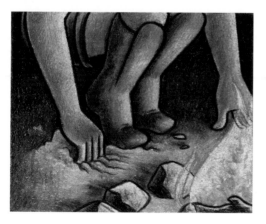

161

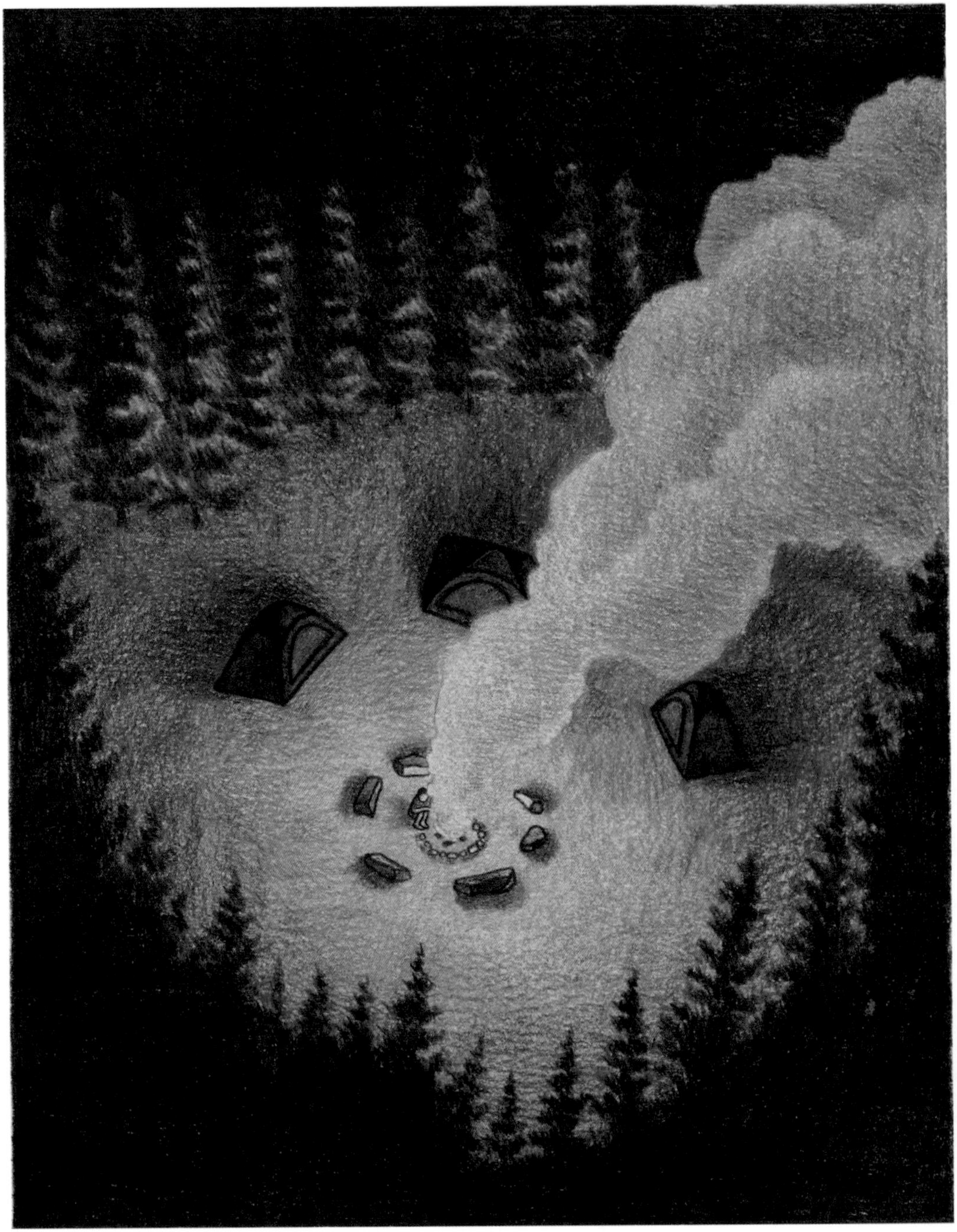

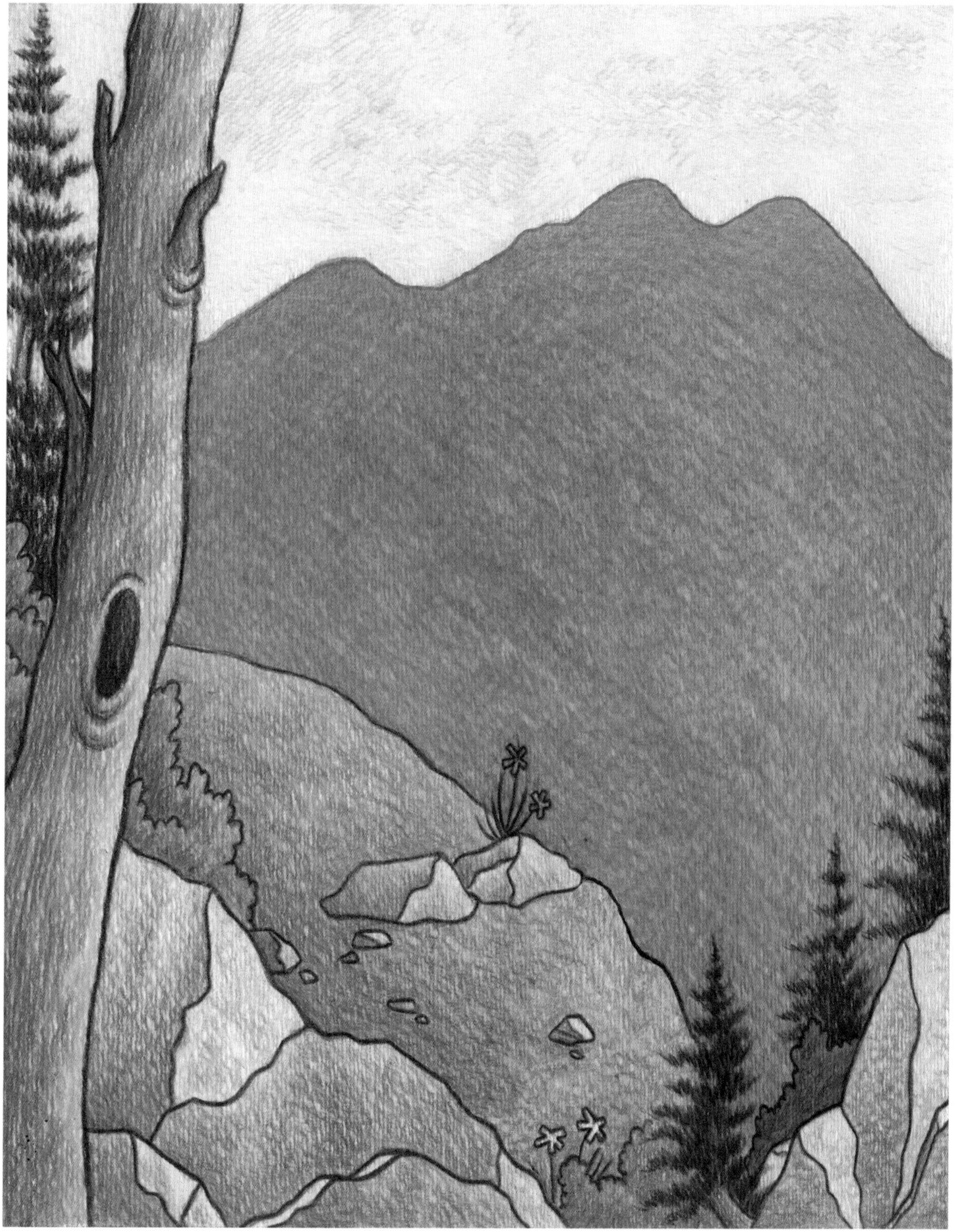

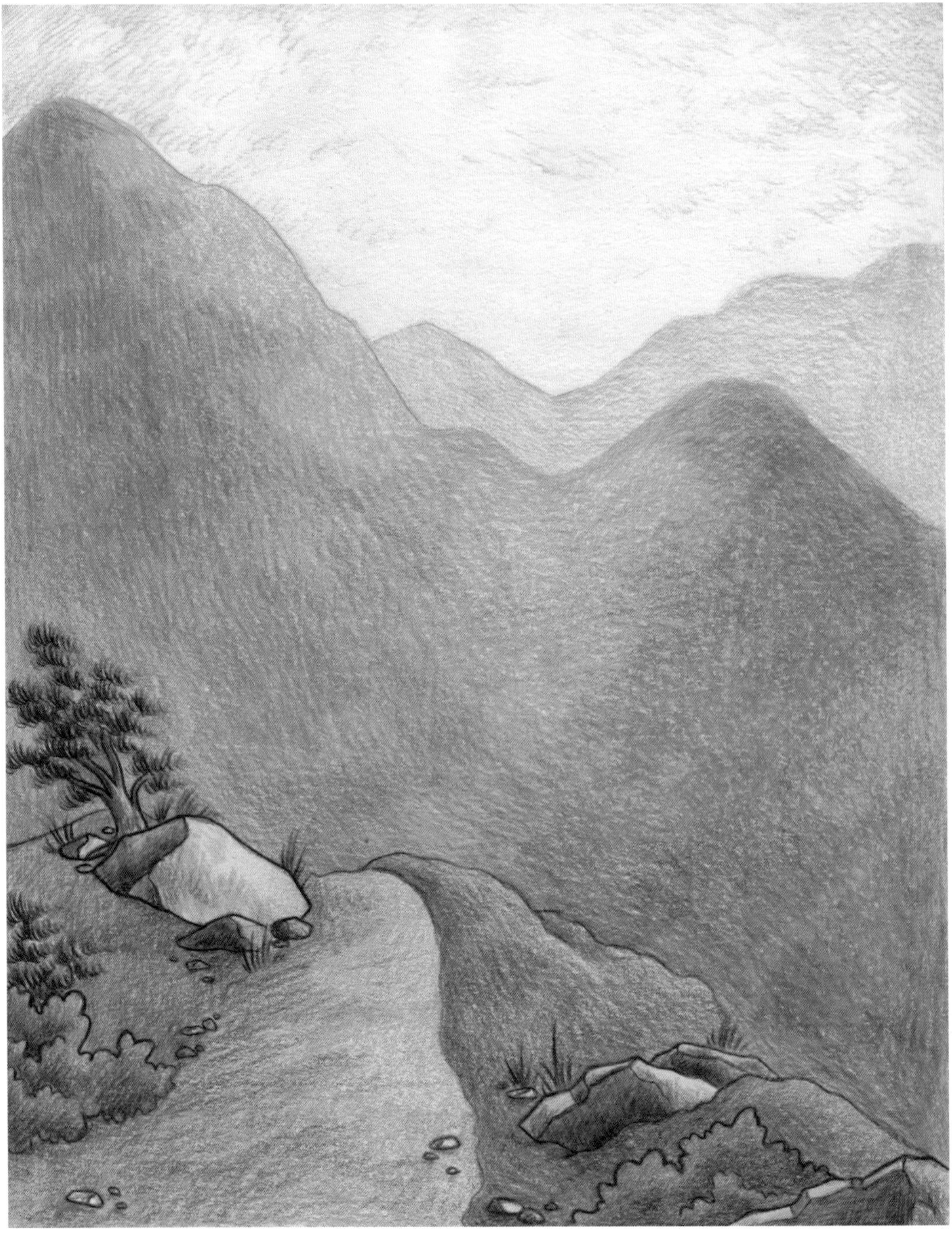

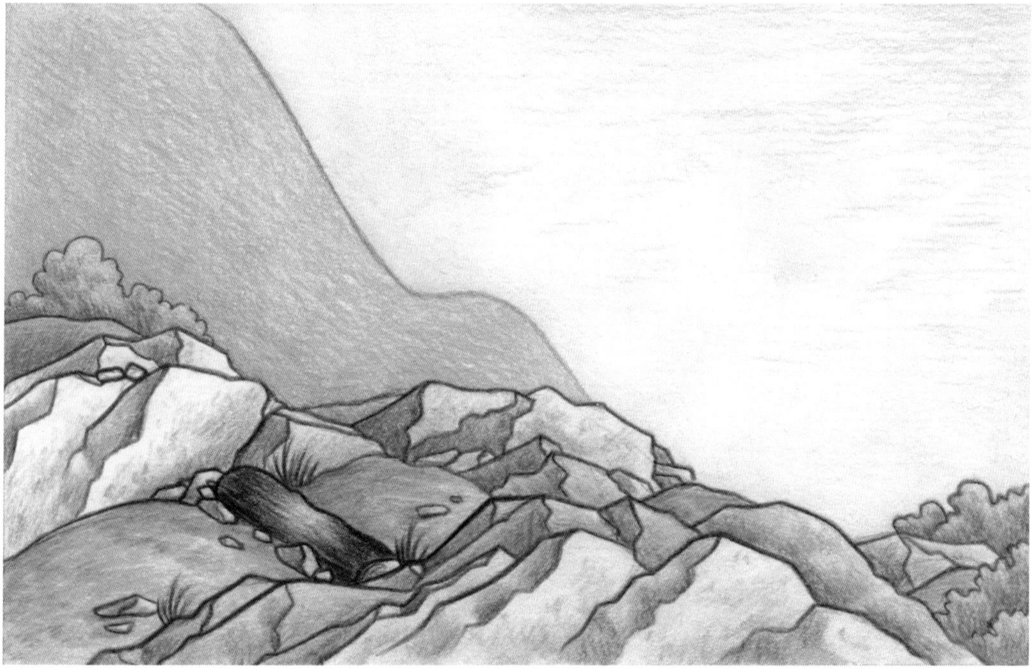

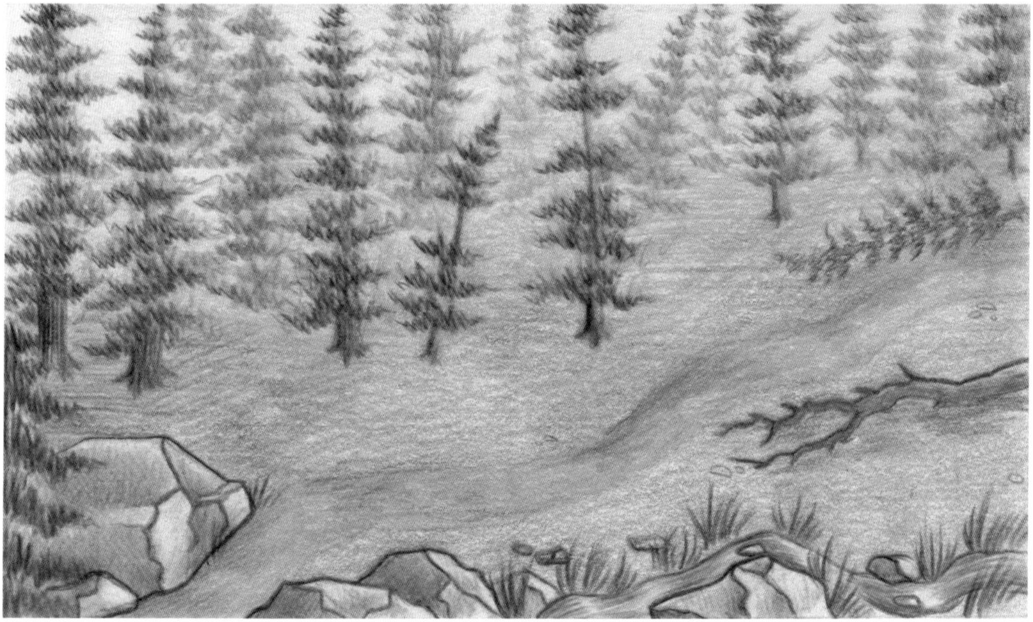

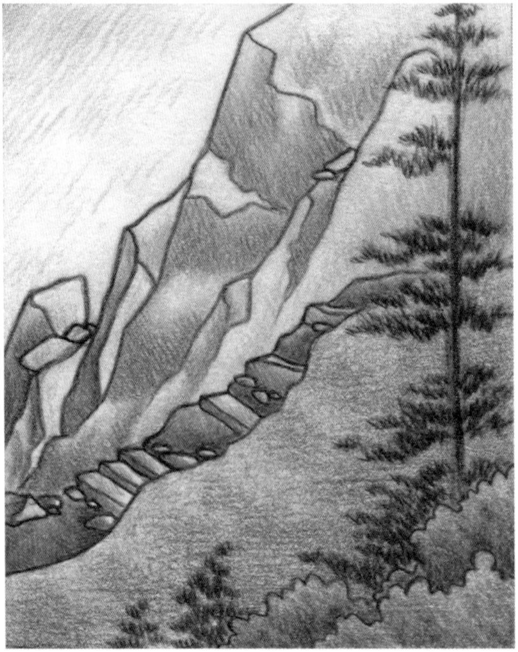
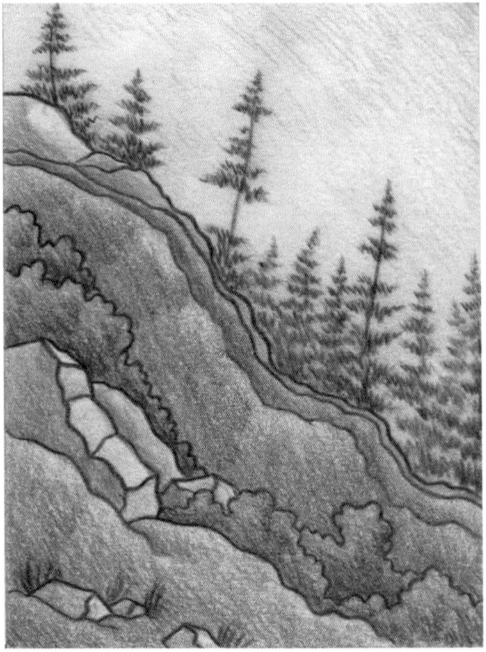
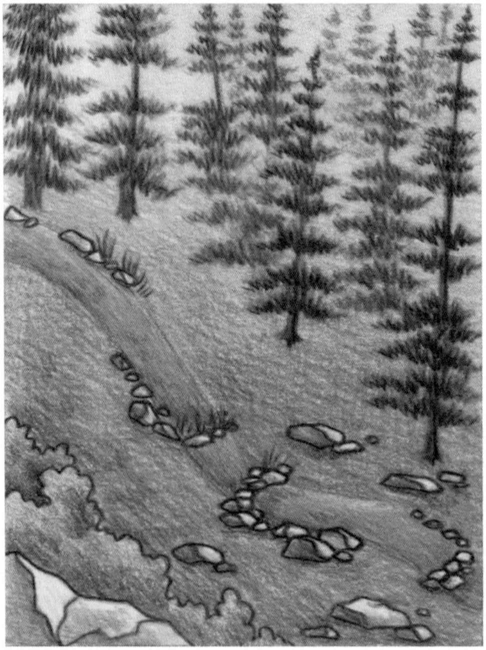
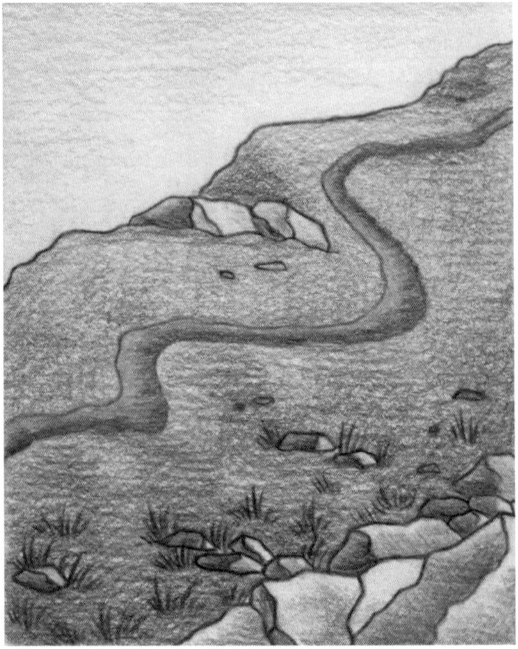

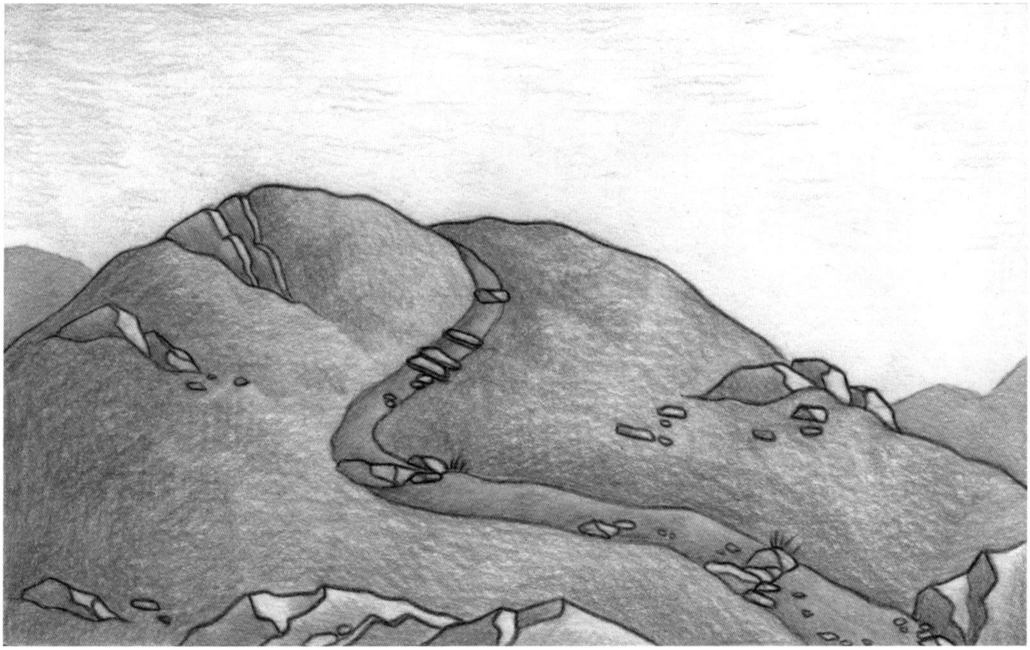

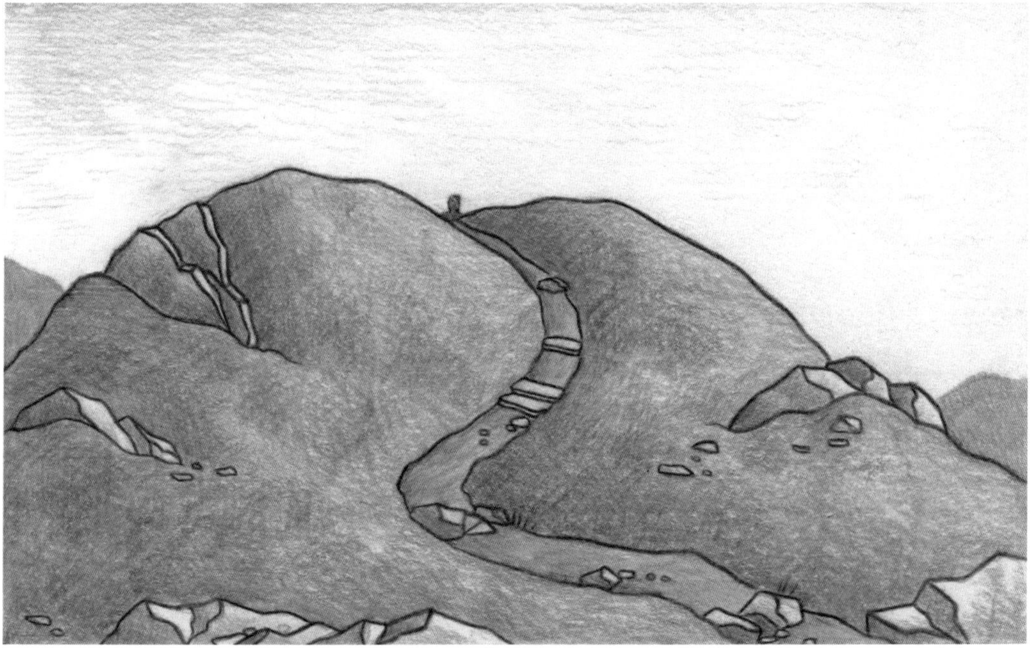

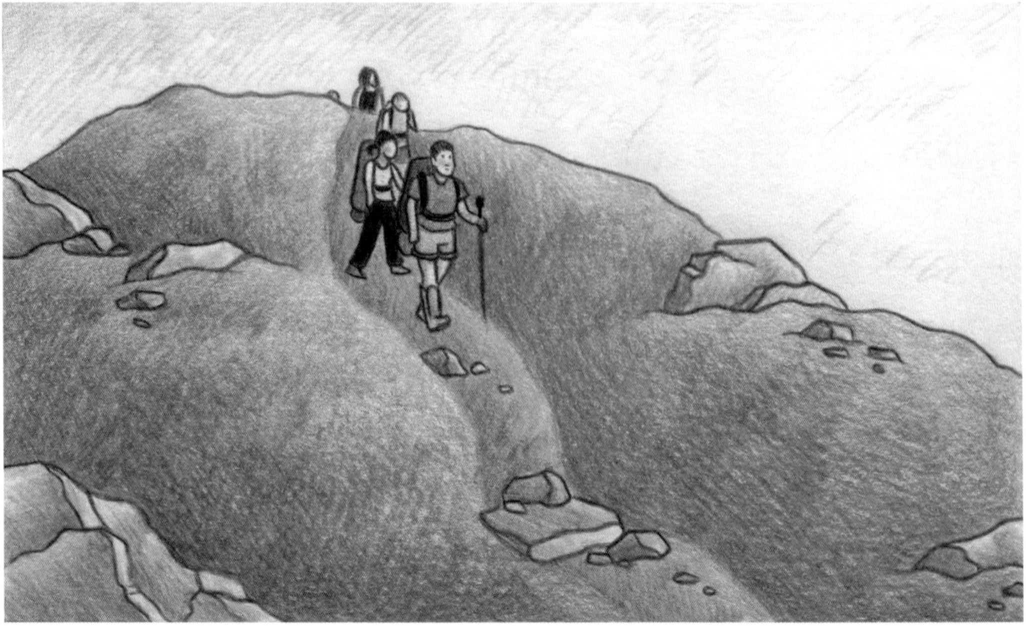

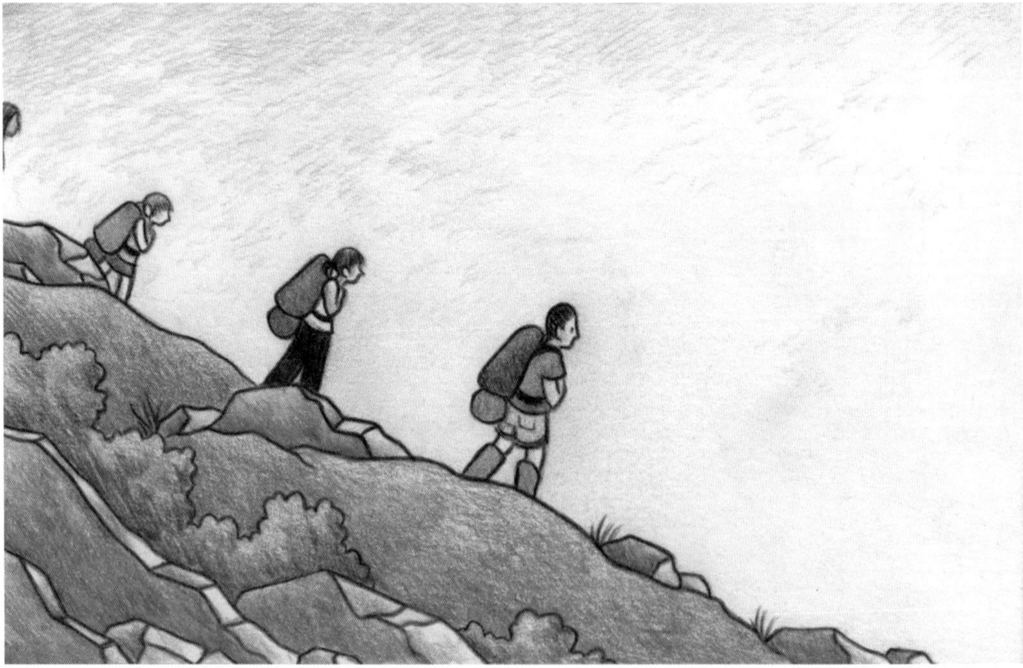

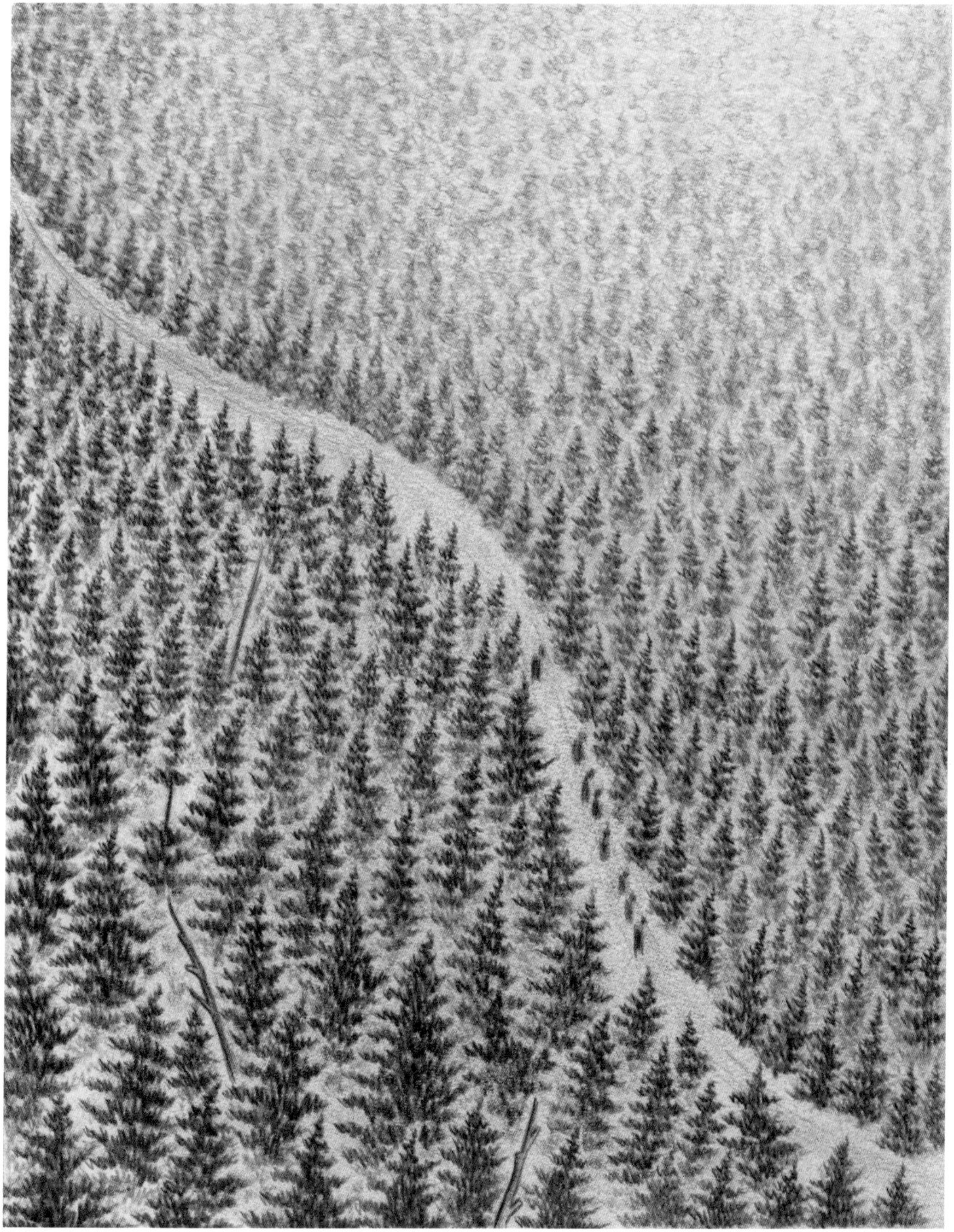

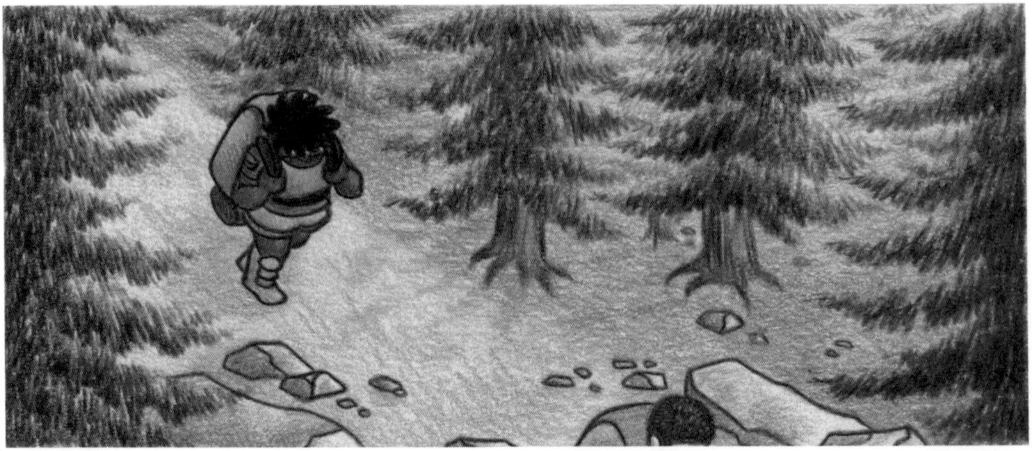

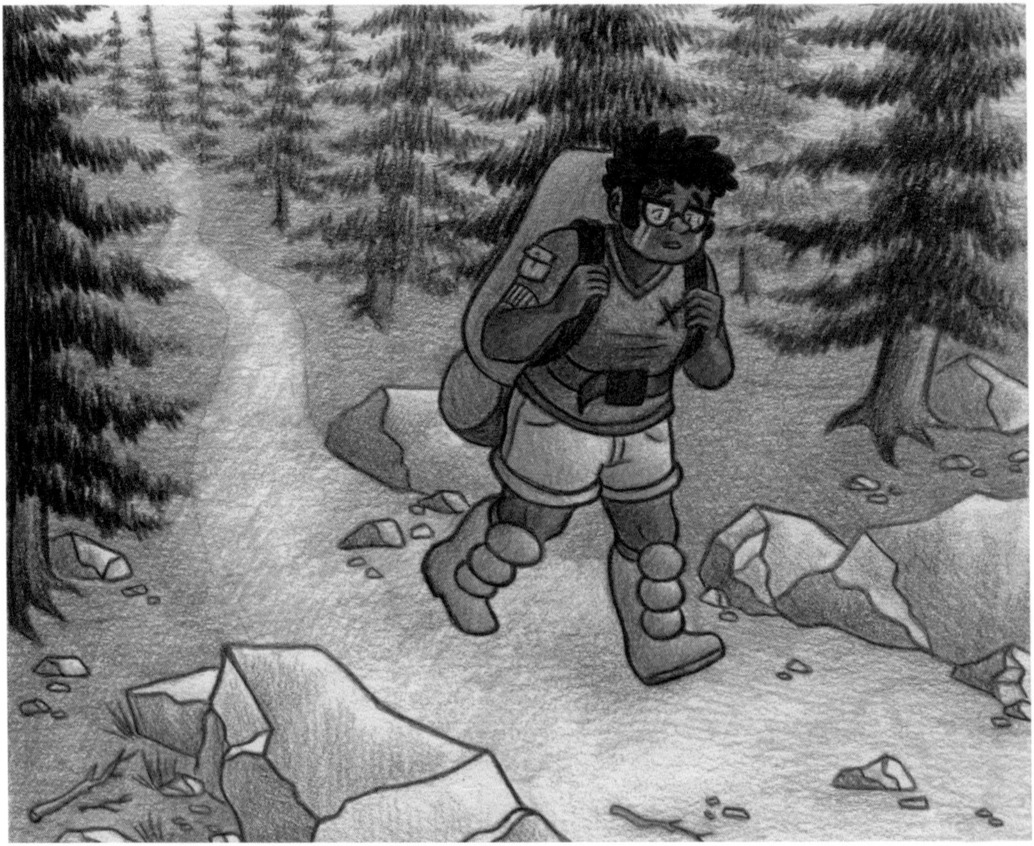

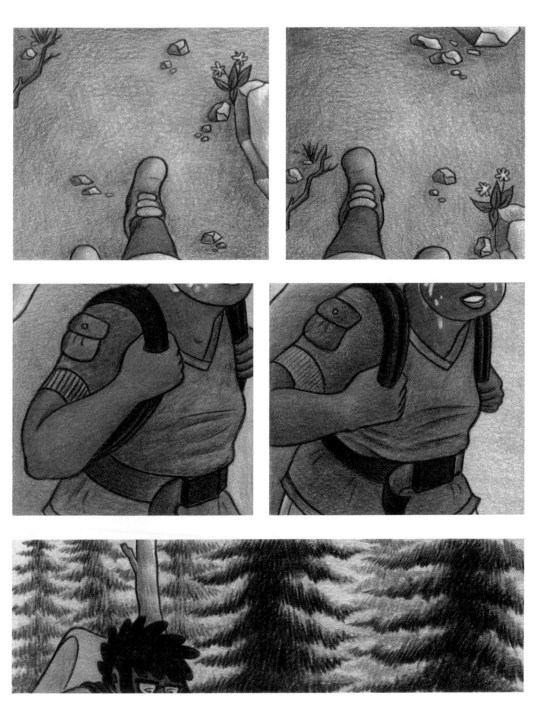

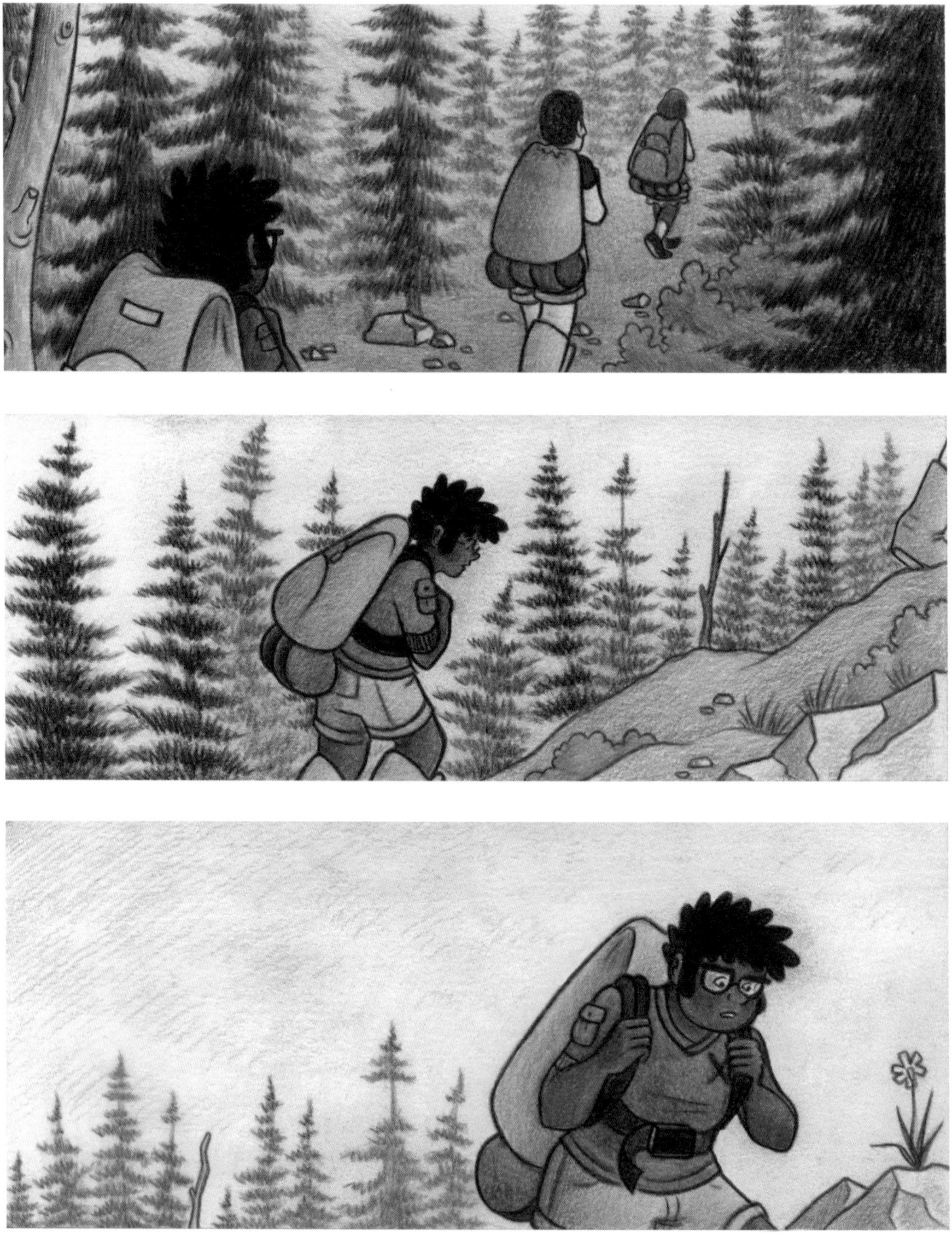

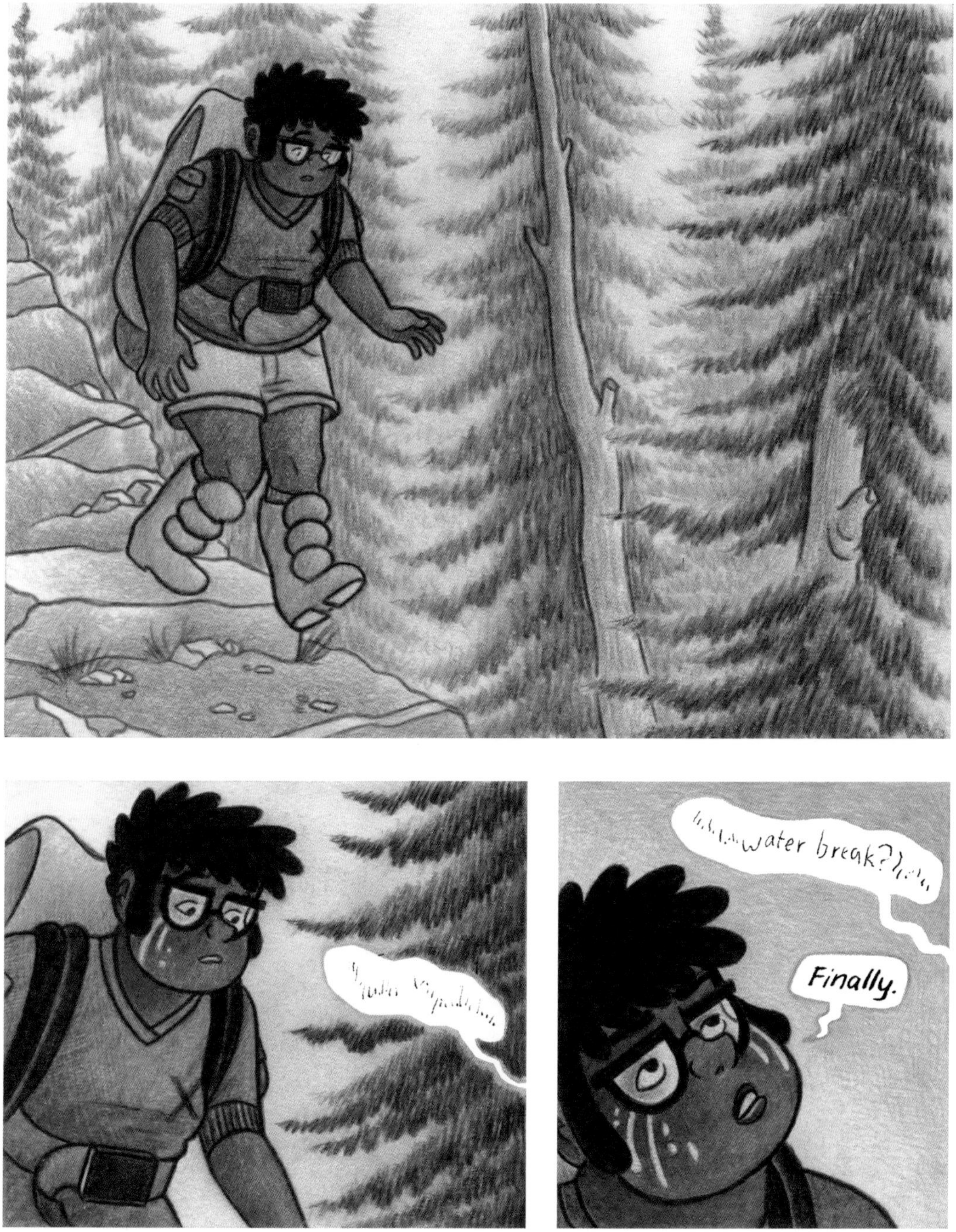
water break?
Finally.

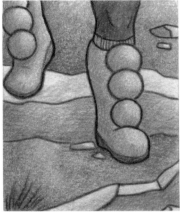

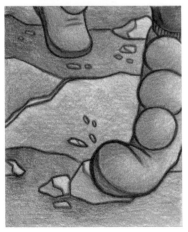

174

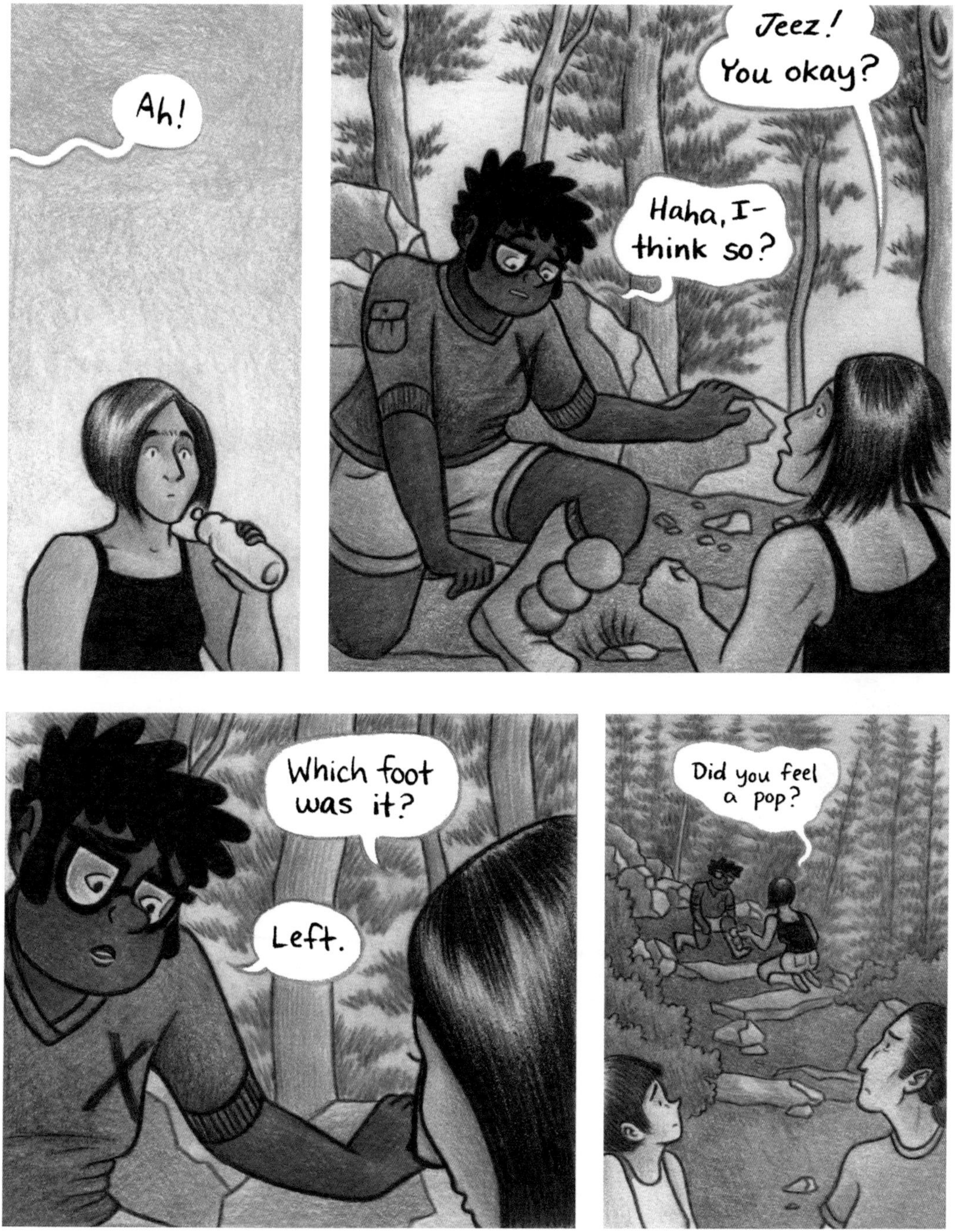
Ah!
Jeez! You okay?
Haha, I- think so?
Which foot was it?
Left.
Did you feel a pop?

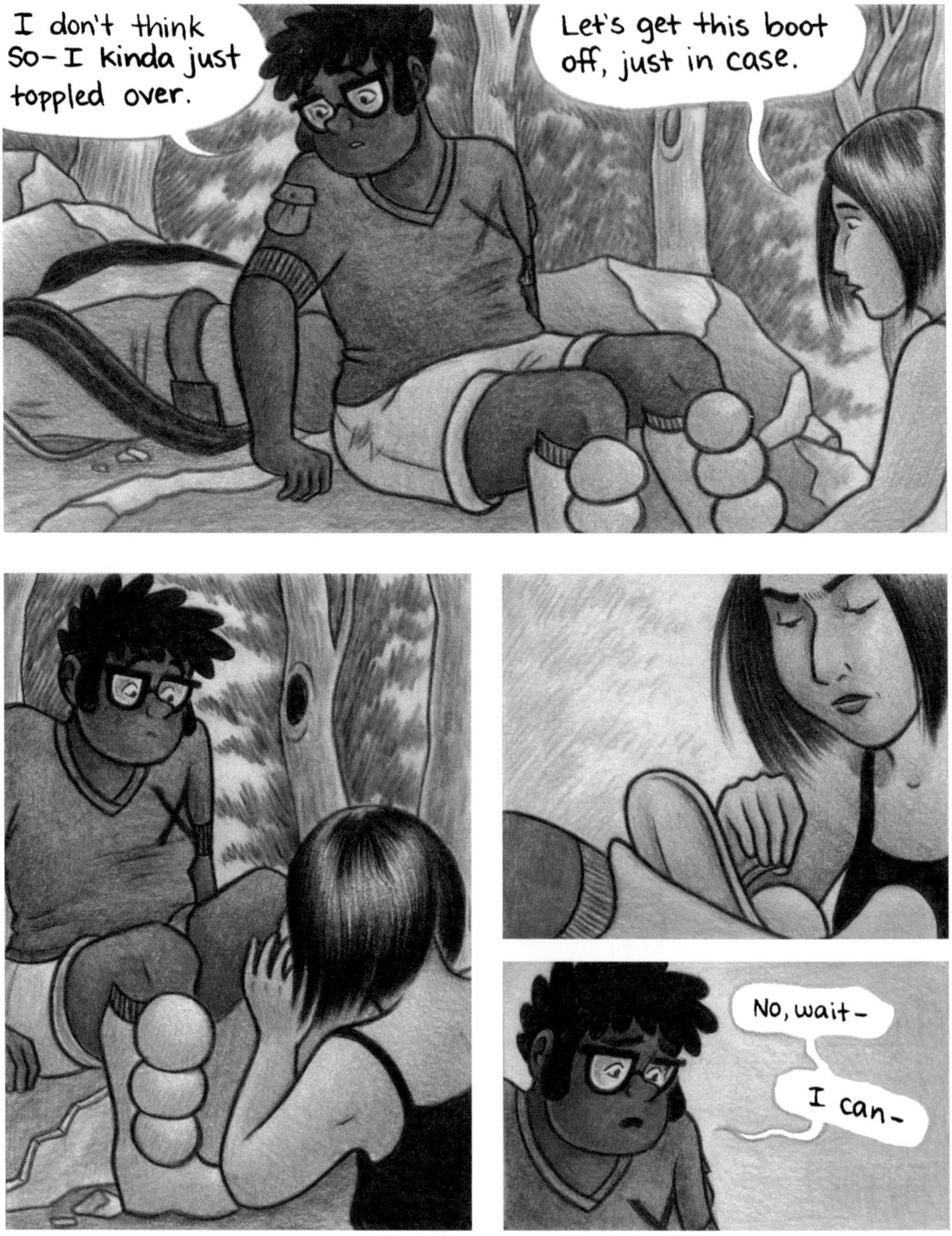
I don't think So-I kinda just toppled over.
Let's get this boot off, just in case.
No, wait-
I can-

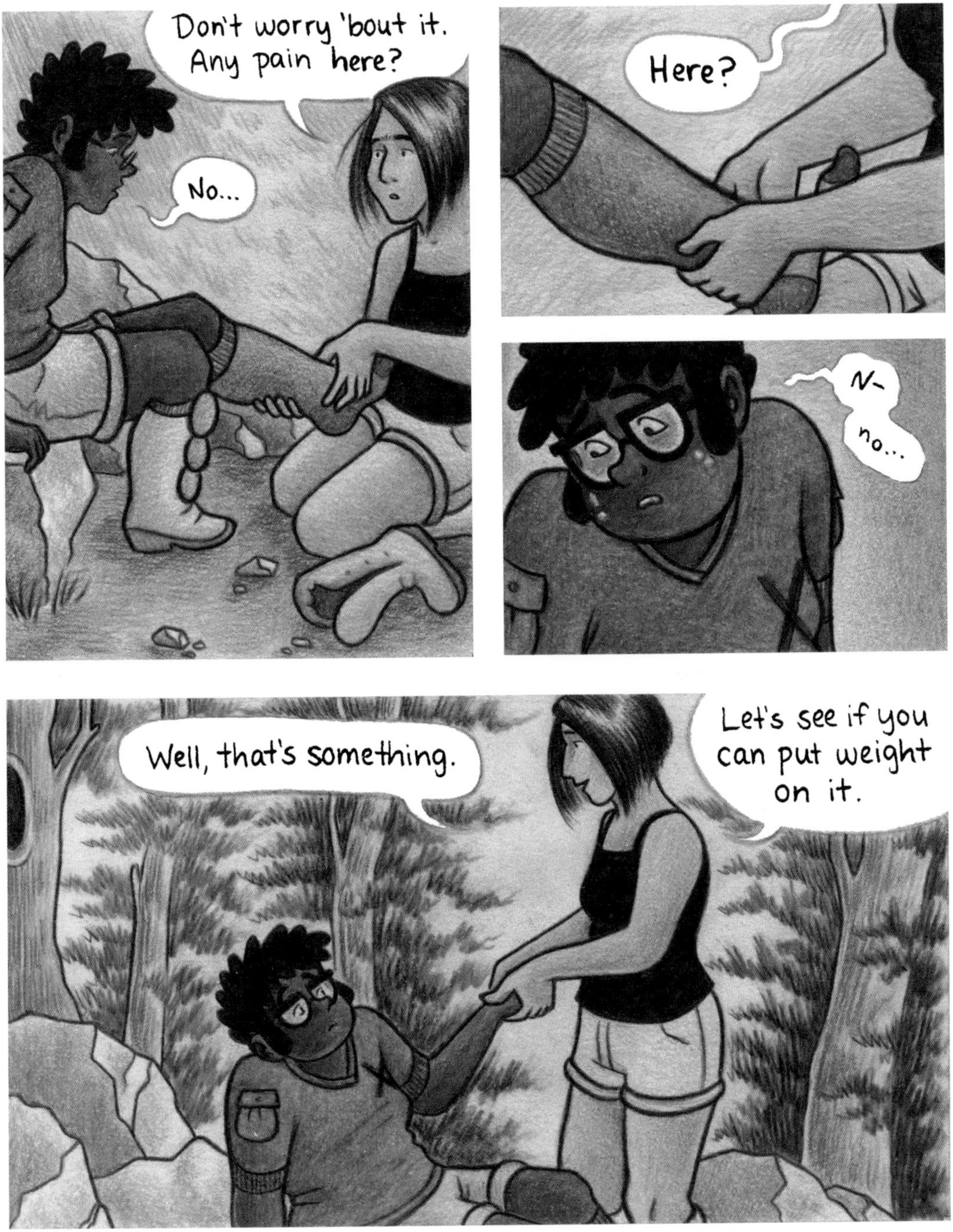
Don't worry 'bout it. Any pain here?
No...
Here?
N-
no...
Well, that's something.
Let's see if you can put weight on it.

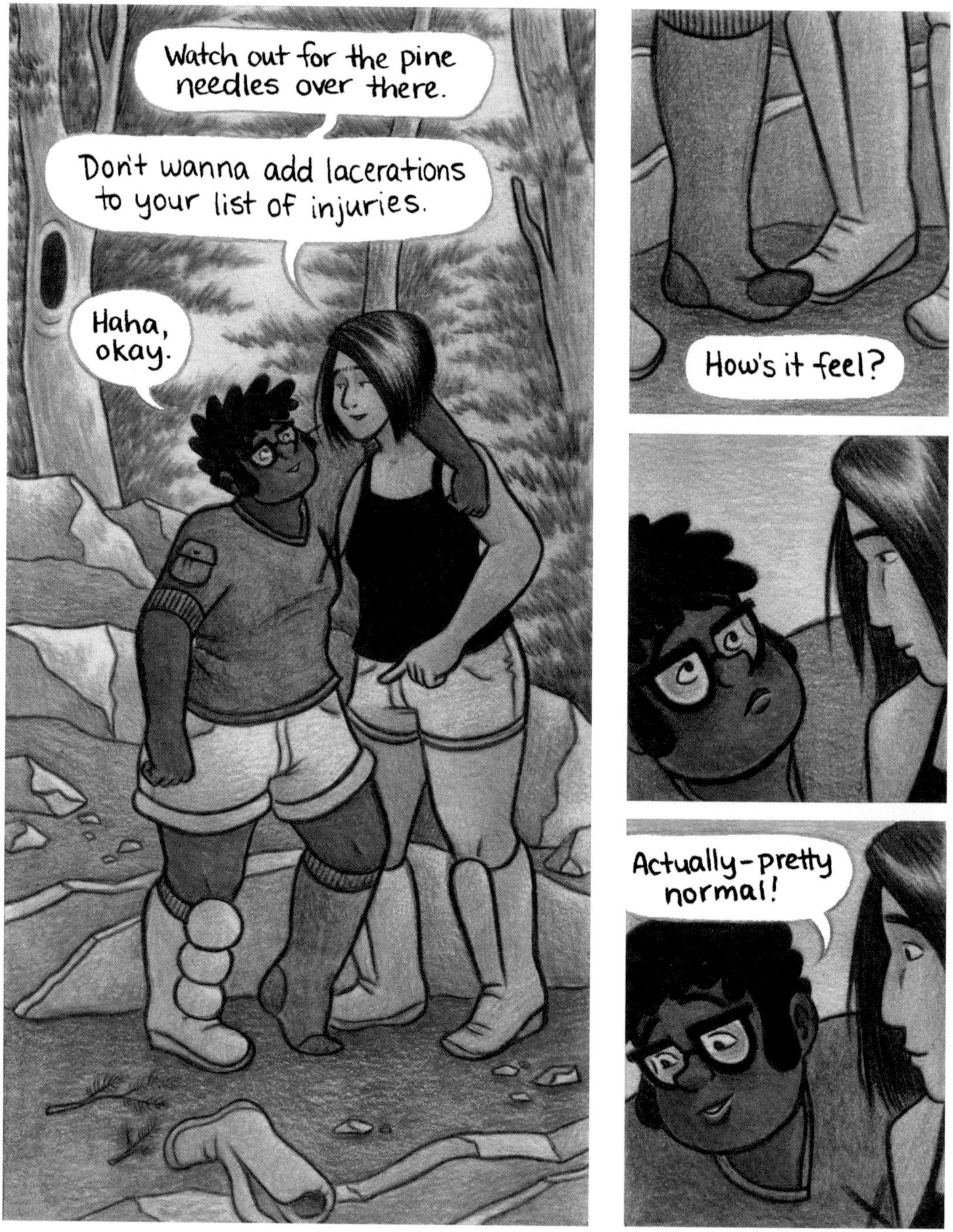
Watch out for the pine needles over there.
Don't wanna add lacerations to your list of injuries.
Haha, okay.
How's it feel?
Actually-pretty normal!

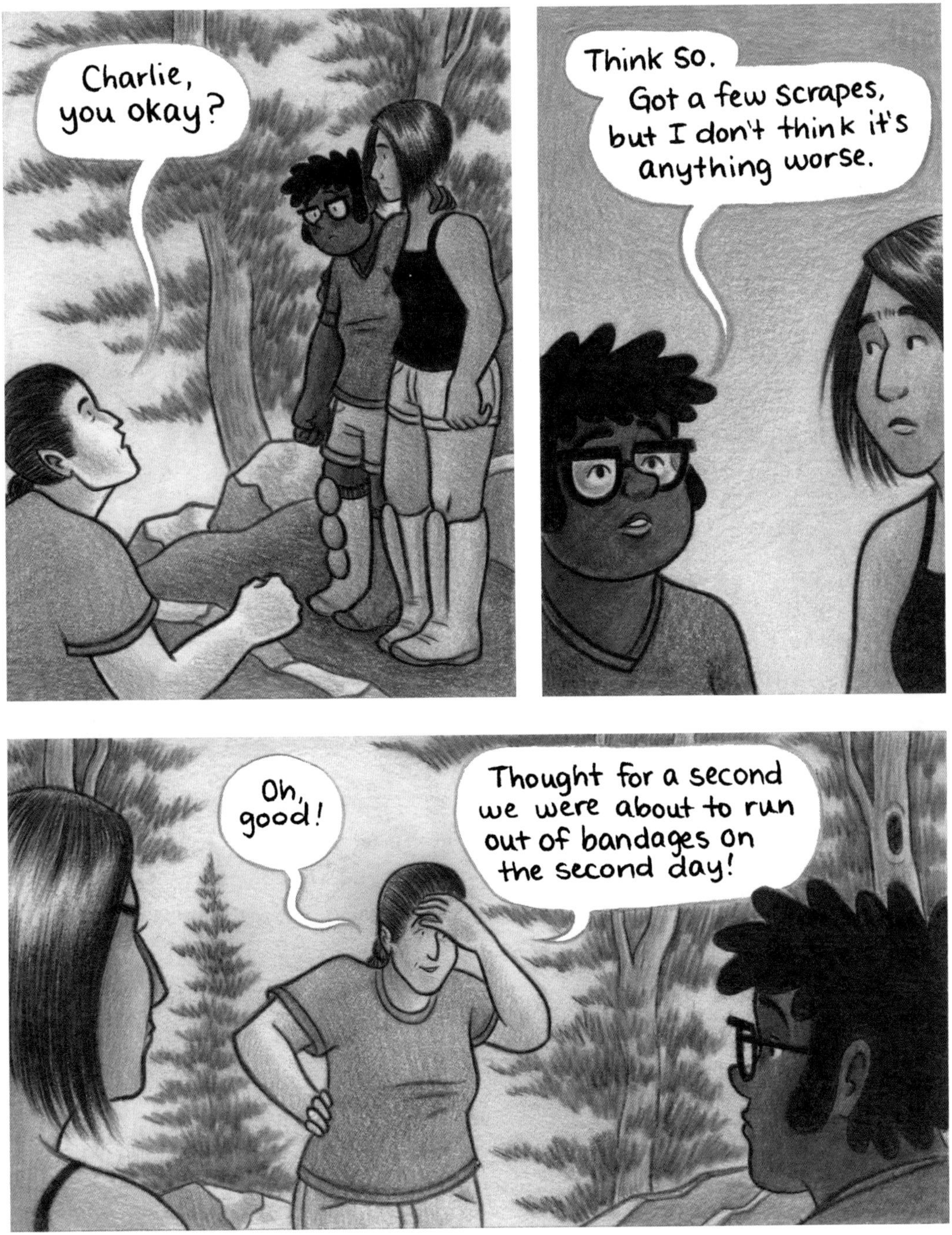
Charlie, you okay?
Think So.
Got a few scrapes, but I don't think it's anything worse.
Oh, good!
Thought for a second we were about to run out of bandages on the second day!

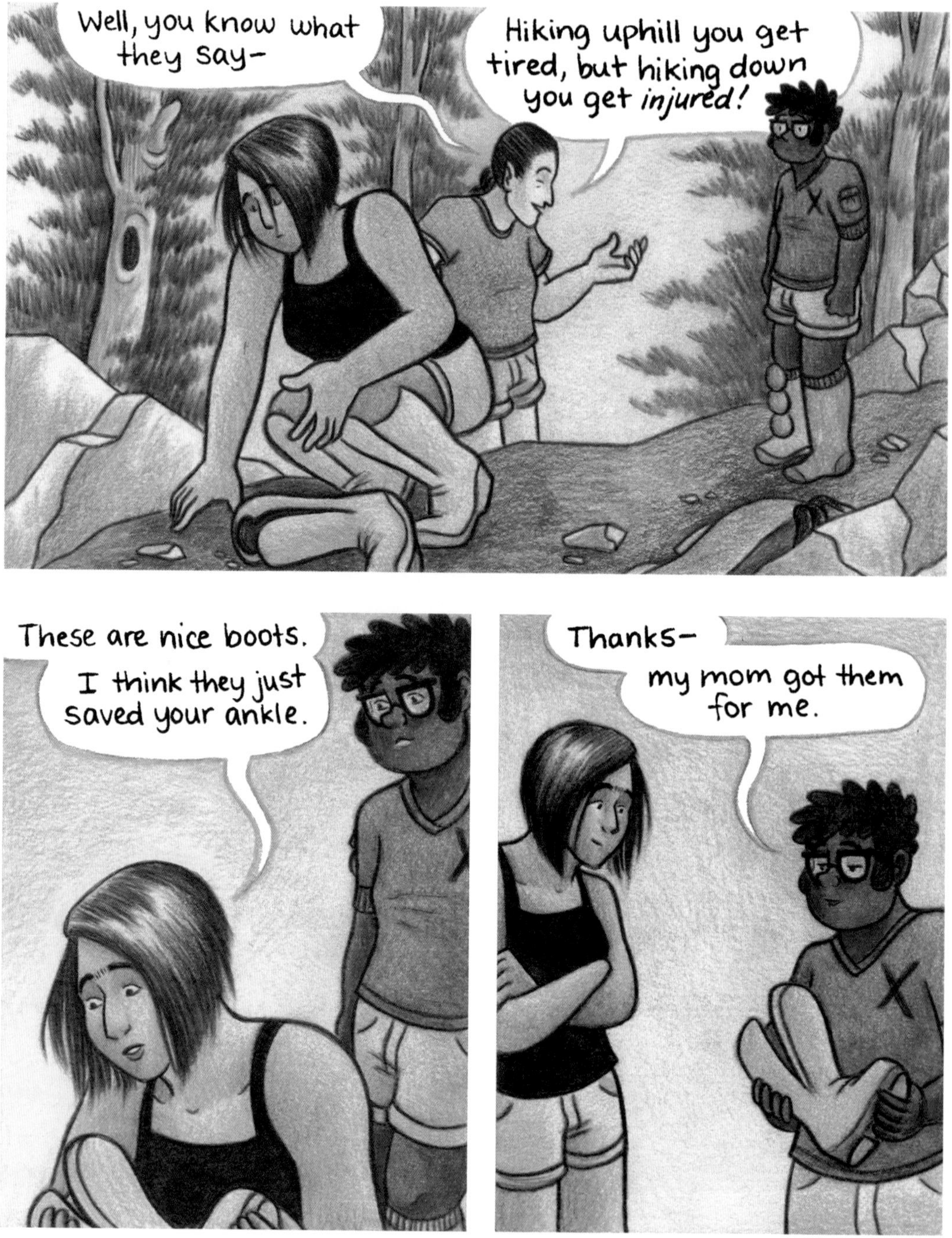
Well, you know what they say-
Hiking uphill you get tired, but hiking down you get *injured!*
These are nice boots.
I think they just saved your ankle.
Thanks-
my mom got them for me.

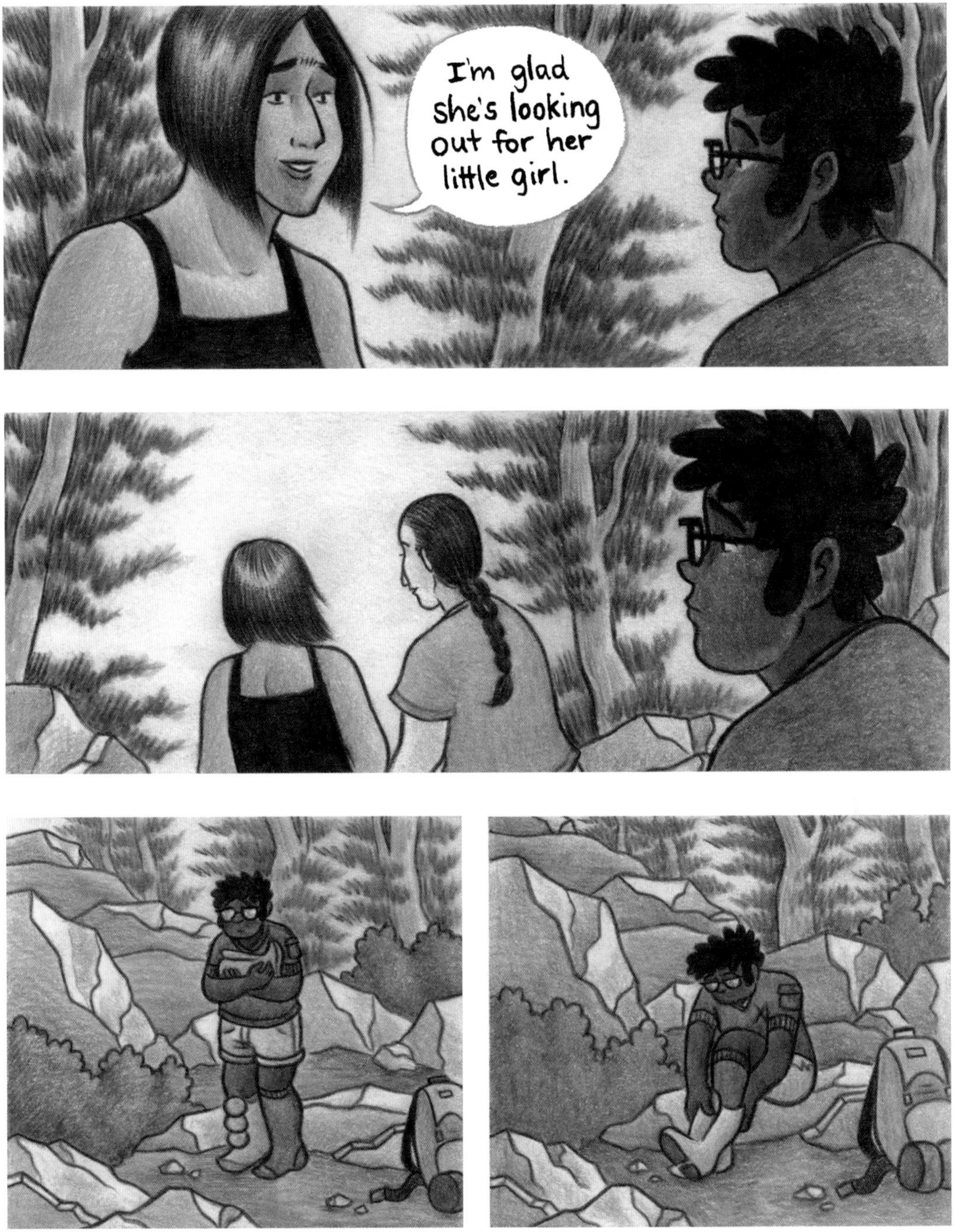
I'm glad she's looking out for her little girl.

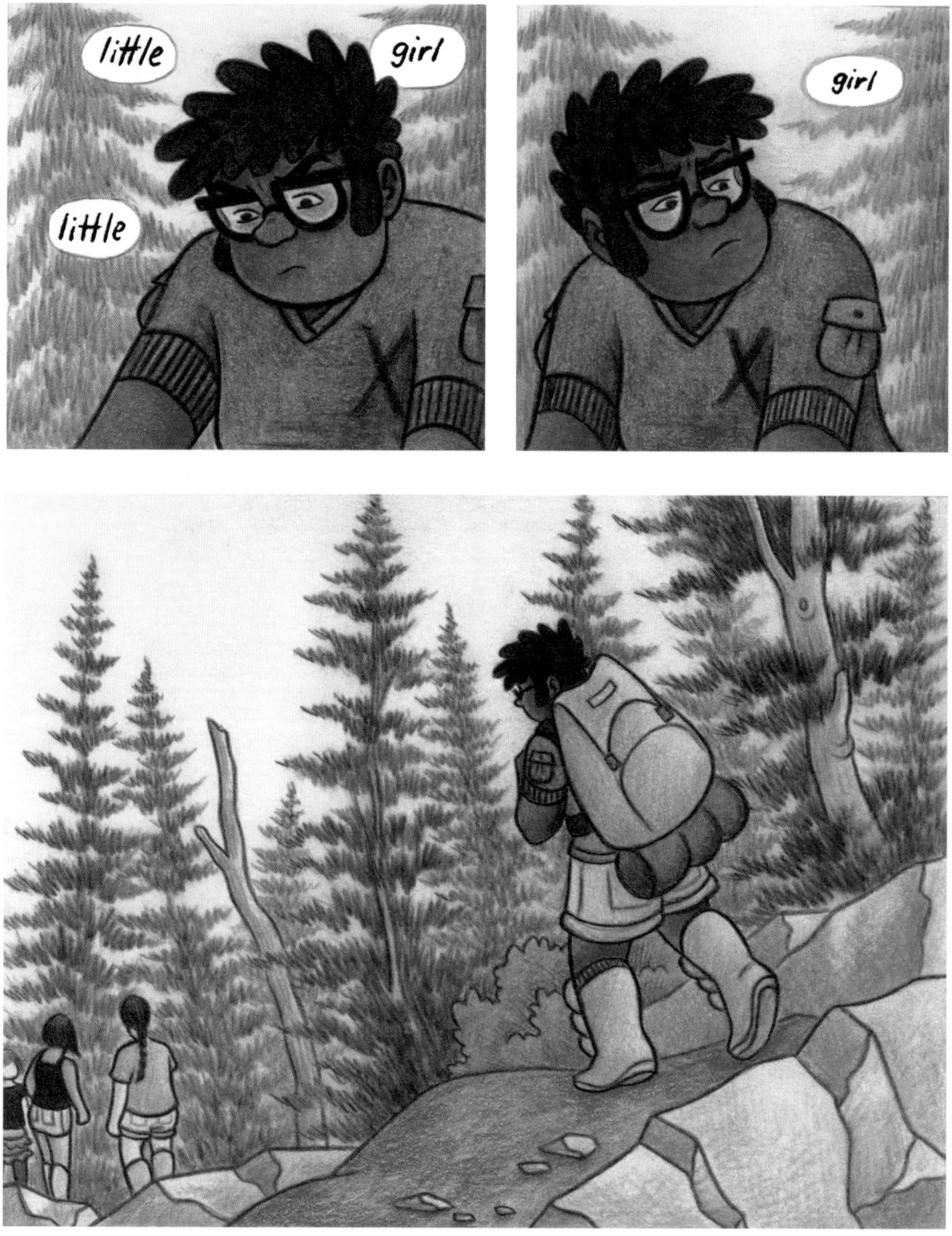
little
girl
little
girl

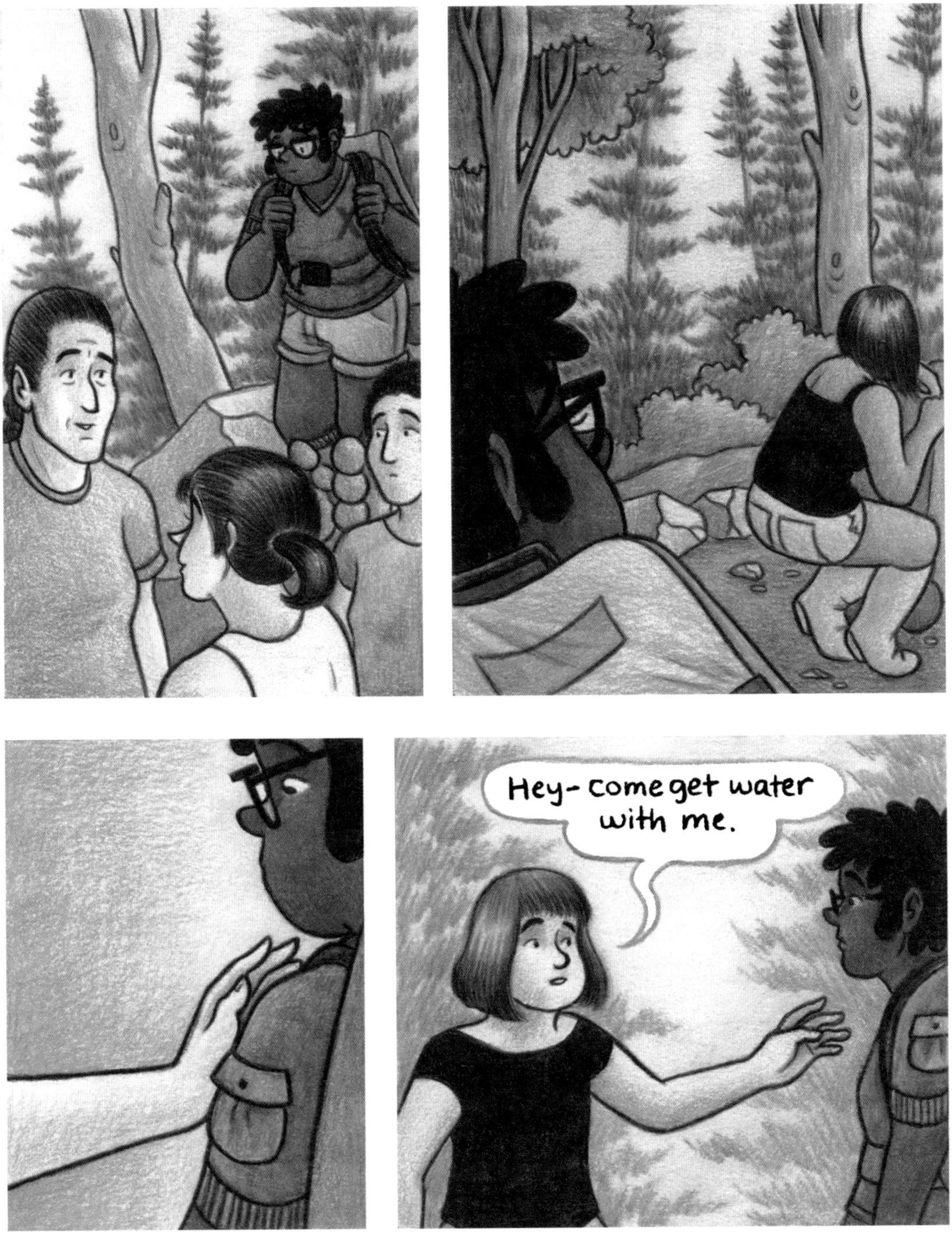
Hey- come get water
with me.

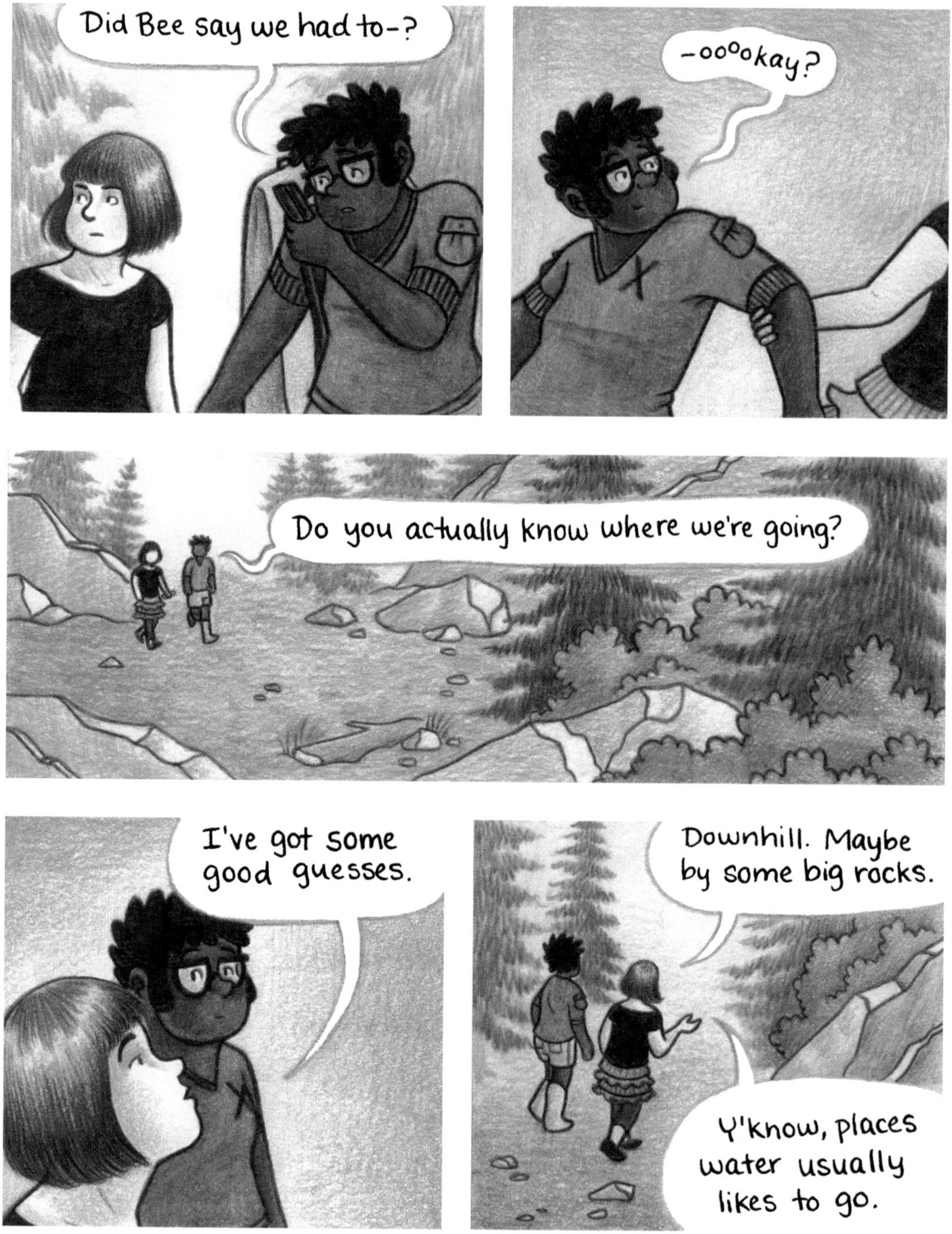

Did Bee say we had to-?
-oooOkay?
Do you actually know where we're going?
I've got some good guesses.
Downhill. Maybe by some big rocks.
Y'know, places water usually likes to go.

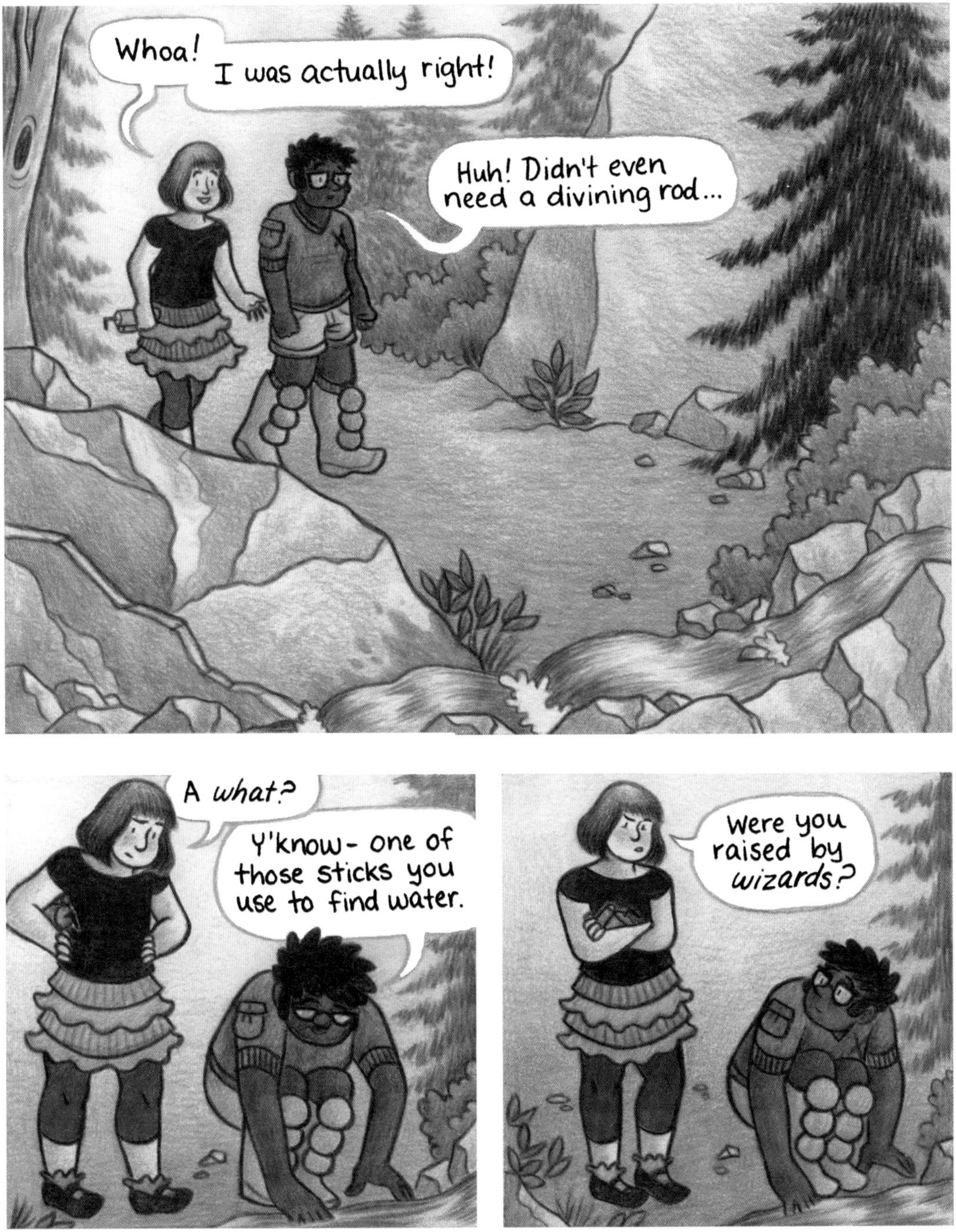
Whoa! I was actually right!
Huh! Didn't even need a divining rod...
A *what*?
Y'know- one of those sticks you use to find water.
Were you raised by *wizards*?

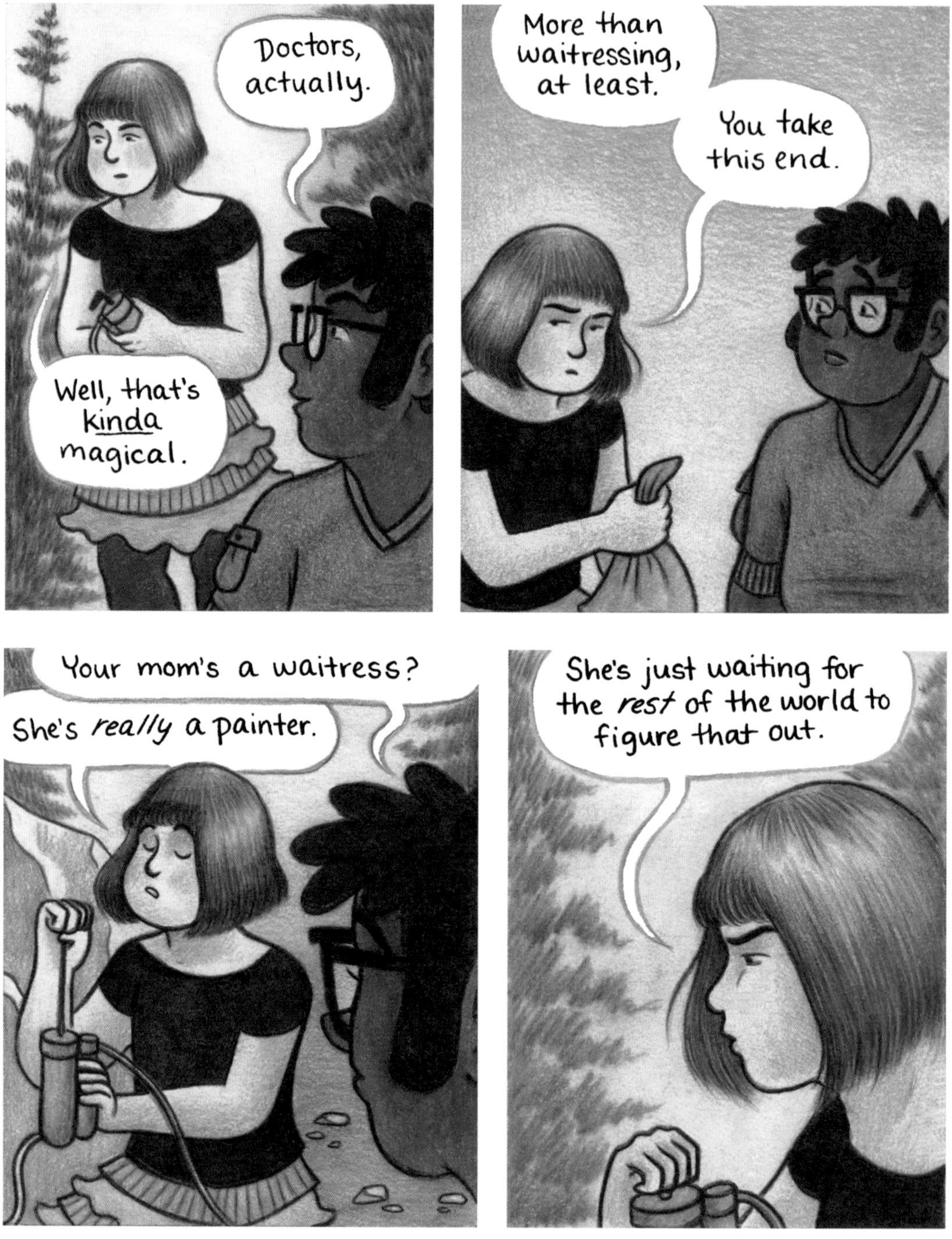

Doctors, actually.
Well, that's kinda magical.
More than waitressing, at least.
You take this end.
Your mom's a waitress?
She's *really* a painter.
She's just waiting for the *rest* of the world to figure that out.

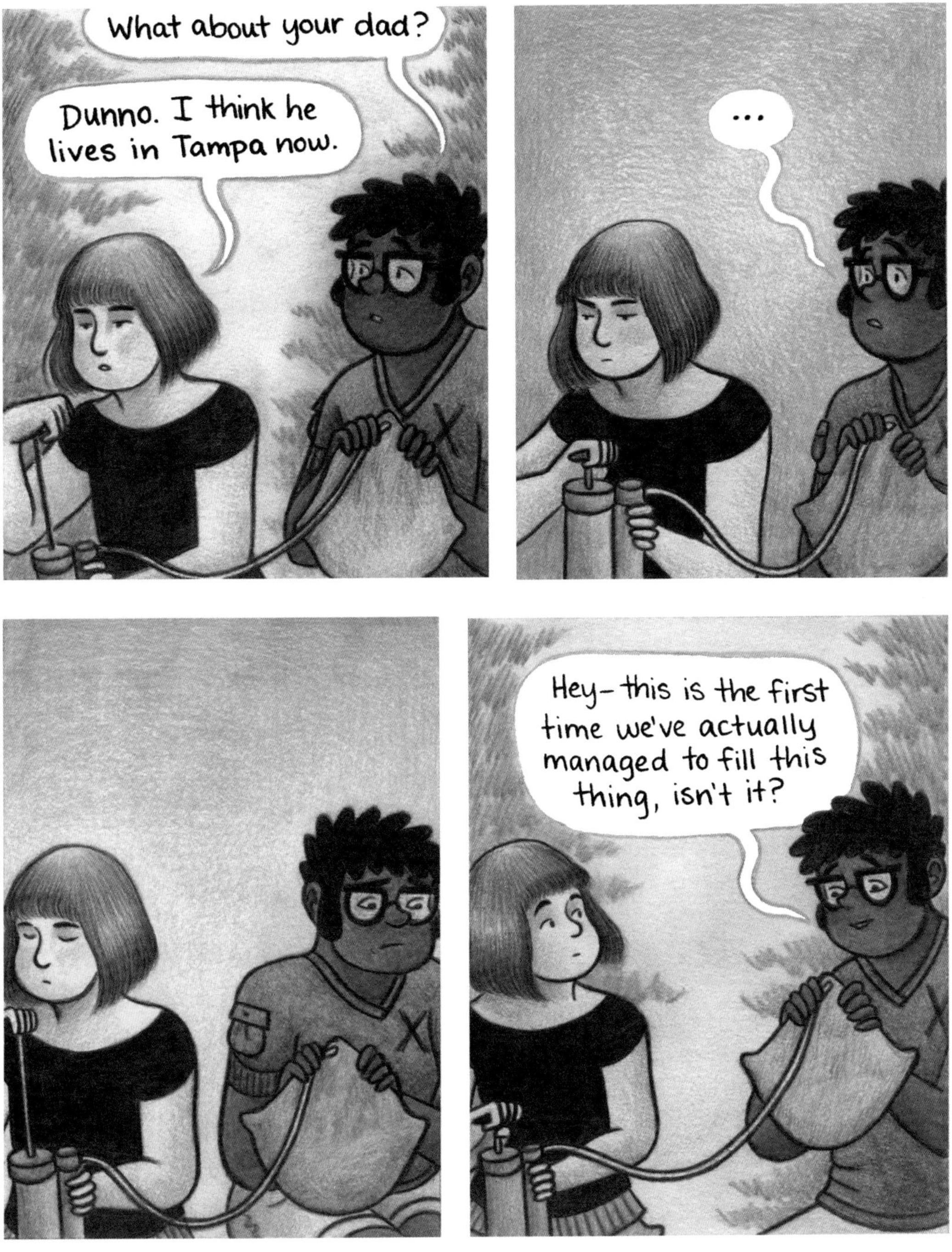
What about your dad?
Dunno. I think he lives in Tampa now.
...
Hey— this is the first time we've actually managed to fill this thing, isn't it?

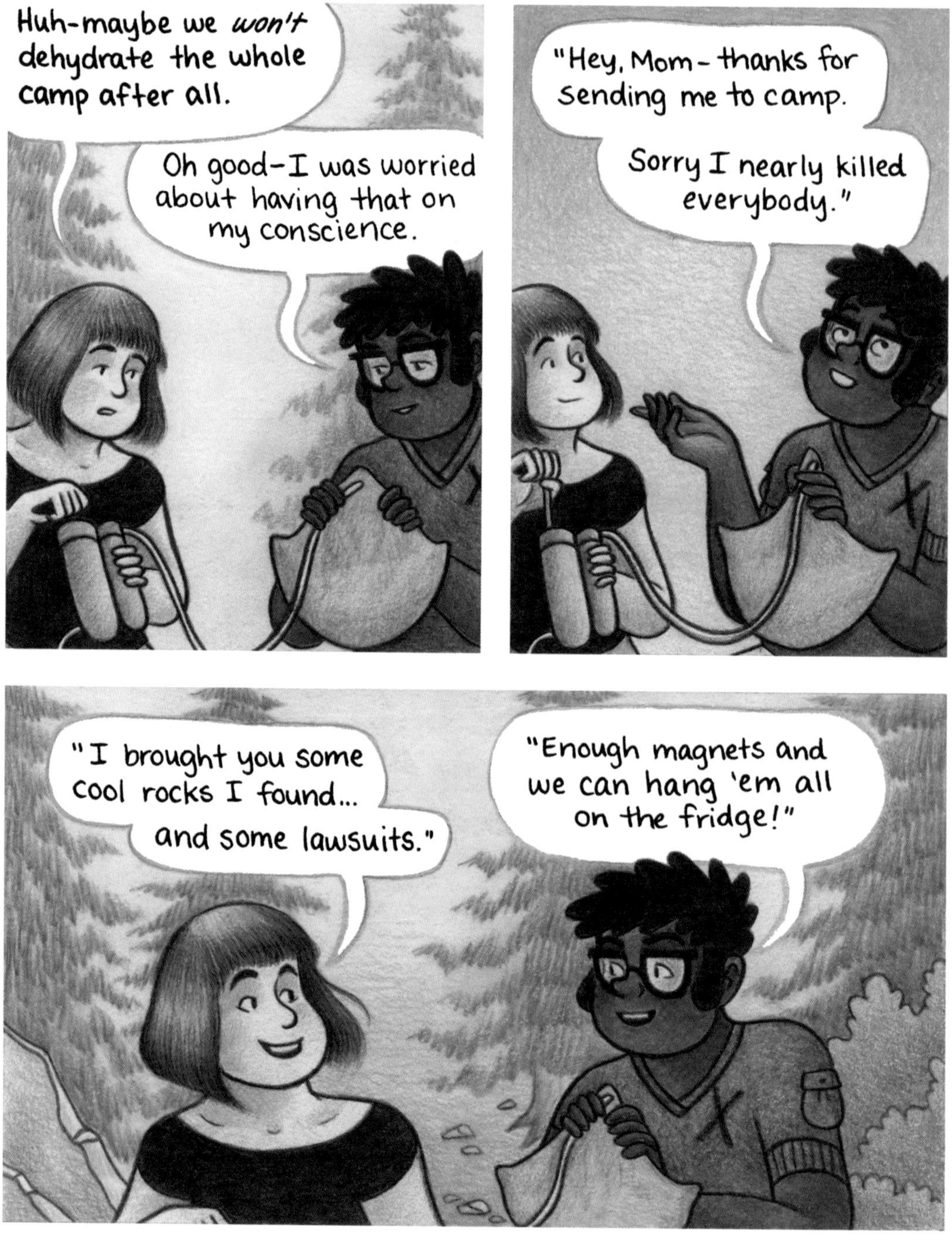

Huh-maybe we *won't* dehydrate the whole camp after all.
Oh good-I was worried about having that on my conscience.
"Hey, Mom-thanks for sending me to camp.
Sorry I nearly killed everybody."
"I brought you some cool rocks I found...
and some lawsuits."
"Enough magnets and we can hang 'em all on the fridge!"

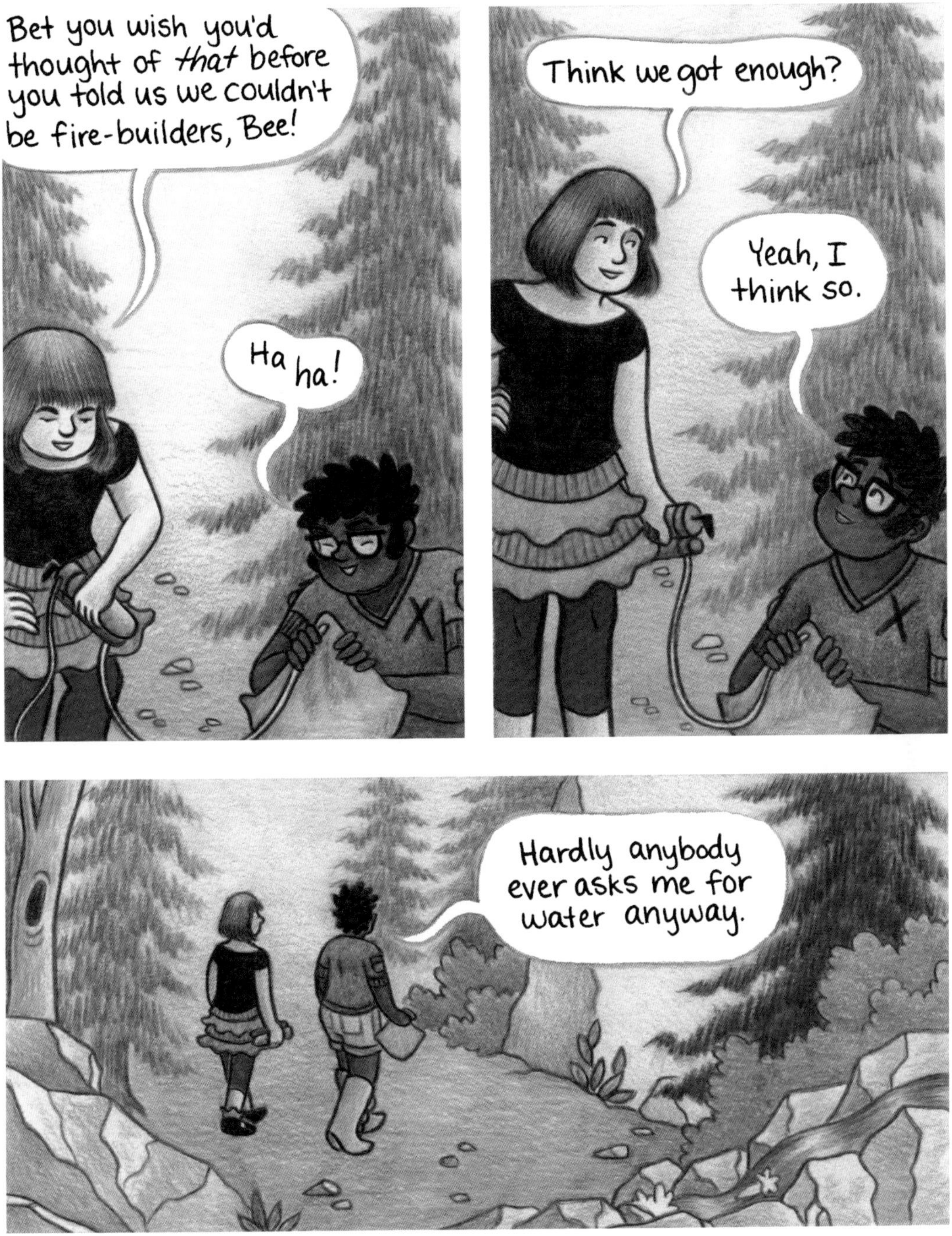
Bet you wish you'd thought of *that* before you told us we couldn't be fire-builders, Bee!
Ha ha!
Think we got enough?
Yeah, I think so.
Hardly anybody ever asks me for water anyway.

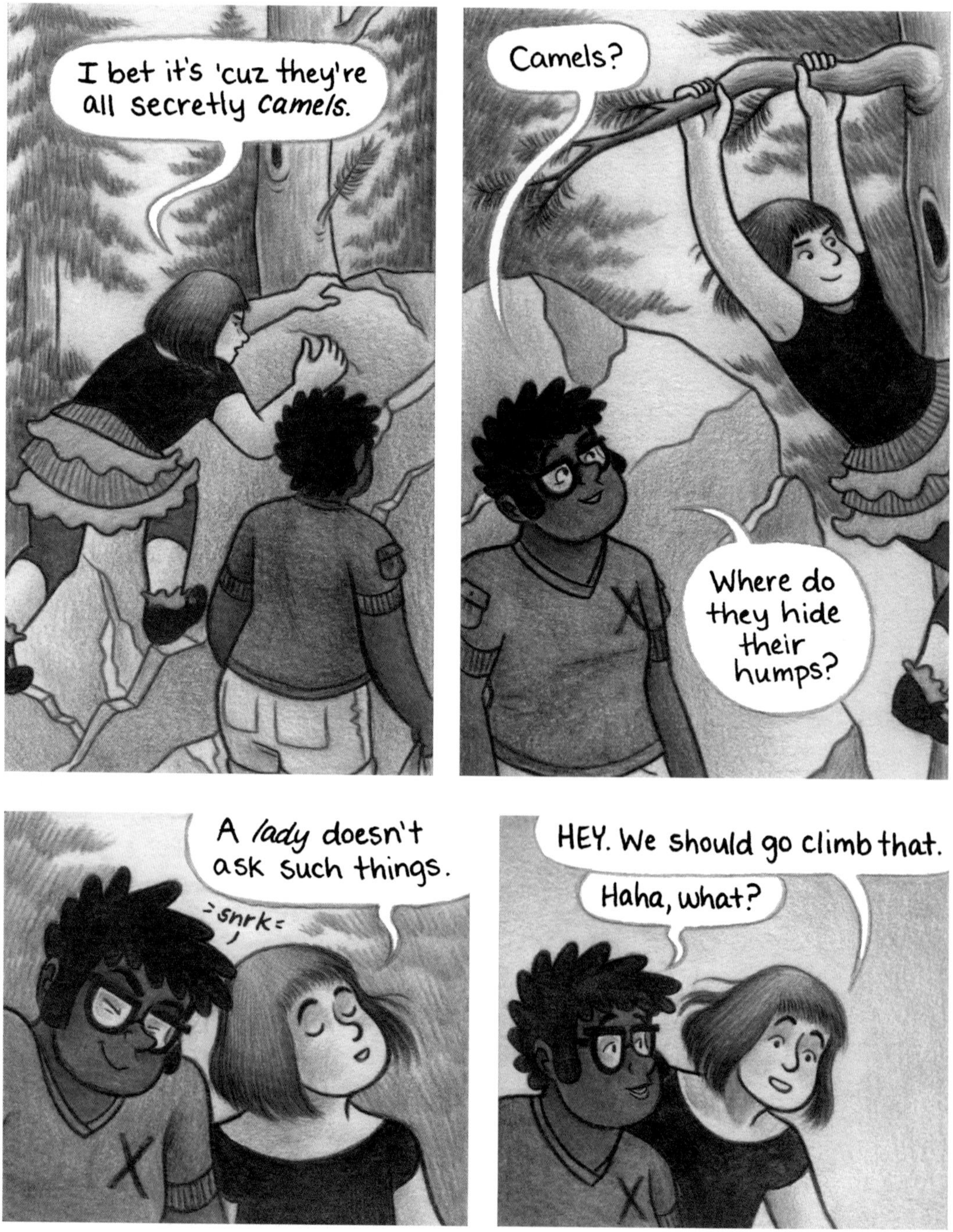
I bet it's 'cuz they're all secretly *camels*.
Camels?
Where do they hide their humps?
A *lady* doesn't ask such things.
=snrk=
HEY. We should go climb that.
Haha, what?

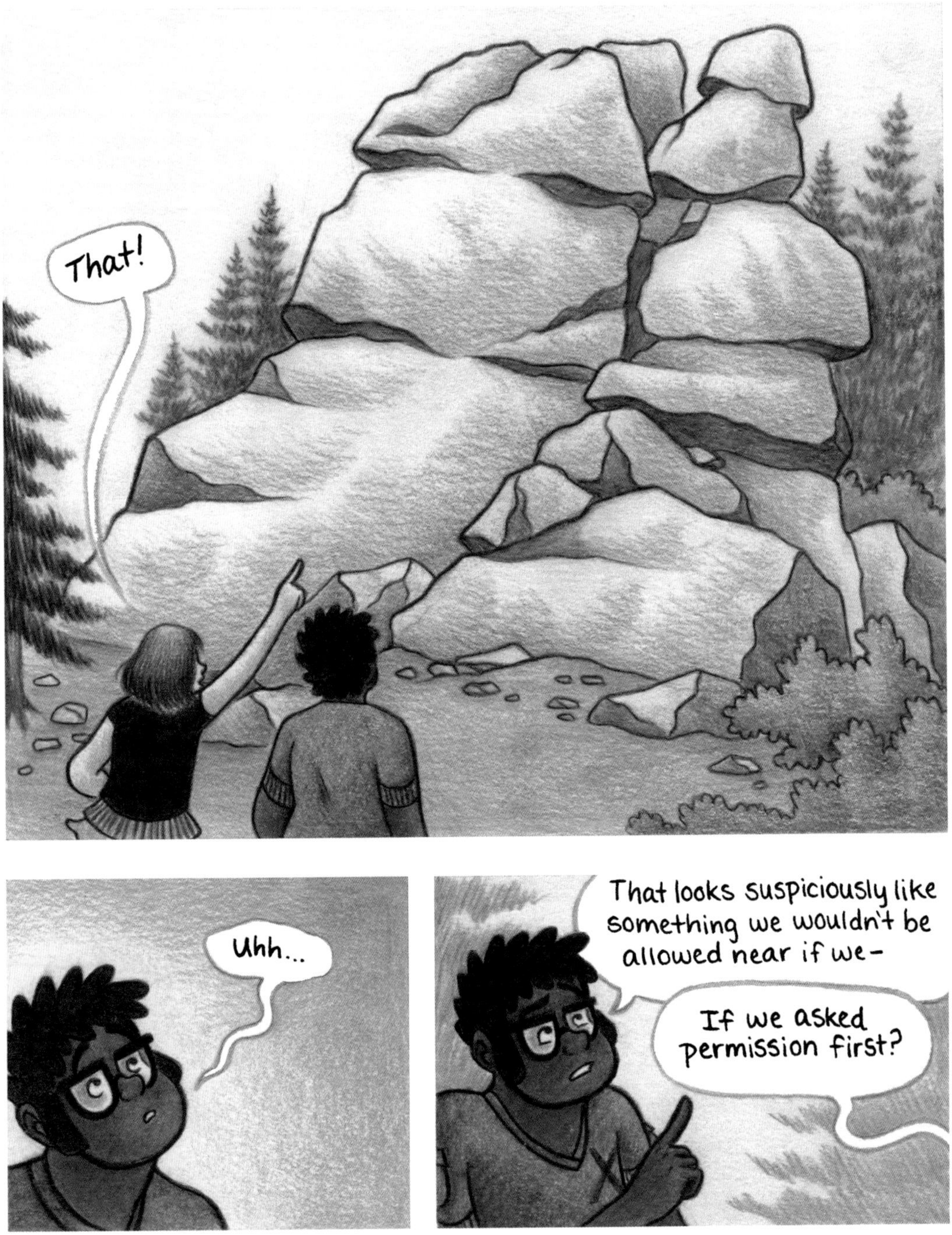
That!
Uhh...
That looks suspiciously like something we wouldn't be allowed near if we-
If we asked permission first?

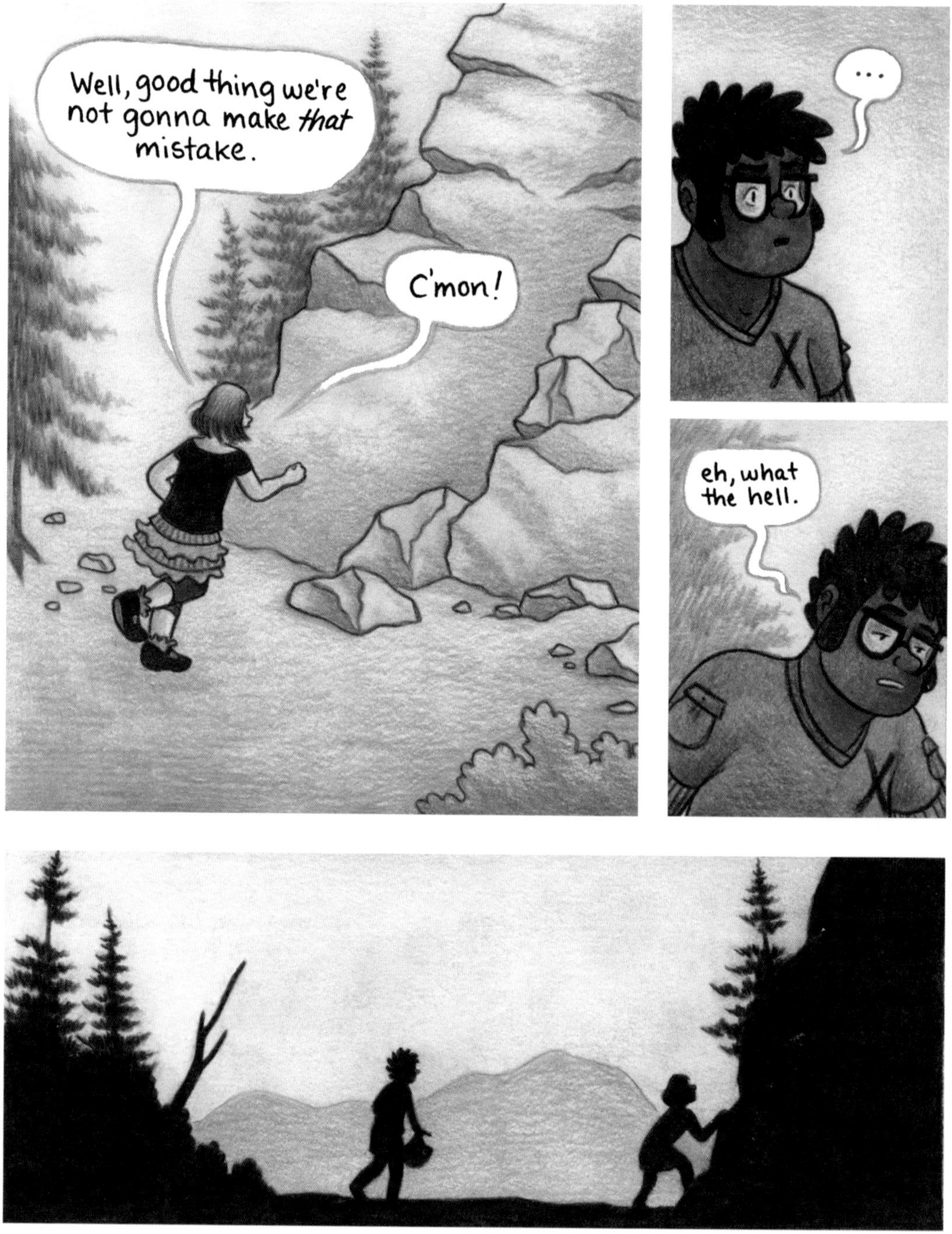
Well, good thing we're not gonna make *that* mistake.
C'mon!
...
eh, what the hell.

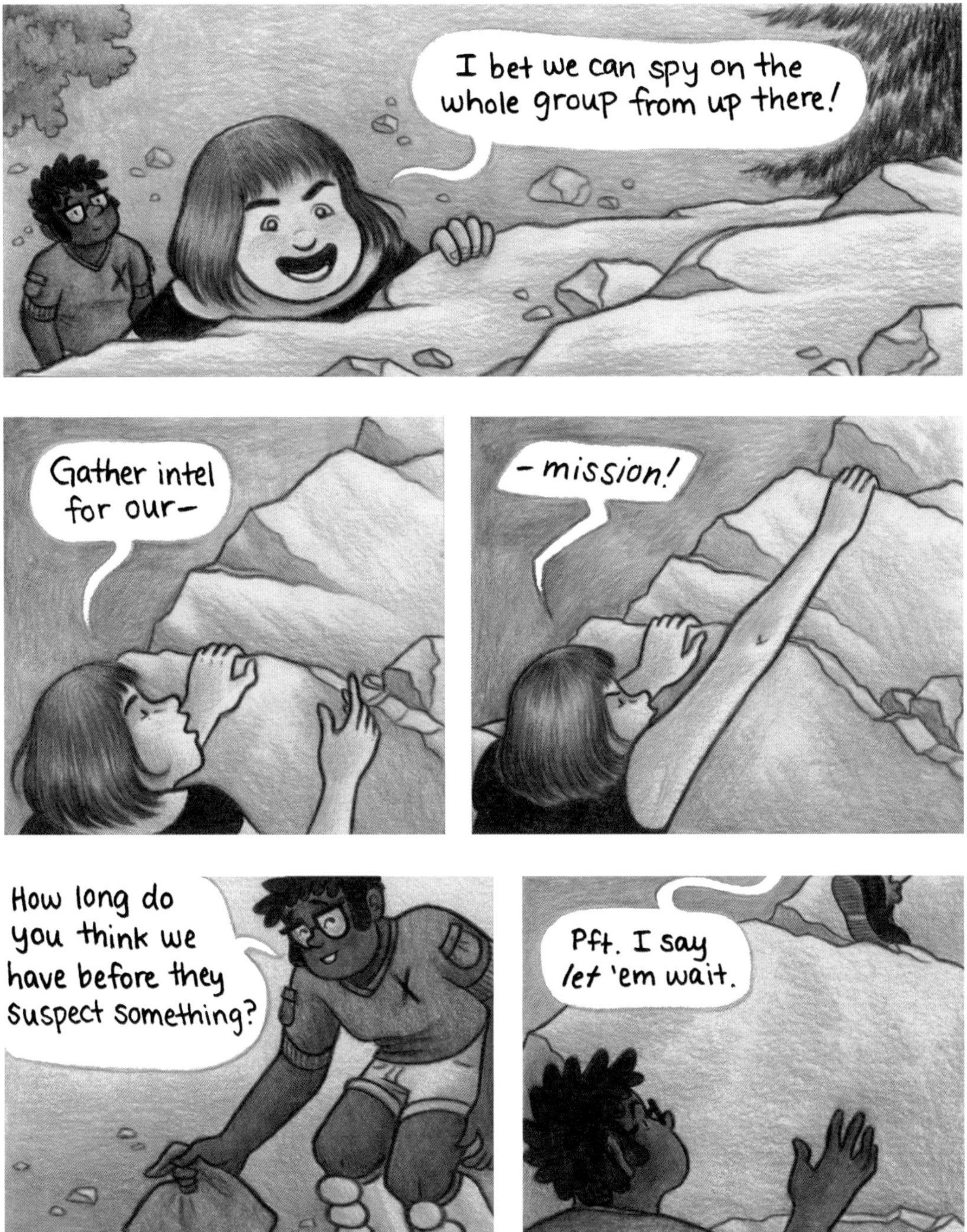
I bet we can spy on the whole group from up there!
Gather intel for our–
–mission!
How long do you think we have before they suspect something?
Pft. I say *let* 'em wait.

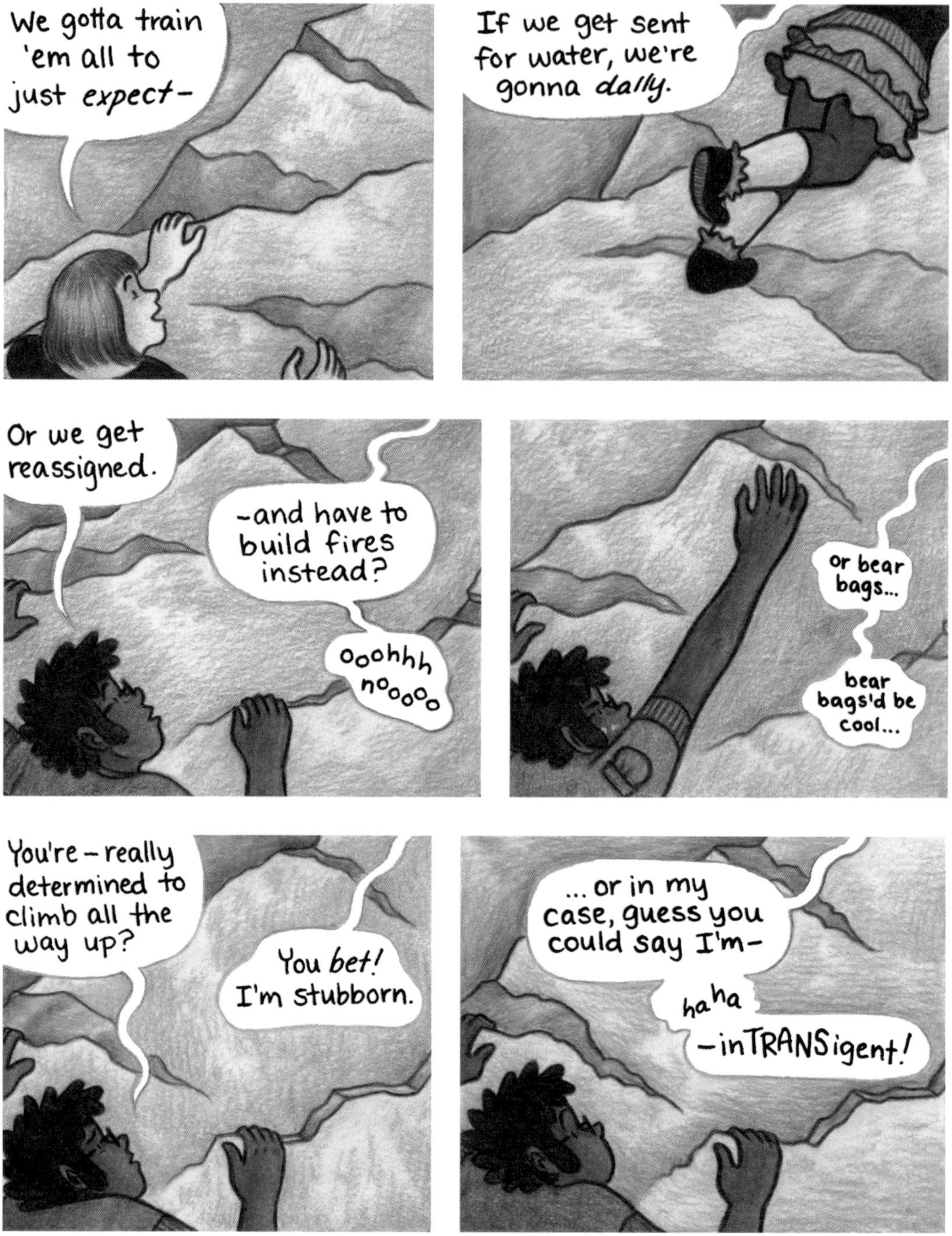
We gotta train 'em all to just *expect*-
If we get sent for water, we're gonna *dally*.
Or we get reassigned.
-and have to build fires instead?
Ooohhh nooooo
Or bear bags...
bear bags'd be cool...
You're - really determined to climb all the way up?
You *bet*! I'm stubborn.
...or in my case, guess you could say I'm-
haha
-inTRANSigent!

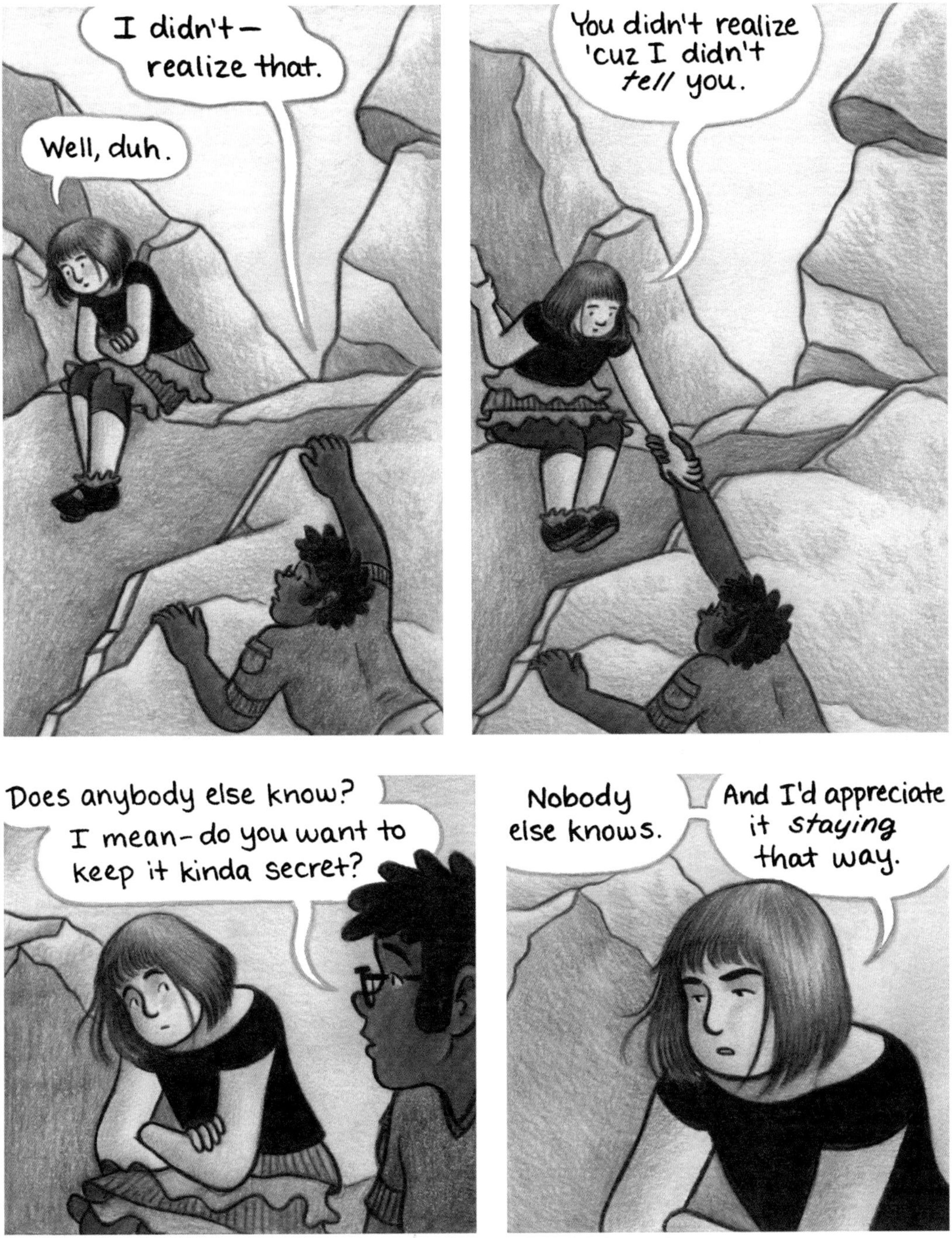
I didn't— realize that.
Well, duh.
You didn't realize 'cuz I didn't *tell* you.
Does anybody else know?
I mean—do you want to keep it kinda secret?
Nobody else knows.
And I'd appreciate it *staying* that way.

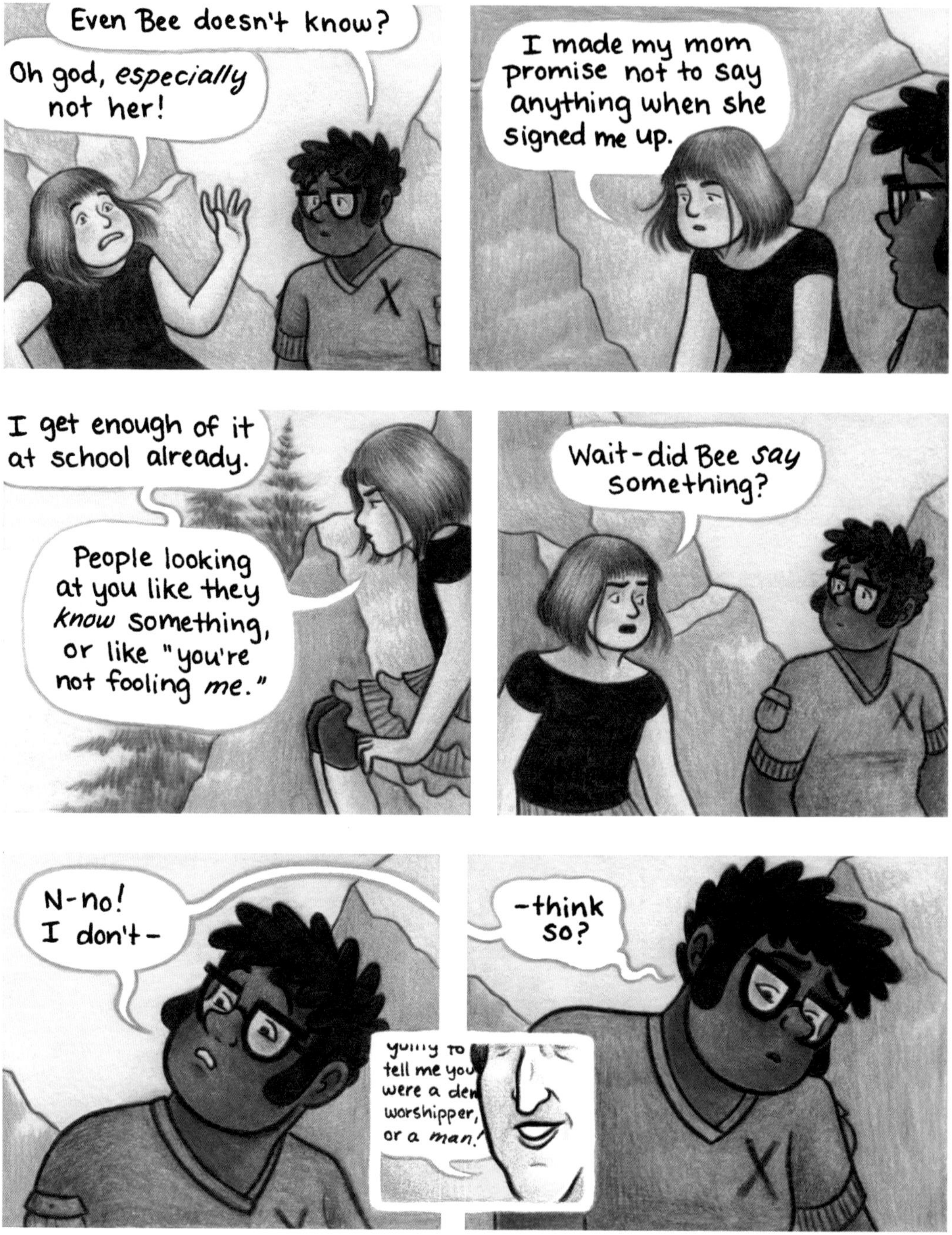
Even Bee doesn't know?
Oh god, especially not her!
I made my mom promise not to say anything when she signed me up.
I get enough of it at school already.
People looking at you like they know something, or like "you're not fooling me."
Wait-did Bee say something?
N-no! I don't-
-think so?
tell me you were a de
worshipper,
or a man!

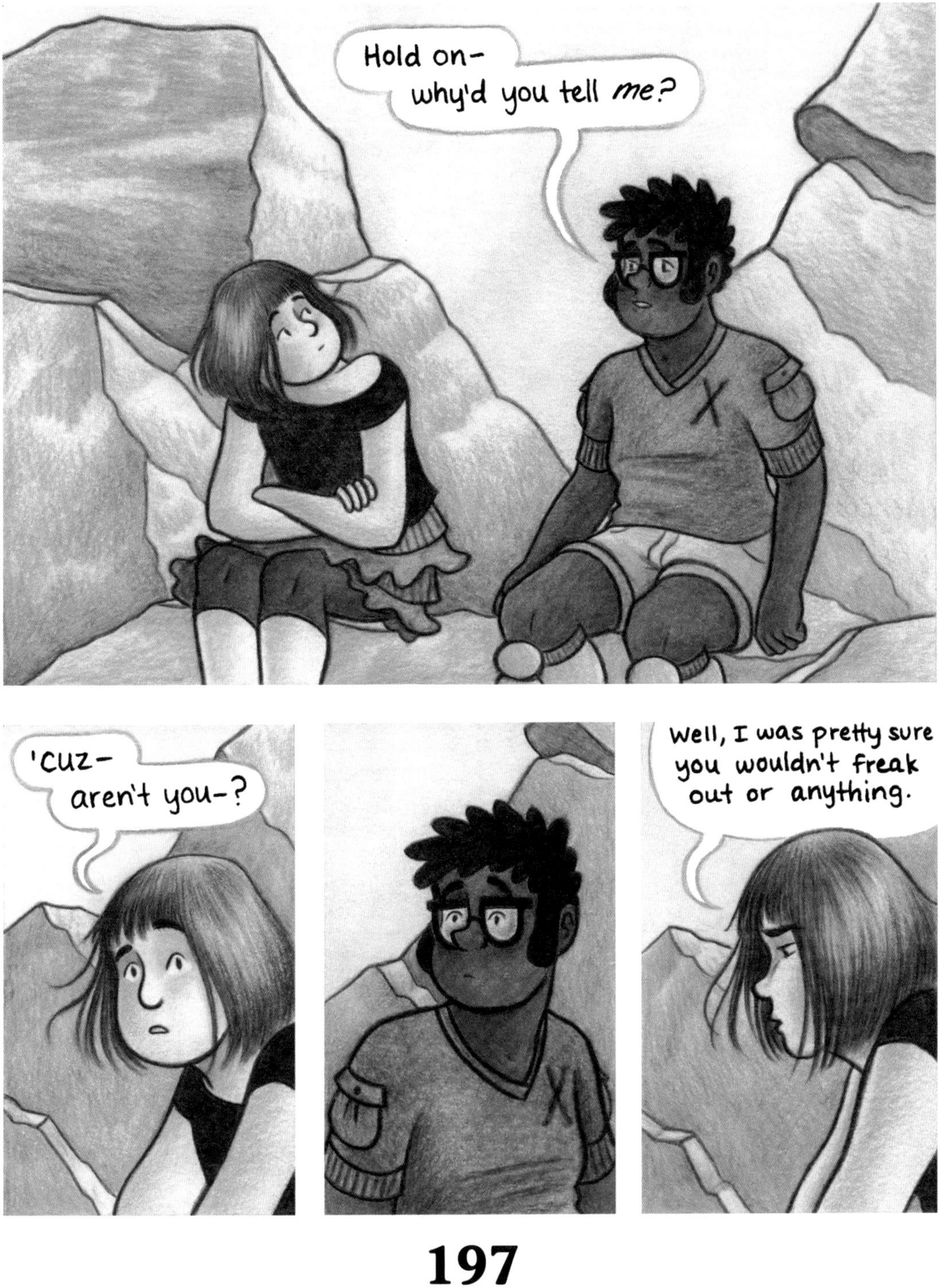
Hold on-
why'd you tell *me*?
'cuz-
aren't you-?
Well, I was pretty sure you wouldn't freak out or anything.

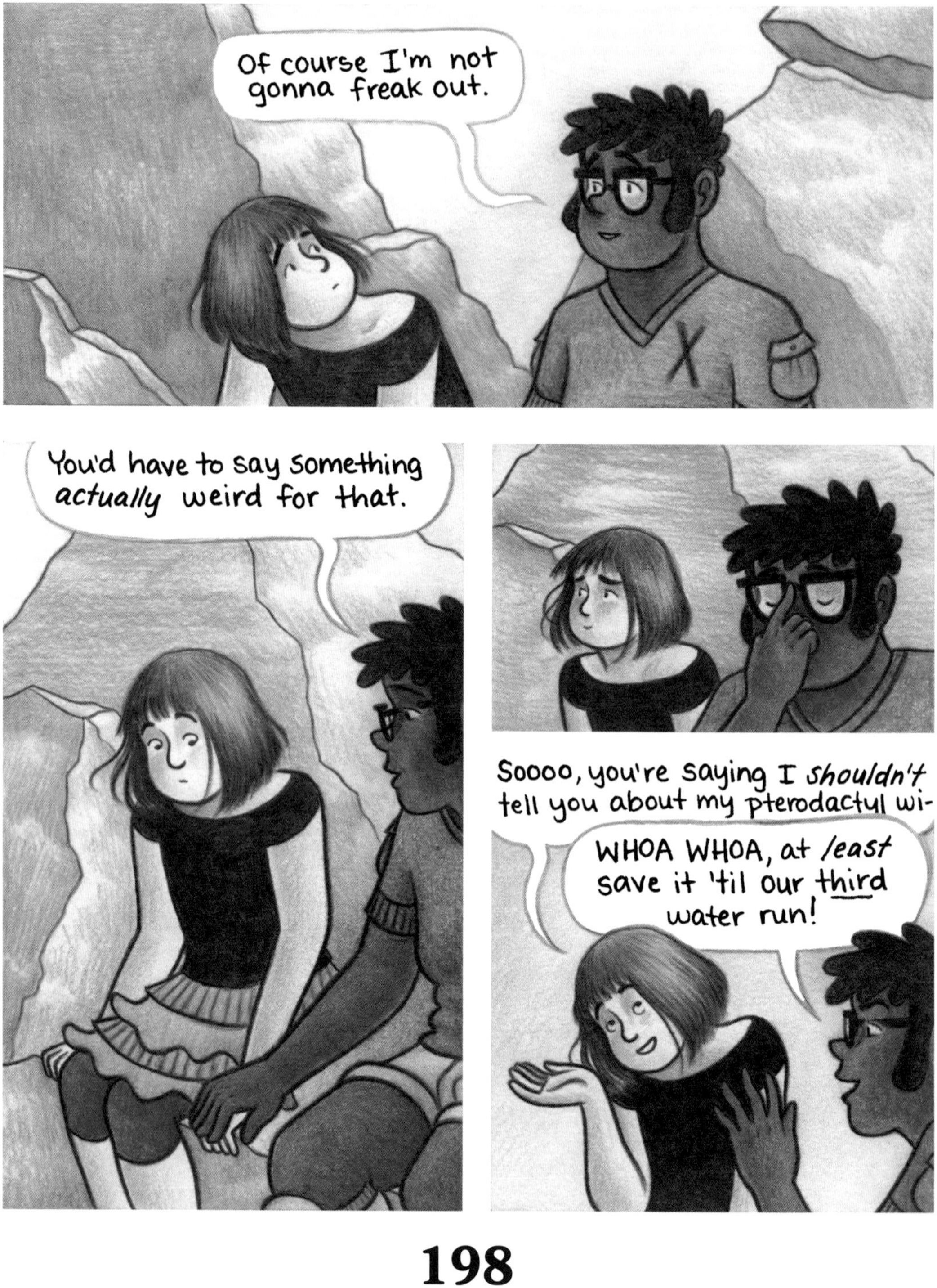
Of course I'm not gonna freak out.
You'd have to say something *actually* weird for that.
Soooo, you're saying I *shouldn't* tell you about my pterodactyl wi-
WHOA WHOA, at *least* save it 'til our third water run!

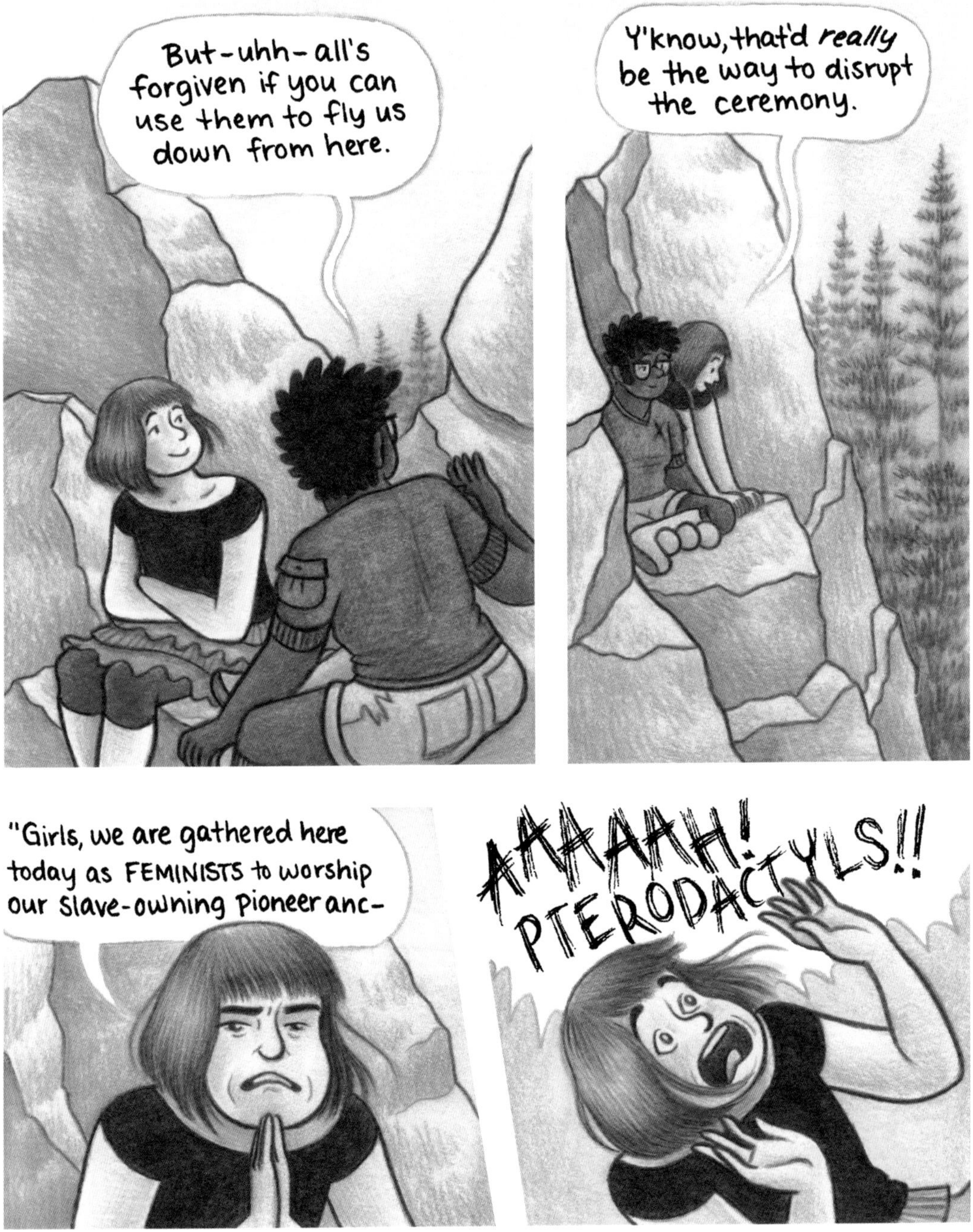
But-uhh-all's forgiven if you can use them to fly us down from here.
Y'know, that'd *really* be the way to disrupt the ceremony.
"Girls, we are gathered here today as FEMINISTS to worship our slave-owning pioneer anc-
AAAAAH! PTERODACTYLS!!

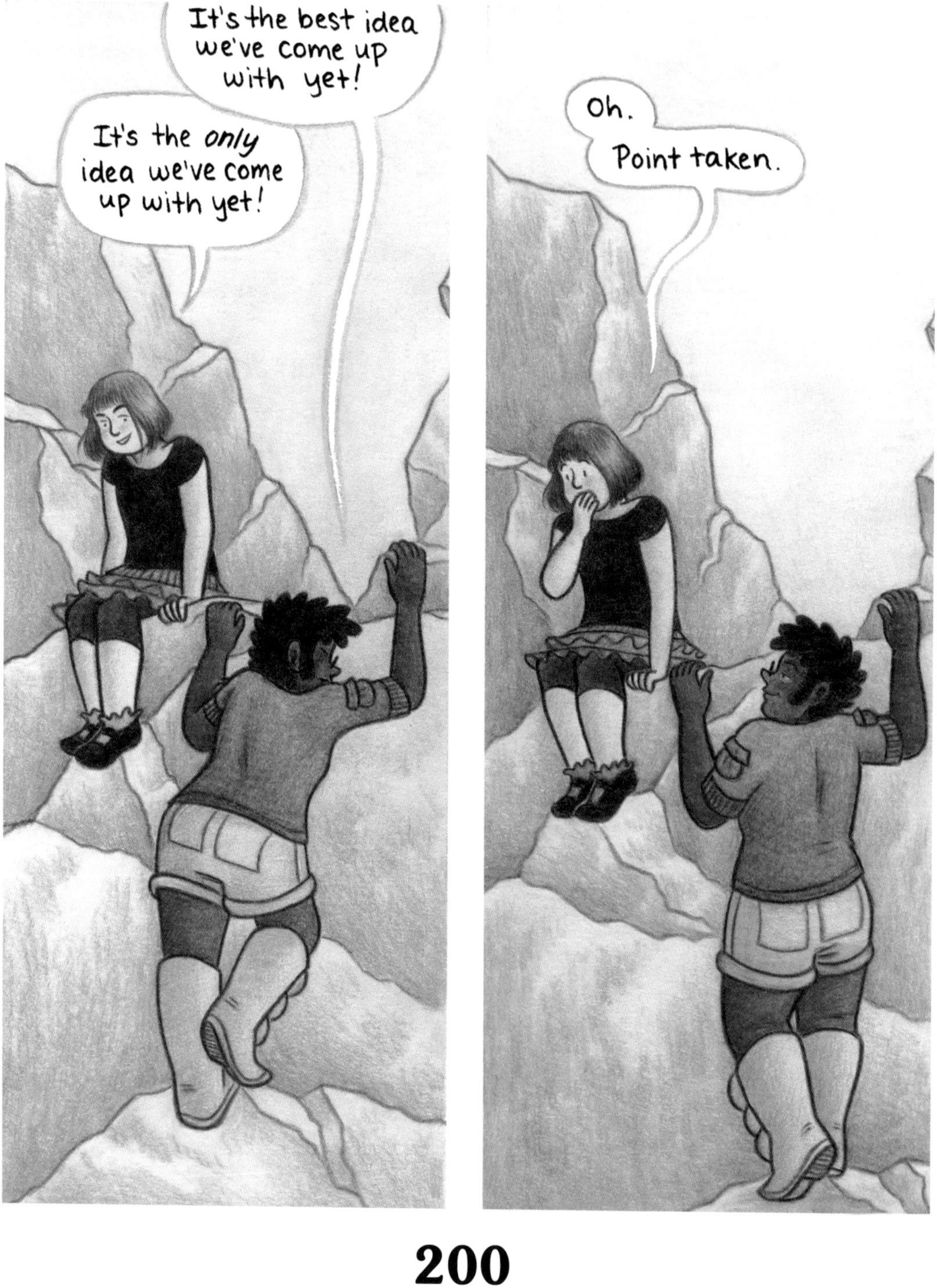
It's the best idea we've come up with yet!
It's the *only* idea we've come up with yet!
Oh.
Point taken.

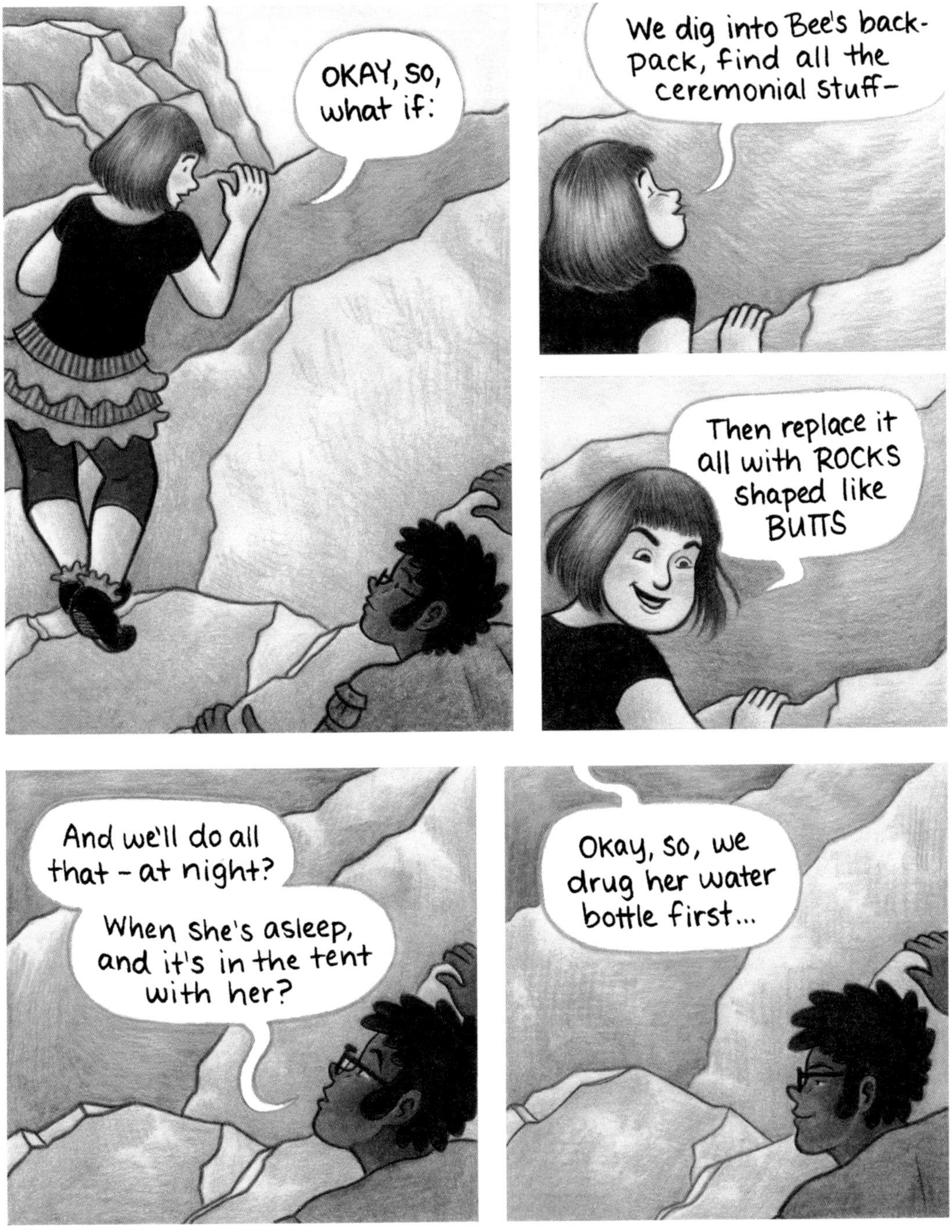
OKAY, SO, what if:
We dig into Bee's back-pack, find all the ceremonial stuff-
Then replace it all with ROCKS shaped like BUTTS
And we'll do all that - at night?
When she's asleep, and it's in the tent with her?
Okay, so, we drug her water bottle first...

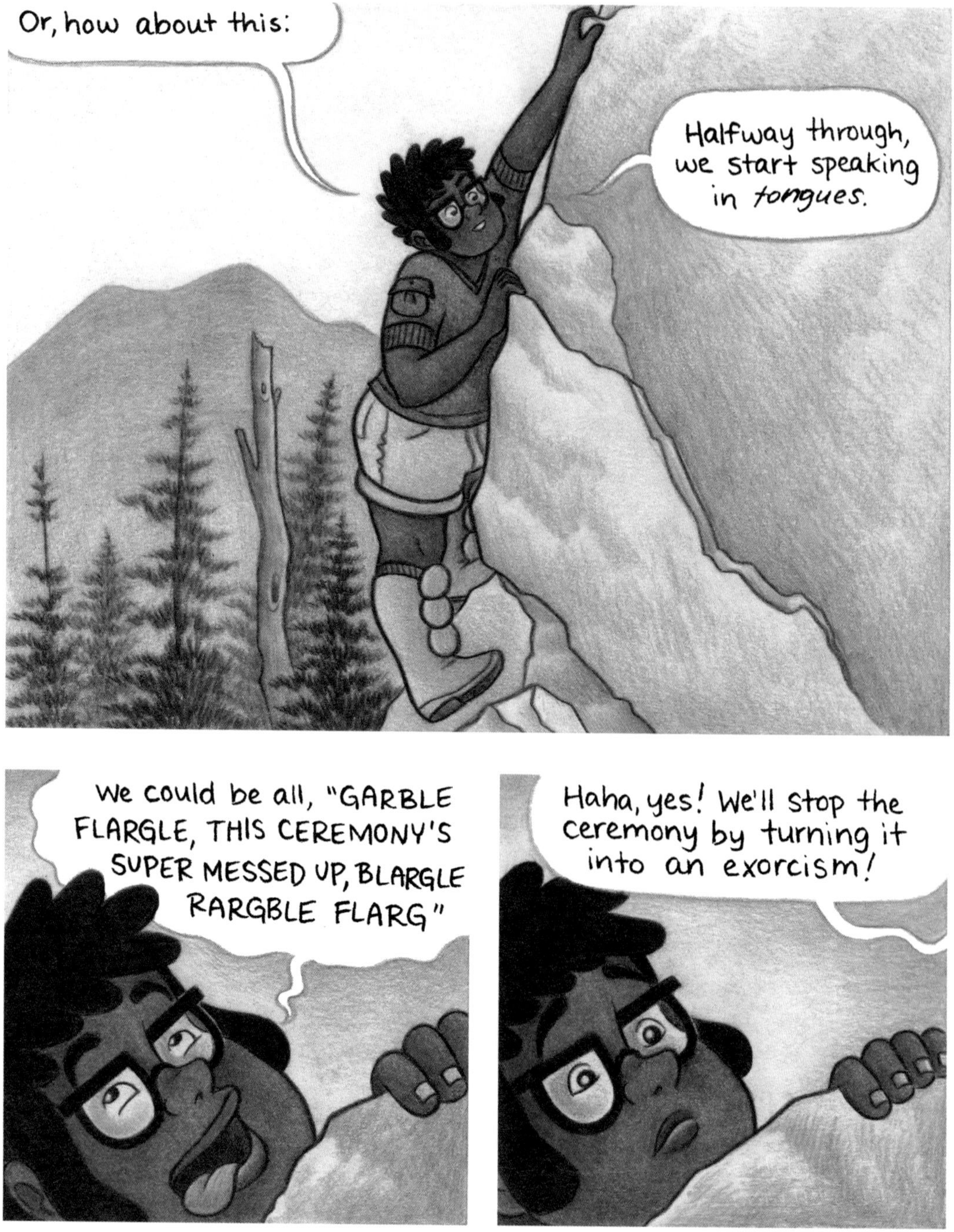
Or, how about this:
Halfway through, we start speaking in *tongues.*
We could be all, "GARBLE FLARGLE, THIS CEREMONY'S SUPER MESSED UP, BLARGLE RARGBLE FLARG"
Haha, yes! We'll stop the ceremony by turning it into an exorcism!

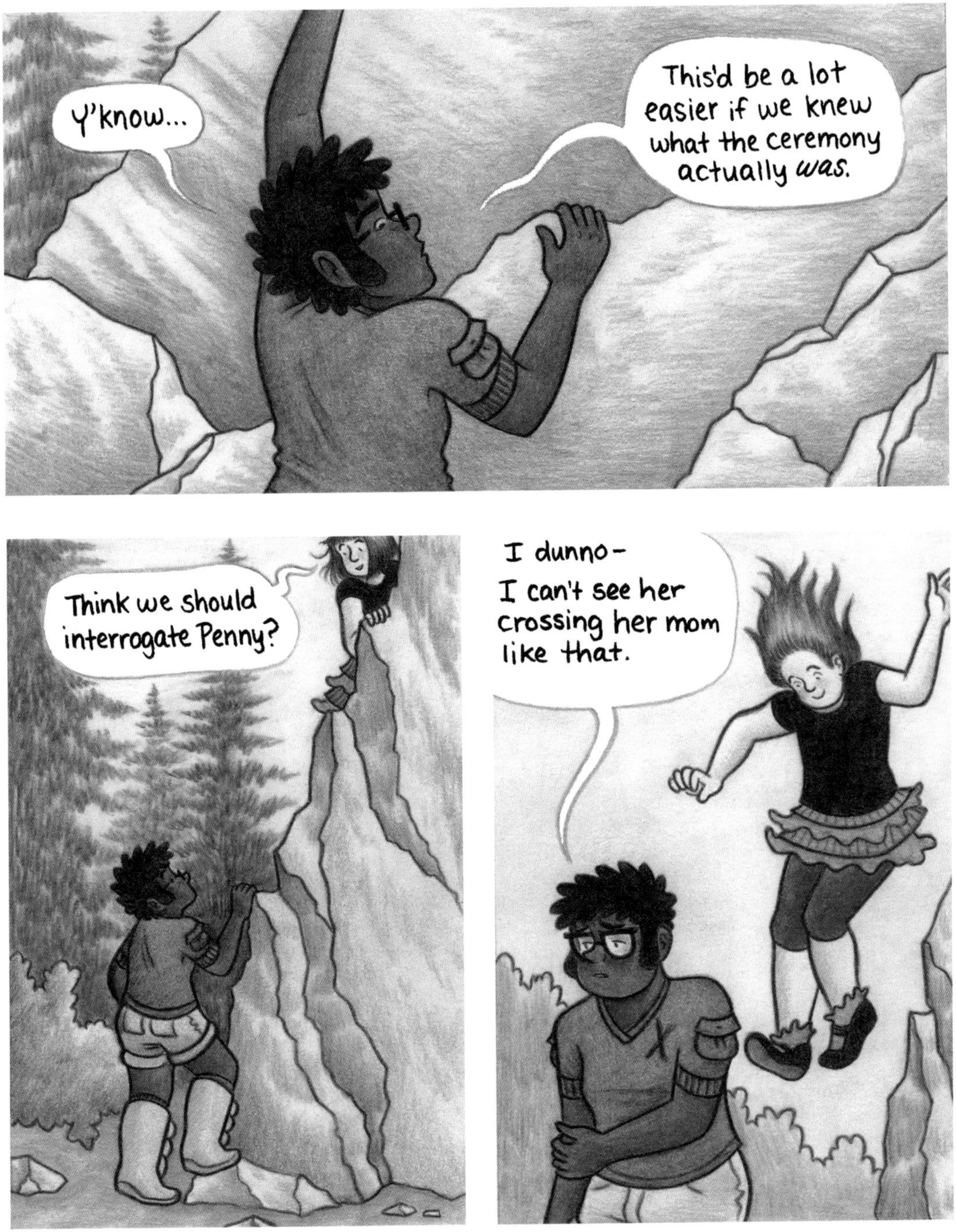
Y'know...
This'd be a lot easier if we knew what the ceremony actually *was*.
Think we should interrogate Penny?
I dunno-
I can't see her crossing her mom like that.

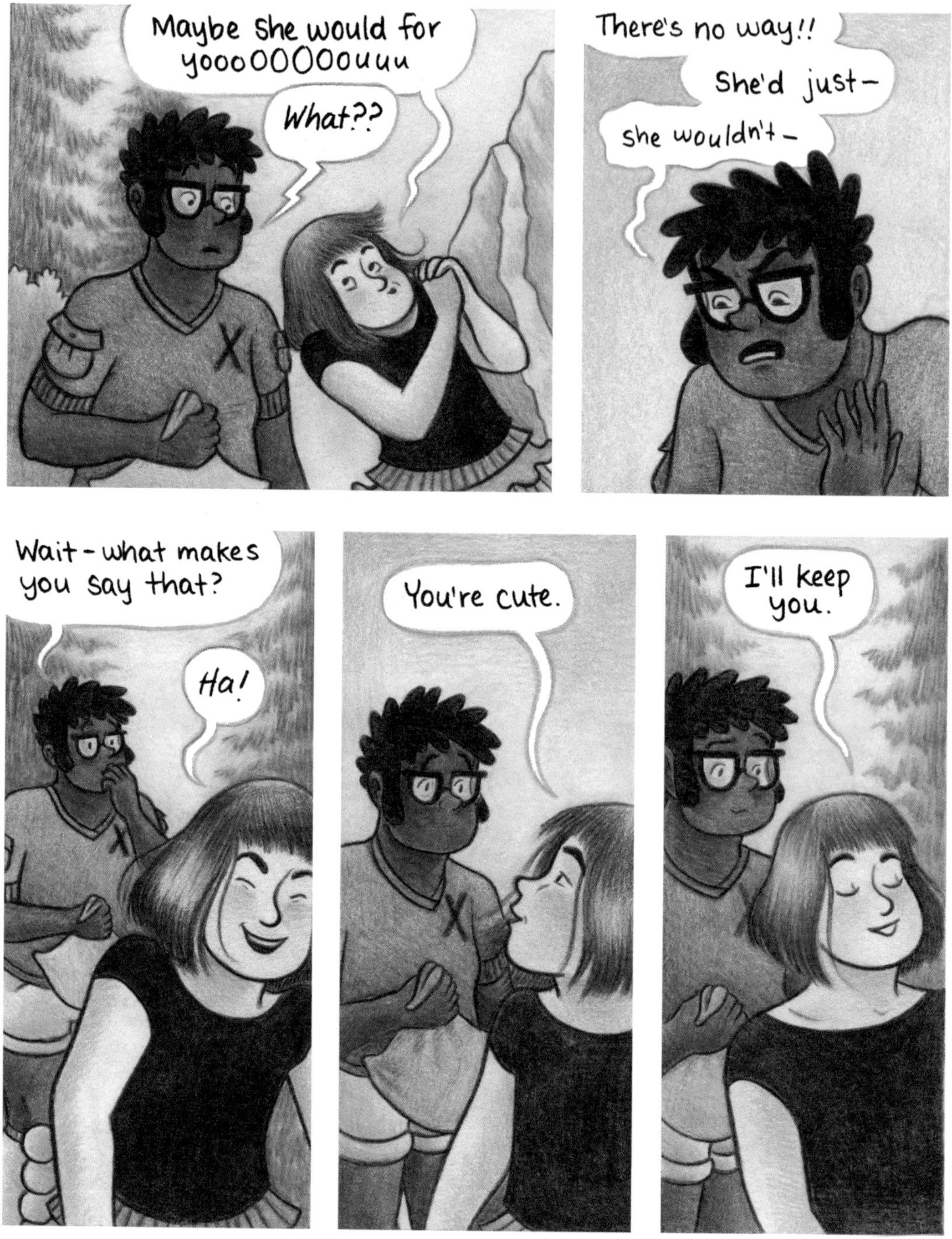
Maybe she would for yoooOOOOouuu
What??
There's no way!!
She'd just-
she wouldn't-
Wait - what makes you say that?
Ha!
You're cute.
I'll keep you.

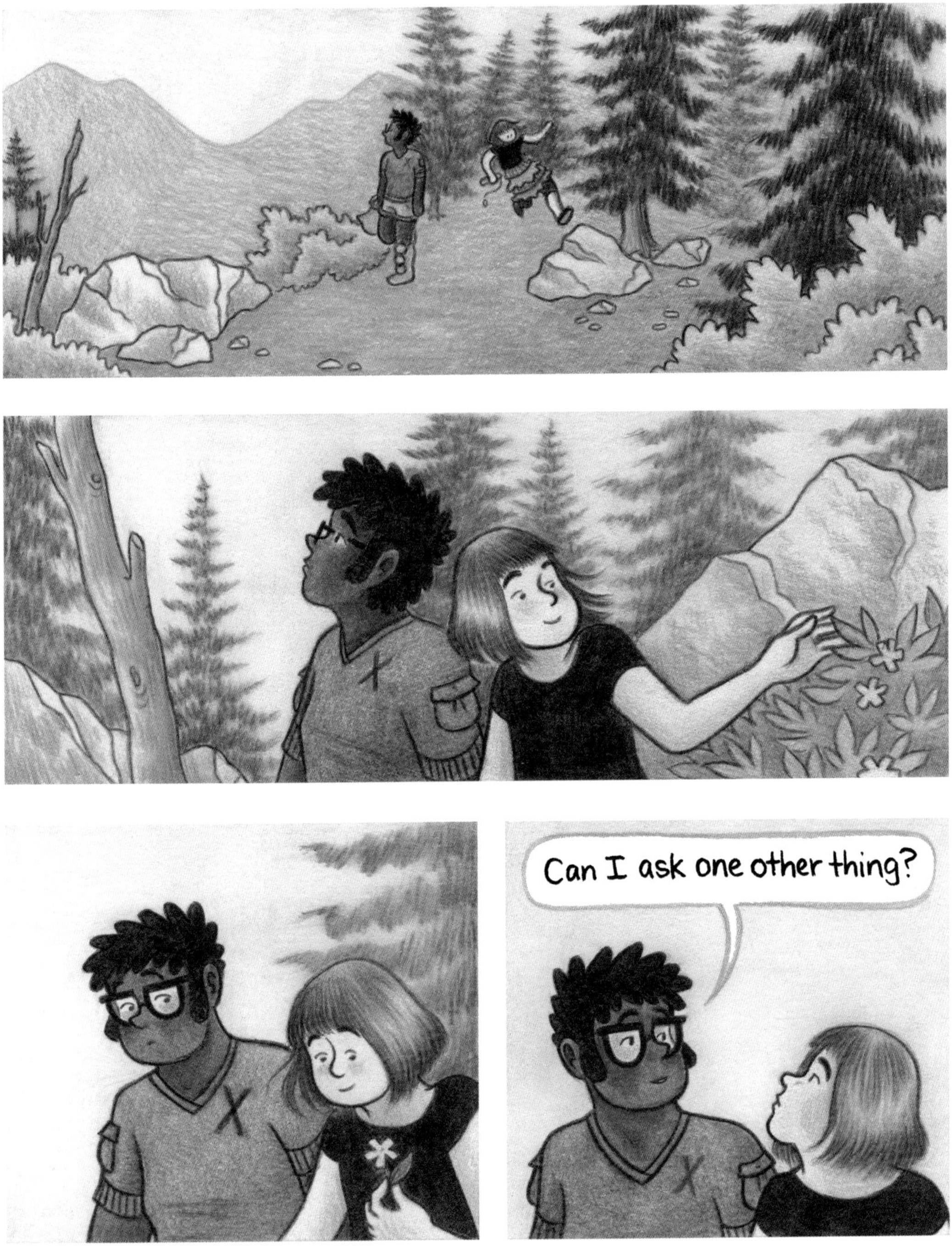
Can I ask one other thing?

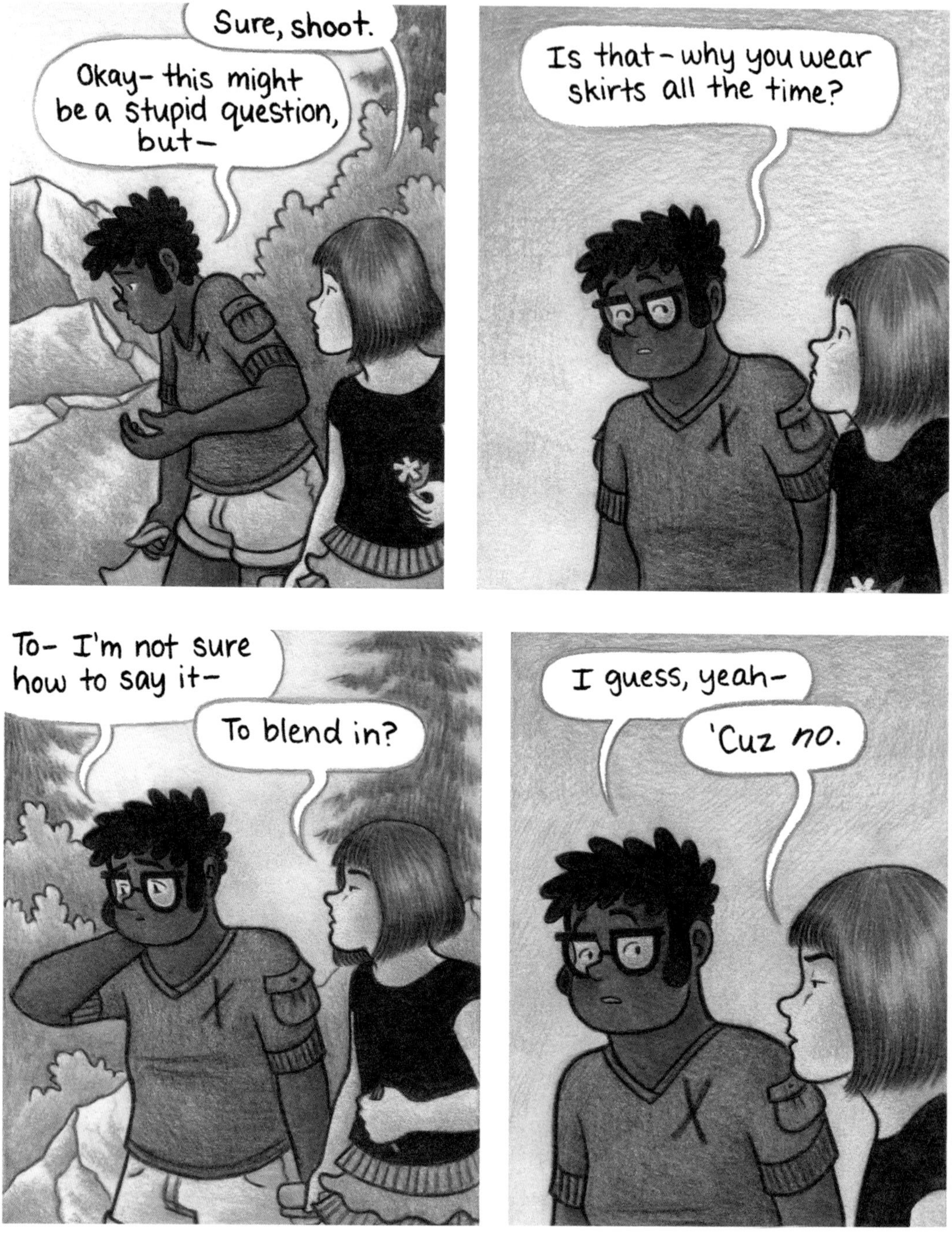
Sure, shoot.
Okay- this might be a stupid question, but-
Is that- why you wear skirts all the time?
To- I'm not sure how to say it-
To blend in?
I guess, yeah-
'Cuz no.

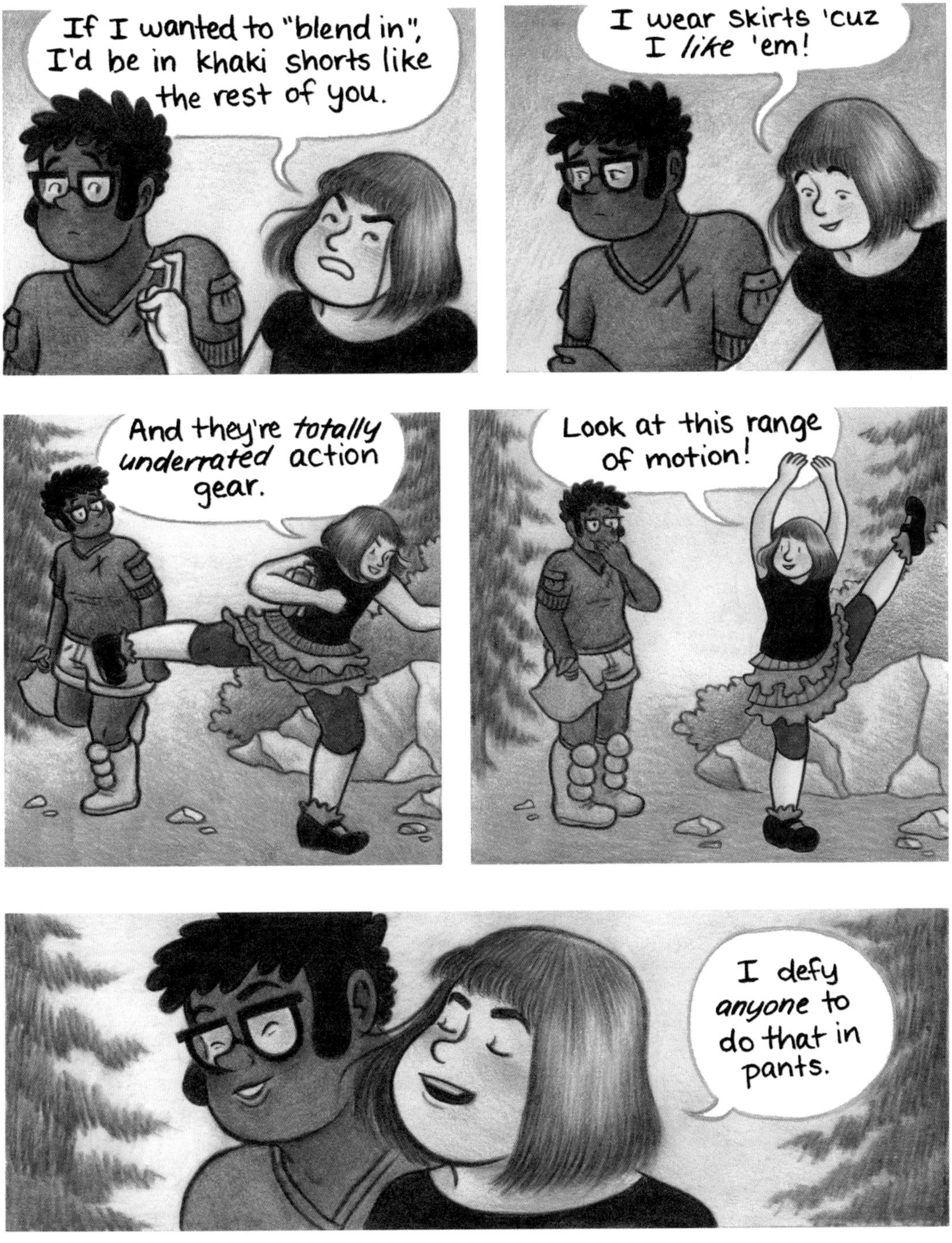
If I wanted to "blend in", I'd be in khaki shorts like the rest of you.
I wear skirts 'cuz I *like* 'em!
And they're *totally underrated* action gear.
Look at this range of motion!
I defy *anyone* to do that in pants.

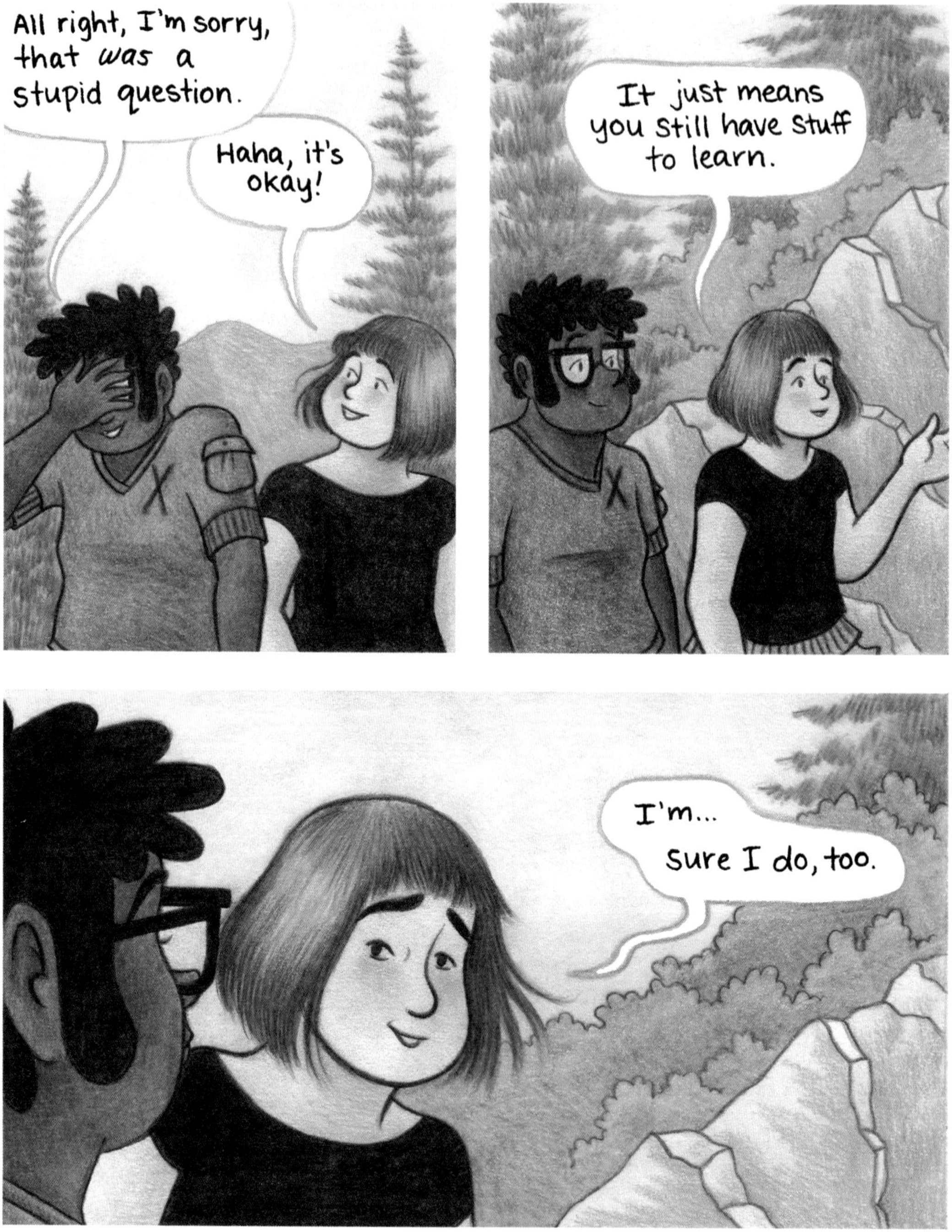
All right, I'm sorry, that *was* a stupid question.
Haha, it's okay!
It just means you still have stuff to learn.
I'm...
sure I do, too.

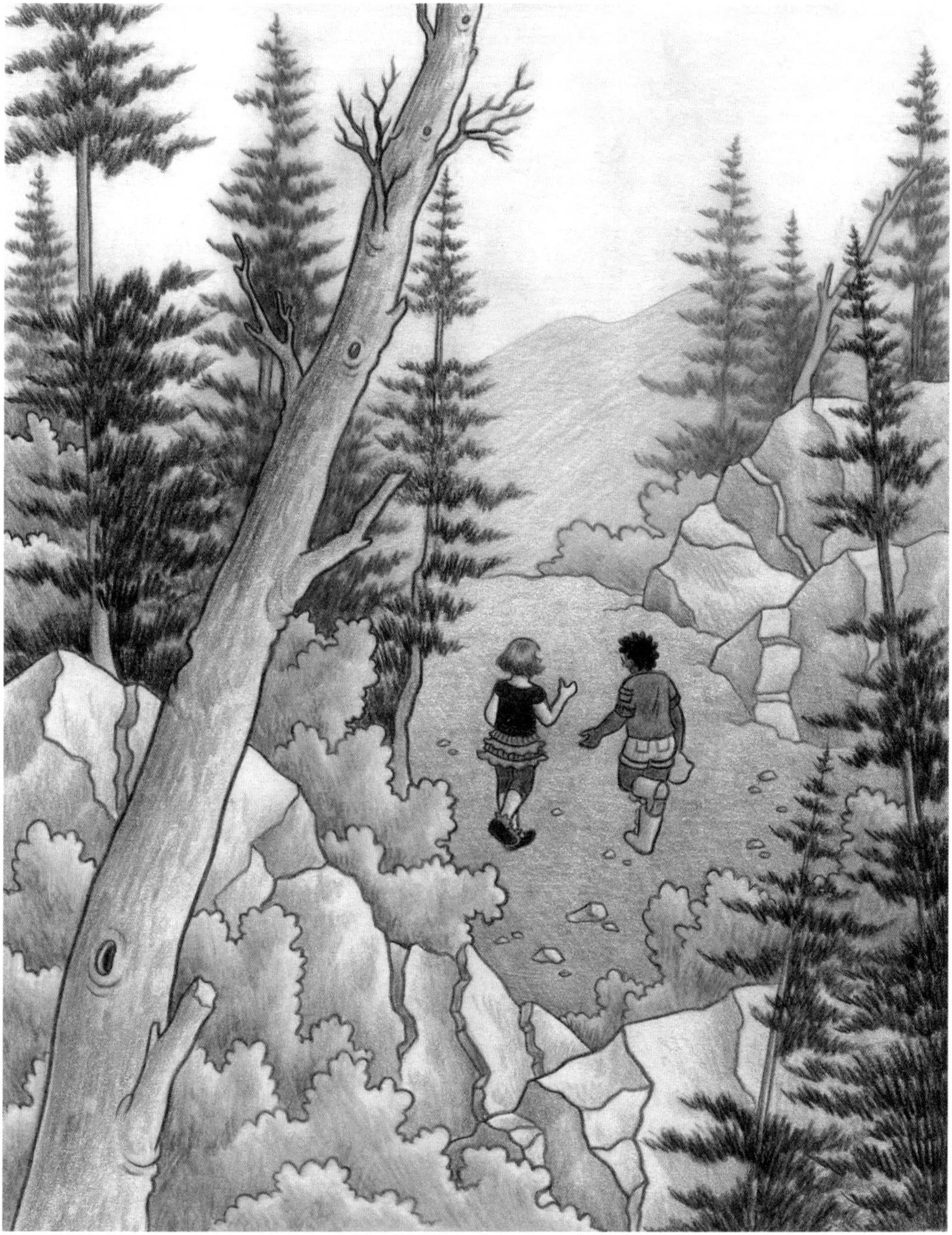

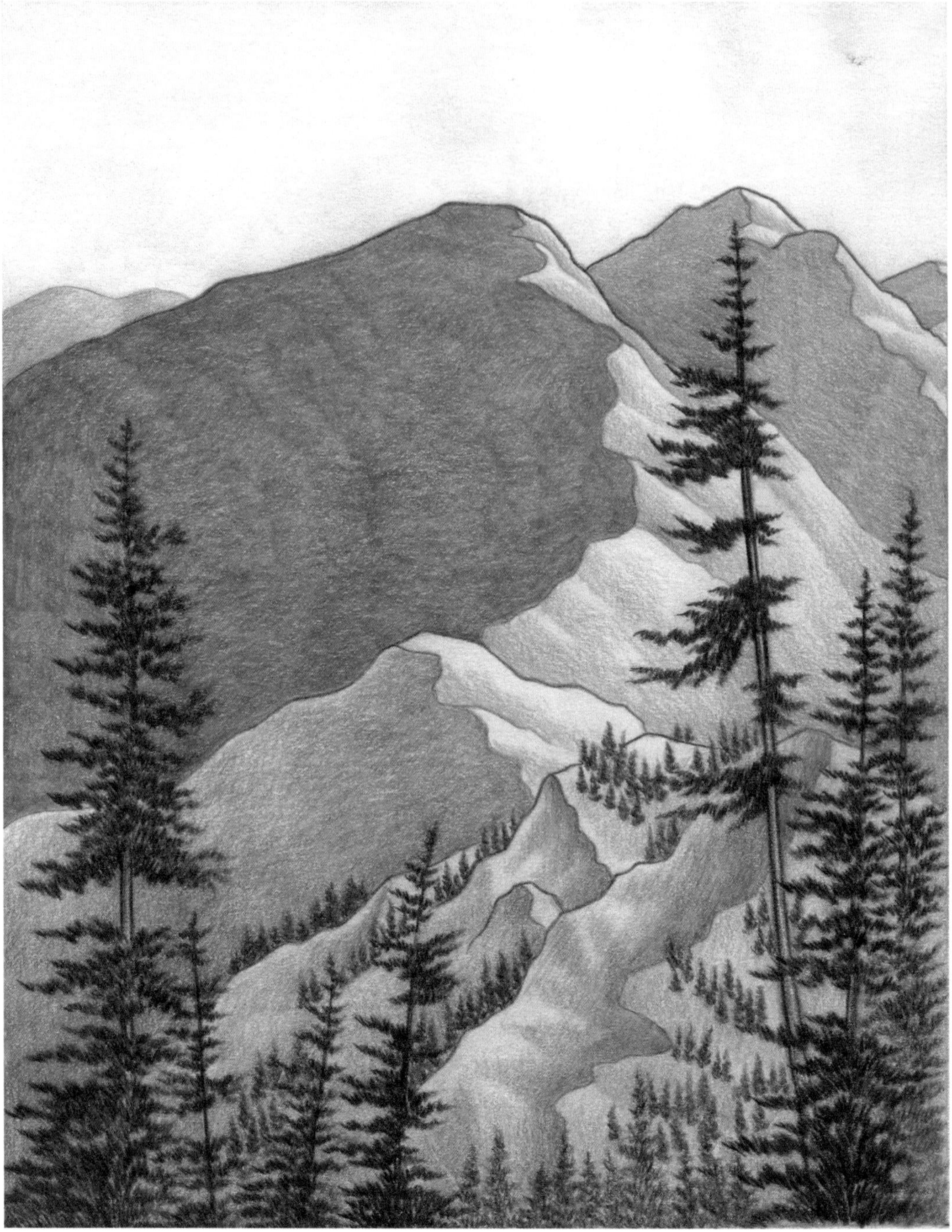

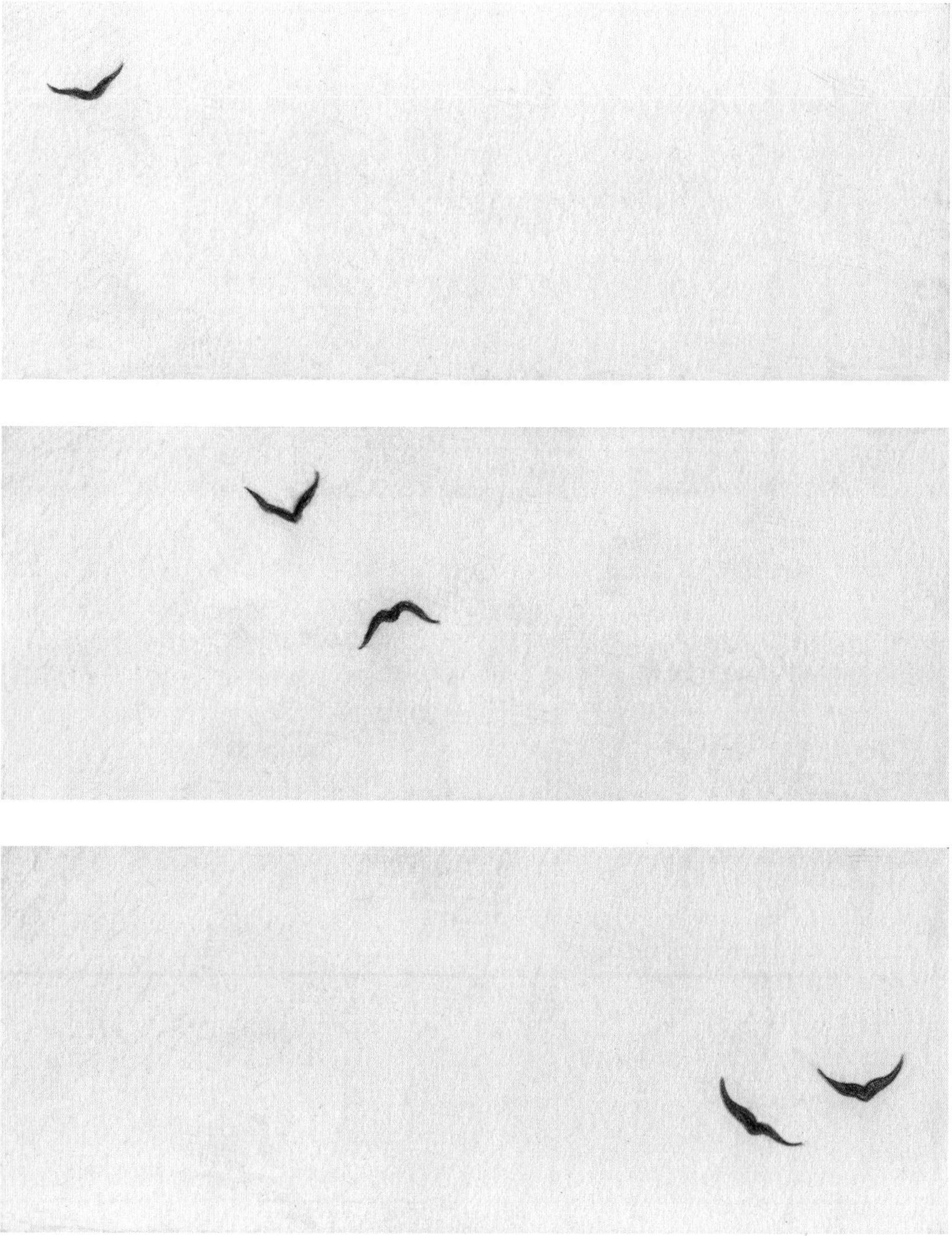

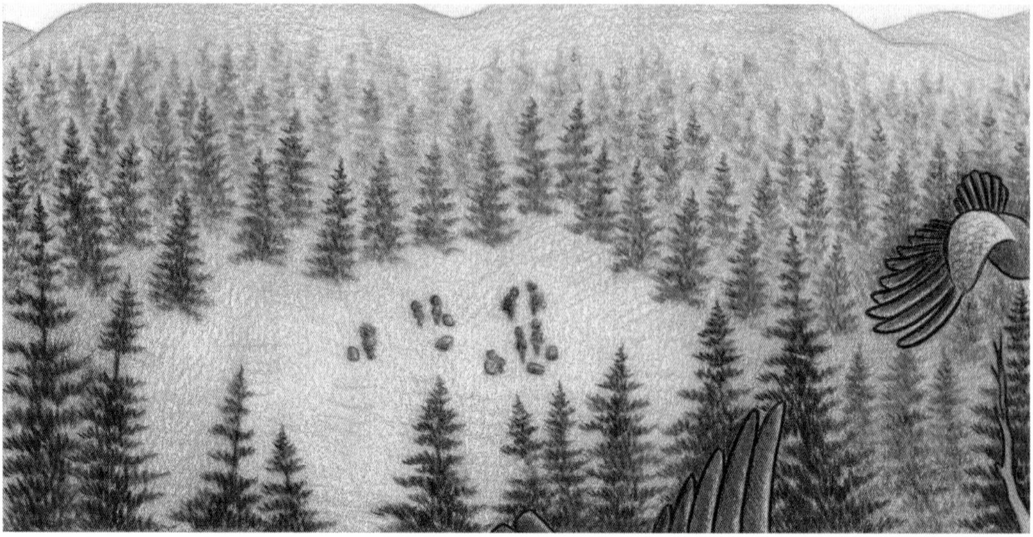

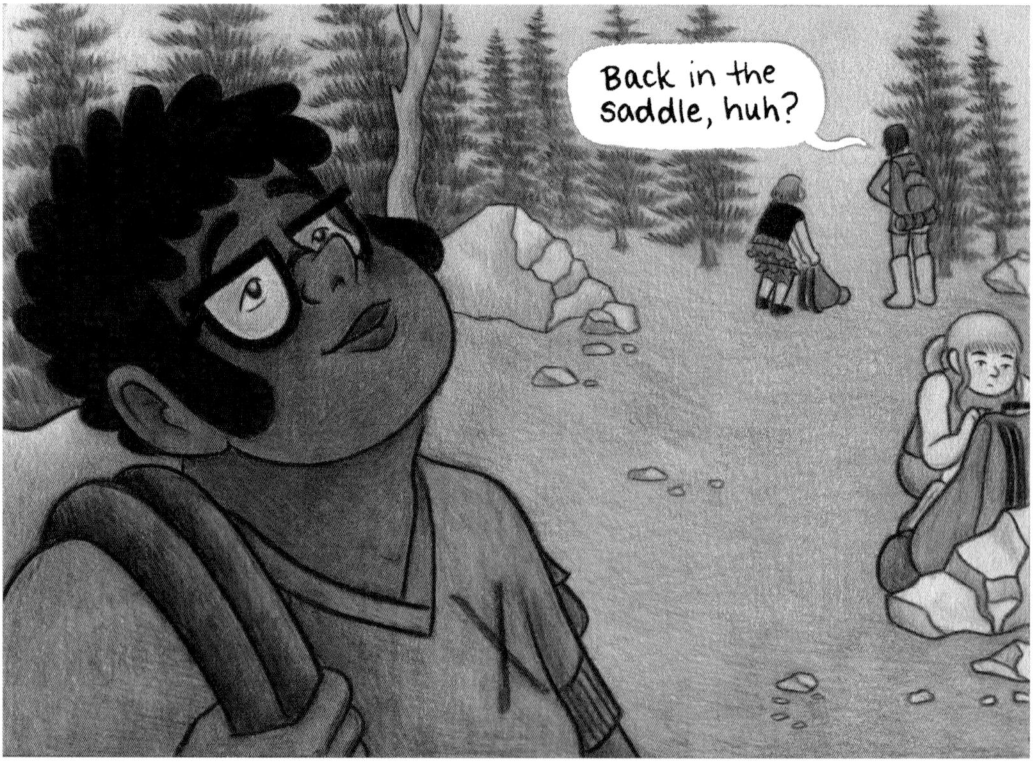
Back in the saddle, huh?

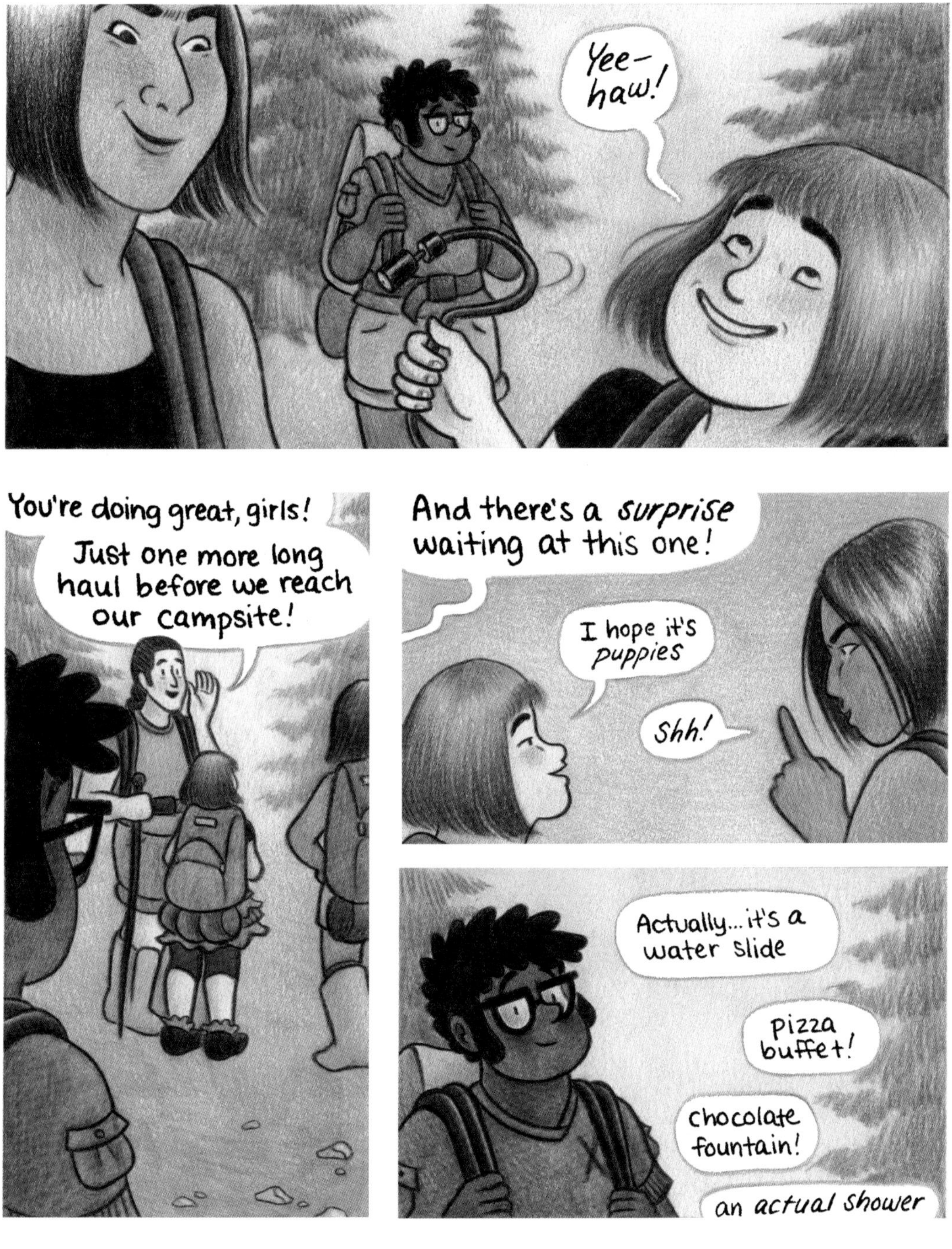
Yee-haw!
You're doing great, girls!
Just one more long haul before we reach our campsite!
And there's a *surprise* waiting at this one!
I hope it's *puppies*
Shh!
Actually... it's a water slide
pizza buffet!
chocolate fountain!
an *actual shower*

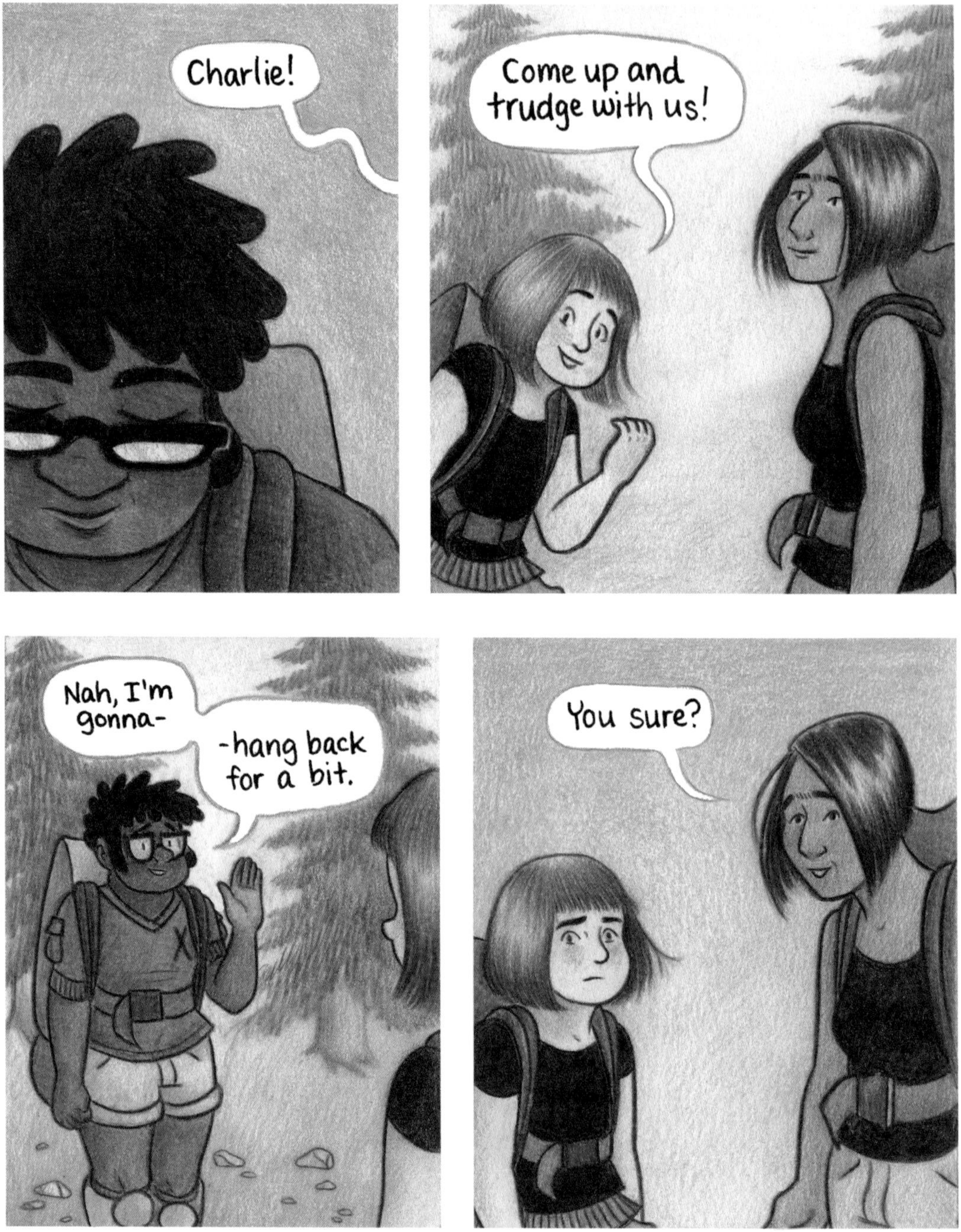
Charlie!
Come up and trudge with us!
Nah, I'm gonna-
-hang back for a bit.
You sure?

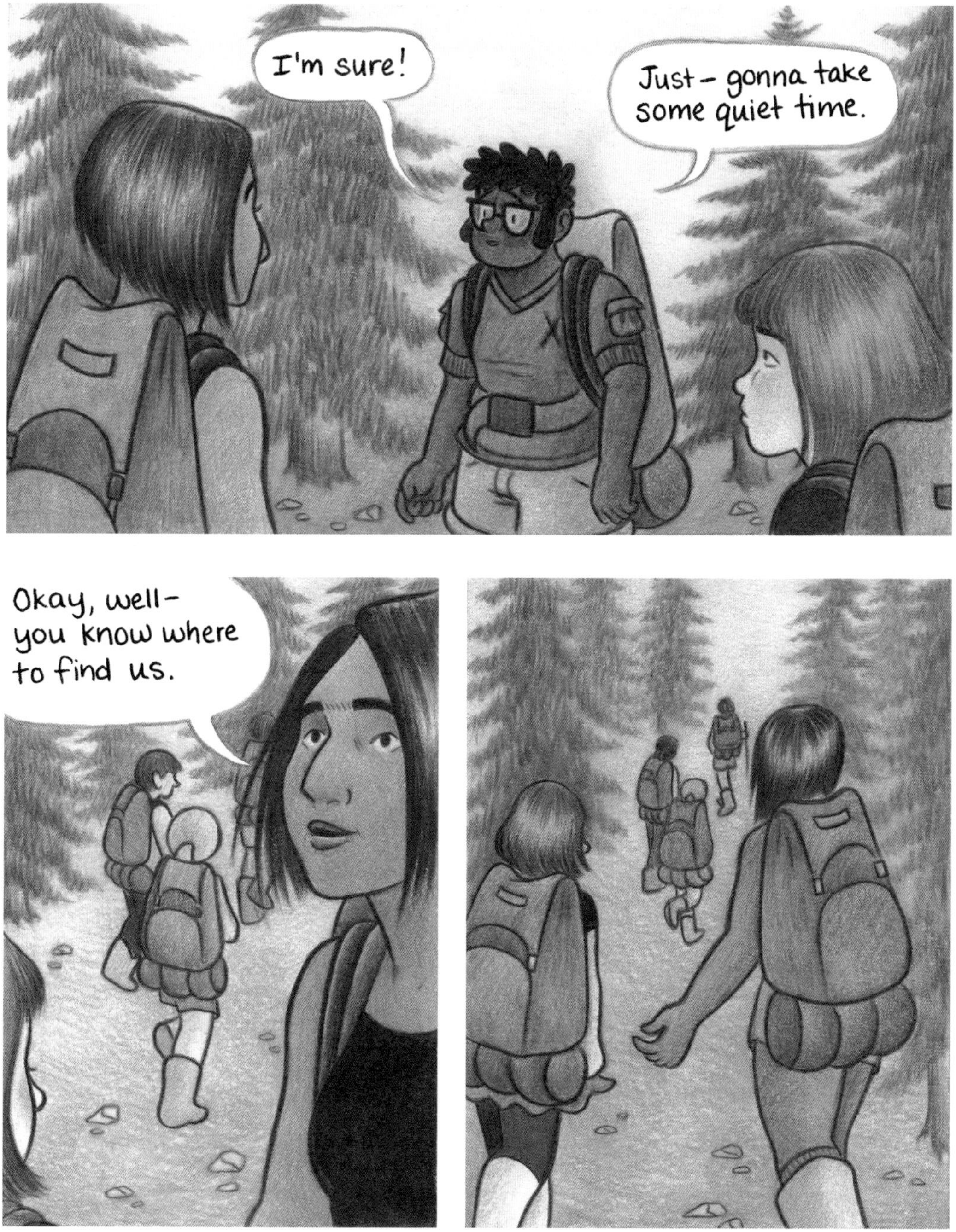
I'm sure!
Just- gonna take some quiet time.
Okay, well- you know where to find us.

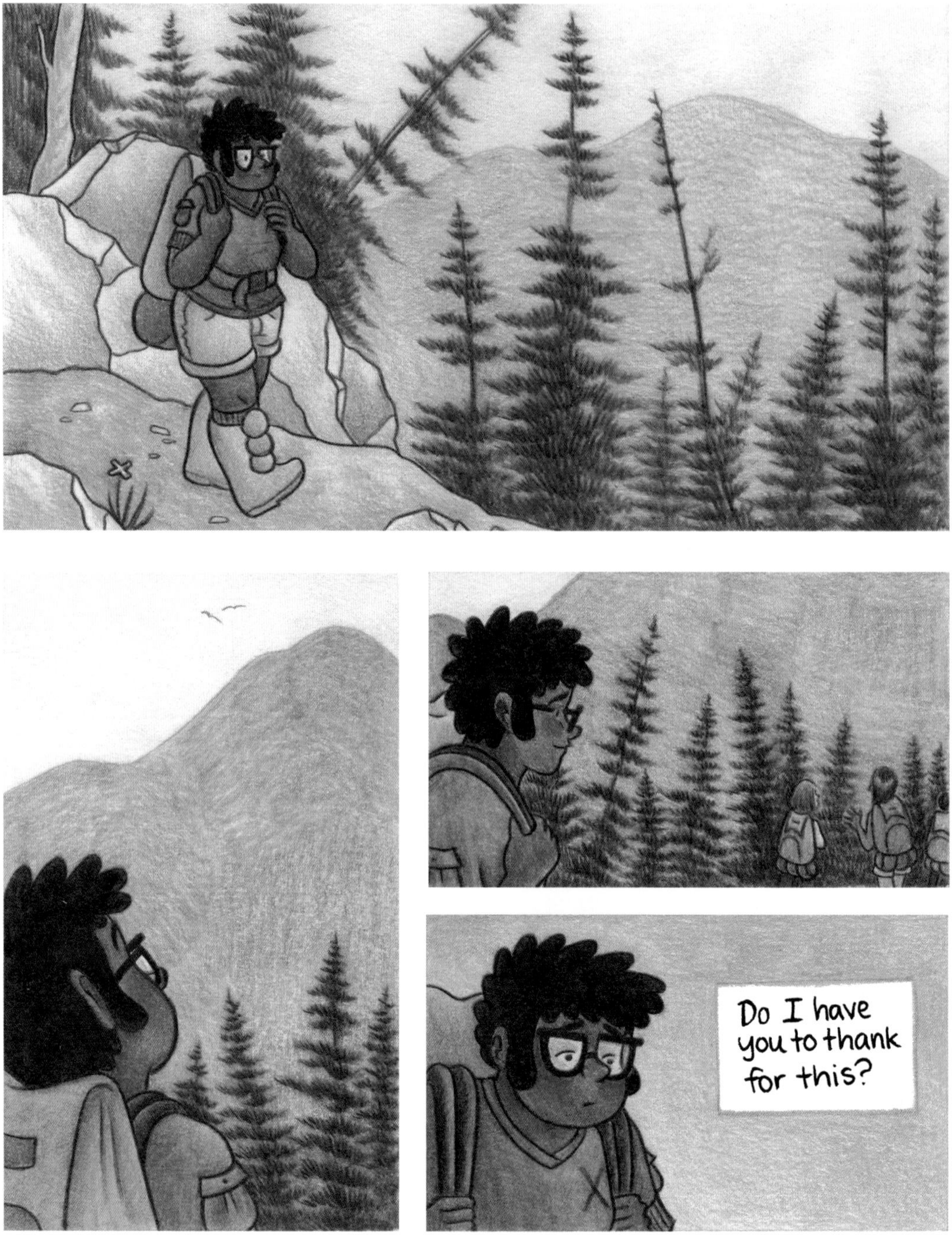
Do I have you to thank for this?

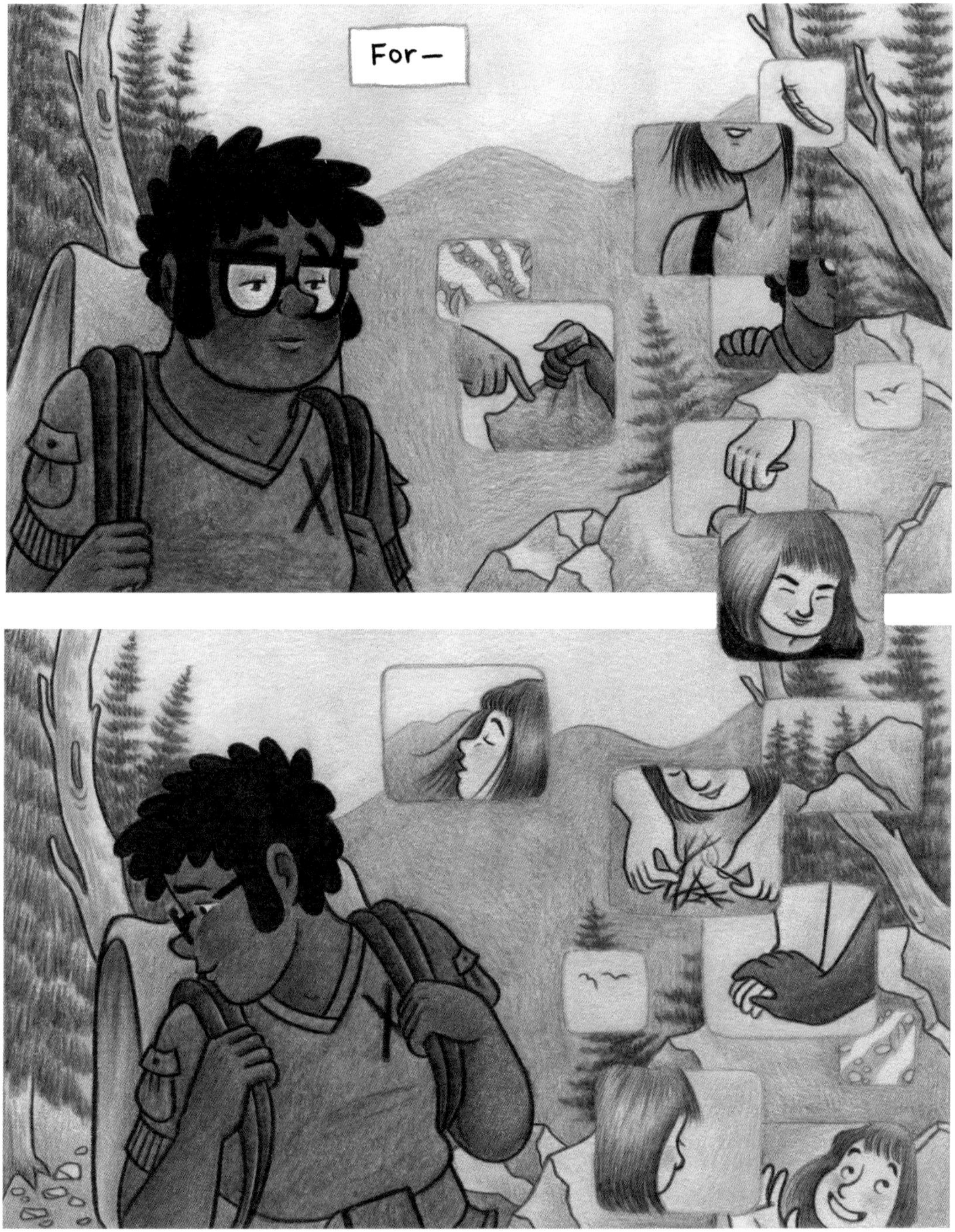
For—

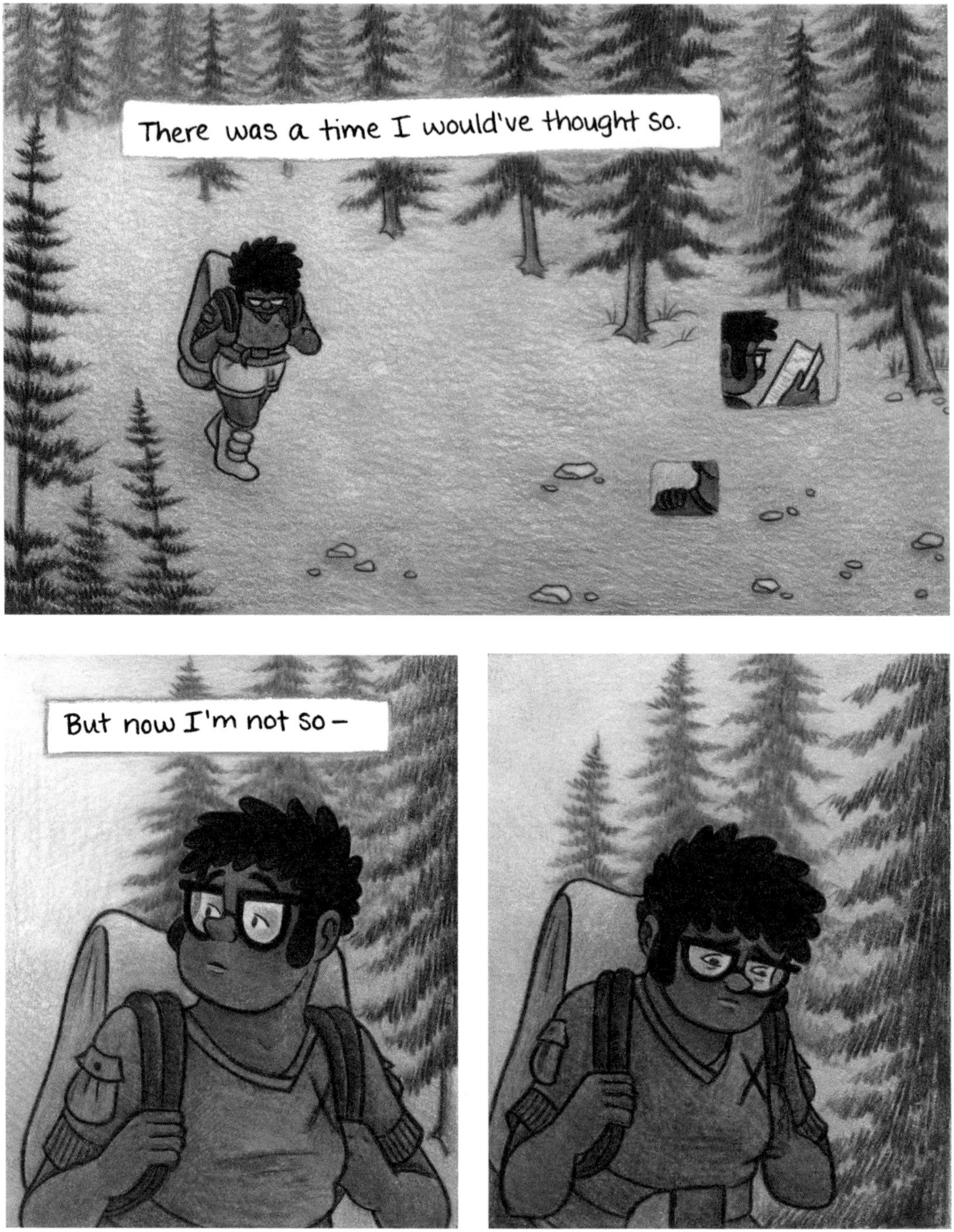
There was a time I would've thought so.
But now I'm not so—

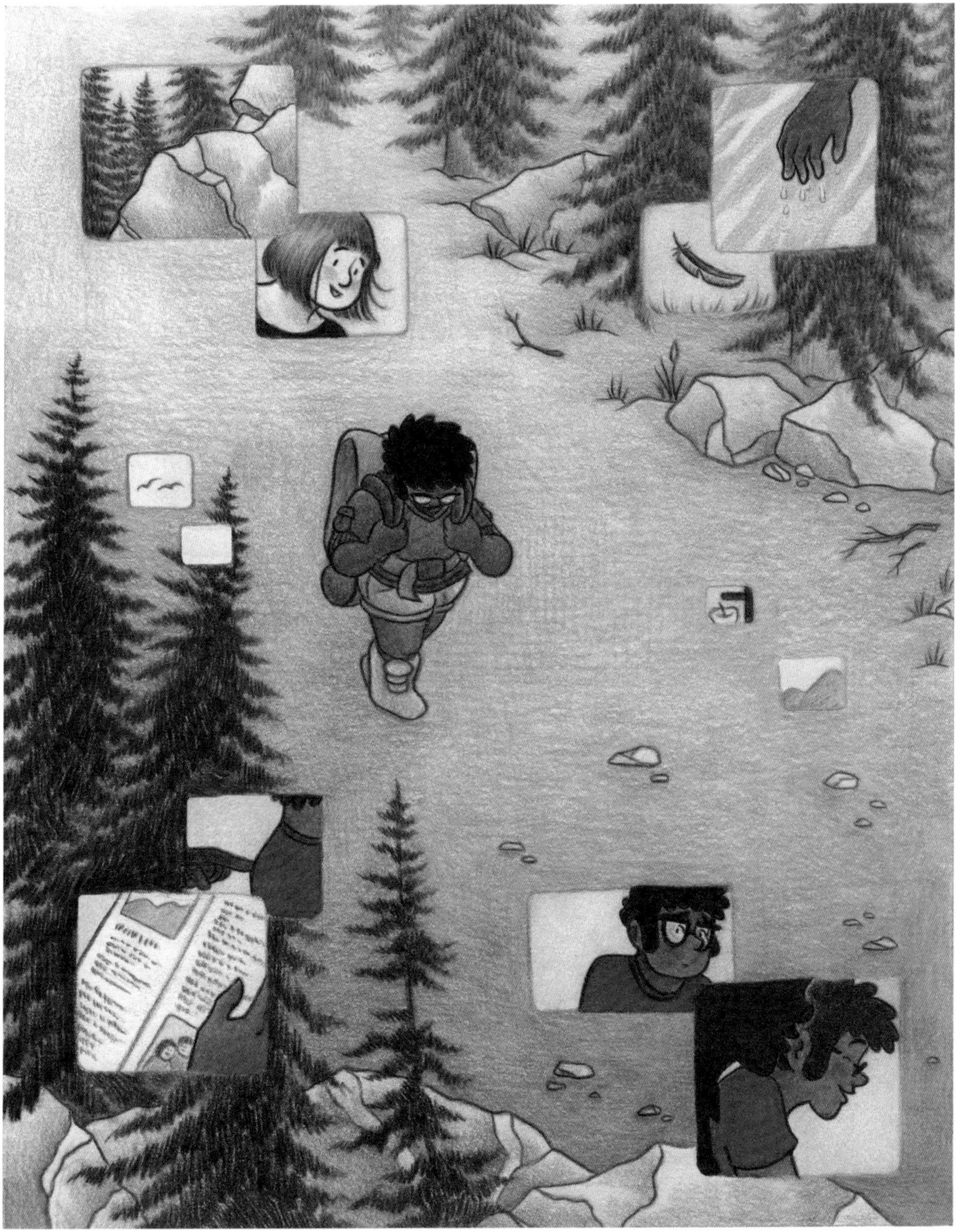

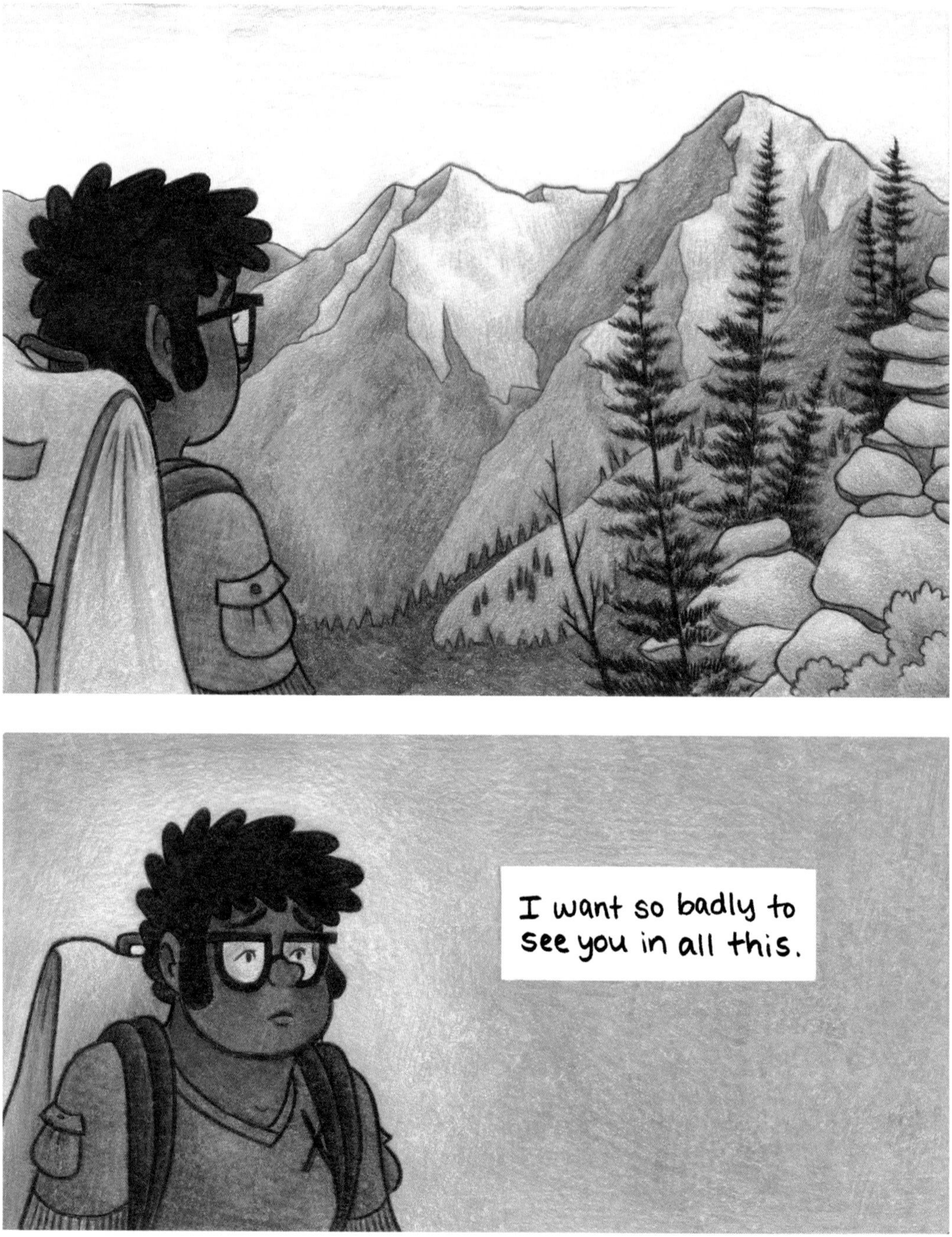
I want so badly to see you in all this.

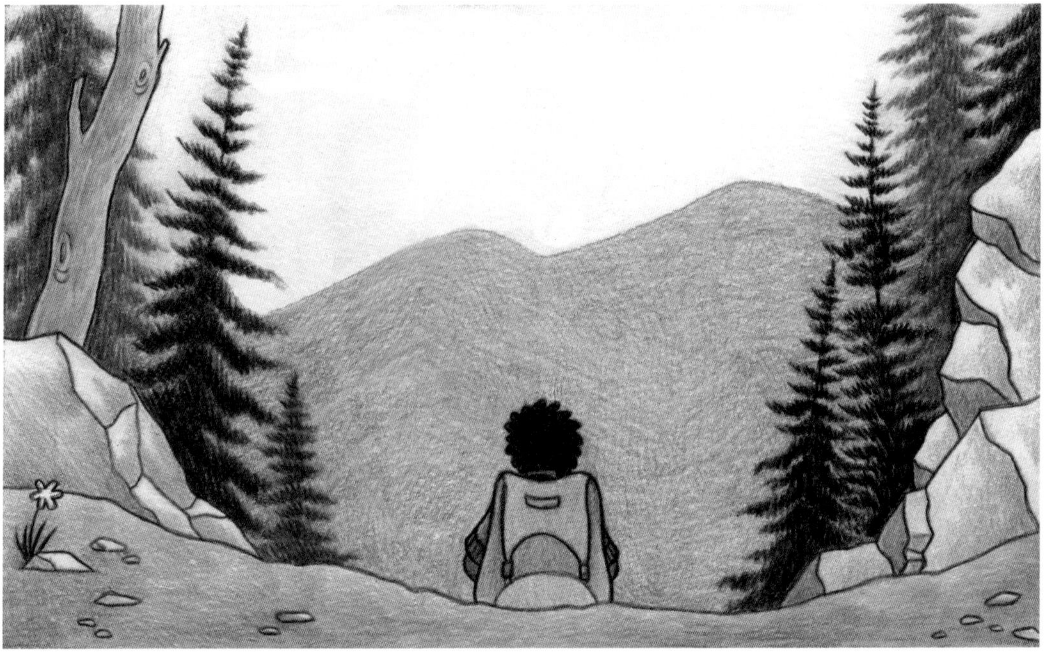

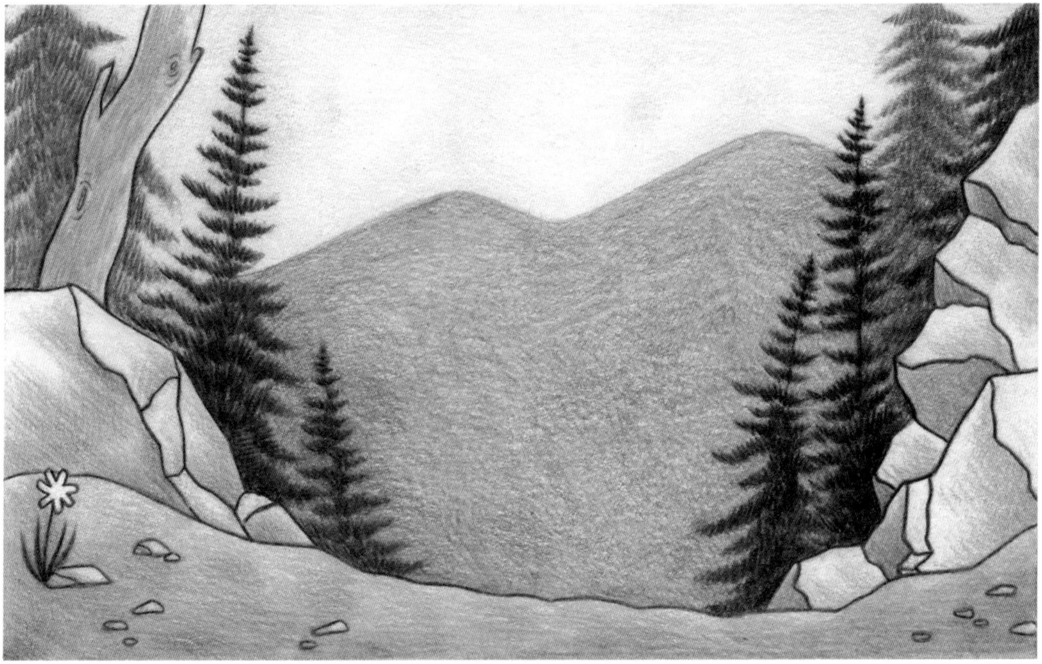

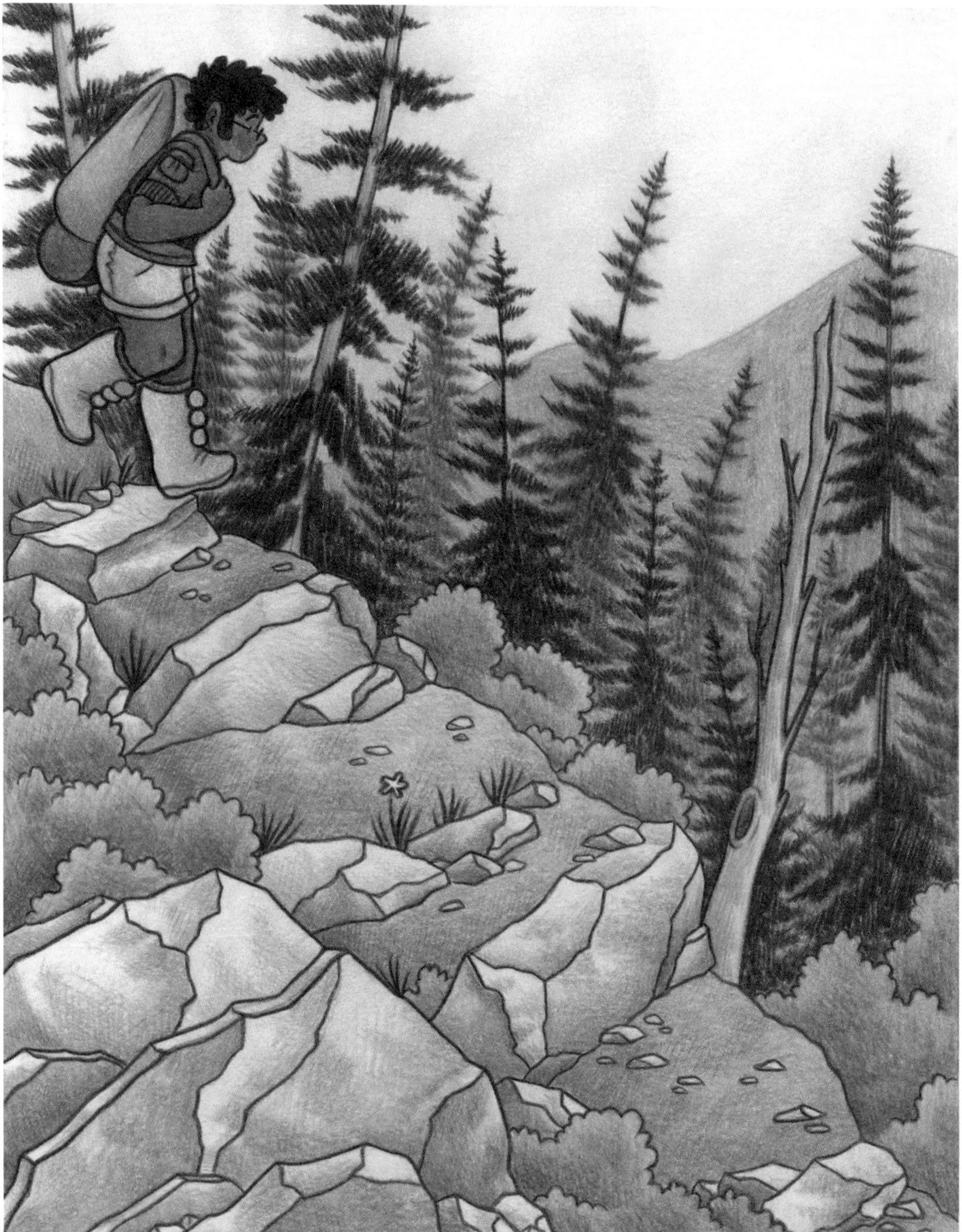

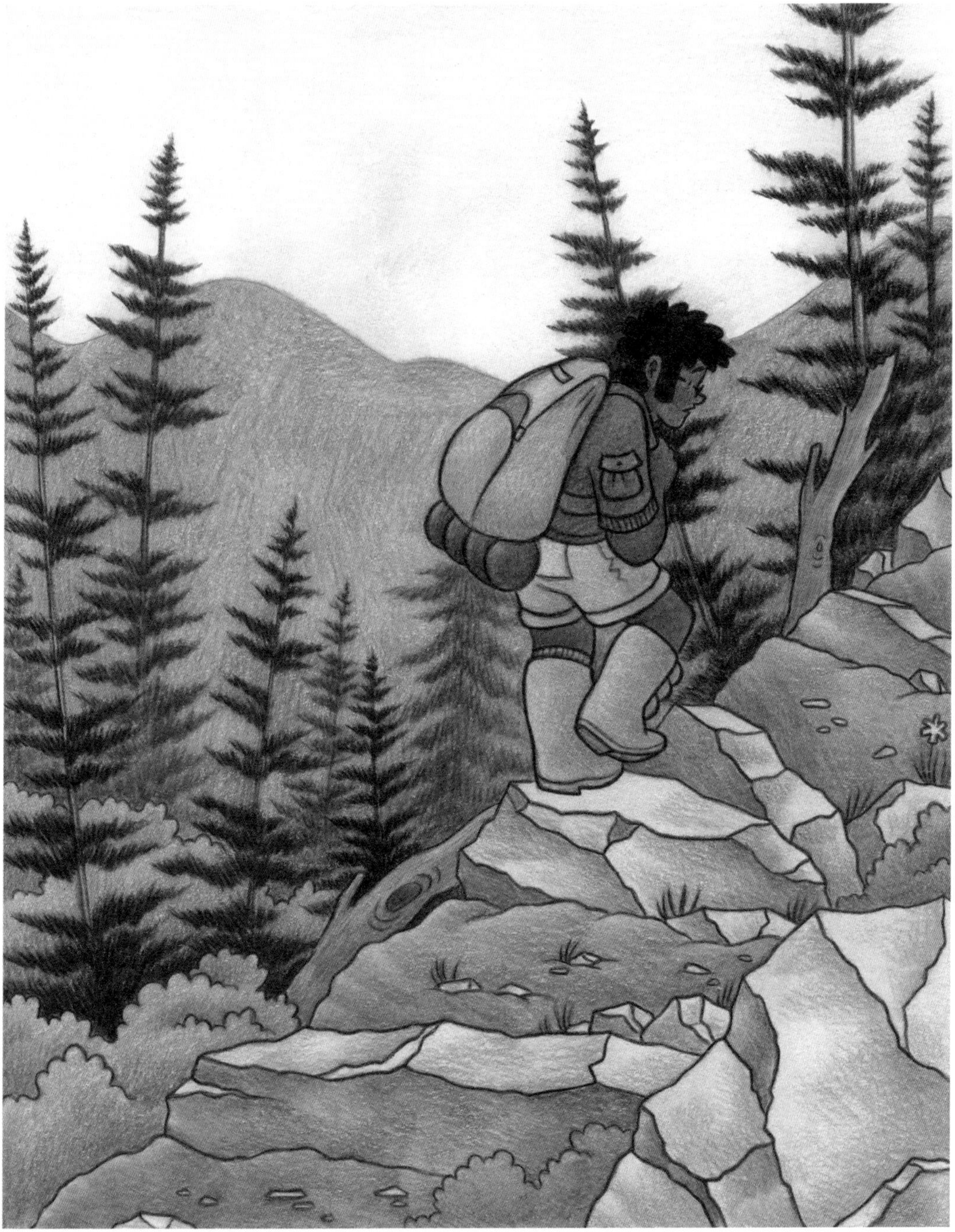

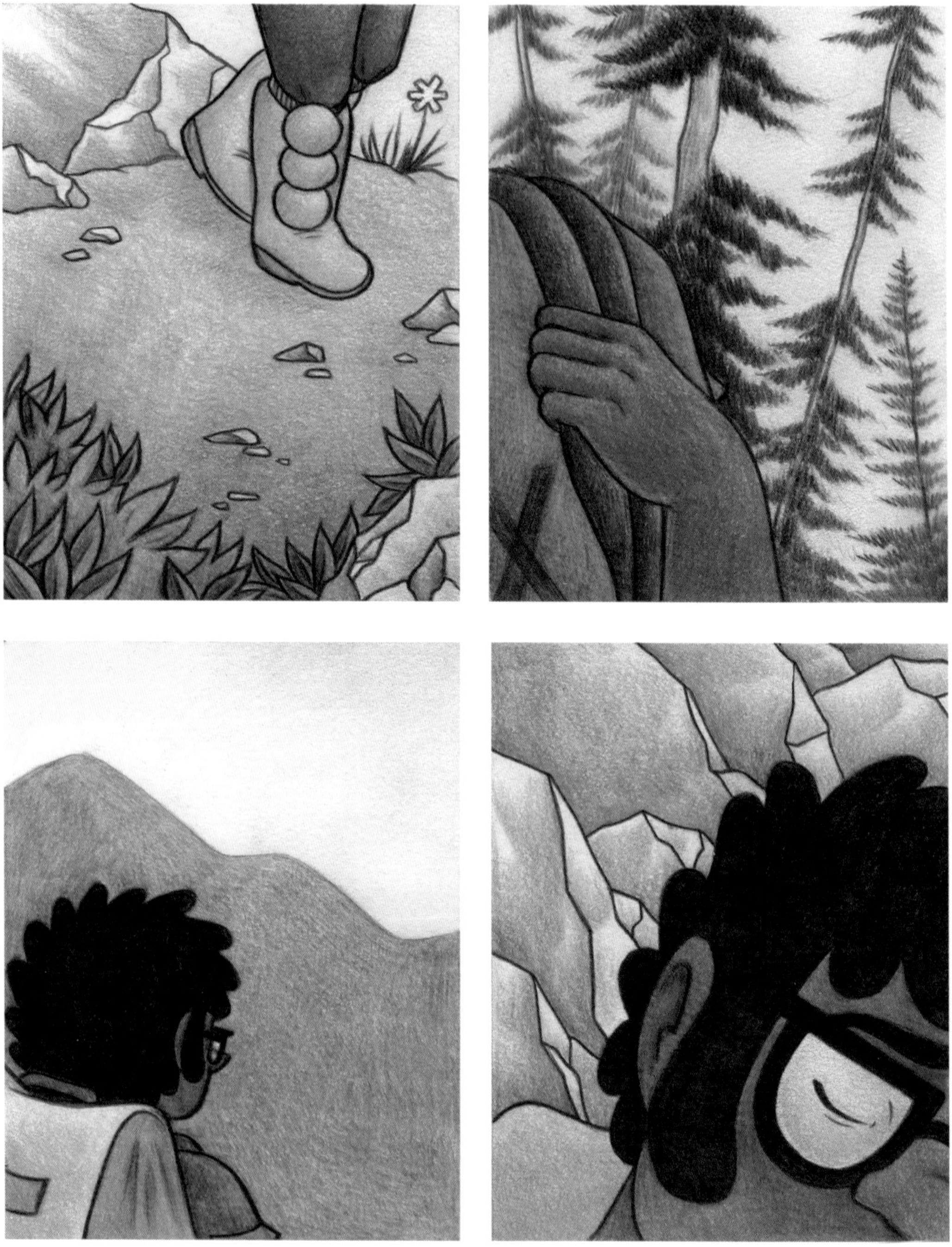

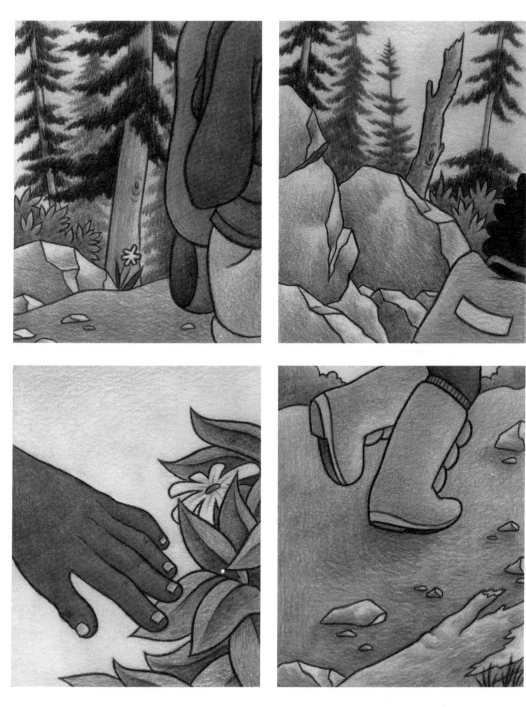

225

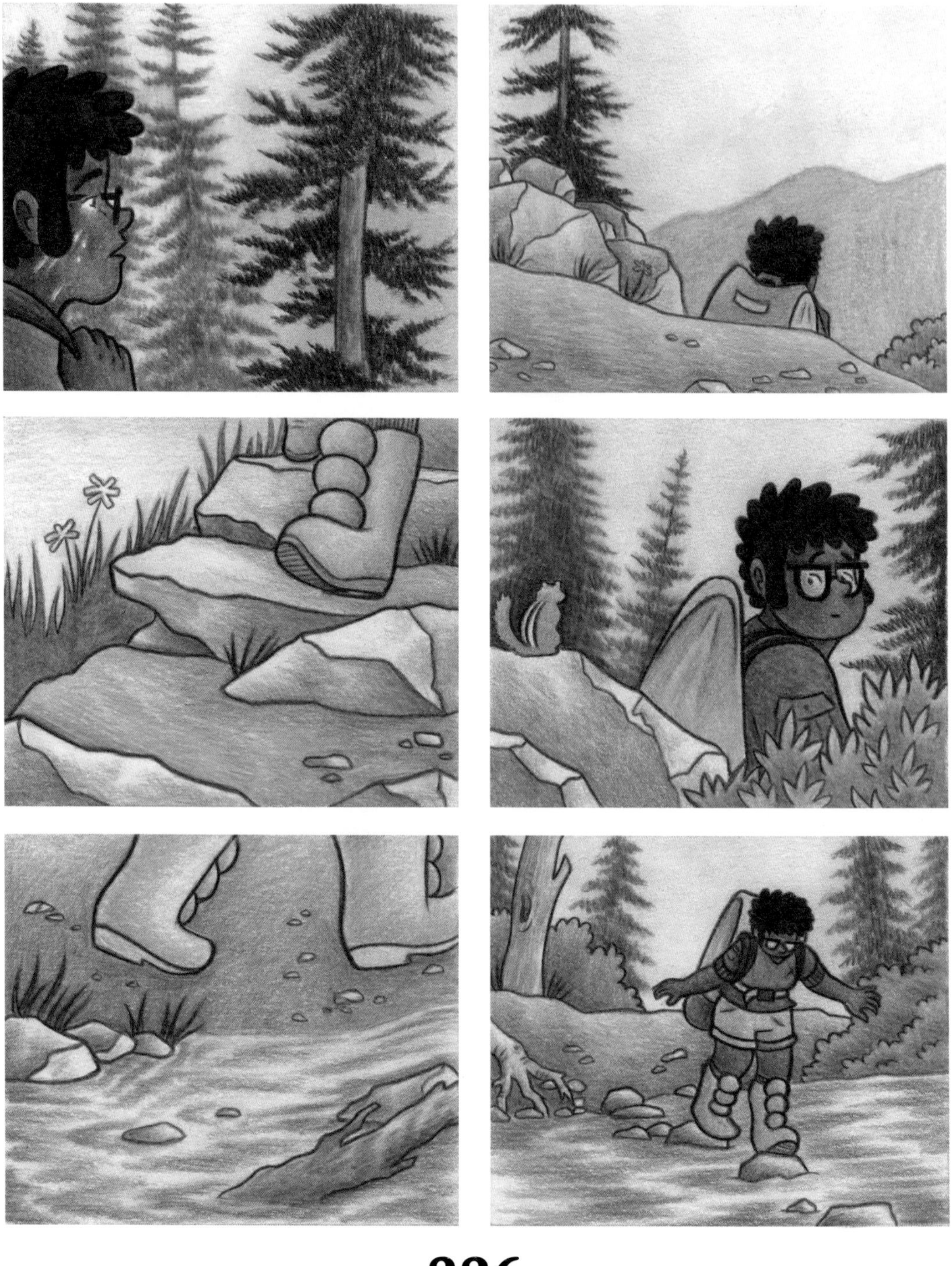

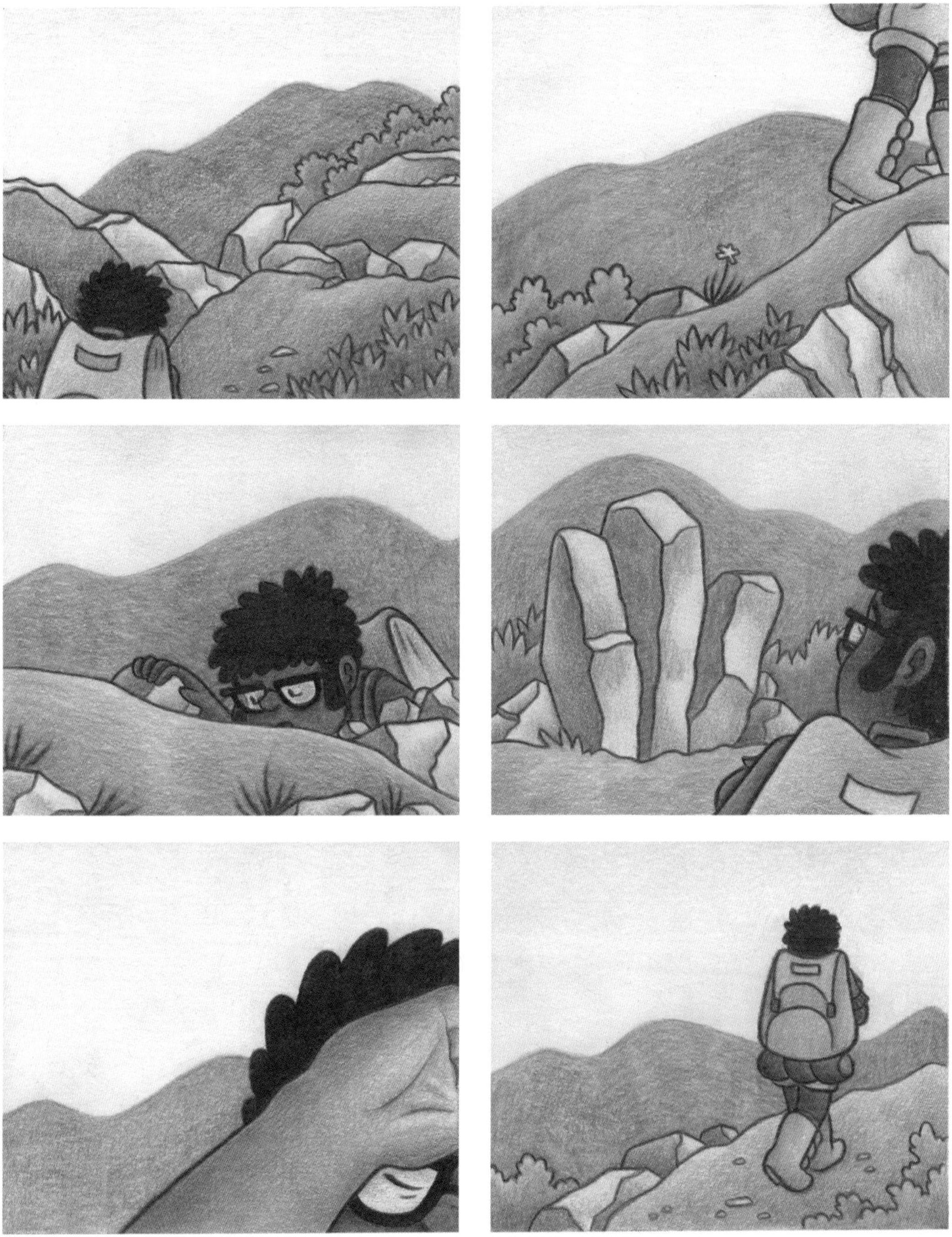

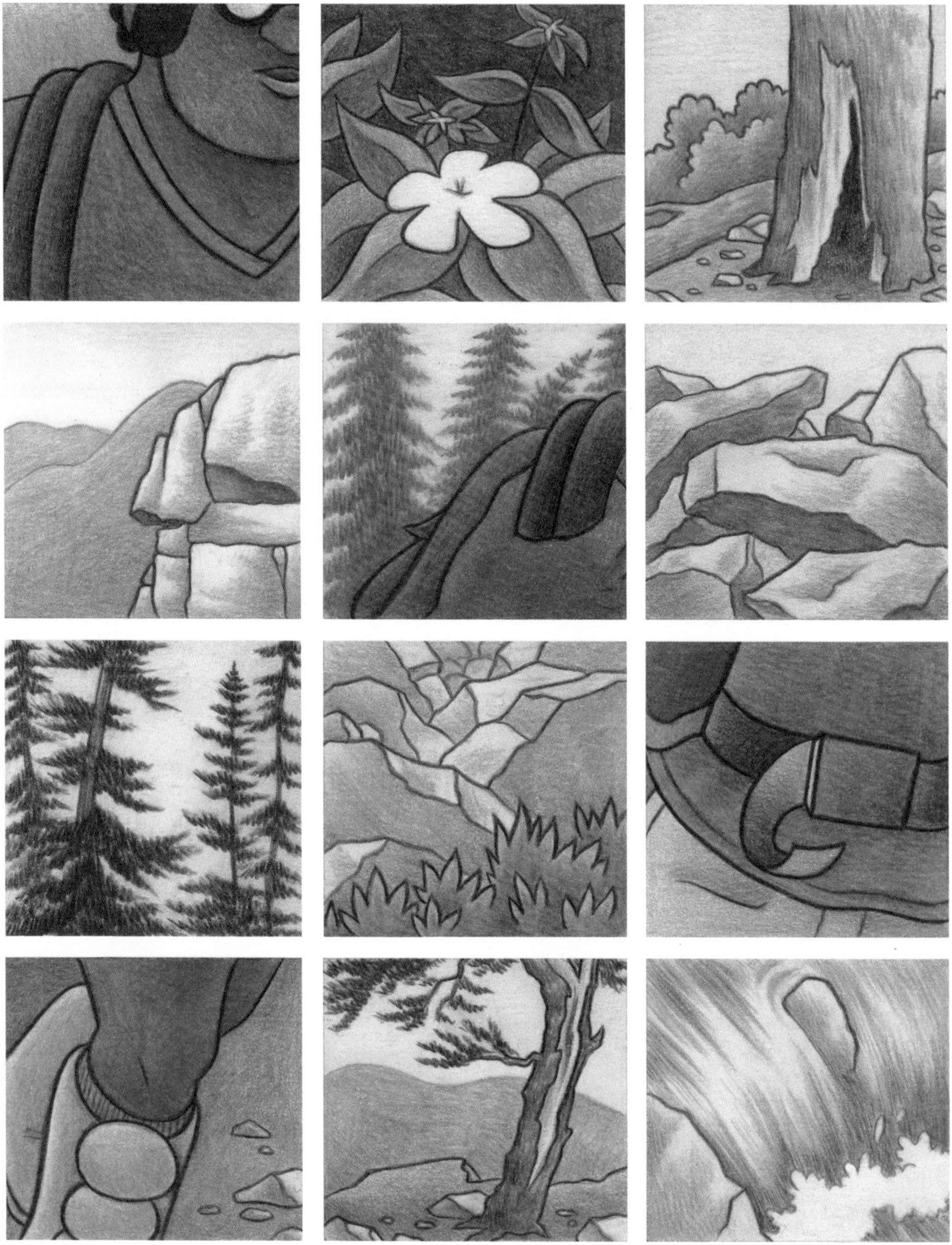

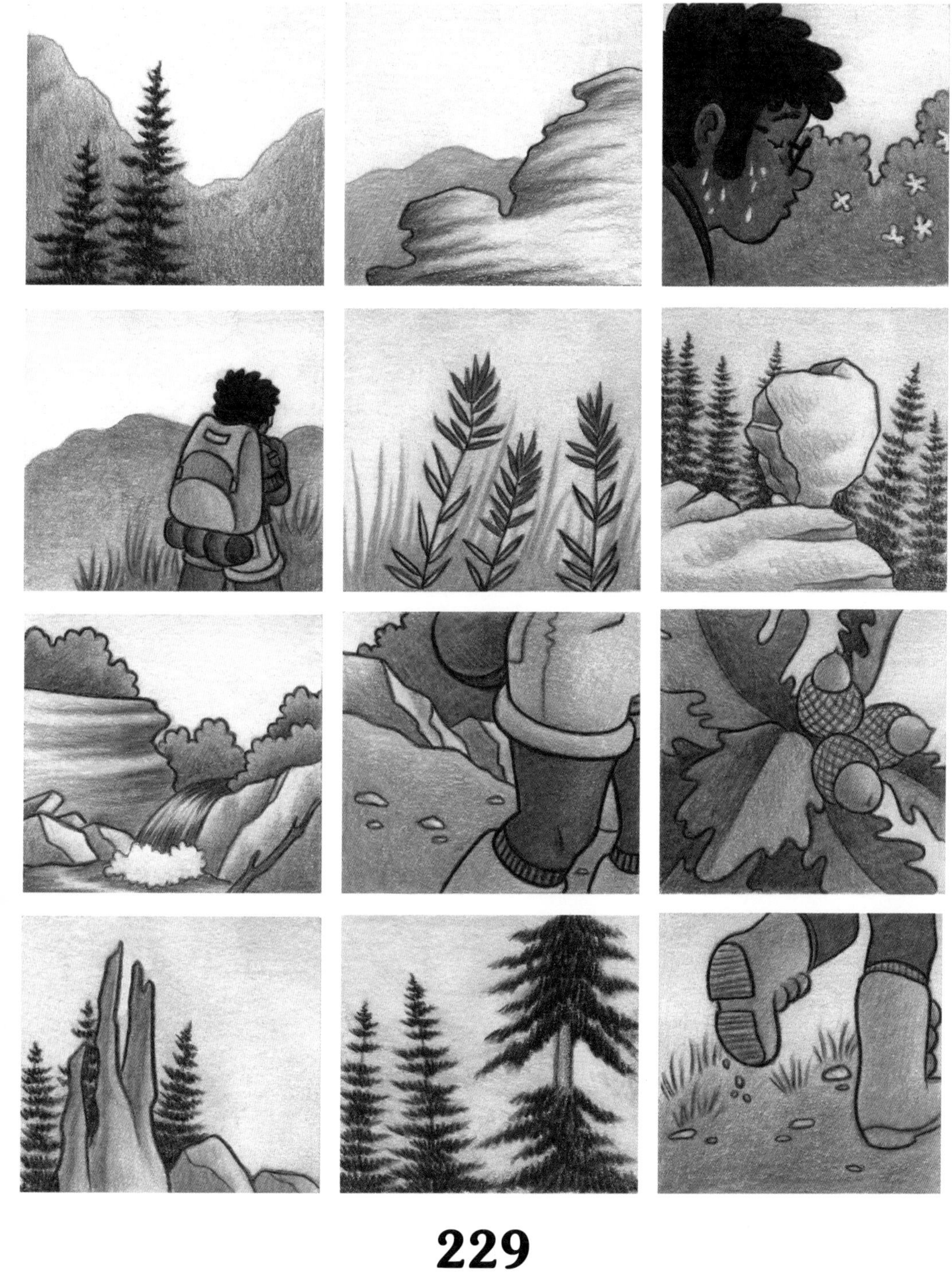

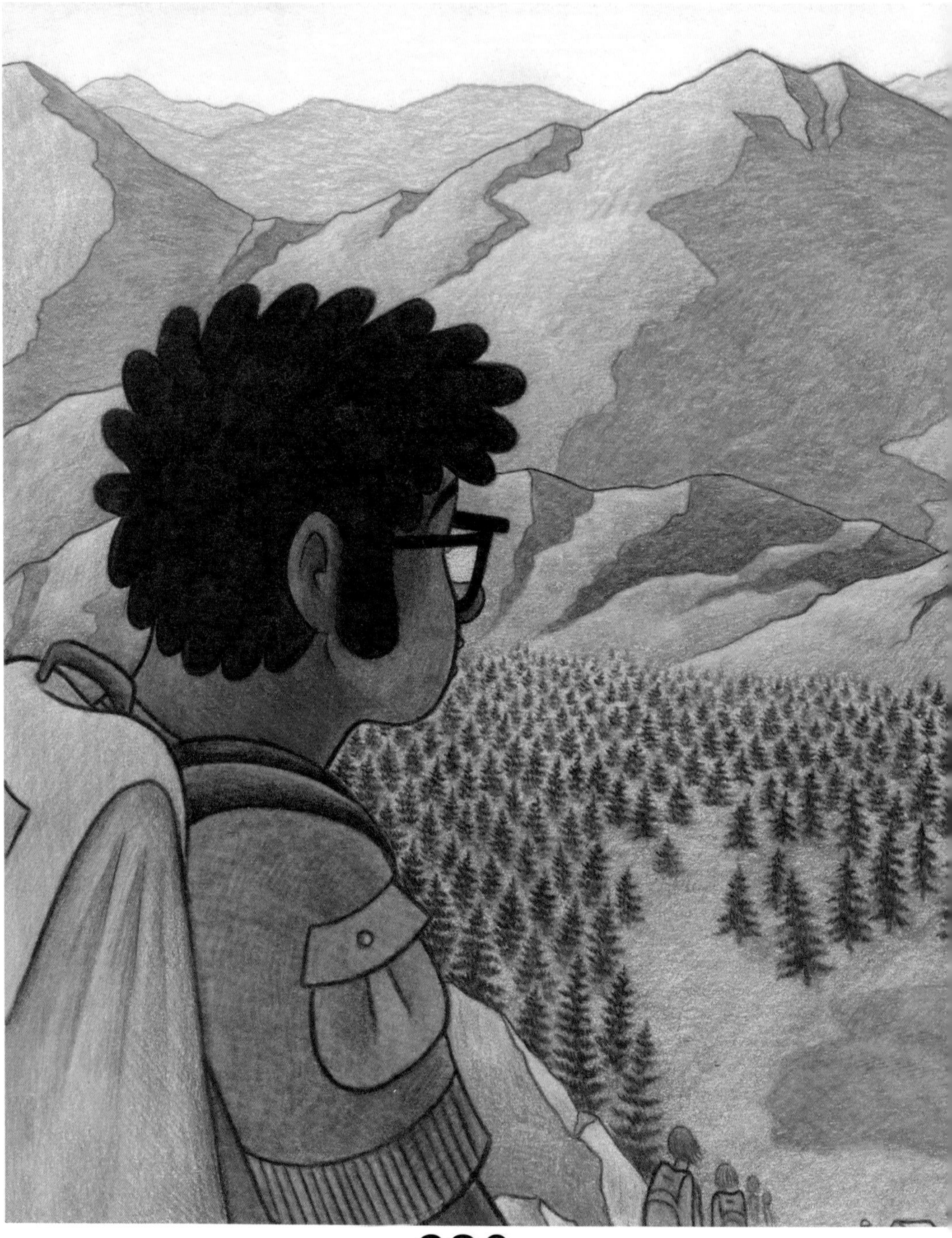

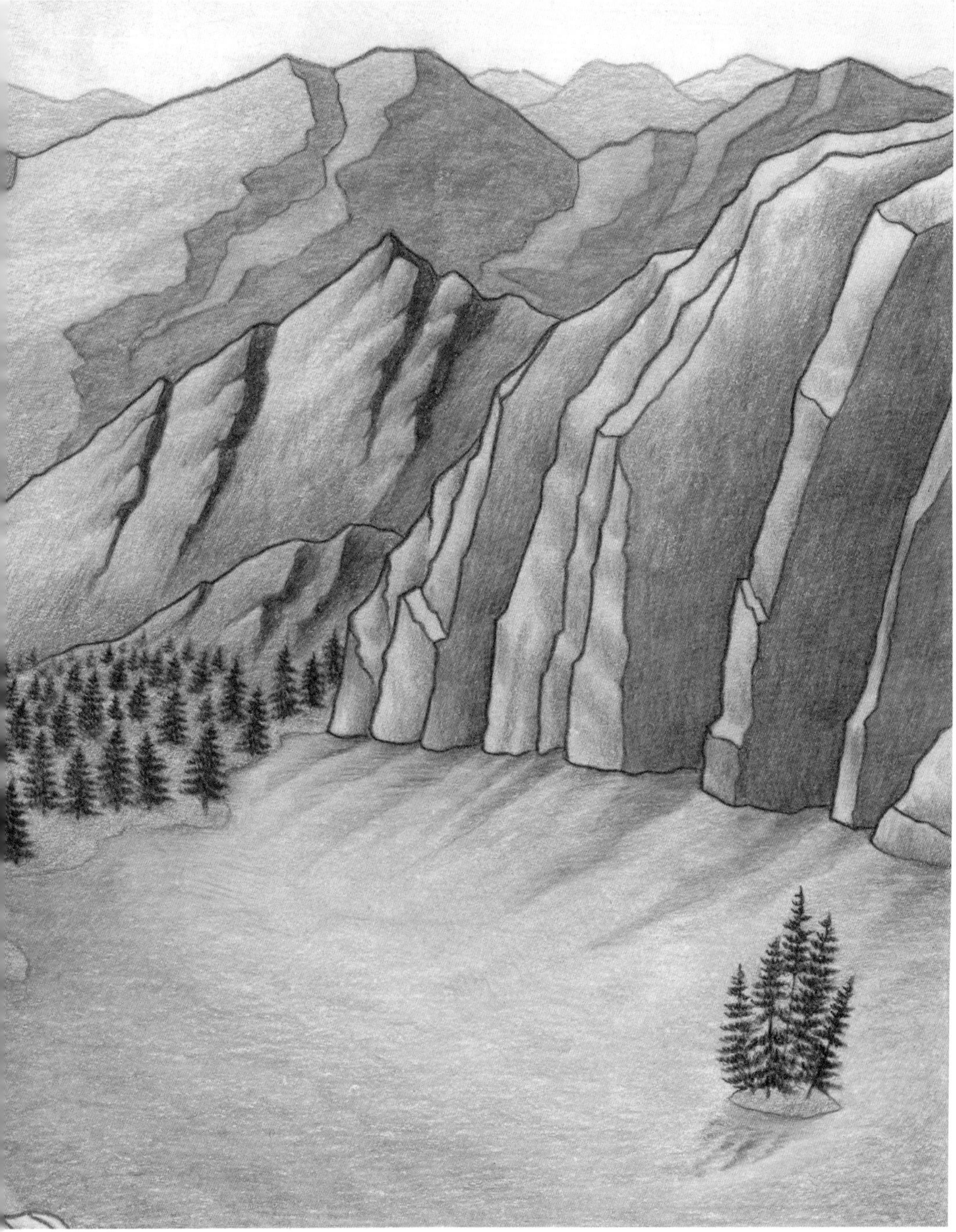

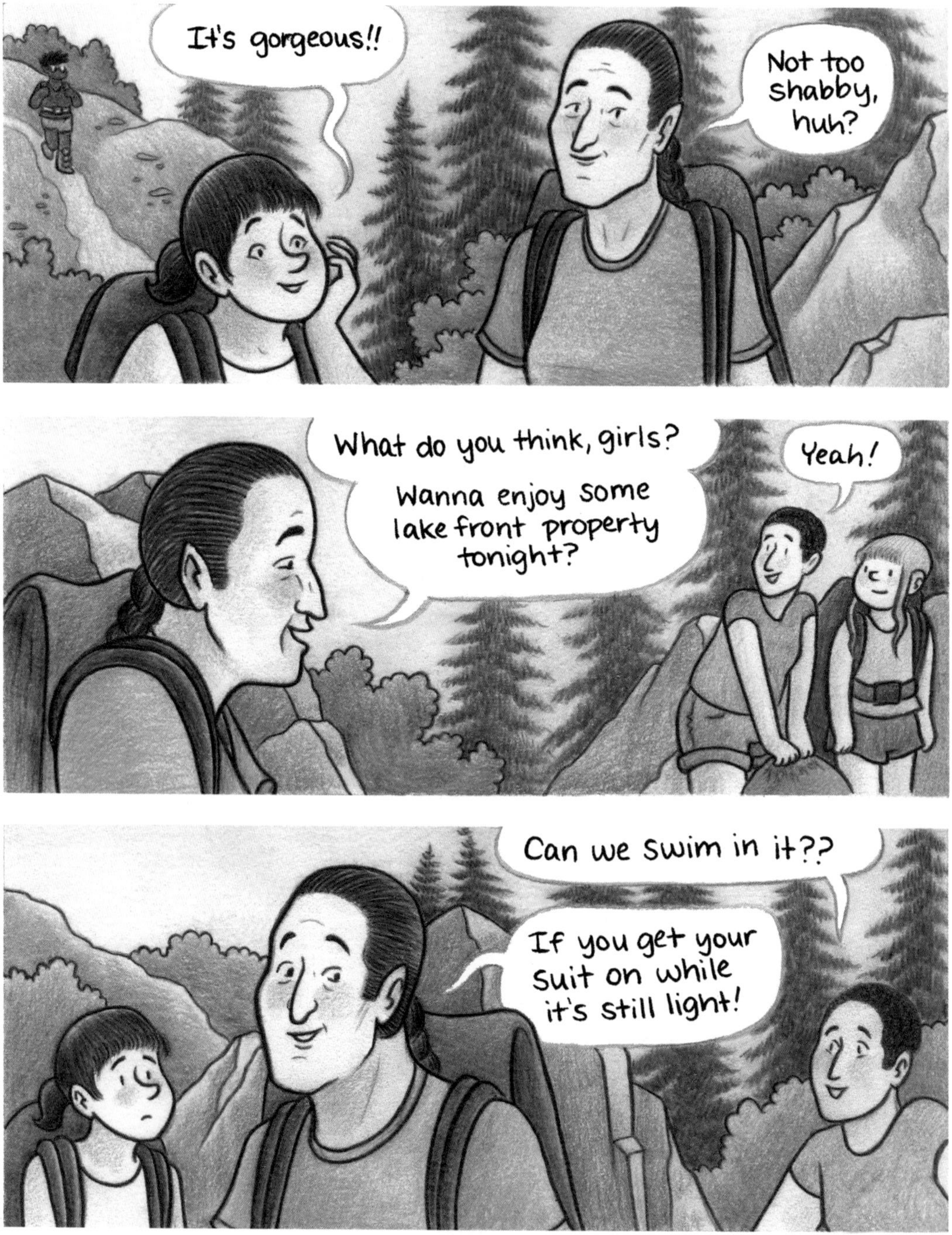
It's gorgeous!!
Not too shabby, huh?
What do you think, girls?
Wanna enjoy some lake front property tonight?
Yeah!
Can we swim in it??
If you get your suit on while it's still light!

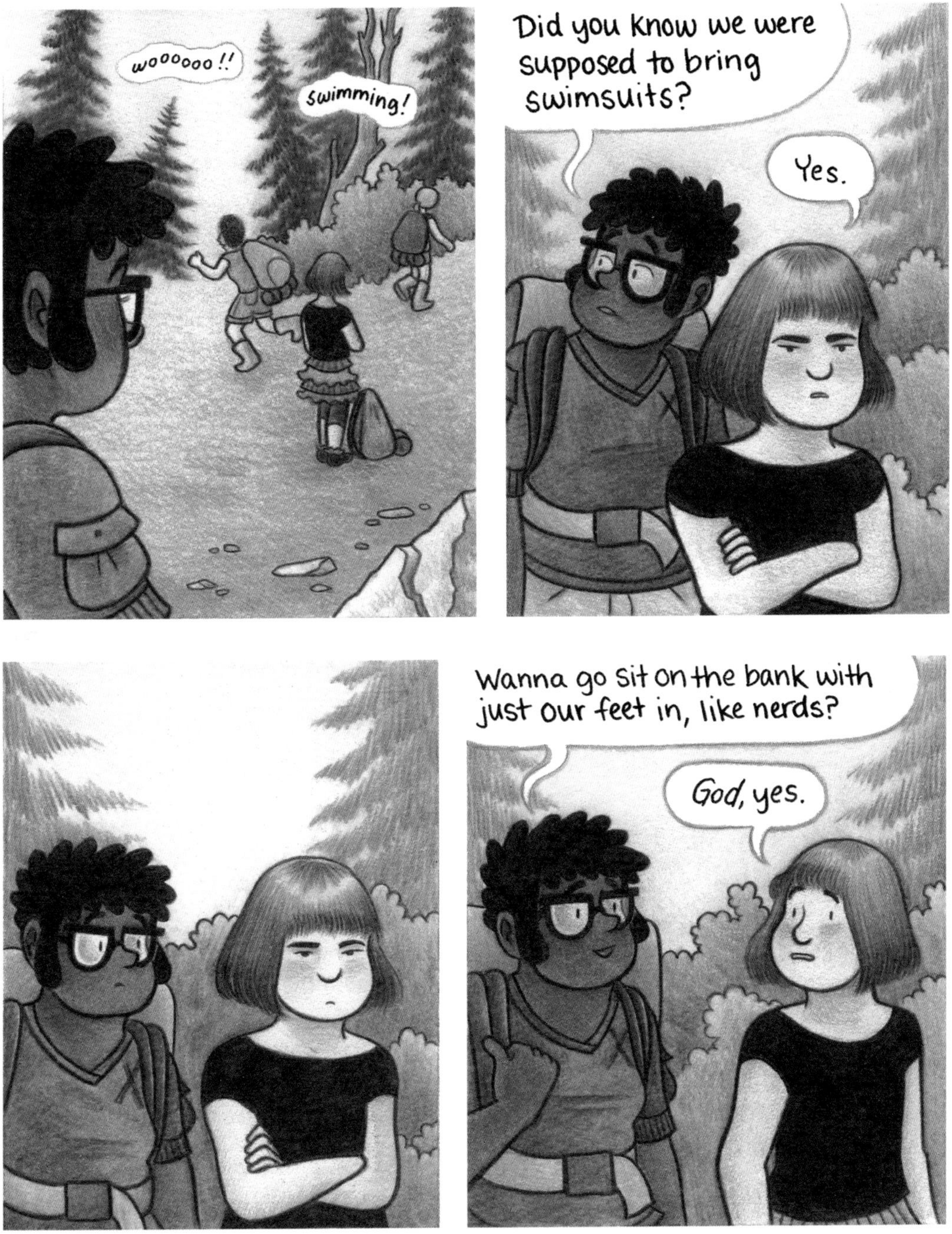
wooooo!!
swimming!
Did you know we were supposed to bring swimsuits?
Yes.
Wanna go sit on the bank with just our feet in, like nerds?
God, yes.

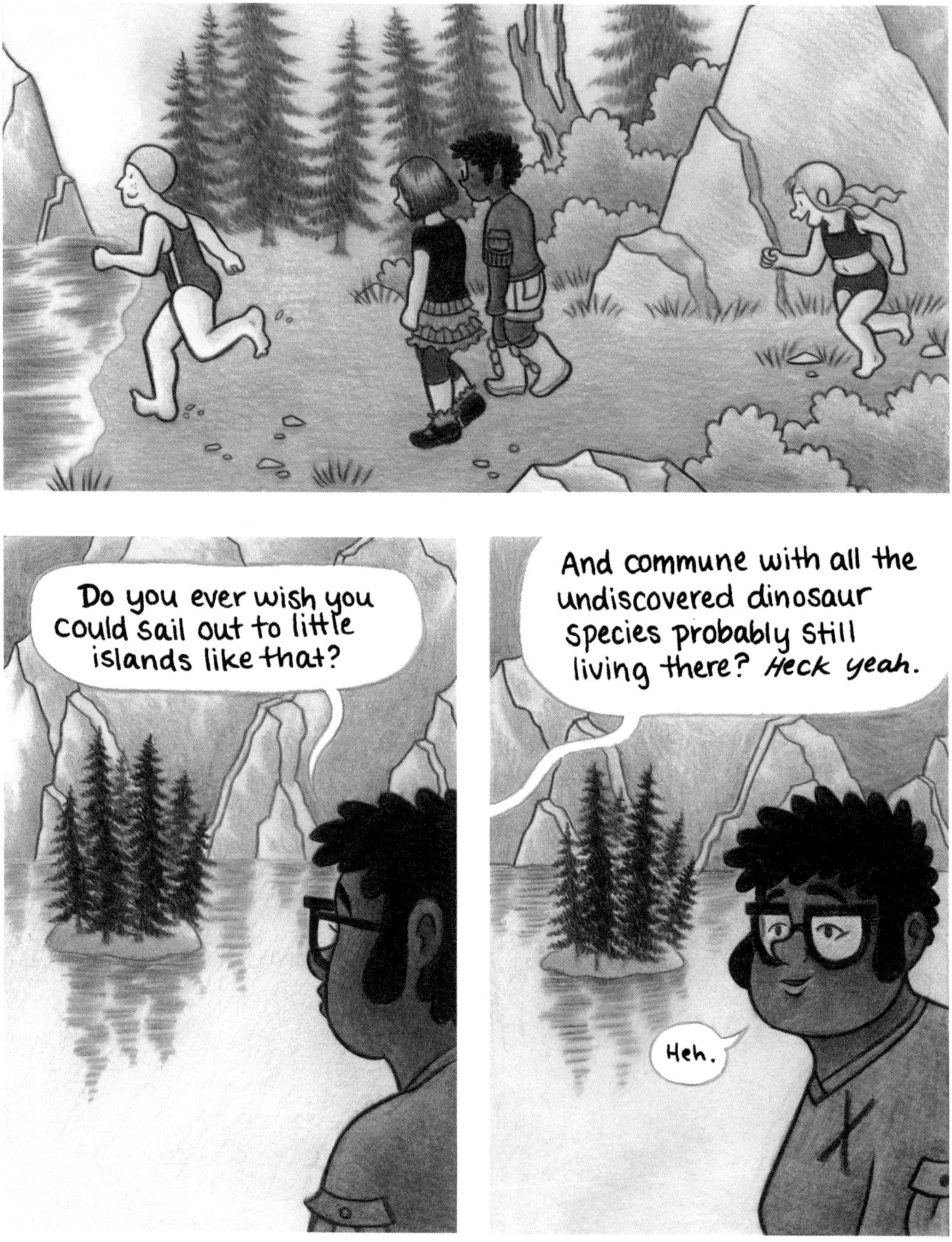
Do you ever wish you could sail out to little islands like that?
And commune with all the undiscovered dinosaur species probably still living there? *Heck yeah.*
Heh.

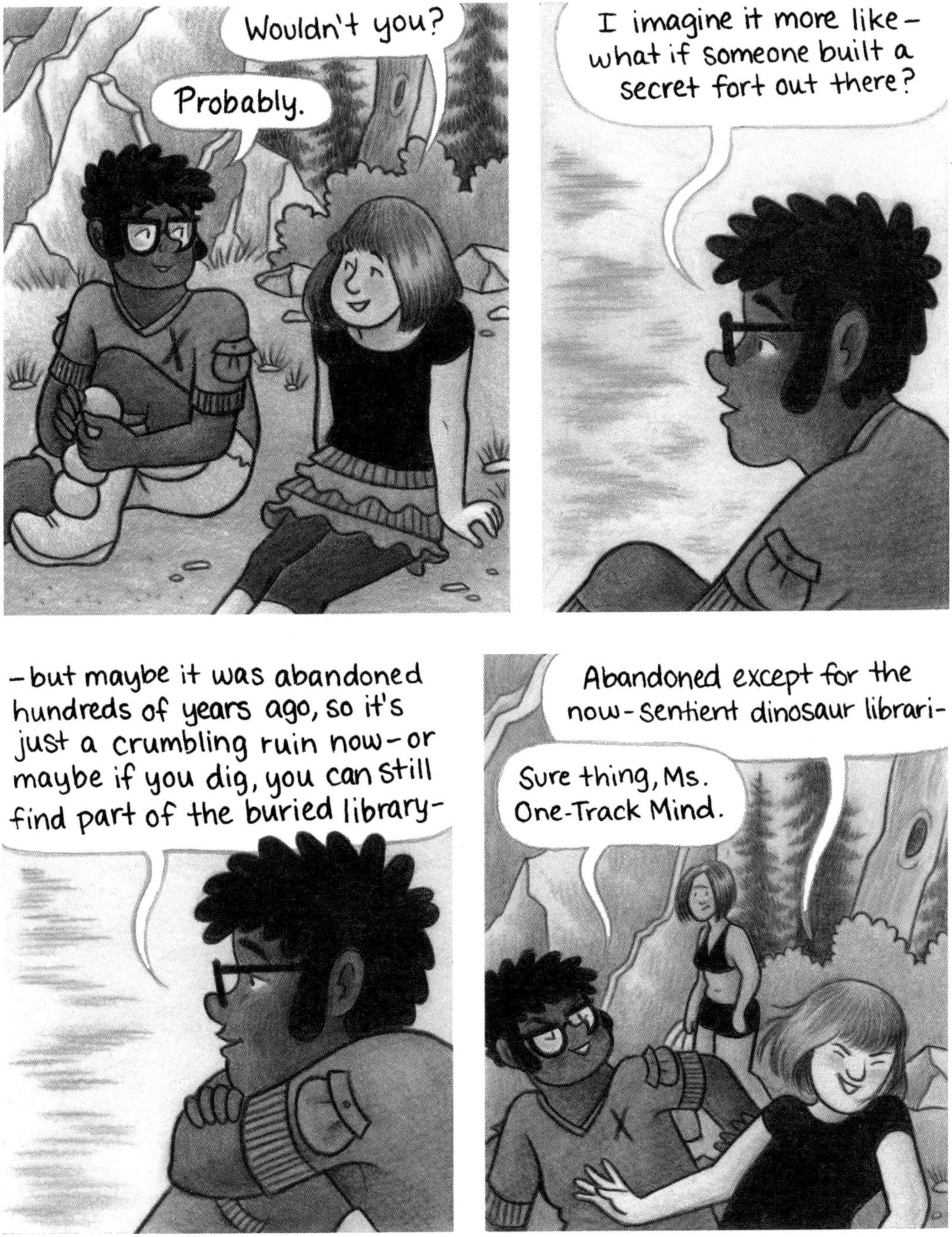
Wouldn't you?
Probably.
I imagine it more like—what if someone built a secret fort out there?
—but maybe it was abandoned hundreds of years ago, so it's just a crumbling ruin now—or maybe if you dig, you can still find part of the buried library—
Abandoned except for the now-sentient dinosaur librari-
Sure thing, Ms. One-Track Mind.

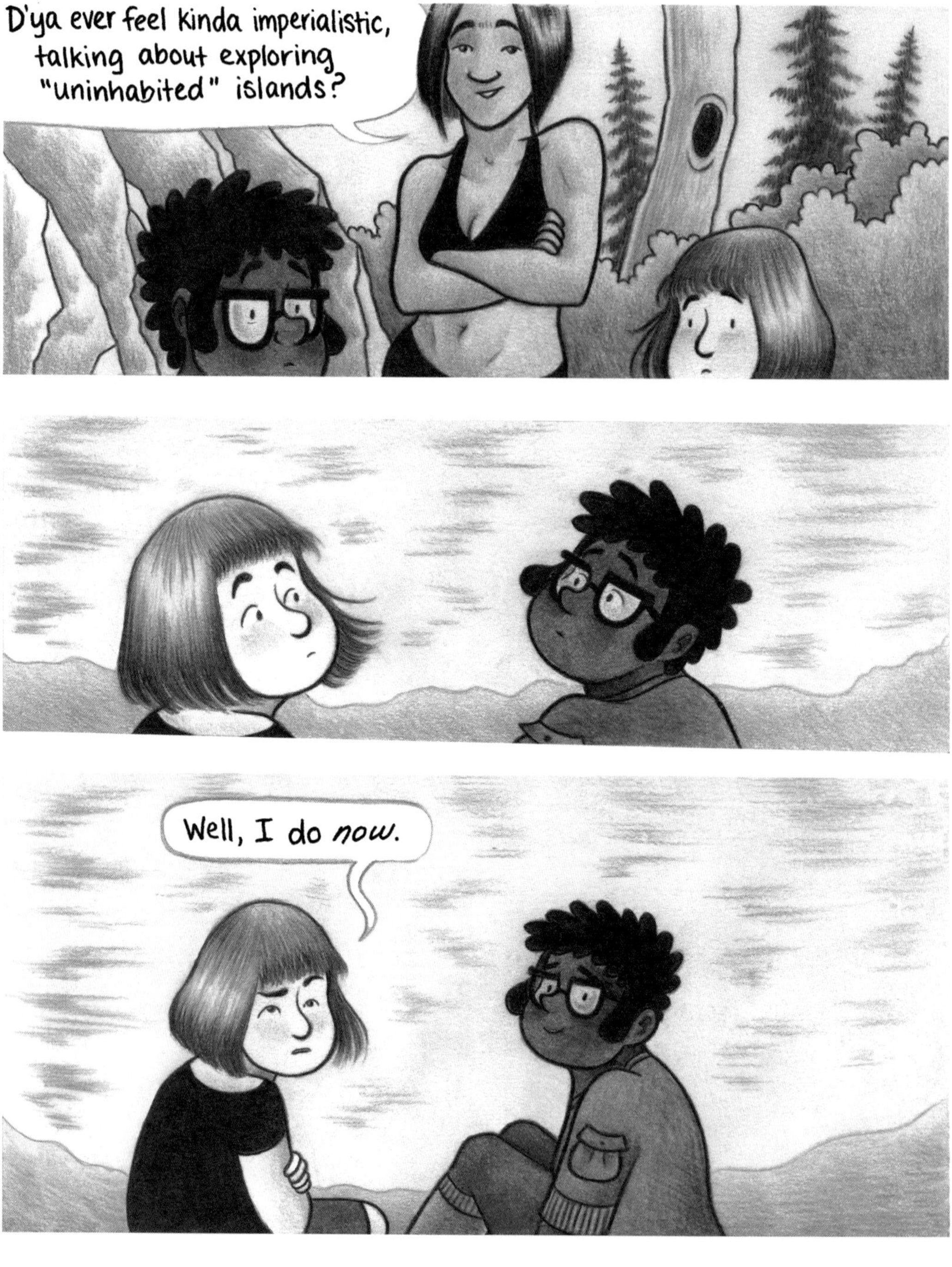
D'ya ever feel kinda imperialistic, talking about exploring "uninhabited" islands?
Well, I do *now*.

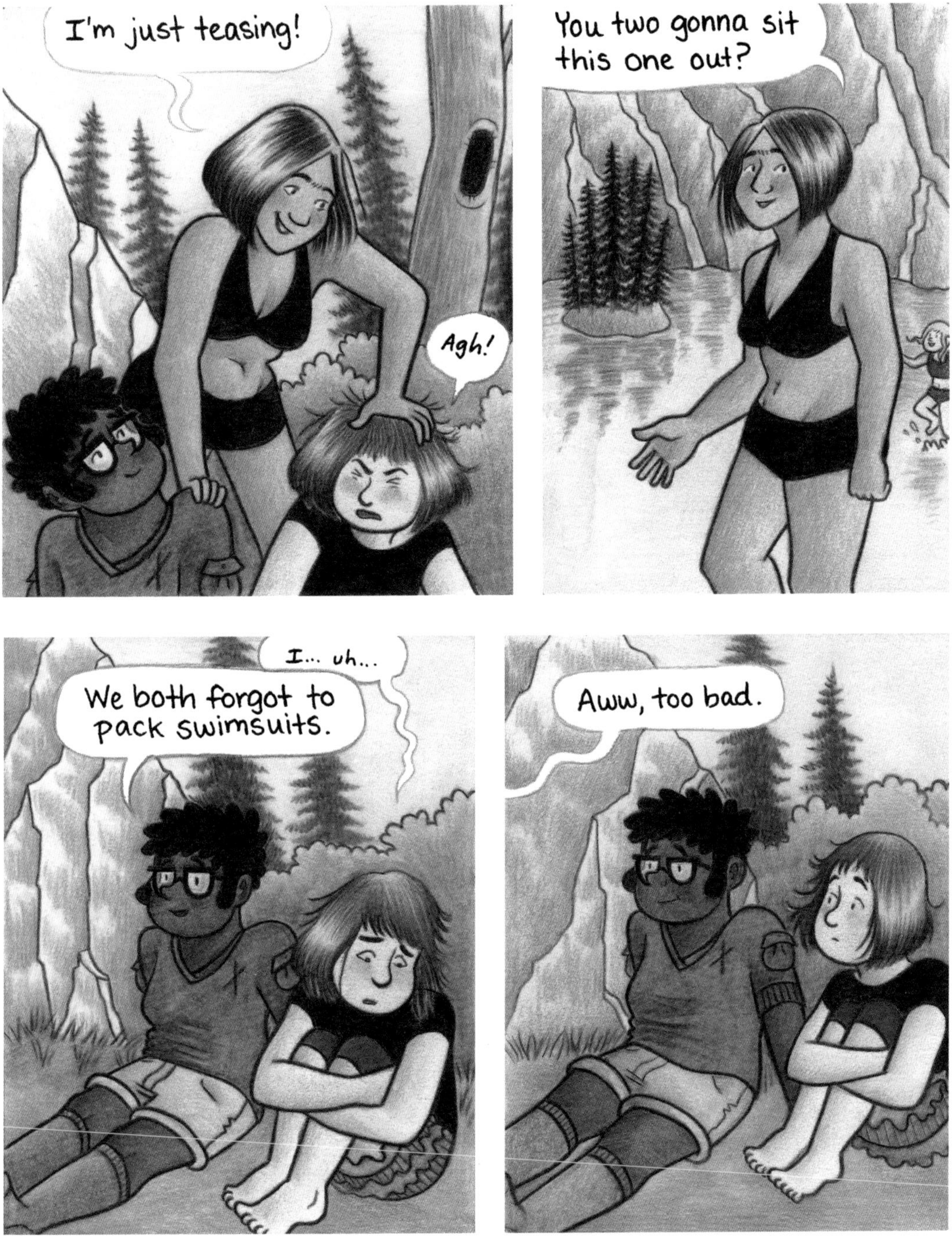
I'm just teasing!
Agh!
You two gonna sit this one out?
I... uh...
We both forgot to pack swimsuits.
Aww, too bad.

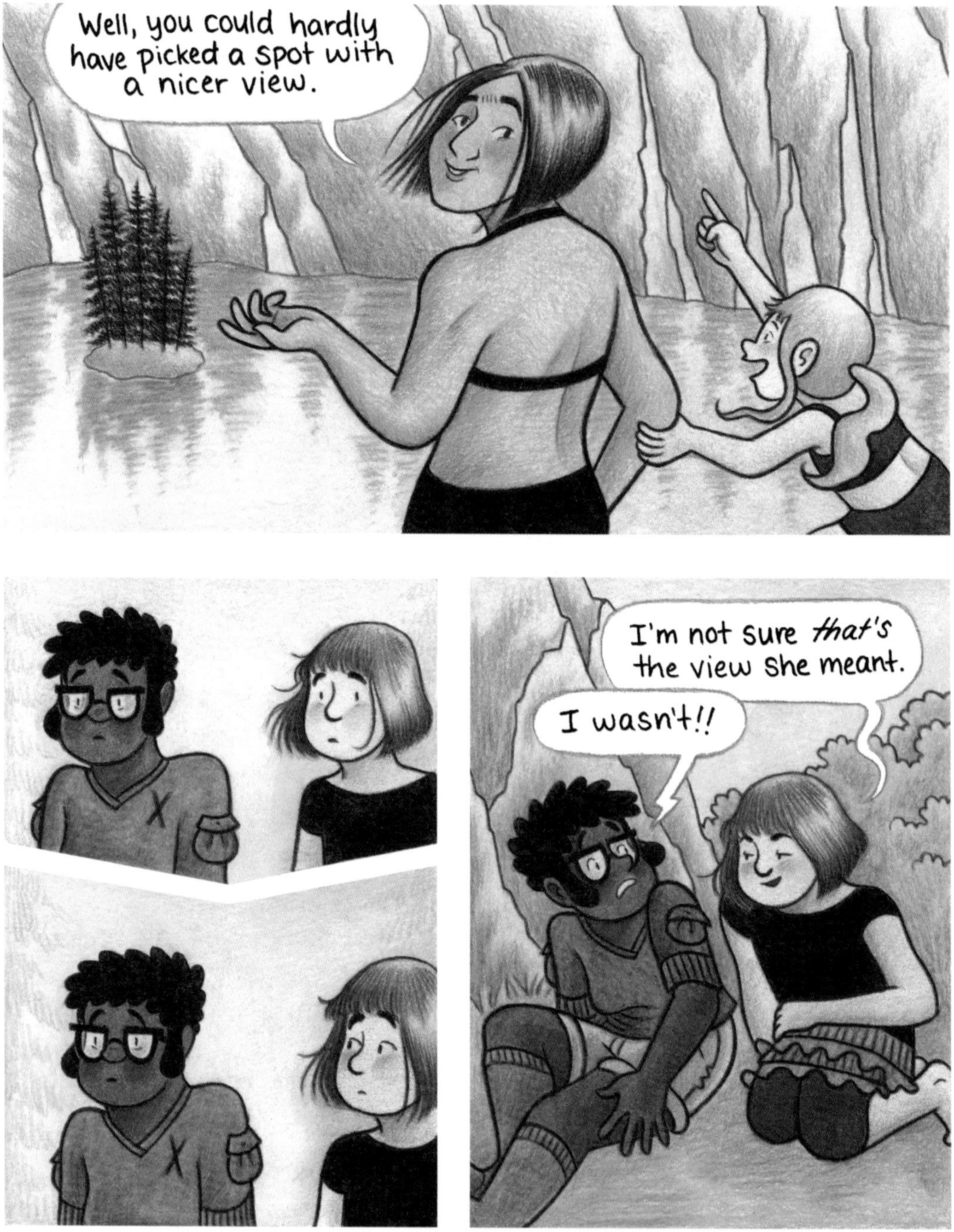
Well, you could hardly have picked a spot with a nicer view.
I'm not sure *that's* the view she meant.
I wasn't!!

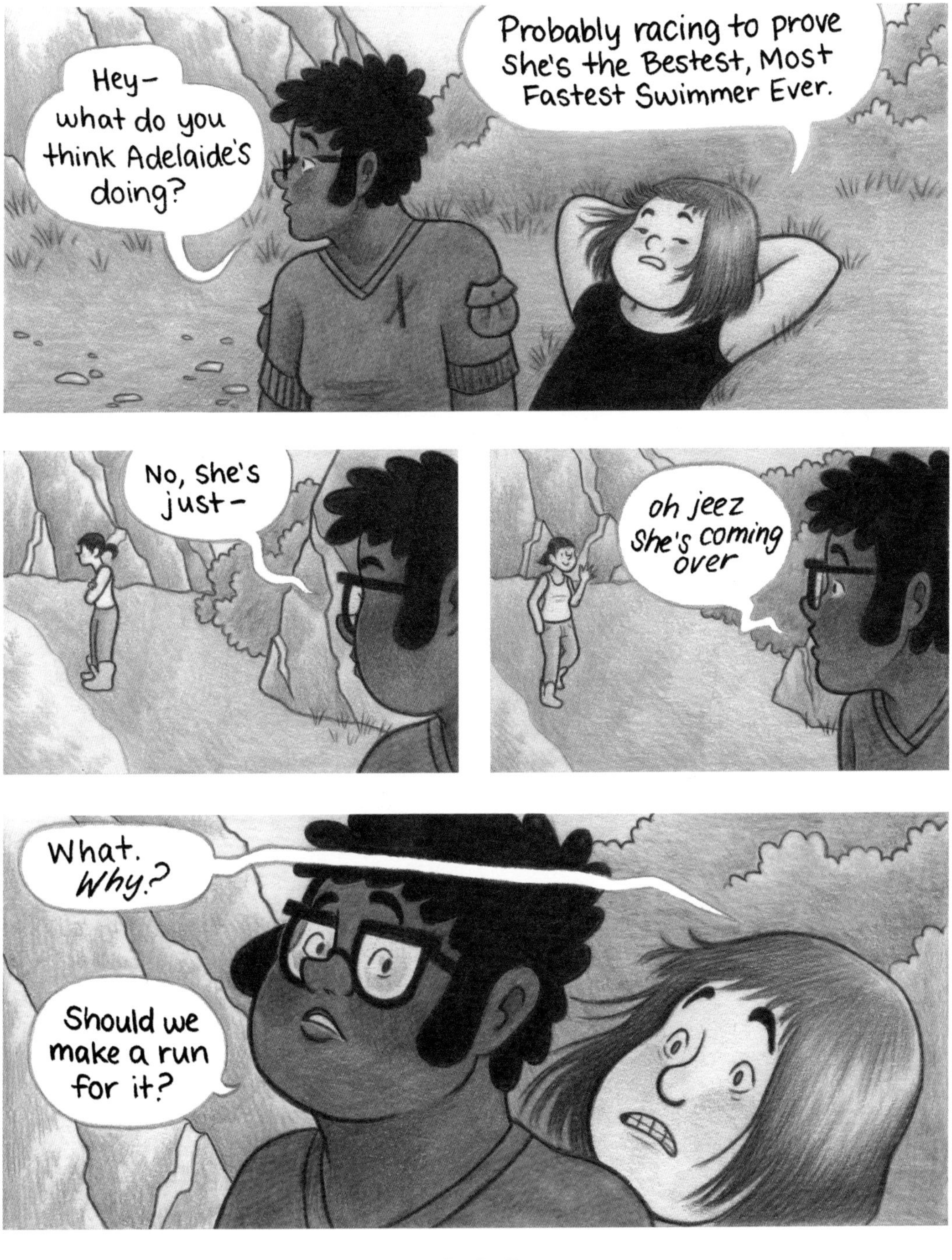
Hey-
what do you
think Adelaide's
doing?
Probably racing to prove
She's the Bestest, Most
Fastest Swimmer Ever.
No, She's
just-
oh jeez
She's coming
over
What.
Why?
Should we
make a run
for it?

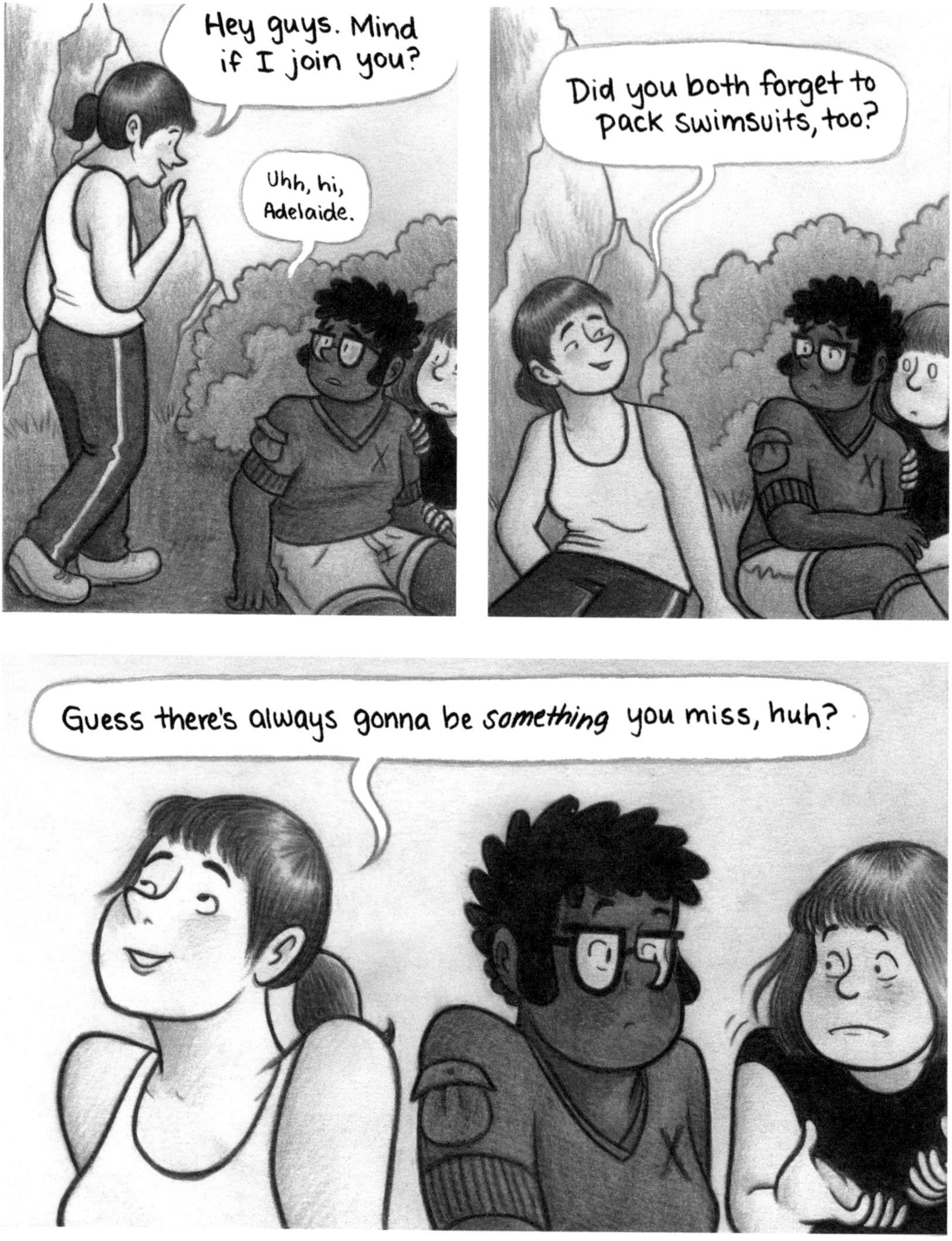
Hey guys. Mind if I join you?
Uhh, hi, Adelaide.
Did you both forget to pack swimsuits, too?
Guess there's always gonna be *something* you miss, huh?

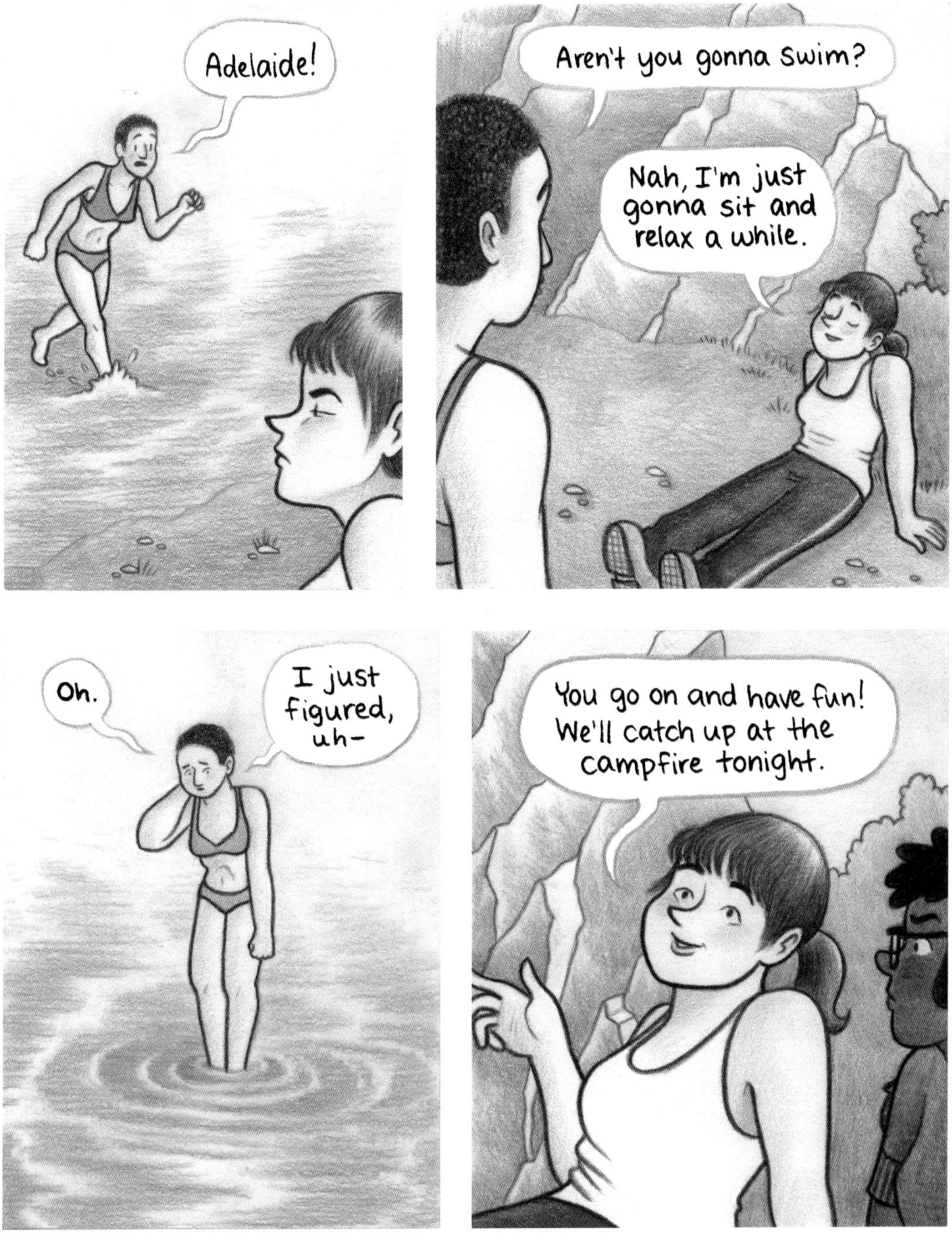
Adelaide!
Aren't you gonna swim?
Nah, I'm just gonna sit and relax a while.
Oh.
I just figured, uh-
You go on and have fun! We'll catch up at the campfire tonight.

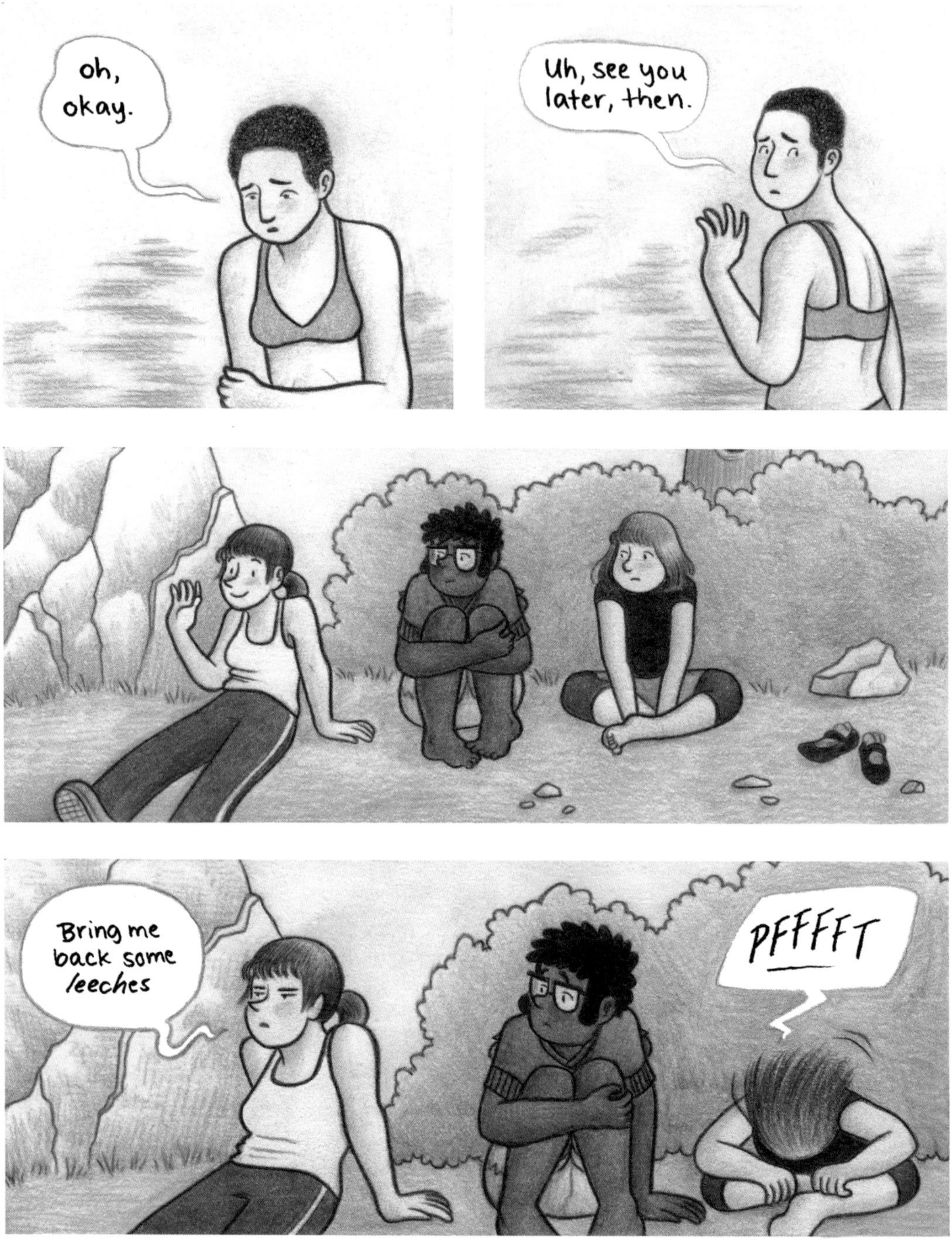

oh, okay.
Uh, see you later, then.
Bring me back some leeches
PFFFFT

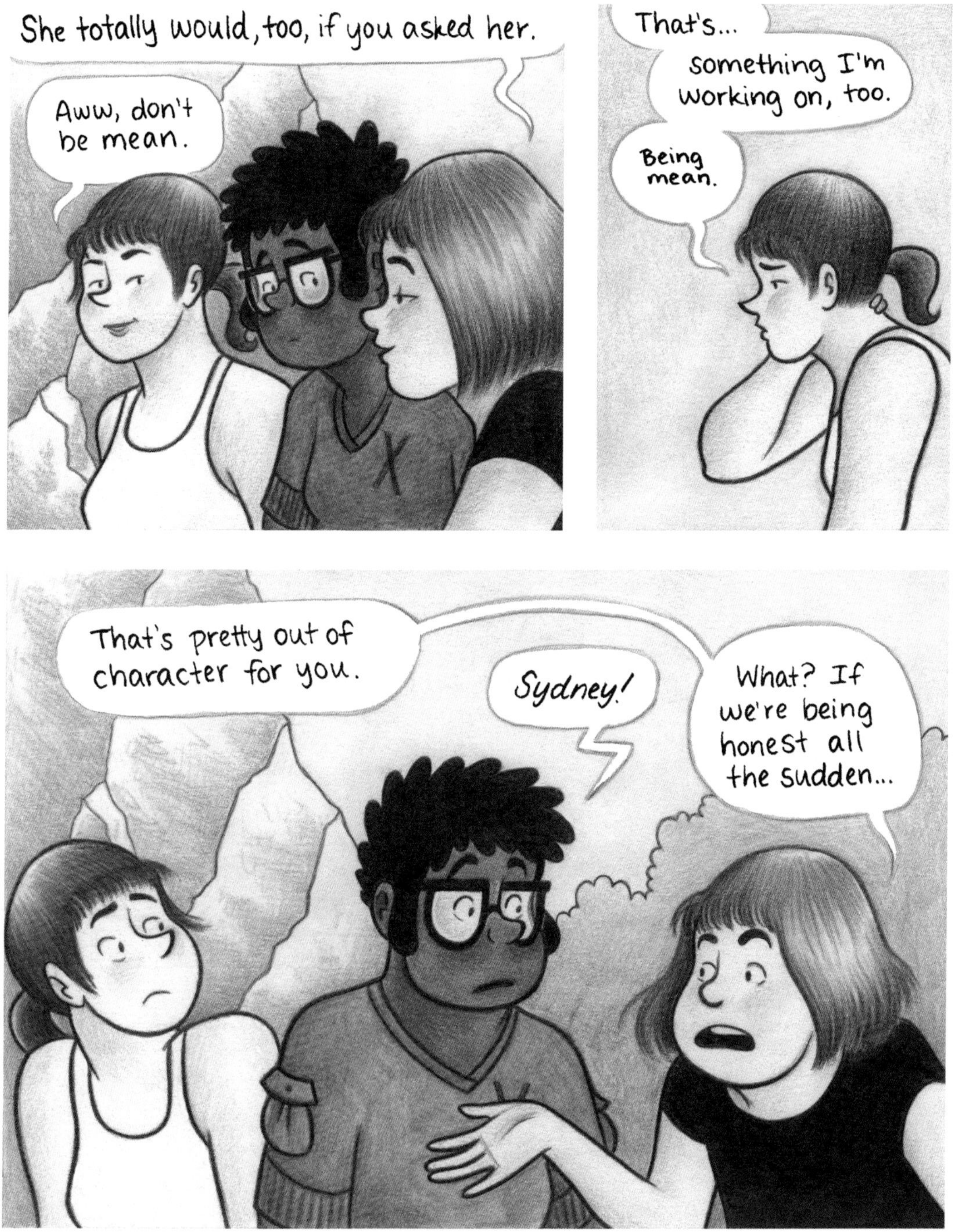
She totally would, too, if you asked her.
Aww, don't be mean.
That's...
something I'm working on, too.
Being mean.
That's pretty out of character for you.
Sydney!
What? If we're being honest all the sudden...

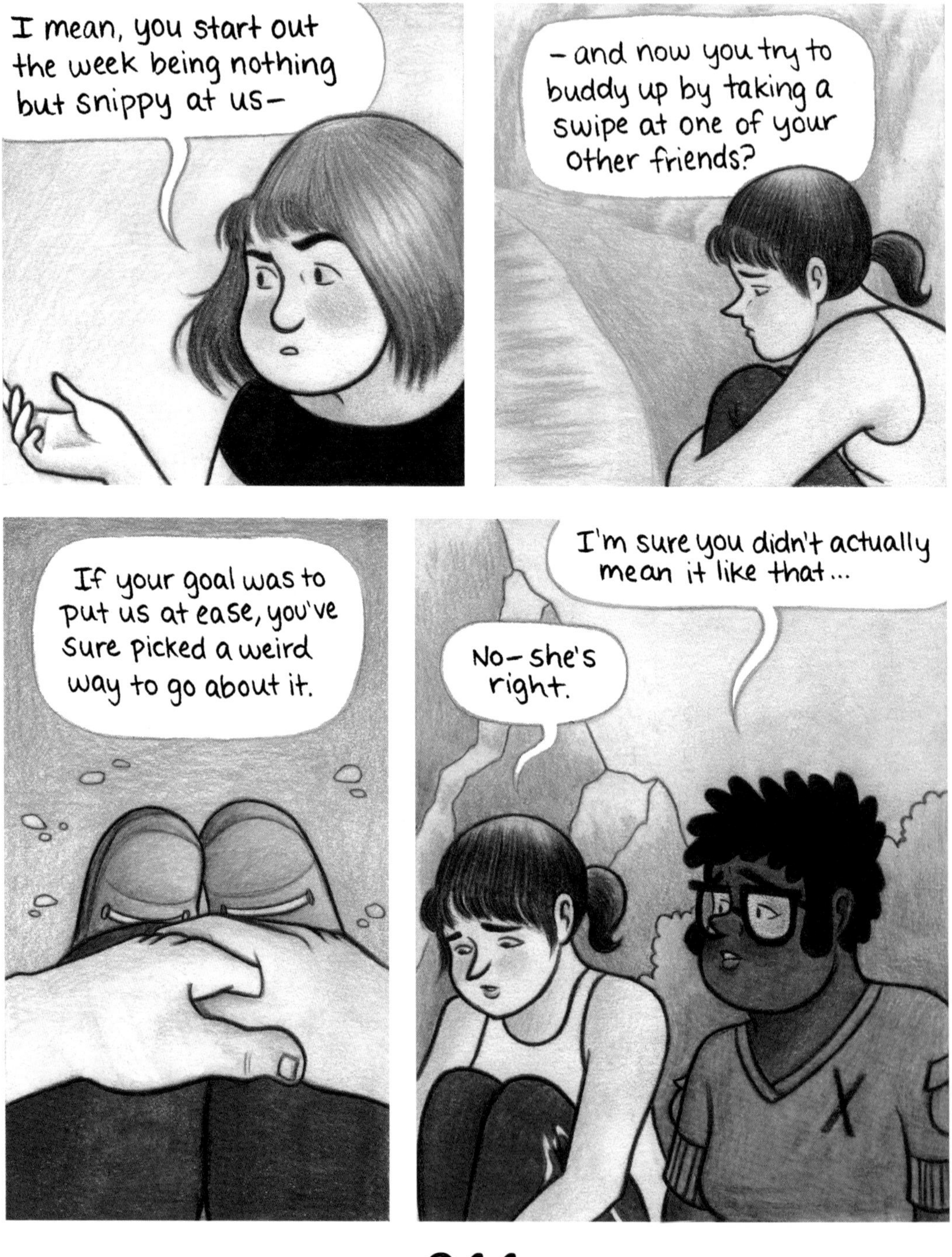
I mean, you start out the week being nothing but snippy at us–
–and now you try to buddy up by taking a swipe at one of your other friends?
If your goal was to put us at ease, you've sure picked a weird way to go about it.
I'm sure you didn't actually mean it like that...
No–she's right.

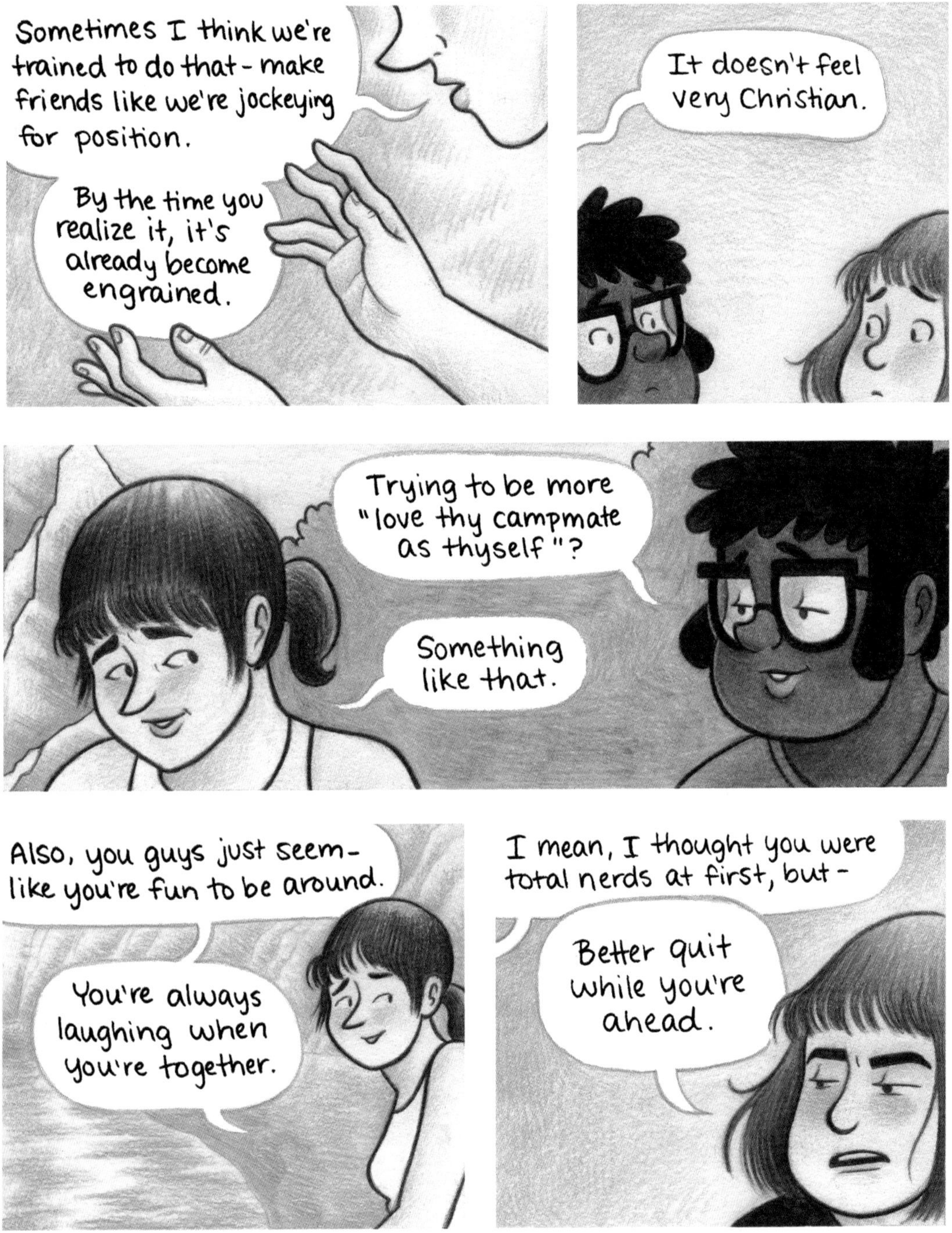

Sometimes I think we're trained to do that - make friends like we're jockeying for position.
By the time you realize it, it's already become engrained.
It doesn't feel very Christian.
Trying to be more "love thy campmate as thyself"?
Something like that.
Also, you guys just seem- like you're fun to be around.
You're always laughing when you're together.
I mean, I thought you were total nerds at first, but-
Better quit while you're ahead.

Agh, sorry. Did it again.

Haha, it's okay!

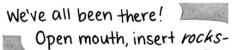

We've all been there! Open mouth, insert *rocks*-

ow!!

I mean, right, God wants us to forgive and forget.

I'm sure he said that to some old guy in a desert once.

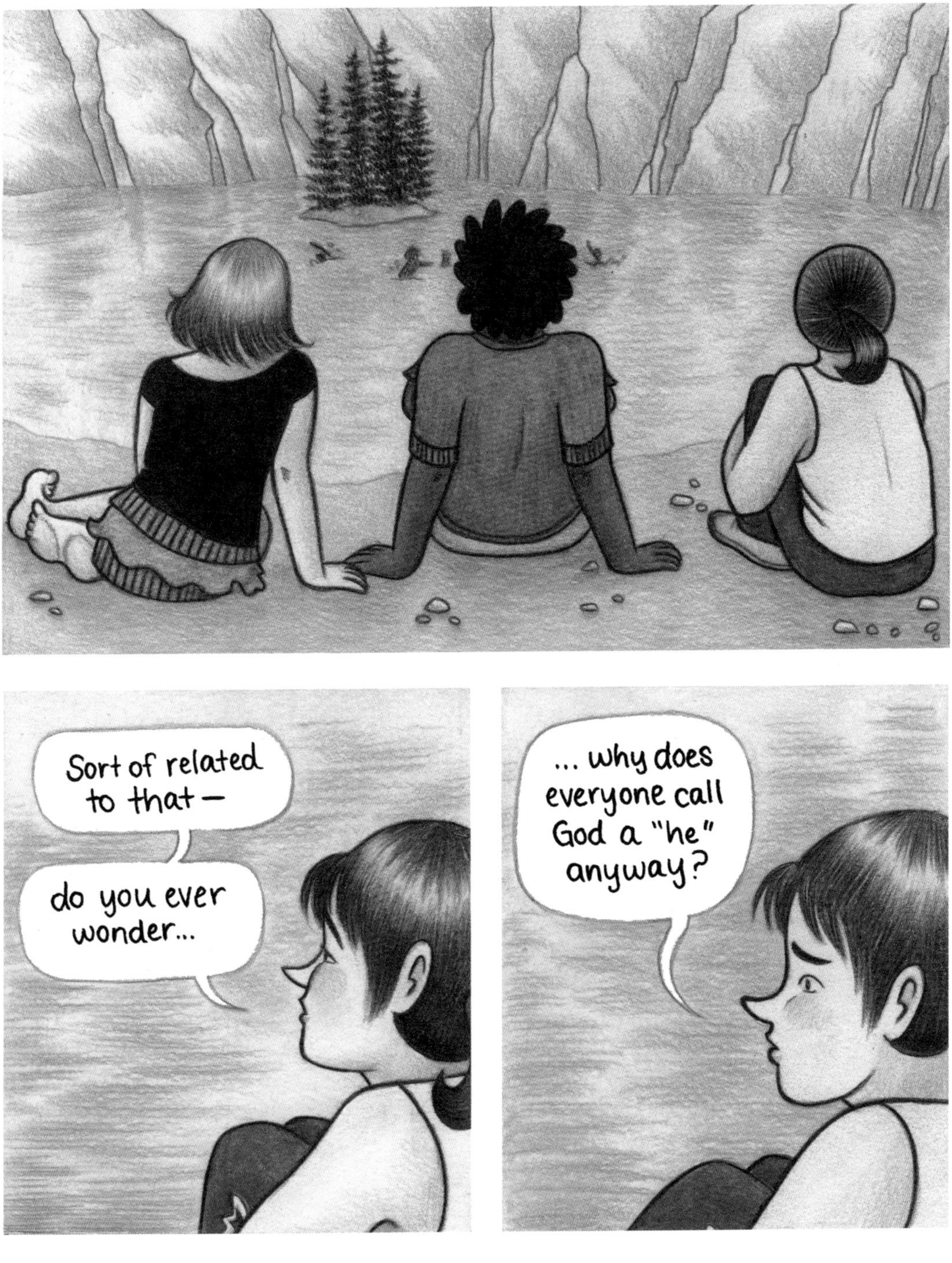
Sort of related to that—
do you ever wonder...
... why does everyone call God a "he" anyway?

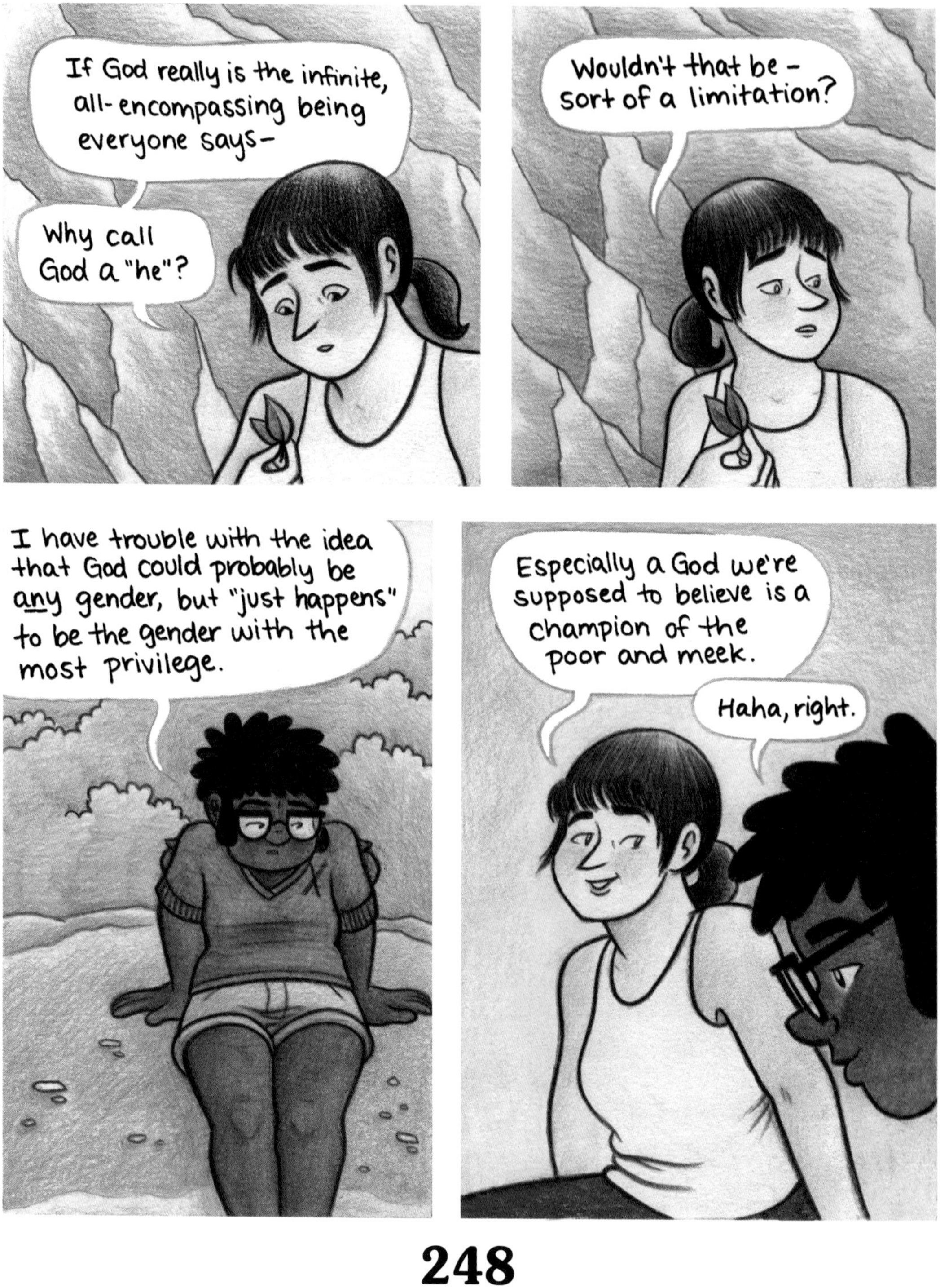
If God really is the infinite, all-encompassing being everyone says-
Why call God a "he"?
Wouldn't that be - sort of a limitation?
I have trouble with the idea that God could probably be any gender, but "just happens" to be the gender with the most privilege.
Especially a God we're supposed to believe is a champion of the poor and meek.
Haha, right.

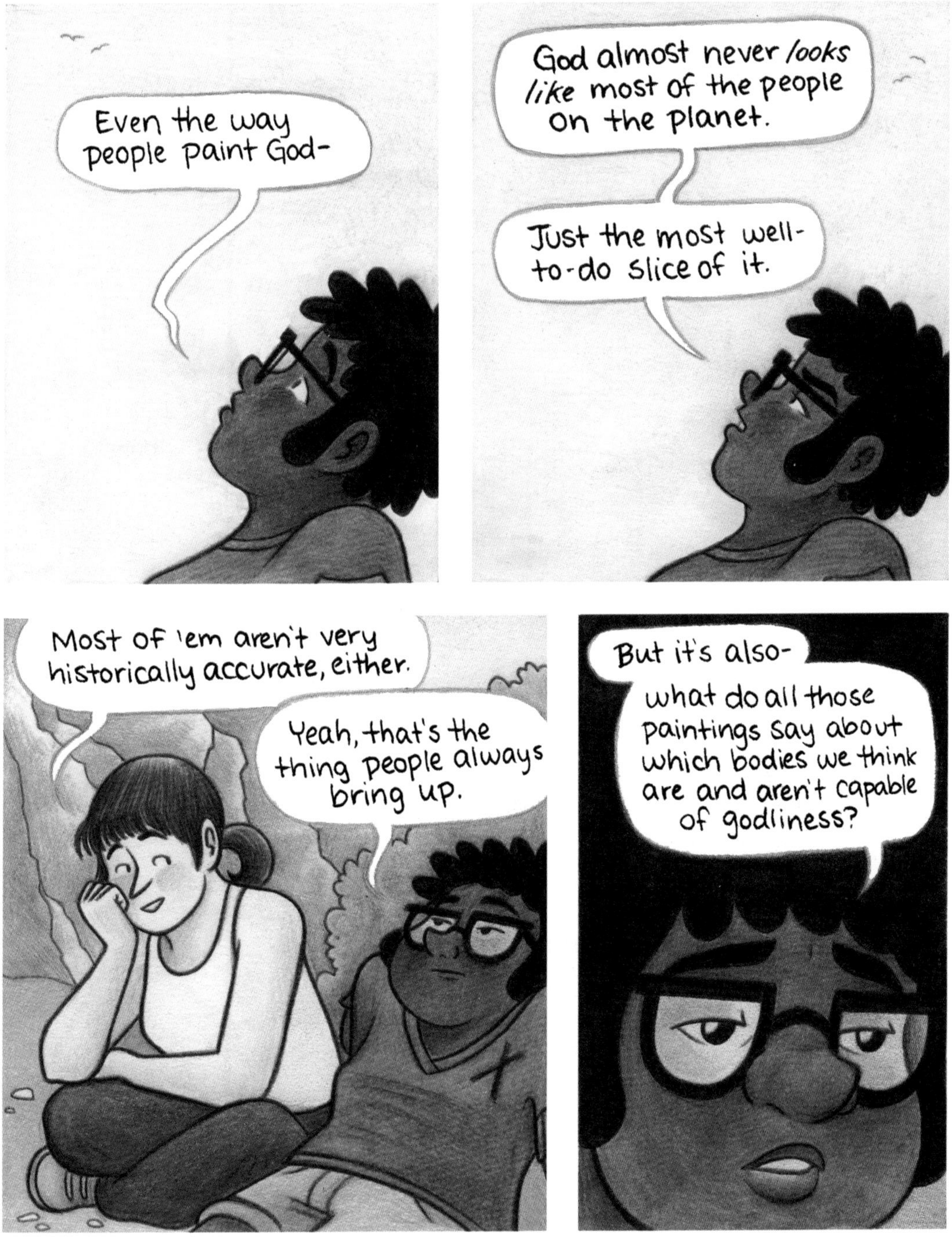
Even the way people paint God-
God almost never *looks like* most of the people on the planet.
Just the most well-to-do slice of it.
Most of 'em aren't very historically accurate, either.
Yeah, that's the thing people always bring up.
But it's also-
what do all those paintings say about which bodies we think are and aren't capable of godliness?

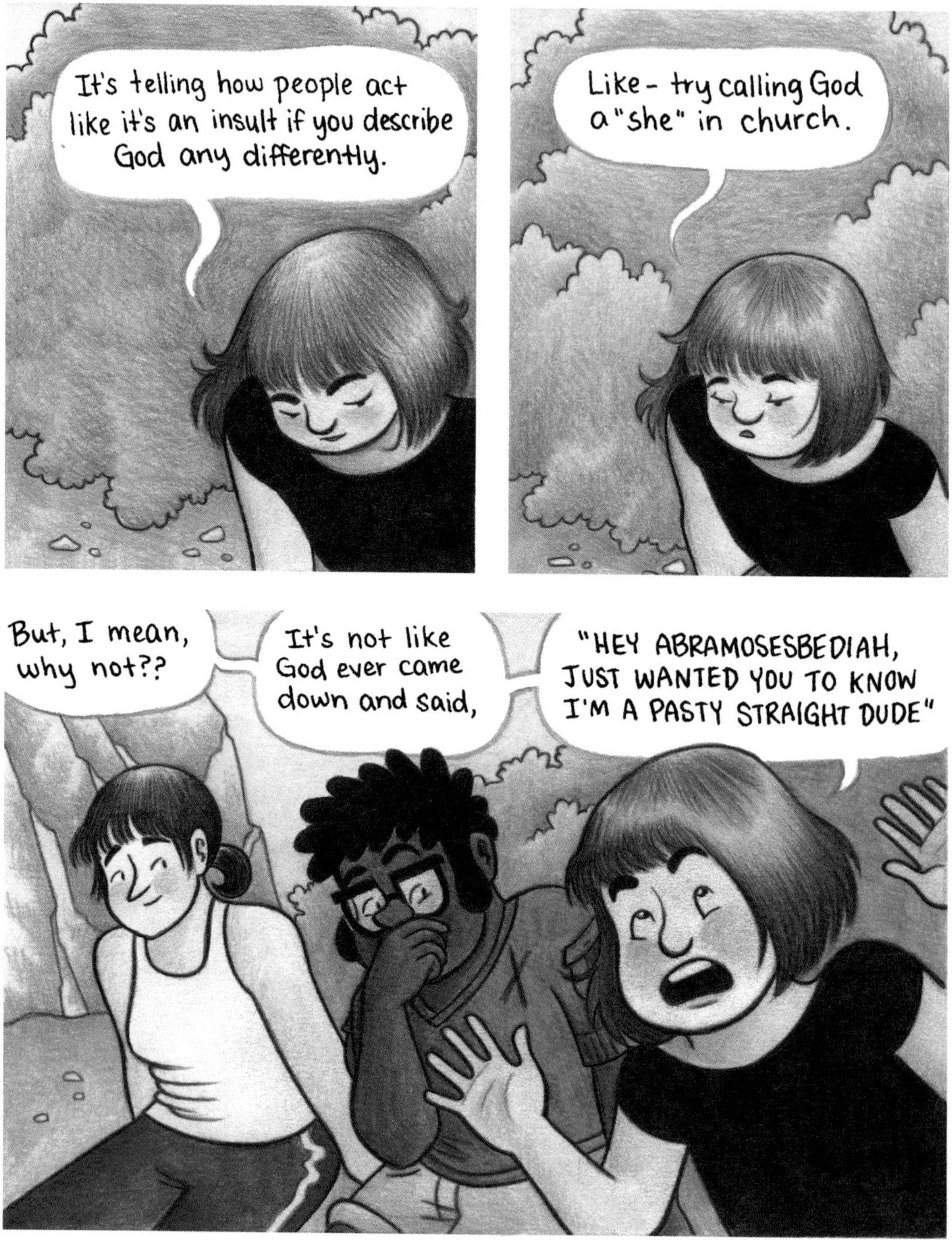
It's telling how people act like it's an insult if you describe God any differently.
Like - try calling God a "she" in church.
But, I mean, why not??
It's not like God ever came down and said,
"HEY ABRAMOSESBEDIAH, JUST WANTED YOU TO KNOW I'M A PASTY STRAIGHT DUDE"

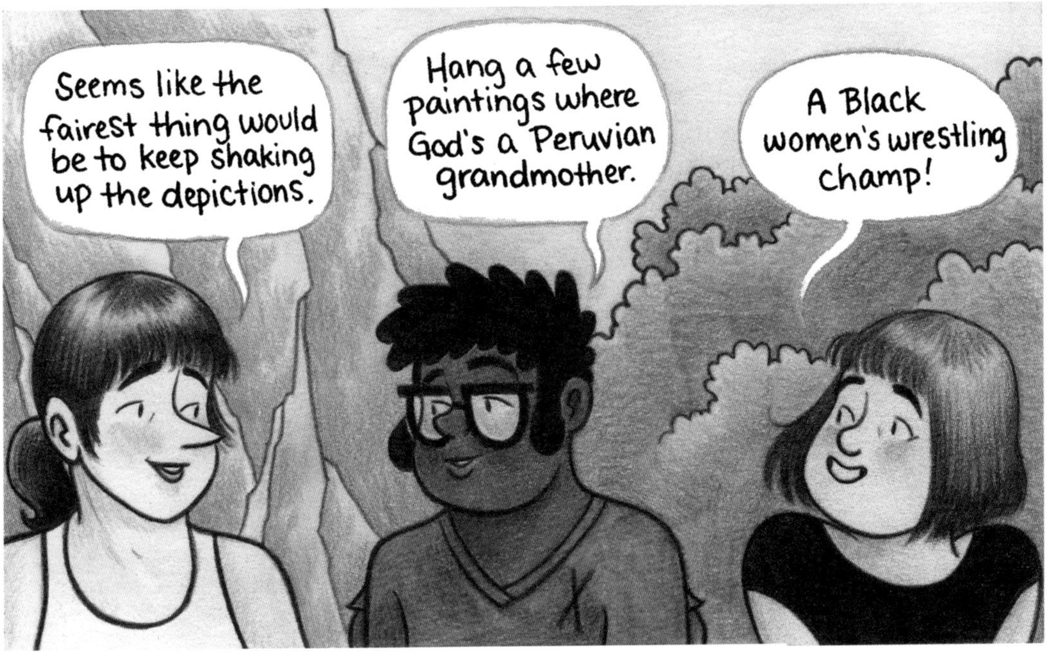
Seems like the fairest thing would be to keep shaking up the depictions.
Hang a few paintings where God's a Peruvian grandmother.
A Black women's wrestling champ!

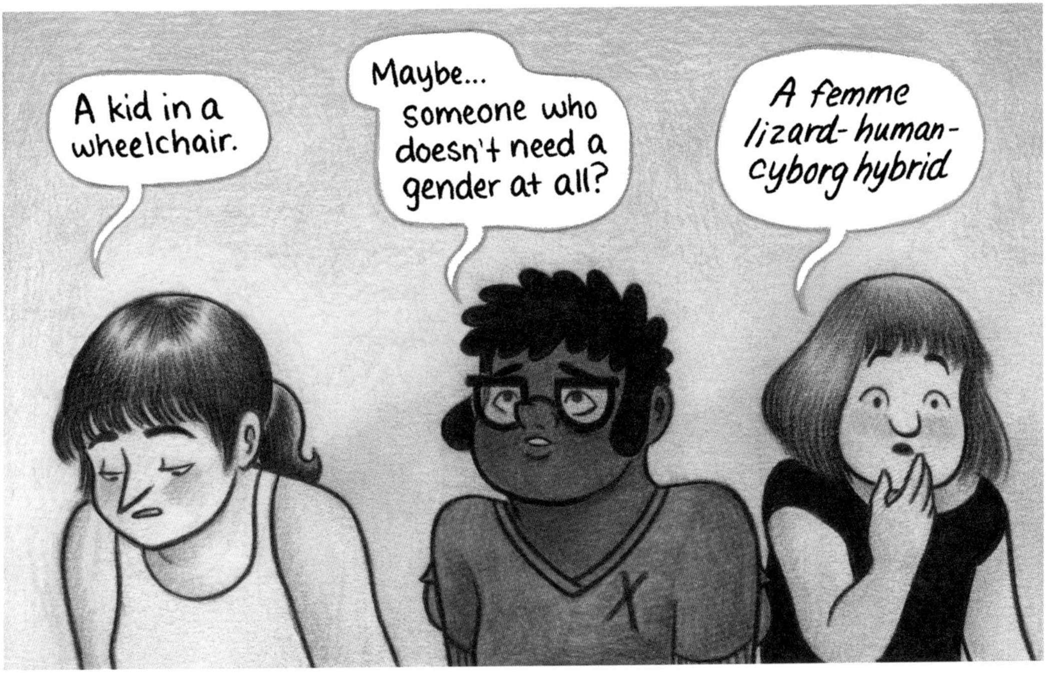
A kid in a wheelchair.
Maybe... someone who doesn't need a gender at all?
A femme lizard-human-cyborg hybrid

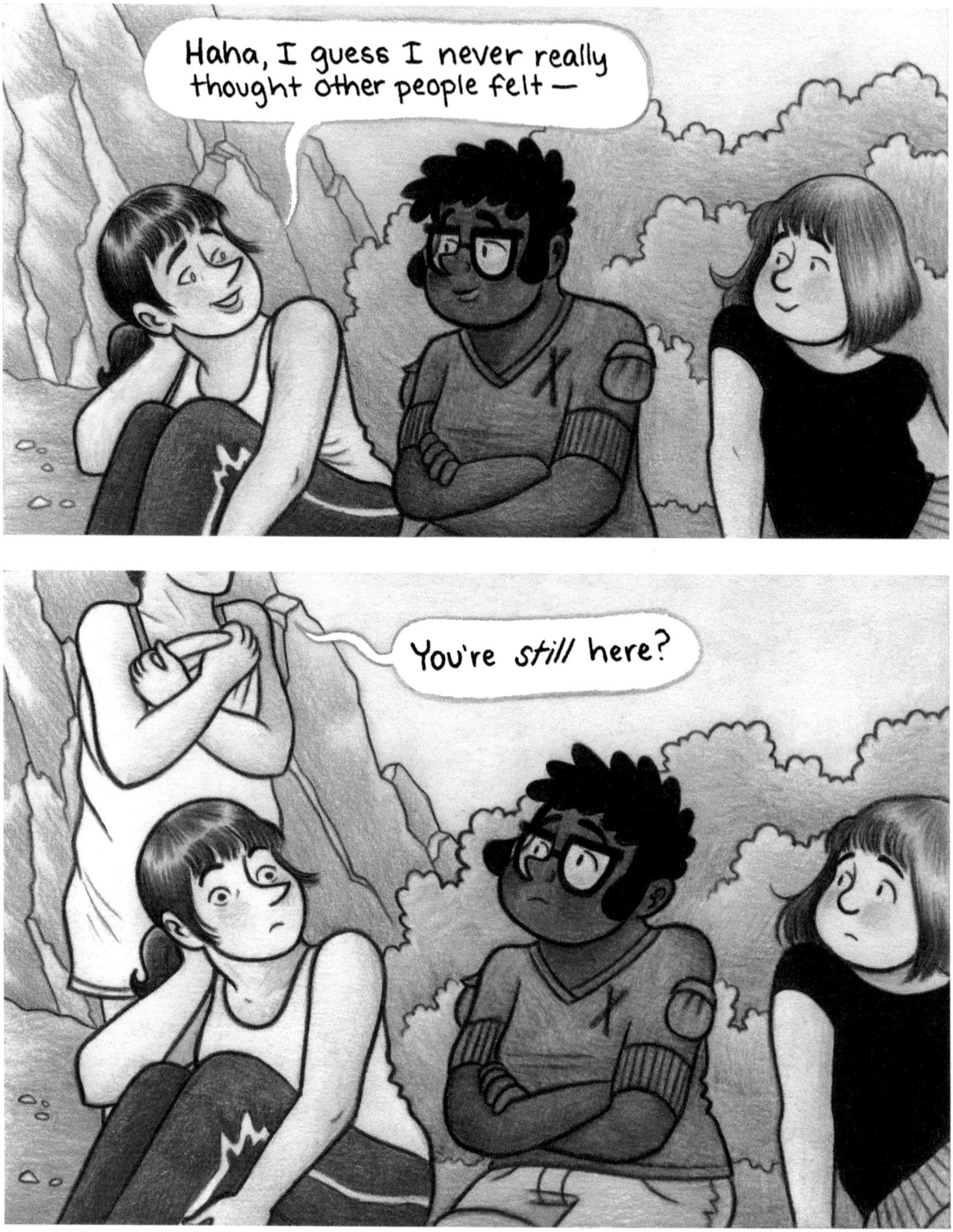
Haha, I guess I never really thought other people felt —
You're *still* here?

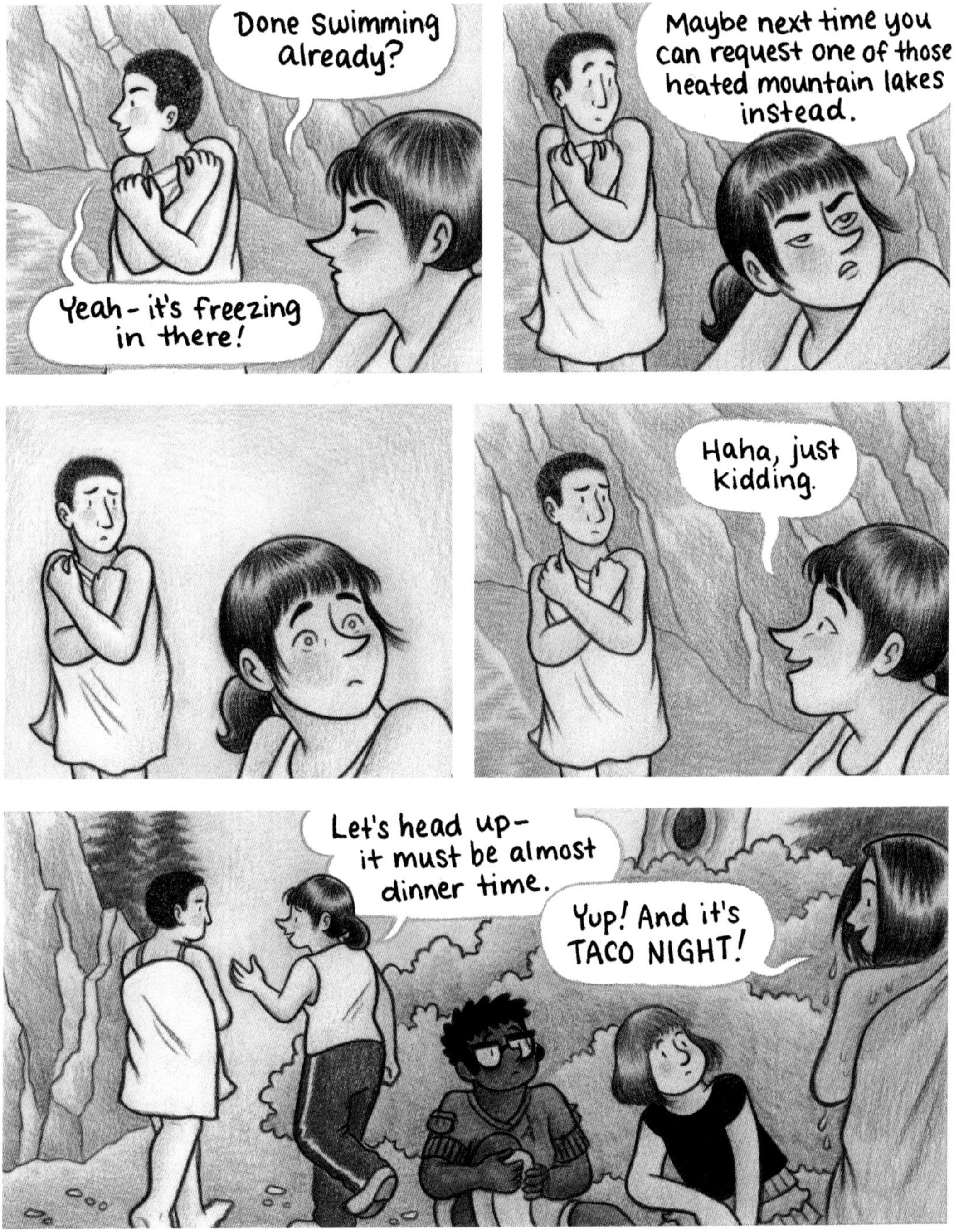
Done Swimming already?
Yeah- it's freezing in there!
Maybe next time you can request one of those heated mountain lakes instead.
Haha, just kidding.
Let's head up- it must be almost dinner time.
Yup! And it's TACO NIGHT!

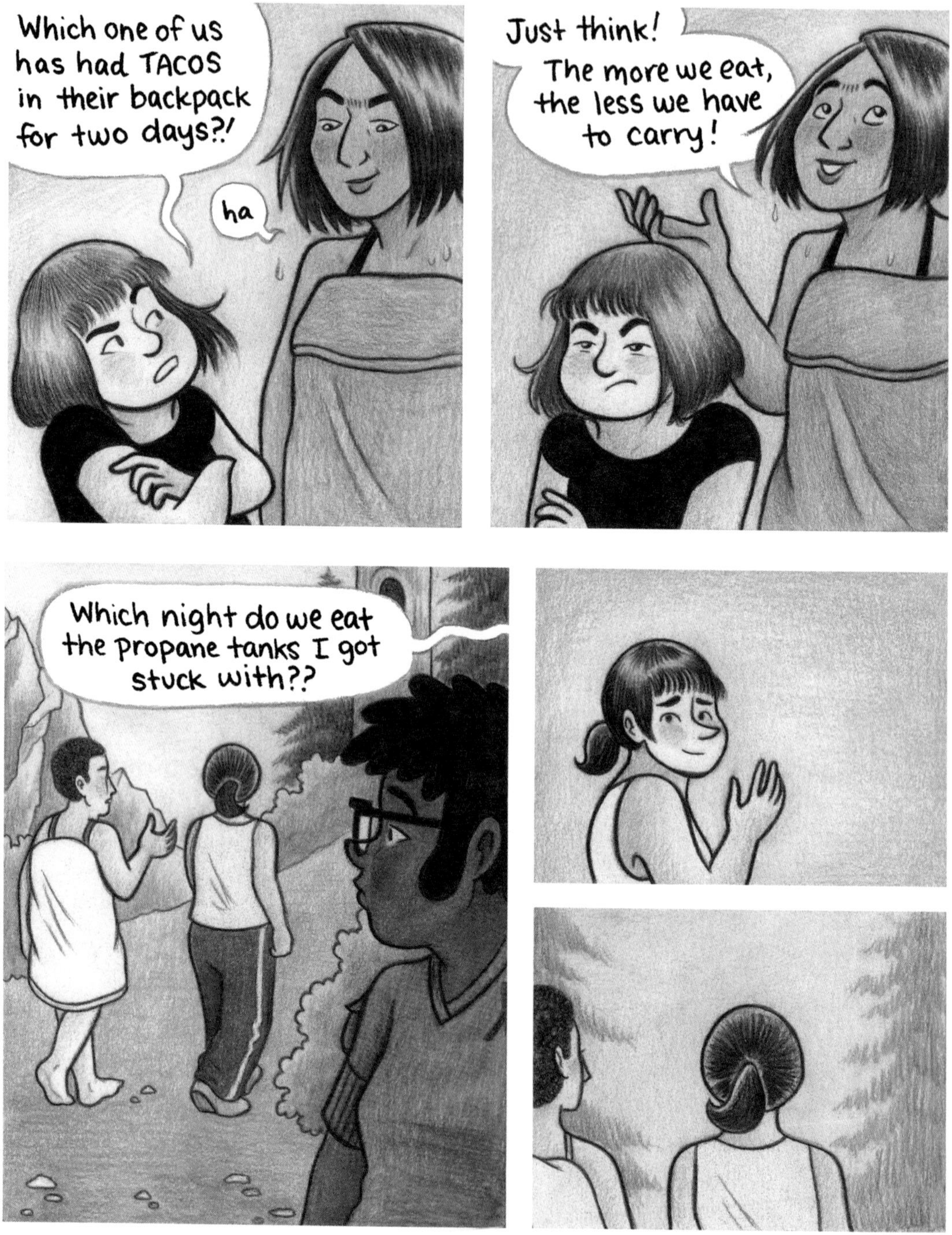
Which one of us has had TACOS in their backpack for two days?!
ha
Just think!
The more we eat, the less we have to carry!
Which night do we eat the propane tanks I got stuck with??

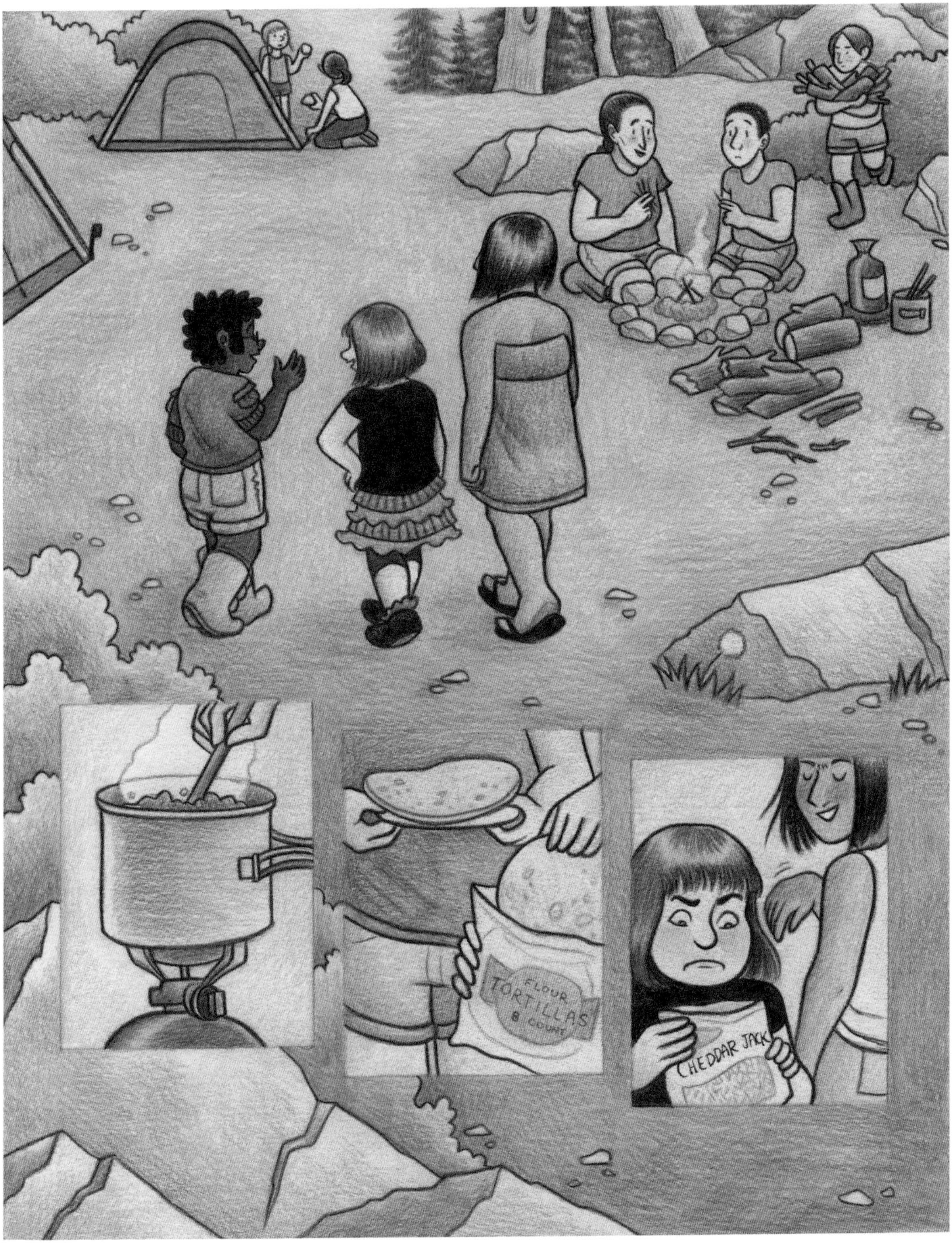
FLOUR
TORTILLAS
8 COUNT
CHEDDAR JACK

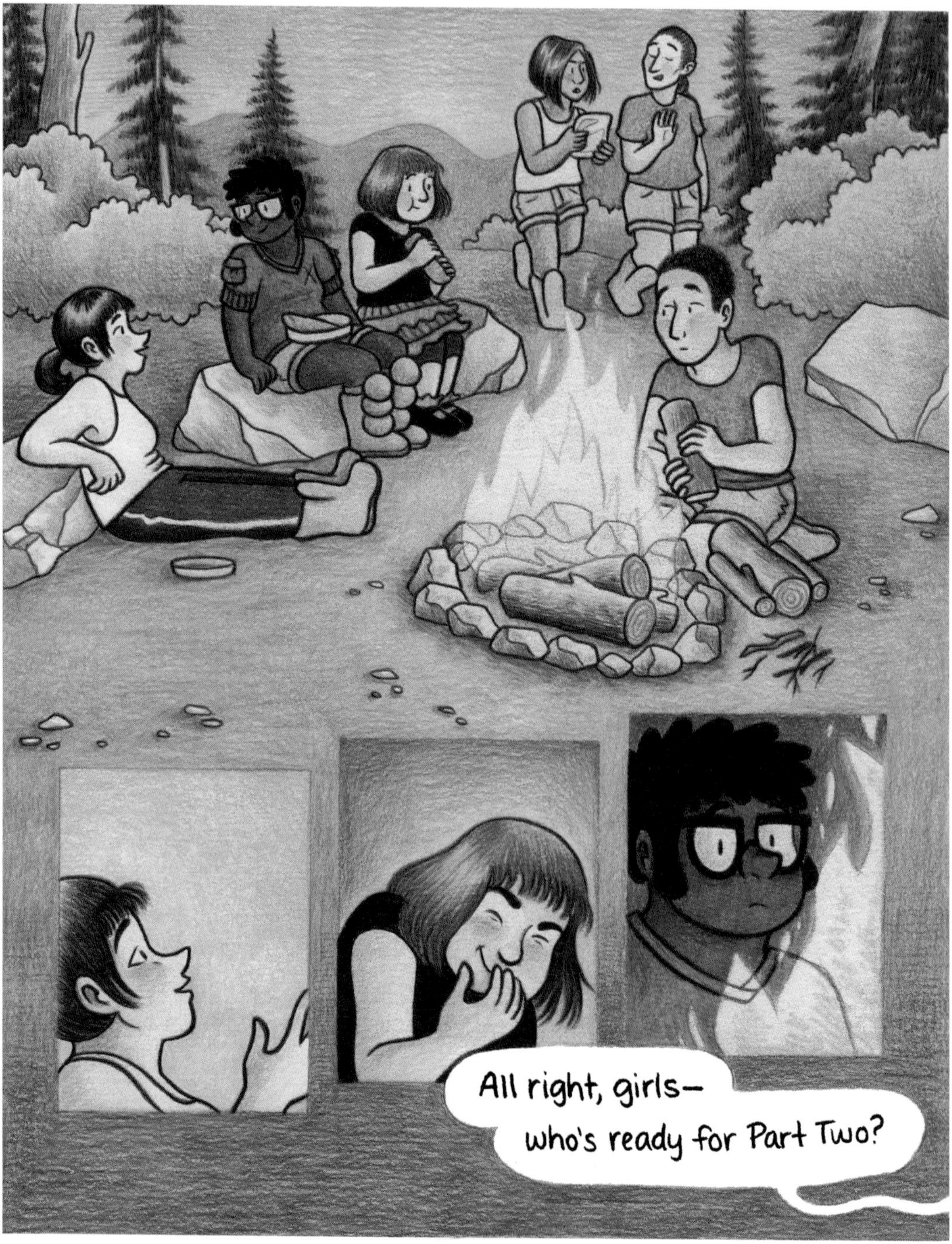
All right, girls—
who's ready for Part Two?

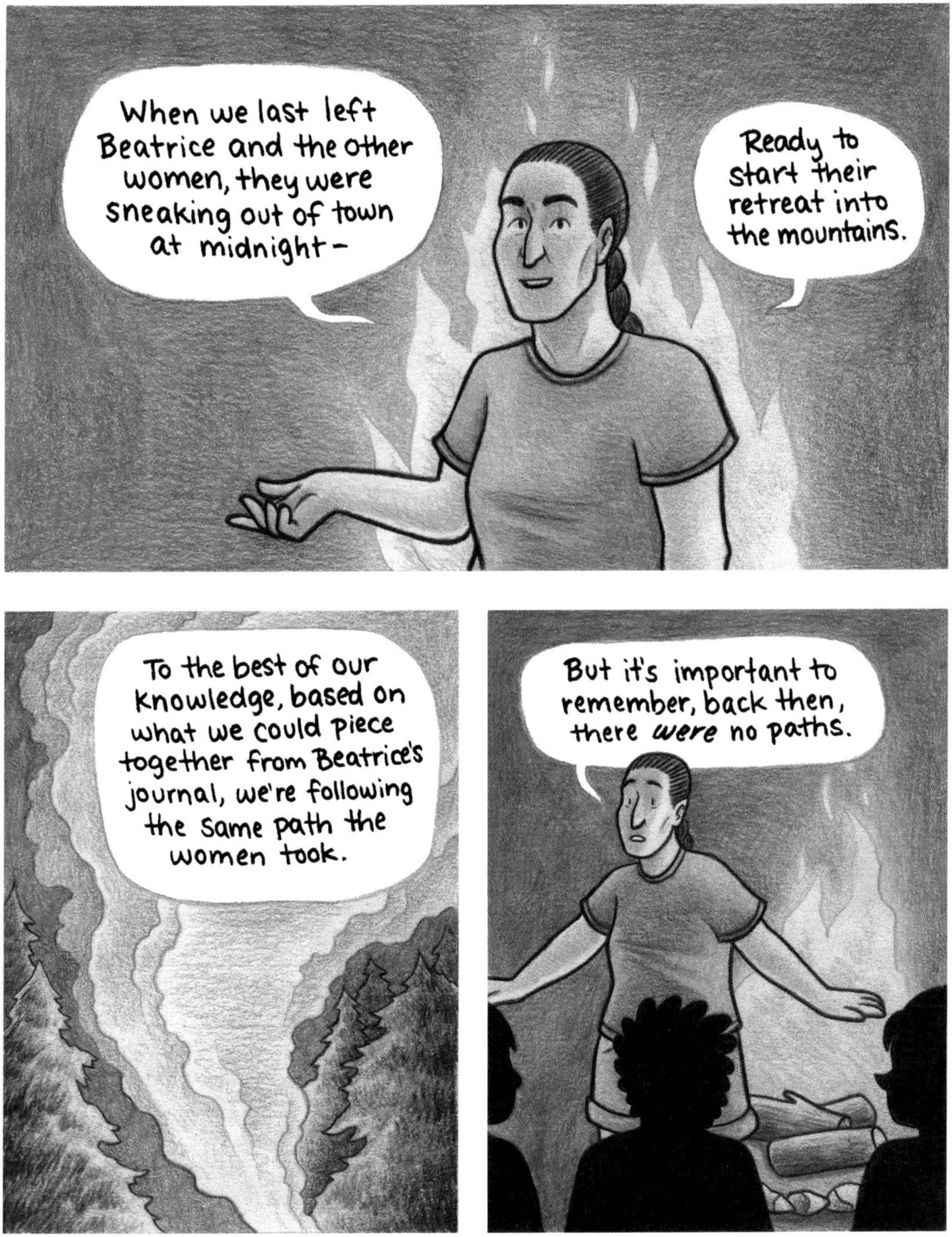
When we last left Beatrice and the other women, they were sneaking out of town at midnight-
Ready to start their retreat into the mountains.
To the best of our knowledge, based on what we could piece together from Beatrice's journal, we're following the same path the women took.
But it's important to remember, back then, there *were* no paths.

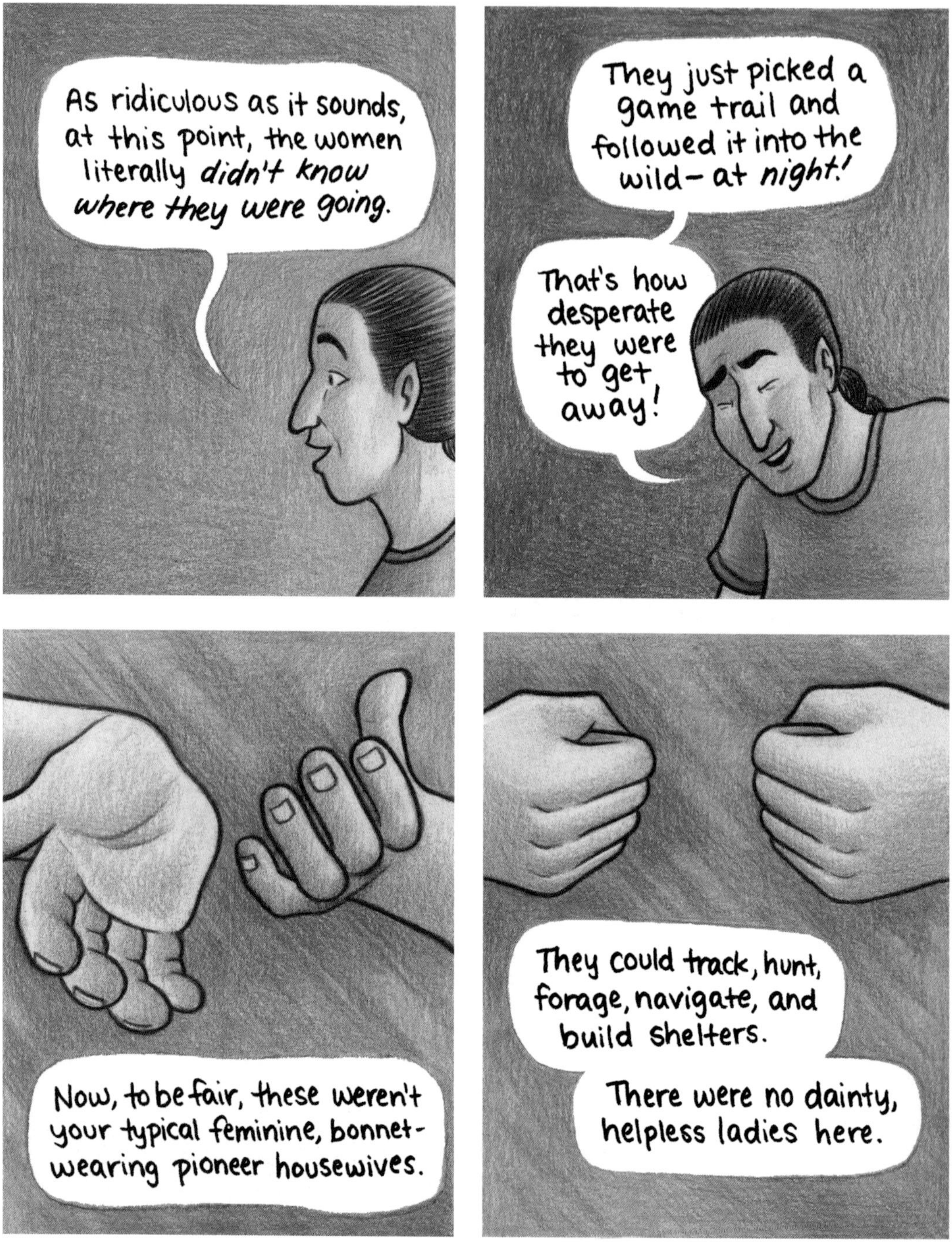
As ridiculous as it sounds, at this point, the women literally *didn't know where they were going.*
They just picked a game trail and followed it into the wild—at *night!*
That's how desperate they were to get away!
Now, to be fair, these weren't your typical feminine, bonnet-wearing pioneer housewives.
They could track, hunt, forage, navigate, and build shelters.
There were no dainty, helpless ladies here.

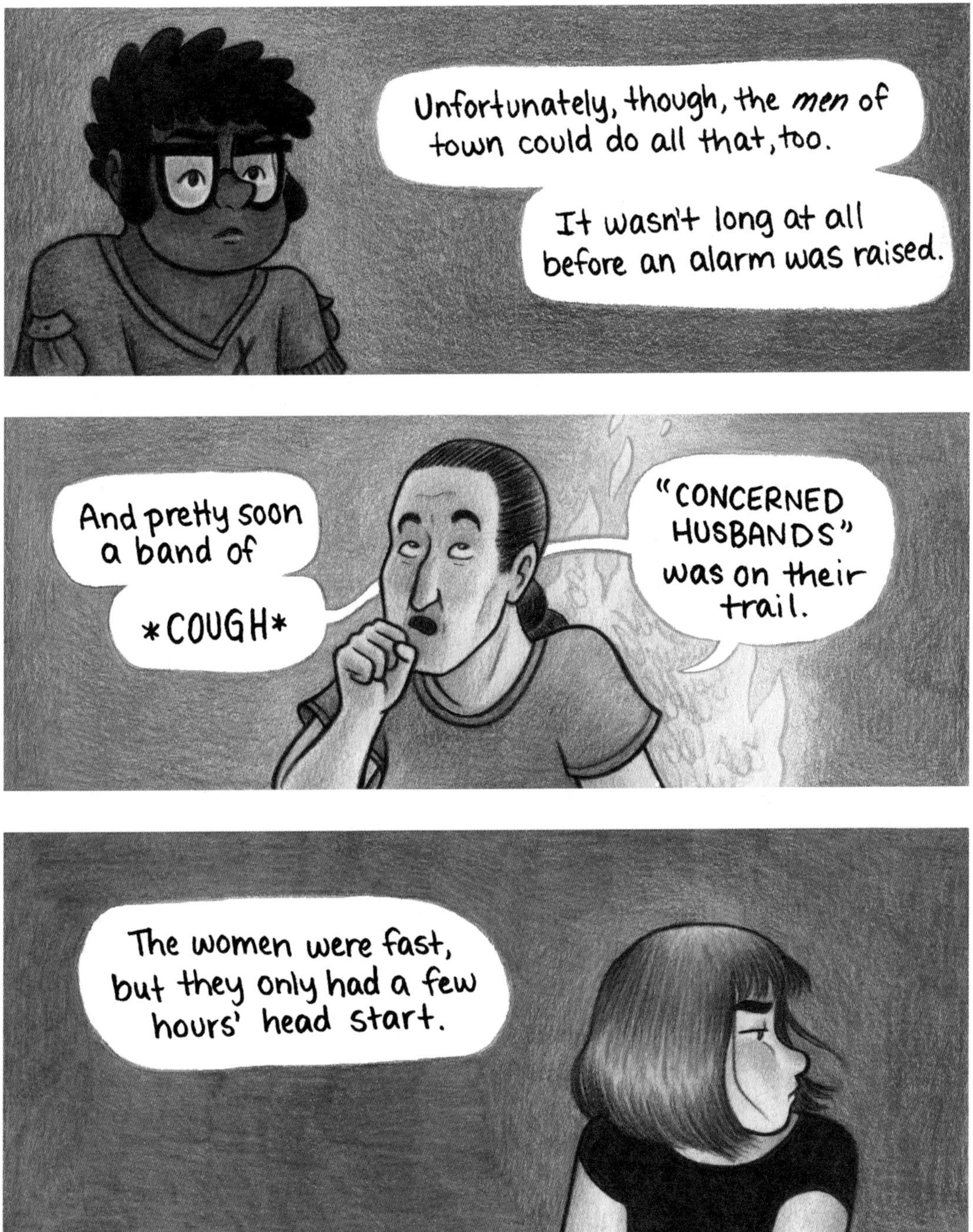
Unfortunately, though, the *men* of town could do all that, too.
It wasn't long at all before an alarm was raised.
And pretty soon a band of
COUGH
"CONCERNED HUSBANDS" was on their trail.
The women were fast, but they only had a few hours' head start.

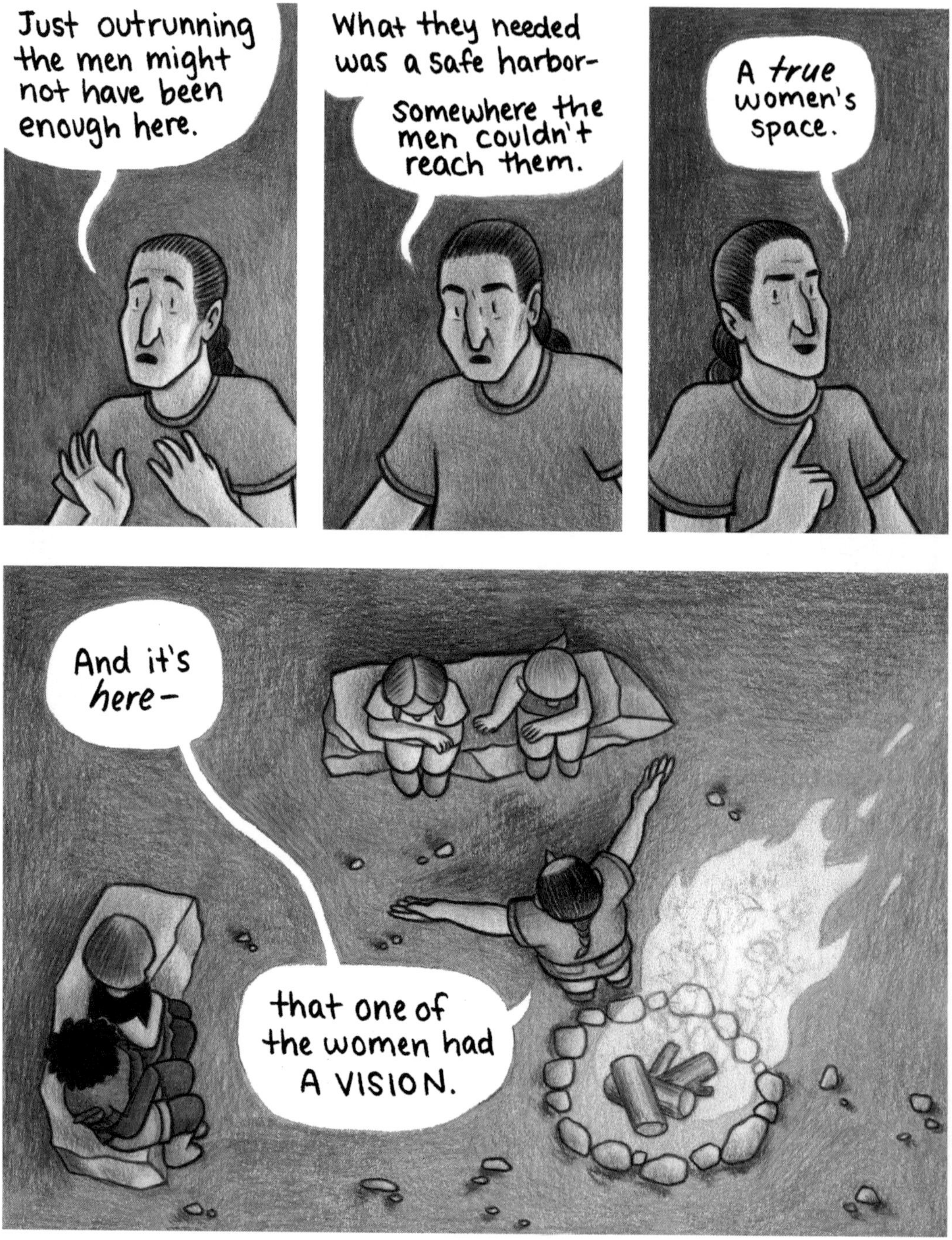
Just outrunning the men might not have been enough here.
What they needed was a safe harbor-
Somewhere the men couldn't reach them.
A *true* women's space.
And it's *here*-
that one of the women had A VISION.

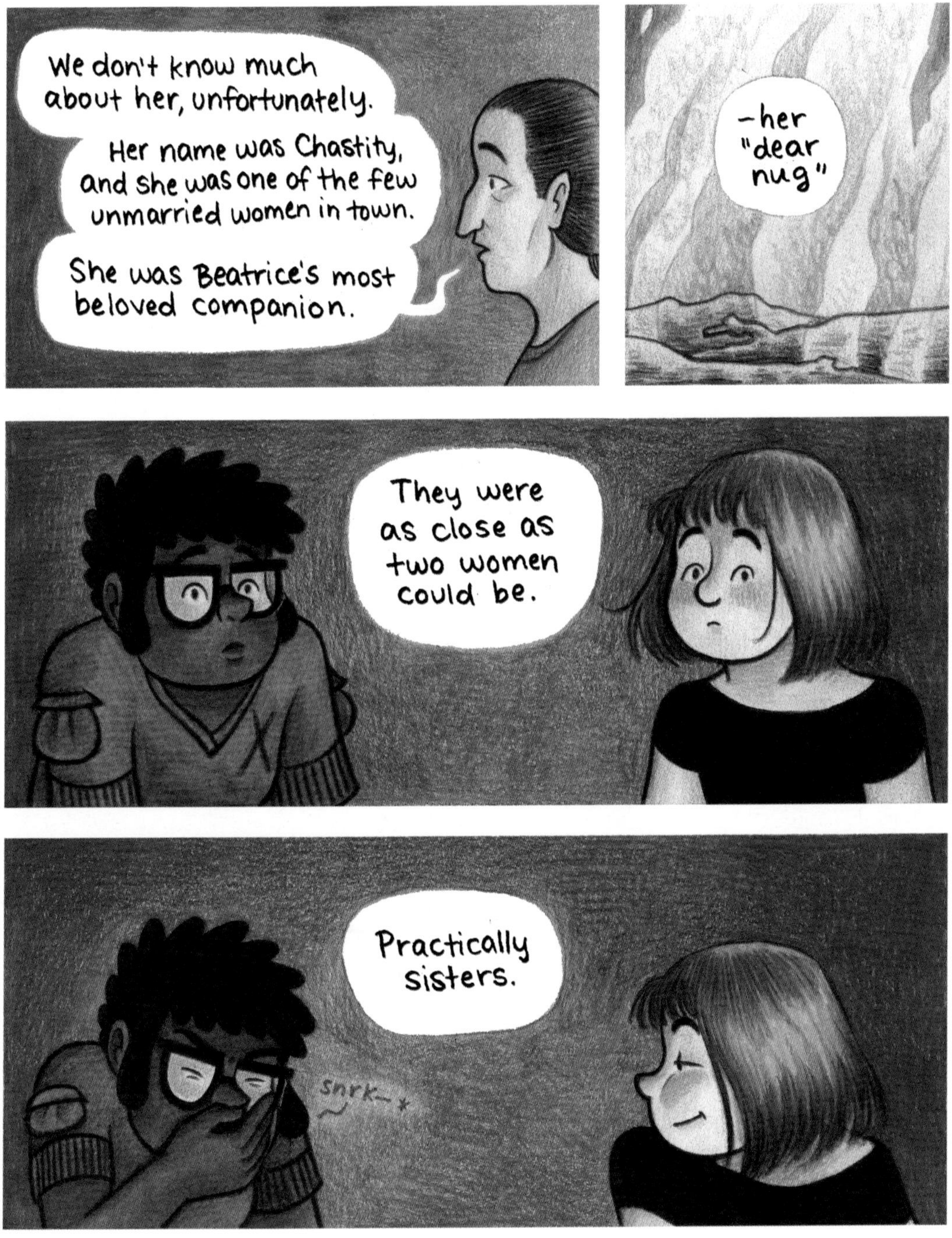
We don't know much about her, unfortunately.
Her name was Chastity, and she was one of the few unmarried women in town.
She was Beatrice's most beloved companion.
-her "dear nug"
They were as close as two women could be.
Practically sisters.
snrk-

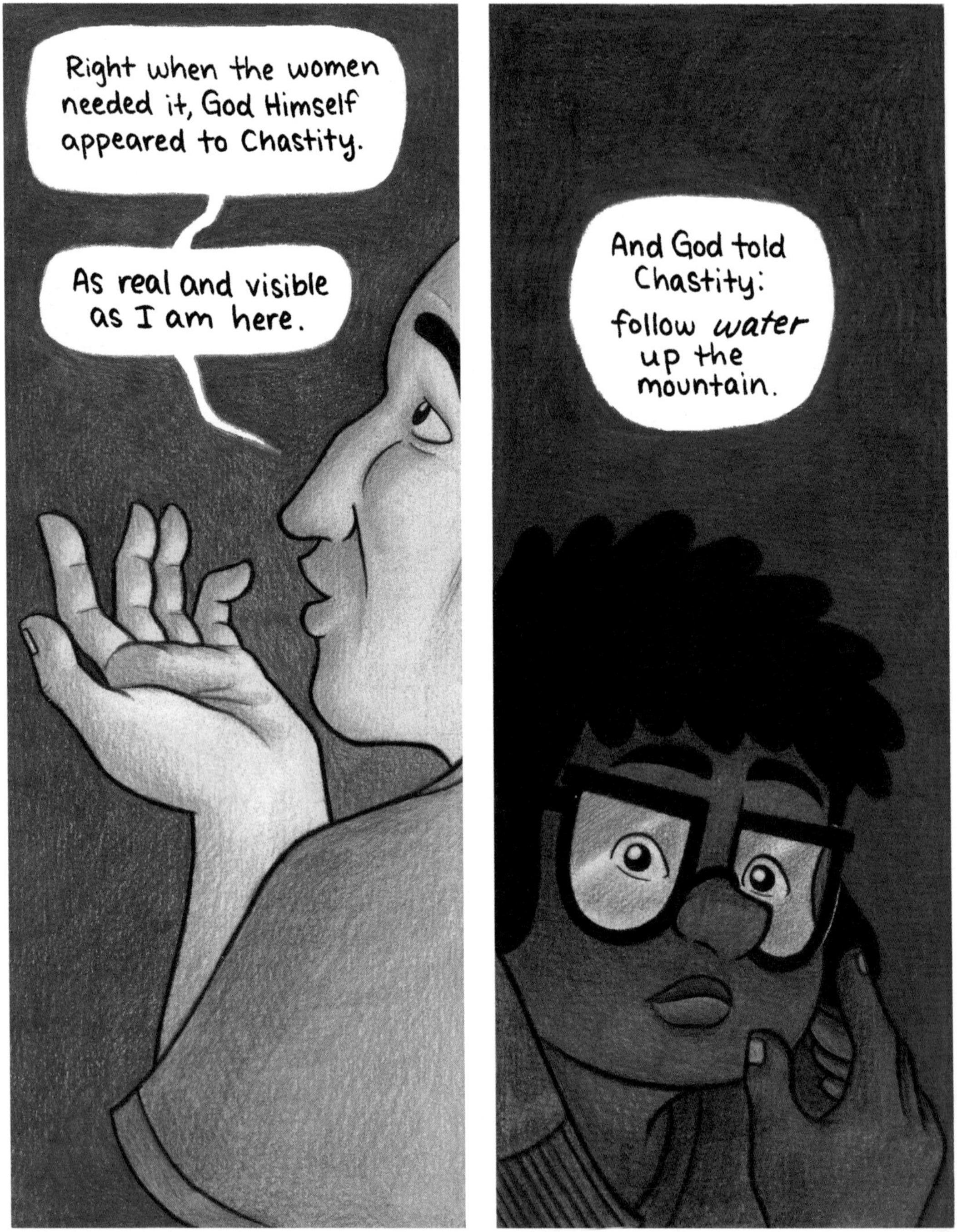
Right when the women needed it, God Himself appeared to Chastity.
As real and visible as I am here.
And God told Chastity: follow *water* up the mountain.

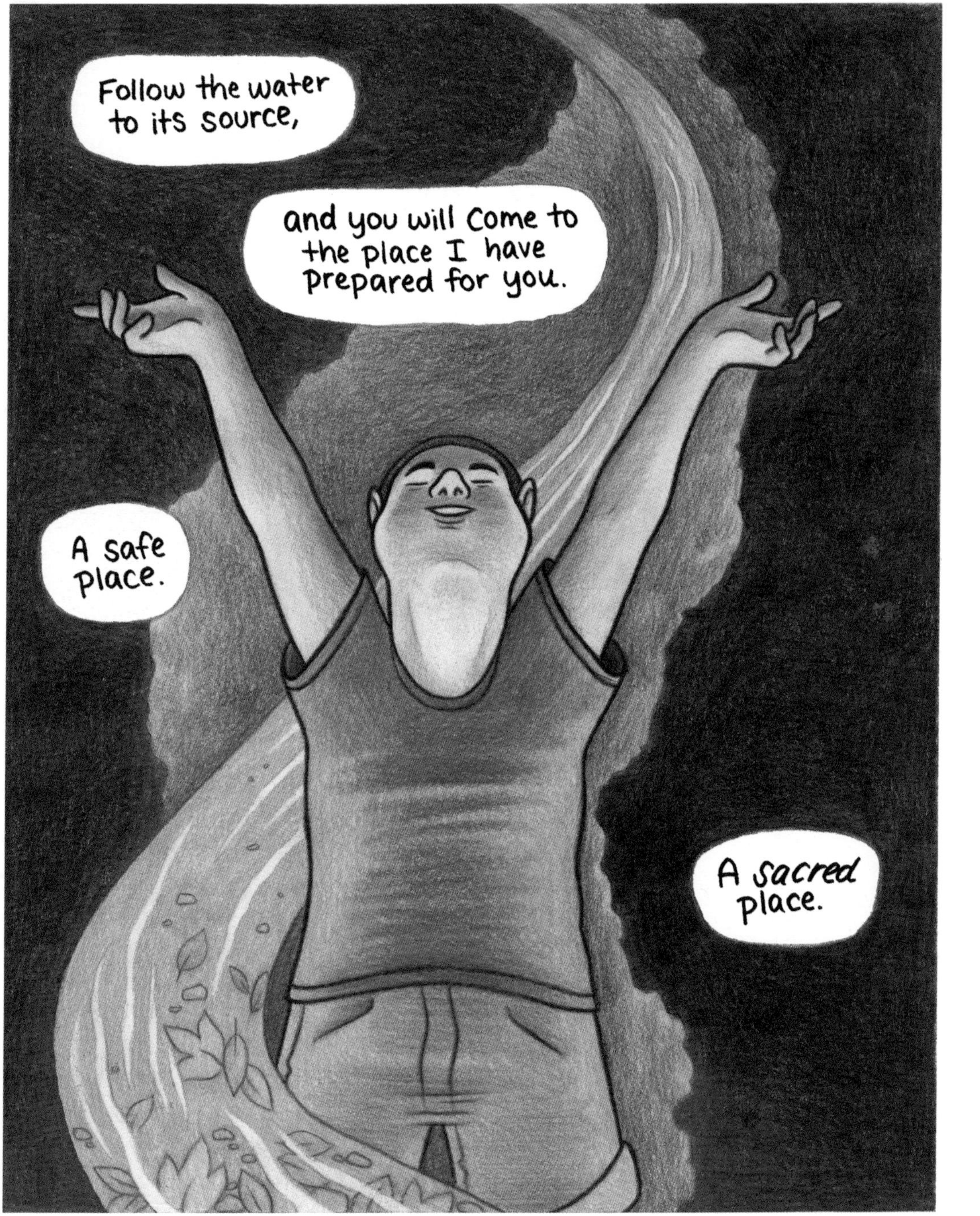
Follow the water to its source,
and you will come to the place I have prepared for you.
A safe place.
A sacred place.

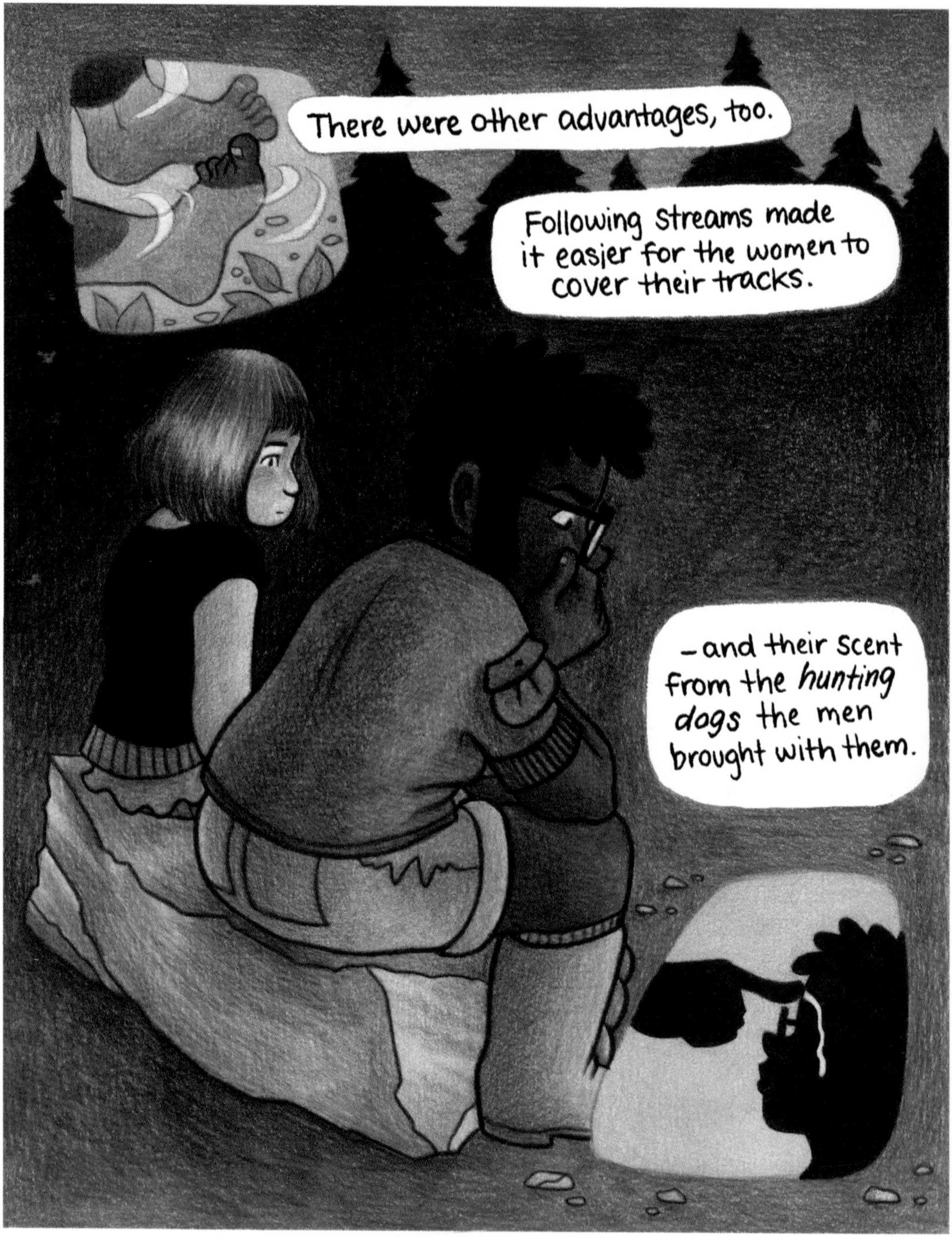
There were other advantages, too.
Following streams made it easier for the women to cover their tracks.
–and their scent from the *hunting dogs* the men brought with them.

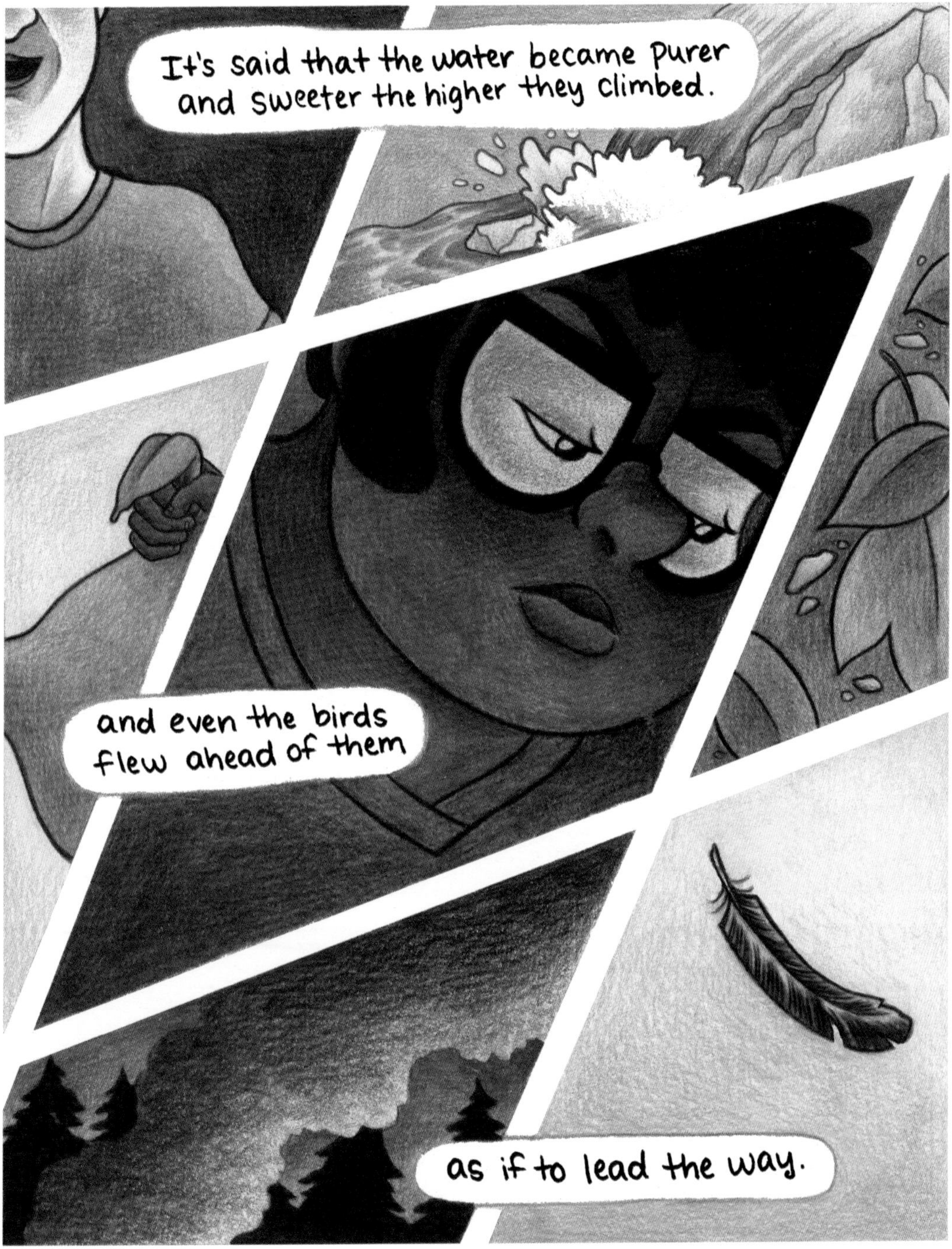
It's said that the water became purer and sweeter the higher they climbed.
and even the birds flew ahead of them
as if to lead the way.

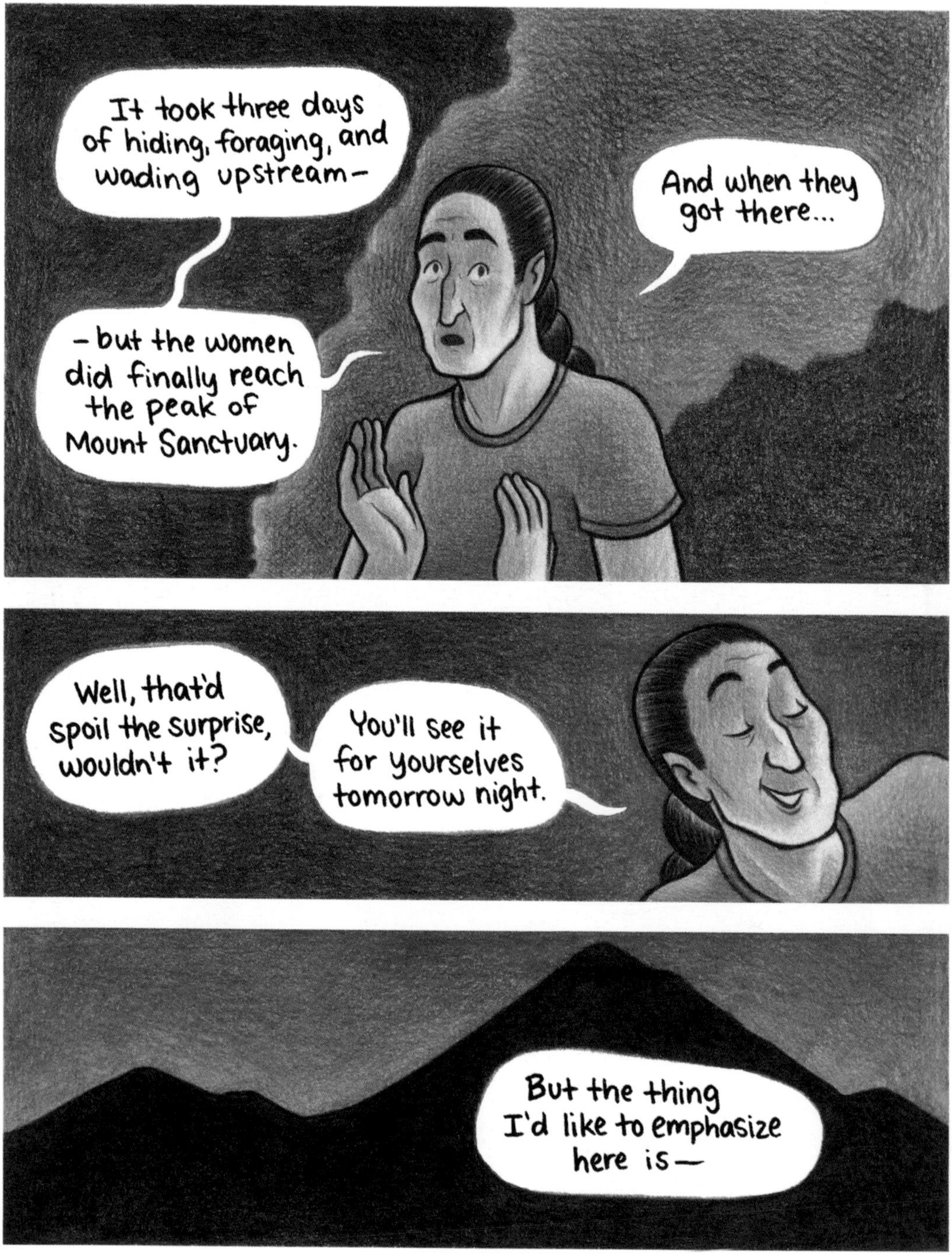
It took three days of hiding, foraging, and wading upstream—
—but the women did finally reach the peak of Mount Sanctuary.
And when they got there...
Well, that'd spoil the surprise, wouldn't it?
You'll see it for yourselves tomorrow night.
But the thing I'd like to emphasize here is—

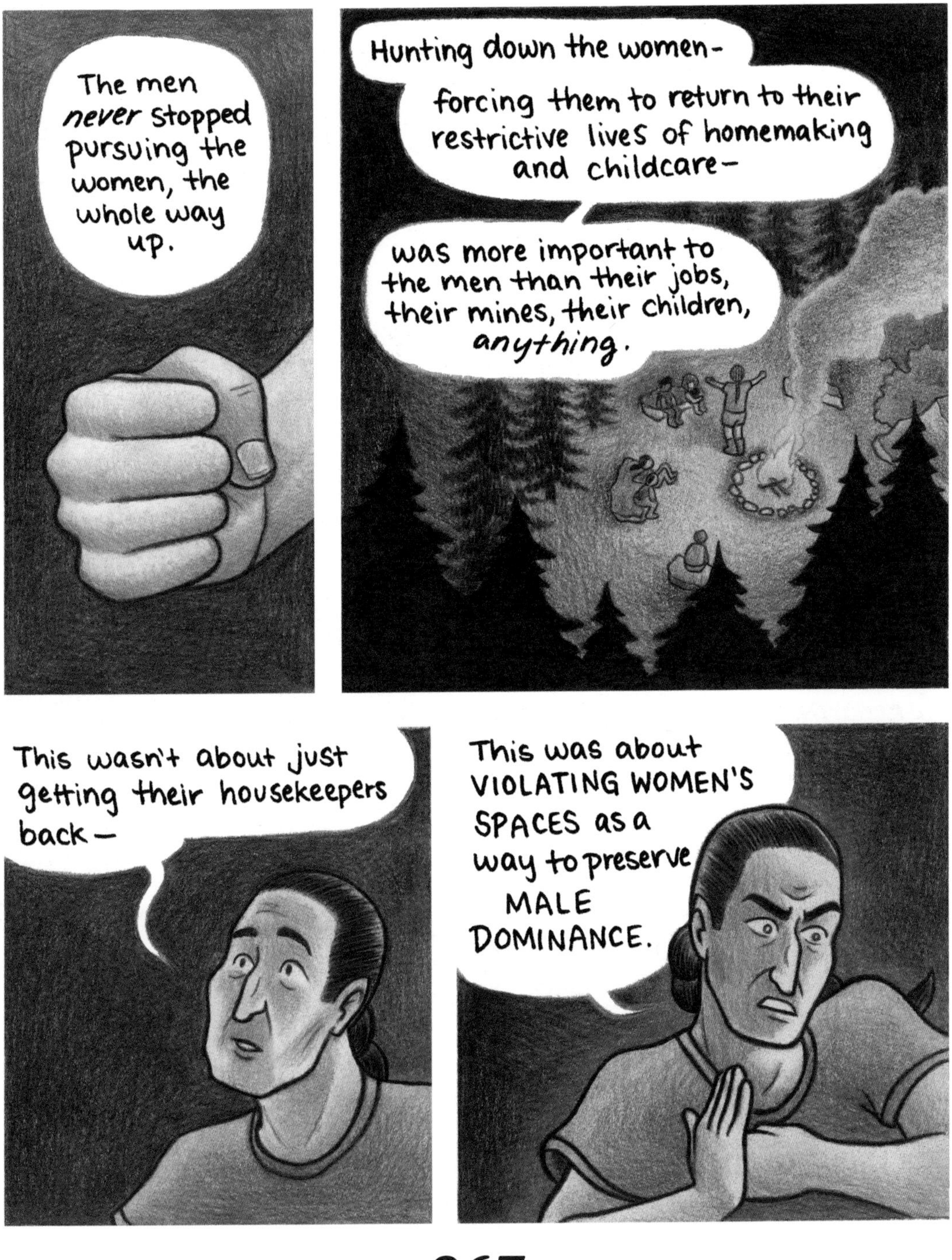
The men *never* stopped pursuing the women, the whole way up.
Hunting down the women-
forcing them to return to their restrictive lives of homemaking and childcare-
was more important to the men than their jobs, their mines, their children, *anything*.
This wasn't about just getting their housekeepers back—
This was about VIOLATING WOMEN'S SPACES as a way to preserve MALE DOMINANCE.

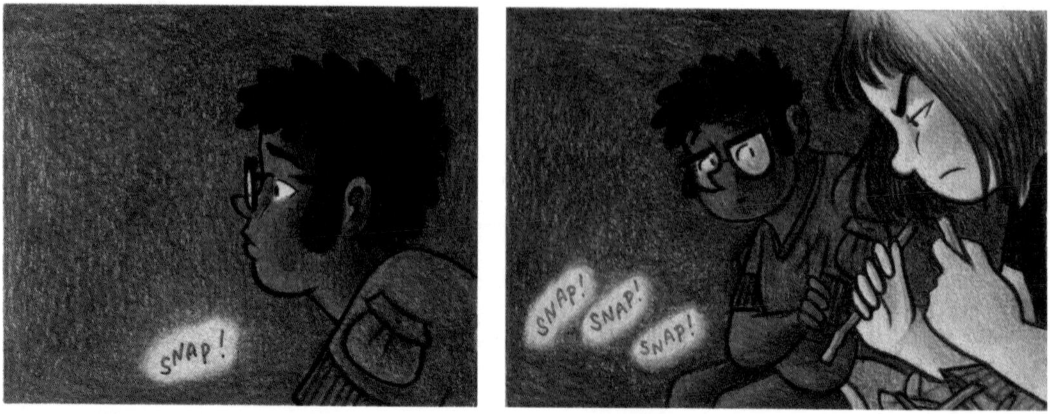
SNAP!
SNAP!
SNAP!
SNAP!

Simply put, the men just couldn't *stand* the thought that

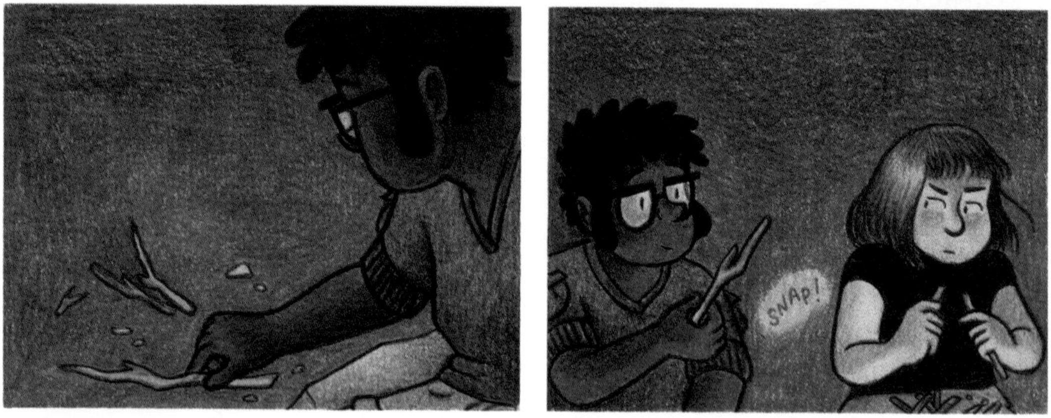
SNAP!

there were spaces where they *weren't allowed in*—

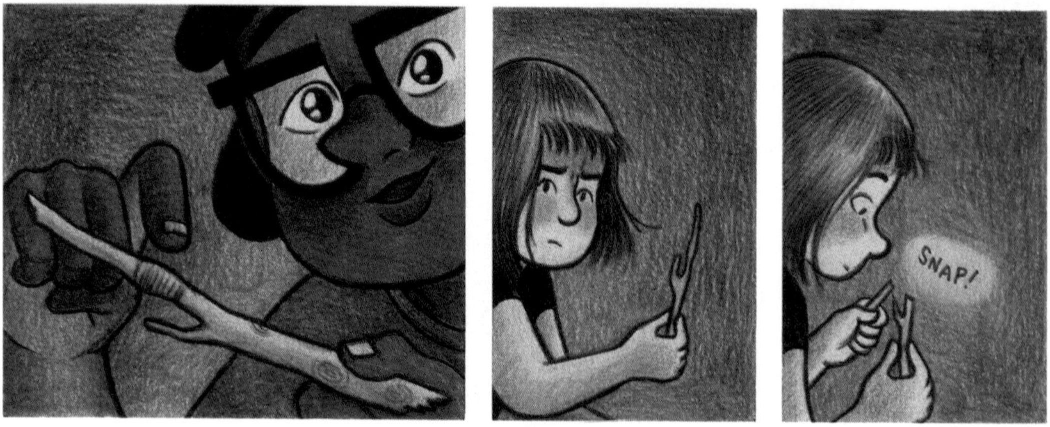
SNAP!

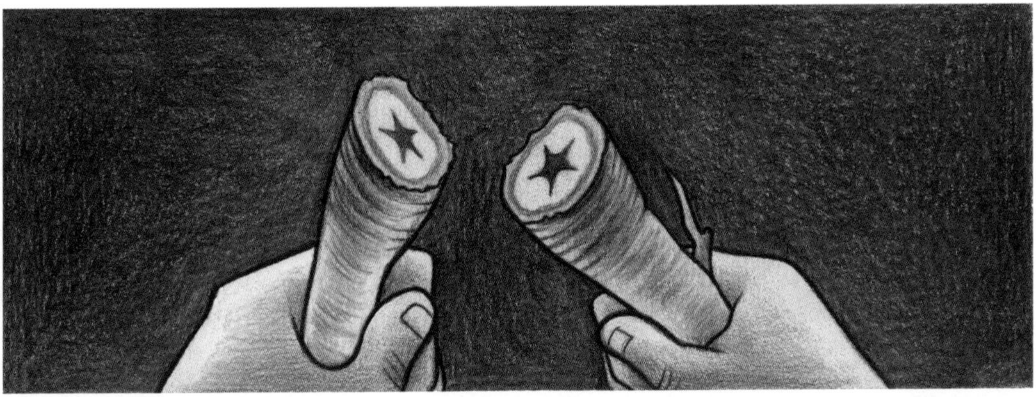

But God Himself, it seems, is a believer in the sanctity of women's

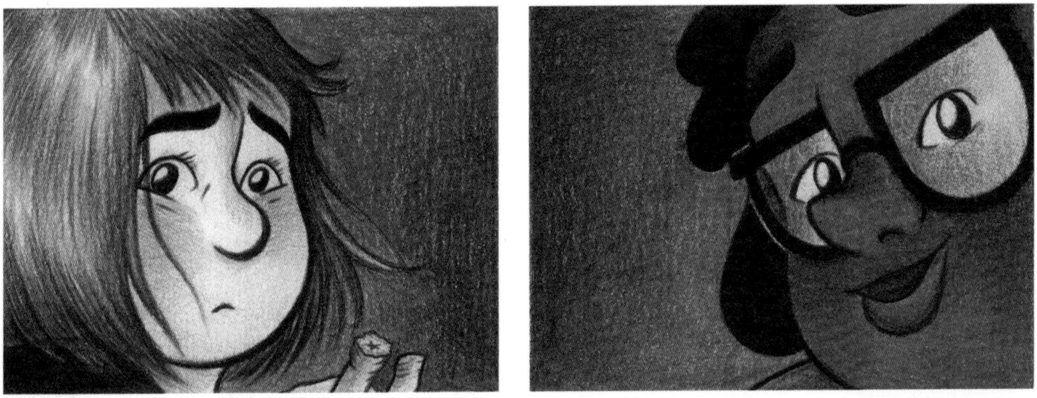

spaces. He protected and sheltered the women, the whole way up.

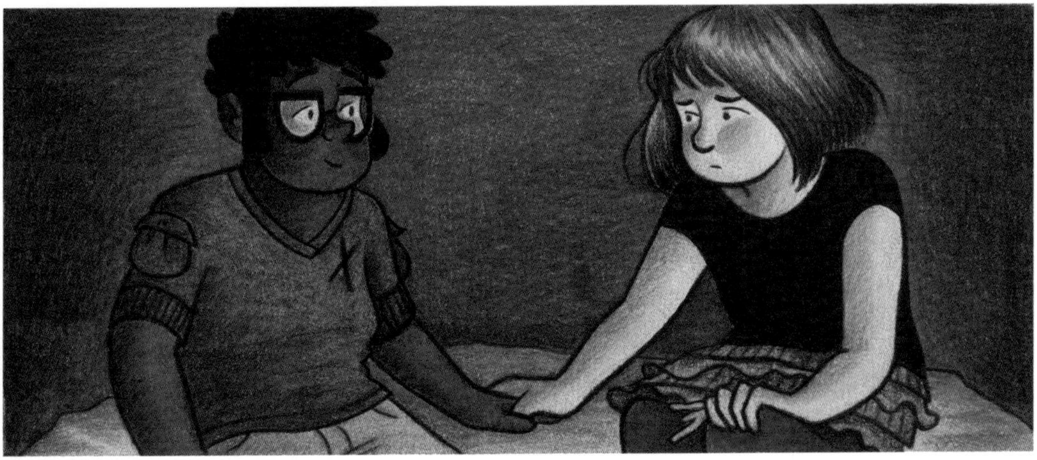

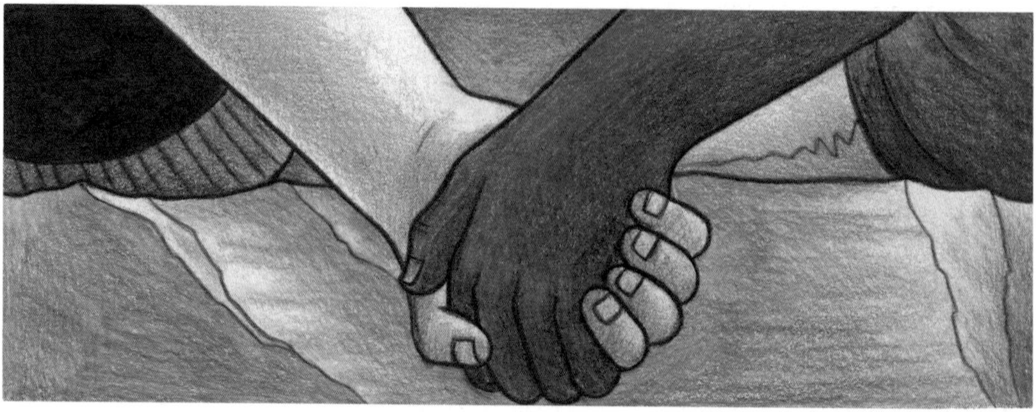

Our God *is* on our side.

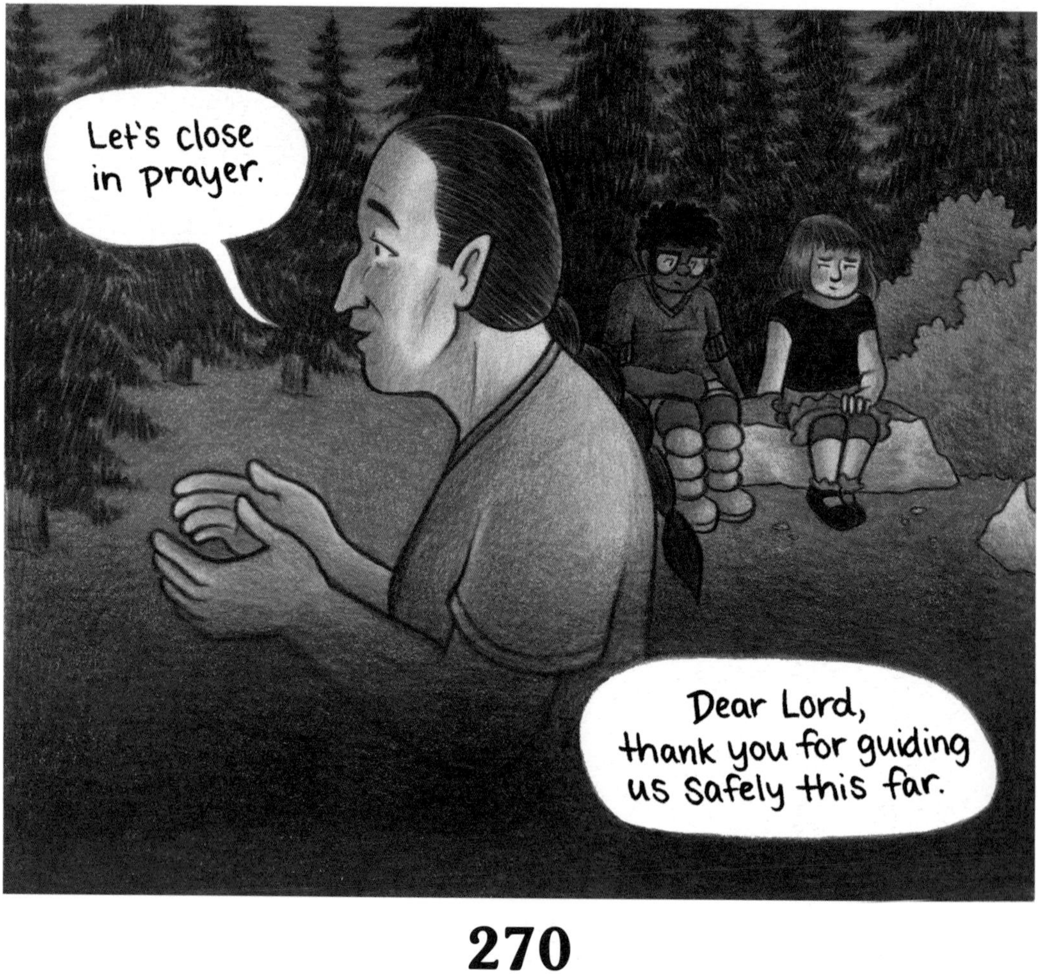
Let's close in prayer.
Dear Lord, thank you for guiding us safely this far.

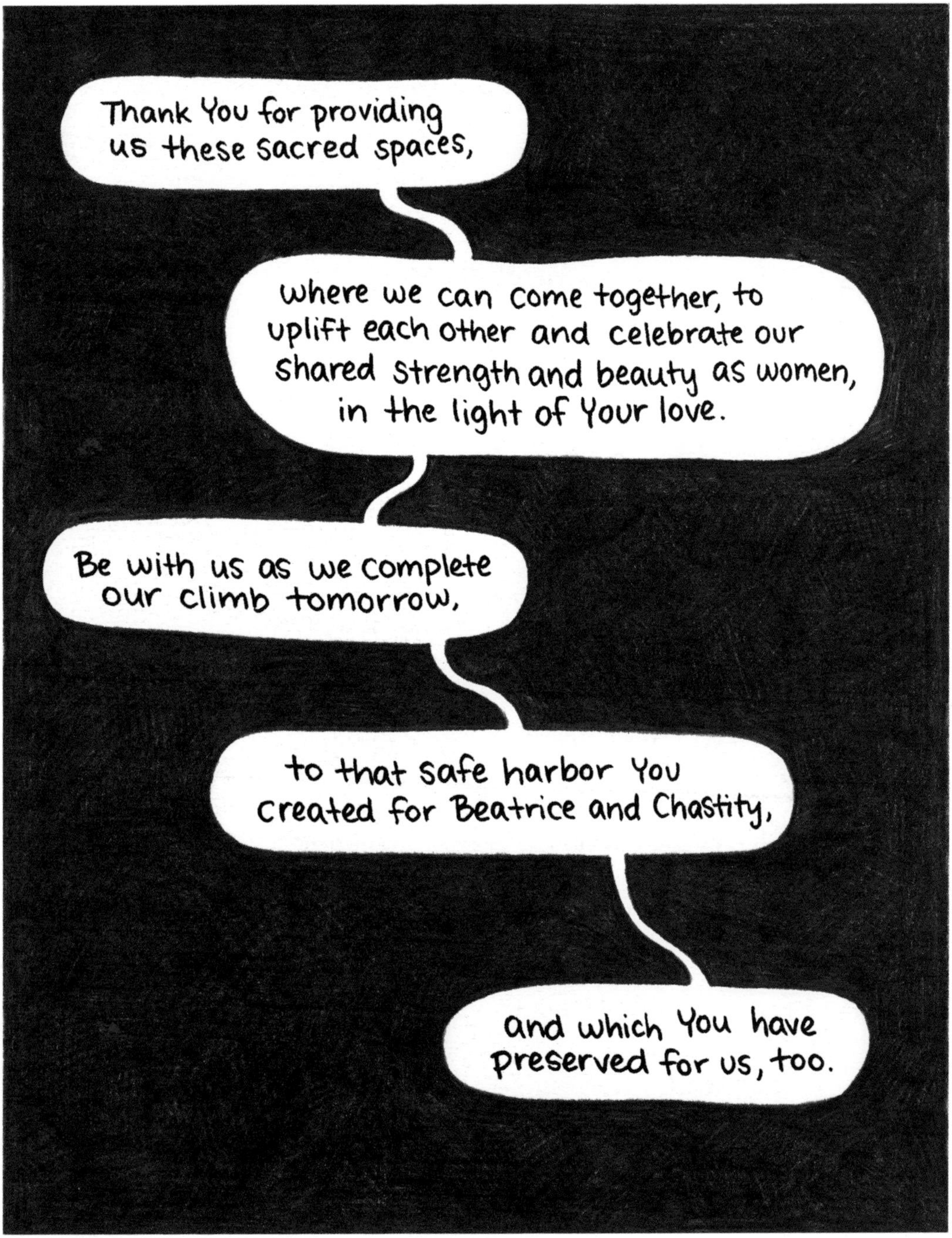
Thank You for providing us these sacred spaces,
where we can come together, to uplift each other and celebrate our shared strength and beauty as women, in the light of Your love.
Be with us as we complete our climb tomorrow,
to that safe harbor You created for Beatrice and Chastity,
and which You have preserved for us, too.

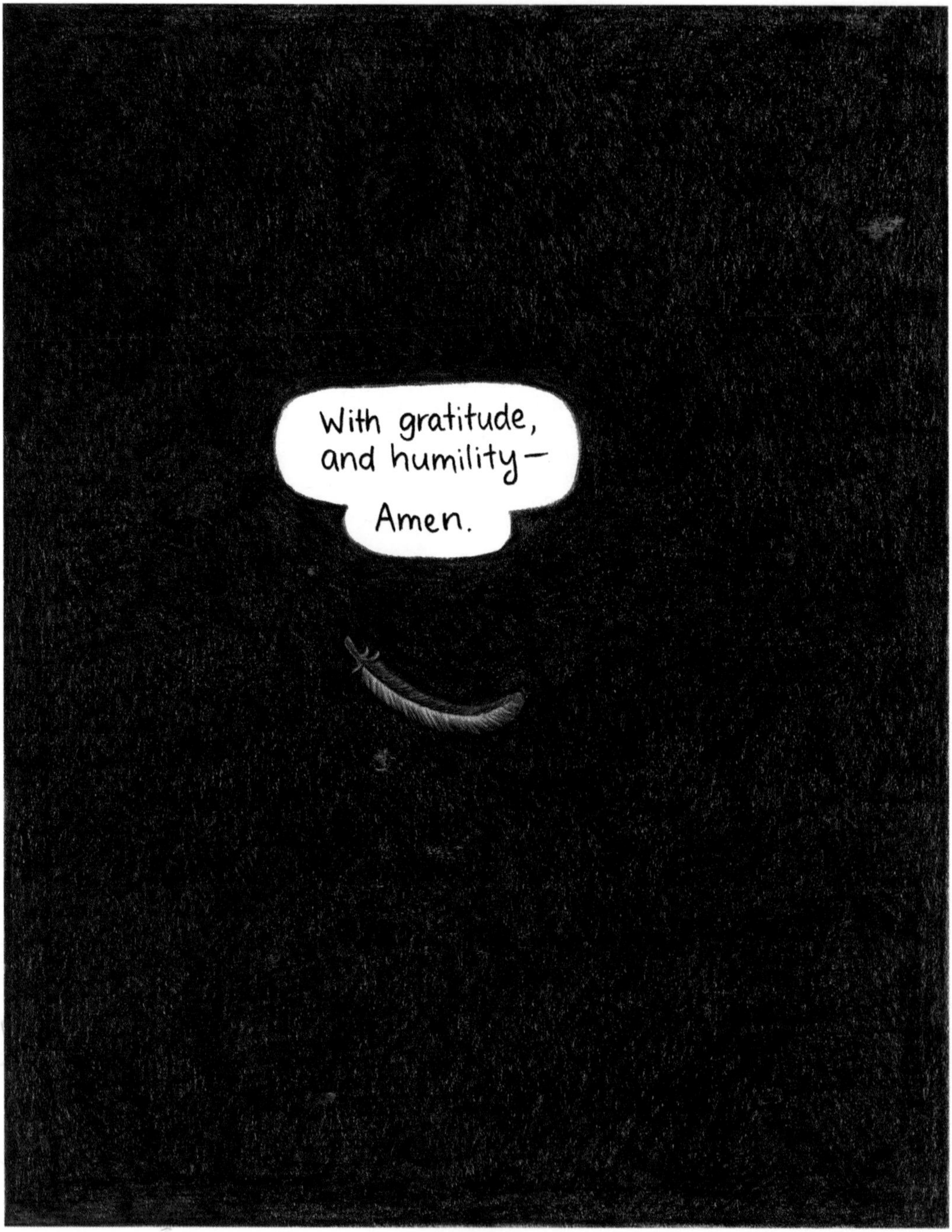
With gratitude, and humility—
Amen.